"A sweeping chronicle of wealthy Atlanta gentry ruined by their privileged destinies."
The New York Times Book Review

"Every bit as fascinating as the story of Scarlett and Rhett. . . . It is the story of 1940s Atlanta and how it grew. . . . Filled with interesting people, a wonderful plot and a grand sweep of history through the South's No. 1 city. The ending is superb. . . . *Peachtree Road* is a winner."
Detroit Free Press

"Siddons masterfully uses the story of Lucy, Shep and their generation to present a richly detailed portrait of an Atlanta in transition, lurching uncertainly, then speeding rapidly, towards its position as capital of the Southeast."
The Dallas Morning News

"Like Faulkner and Conroy, the author cannily manipulates the reader, unfurling familial horrors with just the right degree of psychic tension. . . . *Peachtree Road* tantalizes its way to triumphs."
The Miami Herald

PEACHTREE ROAD

Anne Rivers Siddons

BALLANTINE BOOKS • NEW YORK

For Lee, Kemble, Rick and David
My main men

And for Betsy Fancher

Acknowledgments

The fruits of many lives, minds and hearts went into the making of this book, and I am profoundly indebted to each one. The authors of more books, newspaper and magazine articles than I can count deserve—and have—my gratitude, and the support and forbearance of more friends than I knew I had have kept the essential fires burning.

Special thanks are due to the dedicated and tireless staff of the Atlanta Historical Society, and to the many generous friends who shared their stores of Atlanta lore with me, especially Ham Stockton, David LeBey, Dick Williams, Betsy Fancher, Patsy Dickey and Marty Yarbrough;

And to Emily and Joe Cumming, who shared the magic of Tate colony and the richness of their lives; Emily's story of the deer's leap is, I think, a special point of light in these pages;

And to Alex Sanders, whose extraordinary anecdotes have been shamelessly purloined, as have the lifelong memories of my incomparable typist and dear friend, Martha Gray;

And to my beautiful friend Virginia Schneider, gone now, who showed me what Atlanta could be at its best;

And to my husband, Heyward, who knew this book would happen and never let me forget it;

And to my agent and editor, Ginger Barber and Larry Ashmead, who helped it happen at each step along the way.

And finally, and with love and gratitude, to my friend Pat Conroy, who, on an autumn Saturday two years ago, made me see that it *could* happen . . . and should.

Thanks, guys. I love you all.

Anne Rivers Siddons
February 1, 1988
Atlanta

Some of the time, going home, I go
Blind and can't find it.
The house I lived in growing up and out
The doors of high school is torn
Down and cleared
Away for further development, but that does not stop
me.
First in the heart
Of my blind spot are
The Buckhead Boys. If I can find them, even one,
I'm home. And if I can find him   catch him in or
around
Buckhead, I'll never die; it's likely my youth will walk
Inside me like a king.

—JAMES DICKEY
"Looking for the Buckhead Boys"

PART
ONE

PROLOGUE

THE SOUTH KILLED LUCY BONDURANT CHASTAIN VEN-ABLE on the day she was born. It just took her until now to die. It was a textbook murder, classical in concept, faultless in execution; a work of art, really, as such things go. And no wonder. It's what we do best, kill our women. Or maim them. Or make monsters of them, which may be the worst of all.

I was thinking of that as I stood by Lucy's grave in the Bondurant plot in Oakland Cemetery this afternoon, in the pale lemon sunlight of a Georgia autumn. Of that, and of many other things, this being the accepted time and place for reflection: a quiet burial in an old cemetery where your family and friends and everybody you know lie, or will. One of the other things I was thinking was how contented and tranquil I always feel here; mindless almost. I have always loved Oakland. Lucy and I played together here as children, forty-odd years ago.

It is not that I am morbid, although there would be plenty of people in our crowd to dispute that. To our collective mind, morbid is synonymous with "funny," and there was not one of the people gathered here today, me included, who would not agree that Lucy's cousin Shep Bondurant is "funny." But morbidity is not the direction my aberration takes. Rather the opposite, I think. I'm pretty cheerful and optimistic, in the main, even if I don't go out anymore, or hardly. If I were morbid, I expect I would be dead by now.

No, Oakland is not, to me, a place of shadows and stagnation. Not even of death. There is an air of ongoing bustle and life to it, in a silent and unseen way, of course, which is extremely at-

3

tractive, in the manner of all places where like people dwell close together in harmony of purpose. The people here have their own grand, small mossy mansions, jumbled close together on tiny green, shaded lawns, and a tangle of brick streets threading the high hills, and fine old oaks and magnolias, and a great brick wall to keep out the riffraff, and a splendid view of Atlanta to the northwest, and uniformed servants to tend their lawns and streets and dwellings. That these citizens are all dead has always seemed to me quite beside the point of Oakland. The point is that its denizens are together, as they were in life, and safe, and that they will never, for all eternity, have to deal with the one thing that they detested and feared most in their lifetimes: the increasing intrusion into their ordered world of trash and tackpots. They have left all that to us who only visit them here, and there were not a few of us in the knot of handsome, seemly people gathered to send off Lucy this afternoon who will be relieved to join their sheltered ranks. In the core group of Old Atlanta, of whom I speak, the ecstasy of Heaven is surely incidental to the insularity of Oakland.

Our crowd has always been in and out of Oakland almost as frequently and easily as we enter and leave our homes and clubs. From the time we were small children, Lucy and I were brought here on picnics, and before the city got strict about closing hours and vandalism, it was a prime spot in which to park and catch some monk—a cloying term somebody in my crowd devised for necking, which caught on and became the rage for several years. Lucy always swore that it was here that she and Red Chastain first made love, on top of Margaret Mitchell's grave, on a spring night after a Phi Chi dance when she was sixteen.

"I swear the earth moved, Gibby," she said. "Old Red thought it was his incomparable fucking, but I'm sure it was little old Peggy Mitchell applauding."

I doubt that it really happened, though I know that Lucy was sleeping with Red by then, and Margaret Mitchell's grave would have been just the sacramental fillip she would have chosen to mark the occasion of their first coupling. For one thing, Lucy was a baroque and gifted liar, and for another, Red was like a cat about his creature comforts, and would never have fucked on any but the levelest of ground, and then only atop the pristine Chatham blanket he kept in the trunk of the MG for such occasions. It's even unlikely that he would have done it out of doors, having as he did access to any number of bachelor apartments around town, unless Lucy had brought him all the way to the brink before he could assess the alternatives. That *is* credible. Lucy had half our crowd lifting bumpers by the time she was twelve.

Oakland Cemetery hasn't changed much in the hundred and thirty-odd years it has sheltered Atlanta's favored dead. It is the city's proud claim that all classes of citizens lie here, from poor black and unknown potter's field inhabitants to Atlanta's silkiest gentry, the ones who built the ornate Victorian mausoleums, whose names can be found on a great many municipal streets, parks and buildings. Strictly speaking, this is true; for four years, until Westview was built, Oakland was, so to speak, the only game in town, and indeed, a few blacks of some distinction *are* here, usually at the behest of the white families for whom they or their progenitors toiled. There is, too, a separate Jewish section, an area devoted to the Confederate dead, many of whom fell at the Battle of Atlanta, and an Irish quarter, tactfully dedicated to the Hibernian Rifles of our cherished War. But over the years our crowd has largely usurped Oakland for its own, and now very few tackpots or trash are honored here.

For all its homogeneity, it is an eccentric place, and I think that is why I am so fond of it. I can just hear my mother, who lies here, refuting that: "What a thing to say, Shep. These are our own people. The funny people are all at Arlington." But Oakland has bite and particularity and an air of raffish festivity to it, an orneriness that calls out to me, my mother notwithstanding. Among its ubiquitous angels and lugubrious inscriptions are the graven images of the venality and pragmatism that are the soul of this city, and their robustness bids to far outlive the crumbling cherubim and the soot-weeping eggs and darts. One progenitor of a prominent family has his Ph.D. inscribed on his mausoleum. Another has had replicated on his the facade of his fine Greek Revival earthly mansion, complete with street number, lest anyone confuse it with someone else's.

My favorite has always been that of the Smith family, one of whose members, a Jasper N., had himself carved life-size and set foursquare atop his mausoleum, hat on knee, gazing to the northeast at the fine view to be had of the city. In life, local legend says, Jasper refused to wear a tie, and in death he has not capitulated. That he gazes now, not at the city's skyline, but at the Martin Luther King Metropolitan Atlanta Rapid Transit Station and the new Piggyback Rail facility of the old Fulton Bag and Cotton Mill, does not seem to disturb him. He can no longer see Cabbagetown, the rank warren of old wooden shanties that grew up around the mill, and for that he may be grateful. I would be, profoundly. I have not seen Cabbagetown since a bitter cold day more than twenty-five years ago, and after today, I will not willingly come this near to it again, not until it is my turn to take up residence at Oakland. Cabbagetown was the catalyst that finished transforming me into what is known, euphemistically, as a recluse, though it by no means precipitated the journey. I suppose you might say I was genetically programmed for that.

The Bondurant mausoleum, my own family's port of embarkation, lies on the crest of one of Oakland's many hills, shaded by a giant magnolia and a leaning, fruitless old holly. It is unprepossessing as the mausoleums there go, as spare and chaste and linear as the old scholar, my grandfather, who erected it. But it has a magnificent situation, being adjacent to the site of the long-ago mayor's house from which General John B. Hood watched the Battle of Atlanta. Why that exercise in ignominy should so please my family I have never understood, but it did, especially my mother. Not herself a native Atlantan, she could and always did manage a tear when we visited the plot, and she would always say, "I can actually see the smoke and flames and hear the cannon. It just smites my heart."

"Your heart gets itself smitten over some pretty odd things," my father said on one of those occasions.

"We'd all be better off if yours got smitten over anything at all," she replied.

I can see in retrospect that both of them were right.

Now, over the hulking carcass of the MARTA station and the dreary jumble of the rail yards, you can see the towers of commerce that have made us the hub of the Sunbelt, the undisputed capital of the Southeast, the crossroads, as it were, of the country: a grinding, jostling, hustling megalopolis of nearly three million people in a vast metropolitan area encompassing eighteen counties, spread out on our high green Piedmont plain under a stinking canopy of dull bronze, cupped between Kennesaw Mountain to the west, Stone Mountain to the east, the foothills of the Blue Ridge to the north, and still seeping south like the yolk of an undercooked egg.

Some of our downtown and midtown structures—the Trust Company of Georgia Tower, the First National Bank Building, the Georgia-Pacific Building, the Westin-Peachtree Plaza, the bone-white spires of Peachtree Center, the IBM Building—are very tall. That, to my eye, is all they are: tall. They scrabble and paw at the sky like pale, thin, unformed adolescent fingers. They are without distinction, except for their much-vaunted height. They are abrupt and nervous. It is a nervous skyline. The jangled skyscrapers do not let the observer forget that it was not the deep, rich arteries of the slow old rivers, but the thin, jackrabbity, stinking, robust veins of the railroads that were, for Atlanta, both nourishment and metaphor. From the very beginning, it was destined—or doomed, depending on your point of view—to be a business town.

And it's a money town. Oh, very much a money town. Like height, money is the other conspicuous thing that we have. My lifelong friend Charlie Gentry told me once, at a fund-raising luncheon at the Commerce Club before I stopped going out, "Money is the aristocracy in this town, no matter what you hear at the Driving Club. Money and property. It sure as hell isn't the old families. None of us were here more than a hundred and fifty years ago. There wasn't even an outhouse to piss in until then. And the few of us who have been here since the beginning came from somewhere else—Savannah or Charleston or Richmond, where they really know about old. No wonder we holler so about gumption and guts. It's what we have instead of blue blood."

Charlie, God love him. He was right, of course. He would know. Without any real money himself, he became one of the quintessential money and power brokers in the city. Most of us, plus the tackpots and the Texans and the Arabs we purport to scorn, came courting Charlie Gentry sooner or later. He took it in his stride and did his best for us, understanding precisely from whence we came. Money and business is and always was our ethos. Not creativity or artistic sensibility or even charming, cultivated decadence. Just business. In Atlanta, if it is good for business, it is as good as done.

I have never particularly liked that about Atlanta, but I concede that it has given us an extraordinary vigor, and I have certainly feasted on its fruits. I am not ungrateful, just unengaged. Atlanta has never sung to me. One of the deepest bonds I shared with Lucy was the way we both felt about the city: Neither of us liked it very much, but neither of us wanted to leave it, either. I remember once, late into the cataclysmic sixties, when she asked me why I stayed, I surprised myself with quite a succinct little précis: "It's passionless, calculating, self-satisfied, intolerant, insensitive, uncultivated, vulgar, even soulless . . . but it's alive! God, Lucy, the energy in this town! And it's just so beautiful, parts of it. But mostly, it's mine. It's what I know. It's the card I drew; it's what I'm invested in. I *know* this place. I'd never know another place or other people like I do this."

"Is knowing so important?" Lucy asked.

"Yes," I said. "For some reason, knowing is everything."

"Hell, Gibby," Lucy said. "Knowing doesn't amount to shit. It doesn't change the way things are."

Lucy was early, and ever, a realist.

At a party once, again in those days when I was still going out, a smart, thin woman with a deep, leathery tan and the unmistakable smack of that New York–Palm Beach axis in her voice asked me, discontentedly, where you had to go to find Old Atlanta.

"They certainly aren't at any of the parties I've been to, and I've been to every decent party this entire winter," she said.

I looked around the drawing room of the big house, a beetling ersatz Norman in one of those frightening developments out on the river where florists' and caterers' trucks are lost by the thousands. The Chattahoochee Triangle, we call it. Everybody there was what the old ladies in my crowd would call tackpots, and every other one seemed to be a lawyer. I didn't know anybody; I had come with clever, Jewish Marty Fox, whom I had just hired to help me sort out my father's estate, and whom I liked enormously. The talk of deals and money had bored me, but the hors d'oeuvres were spectacular, and the host had provided a fleet of minivans to shuttle guests from their cars to the house, and there was more décolletage in the room than I had ever seen, except at the strip shows we used to sneak into Manhattan from Princeton to see.

"Funerals," I said. "Most especially funerals at Saint Philip's or All Saints or Saint Luke's. Or Oakland Cemetery."

"You mean they're all dead?" she said, staring at me belligerently, to see if I was making fun of her. I was not.

"No. I mean the only time I ever see what I guess you'd call Old Atlanta all together in a group is at a funeral or beside somebody's grave at Oakland."

"Or at the Driving Club or the Capital City Club or Brookhaven," I did not say. The woman would never find out for herself. Those were still the days when new money, no matter how much there was of it, didn't get into the older clubs. This, like almost everything else, has changed now, of course, and it's one change of which I heartily approve—or would, if I still went to the clubs. Those pretackpot days at the Piedmont Driving Club were among the most astoundingly boring in the history of the world.

I had spoken the truth to the leathery lady, however facetiously. There we all were this afternoon: Old Atlanta en masse, or what passes for it. The quick of it, as well as the dead. A dwindling handful of men and women, young and old, who had lived within a four-mile radius of each other all their lives; grown up together, gone to school and college together, flirted and danced with and courted and married each other, godparented each other's children, laughed and wept and partied with each other, loved and sometimes hated each other, mourned and buried each other. Rich, or what the world calls rich, a good many of them. Incomprehensibly rich, a few of them. Once, all-powerful in the smaller arena that was the Atlanta of their prime.

There beside Lucy's grave today we had a past and present

mayor, a governor, an ex-governor, a United States senator; men
who had built family mercantile and service businesses into international concerns, men who had made literally millions from
Coca-Cola, either directly or indirectly, men who had dramatically altered the face of the South and in some cases the nation
with their monolithic urban and suburban developments; men
who had, almost single-handedly or in concert with five or six
of their peers, brought to the city, in the fire-storm decade of
the sixties, a major league sports arena, five professional sports
teams, a great, dead-white marble arts center and a world-
famous conductor to inhabit it, a world-class international airport, a state-of-the-art rapid transit system, a freeway system to
boggle the mind, unparalleled convention facilities and the people to fill them—and the peacefully integrated school system that
lured in the industry to fuel it all.

They are a superannuated, largely toothless pride of old lions
whose days of glory are past, perhaps, but their turf is still that
cloistered world for which they wrought everything, and it is still
inviolable, even if it is shrunken now, and teeters sometimes on
its foundations. And they still move with grace and ease in it.

And their wives, old now, too, but still chic in the soft, pastel
way of their primes, and their widows; equally smart, equally
erect and slender and expensively and unobtrusively dressed—
all there. And their sons and daughters: us, my crowd, Lucy's
and my contemporaries, our own ranks thinned and wounded,
our faces surprised with middle age. And even their grandchil-
dren, a few of them. Our children. I saw Sarah Gentry's two
quicksilver daughters, and Little Lady Rawson's lone eighteen-
year-old Circe, and Lelia Cheatham's tall, gangling sons. And
Lucy's daughter, Malory, stricken and smeared with grief but
still looking so heartstoppingly like her mother in her own first
youth and slender, smoky beauty that my eyes stung with it.
Malory, standing for the moment with the other women, apart,
as they always seem to be in groups, from the closed ranks of
their men. Malory . . .

The women were an attractive lot, I thought, not for the first
time. They were all still soft-faced, soft-voiced, poised, and they
talked today in low voices with each other, smiling sometimes
over at their men. Without being in the least physically similar,
they gave an impression of agreeable sameness. I knew, of
course, that they were as varied as the women in any comparable
peer group; that the sameness was merely protective coloration,
a softly buffed armor they acquired along with their charm
bracelets and white debut frocks when they came of age in the
big old houses off Peachtree Road.

My eye caught a flash of red in all the quiet taupes and navies, and I grinned involuntarily at the openly defiant scarlet chiffon scarf around the strongly modeled brown throat of Sarah Cameron Gentry. None of the girls in our crowd had liked Lucy worth a damn, and Sarah, of all of them, had had good reason. Too well bred to rejoice on this day, Sarah was nevertheless flying all her flags. Small, staunch, perfectly made Sarah, also my friend from infancy, and once, more than friend. In an earlier time, I might have married Sarah, and thus been saved. In an earlier time, and a better one. . . . Sarah caught my eye and gave me a slow amber wink. Her dark head is threaded now with gray, but it is still the springy, cropped tumble of mahogany curls that she has worn since girlhood. She always kept it short for her swimming and diving. Her body still retains its fine, shapely, flat athlete's muscles, and I still remember with pleasure the pearly sheen of baby oil and iodine on her golden back, and the music and grace of her racing dives off the board at the Driving Club pool.

I wondered if Sarah still dived and swam. I have not been to the club for a very long time.

Over to the left of the women, us. That most endangered of species, the masculine remnants of Old Atlanta, far outnumbered even in middle age by our widows and daughters. Speaking to each other in that peculiar shorthand of ours that marks and dates and explains us: "How are you, suh?" "Good to see you, suh." That "suh" is not politesse; it is our crowd's familiar. We use it among ourselves as the French do their familiar "tu."

A few rich old men who changed a world. And finally their sons, who to my mind, no matter what our collective accomplishments, never were a patch on them.

The Buckhead Boys.

An intense female journalist, who was not one of us but would have died to be, wrote an article about us once, in *Cityscope* magazine. It was overheated and romantic in the extreme, and caused no end of scornful amusement in our ranks, but I have always thought that it did manage to capture something about us that was valid, a kind of oversimplified truth. No one I know agrees with me about that.

Back there, the woman wrote, *in that dreaming cradle slung between Depression and Camelot, there was, in Atlanta, a golden group of boys and girls called the Pinks and the Jells. They were, most of them, the scions of the great merchant families that had built Atlanta back from the ashes of the Civil War, and if the raw young city could be said to have an aristocracy, these were its heirs and heiresses, its best and brightest . . . and its natural victims.*

Their fathers were the power structure of that youngest and least typical Southern city, the movers and shakers, the "club". . .

the bank presidents, the heads of the great utilities, the newspaper and radio empires, and the family-owned businesses that had grown with the city into mid-century monoliths. These fathers were the men who took the reins of the stagnant city in the dying years of the Depression and flogged it with money, muscle, single-mindedness, and pragmatic guile to the brink of what became known at the end of the incendiary 1960s as "the next great international city." Their sons, the children of that endless, golden time, became the men who, prepared or not, took up the torches that would light the city and the entire South into an unimaginable new world called the Sunbelt.

Their daughters became the women who ran the great homes and schools and children and charities of that time of transition, and who flourished like roses on its graceful trellis . . . or who did not, and paid dearly.

James Dickey, who was one of them, called them the Buckhead Boys. Not all of them survived the appellation and all that it implied.

Theirs was a rigidly masculine world of money, privilege, grace, ritual, preening foolishness, high spirits, and low expectations. They were not groomed for their future roles as power brokers because it was taken for granted that they would slide as easily into them as their fathers had into their own earlier and simpler niches. They remained children for a very long time. They were probably genuinely loved and certainly indulged. Most of them would have told you that they had wonderful childhoods and adolescences.

Insular, careless, totally and imperviously self-assured, chauvinistic in the extreme, naive and unsophisticated, arrogant, profoundly physical rather than introspective, largely unburdened by intellect, and almost laughably White Anglo-Saxon Protestant, they were as cohesive as cousins and as stunningly insensitive as young royalty. They were oblivious to anyone and anything outside their charmed circle of prep schools, high school sororities and fraternities, drag racing, endless formal dances, summer camps, drugstores and drive-ins and hangouts, orchid corsages and staglines and cut-ins, country clubs and Cokes and crinolines, and later, debuts and Junior League and Assemblies and Rabun Gap-Nacoochee and Tallulah Falls and Germans and Nine O'Clocks and Georgia Tech and branch water and bourbon . . . endless, endless bourbon.

It was a beautiful, bountiful, exuberant, frivolous, snobbish, and silkily secure kingdom, and it was then, as it is still, a very small and strictly delineated world, perhaps no more than four miles square, in a green northern suburb of Atlanta called Buckhead. And yet out of it came the men, and indirectly the women, who, rather to their own surprise, would change forever the definition of the word "South."

But it was a world with hidden reefs and shoals that could, and did, wreck the unwary, the deviate, the maverick, the vulnerable or gentle or complicated or different ones.

The Pinks and the Jells. The Buckhead Boys and their girls. The small, powerful and sometimes doomed group of people who were born into a very dense, rich, small and unassailable world, therein to move for the entirety of their lives, in which their primary artery, metaphor, and pathway of the heart was Peachtree Road.

More than any of us, Lucy hated that article.

"It's sentimental shit, Gibby," she snorted. "The worst kind of junk, because it has a little streak of truth to it. That silly woman didn't dig any further to get down to where all the real truth of us was. Jim Dickey's the only one who ever did that, and nobody reads poetry in this town. Oh, hell, who would have told it to her, anyhow? But this kind of stuff is kiss-off shit."

As I have said, Lucy was an utter realist. She had a bone-deep knowledge of how things really are. She had it even as a very small child; learned it early, learned it cruelly and indelibly. It is a terrible burden, this gift of truth, especially for so fragile a child as Lucy Bondurant was, but I suspect it was the source of her great charm. She stood apart with it like wildfire on a mountain of blasted stone.

I suppose you could also say that it finally killed her. Brought her there to lie among all those other Bondurants, next to a stone for an unlikable aunt that reads, "She stood foursquare to all the winds that blew." Lucy would have laughed at that, her rich, pouring, froggy belly laugh. In all her life, Lucy was not, for one instant, foursquare to anything. She was all dazzle, shimmer, movement, smoke and light.

There were so many Bondurants at Oakland Cemetery this afternoon, most of them, thank God, safely belowground. My grandmother and grandfather, Adelaide and Sheppard Gibbs Bondurant. My great-aunt Lorena. The aforementioned foursquare Aunt Eugenie. Olivia Redwine Bondurant and Sheppard Gibbs Bondurant, Jr., my mother and father. A small, sad row of newly born and perished infants, all but one of their stones kin to so many in the old cemetery, dating from the days of typhoid and smallpox and diphtheria. Lucy's small brother, Jamie. And aboveground, her narrow Ferragamos gleaming in the dust of early October, old Willa Bondurant, standing now like a lacquered chimera with the other women, on the arm of her surviving daughter, Adelaide. Little Lady Bondurant Rawson, Lucy's younger sister. The "good" one.

Lucy herself.

And me, Sheppard Gibbs Bondurant III. The last Bondurant. Or am I? This is and will likely always be the central mystery of my life.

Lucy's second husband, Jack, does not lie in the Bondurant plot beside her. He is buried in the Venable family plot outside Nashville. Even if he had not died first, he would not have been there this afternoon, in that most essential of all Bondurant countries. He never had any use at all for the Bondurants— including, I think, me—and there was never any question of his lying here beside his widow. I know that his sons came and took him home for burial, but I am not sure when they did so. I had liked Jack, but the moment he was gone it was as if his life had never rippled the surface of ours, mine or Lucy's. I did not go to his funeral, and she did not either.

His widow. The widow Venable. I cannot think of Lucy like that, though of course, technically and for a short time, she was. The word sounds so tissue-dry and alone, and Lucy was never, in her entire life, alone. It was what she feared most, aloneness, and what she spent the whole of her life holding at bay. She did it well.

The other thing she feared above all else was death itself, which is why I find it impossible to connect her with what we buried in Oakland Cemetery this afternoon. I saw her after her death, and even though they say that only the viewing of your dead can bring the healing reality of it home to you, that poor spilled and slackened mannequin had absolutely nothing to do with Lucy, and so I felt no grief then, and have not yet. It is a great relief, though I don't suppose I can expect it to last. Still, it always seemed to me that Lucy and death were such anathema to each other that the sheer force of the aversion might, after all, keep them apart.

Once, when Lucy had first come to the Peachtree Road house, my mother's altar guild met in our drawing room and one of the women brought slides of the American cemetery in Rome, where a kinsman of hers was buried. Lucy and I had been permitted by old Martha Cater, who took care of us, to creep just inside the room and sit quietly in the hot, mote-dancing August gloom to watch the show. About halfway through, after flash after flash of tombstones and mausoleums and angels and cherubim and classical fragments that far outshone Oakland, Lucy began to cry. Before Martha could whisk her out of the room she was sobbing aloud, and by the time she had been tucked into her bed in the small third-floor bedroom next to mine, she was screaming. It was the first of the terrible, inconsolable fits of hysteria that quaked her childhood. All anyone could get out of her was "I'm so afraid to die! I'm so afraid to die!"

Another time, perhaps two years later, when she was seven and I was nine, I was lying in the hammock on the veranda of the summerhouse, as I so often did, thinking of nothing but being drowned in the dapple of light and shade falling through the latticework, when Lucy appeared silently beside me. I knew she had been swinging alone on the swing set by the goldfish pond. She did that for hours on summer days, humming tonelessly to herself, mesmerized and lost. When I looked up, her face was even whiter than it usually was, and her October-blue eyes were all pupil, almost mad-looking. Her hair was smoke around her head.

"You know what, Gibby?" she said. "I think there isn't any God."

I was shocked, force-fed little Christian that I was then.

"Of course there's a God, stupid. You'll go to Hell for talking like that."

"No. If there's not any God, there's not any Hell."

"Well, where do you think you'll be when you're dead then, if there's not any God or Heaven or Hell?" I was beginning to smell trouble, and flinched from it.

"Nowhere. That's where. I won't be anywhere, and you won't either. There'll just be . . . nothing. That's all there is. Close your eyes and think about it, Gibby. Black, black, black nothing always and forever, without any end . . ."

I did, and gradually, as she chanted, the red weight of the sun on my eyelids cooled and lightened, and the heat went out of the June day, and suddenly I was floating frozen and suspended and paralyzed and utterly, totally alone in a howling black void for which there was no help and to which there was no end. Tears of fright and despair stung my eyes, and when I opened them the world spun sickly, and my heart hammered with the first and still worst real terror I have ever known.

Tears were standing in Lucy's eyes, too, and her chest was beginning to heave with the onset of one of the dreadful, mindless screaming fits.

"Anything is better than dying," she said, and there was that familiar knife-edge of panic in her voice. *"Anything!"*

"Lots of things are worse than dying." I parroted my mother and some of the women who visited her in the afternoons. "Dishonor, and being poor, and being conquered, and being tacky, and rape are all worse than dying."

"That's bullshit," she said shrilly. It was her favorite word that summer. "Any of those things is ten million thousand times

better than being dead and nothing! The one thing I couldn't
stand is for there to be nothing!"

"You wouldn't know it if there was nothing," I pointed out,
deliberately pedantic, trying to avert the spell with obtuseness.
But my own heart still bucked and tore with the terror she had
planted there.

It worked, though. "I would too," she said mulishly, and her
chin went up, and the tears receded. Lucy did not like to be con-
tradicted.

I laughed, I remember. But now, deep in those middle-life
night horrors that bring me up sweating out of sleep, my mouth
already tasting that primal nothingness, my heart old with the
burden of its truth, sick and corrupted beyond healing or redemption or resurrection and separated forever from the time
that I did not know it, I see that she was right. That that is what
death truly is, that awful and unending nothing and the eternal
knowledge of nothingness. Not life, but death everlasting.

As we were gathering ourselves this afternoon to leave Lucy
to begin her long residence, I felt rather than saw the eyes of
the women on me, and I heard old Mrs. Dorsey say to Mrs.
Rawls, in the flat nasal shout of Atlanta's wellborn deaf, "I hear
Shep is taking it mighty hard. They always were as close as
twins."

I grinned inwardly.

"Sucks to you, Mrs. Dorsey," I said under my breath. "You're
going to be one bored old sow now that you don't have Lucy
Bondurant to kick around anymore."

She was right, though, if not in the way she thinks. But what
the hell. Let her keep the thought. I get points for being sensitive
and wounded, which may buy me another unmolested chunk of
solitude. Lucy and I did have an extraordinary and uncanny
closeness, unlike anything else in our lives. It was eerie. I didn't
always like it. Sometimes I out-and-out hated it. But there it was.
I could always see into and through Lucy's mind. When she was
young and beautiful and heartless, I was her heart. Later, in the
times when she was essentially mindless, I was her mind. I don't
know now what I'm going to do with all this leftover Lucyness.

Sitting here in the old summerhouse behind the Peachtree
Road house where I was born and which I have owned for more
than a quarter of a century, and which I have entered only a few
times in almost as many years, it occurs to me that when this
level, pleasant numbness lifts I may find that I can no longer live
in a world where Lucy is not . . . though not, again, for the reason
that Mrs. Dorsey and Company will espouse. It simply may not
be possible. If not, I think I know how I'll arrange things. Lucy
would applaud the wit, irony and sheer appropriateness of it. It

would match in artistry the panache of her own exit. If it comes to that, will it be the end of the Bondurants? As I said earlier, I'm not apt to know that, whether I stick around or let myself out by the back door. In either case, it scarcely matters.

It is seven o'clock, and the shadows of the old oaks and hickories in the back garden are falling across the summerhouse and the veranda. The grass beyond that, around the empty oval of the fish pond, is dry and matted and bleached with the heat of September just past, but the shadows have in them the cold blue of winter coming on. Marty needs to get after the lawn service again. Everything looks used and dusty, as it always does in Atlanta in Indian summer. From the looks of the mounded acorns in the grass, and the continuous pelting of them on the old slate roof of the summerhouse, we're going to have a cold winter, and a long one. I think the image of Lucy lying faceup to the winter—she who so hated cold that she used to weep with despair at the simple fact of February—would be more than I could bear, except that the scotch is working now, and instead of muddling my head into sentiment, it is sharpening it out of maudlinism. Liquor has always clarified things for me. It's probably why I drink so seldom.

I should know soon what is going to happen to me.

Old Willa Bondurant was the last of the women to pass by me on her way out of the cemetery. She is almost perfectly preserved, mummified in her beauty, as is Little Lady, who held her mother's mottled, birdlike arm as carefully as old Dresden. Only, unlike Little Lady, by age instead of alcohol. Willa has always taken exquisite care of herself. She stopped and smiled at me, a Junior Leaguer still with her simple black dress from Rich's Regency Shops and her pearls and her "little heels," and the throaty, slow "Old Atlanta" accent which she perfected early in her tenure in the house on Peachtree Road. Of all its occupants, she alone prevails there now. I knew she would go back to it from the cemetery, to a fire in the little sitting room and her endless cigarettes and afternoon sherries and bridge games and charities and the company of imperious old women.

Even before she opened her mouth, I knew she was going to say something so terrible that it would, forever after, divide time.

Oh, yes. We make our own monsters, but they inevitably have their revenge.

CHAPTER
ONE

LUCY CAME TO LIVE WITH US in the house on Peachtree Road when she was five and I was seven, and before that April day was over I learned two things that altered almost grotesquely the landscape and weather of my small life. I learned that not all women wept in the nights after the act of love.

And I learned that we were rich.

That those tidbits of information should literally change a world seems perhaps a bit strange now, when children of seven digest with equanimity the daily disclosure of the sexual peccadilloes of politicians and television evangelists and the felonious traffic in billions by arbitragers and governments. But the Buckhead and Atlanta of that day were infinitely smaller principalities than now, and my own cosmos within them was minuscule. I literally had nothing with which to compare my life, and so assumed, in the manner of cloistered only children, that everything and everybody else was as we were.

I knew that my mother cried at night after having intercourse with my father, because I had slept since my infancy in a small room that had been intended as the dressing room for my parents' bedroom, and I could hear clearly each muffled grunt and thrust of that mute and furious coupling, each accelerating squeal of bedsprings, each of my father's grudging, indrawn breaths. From my mother I heard nothing during the act, but each time, without fail, that he finished with a snort and began to snore, her weeping would start, and I would lie, muscles stiff and breath held with dread and unexamined fury, waiting for her to stop. I knew precisely how long she would cry, and when the weeping would cease on a deep, rattling sigh, and when the

17

traitorous springs would creak once more as she turned over into
sleep, and only then would I unknot my fists and let myself slide
into sleep, following her.

I cannot ever remember wondering what it was that they did
in the nights that occasioned the strange hoarse cries, and the
alien weeping—for at all other times my mother was one of the
most self-possessed women I have ever known. I knew what transpired in their bedroom from the time I could barely walk,
though I had no name for the act until Lucy came, and even
then only the shadowiest notion of its import. My mother never
closed the door between our rooms, and never allowed my father
to close it, and for a few weeks and months when I was about
two and had just learned to wriggle over the bars of my crib and
toddle to the threshold of their bedroom, I watched that darkling
coupling.

It must have frightened me to see the two great titans of my
existence grappling in murderous silence on the great canopied
tester bed, but I never ran into the room and never cried out,
and I do not know to this day whether they knew I was there.
How they could have avoided at some time or other raising their
heads to see my small, stone-struck figure silhouetted in the
sickly glow from my Mickey Mouse night-light I cannot imagine, but neither of them ever gave the smallest sign, and I would
hang there night after night, a small Oedipal ghost haunting in
despair a chamber where he was not acknowledged.

After a time I stopped going to the door to watch, and soon
was no longer afraid, but I never slept until they were done, and
I never lost the feeling of violation that the sounds gave me, or
the resulting bile-flood of guilty rage at them. Even then, something cool and infinitesimal deep within me knew that I was
being burdened and exploited as no child should be. Oddly, it
was never at my father that the jet of my little fury was directed,
but at my mother. He was a massive, tight, furiously simple, red
and white-blond man who vented his considerable tempers and
passions directly, whenever and wherever they happened to
erupt. As useless to feel rage at him as at a volcano, or a broken
water main.

No, it was my mother, the cool, slender, exquisite and infinitely aware vessel for his passions, at whom my anger steamed.
It seemed to me that no one so totally self-defined and perceived
and carefully calibrated as my mother should allow anything
done to her person that would cause weeping, and I was angry
at her both for the tears and for making me listen to them. But
since my parents were all there was, for practical purposes, to
my world, and since I loved my mother and feared my father
passionately, I neither admitted the anger nor shut the door. I

simply moved, for the first seven years of my life, in a dark and decaying stew of unacknowledged sexuality and anger, and neither cursed the darkness nor thought it out of the ordinary until Lucy Bondurant blew it away on a gust of her extraordinary laughter. On the surface, to the rest of the small society in which I moved, I must have appeared the most unremarkable and ordinary of small boys.

It was for the same reason that I did not know we were rich: There was nothing and no one who appeared different from us Bondurants in the entire sphere of my existence, and where there is no concept of poor, neither can there be one of rich. There were, of course, Shem and Martha Cater, who lived over the old stable-turned-garage behind the house and worked in the kitchen and pantry and drove the Chrysler and answered the door and sometimes served meals in the big dining room when people came to dinner, and there was Amos, who worked in the yard, and Lottie, who came in to cook, and Princess, who brought the hand laundry, fragrant, silky, and still warm, in a rush basket.

And there were the dark men and women who worked in the houses and gardens and drove the cars and served the dinners of the few other families in the big houses on and just off Peachtree Road to which I had ingress—as familiar to me as anyone else in my world, known to me by first names as were my few small friends. I knew that these dark people were not like us and did not live as we did, but I did not think of them as poor. I thought of them as Negroes. The one had nothing to do with the other. I liked them, many of them, as well as my own friends, and much better than the white adults, for they neither asked of nor gave to me anything; did not in any way remark me, except as a not disagreeable part of the furnishings of that beautiful and insular and ridiculous fiefdom in which they served.

I knew about poor in the abstract; poor was the starving children in, for some reason, Albania, whom my mother bade me consider whenever I did not eat my dinner. But I did not know where Albania was and neither, I don't think, did my parents, or at least my mother, for once, when I asked, over the cooling drumstick of the chicken that had only that morning flopped hysterically around in the backyard after Shem had hatcheted off its head, where Albania was, my father laughed his loud and mirthless laugh and jerked a stubby red finger at my mother and said, "Ask your mother. She thinks it's down south there just past Griffin. Got kinfolks there that she's never seen because her papa didn't think they were fit for her to know."

My mother, who had been born and raised the doted-upon, joyless and Christ-haunted only daughter of an unworldly and

comparatively wealthy man and his pale effigy of a wife in tiny
Griffin, Georgia, thirty miles safely to the southeast of Atlanta,
where the Redwine family's downtown slum real estate holdings
lay, smiled sunlessly at him.

"Your papa is being funny," she said. "Albania is in Europe
and they're poor because they're oppressed and conquered."

"Who oppressed them?" I asked.

"Soldiers. The army," my mother replied.

"But what army?" I persisted. Like all children of ordered
worlds, I was starved for drama, and this had the authentic ring
of it.

"Yes, Olivia, what army? Tell us," my father said, grinning
his angry wolf's grin.

"Tell us, tell us," I chimed, light-headed in relief and gladness
that the grin was not directed at me.

"It was . . . their own army," my mother said decisively. "It
was a civil war. Like our own poor South suffered, brother
against brother. The worst kind of war, the worst kind of suffering. Albania is as desperately poor as Atlanta and the South were
once. That chicken on your plate would feed a family of Albani-
ans for a week."

"Why don't we send it to Albania then?" I said, choking with
the appreciation of my own wit.

"Albania is not on your mother's list of charities," my father
said. "Don't have a ball or an auxiliary or a fashion show to their
name. Not on the Junior League's roster or the Driving Club's
calendar."

My mother rose from the table with that peculiar boneless,
amphibian grace of hers that always reminded me of a salaman-
der or a newt or something wet and flashing beneath the surface
of water, and left us sitting sheathed in the ice of her disapproval.

"I think both of you are coarse," she said, not turning her
head. She was not just talking. She meant it. "Coarse" was the
worst epithet in my mother's strictured vocabulary, and I spent
a great deal of my early childhood struggling against the vast
natural coarseness rampant in my nature.

I was, I remember, profoundly ashamed of my bowel movements and my frequent thin and reflexive vomitings and asth-
matic gaggings, because she would leave the room and summon
Martha Cater to attend to me in my disgusting state, and though
she never said as much, her sighs and silence were freighted with
the implicit blight of "coarse."

My father grinned at her departing back, but I did not. Flinty
comfort though she might have been to me, my mother was the
artery that connected me to life. My friends, some of them, like
Sarah and Ben Cameron around the corner and down Muscogee

Avenue, had parents different from mine, laughing young parents who sang and danced and spun them around and hugged them in public, but I merely thought those other parents a caprice of nature, or the luck of the draw, like blue eyes instead of brown ones, or freckles. It did not occur to me to aspire to them. Olivia Redwine Bondurant was all I knew personally of nurturing. I ate the chicken.

My father was right, though; we were not a family long on noblesse oblige. Perhaps our noblesse had been too recently acquired, even by Atlanta standards, to feel the need for oblige. It is an oversimplification, but a serviceable one, that in the Atlanta of that day there were basically two types of gentry: those involved in acquiring largesse and those involved in expending it. Some, like the families of Dorothy and Ben Cameron, Sarah and young Ben's parents, were the latter; their families had, for three generations, been deeply involved in the fortunes and lives of the city, and their sense of privilege as a vehicle for service ran deep and strong. The Bondurants were the former.

I could not articulate it then, of course, but our house, beautiful and graceful though it was, was a house of delicate skewedness and aberration. Too many reined passions thrummed there, too many unfed hungers, too many unvoiced fears and unmet needs and marrow-deep repressions. My parents were not clever or active or happy people; did not fit foursquare into the world they had achieved with Redwine money and land and Bondurant guile and acumen. Neither was a native Atlantan, and though there were, in their set, relatively few of those, still, neither Olivia nor Sheppard Bondurant ever felt quite comfortable in the huge house that had been their entree. They did not wear their mantles of aristocracy, such as they were, naturally and lightly, for they were purchased garments and not heirloom ones, and my mother, at least, never forgot that. She, who might have reigned supremely and effortlessly back in tiny Griffin, had painstakingly scaled the pinnacle of the uppity city to the north, and she clung there in faultlessly concealed terror which had, early on, turned her rigid.

My father, who had been as a boy sublimely content and at home in the rough, hard-drinking, hunting and fishing masculine society that formed Fayetteville, Georgia's, small upper crust, was perpetually clumping and red-wristed and truculent in the urban clubs and drawing and dining rooms, which he perceived as effete. She came to think that she had married beneath her and that the vitality and exuberance that had first won her had become the barnacles that weighted her heart and slowed her trajectory through the society of Atlanta. He came to feel that the delicacy and distance and sheen of family substance that had so charmed him had been forged into the weapons with which she cut him off from his kind and kept him isolated at politely hostile club dances and bridge evenings and benefit dinners. She had brought a considerable family fortune to their marriage as a dowry, and with part of it he had bought the house on Peachtree Road and the rural property to the west and north of the city which, coupled with the wretched downtown holdings her family had bequeathed to her, had increased that fortune nearly tenfold. She thought he had used her shamelessly, and he thought she scorned and failed to appreciate him. Both were right on all counts.

That no one else who knew them perceived them as the misfits they secretly felt themselves to be—for no one around them was introspective or sensitive enough to do so—did not occur to them, and would not have mattered if it had. Their distortions were interior ones, and they lived inwardly to those crooked measures. It was inevitable that from the beginning, I would be what my mother called Sensitive (always seeming to speak the word in capital letters) and my father called sissy.

"You're going to make a goddamned preacher of him, Olivia," he would bellow, when he found me totally immersed in reading my way through the Bible, not comprehending that it was the glorious, plum-tasting language of King James and not the precepts contained within that drew me to the Good Book. I did know this, faintly, but could not, in the presence of all that red-faced congestion, explain it, and he would stump away into his study, muttering over his shoulder to my mother: "Always coughing and squinting and fumbling when he tries to play football. Puking up his guts when he tries to put a worm on a hook. Howling like a hound when I put him on a horse. Hell, he can't even keep up with little Sarah Cameron playing kick the goddamn can, and she's not knee-high to a grasshopper. He's never going to have any gumption if you let him keep his nose stuck in a book like that."

"He's Sensitive, that's what he is, Sheppard," my mother would say, brushing the lank comma of white-blond hair that was my father's legacy to me off my forehead, and exposing the hated glasses with the flesh-colored plastic rims. By the time I could read she had given up being disgusted at my bodily functions and had become passionately, breath-suckingly protective. "You wouldn't know about sensitivity, of course, but it's what makes my daddy the man he is, and I prize it in my son more than anything in the world."

I would stare elaborately and sensitively into the pages of the Bible, not looking at my father, but inside I was smirking openly.

I would have, then, bought my beautiful mother's approbation with any coin available to me.

It's funny about love: I can see now, looking back on the child that I was, that it was love that I needed more than anything in the world. Unconditional, eternal, immovable love. Of course it was. Her love mostly, but at that point, anybody's would have served. But I don't think I ever sought it. I waited instead for it to come and blow me across the face of the world. And it did not come until Lucy did. That was always her best gift to me, her primary health and her strength—that tornado of love and approval. And it was in the withholding of it that my mother both cursed me and stamped me forever hers. I still wonder if she could have possibly known what she was doing.

Both of my parents were right about me. I was both sensitive and a physical coward, being possessed, as many precocious only children are, of a soaring and vivid imagination that could illuminate in excruciating clarity the scope and detail of all the dangers the world was fraught with. I was also, like Lucy, that most vulnerable and creative of creatures, a total realist, and, I suppose, a pretty perceptive one. Those qualities enabled me to see all the perils of my world and know them for precisely what they were. It did not make me a comfortable child to be around, for adults or most of the other children I knew. Most children are one-celled and barbaric little sentimentalists, and can sense otherness and know it for the alien thing it is, even if they cannot comprehend it. This did not leave me friendless, but it left me essentially without peers, and the only two close friends I had at that time—Pres Hubbard, who was lame from a bout of infant polio and wore a clanking leg brace, and Charlie Gentry, who had childhood diabetes—were the only two among us who shared the sideline with me. Unlike me, they both had gumption aplenty, but could not exercise it. I was content that my handicap was in my spirit, as my father contended, as long as it excused me from the world of terrifying proper boys' activities he envisioned for me.

But still, I castigated myself bitterly and endlessly, if silently, for failing to like most of the things my companions did and for failing to please the great masculine elemental who towered and roared over my childhood like red Cronus over the embryo world. And dimly, dimly, I felt the lapping of a futile rage at my mother, who had so early doomed me to be Sensitive, and at my father, who would not, perhaps could not, rescue me from her. And hated and feared that rage, and felt the guilt of it festering in my soul like shrapnel. It was not, for a child, the most nurturing of worlds, even in its unabashed privilege.

But oh, the seductiveness, the symmetry, the immutability, the

sheer, heart-drugging beauty of that world! Especially in those
days before it became chic and accessible and throttled with traffic and roving schools of the upscale, pleasure-bent young, Buckhead was one of the most beautiful places on earth. Oh, not the
business district, such as it was; it was then, as it is now, a random, jury-rigged and jerry-built shamble of small shops and
businesses, banks and offices, loading docks and parking lots,
drugstores and cafés and service stations and a few banal brick
government edifices, webbed and festooned with electric and
telephone lines and wires and an eye-smiting array of signage.
No, I mean residential Buckhead, that cloistered, deep green rectangle of great old trees and winding streets and fine, not-so-old
houses set far back on emerald velvet lawns, carved out of deep
hardwood forests, cushioned and insulated from the sweat,
smells and cacophony of the city proper, to the south, by layers
of money. No one has ever been quite sure what the official
boundaries of Buckhead are, but for many years my own personal Buckhead was that four-odd square miles bounded on the
south by Peachtree Creek, the north by West Paces Ferry Road,
the west by Northside Drive, and the east by Peachtree Road.

Peachtree Road . . . It is to me a name with far more scope
and resonance to it than its dozen or so meandering miles of asphalt should rightly command. The restless, well-heeled floods
of people who come to Atlanta each year now to meet and con-
vene and visit and do business think they are seeing Atlanta
when they see Peachtree Street, but they are not. Visitors visit
on Peachtree Street. Atlanta lives—or did—on and just off
Peachtree Road. As little as I love the city now, I still, perversely
and despite what it has become, love Peachtree Road. To me it
encompasses and personifies all that is particular and powerful
about the city, as well as all that is abstract and illusory and
beautiful. Even its ugliness—and much of it is simply and profoundly ugly—seems to me to be rich, deeply textured and
unique to Atlanta. Admittedly I see it now through the scrim
of childhood, but I do not think it looks like anywhere else on
earth. The very name of it rings in my heart like a bell. And still,
to my eyes, the most beautiful and singular point on all of
Peachtree Road is the house at 2500, where I was born and have
lived for the entirety of my life.

These, then, were my worlds in that portentous spring that
Lucy came to us: the larger one of Buckhead proper and the
smaller of 2500 Peachtree Road. Worlds that had, despite the
dearth of real and sustained love, a kind of charm and promise
that I have never found again anywhere. And one of the sweetest
and most solemn promises was that they would never change.
I don't know why I thought that, but I always did in those earli-

est days. I think perhaps that the very contrast of banality and beauty in those two worlds served to give them heft and the authority of permanence.

So when the telegram came, in early April, from my aunt Willa Bondurant, saying that Uncle Jim had left them in New Orleans and she had no choice but to come to us and bring her children, it was a cataclysm of enormous proportions, not only to my mother and father but to me. Whatever my scant status with them, it had, so far, at least been that of only child. The thought of sharing my house and their attention engendered in me a rage so murderous that I could only deal with it as I had learned early to deal with all things that threatened. I shoved it completely out of my mind. By the morning after the telegram, the tattered little band of my unfortunate kin had never, for me, existed.

Even on the day of their arrival, even after my deep-sighing, eye-rolling mother had had Martha Cater make up the extra bedrooms and my stomping, red-faced father had dispatched Shem to the Greyhound bus station with the Chrysler, I was unruffled. I knew absolutely and to the core of me that no alien, white-trash aunt—my mother's overheard epithet—and cousins would appear in the round foyer of my domain out of the luminous green night. I could repeat word for word the message that would come soon by telephone or telegram: "So sorry but all your relatives have been killed in an accident and therefore can't come." I knew how the voice would sound saying the words, and what my words of wisdom and comfort would be to my father, whose younger brother's wife and children these were. I could only think of my uncle Jim as that, my father's brother, for I had never seen him, and had no sense that anywhere in the world did I have a tall, drowsy-eyed, blond young uncle who was the obverse, the fatal, radiant side, of my father, and whom in time I would grow to resemble almost uncannily. There was no photograph of James Clay Bondurant in our house, and few words about him ever passed my father's lips. My mother spoke of him once in a while, but not in words intended for my ears, and even though I only half heard them, I could hear in her voice when she spoke of him something that was not there at other times. It was only in this way, and almost subliminally, as is the way of children, that I knew that my uncle Jim had a kind of dark importance in that house that was all the more disturbing because it was unnamed.

When the doorbell rang, then, I pounded downstairs behind my mother in full expectation of opening it to the lugubrious face of the telegram messenger, and so the four figures who stood there with the twilight falling down over them were as shocking and aberrant to me as murderers or trolls. I could only stare at them, my heart banging so loudly in my ears that I could not even make out my mother's words of welcome, which were, in any case, crisp and short and soon ended; I could hear my father coming heavily down the stairs behind me. But the four did not move, and I could not speak. The moment seemed to spin out forever.

The first clear thought that struck me was that my aunt Willa assaulted the eye and nose and ear simultaneously, though not, to me, unpleasantly. She had hair so black it shone blue and purple in the light over the front door, and she wore garnet lipstick and nail polish "laid on with a trowel," as my mother said to someone over the telephone later that evening, in a low, only half-amused voice. She smelled powerfully of the acrid sweat of travel and nervousness, though this was masked with a friendly, evocative scent that I always associated with Wender & Roberts Drugstore at Christmastime.

"Evening in Paris, a ton of it," my mother further instructed her phone friend.

My aunt Willa's face was blanched and chalky with powder and fatigue, and there were tiny, clumped beads of blackness at the ends of her long eyelashes. Her eyes were the pure, impossible blue that coal fire makes when it has burned itself almost out. She wore a print rayon dress with a peplum that accentuated her willow-wand waist and the rich swell of her hips and breasts, and her long, slender legs were bare and dirty. She tottered lamely on towering sling-back heels, and her toenails were the same dried-blood red of her lips and fingernails. I found her powerfully, magically glamorous, there in that dim foyer with its dim old Oriental rugs and dim, stained stucco walls and dim, ornate old gilt-framed paintings of my Redwine ancestors. Dim, dim . . . Suddenly it seemed to me that, until these four maniacally unknown people had walked in out of the warm April night to light my foyer into rawness and vitality, my whole life had been dim.

I saw next that my aunt held a cherubic little blond boy of less than a year in the crook of one arm, and by the other hand held an equally angelic little girl of, perhaps, three, solemn and sweating and overdressed in a fuchsia velvet coat, bonnet and leggings. Behind her, with one hand on the small girl's shoulder, a girl taller than I, but obviously younger, stood, staring directly at me with her mother's extraordinary blue eyes, and something looking out of them flew into and through my own and straight into my heart with a directness and force that felt as though I had swallowed a fire-tipped arrow. I blinked and gulped soundlessly, like a fish drowning in air, and then, surprising myself profoundly, grinned.

The girl grinned back. Her hair was the pure, clear dark of cold winter creek water over fallen leaves, and it flew loosely around her narrow head like corn silk. Her lashes were sooty cobwebs on her pink-flushed cheeks, and she was tall and willowy like her mother, with long limbs and small hands and feet and a whippet waist. She was standing still, but she looked as if she had been in motion all over and had just settled to earth. She wore corduroy overalls and dirty saddle shoes.

Of all the people assembled in the hall, she was the first to speak.

"Something stinks," she said in a voice that was slow and rich, like music, like dark honey.

"Lucy!" my aunt Willa said, scandalized. She had a flat, nasal drawl. My parents looked at each other, and then at the girl.

"Sure does," I said back, joy caroling inexplicably in my veins. "It's Martha in the kitchen. She's cooking lamb for our dinner. Ugh!"

"Smells like she's cooking dog," Lucy Bondurant said, and laughed, a dark silk banner of a laugh, and I laughed, and even when the adults had made us both apologize, and sent us upstairs to the screened porch to "calm down until you can act like a lady and a gentleman," we continued to laugh. It was the first real laughter I could remember in the house on Peachtree Road. It was the first, last and longest thing I had and kept of Lucy: her laugh.

When we had stopped laughing, she said, "Are you all the children there are?"

"Yes," I said, somehow ashamed of it.

"I guess she must not have liked it when your daddy got on her then," Lucy said matter-of-factly.

"What do you mean?" My skin actually prickled with the portent of something coming.

"Well, my mama used to laugh and holler when Daddy got on her, and there's three of us. There's just one of you, so I guess your mama didn't like it and quit doing it, or there'd be more of you."

"She didn't quit," I said. It was suddenly very important to tell Lucy about the nights in the little dressing room when my mother wept. Shame fled and indignation flooded in. "He gets on her all the time, but she doesn't laugh. She cries. She cries almost every night. I know because I sleep right in their room."

She looked at me in blue puzzlement.

"What for?" she said. "Why don't you have a room of your own, as rich as y'all are?"

"Rich?" I said, stupidly.

"Sure. Why do you think we came all the way down here? Now we're gon' be rich, too."

It was too much, too much of suddenness and strangeness and revelation, too much of promise. My stomach heaved and flopped, and I ran for the bathroom and was sick, and Martha put me straight to bed, so that whatever else transpired that evening, I missed it, and I was still queasy and spinning when my mother came up to telephone her friends and tell them about the invasion of the infidels. It was a long time, late, before I slept.

But I did sleep, finally; slept that night in a different country, one where we were rich and therefore different from other people, and in which women laughed and shouted aloud their pleasure during the act of love.

A country where, now, Lucy was, and therefore all things might be possible.

I slept in a safe child's sudden and simple, lightless peace, and when I awoke in the morning it was to joy.

I have said that I do not go out anymore, but that is not precisely true. I do go out, almost every night. After the last of the light has gone and the streetlights come on, no matter what time and what season it happens to be, I put on my Nikes and I slip out of the summerhouse into the welcoming darkness and I run through Buckhead. I run for miles, some evenings as many as fifteen or twenty, some evenings just four or five. I am never sure when I set out which of my many routes I will take; my feet seem to make that decision for me when they touch the pavement of the sidewalk along Peachtree Road. But I always cover the same territory. It is the country of that long-ago Buckhead in which, as the Book of Common Prayer says, I lived, moved and had my being. Oh, yes, I run, and I suppose many people must see me, a tall, slight man whose thinning hair in the streetlights might be blond or might be silver; not young, but with the long-loping resilience of the runner. It doesn't bother me that I am visible to them; it is not from their seeing of me that I hide during the daylight, but from the seeing of them. I run; I run through a landscape that existed forty-odd years ago. I run for my life.

Pounding silently and steadily through a swelling spring night, or a star-chipped black winter one, I can tick the street and proper names off like rosary beads in the hands of a devout old Catholic, without thinking, without questioning the sense or import of them. The names are my catechism. Whatever is raw and ragged and new and intrusive I don't see; I am running, as I said, for my life, but it is the life that I had then.

Right and down Muscogee, past the Camerons' house, Merrivale House, they called it, after Dorothy's family seat in Dorsetshire: 17 Muscogee Avenue. It was built in 1921 by Neel Reid, a classical architect in whom Atlanta has always set great store, whose years abroad studded Northwest Atlanta's wooded hills and ridges with Renaissance, American Georgian, Federal, Greek Revival, Baroque and Italianate estates of uncommon style and substance. These suburban villas, as they were termed, were designed to be summer homes in some cases, and highly visible showcases for their owners' soaring positions in others. At the time most were built, in the late teens and twenties and on into the thirties, entertaining and gardening were two of Old Atlanta's overweening passions, and formal reception and dining rooms and extensive, formally landscaped grounds were *de rigueur*. Most of the houses had, and many still have, vast acreages of gardens, all flowing together, mile after mile, so that whole streets seem in the spring to be one great lapping surge of color.

It is that great amplitude of space, and the random, puckish cant of the wooded hills, and the sheer scope of the surf of azaleas and dogwood and flowering trees that make the spring here a neck-prickling and breath-stopping time. Traffic along the narrow old streets in April is near critical mass, and many a grand dowager curses now the splendor she and her yardman labored so mightily to achieve when both were young. I remember vividly the gardeners and yardmen of all these old estates. Most of the children in my crowd took their first steps tottering after the impassive black yardmen and their wonderful arrays of tools and treasures.

I do not, on these night runs, see the fleets of minivans and the Davey Tree trucks that keep the gardens up now. If they are kept up at all. Many of the old houses are falling to the glittering, trashy condominium developments that are littering Buckhead. Others are going like hotcakes to the Arabs and the tackpots, who are the only ones who can afford to keep them up. They are occupied now, many of them, by elderly widows, and the cost of heating and cooling and maintaining them is just too prohibitive, the money being offered just too much. In 1907, when the first trolley line from downtown to Buckhead was laid down, you could buy land on West Paces Ferry Road for ninety dollars an acre. Now it's going, some of it, for nearly two million. Old Dorothy Cameron, in the last years before she moved from the Muscogee Avenue house, paid ten thousand annually for taxes alone, and by that time she and Ben were far from wealthy. It was heart and breeding they had in the end, not money.

Ironic, that it was money that built Buckhead, and it is money that is killing it.

But I do not see the Sotheby and Harry Norman and Buckhead Brokers signs, the dark windows, the encroaching weeds where once lawns the color and texture of good billiard tables rolled away. I see, instead, Sarah and Ben and me, in the back garden of 17 Muscogee, running through the dazzling shower from the hose held by Leroy Pickens, the Camerons' driver, as he washes the identical black Lincoln limousines that Ben Cameron kept. The fine spray rainbows off fenders and tall, mullioned windows and our sleek, tanned hides, tasting warm and metallic and somehow like the red clay of North Georgia, and butterflies dance in the little picking garden, and a hummingbird strafes the roses beyond, just coming into bloom in the formal garden where the gazebo sits, and a fat black crow struts along the high stone wall that snakes around the front courtyard and the boxwood parterre by the sun porch.

"This is the way my daddy takes a bath," Ben says, leaping high into the shattered rainbow of the water and contorting himself extraordinarily, so that, for a moment, pinned at the apex of the leap against the melting blue of June, he looks fantastically like some slender, small Cossack dancer, or a creature entirely formed of air and dazzle, like Ariel.

"No, like this," small Sarah chimes, and throws herself high against the blue, curved into a beautiful, brown, unconscious arc like an otter entering water. In that moment Sarah foreshadows the lithe and lovely water creature she will become.

I collapse in laughter in the spray, because the thought of anyone's parents taking baths at all, even Dorothy and Ben Cameron, Senior, whom I adore, is beyond conception.

"How does your daddy take a bath, Shep?" Ben Cameron says. "I bet he wallows and snorts like a warthog!"

And he mimes that action expertly, so that we see as clearly as if we stood before it the grunting, furious beast, and the stinking, slimy mud, and the vast African plain stretching away. Ben is not being cruel; the analogy of my tight, massive, red father in the mudhole is uncannily apt. And in fact, Ben and Sarah have actually seen a warthog in a mudhole, on a trip to Africa with their parents the preceding spring.

But the laughter drains out of me. I think about it, and then I say, "I don't think he takes baths." For the thought of my father wet and naked is light-years beyond my mightiest imagining. I shrink even from the attempt.

"Then he sure must stink," Ben crows, and collapses in helpless glee.

Sarah stops her capering and glares at him, her great brown eyes thunderous.

"Shep's right," she says. "You can just stop laughing, Ben Cameron, because I happen to know that Mama and Daddy

don't really take baths, either." She turns her eyes to me, and
I feel the healing and benediction that flow from them.

"We were just making it up, Shep," she says. "My mama and
daddy never, never, never, *never* take baths, *ever.*"

It is an enormous, towering, glorious lie. We laugh, and Leroy
Pickens laughs, and water chuckles, and their Scottie, Yappie,
does just that, and I run on past this now-dark house that I have
always thought, of all the estates in Buckhead, the most romantic.

Left on Rivers Road, past the Slatons' white wooden Federal.
I see Alfreda, small and darting and avian in many crinolines,
getting into Tom Goodwin's 1935 Chevy, which is bereft of fenders and top and muffler, to go to a Phi Chi dance. Tiny Freddie,
as pretty as she will ever be, her hand on Tom's arm tight with
promissory possessiveness.

I am with Lucy in the backseat of the Chevy—for it is in the
days before the advent of Red Chastain—and Freddie's sharp
little eyes take in the small forest of orchids on Lucy's dress and
wrist and in her hair. They are not mine; they have been sent
by the dates she will have for the dance and the breakfast after
that, and by her general admirers. It is a barbaric custom, but
an immutable one. Freddie wears only Tom's small purple
bloom. His father is not in the same financial league as most of
ours, and groves of opulent white orchids are forever beyond
Tom. Freddie's face goes tight and hard.

"Goodness, Lucy, you look like a fruit salad," she says
sweetly, the acid of have-not thin and virulent in her voice. Poor
Freddie, she is forever being propelled by her great, formless
wanting into competitions where she is outclassed and out-
matched.

"I guess I do," Lucy says in her lazy, smoky drawl. "And you,
sweetie, look like an empty salad plate."

It is a clear victory. Freddie is silent in her pain and rage for
the rest of the drive to Brookhaven Country Club. The back of
Tom's neck is dull red, and I glare sternly at Lucy. I am in my
Saint Shep the Defender mode, and feminine pain, even Freddie's, is anathema to me. She glares back and then grins.

"Tough titty," she whispers. And reluctantly, I grin back.

I run right onto Peachtree Battle Avenue, divided by its
wooded park. It is, I think, spring: April, with the new leaves
point d'esprit—tender and lacy—and the white stars of the dogwood incandescent in the streetlight. Streetlights through new
green . . . they hang over my childhood and pack my heart tight,
the small, perfect icons of the urban child. On down past Wood-
ward Way, and up Dellwood to the right, past the huge, Ad-
amesque pile where Carter Rawson's family lived. He and Little

Lady still live there; the house is awash with light now as it must
have been then, though I did not, in those years, know Carter.
Indeed, I never went into the house at all until the engagement
party that Carter's parents gave for him and Little Lady, and
so what I see now is the long, exquisitely proportioned formal
boxwood garden behind the house, leading down a central allée
to the domed Ionic gazebo, where Little Lady stands beside Carter framed in Cape jessamine and columns, glowing like a Dresden shepherdess.

"Hello, Mrs. Draper," Little Lady says sweetly to a formidable, tanklike matron, fluttering her famous feathery, gold-tipped
lashes. "Hello, Mrs. Dorsey. You're mighty sweet to come share
this happy day with Carter and me. We hope you'll be our very
first visitors when we get back from Sea Island. We just *love* the
beautiful toast rack; I know it's a family piece, isn't it?"

And two old ladies, finally, smile, and Little Lady is launched
like a rocket into the ionosphere of Atlanta society.

"Shit," says Lucy, who is behind me on Red Chastain's arm,
under her breath. "What's wrong with this picture? I know.
There's no background music. Ought to have an orchestra squat-
ting behind the bushes over there. Playing 'Fascination.' "

Right on West Wesley and left on Habersham, and a long lope
up to Tom Goodwin's much smaller house on the right, a neat
brick and frame that was built not by Neel Reid or Philip Shutze
or anyone else likely to be known in Atlanta, but by a contractor
whose firm was a client of Tom's father, the owner of the city's
first advertising agency. Tom's family has some money, but not
enough, and some background, but not enough, and the house
is not nearly grand enough to keep the Goodwins securely in the
pantheon in which they teeter. But the location is beyond reproach, and that Habersham Road address and the prospects of
one day commanding it will eventually win for Tom the birdlike
little hand of Freddie Slaton. Better, I guess, that his father had
gone on and bought an affordable bungalow safely across
Peachtree Road in Garden Hills, and so beyond the pale.

Right onto the major artery that is West Paces Ferry Road.
It runs out to the river, where Hardy Pace did, indeed, operate
a ferry, and has now become one of the Northside's most lamen-
tably snarled traffic arteries from west to east. But in the time-
stopped nights in which I run, all that can be seen in the darkling
woods are the lights of the few big houses on either side. Where
the new governor's mansion—Geek Revival, it is not so fondly
known as in some circles—sits now, these thirty years later, there
is in my eyes only forest. The great pile of stone just down from
it is still the Grant family home, and not the Cherokee Town
Club, that unsuccessful pretender to the Driving Club's throne.

Woods, and the smell of honeysuckle and heartbreak, and warm
tar in cooling night air, and late-mown grass . . . and ahead, the
scattered lights and occasional sibilant, swishing traffic sounds
of Buckhead proper.

Gaining the familiar intersection of Peachtree, West Paces
Ferry, and Roswell roads is like coming out of black, raging
Midgard into the eternal radiant whiteness of Valhalla. It has
always been so to me. It is all there in that one shabby 1950s
crossroads, life and succor and promise and a kind of secular
immortality. What power those few dim, perfunctory, yellow
and pink and blue neon lights have for the myriad ghosts who
flutter like moths around Buckhead! Jim Dickey wrote about it
in "Looking for the Buckhead Boys"; that poem took the top
of my head off when I first read it, and I tried to find Jim to call
him and tell him what it meant to me, but he was out of the state
and the South, his sister said, and probably wouldn't be back
anytime soon. Jim knew what it took to survive Buckhead: a kind
of distance not measured in miles.

He wrote:

> First in the heart
> Of my blind spot are
> The Buckhead Boys. If I can find them, even one,
> I'm home. And if I can find him   catch him in or around
> Buckhead, I'll never die; it's likely my youth will walk
> Inside me like a king.

Yes! And I quicken my steps and run into Buckhead. On my
right, Wender & Roberts Drugstore, and Lane's, and just across
the street in the arrow tip formed by the confluence of Peachtree
and Roswell, Jacob's Drugs and Madder's Service Station and
above it all the great moon of the Coca-Cola sign. Just past Roswell,
the Buckhead Theatre, with the balcony upstairs for the
Negroes lucky enough to have the nights off from the big houses
all around. I don't think, excepting servants, there was another
black head in North Atlanta in those days. I can see us all, a
flock of us, jostling and crowing and knuckling each other on
the biceps, walking from Wender & Roberts across the street to
the midnight movie. Just up East Paces Ferry there was the taxi
stand where even the smallest of us could reach far up to the
counter with a penny and receive, in exchange, one cigarette.
And Burt's Bottle Shop, where a lank, depressed bear languished
in a cage out in the weedy, cinder-block-littered back.

Across the street where the monolithic and hideous Buckhead
Plaza is going up now (unseen, unseen!) was a miniature-auto
racetrack, on whose grassy infield Caroline Gentry, Charlie's lit-

tle sister, used to tether her pony and cart after driving it in from
the Gentrys' sprawling, stained stucco on West Andrews. From
there she'd cross the street to Wender & Roberts and meet, illicitly, Boo Cutler and have a fountain cherry Coke and a package
of Tom's potato chips, and they'd go to the afternoon show at
the Buckhead Theatre and neck. Nobody, not Mr. and Mrs.
Gentry, not Caroline's Sunday school teacher, not her teachers
at North Fulton High, not Charlie himself, could break that
match up.

Boo Cutler. With the drooping-lidded blue eyes and the
spoiled, corrupted baby's face and the bubblegum-pink underlip
and butter-yellow crew cut and the fastest '48 Mercury in the
South. Boo of the legends and the homeroom whispers: That he
ran shine down from Hall County to South Georgia on weekends, and had been shot at many times by police and agents, but
never hit. That he had laid more than fifty women by the time
he was old enough to drive, and one of them taught at North
Fulton. That he had a shotgun in the trunk of the Mercury with
notches in it that represented the number of Negroes killed on
back country roads in wire-grass South Georgia. That he had
done it with a cow.

It was the literal truth, I think, that he ran shine; at any rate,
I remember one night when I was fifteen and he was sixteen the
word went out that Boo was coming through Buckhead from
up in Hall at precisely midnight with a load, and that he had
vowed to be going a hundred and twenty when he did it, and
that he didn't care what cops were waiting for him, the Merc
could take them all. It was in the late fall, I remember, on a Friday night after a home football game, and we all told our parents
we were going to the show, and we went and stood out of sight
around the corner on East Paces Ferry and Peachtree in the silent cold, waiting for him. There was, as usual for that time of
night, virtually no traffic and few lights except for the marquee
farther up at the movie house, and the wind was high and prowling, abroad in the sky, and the silence rang with our efforts to
hear his engine. At first, when we did, it was so high and keening
that we just thought the wind had intensified. And then Snake
Cheatham said, "It's him. That's him."

And we came out of the lee into the full stream of the wind,
eyes tearing, and we heard and saw Boo Cutler coming like a
devil out of Hell down the empty middle of Peachtree Road, the
few sickly streetlights catching the flying Mercury and flinging
it along, its engine screaming full-throated and terrible and wonderful.

We did not speak. He was past us and gone down Peachtree
Road before we could comprehend the splendor and speed of

him, the Merc riding so low that the exhaust bit great fountains of sparks out of the pavement, and before we could even turn our heads to test the new sound, a DeKalb County black-and-white flashed past impossibly far behind him, its siren sounding thin and mewling in contrast to the Mercury's Valkyrie cry. Both were gone into the silence in an eye-blink, and we did not speak for a moment.

"Jesus Christ, he must have been doing a hundred and forty," Tom said weakly.

"I just creamed my jeans," Charlie said reverently.

I remember that I cried, silently in the sheltering dark, and was ashamed of it, but not so ashamed that the memory of that perfect moment does not still have the power, all these years later, to bring tears of joy and thankfulness to my eyes. It was, in its fullness, as round and whole as an egg.

Boo Cutler, Charlie . . .

Buckhead is called that because a man named Hardy Ivy mounted, in 1838, the head of a buck on a tree over his tavern and crossroads store, and the name stuck among the settlers who met there. The tree on which the grisly trophy hung still stands in the parking lot of a liquor store. Hardy paid $605 for the land that makes up the core of Buckhead, 202 acres where the race-track sat, and then Sears, and where now Buckhead Plaza is going up. We always heard that there was gold buried in a box under that earth, put there by an old man and his slave during the siege of the city to the south, "out yonder so the damn Yankees won't get it."

It was an auspicious omen. Buckhead has always been known, proudly, as the wealthiest unincorporated suburb in America, whether or not the appellation was true. It remained unincorporated only because a stubborn little town also named Buckhead, in Morgan County, refused to surrender its charter and let Buckhead have the name officially, else it would have, early on, been a town proper. It has always considered itself apart both in spirit and in fact from the pushy giant directly to the south, and fought annexation tooth and nail. I remember that when I was ten, the community trounced one attempt and staged a mock funeral, featuring three caskets labeled Mayor Hartsfield, the Atlanta *Journal* and the Atlanta *Constitution,* and bore them proudly down the middle of Peachtree Road to the strains of *Finlandia* played falteringly by the North Fulton High marching band. It wasn't until 1950 that the city got us, and it remains to many Buckheaders still alive a catastrophe of only slightly less magnitude than the one wrought by General Sherman.

Well. I run out of the beneficence of central Buckhead, then, and back into the dark, pounding south on Peachtree Road. In

that earlier country, a dying straggle of stores and businesses
stood on either side, and directly beyond them on my left, the
subdivision of Garden Hills: firmly middle-class, agreeable and
substantial, but another world entirely from the kingdom on the
other side of Peachtree Road. It was not until I began high
school at North Fulton High, off to my left down Delmont, that
I came to know anybody who lived in Garden Hills, and though
we children were not, that I remember, snobs in particular—at
least not about where people lived—it was as if, in my early
childhood, Peachtree Road was as impenetrable and decisive a
dividing line as Hadrian's Wall. Later on, I got to know and like
many of my schoolmates who lived Over the Line, and one,
A. J. Kemp, became, after Charlie Gentry, perhaps my best
friend. But in that first country of childhood, none of us
crossed—or wished to—the Rubicon.

On down Peachtree Road I run, past North Fulton High and
Garden Hills Elementary, both out of sight on my left; past, on
my right, Saint Philip's Church, where we went in perfunctory
piety each Sunday when it was still a small parish church; past
Second Ponce de Leon (Baptist and just a bit below the salt) and
the Cathedral of Christ the King (Catholic and resoundingly so);
past the last commercial lights and down into the dark of, now,
only sleeping houses. Big houses in a line on my right, like the
ones on the cloistered streets behind them; houses that could and
did shelter princelings and sit out, for an incredible number of
years, the siege of the city to the south. Mostly mellow, rosy
brick, these few Peachtree Road houses were, two- and three-
storied and black- or green-trimmed, some with columns and
some with Adam fanlights and fine Georgian facades. Safe, sleeping there in the dark. Safe and dignified and beautiful.

And the last before you reached Muscogee Avenue and the
safest and most dignified and, to me, always the most
beautiful . . . my own: 2500 Peachtree Road.

Looking back, it might seem that, in light of my hungry and
strictured childhood in that house, my passion for it borders on
self-destructiveness. The sane thing to do, for anyone with the
slightest bent for survival, would have been to draw in his head
and deny in spirit the walls that starved and imprisoned him
until the earliest possible opportunity for escape presented itself,
and then to leave them behind with no regrets and a singing
heart. But those stout, sheltering brick walls were never oppressive to me in themselves; indeed, they were sanctuary and solace
whenever my eye or mind fell upon them. And though I did leave
them at an early juncture, it was with—for the house, at least—
an almost physical stab of sorrow. And when I came back, even
though the return was not initially of my own choosing, my heart

gave the same small, glad wing-waggle that it always did when I rounded the long curve past Peachtree Battle going north and saw again those soft-rose bricks and the sweetly hipped roof.

It always seemed to me in that house of infinitely lovely proportion and abundance of clear light that, no matter what miasma of disharmony prevailed at the moment, anything so beautiful could not be in and of itself hurtful, but was merely sleeping under some spell soon to be broken, and when it waked, the happiness that would come flooding in would be mythic in its scope, out of my small imagining entirely. I think the reason I was never really unhappy there is that I waited with such absolute conviction for joy. What child dares see his primal danger plain? Even now, when whatever future I might have imagined for it is past, the house at 2500 Peachtree Road still smites my eyes with its beauty whenever I look at it. I do, several times each day, from the summerhouse.

"Lordee, but it's big, ain't it?" I remember Lucy saying on the first full day she spent in the house. We were standing on the half-moon front drive, looking up at it. Her blue eyes had a dazzle in them not entirely from the sun.

"Do y'all charge admission for folks to come look at it?"

"Why would we do that?" I asked, honestly puzzled.

"Mama says people do in New Orleans."

"Well, nobody does here," I said, defensively.

"I bet you could make a pot if you did," Lucy said. "I'm gon' ask Aunt Olivia if I can do that. I bet lots of folks would pay to come see this house."

"Don't do that," I said quickly, knowing instinctively that my mother would be outraged by the idea. "If you want some money I'll give you some. How much do you need?"

"A nickel," she said promptly.

"Wouldn't you rather have a dime? I've got one."

"No, silly," she snorted. "Nickel's twice as big as a dime."

I gave her the nickel.

The house was designed in 1917, not by Need Reid but by a young architectural student cousin of its first owner, a physician who made one of the early fortunes investing in Coca-Cola bottling equipment, as did so many of the men who built the first of the great Buckhead houses. Indeed, the intersection of West Paces Ferry and Roswell roads is still called Coca-Cola Corners. The young architect died a year after the house was finished, during the obligatory year's study in Florence after graduating from Georgia Tech, attempting to swim the Arno after staying up all night drinking and reading Lord Byron. My mother told me the story when I was barely three; it is one of the very first memories I have: sitting in her lap in a rocking chair in front of the coal fire in her and my father's big upstairs bedroom, rocking back and forth, back and forth as the red firelight leaped over her hands and the dark, seal-sleek curtain of hair that fell over her face and mine together.

"Tragic," she said, rocking, rocking. "Tragic, to die so young and so gifted, so far away from home. You must promise me never to drink, Sheppie, and never to leave your mama. Do you promise me that?"

I suppose I remember it so vividly because it was such a rarity in my small life; she almost never rocked me. In fact, I can't remember another time. Old Martha Cater did, and I am told that my unremembered grandmother Adelaide Bondurant did, but I think I was far too apt to spit up in those first years for my mother's sensitive stomach. I can't imagine why she was doing it that one time; perhaps I was sick with some small childhood affliction that did not involve bodily secretions. At any rate, I promised her then that I would never drink and never leave her. I would have promised her, in that moment of perfect, firelit bliss, to enter a Trappist monastery, if she had asked it of me.

I never forgot the drowned young architect of my house. I did not think his fate tragic, but romantic and somehow unspeakably noble. Muzzily in my mind for years whenever I thought about the house was the thought, "Someone died for this house." That dank and ignoble death in Florence gave it a kind of promissory import, as though set apart from its birth for some special fate.

It is a spare, eloquent American Georgian house of soft rose brick, hip-roofed and stone-quoined, with a row of four gables showcasing the small third-floor Palladian windows, and twin chimneys at each end. The front door is an austere and lovely Federal, with fanlight and sidelights beneath a richly detailed portico supported by thin Ionic columns. A semicircular drive describes a half-moon in front, slicing through a small rectangle of lawn, and a black wrought-iron fence sets it off from the sidewalk along Peachtree Road. Most of its three acres lies behind it, where the long formal garden and lily pool and summerhouse are carved out of a hardwood forest which stretches over to meet the backyards of the houses on Rivers Road. Once behind the house, you would never know, even now, that the traffic of a city of nearly three million pours past virtually at the front door.

Of course, when my father bought the house, in 1930, Peachtree Road was very nearly country, and the traffic was minimal. That was one reason he chose it. Newly come to Atlanta from tiny, rural Fayetteville to the southeast, he was resigned to the fact that his fortune and his future lay in the city, but he was damned if he would live among its humors and noises and hauteur. As for my mother, only the knowledge that Buck-

head was the city's smartest new address lured her out into the
wilds of its northern suburbs. She was one small-town girl who
would have lived in the middle of Five Points downtown if she
could have. But when my father brought her to see the house
and told her that on her left was one of the Coca-Cola Candler
daughters and just behind her on Muscogee a former governor,
she saw the wisdom of it. Besides, the price the doctor's newly
widowed wife was asking was low, and my mother, though a
banal woman, was not a stupid one. And the house was bought,
after all, with her money.

"It's an investment in your future, Sheppie," I can remember
her saying many times when I was small. And it has indeed been
that, if not in the way she envisioned. She meant, I know, for
me to marry and raise an exemplary Buckhead family in it after
she herself had enjoyed the full fruits of its irreproachable address and proximity. She never envisioned it to shelter my self-
imposed exile from the world.

Inside, it was almost classically Georgian: A round, domed,
rotunda-like entrance hall with niches for flowers or statuary
gave on the left onto a vast living room, with a formal columned
porch beyond that, and on the right onto a dining room with
the pantry and service porch behind it and the kitchen beyond
it on the right. Behind the entrance hall lay a soaring two-story
stair hall with a beautiful curved Adam stair ascending five
flights and six landing levels. When I was small, I used to picture
Lucy in her wedding white coming down that stair to meet me
in the rotunda of the entrance hall, and indeed I did see her in
white, years later, descending it, but it was not to her wedding
that she came. That was left to Little Lady, and I have to think
that my aunt Willa began planning it when she first stepped into
the house out of that spring night in 1941.

Behind the stair hall was the octagonal paneled library, which
my father used largely as his study, and though it was a beautiful
and air-washed room, lambent with sunlight, as were all the
downstairs rooms, from the floor-to-ceiling Palladian windows,
I never liked it, and was never allowed to spend much time there.
We sat there for an hour or so on winter evenings, all of us, while
my father and mother and Aunt Willa sipped whiskeys or sherry
before dinner and we children, scrubbed and combed, played the
Victrola or listened to the big Capehart with the volume turned
down. But mostly the family sat, when we were together, in the
small morning room behind the living room or, during the long,
warm springs and summers and autumns, on the comfortable,
slightly shabby lattice-screened porch that ran off to the right
of the library.

Upstairs, to the left of the stair hall, were my parents' bedroom

and bath with a seldom-used sleeping porch off them and the
little dressing room where I slept my furious, captive sleep. To
the right were the two bedrooms that became Aunt Willa's and
Little Lady's, and the small maids' room in which little Jamie
Bondurant slept so briefly. Behind the stair hall, over the library,
was a screened porch where Lucy and I sometimes played on
warm days, before we appropriated the summerhouse.

On the third floor, up a narrow stair, was the low-ceilinged,
musty warren of rooms where the servants refused to stay, which
became Lucy's and my childhood retreat. They were meanly lit
and airless in the extreme, suffocating in the summertime, but
to us they were a refuge to be guarded fiercely, and we shared
them in a kind of bone-and-skin-deep accord, the only secure
burrows we had ever known, until we grew too old for such proximity. Even then, when the wisdom of our separation was apparent even to me, I mourned the loss of those cell-like nests under
the roof, and Lucy wept inconsolably for days.

"What did they think we were going to do that was so bad?"
she stormed to me, in my new fastness out in the summerhouse,
after the incident that resulted in our separation.

"Well, you know," I said, reddening.

"Oh, shoot, that's silly. I don't want to, and you wouldn't even
know what it was if I hadn't told you. I don't even think you've
got your doohickey yet, have you?"

"Go on, now, Lucy, I hear your mama calling you. I've got
stuff I need to do," I said, face flaming.

"Well, even if you did have one, which I don't believe you do,
I wouldn't do it with you," she said, the angry tears beginning
again. "I don't think you'd be a bit of fun. You'd probably cough
or vomit."

Lucy was ten then, to my going-on-twelve, and knew the frail-
ties of my flesh, as well as the deficiencies of my soul, better than
my mother ever had.

The summerhouse! Always, to me, and then to Lucy, it was
sheer enchantment, a place apart both in distance and in spirit,
with the utter and endless fascination that all perfect, miniature
things have for children. It was a complete small house, a near-
replica of the big one, except that it was done in white frame,
with the same hipped roof, black-shuttered Palladian windows
to the floor and a pedimented, columned portico. It was buried
in a surf of old boxwoods and crape myrtles and backed by dense
woods, and a wisteria vine arched over the portico and bathed
the two big rooms inside in a wash of lavender light and fragrance each spring. There was one great room for living and dining, floored in Italian quarry tiles and with a small stone
fireplace, and a smaller one adjoining it for sleeping and dressing.

Behind these rooms were a small bath and a complete, compact
kitchen. It had been built for my grandmother Adelaide, who
came to live with her son and daughter-in-law when my grandfather died, before I was born, but she lived in it for only two years
before she too died, and it was largely unused until Lucy and
I claimed it and moved our daytime base of operations there.
My parents and her mother did not really mind. The furnishings
were too grand for the servants, who in any case had quarters
over the garage, and not grand enough for use in entertaining.
My mother never liked my grandmother's plain, well-used old
family pieces. She had thought once of building a swimming pool
in the garden where the lily pool has always been, and using the
little house as a pool house, but she and my father both were
too fair to take the sun, and I was adjudged too frail, especially
in the summer polio season; so the house became known as the
summerhouse, albeit an empty one that had known, until we
opened it for our play, no summers.

All this, then, had been mine from birth, this overflowing largesse of physical grace and symmetry and seclusion, but it took
the clear, light-sparked blue eyes and strange, silverfish imagination of my cousin Lucy Bondurant to open my own eyes and
heart to its unique place-magic. I do not know what would have
become of me ultimately—a suicide? a stockbroker?—if she had
not come to live with us, but she did, and in one revelatory split
second when she stepped into the foyer of the house on Peachtree
Road and said in her extraordinary, musky voice, "Something
stinks," my star was as fixed in its far firmament as Orion: Joy
and aloneness were mine, in equal measure, gift of Lucy, out to
the distant edges of my life.

CHAPTER
TWO

THEY HAD NOT BEEN IN THE HOUSE a week before it became apparent to me, my spongelike pores newly opened to revelation, that my uncle Jim was to loom over Lucy's life, and therefore mine, like one of those menacing grotesques in Macy's Thanksgiving Day Parade.

I had not thought of him again since the day they came, and then only abstractly, as the author of Lucy's appearance in my life, and no one—not my parents, not my aunt Willa, not Lucy herself—had mentioned him. If Little Lady wept for her father, or lisped his name, we did not hear it, for she spent her days in the second-floor bedroom-nursery hastily fashioned by my mother and Martha, attended by Martha's teenaged daughter ToTo. Little Jamie, a happy child, did not cry at all, for his father or anyone else. For a small space of time it was as if Jim Bondurant had never existed.

Then, around four o'clock in the afternoon of the fifth day they had been with us, Martha Cater put her head into my newly acquired little third-floor cubicle, where I was just yawning my way out of an enforced nap, and asked if I knew where Lucy was. I did not. She had been put to bed in her new room, next to mine, at two o'clock, as had become the custom, and had fallen asleep before I did. I knew that because she had not answered the last of the sleep-silly questions I had called in to her. I had drifted off soon after.

No one downstairs had seen her either, and a quick search of the immediate back garden did not turn her up, and so Martha went muttering upstairs to my mother in her bedroom and my aunt Willa in hers. In those first days, Willa Bondurant spent all the time when she was not bidden into my parents' presence, such as breakfast, lunch, cocktail time and dinner, in that room, with her children. I don't know what she did there—her nails and hair and sparse clothing, probably, for each evening's manicure and hairdo excelled in splendor and intricacy the previous day's, when she appeared downstairs on the "good" porch for afternoon drinks, and her clothes were as faultlessly pressed as they were startling in cut and pattern. I know she did not read.

Mother and Aunt Willa were sufficiently alarmed at Lucy's absence to come down in dressing gowns and slippers, Mother only halfway through her careful evening's makeup, Aunt Willa as fully anointed as a Kabuki dancer. Not wanting to disturb my father in his study, they sent Martha back upstairs to look into all the imaginable hiding places that the house harbored, and me out to the back garden and the summerhouse to search. They themselves stood on the back veranda calling softly, "Lucy! Lucy Bondurant! Come in the house this minute!" I could hear their voices spiraling up, intertwined, the soft drawl and the metallic kitten's mewl, as I riffled aside bushes and vines and walked through each room of the summerhouse.

"You ought to come on out now," I said aloud, for I felt sure that Lucy was somewhere in the vicinity of the summerhouse. "You're really going to be in the soup if my father gets mad at you."

But there was no answer, and my own voice in my ears frightened me somehow, and I did not call again. I went back to the house in defeat.

Mother called Shem Cater then, and he beat his way through the dense woods, newly greened and swollen with spring, all the way over to Rivers Road, and even asked at the back doors of some of the nearest houses, but there was no trace of Lucy. By the time my father, attracted by the subdued furor and ready for his six o'clock bourbon, came out of the library and around to the porch, the light was seeping out of the afternoon and the shadows were going long and blue. He and Shem took the Chrysler out and canvassed Buckhead, up one winding, green-canopied street and down another, pulling up before the big houses at the end of the long drives. Shem would wait while my father knocked on each door in turn and asked if anyone had seen a thin, dark-haired, blue-eyed five-year-old in corduroy bib overalls and saddle shoes. No one had.

I was in agony, drowned in mute pain. It was my first experience with loss, for I had, somehow, never had the common child's fantasy that my parents would die and leave me, and there had been no one else in my life whom I had valued, at least not directly and particularly. I had never had a pet, so never had

lost one, and had not known a name to put to the uneasiness
that the death of my little-known grandfather Redwine had left.
But Lucy was the perfect hostage to fortune. She had blown into
my life like a radiant whirlwind, bringing liberation and laughter
and childhood with her, and I had fallen without a shot being
fired. Moreover, I had accepted the new state of joy she had
brought as the secret in the house for which I had waited so long,
and it had never even crossed my mind that I could lose it. Now
I tasted for the first time vulnerability and frailty and the terrible,
casual power of the world, and the fear and outrage howled so
powerfully in me that I could only crouch behind the striped
canvas glider, arms around knees, head down, thinking of all the
things that could have happened to Lucy.

My mother was tight-lipped with annoyance and, I suppose,
a sort of worry, and my father was openly exasperated. Aunt
Willa seemed more embarrassed than upset.

"I'm gon' tan her hide when I get my hands on her," she said
over and over, looking sidewise at my still-faced mother and up
under her spiked lashes at my father. "She's a willful child; takes
after her daddy. But she don't do this kind of thing, usually.
Lord, I hope she hasn't gone off with a man. She loves men, and
she ain't . . . isn't . . . afraid of anything in shoe leather. I've
told her and told her, but it looks like she just doesn't hear
me. . . ."

"There aren't any men around here who would hurt her," my
mother said icily. "We know everyone in the neighborhood, of
course, including the servants. She would be quite safe with anyone she happened across."

"Well, of course she would," my aunt Willa said, reddening.
"I didn't mean I thought anybody you all *knew* would . . . you
know . . ."

"I do know. You can put your mind at rest about that," my
mother said, and Aunt Willa fell silent.

But I didn't know, and the unimaginable and unnamed thing
iced my heart and lungs so that, behind the glider, I struggled
for breath, and the world grew overly bright and buzzing for a
moment.

It was full dark and my father was on his way to the telephone
to call the police when Lucy came drifting up from the garden,
hair wild and caught with bits of leaf trash and eyes smoke-dark
and large. Even in the green darkness I could see the white sweetness of her smile.

She did not tell us where she had been, except to say, "Back
there." Even after Willa had taken her by her thin shoulders and
shaken her until her head flopped on her neck like a chicken's,
and had spanked her with a ferocity that finally prompted my

father to say, "That's enough. It's all right," she did not say any more than "Back there," and she never did after that. She did not seem to understand why she was being punished.

When Aunt Willa had finished spanking her and let her hands fall, breathing hard, Lucy looked up at her, white-faced and dry-eyed, and said, "Will you hug me now, Mama?"

"Of course I won't hug you," Aunt Willa shrilled. "You been an awfully bad girl. Like to scared us all to death, and your uncle Sheppard out in the car looking all over for you, and dinner ruint. . . . Bad girls like you don't deserve hugs."

"Daddy hugged me all the time," Lucy said, more to me, hovering in the background, than to her furious mother.

"No, he didn't," Willa said. "He never did hug you. You always were a bad girl, and he never did hug you one single time. He hit you, that's what he did. You were so bad he hit you every time you turned around."

Lucy cried then. Her blue eyes slit shut in anguish, and her hands flew to her mouth.

"Not any more than he hit you!" she cried, whirling away from us. "Hit you lots more'n he did me!"

"LUCY!" Aunt Willa shrieked, but Lucy was gone up the stairs into the dimness of the second floor. We could hear her small feet beating a diminishing tattoo of woe.

I could not look at my aunt Willa's mottled, dull-red face, so I looked at my father. He grimaced in distaste. I looked at my mother. Incredibly, she was smiling, a full, slow smile. I had not seen that smile in nearly a week. She laid one slim hand on my aunt Willa's arm.

"Come on up to my room with me, Willa," she said in her slow "Atlanta" accent. "I have a few things in my closet that I never wear anymore. I think they'd look awfully pretty on you. Martha will see to Lucy."

Only then did I look full at my aunt Willa. Before the black lashes dropped down, I saw in her eyes a pure and living hate.

"Thank you, Olivia," she murmured.

A long and terrible symbiosis had begun.

I followed Lucy upstairs and waited until I heard Martha leave the little bedroom, and then I went in and sat down on the side of her bed. She was not crying, but staring straight ahead in the darkness. I could see the fevered blue of her eyes.

"I'll hug you, Lucy," I said. "Do you want me to?"

"Please," Lucy said, in a small, frail voice. "I need for you to so I won't fly off the floor of the world."

This did not sound at all strange to me then, or ominous. I crawled into the bed beside her and put my arms awkwardly around her, and there we stayed, her small bones feeling, under my hands, like a bird's, until the hammering of her heart slowed, and she fell asleep.

Before she did, just before, she murmured to me, "He did too hug me. My daddy hugged me all the time, and he never did the other two, or Mama either. Just me."

I held her until my arms began to ache and prickle, and then I got out of her bed and into mine, slowly and carefully, so that she would not miss the feeling of my arms, and waken. But I knew even then, though I could not have sculpted the thought, that it was not my arms that Lucy sought. It was those first arms, that vanished phantom's arms, and whether or not what she had said as she slid into sleep was true, never again in all her careening life did she find them.

Lucy was by no means the first woman to know the promise and pain of my uncle Jim's arms. He had been pledging and betraying since his birth. Six years younger than my father, Jim Bondurant was, from the moment he slid redly into life in my grandmother Adelaide's bed in Fayetteville, the favored one. His had been a swift and easy birth; my father's long and arduous. His fairness was from the first hour smooth and silvery, his eyes a dark, velvet pansy-blue. My father's blondness was white almost to the point of albinism, his eyes milk-pale and perpetually squinted shut. My uncle Jim's face was rose satin and his smile pure and focused. My father's was mottled with fury and woe, and he bellowed his anguish abroad to a world that he must have, from the outset, perceived as unloving. His features, even then, and more so later, were heavy; my uncle Jim's blade-fine and aristocratic. All his life, my handsome, high-spirited, feckless uncle must have seemed the one for whom my father was the rough, blunt, half-finished model. From his birth, women rushed to grant his wishes and win his magical sweet smile, and wept when he left them. In all his life, James Clay Bondurant found no good reason to stay and confront rough weather. Fair skies always lay, for him, as near as the next valley.

My father, reduced to battering his way through life with ham fists and furious red face, must have hated him, must have welcomed, even as he deplored aloud, each scrape and escapade that brought tears to my grandmother Adelaide's eyes. But to his credit he did not excoriate his brother, to his parents or anyone else, and it was finally his taciturn loyalty, his rocklike *thereness,* that won for him the grudging accolade from old Adelaide: "He's a good boy, a good steady boy. And he's a money-maker."

This she said to a group of ladies gathered in the drawing room of her son's great house, during her short stay with him and my mother just before her death. By this time my father was on his way to real wealth, and she had not heard from her younger son in more than five years. The periodic checks that were dispatched to him to cover the series of disasters and false starts that were his life went now, not from her, but from my father. She did know that he was married, but she died without knowing—for she would, finally, not permit his name to be spoken in her presence—that he had a daughter Lucy who was said to be the image of her as a child. It must have been gall and wormwood to my aunt Willa that the old lady died before the birth of the granddaughter who was her namesake—though by that time Willa Bondurant must have grasped that a veritable platoon of small, white-blond Adelaides would not have melted her mother-in-law. Perhaps she used the name Adelaide because she thought that candy-box Little Lady would cut some future ice with my father, the only Bondurant left by then who might conceivably throw her a lifeline. He was, after all, a money-maker.

In the Atlanta of that day, as in this one, that was perhaps the highest accolade you could pin on a man. I can remember lying on the floor behind the Capehart, my warm winter nest, as my mother talked with a group of her bridge ladies one roaring January afternoon when I was very small. I don't know who they were talking about, and I don't know why their words pricked my ears, but one of the women said, "Well, I know he's sorry in a lot of ways. I was there when he peed in the punch bowl from the Driving Club stairs. I went with Laura in the ambulance when they took him to Brawner's this last time. He's a drunk and a rooster. But whatever else you say about him, you can't say he's not a money-maker."

My ears pricked further: Here, then, was another signpost on the way to the baffling country of adulthood. A money-maker. I filed it away, along with Gumption and Respect for Women. I already had a surfeit of the latter, but I thought it highly unlikely that I would ever attain the former two.

I have come to think that the store we set on making money here is not so much a purely materialistic trait as it is a reflexive twitch left over from the poverty and humiliation of defeat and occupation after the Civil War. We had seen that witless gallantry and conviction were not enough to save our land and homes. We had seen that they could be smashed by armies of superior wealth and strength, and bought by carpetbaggers of superior means. The defeat left us with a near-genetic hangover of fear and inferiority and truculence—and yes, guilt—which, it seemed, only the balm of money could soothe. Crass as this trait undoubtedly is, it also built us back a viable city in a very short time. Very few Southerners, no matter how blue their blood or high their ideals, will, in their deepest hearts and souls, truly scorn a money-maker.

And so that obedient and industrious money-maker, my father, must have felt at least a small snake-slither of satisfaction at the spectacularly destructive trajectory in which his wasted younger brother launched himself. After flunking out of the University of Georgia and being expelled from Emory at Oxford for drinking, Jim Bondurant had been sent to Georgia Southern College in Statesboro, in Bulloch County, then a minimal little school on Georgia's sun-punished coastal plain. The nearest city was Savannah, some sixty miles away, and since almost the last act my grandfather Bondurant performed before his death was to take away his youngest son's automobile, the spoiled young demigod was a captive in this arid wire-grass Lilliput. He had, he felt, only one recourse. He proceeded to fuck his way through the scant female contingent of the student body.

He met Willie Catherine Slagle, a freshman in home economics on a scholarship from her local Optimists' Club, when he was a senior. She was the improbably lush daughter of a shiftless chicken farmer in a nearby hamlet so small and hookworm-poor that it had no name, and by the time she got to college and secured for herself a job waiting tables in the town's lone, dingy soda shop, she would have done anything to escape the ramshackle pens and coops and stinking carcasses and burning feathers that were her life—including sleeping with the handsome, said-to-be-rich young man from a fine family near Atlanta who swept her off her tired little feet.

By the time she found that she was pregnant, Jim Bondurant's graduation was nearing, and his newly widowed mother was showing signs of welcoming him back to her ample bosom and dowering him with funds sufficient to "give him a little start in business." Knowing full well what the advent of a pregnant, poor white trash daughter-in-law would do to that nest egg, he refused to marry Willie. Well, said Willie Catherine Slagle pragmatically, then she would, of course, have to kill herself, but not before she had gone to see his mother in person and told her about the grandchild soon to be murdered.

"I'll pay for an abortion," Jim said hastily.

"You don't have the money for that," Willie Slagle said calmly. She kept her spectacular blue eyes cast down on her folded hands. Things were not going, on the main, too badly.

"I'll get the money," he said.

"Yes," she smiled. "You do that."

She knew what would happen when he asked his mother for money, and it did. Essentially a slow-witted young man who had never needed to employ guile or deceit in his dealings with his

mother, he called her and told her what he needed the money
for. To his outrage and utter surprise, she hung up on him. Willie
Catherine Slagle kept on smiling and pressed her good rayon
dress.

They were married by a justice of the peace in Savannah in
May, the afternoon of his near-miss graduation. Jim was not displeased with his new wife. She was possessed of a true, if conventional, peasant beauty, and her untutored farm appetites were
overwhelming. Furious that his mother had refused to bail him
out of this last boyish scrape, and bitterly homesick for the glittering urban arena of Atlanta, he saw in the fecund Willie Slagle
a source of both endless sexual delight and just retribution. He
kept her rolling happily in the spavined bed of a down-at-heel
tourist court all of their honeymoon weekend, bought her two
new dresses and a pink rayon negligee at the Sears Roebuck in
Macon on their way back north and finally, on a tender night
in late May, presented her at the front door of 2500 Peachtree
Road, where his brother and dark, languid sister-in-law and,
lately, his mother lived.

An uppity, ashy-gray Negro man answered the door and said
that no one was at home. Since he could see lights in windows
and curtains upstairs stirring, he knew this was not true. He
yelled and cursed at the Negro man, and Willie Catherine, shivering in her flowered silk despite the balmy spring evening, began
to cry. She held her hands protectively over the hard little
mound of her belly. Eventually the Negro man closed the great
door in their faces, and before Jim could double his fists to hammer on it, his wife took his arm and jerked him away from there.
The old Bondurant place in Fayetteville had been sold, so he
could not take her there. For the first time in his life, Jim Bondurant was forced to fend for himself. He never got over the shock
of it.

He got a job ineptly pumping gas in a Decatur service station,
but lost it almost immediately because he could not conceal his
distaste for the oil and grease and customers, and appeared to
them to be fully as arrogant as he was. It was mid-Depression,
and jobs were scarce for even the most qualified and able of
young men. Jim, Willa (as she had taken to calling herself immediately upon becoming a Bondurant) and tiny Lucy, who arrived
that murderous red September, drifted from city to small, wasted
city around the Southeast, staying in a succession of dismal
rooming houses and attic apartments. Kewpie doll Adelaide
came along when they were living in Charlotte and Jim was
working, when he did work, as a freelance house painter. Two
years after that their first son and last child, James Clay Bondurant, Jr., was born in Greensboro, North Carolina.

By this time little Jamie's father was not working at all. He was, instead, drinking his way steadily across the Southeast toward the Mississippi River, alternately striking and smothering with caresses his children and his wife. In time, Willa and the two younger children took to cowering away from his fists in a groveling terror that maddened him, so he no longer caressed them, but only smote. But smoky, quicksilver Lucy, his oldest daughter, took his blows with averted dry eyes and a small-smiling silence that was oddly soothing to him, and turned after each beating with slender, bruised white arms held out to him, and his heart would turn over with a raging love for her, and he lavished on her all the caresses that the rest of his fearful family abjured. Pain and love, love and pain . . . dark twins which were, by then, all that he could give, and all that Lucy could accept.

A few months into 1941, Jim Bondurant left for New Orleans to look for work, said to be more plentiful there, and soon after wired Willa and the children to give him three days to find them a place to live, and then catch the Greyhound and come. When they arrived at the New Orleans station, he was not there, and there was no message, and after waiting for almost nine hours, until it was quite dark, it was apparent to Willa Bondurant that he was not coming at all. And he did not, then or ever, and it was the last that any one of them ever saw of him.

Willa called Sheppard Bondurant in Atlanta with her last nickel, and Travelers Aid bought the midnight tickets that sent them grinding through the flat, humid, mosquito-plagued fields of Louisiana toward the gullied and scrub-pined red hills of the Georgia Piedmont Plateau. Shem Cater met them at the Greyhound station that evening, in Sheppard's big car, and brought them in the twilight to the house on Peachtree Road. Sheppard and Olivia were not with him; Willa had not thought that they would be. She was, by then, as bereft of worldly goods as an animal, and as unself-pitying. She had four cents and a roll of butterscotch Life Savers in her purse. The children had not eaten since breakfast, in Mobile.

It was a journey measured in immensities. Somewhere during it, in that endless fugue of flying miles, Willa Slagle Bondurant stopped crying and began planning. Driving through the luminous, cloistered northwest quadrant of Atlanta in the backseat of the big car, she marked with a coldly assessing eye the architecture, landscaping and details of each great house they passed. When she walked into 2500 Peachtree Road, she was determined to do whatever it took to ensure that she never left it again.

All this I learned from Lucy years later, during one of the rare times when she spoke of the life she had had before she came to Atlanta. It was the last time we were together up at the mountain house at Tate, and we had talked so easily and about so much of the past, and with such a genuine benison of rancorless remembrance, that I was not at all surprised when she segued into the night of that awful bus ride. Though only a few miles separated them, Lucy did not often speak, in those last years, of her mother.

"You have to hand it to her," Lucy said that night on the mountain. "Not a cent to her name, no education to speak of, no family, no future . . . nothing but her and us three children. And she'd been to the house before, remember, and they'd turned her away. She had to be terrified. And she was; when I finally fell asleep, about Biloxi, she was still crying. But when I woke up, at Mobile, she was putting on lipstick and fixing her hair, and she had that little Mona Lisa smile on her face. When I asked her what she was smiling at, she said, 'The future. We're going to have a fine future in that big old house.'

"So I said, 'When we gon' leave it?' You know, because we always left every house we stayed in. And she said, 'We're not.' "

Willa was as good as her word. She shoehorned herself into the life of the house with a persistence as seemingly effortless as it must have been enormous. She smiled. Endlessly and charmingly, she smiled. She pleased whenever an opportunity arose. She was helpful, modest, grateful, unassuming, dutiful, deferential to my mother, girlish and just short of adoring to my father. And from the outset, as if to make up for my mother's distance, he seemed to me to be uncharacteristically warm to the beautiful, flat-voiced, lushly built farm girl who was his sister-in-law, and to her children.

I know that his manner was unusual enough for my mother to mark it; I saw in her eyes, before the sooty, feathery lashes came down over them, something as nervous and darting as a small wild animal, when she looked at my father and my aunt Willa in those first long evenings. But the strangeness did not bother me; indeed, I was glad for it. Some of his new benevolence seemed to spill over onto me, and for a long space of time after they came, I was no longer the focus of his discontented stare and probing questions at meals. I was happily engaged, heart, soul and mind, with Lucy.

We did not run wild. Aunt Willa tended her children well. She stayed out of the way of the household as she must have sensed quickly my mother wished her to do; accepted with comely murmurs of appreciation the cast-off clothing my mother found for her; smiled and accepted with grace and modest pleasure the weekly "Of course, you'll be our guest at the club this Sunday for lunch" that Mother proffered, never failing in all the

years I heard her extend the invitation to accent the word
"guest"; accepted with small, real pleasure the single sherry my
father poured out of the bottle he kept on the liquor tray in the
library, each evening before Martha stumped in to announce dinner; kept her children out of sight of the adults except when they
were washed and brushed and dressed and drilled to come and
murmur their polite hellos and thank-yous to my parents . . .
and she learned.

She learned prodigiously and constantly, by rote, through her
pores and fingertips, with a wary animal's untutored cunning,
how to become a woman to match the house. Within a year, by
the time World War II had taken our minds off slow and graceful
rituals and taken many of the men from the great Buckhead
houses, she had largely accomplished her mission. My father,
whose blood pressure and flat feet kept him out of the army, re-
marked and applauded the sea change. Even my mother, whose
shuttering lashes concealed the eyes of a harpy eagle, could find
in Willa by that time little of the awkward, vulgar, overdressed,
rankly sexual young woman who had alighted in her foyer a year
before. Reluctantly, and at my father's insistence, she began to
introduce my aunt Willa into the sanctity of her garden club,
bridge circle and a few selected lesser charities. It was, in retrospect, a stunning achievement. What it cost Willa Slagle Bondurant might never have occurred to me if I had not seen so clearly
and with such a palpable shock the living adder of hatred that
had stirred in her eyes on the night Lucy first ran away, when
my mother had bidden her to come upstairs and be dressed in
the first of a long succession of cast-off garments from the closet
of her enemy.

Now, even more than ever, tides ran through that house that
I sensed had the power to capsize and sink us all, deep-running
tides that obeyed some great moon whose name I did not know.
I don't know if the adults in the house were aware of them,
though on some level I think they must have been. How could
they not be, when all three of them seemed involved in some
slow, formal, highly stylized waltz of manners? The oblique
looks sent and received, the silences spun out at meals and over
cocktails, the conversations that seemed freighted with some import far weightier than their actual words merited, the laughter
that rang, to me, utterly false. Sometimes it seemed to me that
a kind of crazy power shimmered loose in those rooms like a
haze of lightning, seeking a place to come to rest.

I don't know why my father smiled so benignly on my aunt
Willa, especially in the presence of my mother; it was totally
alien to him to notice, at least openly, other women. Revenge
on the will-o'-the-wisp brother and the wife gone cold? Simple

lust? I don't know why my mother, noticing it, smiled her secret smile and drew the shutters of her lashes down over her eyes. This new arcanum of theirs was as unfathomable to me as the old legerdemain had been. I do know now, and I suppose I sensed then, what my aunt Willa was about. Of them all, she was the simplest, the most direct, the least oblique. It should have made me easier in her company, but it did not then, and it does not now.

Lucy felt the subterranean surges as keenly as I did, but being vastly more at home with nuance, simply shrugged her thin colt's shoulders and said, "Don't pay any attention to them. If they think you think they're actin' funny they'll get all over you."

And so, on the main, I didn't. That spring was altogether too dazzlingly, burstingly full of Lucy.

The bond that had leaped into life between us that first evening in the foyer deepened steadily. On the surface, I suppose, our temperaments could not have seemed more divergent: I was shy where she was gregarious; cosseted where she was, of necessity, used to fending for herself; physically clumsy and crippled by asthma (and my mother's fear of those terrible clawing, choking attacks) where she was bird-slender, swift and agile; timid where she was fearless. But our needs and hurts met and knew each other with absolute fidelity. Both of us bore the indelible stigmata of difference. Both of us knew the terrible, unpayable penalty, in our small worlds, of our essential inability to adhere to the rules. This kinship made her, to me, irresistible.

And then, there was her beauty. It was clear from the outset that both my aunt Willa and my mother greatly favored Little Lady and young Jamie, but I could never understand why. To me, my cousin Lucy was by far the most interesting and beautiful creature I had ever encountered.

There was a light, an aura, a sort of halo, like streetlights sometimes wear in mist, that lay at times around Lucy Bondurant. I saw it that first evening, and it did not fade for me until the end of her life. She drew eyes to her, even in the company of rose-gilt Little Lady, who was a much more conventionally pretty child. Lucy's looks were, I heard my mother say once, her mother's looks, the Slagle woods-colt looks. Blond Little Lady and Jamie, on the other hand, were obviously Bondurants, icons of the vanished Jim. Perhaps that was the reason my mother was cold to Lucy from the first, as cold as she was to Aunt Willa, while she was warmer, if not affectionate, to Little Lady and Jamie. And maybe it was because Lucy was, from the beginning, too vivid, too alive, too *much*, for the eminently proper mistress of the house on Peachtree Road.

Lucy was animated, vibrant; life seemed to brim and leap in her so that her transparent skin could scarcely contain it. All her life, the small blue pulses that beat in her throat and temples seemed to me to be the drums of a sort of special vitality, which she possessed in greater measure than most mortals. Her laugh was rich and deep and almost bawdy, and she found things funny that would and did terrify most children of her age, and horrify most adults.

She was ferociously bright, possessed a quirky, silverfish intelligence that soared and looped and doubled back upon itself; her mind described its own windborne ballet, which few people in her life but I ever really followed. She was an accomplished and amusing liar, telling herself and whoever would listen wonderful, towering, complex tales of intrigue and adventure, in which she was perpetually the rescued heroine, the saved damsel in distress. She was a dreamer, a firebrand, a small poet, a great reader. She taught herself to read when she was three, and by the time she came to us had spent a great deal of her life in trees and under back porches in the various mean homes Uncle Jim and Aunt Willa inhabited, lost and safe in books beyond her age but not her ken.

As that spring swam into and through summer and toward the crisper hummock of autumn, I was as nearly totally happy as I have ever been in my life, and perhaps will ever be again. Who could not love Lucy?

On an autumn evening when it had just turned cool enough to have a fire in the library when we gathered for drinks there, my aunt Willa came into the room a little later than usual, and I saw my mother lift her head and flare her nostrils, as if she smelled on a faraway wind something sharp and alien and dangerous. Aunt Willa looked especially pretty to me that night. Her cheeks were pink with a stain that had not come from her rouge cake, and her jewel-blue eyes were very bright. She had on a dress I had never seen before, a very plain, soft blue wool which fitted her beautiful body like water, but not, as the clothing she had brought with her from New Orleans had, like paint. The difference was enormous. I could see it in my mother's eyes, and my father's.

"I have something to tell you all," she said, her voice lilting out of its flatness with practice and excitement. She did not sound at all like the woman who had first come to our door. We looked at her silently.

"I have gotten myself a job!" she said, and broke into laughter, a small gurgle of pure pleasure. "I am, as of right now, a saleswoman in Better Foundations at Rich's. I start in the morning, and I'm going to be making twenty dollars a week, with benefits and an employee discount. Now what do you think of that?"

We stared at her, all of us. My mother spoke first.

"You certainly didn't have to go and get a job selling corsets to God knows who, Willa, not to mention all my friends. You know that it's been my . . . our . . . pleasure to share what we have with you."

Aunt Willa's smile wrapped my mother in light and venom.

"I'll never forget your generosity, Olivia," she said, in her new, many-leveled voice. "But my mama used to say that sooner or later every tub has to get on its own bottom. And it was time for me to get on mine. I could not impose on your and Sheppard's generosity any longer."

I goggled. I had never heard her mention a mother, a life of any kind, before the one she had shared with my uncle Jim.

"I know you mean well, Willa, but you need to consider how it will look, your going to work, when you're living in your own family's house. . . ." My mother paused delicately, and smiled. There was no warmth in it.

"What Olivia means is that her friends in the Junior League will think that we made you go to work," my father said, getting up from his big leather chair with his whiskey and coming across the faded Oriental to kiss Aunt Willa wetly on the cheek. "Don't pay any attention to her. It shows a lot of grit and gumption, and I'm proud of you. Besides, it's a mighty pretty bottom that tub of yours is sitting on."

Lucy and I looked from one to another of them, still mute with surprise and interest and that back-of-the-neck radar with which children are necessarily endowed, which tells them to be silent or risk peril. Aunt Willa smiled, her lashes down over her blue eyes, but she said nothing, and neither did my mother. But her dark eyes blazed up as if kerosene had been dashed upon a fire, and I felt, rather than heard, the great ponderous grinding of a shift in the balance of power.

CHAPTER
THREE

"**I**S THAT THING REAL?**" Lucy whispered loudly to me, over the cicada-buzzing and giggling, in the Camerons' back garden, of a small group of children.

We were seated on folding bridge chairs in a semicircle in the paved rear courtyard, watching tall, black Leroy Pickens lope in circles holding a tether, on the other end of which trotted a very small, tarted-up Shetland pony with a monkey astride it. The monkey's owner, a swarthy, gypsyish young man with a full mustache and a rakish red bandanna, watched suspiciously from the edge of the formal boxwood maze. The white sun of August burned into small necks and arms, and wilted starched organdy and dotted swiss; the handful of adults had long since retreated to white wooden lawn chairs under the pergola roof, where small Glenn Pickens, Leroy's son, his red tongue protruding from between his white teeth, passed a tray of Tom Collinses.

"What do you mean, is it real? Is what real?" I whispered back, in rare annoyance. For the last hour or so, Lucy had been acting as sulky and obdurate as the prim, evil-eyed pony. I did not know what was the matter with her, and was vaguely embarrassed and angry, because I had wanted this small society to be as enchanted with her as I was, and thus envious of me. Before she came, there had never been any cause for that.

"That stupid pony," she said, not bothering to lower her voice. "And that stupid monkey. They must not be real. All they can do is run around in a circle."

Heads turned to look at us, including those of my parents and her mother, and Ben and Dorothy Cameron. Ben winked at us, and Dorothy's smile wrapped us both in warmth and favor. No

56

one from the Peachtree Road house smiled or winked. My father looked blank and formal, and my mother smiled the small, superior smile she kept strictly for Aunt Willa and her children, and Aunt Willa herself, diaphanous and splendid in white voile and a big-brimmed, flower-trimmed hat that had Rich's Wood Valley Shop written all over it, glared at Lucy out of eyes gone ice-white with anger. Ben Cameron, Junior, my age and as copper-haired and freckled as his father, glared at her too, but Sarah, his sister, whose sixth-birthday party it was, blushed furiously, and her golden-amber eyes filled with tears. Lucy ignored all the looks and began to scratch absorbedly and ostentatiously at a mosquito bite on her elbow.

The monkey did a somersault on the pony's back, and the children, Lucy excepted, all clapped and cheered.

"Don't be dumb," I said furiously between my teeth. "Of course they're real. Haven't you ever seen a pony or a monkey before?"

"Just about a million times," Lucy said boredly, but with red rising smartly in her neck and cheeks, and her blue eyes narrowing. "I had a pony and a monkey both when we lived in Charlotte. My daddy got them for me. Nobody else but me could play with them. They could do lots more stuff than run in circles. That's why I thought those weren't real."

I knew then that she had, in fact, never seen a Shetland pony or a monkey before, and that the wonder of seeing them was, for her, murdered by the fact that it took place in the garden of, and at the party of, another little girl who was a figure of some unknown but real importance in my life. For when we had rounded the sun porch to the back garden where the party was beginning, small Sarah Cameron had run up to me with her wide, incandescent smile and her sherry eyes glowing like candles, and her mother had hugged me with the easy warmth and affection that she lavished on all of us. Lucy, who had been gleaming and chattering all morning in anticipation of the party, began to go quiet then. That the cold wings in her eyes were not those merely of envy, but of a kind of fear, was a precocious insight for a seven-year-old boy to have, but from the beginning there was little about Lucy that I did not ken. My anger faded and I took her hand. I did not have words to comfort her, but I knew that my touch usually had the power to dispel whatever demons were threatening her.

A shadow dropped down over us, and Ben Cameron squatted beside us, rocking on his heels, gray Scot's eyes and red hair giving back the sun in splendor. He was a tall man, younger than my father, wiry and knotted with an athlete's muscles, and he wore white duck pants and white shoes and a blue, open-collared shirt with the sleeves rolled up his prodigiously freckled fore-arms. He had, for some reason, a striped necktie knotted around his waist. I thought he looked wonderful, gay and accessible. He put his arm around Lucy's shoulders and smiled his magical smile into her face, and after a wavering moment she smiled back.

"Everybody knows Charlotte ponies and monkeys are the best in the world," he said. "These are just in training to get good enough. When they shape up, we're going to ship them off to Charlotte. I bet they won't ever be as good as your pony and monkey, though."

Lucy looked up at him through her inky lashes and smiled, and was, at that moment, pure Willa.

"No," she said.

The clouds rolled off her face then, and for the rest of the afternoon she was the center of the group, darting in and out of the shrubbery and woods playing hide-and-seek, pinning the tail on the donkey with sure, swift grace, spilling as much ice cream as anyone else on the elaborately ruffled Rich's frock Aunt Willa had brought home for this, her daughter's debut into the small society of junior Buckhead.

She had met one or two of the neighborhood children over the spring and summer she had been with us, but this was the first group she had been in, and it was not a large one. Though we ran with a much larger pack of children at E. Rivers Elementary School, on the corner of Peachtree Road and Peachtree Battle Avenue, during the fall and winter, none of the young of those golden roads and houses saw much of one another in hot weather. Polio stalked the canyons of Buckhead as relentlessly as it did the warrens of Cabbagetown and Vine City in those long, deadly summers, and the fear of it was never out of any-one's mind. My friend Pres Hubbard, who lived on Chatham Road, had gone white and quiet one afternoon several summers before, and complained of a headache, and the next day he was in Crawford Long Hospital in an iron lung. Pres was lucky. He walked now with a heavy iron brace, but he walked. Alfreda Slaton's small sister had died two years ago of infantile paralysis.

By the time some of the red anger began to go out of the afternoon and the adults put down their tepid glasses and rose to leave, Lucy had, with her physical daring, her infectious laugh and her light-spilling blue eyes, gathered a crowd around her that would, with some defections, remain there until high school. I had heard her say more than once that afternoon, "Hey, I know a story," and seen them all—Freddie Slaton, Snake Cheatham, Tom Goodwin, Charlie Gentry, Pres Hubbard, even young Ben Cameron—gather close around her. Only Sarah Cameron did not succumb, pressing close to her mother's side, her huge eyes shadowed and grave on Lucy. I was as proud of Lucy in that moment as I have ever been. She was a hit, and she was mine. Vindication ran sweetly in my veins.

But that night she had one of her terrible nightmares, and after Martha Cater had soothed her wild crying and sponged the sour sweat of panic off her and settled her back in her bed and gone back to her own room, leaving Mickey glowing staunchly from the baseboard of Lucy's cubicle, she came and slid into my bed with me.

"Hey, Gibby," she said—for she had begun to call me that immediately upon finding that my middle name was Gibbs— "are you awake?"

"What do you think, after all that?" I said. I moved over toward the wall to give her room, and she burrowed against my side like a small animal.

"What were you dreaming?" I asked.

"I dreamed . . . that I went over to the Camerons' house to play and I went inside and it was dark, and I couldn't find anybody, and then I heard them in back and I went back there and they were all there, grinning at me and holding out their arms to me . . . but, Gibby, they were all . . . dolls."

"Dolls?" I could not imagine what there was in the image of toys that would set Lucy to shaking and screaming, but the fine tremor still had not completely gone out of her arms and legs against mine, and her tear-thickened voice was not completely steady.

"Yeah. You know, dolls. Big ones, with strings hanging off of 'em, walking all jerky and talking funny. Like that place we went when I first came."

Puppets. My parents and Aunt Willa had taken me and Lucy to a much-heralded children's puppet show at the old Erlanger Theatre down near the Fox that spring, just at Easter, and I remembered then that Lucy had not liked it. I thought of Ben and Dorothy Cameron, of Sarah and Ben Junior, smiling painted smiles from the darkness of the vast, shadowy sun porch where they lived during the summers, wooden arms stretched out avariciously. The image was terrible.

"Did they chase you?" I said.

"No. They didn't do anything. But I knew they wanted me."

"Why would that be so bad?" I asked, to reassure both of us. "They're real nice people."

"Because," she said. "They weren't real."

As she often did, Lucy had gotten hold of an essence that had, in her starved and vulnerable heart, been skewed and magnified into something dangerous. The Camerons were such an exem-

plary, whole and healthful family that it was not hard to see that
they might appear, to some few original eyes, simply unreal.
They were not that to me, but they were, perhaps, hyperreal.
Supernormal. And they were revelatory. Willa Bondurant
brought to the Peachtree Road house, already askew, her own
poverty of soul, and Lucy's deep starvation darkened the stew.
I would not have known lightness, grace and normalcy if it had
not been for the household of Dorothy and Ben Cameron, and
their children, Sarah and Ben. I said that to Sarah once, years
later, in the paneled drawing room of the house on Muscogee
Avenue, after a funeral.

"You all showed me everything I ever knew of lightness and
straightness," I said. "You were my models for how sane, normal, productive people act, for how well privilege can be used.
I really think you all—your mother and dad, especially—are the
reason I'm just a little funny and not dead myself."

Sarah's eyes were red from weeping, but she smiled. It was
not a smile of amusement.

"If you can say that after today," she said, "then you must
be worse off than anybody ever thought."

"It wasn't aberration that did this, Sarah," I said. "It was the
times. It was the town. In another place he'd have seen options
he could have lived with. In another time, maybe, he could have
done it here."

They were, Ben and Dorothy Cameron, as close, to my mind,
as Atlanta can come to producing aristocrats. Benjamin Aird
Cameron's family had come from Scotland to Virginia before the
Revolution, to Atlanta the year it was founded and back to Atlanta before the ashes were cooled, to begin rebuilding the city.
Dorothy Chase Cameron's family hailed originally from Dorsetshire, England, and it was a copy of the Chase manor house,
which her father had built on Muscogee, into which she and Ben
moved at his death. Merrivale House, it was named, after that
first one, though only outsiders called it that, never the Cameron
family.

I never knew a family so vital and energetic and so devoted
to—even infatuated with—each other. They played together
endlessly: rode their bicycles around Buckhead and deep into the
surrounding country together, played tennis and swam together
at the Driving Club, played badminton and croquet on the satiny
lawn beyond the box maze behind the house, performed so many
family plays and pageants and skits and spoofs and entertain-
ments that their cottage in the old colony up at Tate had a min-
strel's gallery built into it just for that purpose. In the long
evenings of winter they read aloud to one another and listened
to music on the big Capehart that was a twin to ours and the

ones in half the Buckhead houses—popular songs and light classics and show tunes, for they were not intellectuals; I was well established at Princeton before I encountered families who were truly intellectually cultivated—and they even had a sort of family band. Dorothy played an accomplished, if conventional, piano, Sarah was not half bad on the flute, Ben played the saxophone, and Ben Junior the clarinet. It was from noodling around on his instrument in the long afternoons of our later boyhood, and tasting the slick-sweet taste of the bitten reed, that my lifelong passion for the clarinet was born. It was as if I could taste the sweet marrow of music sunk in the long ebony and silver cylinder, though, for a long time, I couldn't get it out.

They gave off, when together, a kind of soft, clear light, a diffuse energy born of love, mutual admiration, curiosity, endless appetite for the charmed lives they led, and above all, a respect for each other which was, to me, totally seductive. I knew about love; it was, even if canted and lamed, what I felt for my mother. But the Camerons were the first people to show me that respect and love could go hand in hand. So far as I know, so far as the world knows, none of them ever did anything to damage that respect in the others' eyes. Even after what happened to Ben Junior, there was no betrayal of respect; only bewilderment and grief.

And the light that they gave off fell, as naturally and abundantly and indiscriminately as the light from a star, over the people who came close to them. I always felt, in the presence of the Camerons, more than I was . . . or possibly, all that I could be. I will never understand why, in all her life, Lucy did not feel it, but she didn't. She used to say, even after we were grown, that an hour in the company of Ben and Dorothy and, to a lesser extent, Sarah made her want to go home and take a nap.

Looking back, I can see what she meant, even if I do not agree with her. I remember a night late in the summer Lucy came, when she and I had been taken over to the Camerons' house by our parents for an early supper and badminton in the back garden. After the last game, when the adults had collapsed on lawn chairs with drinks and the first fireflies were winking in the cutting garden, Sarah and Ben broke into one of their impromptu "shows," presenting, with uncannily synchronized steps and gestures, a pantomime of Gene Kelly and Vivienne Segal in *Pal Joey.* Dorothy and Ben Senior had taken them to see it in New York at Easter that year, and they had been utterly beguiled with the dark, glinting Rodgers and Hart arcana. My mother, who had not seen the play but had heard of it, had been scandalized by the Camerons' exposing their children to such steamily suggestive goings-on, and having those exemplary children present

them to her flushed face kept her on the telephone to her circle
for days afterward. She listened that night in tight-lipped silence
as Ben Junior and Sarah wriggled and leered their way through
"I Could Write a Book," "Bewitched, Bothered and Bewildered" and worst of all, "Zip," and gave Ben and Dorothy a sidewise glare of honest outrage when they laughed and applauded.
Aunt Willa kept her dense lashes modestly over her eyes, and
my father swallowed his bourbon in silence, but I was enchanted,
and even Lucy laughed and clapped her hands.

When at last Ben and Sarah took their bows and made as if
to sit down, Dorothy and Ben Senior jumped to their feet and
pulled me and Lucy with them, and ran out to the smooth grass
of the badminton court.

" 'Hut-Sut Rawlson,' " Dorothy Cameron cried, and she and
Ben and the Cameron children swung into a mad, syncopated
version of that witless doggerel, which in an eye-blink had me
and Lucy shucking and jiving right along with them.

"Hut-sut Rawlson on the rillerah and a brawla, brawla soo-
it," we six bellowed into the fast-falling dark of Muscogee Avenue. "Hut-sut Rawlson on the rillerah . . ."

We were wonderful that night, magnificent. It was as if our
twelve hands and feet were synchronized by some unseen master
choreographer, and our voices silkened and silvered by a con-
summate cosmic musician. I could not and cannot sing, and
Lucy never could carry a tune in a bucket, but that night it
seemed to me that the world should have paid pure gold to see
and hear us. We performed "Hut-Sut Rawlson" again, and then
"The Music Goes Round and Round," and finished up with a
great flourish with "Three Little Fishes."

When we were done, sweating and gasping and laughing, Dorothy hugged us and said there was no doubt in her mind we both
had an unlimited future on the stage, and we danced on joyful,
clumping feet all the way home, where our grimly silent parents
banished us immediately to bed.

"I think living at the Camerons' house must be the most fun
there is," I said as we turned off Mickey and crept into our beds.

"Shoot, I think they are the silliest grown-ups I've ever seen,"
Lucy said. But I just grinned into the darkness. I had felt the
music and joy in her, there on the lawn behind Merrivale House.
It was only later, back inside the dark-souled walls of 2500
Peachtree, that the spell of the Camerons left her.

As close as they were, the Camerons encouraged in one another the development of individual gifts. Young Ben, besides
being a musician of some skill, was the sort of workmanlike, un-
temperamental athlete his father had been, a perfect team player
and content with that role despite his impetuous nature and

flamboyant grace, and knew practically from infancy that he would become the visionary architect he eventually did. Sarah's talent for drawing and painting was the stronger of their gifts; she was truly talented, and endeared herself to her parents and their friends by painting odd and hauntingly lovely little portraits and landscapes and giving them as gifts. In grammar school, she did a brisk and profitable business drawing naked women and rearing horses on commission, until her mother discovered the thriving cottage industry and put a stop to it. She had the obligatory Saturday afternoon lessons in watercolors and pastels at the High Museum of Art, and more than one teacher called Dorothy Cameron and urged special tutors, serious study and consideration of one of the really good schools of art in the East or abroad for her.

But Dorothy did not like the thought of a self-serving artist's life for her daughter, and sunny, biddable Sarah, by then in love with her family and her world and her near-amphibian swimming and diving, did not push for the studies. I often wonder what the world lost when Sarah laid aside her brushes and strode to the end of the Club diving board. It is hard for me to mourn the loss totally; the memory of her small, perfectly shaped body suspended at the top of its lovely arc like a swan in flight is one that I will never lose.

If it did not sound so gummily, cloyingly banal, you might say that the Camerons en masse personified the ideal of noblesse oblige. Ben's grandfather made the family fortune in the manufacture of a popular and virulent patent medicine, and Ben's father and Ben himself tended it well, and so by the time he had married Dorothy and begun his family, he was free to devote himself to civic and political endeavors that had the very real power and weight of a considerable personal fortune behind them. Soon after Sarah graduated from college, in 1960, he was elected mayor of Atlanta, and held its helm sensitively and surefootedly through the most explosive decade of growth and upheaval it would ever know. His thatch of hair, rusted iron-gray by then, and his freckled, fine-boned face became almost as familiar in the national media as the chestnut shock and white grin of the young president who admired and lauded him. More than Atlanta would eventually come to mourn his decline and death.

Dorothy Cameron was a small, straight-spined, beautiful woman with the thick, dark hair, warm, sherry-brown eyes and straight black brows that became her daughter's. She was intelligent, outspoken and carefully, if not deeply, cultivated; a bit prepossessingly high-minded for the far earthier society of Atlanta in which she moved; a fierce, self-proclaimed Jeffersonian democrat. Her caustic humor saved her from the impossibility of utter

worthiness, and her energy and awesome concentration were a
good foil for Ben's lazy grace and catlike physical indolence. She
was a tireless volunteer worker, and her pioneering program at
the city's massive charity hospital, Grady, became the model for
other hospital volunteer programs all over the South. She toiled
tirelessly in auxiliaries, leagues, committees, task forces and
study clubs.

I can still see Dorothy Cameron, as vivid and commanding
as an actress in her Red Cross uniform, looking out from the
pages of the Sunday society section of the Atlanta *Journal-
Constitution,* seeming beside all the other women in their ball
and benefit gowns as intrepid and otherworldly and androgynous
as a young Joan of Arc. Unlike the other adult women in my
world, she did not like formal social occasions, and though she
dutifully attended them, and invariably looked marvelous in her
austere, handmade gowns and shoes, she would not have been
there if she had not been on some committee that required her
presence. The other women must have known it. Looking back,
it is clear to me why not many of them liked her, and also why
so many of their husbands and all of their children did. For to
a youngster, we all adored her.

The winter I was ten and Lucy eight, Atlanta had one of the
rare, magical snowfalls that come along perhaps once a decade.
We have small, spitting snows nearly every winter, but the genuine, deep, creaming big ones come so seldom that when they do
the entire city halts with both the breath-held blue sorcery of
it and the utter impossibility of getting around. On the evening
after this one, Lucy and I were both in our beds with the beginnings of tedious, dripping colds brought on, no doubt, by our
stubborn refusal to come in out of the silent, lapping white back
garden when our mothers called us.

"I hope you're both happy," my mother said, closing the door
on us. "You're going to be stuck in that attic until the last cough
is coughed, and you'll miss days and days of school, and have
to make them all up."

By that time the snow was effectively ruined for us, and we
were just drifting into fretful, feverish sleep when the door
opened again and my glaring mother came into the room, followed by Dorothy Cameron wrapped in her fur coat and
swathed in scarves.

"I've told Mrs. Cameron you're both sick with colds, but she's
talked me into letting you do something I'll probably regret forever," my mother said. "I don't know why I listen to her."

"I'll take all the blame," Dorothy Cameron said. "And we'll
personally pay the doctor bills if they get sick. But I don't think
they will. I think this is the perfect cure for what ails them. Get

up, you two, and put on your warmest coats over your pajamas, and your galoshes, and your hats and scarves and mittens, and come on with me. I'm kidnapping you."

We did, silent and solemn with the weight of doing something my mother so obviously disliked, yet with her approval. We could not imagine what awaited us downstairs.

What did was, wonder of wonders, an old-fashioned sleigh with two chestnut horses in harness before it, stamping and jingling on the semicircular drive in front of the house, a mummy-wrapped Ben Cameron at the reins and swaddled-to-the-eyebrows Ben Junior and Sarah behind him. We gaped in absolute and perfect awe.

"Come on!" Ben cried, gesturing with an elegant black whip. "I borrowed them and the sleigh from George Haynes over at the stable at Chastain Park, and I've got to get them back in a couple of hours. Let's make tracks!"

And we did. Under a high, sailing, white galleon of a moon, which came riding down the star-strewn sky on a vast, skirling night wind, we made magical, enchanted snow-tracks all over a ghostly Buckhead: straight up Peachtree Road where virtually no automobile traffic could pass, out a white, deserted West Paces Ferry, down winding, silent Habersham to West Wesley and Peachtree Battle, and up Peachtree again to our house. We four children were too rapt with exaltation and strangeness to utter a word above a whisper, and the sounds of the horses' chiming bells and the scrunching clop of their iron-shod feet and the low voices of Ben and Dorothy Cameron talking to each other and occasionally breaking into soft snatches of song were the only ones in all that hushed, bewitched silver and black night.

When we got back to our house, my mother received us grimly and sent us off to bed, and as we pattered up the stairs I heard her say to Dorothy Cameron, "I hope it was worth it. They're going to absolutely perish of pneumonia."

"No they're not," Dorothy said, laughing. "I guarantee they won't. But it would be worth it, almost, if they did."

We did not get pneumonia, of course, and our colds never materialized. And she was right. That magical night sleigh ride was worth . . . everything. Neither of us ever forgot it. Dorothy Cameron always knew what was important, and she gave well and widely the gift of imagination and acceptance. Sarah is very like her.

Dorothy and Ben were, rather surprisingly for their day and backgrounds, ardent champions of the Negroes and their cause. Dorothy did not have a shred of Lady Bountiful in her makeup, nor Ben of the massa, and so they were permitted the classic dichotomy of both espousing black needs and having in their home black servants. The result was that the black families who served in and lived behind most of the big houses were accustomed to dropping by, during their times off, to pass the time of day with whatever Cameron was around. I think the tendrils that reached out to the sad black ghettos from these taproots in the Northwest were one of the strongest reasons why Ben Cameron was able, almost single-handedly among the whites who labored to do so, to quell the incipient race riots that threatened his city in the sixties, by the simple expedient of going into the hot streets and talking to the furious mobs. During one of them, potentially the worst, he went, alone except for young Glenn Pickens, into the melee, climbed atop a parked automobile and talked for hours to the angry and frustrated crowd, all of whom knew who he was and many of whom knew him personally. Until the very end of that bitter time, Ben Cameron kept Atlanta the city that, as it had always boasted, "was too busy to hate." On the surface, at any rate. What went on below it, in the dark, roiled waters there, was another matter entirely, and Ben Cameron would have been the first to acknowledge that. In those days, surfaces, if they kept the first match from being lit, were enough at least to serve.

"This kid at school says Mr. and Mrs. Cameron are nigger-lovers," Lucy said at dinner one night during the early days of her stay with us. She had just entered the first grade at E. Rivers, and was finding the society of other children both a baffling and a stimulating thing.

"He says Mr. Cameron sleeps in the bed with a nigra lady, and Mrs. Cameron hugs and kisses Leroy Pickens all the time. He says his mama said Ben and Sarah are probably Leroy's children."

"Lucy!" Aunt Willa hissed, cutting her eyes at my mother. "You know I don't like that kind of talk."

"Well, I didn't say it, this kid did," Lucy said.

"What little boy was that, Lucy?" my mother said interestedly. There was a glimmer of something amused and avid in her dark eyes, like a fish far down in dark water, and all of a sudden I wanted Lucy just to be quiet. But I knew that she would not be.

She wasn't.

"I don't know his name," she said. "He's a funny-looking kid with scabs around his nose and a fat fanny. His folks' nigra driver comes for him in a big old car every day. I beat him up."

This time the outrage was evident in my mother's dark, beautiful face.

"We don't beat people up in this house, Lucy," she said. "I

think that was little Todd Beauchamp. I'm going to have to call his mother and apologize for your behavior."

"Wasn't in this house," Lucy said earnestly. "It was on the playground. I had to beat him up, Aunt Olivia. It wasn't true. I mean, I know Mr. and Mrs. Cameron love the nigras because they said they do . . . gee, so do we, don't we? I mean, Shem and Martha and all . . . but they don't sleep in the bed with them, or hug and kiss them. And Ben and Sarah aren't Leroy's children. I asked."

"LUCY!" Aunt Willa out-and-out squalled.

"Oh, for goodness' sake, Willa," my mother drawled, her amusement at the thought of Lucy asking the totally exemplary Dorothy Cameron if she hugged and kissed Leroy Pickens apparently outweighing her disapproval of the thrashing of fat Toddy Beauchamp.

"Everybody knows Ben and Dorothy are funny about the Negroes. It's no wonder the children pick it up."

Indeed, Ben and Dorothy's friends paid little heed to their crackpot sentiments, which would have gotten any other Atlantans drummed so rapidly out of the Driving, Capital City, and Commerce clubs that their seersucker coattails would have smoked. The Camerons, particularly Dorothy's side, had always been "funny." Old Milliment, Dorothy's mother, that martinet of eminent respectability, had once ridden a white horse at the head of a column of suffragettes straight down Peachtree Street during a Fourth of July parade, black hair flowing down her ramrod back, in the middle of a difficult menopause. Later, long before it was seemly for ladies to drive themselves into town for shopping, she would take out her huge black Cadillac each Tuesday—the traditional Buckhead chauffeur's day off—and drive herself, leaving carnage and mayhem in her wake, never looking back. She lived, after her husband's death, in the Cameron guest house behind the box maze, and for many years had living with her there a younger, unmarried sister who was a dwarf. Neighborhood children swore that Miss Callie, as the tiny woman was called, did not live in the guest house at all, but in a huge doghouse out behind it, fitted out with doll's furniture and screened and shielded with honeysuckle.

"She has a teeny little bathtub and she uses a baby's potty chair," Lucy once told a breath-held group of ladies at one of my mother's endless committee luncheons. "Her doo-doo is like a little ol' chicken's."

But as Sarah and Ben Cameron had vivid imaginations and Lucy was a liar of no small reputation and it was known that I would parrot whatever Lucy said, this was given little credence. I myself never saw the doghouse, but it might have been true.

Any dwarf sister of old Milliment was bound to be eccentric
enough to demand one and see that it was obtained. There was
and is, in old Atlanta, an eccentricity that is tolerated, even cherished, and an eccentricity that will never be countenanced. Ben
and Dorothy were of the former. Lucy came to be of the latter.
There are not many people left who know the difference.

In addition to all their closeness, their talents, their kindness,
their charm, their worthiness and good works and their infinitely
engaging gregariousness, Ben and Dorothy Cameron had traveled almost all over the world, often taking young Ben and Sarah
with them. The result was a family that would, in its attractive-
ness and wholesome worldliness, have been at home and welcome in a far more sophisticated arena than Atlanta. Given their
very fullness, I suppose I can see, after all, why Lucy in her emptiness and hunger flinched away from them, shied like a colt at
their bounty. But to me, they shone like the sun, and I loved
them with an uncritical and grateful heart.

I think it was the dark side of Lucy that shrank from the Camerons' light. I know that we all have our dark sides; no one is
shadowless. But I came to think, in that first year, that there was
an actual darkness, a real shadow, that lay over Lucy. You didn't
see it often, because she was almost always in motion, flying in
radiance, moving in a wind of light. But it waited for her, off
in the edges of the sunlight, and when it swept over her it was
unmistakable, like the shadow of wings.

I saw it once, darkness visible, lightlessness tangible. It was
in the fall of that year, a warm stretch of Indian summer days
after an early frost that had left the hardwoods afire, when we
all went up to the cottage at Tate for the weekend. We had not
taken Willa and her children there before, even though it would
have made, in its coolness and isolation, a perfect fortress against
polio. My mother never liked the Tate cottage, and I know that
she did not want to take Aunt Willa there. I heard her telling
my father once, "If you think she's conspicuous here, wait till
you get her up at Tate. A sore thumb doesn't begin to describe
it."

Even I could understand what she meant. The little colony
of summer places up in Pickens County, about an hour's drive
to the northwest, was so unfashionable and simple that most
Atlantans who did not have homes there would not know it existed. That is why, of course, it was, and is, thought to be so exclusive. The families who summer there are, for the most part,
the descendants of the original owners, the colonists who made
up the Tate Mountain Corporation and built the old houses and
the golf course and the lake and dam and dock and boathouses.
It is extremely hard to buy into Tate if you have not always been

grounded there, and we acquired our cottage only because it was part of the package the doctor's widow offered us. Even then, I wonder if my parents would have been accepted if the other colonists had not known that the old lady needed a quick sale. As it was, though the other residents were cordial to us, they were never really warm, and my mother was not one to either miss that nuance or forgive it. I think my father might have eventually found a haven there, with his knowledge and love of fishing and the outdoors, but after the first two or three visits, my mother refused to go back, until Aunt Willa and her children came to us, and so the house mainly sat idle in its grove of fine hardwoods on the flank of Burnt Mountain, and we went, in the summers, either to Sea Island or to Highlands.

"You couldn't get a decent game of bridge in Tate if your life depended on it," my mother would say, "and your name is mud from the word go if you don't want to dig in the dirt or tromp around after birds and beavers or freeze yourself in that damned little lake."

And she was right. There was plenty of socializing in Tate, down at the swimming and diving dock, or on the golf course, or walking in the cool mornings and evenings around the lake, or even at the late-afternoon ice-crackings, as they were called, on screened porches and before vast stone fireplaces. But these gatherings centered around a communal life in the mountains that was generations deep, rooted in the original families, rich in anecdotal lore from summers long past. Suppers were family affairs and bedtimes early, and in the daytime, activities ran to supervising children's play or gardening or ambling, to desultory golf or serious canoeing and swimming. All of it was extremely plain, even austere; there was not a pair of high heels or a tie in the entire colony, and there has never been even one telephone. I think, now, that the Elliots' cottage has an old black-and-white television set, but they do not use it except for Braves games, which are old Mr. Elliot's passion, and the Saturday gardening show on the educational channel, which is Mrs. Elliot's. The Camerons' log cottage is one of the largest and oldest, and was the center, from June on, of a constant stream of children, eddying and swirling around Ben and Sarah. Tate might have been created with the Camerons in mind.

My aunt Willa, true to my mother's prediction, did indeed fit into Tate, on that one autumn weekend in 1941, like a peacock in a sparrowcote. She ruined her new Newton Elkin heels in the red mud at the front door, was routed from the rudimentary bathroom by the resident scorpion, nearly froze in the chill night in her flimsy peignoir and ended up sleeping in one of my father's ripe old flannel shirts, and was badly frightened by the thin, shuffling she-bear who foraged on weekends in the colony garbage cans.

In the glorious blue and gold morning, when the sun broke free over Burnt Mountain and turned the woods to yellow wild-fire, she came red-eyed and shivering down to breakfast only to find that my father had taken us children on a hike to see the beavers and my mother had gone back to bed and let the fire die out, and when she tottered desperately out into the rutted little road that encircled the lake in search of another human face, she met none. We were the only family there. Most of the other cottages had been closed before the first frost. Aunt Willa was near tears by the time we came back and built up the fire and my mother arose to set out our hotdog lunch. We went back to Tate a few times during my childhood, but Aunt Willa never again in all her long life set foot on Burnt Mountain.

But from that first day, Lucy adored it, almost as much as she did the summerhouse, and even though she was not taken there with any regularity during her childhood, we did go on occasion, and Lucy never forgot those visits. I let her have the keys whenever she liked after we were grown, and I think she spent quite a bit of time up there. Malory loved it, too, in her turn. After she was born we went fairly often. That is why after my parents died, I never sold the Tate house, and why I probably never will. It is entirely possible that I will never see it again, but it makes me happy to think of Malory's young-willow height and slenderness, so like Lucy's, vivid as a live flame against the green of Burnt Mountain.

On the second evening we were there, that first autumn, there was a meteor shower, and Lucy and I bundled up and took blankets and went down to the dock to watch it. We lay on our backs, utterly silent as the very sky above us arced and bloomed, and when it was over we decided to walk around the lake, so as to prolong the magic. We walked quietly, without speaking. The silver spell of the teeming sky was too recent and close for words. I remember that there was a huge white moon, hanging perfectly full and so low that it seemed to rest on the top of Burnt Mountain, and the whole world was black and silver, like a photographic negative. Where the road and lake and meadow lay in the clear, it was as if the world was flooded in a kind of cold, burning radiance, but in the shadows of trees it was as thick and black as ink. Magic. That night it was just magic. It took your breath; you wanted to whisper. Something old as the world and outside it entirely walked that silver road with us. Lucy, skipping a little ahead of me, was bathed in silver; the radiance seemed to flow off her like phosphorescence does off your skin when you're in a warm night ocean. I knew that something enormous and awesome was going to happen. How could it not?

There is one point on the road, on the far side of the lake, where the old mountain highway runs right alongside it, but it is higher than the road, about twelve feet; it hangs over the little lake roadway. But you can't see it, or the bank that leads up to it, for the enshrouding trees. The lake road lies black there, deep in tree shadow. It looks as if you're approaching a tunnel. All of a sudden I did not like the look of it, that troll's tunnel, and I said to Lucy, in a small voice, "Let's go back the other way. I left my flip down on the dock."

"No you didn't," she said, not looking back. "Your flip's in your pocket. You're scared to go through that dark place. Scaredy, scaredy, scaredy-cat!" And she ran ahead, trailing silver, and headed straight for the blackness. Suddenly I was so frightened that I could not even get my breath to call out to her. Something was so heavy in the air that it crushed my chest. I began to trot after her, but it was as if my feet were mired in concrete.

And then, just the instant before she plunged into that black tunnel, an enormous, flying . . . I don't know, *shape,* a great, black canopy of shadow . . . came flying over her, just over her head, like a curse falling down on her out of the sky. And then she was gone into the tree shadow, and I heard a dull little crack and a kind of scream, and then nothing.

My heart literally stopped. I could not move my feet. My legs were ice water. I did not know what it was; it was not like anything from the world. I called out, a thin bleat of fear, but she didn't answer, and then I heard something crashing down through the underbrush toward the lake, and a deer came leaping out and crossed the road and flew on into the woods at the water's edge. That's what it had been—a deer from up on the road above us, frightened by a car. I saw headlights swing over us then, and heard an engine swell and die. The deer had bounded down the bank and jumped right over Lucy and run on into the woods, and the crack I heard had been its hoof, glancing off her cheekbone. It half stunned her for a moment, and laid her cheek open. We had to take her into Jasper and get it sewn up. She was so proud of the scar it left; she had it all her life. She didn't cry when it happened and she didn't cry while the doctor was working on it, and she was only five. It was Aunt Willa who cried, loudly and in, I think, vindication. It was the dot over the *i* of her distaste for Tate.

I have never forgotten that night. It was so mythic, so somehow like an omen. It left Lucy stamped with the mark of otherness.

"How like Lucy, to have her own private omen," Sarah Cameron said much later, when I told her about it. She was, by then, less than altogether enchanted with Lucy.

But for Lucy and me, the night of the deer remained a part of our private mythology. For though, as I have said, we were, both of us, sad-eyed small realists, still, what child does not make myths of its life? How else could it be borne?

We talked of it so often that fall and winter that our parents finally told us we were being tiresome; that nobody wanted to hear any more about the deer that jumped over Lucy up at Tate. But by that time it did not matter, for there came a Sunday afternoon in December when we were sitting around the Capehart in the library, waiting for Shem to bring the car around and take us to the Driving Club for lunch, and a voice broke into the program of music to tell us that Japanese planes had bombed Pearl Harbor, in the Hawaiian Islands.

I remember clearly that my mother cried, and my aunt Willa gave a little squeal, and my father put his hands into his pockets and walked to the window and stood with his back to us, looking silently out into the leafless back garden.

But Lucy jumped to her feet, red flags snapping in her cheeks, blue eyes blazing up like flung diamonds. She stamped her feet on the old Oriental; she hugged herself and danced around like a marionette. And then she ran to me and flung her arms around me, her silky hair whipping across my face.

"That's where he is!" she shouted, and her voice caroled like flutes and bells with joy. "That's where my daddy went! He didn't leave us! He went to the war!"

And from then on, until the day in August four years later when the church bells and fire sirens of Buckhead called out to tell us of V-J Day, we followed the war, and Lucy was as happy as she would ever be.

CHAPTER
FOUR

OVER THAT FIRST YEAR OF FIGHTING there hung and still hangs a bright scrim of excitement, exhilaration; of pure, jingoistic glamour that emanated, for me, as much from Lucy's mind as it did from the whole war ethos of America in those early days of conflict. World War II was, to most Americans except those actually embroiled in it, an extremely romantic war. It had all the ingredients of a Tennysonian epic: a clear-cut moral imperative, highly visible forces of light and darkness, simple and larger-than-life heroes and villains, sacrifice, sanctioned violence, brave men fighting and dying for home and country, brave women waiting until they came home again. It was irresistible. There was not a living soul in America and Atlanta and Buckhead who was not caught up in the glittering web of that war.

And Lucy was the greatest acolyte it had. Much later she would write a fine little essay on those first days of war in Atlanta, called "The Last of the Great Ruffled Wars," and in it catch some of the muddleheaded chauvinism that kept us as a city and a nation from perceiving the howling horrors under the ruffles. But in that first war year of 1942, no American, large or small, stuck to a radio or pored over newspapers and magazines with such single-minded ardor as small Lucy Bondurant, of 2500 Peachtree Road, Atlanta.

I stuck and pored beside her, willingly, and the glamour and power of it, that beat in her head like great wings, soon engulfed me. For that first year, we did little, thought little, said little that did not have its genesis in the war.

Buckhead was a small village still, then, and so the feathery wing tips of the war that reached out to brush a Buckheader touched, inevitably and personally, someone we knew. Early in 1942, a Buckhead boy, the son of a clerk at Cantrell's Grocery Store on Roswell Road, was shot through the throat in the Solomons, and all of us turned out to call on his parents, and to stare solemnly at the gold star, Buckhead's first, in the window of the little bungalow on Mathieson Drive. Then a lifeguard from the Garden Hills pool died, and a track star at Boys' High, and soon there was a small colony of gold stars.

They were, all of them, our very own dead. Later, a very few of the fathers of our small friends went to fight, leaving from the great induction center out at Fort MacPherson, in Southwest Atlanta. But the majority of them did not. Married men with families did not go to the early war, and when, later, they were needed, it seemed that in Buckhead, business empires needed them more. In most cases this was true. Few strings were pulled in North Atlanta to avoid fighting. The insular, truculent Southerner, violence never far under the surface courtesy and indolence, has always known that he fights better and with more savagery than other Americans; he does not shirk a chance to spill blood in the name of honor. The epithet "essential business" that most of our fathers wore was true. So there was, in those first winter evenings of war, around Buckhead dinner tables and radios, in libraries and drawing rooms, a full complement of sober young men listening with their women and children. When I think of my family as a family, as a group of people unified by blood and purpose, I think of those evenings in my father's library, where we gathered to hear H. V. Kaltenborn with the news and to see, in the pages of *Life* magazine and the Atlanta *Journal*, the images of war.

They are still indelible to me: Whole families sprawled lifeless at the entrance to an air raid shelter in Chungking, crushed in a panic to enter. They looked like tossed Chinese dolls: Why were they all naked from the waist down? Why was there no blood?

Boiling black smoke over the slow-toppling towers of battleships, in Pearl Harbor.

Joe Louis in his private's uniform; Veronica Lake, her silky sheaf of hair caught in a drill press, demonstrating industrial safety.

For some reason, a great, forty-foot pile of stockpiled automobile tires in Akron.

The charred head of a Japanese tankman buried in blackened sand at Guadalcanal, the teeth living and terrible in their eternal grin.

The monstrous insect gaze of gas masks.

Afterward, Lucy and I would be banished to our upstairs beds, but we did not mind, for we were free then to talk openly between us until we fell asleep, and what we talked of, always, was the war. Or to be exact, the role in that war of my uncle and Lucy's father, James Clay Bondurant.

For he was everywhere. His face hovered just beyond the great, jovial moon of Roosevelt's in the newsreels at the Buckhead Theatre. "There he is; see?" Lucy would whisper in the dark, poking me, and the anonymous aide would, indeed, become my fabled Uncle Jim.

He was there in the Solomons, and the Philippines, and Burma and Borneo and Singapore; he left Corregidor with General MacArthur and marched with the skeletal dead at Bataan. He almost alone survived; he alone led out the small band of survivors; he alone endured and prevailed. Lucy did not seem to care about the defeats and deaths of those early battles; perhaps she did not take them in. I would say, sometimes, feeling an obscure and smoldering jealousy of the phantom father-uncle who drifted like smoke over those lost battles and never died, "We didn't win that fight, stupid! We lost it! Everybody died. It was a defeat."

"No, it wasn't," she would say calmly. "Everybody didn't die; he didn't die. How could he get his picture in the paper if he'd died?"

"That wasn't his picture!" I shouted once, in rage. "That was somebody you never heard of, who doesn't look a thing like your father!"

"How do you know?" Lucy said. "You never saw him."

"Then how come he never writes to you, if he's such a hotshot hero and he lives through all those battles and gets his picture in *Life* and the movies?"

"He's busy, stupid," she said.

And he was! James Bondurant turned the American tide single-handedly at Midway, in the Coral Sea, and waded ashore with the first wave on Guadalcanal. Soon he skipped across seas and mountains to the deserts of North Africa, and was seen posing in modest glory after finally trouncing Rommel's Afrika Korps. When I pointed out to Lucy that that was a British engagement having nothing to do with American fighting men, she said, reasonably, "Well, then, that's why there haven't been any letters. My daddy doesn't know how to write British."

I don't think Aunt Willa and my parents were aware of Lucy's strange, skewed obsession with her father, at least not for that first year or so of the war. I don't know how they could have missed it; she made no attempt to conceal it from them. The fact is, in that head-spinning, heart-bulging time, the adults at 2500

Peachtree Road were not much concerned with small Lucy Bondurant and her phantom fighting father.

But Aunt Willa eventually caught on to the extravagant fancy, and came down on Lucy like a Fury. I was there when she did. I will never forget it. I'm sure Lucy never did.

It was near Christmas, 1942. We had been at war just over a year. Lucy lay on the floor of the little den on a Sunday afternoon, poring over the Sunday newspaper. I lay in my accustomed lair, half in and half out of the space behind the Capehart, reading a Captain America comic. The desultory talk of the adults, sated with starchy wartime fare at the Driving Club, eddied and surged over our heads.

Bored, I crept out of my nook and ambled over to Lucy.

"What're you doing?" I said. I could see that she was reading, or at least looking at photographs. She was quite proficient with words by that time, but the small newsprint sometimes eluded her. It was raining, and we had been forbidden to go out. The afternoon seemed endless.

"Reading about my daddy," she said. "He's over in Yugo . . . Yugo . . . this place now." Her small finger stabbed a fuzzily drawn map, and then moved to an out-of-focus photograph of the legendary Yugoslavian partisans, men, women and children, swarming out of ambush from a dark forest and into the very teeth of a Nazi panzer column. Lucy's forefinger lingered lovingly on one shapeless and altogether unrecognizable figure in the foreground, arm raised as if to hurl a homemade grenade. Its face was obscured; you could not tell if it was man, woman or large child. I merely nodded and said, "Oh, yeah."

But Aunt Willa was out of her armchair and down on her knees beside Lucy like a lithe whirlwind. She snatched the newspaper from her daughter's grip and crumpled it in her fist. I stared, openmouthed, and Lucy went absolutely still and white.

"Lucy Bondurant, that's a lie and you know it!" Aunt Willa shrilled. "I'm not going to let you sit there on the Lord's day and tell *lies* like that about that no-good, shiftless father of yours! That's not your father! Your father isn't anywhere near this . . . foreign place; those aren't even Americans! He isn't even in the army; the army wouldn't have him! The *German* army wouldn't even have him! If he's still alive he's hiding in some swamp somewhere so he won't have to go in the army; he's the worst coward on this green earth, and you can bet your prissy little bottom he's as far away from it as he can get—if he's even alive, which I doubt. Most likely he's long dead from liquor, or worse. So you just hush your mouth about him. I don't ever want to hear any more of this nonsense!"

She broke off, and looked around her as if coming up out of

deep water. My father had retreated behind his own newspaper, but my mother was looking steadily at Aunt Willa, her long hands knitting silently and competently at something olive drab, a cigarette burning in the ashtray beside her. She smiled, a small, odalisque's smile.

Aunt Willa turned a deep, dull red, and dropped her blazing eyes.

"I didn't mean to yell," she said, not to Lucy, but to my mother. "But I won't have her turning into a little liar."

"We're all under a strain these days," my mother murmured silkily. "I'm sure Lucy was just playing . . . make-believe."

Lucy turned the small white mask of her face from Aunt Willa to my mother.

"No I wasn't," she said. "It isn't make-believe. This is my daddy. I don't care what she says. I don't care what anybody says. He's right there in this newspaper, and anybody who says he isn't is a goddamned liar."

"Lucy!" Aunt Willa shrieked.

"I hate you," Lucy said roundly and evenly to her mother. "I hope your arms and legs rot and fall off and your tongue turns black and chokes you."

She got up carefully from the floor, smoothing out the crumpled ball of newspaper, and walked stiffly and regally out of the room. We could hear her feet, steady and firm, climbing the stairs to the attic, and the muffled slam of the door. I sat silent, my breath stopped.

"I apologize for her," Aunt Willa said. "I'll go and talk to her."

And she left the room, the red still suffusing the back of her slender neck. My parents said nothing. My mother continued to smile.

Lucy would not let her mother into her locked bedroom. She would not even let me in. It was morning of the next day before she opened the door, and then it was as if the ugly incident had never occurred. So far as I know, Aunt Willa never challenged Lucy's fantasy again, and I simply gave up.

More than that, I entered into it. For much of that war, the face of my handsome young uncle was behind all the images of war I carried with me, like a kind of familial pentimento. I knew that she was wrong, but on another, deeper level, the one on which Lucy and I communicated, I believed. We did not speak of this again to my parents or her mother. The fact that they did not see Jim Bondurant did not surprise us. I knew, somehow, that he was given only to Lucy, and by her sufferance, to me: our own totem and her hero.

She was, oddly, never afraid for him, though the possibility of his death in battle was always with me, and I half dreaded, half yearned for the devastating, liberating telegram that began: "We regret to inform you"; the olive drab sedan on the circular driveway; the tall, pale officer at the door. They never came. For four years, despite my developing powers of reason and assessment, I continued to carry with me the certainty of his golden whippet ghost, going ahead into battle after battle like a Viking standard, and when the bells and sirens rang on V-J Day and rock candy came back to Lane's and Wender & Roberts Drugstore, James Bondurant left my pantheon of heroes and soared away out of my head like a falcon. It was, after that, as if he had never been there.

Oddly, the war made of the house on Peachtree Road a healthier place than it was ever again. I suppose that only something on the scale of a world war could loosen our attention from the sucking sands of self and neurosis and coax it outside. But all of us, from Lucy and me to the servants and my parents and Aunt Willa, had a focus for our hungers and energies, and, moreover, one that was universally approved. Lucy and I had our phantom warrior. My father had his essential occupation. My mother and Aunt Willa had war work. I think perhaps it was the first—and looking back on it, only—time in their lives Olivia and Willa Bondurant had the approval of their small society for something that they did, rather than something that they were. I wonder that they did not like the approbation well enough to continue the work, but they did not: Neither, so far as I know, did more than rudimentary volunteer work again for the balance of her life.

But for that time, all the women of Buckhead worked. The women of the larger Buckhead around us, which we saw every day but somehow did not see, went to work for pay; they took over the jobs that the young men had left when they went to war, in offices and factories and shops; they drove taxis and stood behind counters and served food and did laundry and pumped gas. Some of them went to work at the massive new Bell bomber plant in Marietta when it opened; the great mass of the "bummer plant," as it became known, bulked comfortingly over my childhood like a fortress, like an arsenal, between Us and the enemy Them. These women gave up their nylons and silk stockings and wore cotton lisle, or dyed their legs a weeping brown; they wore trousers and bandannas and berets and battle jackets, and some few of the young ones soon wore the uniforms of nurses, or Wacs, or Waves. Everybody, it seems, had a costume for the Great Ruffled War. Lucy received, that Christmas, a hideous Wac's outfit with a flat-topped, brimmed hat, and I got and wore out a small white regulation sailor suit.

The women of the Buckhead we knew, in which we moved, had their own uniforms. They were the smart, somehow immensely flattering uniforms of the Red Cross, and to a woman, the circle my mother moved in and the wider circle of women from the great houses of Buckhead put them on for the duration of the war. My mother went three afternoons a week to Fort MacPherson where she served coffee and doughnuts to homesick young men being processed there by the thousands. I'm sure she was the object of more than one yearning wartime crush. I remember how she looked on those afternoons when she got into the backseat of the Chrysler which Shem brought around to the front of the house: slender, austere, pale and fine-featured, her sleek wet-looking dark hair drawn smoothly up and under the becoming little billed cap, great, dark, drowned eyes somber. She looked the way a young Florence Nightingale should have looked. Even the lipstick-stained cigarette in her fingers did not spoil the ministering purity of her, on those first winter afternoons. Because she was going out to serve in the war that so absorbed me, I adored and admired her, for that little time, as well as loved her. It was the most and the fullest I have ever felt for her.

Some of the women we knew did work for which, had it not been volunteer, they would have held company presidencies or board chairs. Dorothy Cameron directed a pioneer nurses' aid training program for a seven-state area for the Red Cross, a program that became, under her aegis, a national practical-nursing service. She was, that year, Atlanta's Woman of the Year in Defense, and missed her own awards banquet because she was down at Grady holding the head of a pregnant, husbandless young Negro woman volunteer as she vomited into a towel.

"How ghastly," my mother said honestly, when she heard the story. "Isn't that just like Dorothy?"

"Yes, it is," my father replied. "I think she's a pretty brave, smart gal."

"You would," my mother said sweetly.

My aunt Willa did Red Cross work too, partly, I suspect, because she knew instinctively how well she looked in the uniform. She stayed downtown after work two evenings a week, and helped staff a canteen near the bus station, and I know that she left a trail among the cheeky, gum-chewing young soldiers and sailors who flocked there, because not a few of them telephoned her at the Peachtree Road house, and one or two quite literally followed her home. I didn't blame them. Aunt Willa in her battle dress was spectacular. The severity of the uniform both tempered and set off the tropical lushness and humidity of her, and the chaste white collared cuffs and the purity of the cross on her uni-

form were perfect foils for the smoky cat odor that somehow
hung about her, no matter how demure her downcast eyes or
practiced her aristocratic drawl became. Aunt Willa by that time
had nearly perfected the outward armor, if not the inner anima,
of a wellborn Atlantan woman, but there still clung to her like
a spoor something that called out, stridently and urgently, to the
raw, prowling young servicemen.

"Like tomcats to a cat in heat," my mother muttered to my
father after Shem had glared away the second randy youngster
from the portico. "She can buy up the entire Wood Valley Shop,
but she's still as common as gully dirt."

"She's holding down two jobs and raising three children,
Olivia," my father said, "and she hasn't taken a cent from us
since she went to work."

"Why should she?" My mother smiled bitterly. "She has all
those good clothes of mine and a nurse for her children and a
lovely home and good food and a car at her disposal. . . . Why
should she take any more? What more does she need?"

"Maybe a little support from her sister-in-law," my father
said.

"She doesn't need that, either," my mother said. "She gets all
of that she needs from her brother-in-law. It makes me wonder
what else she gets from him."

"I never knew you were jealous," my father said, leaving the
drawing room with what looked to me, hiding with Lucy under
the great foyer staircase in the telephone nook, like a strange,
small smile.

"Don't flatter yourself," my mother said, and went on up the
stairs.

"They're fighting over your mother," I said to Lucy. It was
her idea to lurk under the stairs that winter, to spy on the adults
in the house. I still do not know why she did it. She never seemed
to me then, or at any other time, to be particularly interested
in the comings and goings of my mother, or hers, though she
was interested, almost endlessly, in those of my father.

"Yeah," she said. "I think your daddy wants to get on Mama.
He ought to, too. She likes it a lot better than your mama. At
least, she yells and laughs, instead of crying."

The thought was, to me, quite dreadful, though I did not, then,
understand why. The undercurrents in the house, though over-
ridden by the larger storm of the war, were still there. But I was
enjoying the relative peace of those early war days, and the less-
ening of my parents' hawklike scrutiny that they brought, and
I did not want anything to call those powerful tides out of their
subterranean stasis.

"Come on upstairs," I said, hoping to divert her from the sub-

ject of my father and Aunt Willa. "I got a new book at school.
I'll read some of it to you."

It worked. She was past me and up the stairs like a small deer.
Lucy reveled in the war and delighted in the peccadilloes of the
adults, but she bloomed and thrived on words on a page like a
parched vine in a spring rain.

She was reading proficiently by that time, even though she was
scarcely into first grade at E. Rivers, and she could have read
for herself any book that I brought home. But she loved to be
read aloud to; loved it all her life, and all her life, or most of
it, I spun webs of words out into the air between us, reading
sometimes far into the night, reading through drying and husked
throat and with aching eyes, for the sheer pleasure of watching
Lucy's face as she received the words. She had a way, then, of
looking intently at your eyes and lips as you read, her head tilted
slightly to one side, lips just slightly parted in a smile so that
the nacre of her small, pearly teeth showed through, eyes so suf-
fused with the peculiar, still blue light that tears seemed to be
standing in them. It was the rapt, passionate gaze of the young
novice receiving the ring of Christ; it was a look that gave the
reader the full status and power of a deity. Sometimes she listened to people talking to her with something of that look, and
all her life it entranced people. But it was never quite the same
full, blissful, *receiving* look that she kept for the person who gave
the words of books to her. I don't know if anyone else ever read
to her; I know, when she was small, that no one in the Peachtree
Road house did, and I cannot imagine Red Chastain doing it.
Perhaps Jack Venable, though somehow I doubt that. By the
time he entered Lucy's life his best gift to her was his powerful,
enabling passivity. At any rate, it was my fancy that I was the
only person Lucy ever allowed to read to her, and I would have
read my way through Plutarch's *Lives* for her, if she had wanted
that.

When she had started first grade, her teacher had read the
class a snippet of Kipling's *The Jungle Book,* and Lucy was instantly and utterly captivated. Her face was so incandescent
when she told me about small Mowgli, who was saved from starvation and raised by the wolf pack, that I badgered my mother
to take us downtown to the big gray stone pile of the Carnegie
Library and check the book out. That night, with the aid of
Mickey Mouse and a stolen flashlight, I read the book in its entirety to her, and for the rest of that fall we lived in the enchanted
emerald jungle of those pages. Each evening I reread a portion
of the book to her until she fell asleep, and after school, in the
autumn-gilded honeysuckle thicket behind the summerhouse,
we played endless games of Jungle Book. Lucy sometimes took

the role of Bagheera, the sleek black panther, but most of the time she was Mowgli, and she always accorded me the role of Baloo, the great, fierce, protective bear.

"We be of one blood, thou and I," Lucy would intone endlessly, in a kind of incantatory singsong, through those warm, vivid afternoons. And when we were separated from each other, or met again, we would cry, "Mark my trai-i-i-i-l! Mark my trai-i-i-l!"

One afternoon, when the cicada-buzzing, dry heat of Indian summer had burned so endlessly onto our heads and forearms that we felt time-stopped and weightless in a dusty golden void, Lucy unwrapped the ball of her red sweater and pulled out a kitchen paring knife.

"Let's really be of one blood," she said. "Let's cut our wrists and bleed in each other, so we'll always be blood kin."

The mere sight of the knife made me weak and sick. I knew instantly that she would do it. Lucy often did not seem to feel the pain of a skinned knee or a stubbed toe, and blood meant no more to her than water or Kool-Aid. I knew, too, that she knew that blood and pain weakened and sickened me profoundly. She had never taunted me with it, nor lured me into harm's way. I felt the old pre-Lucy vulnerability and shame wash over me.

"We *are* blood kin," I said. "We're first cousins. We couldn't be any closer kin unless we were brothers and sisters."

"You know what I mean," Lucy said.

I did.

"Lucy, if you think I'm going to cut myself with that thing, you're crazy," I said desperately. "We'll get a whipping if we do it."

"We won't if they don't know it," Lucy said. "How will they know it if we don't tell them?"

"They'll just know."

"Come on, Gibby," Lucy said. "You'll do it if you love me."

She took the small, bone-handled knife, kept keen and glittering by Shem's whetstone, and drew a welling line of red on her fragile, blue-veined wrist. It filled, trembled, and showered down in a cascade of red drops onto the dry earth of the thicket floor, which drank it thirstily and instantly. She stared dreamily at the blood, as if to memorize its course over her arm. Then she raised her light-drowned eyes to me and smiled. She held the knife out.

The dry, burning day quite literally described a slow, stately, shimmering arc over my head, and the scraping song of the cicadas retreated from my ears in a long, sucking surge, as if a tide were going out. A great, faraway roaring remained. I could seem to see nothing but the evil, efficient glitter of the little knife.

"Your turn," she said. I could scarcely hear her through the roaring in my ears.

I turned a blinded, shamed face to her.

"I can't do that," I said humbly. "I can't cut myself. There's lots I'd do for you, Lucy, but I can't cut my arm with that knife. I'd get sick and urp all over you. Or I'd faint. You know that. You know what happened when I got that nosebleed last spring. I was in bed all day."

"You have to," Lucy said inexorably. In her stillness and implacability she was like some pagan priestess, kneeling there in the burning woods with the autumn sun glinting off the knife in her hand.

"I can't," I said. "You might as well ask me to cut my throat."

"I'll do it for you," she said earnestly. "I'll do it real quick, so you won't have time to be scared. You won't even feel it, hardly. It's real sharp. And I'll put my sweater over it, so you won't have to look at the blood. And if you urp I'll clean it up."

"I can't," I said again, in dull despair. The humiliation of the endless moment was complete.

She was beside me in a moment, in a silent, sinuous wriggle like the movement of a snake.

"You have to do it, Gibby," she hissed, in an urgent, sibilant whisper that snapped my tight-screwed eyes open. Her face was paper-white and her eyes blazed, and tears stood in them. She did not, in that moment, even look like my cousin Lucy; she looked like something out of a forest far older and wilder than the one in which we sat; she looked like something that should wear, on her beautiful, narrow head, a crown of living, writhing snakes. I felt my mouth drop open into a slack *O*.

"Do it now," she whispered. "Do it. It will mean that we belong to each other. It will mean that all our lives we'll have somebody who'll come and help us and be with us when we're lonesome, and save us from bad things. When bad things happen and nobody else will save us, we'll have each other to do it. We'll know the other needs us wherever we are in the world, and we'll have to come. If you don't do it I won't have anybody, and one day something bad will happen to me and there won't be anybody to come and save me, and I'll die. If you don't do it, Gibby, I'm going to stick this knife right into my heart, right this minute, and I'll die right here in front of you in awful pain and buckets of blood, and it will be all your fault."

I did it. With the quickness of sheer desperation I pressed the blade deep into my wrist where the little blue delta of veins beat as fast as a snared rabbit's, and the pain was as sharp and sickening as the overripe, mashed persimmons on the floor of the woods around us.

Blood did not drip or trickle; it leaped from my wrist, and flowed, and sheeted my flesh and sated the parched earth so that some of it stood in savage miniature pools and did not soak in. Lucy grasped my wrist quickly and pressed it to hers, even as the pain and nausea and dizziness flooded my veins and climbed, buzzing, up my arms, and flew up to my temples. The thicket spun mightily in the sun, and for nearly an hour after that I lay clinging to the warm earth, afraid that I would vomit my lunch. But I did not. By the time the blood slowed and stopped and Lucy washed it off with the tail of her sweater dipped in the green-scummed water of the stagnant lily pond, my head had cleared and my stomach subsided, and pride and a great, warm sense of owning and being owned flooded over me. As she had said, nobody noticed the cuts, which were, when cleaned and dried, almost invisible, though severe enough so that we both bore the scars always. I think that if they had not scarred, Lucy would have kept at her grisly task until they did. Those small, fine white lines on our two wrists became, forever after, brands of ownership and identity.

The book I brought home that winter night we spied on my parents under the foyer stairs was Sir Thomas Malory's *Morte d'Arthur,* and like *The Jungle Book,* it came to hover over our childhoods with such a weight and mass that it in some ways defined us. Where Lucy had been enchanted by the story of the salvation and deliverance of Mowgli, she went down into Malory with a kind of fierce and full-souled affirmation that suggested a water creature finding, at the last moment before suffocating in the blade-sharp air, the depths of his life-giving sea. I could not read it often enough; I could not read it long enough at a time, to satisfy her. Many nights my head would nod and my burning eyes would close of themselves as the pages blurred before them, and Lucy's voice would jerk me back to wakefulness.

"Wake up, Gibby. You haven't finished this part. Elaine hasn't even got in the boat yet."

"Lucy, it's one o'clock. You've heard this fifty times already. I'm about to die."

"No, Gibby, just this one; just finish this. I have to know what happens. I have to *know.*"

"You do know."

"No, Gibby, *please* . . . " and the distress would be so thick in her voice, a real whimper, that I would go on to the end of the tale before closing the book. There was no story of distress and rescue that she did not hear so often that it became a part of the very fabric of her, no tale of daring and gallantry that did not, invariably, make her eyes shine and the three-cornered kitten's smile dance on her pink mouth. She always thanked me

so genuinely that my fatigue and irritation vanished, and I
counted the heavy head and scratchy morning eyes well spent.

For somewhere in that string of Thomas Malory days, Lucy
had given me my soul, and I knew it. I could never again go back
to being merely a small boy who read aloud to his smaller cousin,
and did, endlessly, her bidding. Malory and his tender, foolish,
beautiful victims were the gift I gave to her. Sainthood was hers
to me.

She said it on one of the first nights I read to her from Malory,
that time the story of Lancelot and Guinevere. When I finished,
I looked over at her and she was sitting bolt upright, light burning on her face like white fire, color coming and going in it.

"They were always saving ladies back then," she said, on a
breath of pure joy. "It was the way a knight had to act. He *had*
to. You're going to be my knight, Gibby, you know that? You're
going to be the bravest and handsomest knight of all, always and
always, and you'll always, always save me. I knew you would
when we cut our wrists."

The simple salvation of identity roared in my head. I knew
then, as I have never really known since, who I was. Sheppard
Gibbs Bondurant III. Knight.

"Well, I'd better start now, then," I said casually, to hide my
flaming heart. "Or I'll end up being the scaredest and skinniest
knight in the world."

"You won't always be skinny," she said. "And you're going
to be very handsome. You're going to look like . . . hmmm . . .
like Lancelot. Or no, more like Galahad, I think. Kind of like
a hawk."

And I gave her the hawklike grin of a golden Galahad, and
loved her in my deepest heart. And when I lay in bed that night,
after she had fallen into sleep and I had turned off Mickey, I
wept silently with the sheer relief of having been given a self.
The shiny bracelet of the scar around my wrist seemed to pulse
with a noble life of its own.

For it was that, in being given and accepting the role of protector to Lucy, all the years of my life as a powerless and completely
irrelevant small boy vanished as if they had never been, and what
was left was pure and endless power. All I was and had been
that was weak and hateful to others, all that was wounding and
shaming to me, became transmuted into power. My obscure and
deep-buried angers were all right, because they became, in that
moment, the righteous wrath of a saint. All aberrations became
divine, because they were the God-bestowed stigmata of a saint.
It justified all I was and would become, would do: I would look
after Lucy Bondurant and scourge through the world anything
that threatened her. Dear Lord, but it was a terrible and seduc-

tive boon that she gave me: to a small boy with nothing, the most seductive of all. It kept me in thrall to more than just Lucy for the bulk of my life; it kept me in a saint's sterile self-imposed exile.

I remember once, when I was long grown, after Ben Cameron had become ill and Dorothy was considering the sale of the Muscogee Avenue house, we talked about that dreadful gift of power that Lucy had given me. It was long after I had stopped going out, except to a very few places, and those mostly at night. Dorothy Cameron's house was one of the places I never stopped going. In those sheltering darks, there seemed to be nothing I could not talk to her about.

"Ever since I discovered that heady, all-powerful feeling of protector and knight-errant to Lucy, I have wanted to be a saint," I said. "Or not so much wanted to be as known that I needed to be. She showed me what a life of power and exaltation that could be. So I did that. I bent everything I had, for a while, toward being a literal saint, the protector of the weak, the helper of the helpless. Saint Shep the Enabler. It started to erode that day out on the river—I'm sure Sarah told you about that—but it didn't really begin to come unraveled until the day of the fire, when I became, in the eyes of this town, not a saint, but a . . . well, you know what they think I am now. And yet the desire, the need, is still there; it's still strong. . . ."

I could feel, in the thick darkness of their sun porch, her great amber eyes on me.

"And so you dropped out," she said in her rich, warm, girl's voice.

"And so I did."

"Not a very saintly thing to do, do you think?"

"On the contrary, Miss Dorothy. Us saints have historically spent quite a bit of time over the years being hermits and eremites and such. Us saints don't have it nearly as good as people think, you know."

"I never thought you had it very good, Shep," Dorothy Cameron said. "On the other hand, I never thought you had it very bad, either."

Dorothy Cameron's great gift to me was that she always knew me for what I was and never stopped both loving and liking me. Lucy's was that, too, of course. But Lucy knew a different person. It always seemed to me a great pity that she could not have acknowledged at least a shadow of that entirely commonplace man that Dorothy Cameron knew so well; it would have spared us endless pain. But she could not. That was, from the very beginning, simply not given to her.

*   *   *

The summer of 1942 was a powerfully hot one, and so humid that doors would not close until autumn, and shoes in closets wore gray-green shawls of mold. The walls of the Peachtree Road house were almost as thick as those of a medieval cloister, and, with the floor-length drapes in the downstairs rooms drawn and the toiling electric fans droning, kept us comfortable during most of my summers there; I cannot remember, before that one, ever being truly hot in that house.

But that summer was different. Day after day dawned milky and tepid, and by noon the entire world was bleached a savage white. Temperatures did not fall below ninety-five degrees more than three or four days after June, and the thunderstorms that came grumbling in from the west almost daily did not break the heat, but only breathed a suffocating wetness into it.

My father and mother and Aunt Willa sat late into the nights on the sun porch, putting off climbing up to the second floor, which was airless and terrible, and Aunt Willa came home from her job at Rich's in the afternoons as wilted and flushed as an infant after a long, sweating sleep, cinders and smoke stuck into the melting icing of her makeup. My father took to working in the library in his shirtsleeves, something he never did before or after, and my mother gradually stopped going out on her rounds of luncheons and bridge. Hardly anyone called, and we did not even have the surcease of the Garden Hills pool or the one at the Driving Club, because the conditions were, we were told over and over again by the radio and newspapers, made to order for infantile paralysis. I suspect we would have broken my mother's edict about Tate that summer, and spent at least two months up there at the cottage, but gasoline was strictly rationed by then, and few people squandered it. My father had a C card, but it was a point of honor with him not to use it often. Confined largely to the house and grounds of 2500 Peachtree Road, Lucy and I slept that summer, by parental dispensation, on mattresses on the summerhouse floor, and virtually lived there with our books and a small radio my father brought us from Buckhead Hardware.

What those nights must have been like for Shem and Martha Cater, in their little rooms over the garage, I don't like to imagine. They never appeared rumpled or cross, as the rest of us did, and I never saw either of them sweat.

"Negroes don't sweat," Lucy told me. "It's because they're so black. They come from Africa where it's a million times hotter than this, and the heat turns them black, and that's why they don't sweat."

That did not sound right to me. "How do you know?" I asked.

"I read it someplace," Lucy said. I knew that she had not,

that I had read everything she had, and nowhere was there any mention of the skin and sweat glands of Negroes. But I did not challenge her. One of Lucy's fantasies had only to come tumbling toadlike out of her mouth before it turned into a pearl of fact, and it upset her genuinely and deeply to be called a liar. I always believed that she knew a truth that transcended the literal one the rest of us were saddled with, and indeed she did seem to get hold of the essence of things in a way few adults I have known ever did. I was not about to argue with her about the sweat of Shem and Martha Cater, and I was not about to ask Martha. Asking remote and thunder-browed Shem was simply beyond imagining.

Martha had her hands full that summer with small Jamie and Little Lady. During the year they had been with us, we had heard and seen little of them, for they had not needed much attention at eight months and three years respectively, and my aunt Willa had cannily kept them out of sight in the rooms allotted to them until she went to work, at which time Martha took over, with her agreeable, dim-witted teenaged daughter ToTo backing her up.

They were quiet, beautiful children, as docile as if they could sense the precariousness of their sufferance in that house, and when they were brought out to join the family at ceremonial occasions such as holiday dinners and Sunday school services and afternoon rides, Aunt Willa always had them scrubbed to polished rosiness and dressed in their starched and ruffled best. They were such attractive children, and such ridiculously obvious little Bondurants, with their rose-gilt fairness and enormous pansy eyes and perfectly wrought small hands and feet, that it was nearly impossible not to smile at them, to touch the satiny, downy surfaces of them. Aunt Willa had taught Little Lady to curtsy, a dreadful, ostentatious little parody of gentility, and to lisp, in her thin, flutelike, nasal drawl, "Thankyouma'am, pleaset'meecha," and though my mother would flinch and my father avert his eyes, they had to respond eventually with approval and murmured accolades, just at all that sheer prettiness.

Little Lady would wriggle then like a toy terrier being petted, and climb up onto a lap, and dimple and duck her perfect little chin and look up under her inch-long, maple-syrup lashes. It was, for a very long time, all that was required of her, and all that was necessary. Everyone who saw her remembered her as a flaxen enchantress, and it was she they meant when they asked my aunt Willa, "How is that pretty daughter of yours?" I could never understand how they could look past the leaping fire that was Lucy to all that pink and white banality, but I truly think the adults of that time never came to see what I first saw, and what soon all the children of Buckhead, especially the boys, eventually did: that Lucy Bondurant was a great, distinguished and disturbing beauty.

As for little Jamie, what is there to trouble the eye and heart about a beautiful baby who never cries? His beauty and sunniness toppled hearts like a perfectly placed bowling ball. Even my mother came to hold out her arms for him to be put into, fragrant and damp and crowing with delight, from his bath. Even my father laid aside his glasses and put down his cigar and held out his arms for little Jamie Bondurant, as he never did for me. I understood, in the wisdom and fullness of my own new status as saint, that it was not possible to be disappointed in something so uncomplicated and unfinished as a baby, and that my father surely knew, as I did, that this tiny male was, beside me, the only standard-bearer for the family name. I knew, too, without too much rancor and hurt, that he sensed that his own issue would refuse or fail that standard. I even conceded, in my innermost heart, that he was probably right. With the favor of Lucy firmly affixed to my knightly sleeve, that knowledge did not give me a great deal of pain.

That second summer, though, the two younger children were miserable upstairs in the heat, and bored and lonely with their mother away during the day, and old enough to chafe within the comfortable prison of their tiny world. A beleaguered ToTo would finally, about two o'clock each afternoon, be driven downstairs by the murderously rising heat, herding her whining, scuffling charges ahead of her like small, fractious geese, and would be forbidden by her exasperated mother to bring them into the kitchen under her feet or let them stray into the library under my father's or the "big" sun porch where my mother lay on her chaise in limp surrender to the July day. That left only the back porch, which for some reason they detested, or the garden and the summerhouse. Since the garden was by that time a blighted Sahara, ToTo brought them into the dim, snake-cool, tiled expanse of the summerhouse where Lucy and I were encamped, and said that if we didn't like it to go tell her mother.

We knew instinctively the consequences of that. Martha was unmaternal by nature, and though a good enough tender of children, not a long-sufferer. Her solution to being harried by small, yangy children was simply to tell my mother that she couldn't get any work done with them underfoot. That produced instantaneous banishment and incarceration all the way around. With no real choice but to let the loathsome Little Lady and Jamie invade our domain at will, Lucy and I spent the summer engaged in creative torture. Not a day passed that we did not inflict agony of body and spirit on the two smaller children sufficient to send them howling and toddling for the house, bent on telling. We would then give ToTo a long, level look and she would uncoil off the sofa, where she slept away the afternoons, and go shuffling after them. She did not protest. ToTo knew that if she could not control the smaller children, if they ran to Martha with their angry bellows and tears, her tenure at 2500 Peachtree Road was over and she would find herself a member of the prodigious household of a shiftless, hard-smacking aunt down in Perry Homes. It was a devil's bargain.

On an endless August afternoon when the heat had turned even the tiled cave of the summerhouse into an inferno, Lucy and I moved our play out into the honeysuckle thicket, where the torpidly stirring air might at least dry the sweat on our bodies. For once we were alone. ToTo slept her usual deadened three o'clock sleep on the grimy sofa, and Jamie and Little Lady, both listless and drugged with too long in the sucking breath of that summer, dozed fitfully on the pallets where Lucy and I slept at night. They had been particularly maddening all day; Little Lady's coy beauty had turned cloying and mule-sullen, and white-faced Jamie had fussed and mewled and scrubbed his shadowed eyes with his fists ever since ToTo had brought them out. He had not slept much at all the night before, she reported aggrievedly, but we took no notice of that. No one had slept well since the monstrous heat had set in.

There was a warren of roomlike partitions under the thicket of the honeysuckle; perfect, child-sized chambers that opened one into another, like a railroad flat. We had named it, for who knows what arcane reason, Dumboozletown, Florida, and had peopled it, invented for it a history and an ongoing narrative line and sealed it off ruthlessly from the advances of the two smaller children. For the space of that summer, Dumboozletown, Florida, was as real to all four of us Bondurant children as Buckhead, and if it was absorbing to Lucy and me, it was absolutely irresistible to Little Lady and Jamie. But we had set around the entire perimeter of the thicket a circle of smooth white stones from the lily pond, and told the two small ones that it was a magic circle and their arms and legs would turn black and fall off if they stepped over it, and they believed us. They would stand outside the circle for hours on end, and cry and wheedle and whine, but never once did they come into Dumboozletown, Florida.

But on this day, perhaps finally maddened with heat and ill feeling, the younger children awoke from their naps, heard us, and tumbled out of the summerhouse and across the veranda and straight over the magic circle into our lair, glaring truculently at us and then all about them, as if waiting for the first of the telltale blackness to begin creeping up their arms and legs.

Little Lady sniggered and crooked her finger at us, and Jamie drew his tow-white brows together in a ridiculous scowl over his blue eyes and thrust out his underlip. His eyes looked weak and squinting, and his nose leaked copiously down onto his chapped upper lip, and his sagging diaper smelled powerfully. They were, at that moment, totally devoid of charm or humanity. I was redly, irrationally angry at them for defying us, but Lucy was utterly enraged.

"Get out of here, you stupid babies!" she screamed.

"Will not," sang Little Lady.

"Won't," droned Jamie.

"Get out right now or I'll beat your heads in," Lucy howled.

"I'll tell Mama on you and she'll put you in a 'norphanage," Little Lady smirked. "She don't like you as much as she does me, anyway. She thinks you're mean and bad. You made our daddy leave home."

"Bad, bad," Jamie sniveled. "Want my daddy!"

Without an instant's hesitation, Lucy swooped, shrieking, down on the two and half pummeled, half pushed them back across the stone circle and out into the sunlight. Her blue eyes looked white and mad, and her smoky hair escaped its loose pigtails and flew free around her blanched maenad's face, and I was profoundly startled and more than a little frightened of her in that moment. Like the original avenging angel of the Book of Genesis, Lucy in her holy fury drove Jamie and Little Lady out of Dumboozletown, Florida.

They went sprawling, and landed in a heap, fetching up against a white wooden garden settee at the edge of the veranda. They lay utterly still for a moment, while the hot-humming earth seemed to stop and listen, and then the great, rattling indrawn breaths came, which meant sky-splitting screams of pain and outrage and the ultimate certainty of our incarceration upstairs in our little cubicles, and Lucy and I looked at each other in dismay. Her breath still shook her chest, and her eyes were white-ringed. It was, after all, they who had broken the covenant, invaded the sanctum, smashed the taboo. But we both knew who would pay.

The shrieks started then, as maddening and repetitious as a berserk train whistle or a stuck siren, and ToTo came stumbling out of the summerhouse. Little Lady had struggled to her feet and was dancing up and down in place, stamping her shapely, dirty little bare feet in rage and frustration, but Jamie lay where he had fallen, eyes closed, uttering short, strange, atonal cries, all on one note, like a dissonant night bird. He did not sound like a small boy who has been thwarted and bumped; he did not sound human. There was a small, dull-red mark on his temple,

vivid against his white skin, and an unprepossessing little smear
of blood at the corner of his mouth, where he had bitten his lip.
Otherwise, he seemed virtually untouched. But he did not get
up and he did not open his eyes.

ToTo picked him up out of the dust and started into the house
with him, Little Lady roaring and dancing along in her wake.

"You all done be in the fire now," ToTo said over her shoulder, not without satisfaction. "You all done hurt this here baby,
an' you know how Miss 'Livia an' Miss Willa suck up over him.
You all not gon' sit down for a month."

Lucy and I went back across the ring of smooth stones, scattered now, and sat down in the last of the string of rooms in
Dumboozletown, Florida, to wait. ToTo was right. The baby
was the undisputed treasure, the crown jewel, of the Peachtree
Road house. Retribution would be swift and certain. We both
knew it would be bad.

"I'm going to say it was me that pushed them," I said to Lucy,
my new sainthood singing sweetly in my veins. "Don't you
worry about it. Nothing's going to happen to you."

Besides its overripe taste of virtue, the offer had a basis in practicality. No one in the house had ever really punished me, certainly not struck me; I had never before had the wit or courage
to do anything that warranted it. I did not think that anyone
would do so now, though I did believe there would be
punishment—grounding or imprisonment somewhere apart
from Lucy, probably, and likely for a long time. I would hate
that, but the saint would endure stoically.

But Lucy always suffered terribly when Willa punished her.
She would not, absolutely refused to, weep or cry out under the
spankings, but they left her diminished and dimmed for days.
And imprisonment simply sent her wild. On the whole, I knew
I could handle it better. And the points I would gain with Lucy
were pure lagniappe.

"They'll know I did it," she said dully. She did not look after
ToTo's retreating back, or at me, but straight ahead of her, into
the hot green haze of the thicket. "Little Lady will tell. ToTo
will tell. Mama will beat me. And then they'll lock me upstairs
forever and ever."

"They can't do that," I said reasonably. "That's not fair."

She looked at me then. The blue eyes were very old.

"They aren't fair," she said. "Why did you think they would
be?"

And so we fell silent. And we waited for them to come and
punish us.

But they did not come. The white fire went out of the day,
and then the red, and soon only the hot, graying ash of twilight

remained, and still no one came to mete out justice for Jamie and Little Lady's sake. It was nearly full dark when we heard the siren, almost eight-thirty, and by the time the ambulance pulled up in front of the house and the running steps of men hit the portico, and we heard the soft, frantic babble of voices in the foyer, the last of the light was gone and the fireflies were beginning to wink in the black woods and garden. The stars seemed scummed with heat, and there was no moon. Before the ambulance door slammed shut and the siren began its long, awful cat's howl, we heard the first katydid begin his song, and after it had screamed away down Peachtree Road, diminishing toward Crawford Long Hospital, the full night chorus was out. We lurched to our feet and began to run.

When we got to the house, our breath high in our throats and thin with dread, no one was there. There was no one on the sun porch or in the library, and none of our parents were in their upstairs bedrooms. I had the insane fancy that everyone was dead, that the ambulance had come for all of them. We trotted around that great hot, empty, darkened house, in and out of room after echoing room, and by the time we reached the kitchen the dread had turned into terror so acute that I was weeping quite uncontrollably with it. Lucy was silent. The kitchen was empty, too, and starkly clean. No food simmered on the vast stove, no dishes sat out. The wrought-iron table on the screened porch was not set for dinner.

Our hair was wet to the roots with panic by the time we pounded up the outside stairs to Martha and Shem's little rooms over the garage and hammered on the door, and it was only then that we learned that little Jamie had been taken to the hospital near death, and that my parents and Aunt Willa had gone with him. Little Lady lay asleep on Martha's narrow iron bed; Martha's gnarled finger to her lips quieted us, and we noticed then, in the stifling gloom, the misery-stooped figure of ToTo, sitting beside the bed, watching over Little Lady.

"Look lak they done clean forgot about y'all," Martha said in a weary whisper. "Go on back to the house an' I'll come fix y'all some supper."

We saw that there were tear tracks on her dark face, like the trail of sticky silver that a snail leaves. She and ToTo were alone with the sleeping Little Lady. We knew that Shem would have taken my parents to the hospital in the Chrysler, behind the ambulance.

She made scrambled eggs and bacon for us, and sat us down at the kitchen table to eat, but we were not hungry, and only picked at the cooling food. Oddly, we did not ask her about the baby's condition; could not. I simply assumed that he had been hurt in some terrible, unseen way when Lucy had pushed him out of Dumboozletown, Florida, and that he would surely die, and that nothing in our world would ever be the same again. I knew with marrow-deep certainty that Lucy thought so, too, but she was very white and mute and did not say, and she never did say afterward. There seemed to me, sitting in the dark of that endless night with Lucy, absolutely nothing in my power, or in anyone's, that could be done to make things right again. It was the first I ever knew of despair, and it remains the worst.

The baby died at 4:15 the next morning, August 11, 1942, and it was not until late afternoon of the following day that anyone thought to tell us that he died, not of Lucy's anger, but of polio. Then and only then did Lucy finally begin to cry, and though my father came belatedly and picked her up and held her on his lap and attempted, stiffly, to soothe her, and though she finally did subside, hiccuping, into silence and then at last into exhausted sleep, only she and I ever knew that she cried, not from sorrow, but from relief.

CHAPTER
FIVE

THEY QUARANTINED US IMMEDIATELY. Even before Jamie's funeral, they separated us from each other and from the rest of the family, and for the two weeks the isolation lasted, I felt as disoriented and alone and outside the human pale as I have ever felt. Even now, when days and weeks go by and I do not see anyone, there is no comparison to that alienation, that sense of being beyond communion and redemption. This solitude is of my own creation. That one was cast around me like an unclean shroud.

Quarantine was not a medical consideration; Dr. George Ballentine, who lived down West Wesley and was a frequent dinner guest in my parents' house, came on that second evening, looking wildly out of character in a short-sleeved shirt and two-tone shoes, examined Lucy and me and pronounced us, so far as he could tell, fit and free of incipient polio. He gave us both aspirins and bade that we be put to bed, but that was merely in consideration of Lucy's exhausted sobbing and my paleness and nausea. He went into my parents' bedroom and spoke with my mother, and then into Aunt Willa's and gave her a shot to ease the terrible, wild crying that had shaken her like a fit ever since she had come back from the hospital. Hovering on the black lip of sleep, I heard him tell my father, who had walked out into the upper hallway with him, that we children should both be all right by the next morning, and to feed us lightly and keep us quiet for a day or two and call him if anything unusual came up.

But when the next morning broke, still, incredibly, as monotonously unchanged in its colorless heat and fetor as all the days before it, it was to find ToTo moving Lucy's few clothes and toys

95

out of her bedroom and into the little rooms over the garage, and the big storeroom at the end of the attic corridor being cleared and aired.

My mother appeared in ToTo's wake, elegant in black eyelet and so pale that her dark red lipstick looked the color of blackberry stain against her fair skin, carrying a breakfast tray for me. I did not like the looks of any of it, and began to scramble out from under my damp sheet preparatory to flight. My mother closed the door firmly behind her and sat down on the edge of my bed. Her brown eyes, so dark that you could never look into them, were heavily shadowed underneath with greenish smears, and her skin looked flat and large-grained. Even her dark hair, which always caught so much light that it looked newly wet, was lusterless.

"Jamie died of infantile paralysis," she said. "Do you know what that is, Sheppie?"

I nodded in silence, looking at her uneasily. I had not heard that "Sheppie" since Lucy and her family had come to live with us and some of the sucking weight of my mother's full attention had lifted from me. It rang with portent.

"Well, then," she said, "you know how bad it is, and why we have to do everything in the world we can to see that you don't get it. And since we don't know where poor little Jamie got it, we're going to have to keep you out of harm's way until it gets cooler. Lucy's going to stay with Shem and Martha for a little while, and we're going to make you a lovely playroom all for yourself up here. We'll bring you lots of books and toys, and Lottie is going to cook everything you like to eat and we'll bring it to you up here. I'll come up and read to you in the afternoons, and sometimes I'll have my supper up here with you, and Daddy will bring you your very own radio and all the new comic books. It'll be just like living in a hotel. You know how you enjoyed staying at the Waldorf that time we went to New York; it'll be just like that."

My eyes began to fill with frightened tears, and I despised them, but I could not will them back. They overflowed and ran silently down into the corners of my mouth. The warm salt of them nauseated me all over again.

"I don't want to stay up here by myself," I said. "It's too hot. It makes me sick. And Lucy can't stay out there by herself while Shem and Martha are at work. She's too little. She gets scared. Why can't she come up here with me, or why can't we just go out to the summerhouse and stay there and not come out till you tell us to? It's mean to make her stay by herself."

My mother put her arms around me and pulled me against her, and I could feel the warmth of the flesh under the eyelet, and the smell of Lily of the Valley, which she always wore in those days. It felt so strange to be in her arms that it paralyzed me, and I did not, somehow, dare to take a breath. I could not remember the last time she had hugged me. I knew that my weak, unstoppable tears were splotching her pretty dress, and I was mortified, but powerless to staunch the flow. I bit my lip so hard that pain reddened the darkness behind my closed eyes, and the freshet abated a little.

"We've lost one little boy in this house," my mother said, with an uncharacteristic fierceness. "I'm not going to lose my own. Maybe I haven't taken enough trouble with you, letting you run wild all summer with Lucy, but that's going to stop now. You're all I have that's really and truly my own, Sheppie, and I'm not going to take any more chances with you."

I blinked, against the fragrant blackness of her breast. What was she up to? I knew I was not all she had; she had a big house, and two big cars, and lots of beautiful clothes, and all that dark, gleaming furniture and those frail, light-struck porcelains and crystal; she had an army of acquaintances almost identical to her, and clubs and parties and dances and luncheons and dinners that she went to all the time; she had my father. I had never considered myself to be in the pantheon of her prized possessions before. I felt deeply uneasy, a small forest creature turning in a circle, smelling rather than seeing the amorphous danger that lay thick in the air around it.

"But Lucy . . ." I began.

"Lucy is going out where ToTo and Martha can take care of her, and where she can't get up to any more mischief for a while," she said crisply. "She's been exposed to polio just like you have, and she's not going to spread it around this house. For all we know, she could be a carrier of some kind—"

"She is not!" I yelled, pulling away from her. "You just don't like her, that's why you're locking her up down there and me up here! She is not either a carrier!"

"You don't know," my mother said coolly, sitting back upright on the edge of the bed. "We don't know what causes polio. Don't sass me, Shep. You can both move back to the summerhouse when it cools off a little, but for right now you're staying here, and I don't want to hear any more about it. A little vacation from Miss Lucy will do you good. I know who pushed that baby down and made him hit his head."

"That was me!" I shouted. "I did that! Lucy didn't touch the stupid baby!"

"That's enough," she said, the familiar ice back in her voice. "ToTo and Little Lady told us what happened. That child is nothing but trouble, and the fact that she's got you lying for her only bears me out. I have to get ready for the funeral now, and I want you to take a bath and put on your good clothes. I'll bring them up after I've finished dressing."

"Why do I have to get dressed up if I'm only going to sit up here dying in the heat?" I said sullenly, mutiny simmering in my heart.

"Because your little cousin has died very terribly and is being buried today, and you can very well show some respect even if you show it by yourself. It's what decent people do. It's time you started learning how to live like the privileged and fortunate little gentleman you are. You were born to breeding and manners, Sheppie, even if you do spend all your time with . . . children who were not. I don't want you to forget that."

She was gone from the room before I figured out that she meant Lucy. I got out of bed and went hesitantly down the dim little hall in the unaccustomed silence. Always, at this stage in the morning, Lucy would be awake and calling out to me as we dressed for our day. But now there was only dust and heat and silence, and her cubicle, when I looked into it, was empty, even the small iron bed stripped down to its mattress. Her clothes were gone from the meager closet, too. Only Mickey lived; someone had forgotten to turn him off, and he glowed happily and somehow terribly there in the void where Lucy was not. The thought struck me that she had died, had died in the night of the polio that had carried off her small brother, and immediately upon thinking it I found myself at the top of the narrow stair down to the second floor screaming, "Lucy! Lucy!"

There was a long and awful silence, endlessly ringing, in which my heart almost knocked me to my knees with its force, and then Martha Cater appeared at the foot of the stairs and glared up at me.

"Hush that yellin', Shep! This is a house of mournin'! I kin hear you all over the downstairs. What you want?"

"Lucy!" I bellowed. "Where is Lucy?"

"She in her mama's bathroom gettin' a bath just lak you ought to be," she said severely. "What the matter with you two chirrun? You a'hollerin' and her a'screamin' lak a fiah engine, and yo' po' folkses tryin' to git ready to go bury that po' little boy. You ought to be ashamed of yo'se'fs!"

I heard Lucy then, over Martha's voice; heard her screams, far away and muffled through several closed doors, though I could not at first make out the words that she cried. But I knew the tone; knew what she was feeling, as I always knew with Lucy. Outrage, betrayal and that ultimate and mindless panic that being pent up always set loose in her. In the midst of her screams I heard my name: "Gibby! I want Gibby!"

Martha turned away in disgust, and I went back to my room and shut the door so that I could not hear her calling me. I knew that if I tried to go down to her I would simply be picked up and carried bodily back upstairs like the impotent small boy I was. My new sainthood had deserted both of us. I did not wish to compound the desertion with humiliation.

"Okay," I said under my breath, fiercely, and yet with a kind of detached calmness. I was absolutely clear in my mind. "Just all of you wait until I get big enough. None of you are going to be able to stop me then. I'm going to take Lucy and go far away from here, and you'll never see either one of us anymore in the world. I don't care how long it takes. I'm going to do it."

And I lay back on my rumpled little bed and folded my arms under my head and began, in a kind of furious peace, that long wait.

It was a terrible time, a hiatus made all the more unendurable because we did not know when it would end. We knew only that freedom would come with the abating of the heat, and it seemed to us, by then, that the very weather that wrapped the earth was in immutable conspiracy against us. Day after day dawned pale and featureless and still; afternoon after afternoon fulfilled the punishing promise of the thick morning. Even the boisterous, ineffectual thunderstorms that had broken the days stopped toward the end of that August, and then there was nothing, nothing, but whiteness and stillness and quiet and boredom and heat. My sharp and particular yearning for Lucy dulled and slumped back into the general, featureless malaise of misery in which I spent my days, despite the daily visits from my mother and sometimes my father, despite the piles of books and magazines and the new radio and the trays of special tidbits that ascended three times a day from the kitchen.

After that first day, I did not hear her cry out for me again, and I stopped asking for her, because the invariable answer to my queries was "She's just fine. Living the life of Riley, reading and listening to the radio and playing games with ToTo." I knew that was not true, but I did not know what was.

Sometime during that first week of mourning, my aunt Willa stopped her wild crying and washed her face and reapplied her makeup and went back to her job, and was much applauded for her pluck and gumption. I had discovered that by lying with my ear pressed against the hot-air register in the floor of the storeroom, which had become my daytime playroom, I could hear, through some elemental magic of physics, the conversations that were held on the sun porch off the drawing room, and I assumed the position whenever I heard a visiting automobile's tires crunching on the gravel of the drive. My mother received her

callers there in those days of formal mourning, as Aunt Willa
had before her duty called her back, and it was in that way I
kept my finger on the pulse of some tenuous reality. It was there,
too, lying on the floor with my ear to that painful grid, I learned
that Lucy was without patronage in the house.

Dorothy Cameron had come to call on my mother that day,
bringing with her some red and green pepper jelly for which I
heard my mother's languid voice thanking her, and it was she
who praised my aunt Willa. My mother brushed the praise aside.

"You'd have thought she was dying herself, the way she carried on up there, with poor Martha hauling trays and the doctor
in and out five times a day," she said. "And then before we know
it, she's downstairs all tarted up and with the makeup on an inch
thick, asking if Shem could drive her downtown; says she's
needed at the Red Cross canteen. Now I ask you! Her only boy
just dead and she's going down and throw herself at that trash
around the bus station! What on earth will people say?"

"Good for her," Dorothy Cameron said, her voice crisp and
edged. "I think she's absolutely right. We *are* at war, you know,
Olivia, and lying around crying isn't going to bring that poor
baby back. The Red Cross needs all the hands it can get. People
will say she's just what she is, a brave woman who puts her country above her own personal sorrow."

"You sound just like Sheppard." My mother's languid voice
was clearly exasperated. "I thought he was going to run right
out and get her a Congressional Medal of Honor. Oh well, I
know her type even if you're too nice to see it, and I know what
men are. Sooner or later she's going to do something so tacky
that even he'll see her in her true colors, and I wouldn't be surprised if he didn't put her right out of the house then."

"Which would be an awful shame for those two poor, fatherless children that are left," Dorothy Cameron said.

My mother did not reply, and I knew that Sarah's mother had
bested her again. For some reason she was a little afraid of tiny
Dorothy Cameron, or at least, respected her enough so that she
would accept with unaccustomed meekness words she would
have flung back into anyone else's face. I knew also that she
would be on the phone to her circle after Dorothy left, reporting
this latest Cameronian breach of decorum.

There was a little silence, and then Dorothy Cameron said,
"How are the children taking it? I haven't seen Shep since it happened. I've thought about him and Lucy. She's a sensitive little
thing. I hope this hasn't upset her too much."

"We're keeping them quiet and apart for a little while," my
mother said, and I grinned an adult's mirthless grin at the enormity of the understatement. "Lucy isn't a very good influence

on Shep, and this little break is doing him a world of good. He's fine; I spend all my afternoons and nights with him, and I've really enjoyed getting to know my little boy again. He's awfully precious to me, Dorothy, especially since I've seen how easy it is for them to just slip away. I'm not ever going to let him run wild again, like he has this summer with that child, that Lucy. There's too much of sensitivity and talent in Sheppie that ought to be cultivated. She's a wild little thing, you know, and not at all stable. Way too big for her britches and spoiled from running loose. Willa hasn't spent a minute with her since the baby died; she's with Little Lady every second that she's home. Now *that* poor baby was just devastated. She hasn't stopped crying yet. But Lucy . . . not a tear, not a word. Oh well. Given the givens, what can you expect?"

"Who stays with Lucy?" Dorothy Cameron asked.

"Why . . . no one, really, I guess," my mother said. "ToTo every now and then, maybe. She doesn't seem to want anybody around her; won't answer if you ask her a direct question; won't even look at you when you're talking to her. So we're just leaving her pretty much alone and letting her sulk. I think she'll soon catch on to how unattractive it is. I don't worry a bit about that child. She doesn't need anybody. If this little spell by herself teaches her a few manners, so much to the good."

I rolled off the register and drew myself up on the floor in a ball of sheer pain. I did not want to hear any more. It was far worse than I had thought. Apart from me, Lucy was without a protector in the house. Her own mother, perhaps sensing the loss of power that Jamie's dying had dealt her, had bent her efforts now upon nurturing and cultivating Little Lady, her only other viable little commodity. My mother had, for some unfathomable reason, bent her whole obsessive attention once again upon me. My already remote father, grieving in his own way over the loss of that tiny male Bondurant, would, I knew, have retreated into the library and pulled his distance in behind him. ToTo was with Little Lady all day. That left only Martha Cater—an already exasperated, spread-too-thin Martha. Lucy had become that for which, it must seem to her, her very birth had marked her: pariah.

Rage filled me and became tears, and as I wept I resolved to go downstairs that night when everyone was sleeping and comfort her, and whoever found me be damned. If they removed me I would go back. And I would go back again. Whatever they did to me, I did not care. Sainthood surged back, strong and simple and sweet.

But I did not, after all, have to put myself to the test, for just after my mother had brought my dinner tray and settled down with me for the evening, my father came into the little room, his face a thundercloud, and said, "Is Lucy up here?"

"Why, of course not," my mother said. "What's the matter?"

"She's not in her room," he said. "She was gone when Willa got in from Canteen, and we can't find her anywhere around the place. Little Lady is gone, too."

"ToTo . . . ," my mother began, half rising.

"ToTo," my father said in profound disgust, "was asleep. It took me and Martha five minutes to wake her up. She wouldn't have heard the Third Army Band if it had gone through."

"Where is Willa?" my mother said.

"Downstairs having a fit." My father bit off the words. "Martha has called George Ballentine, and I've called the police. I'm not going to fool around with that little brat this time."

My blood ran cold with fear for Lucy, but under the ice leaped a tongue of sheer exultation: "Good for you, Lucy! Good for you!"

When they went out of the room and down the stairs I was behind them, and I don't believe they ever did realize that I had, without a word, ended forever that hateful quarantine. Or no, that Lucy had ended it for both of us, when she had kidnapped her younger sister. A missing Lucy Bondurant was one thing, but a missing Little Lady was another matter entirely. We heard the sirens of the first police car before we reached the foyer.

They found Lucy in the Greyhound bus station downtown, pushing a shrieking, filthy Little Lady in her outgrown stroller, waiting for the bus to New Orleans for which Lucy had purchased two tickets. She had, she calmly and freely admitted, stolen the money from her mother's purse and watched and waited until no one seemed to be about, called a taxi and put Little Lady and the stroller into it and been driven to the station. And no, she had had no trouble at all in doing so. It was easy when you knew how.

But where was she going? they asked. And what did she think she was doing, taking her little sister all the way downtown and trying to get on a bus with her?

"I was saving her from the polio so Mama wouldn't cry anymore," Lucy said earnestly, her eyes wide and lambent and impossibly blue. "I was going to find Daddy and he would save her from the polio."

After she had been spanked and sent to bed without her supper, and—much worse, unheard of—scolded soundly and coldly by my father, she sobbed quietly in her little bed up under the eaves, and at first would not answer when I slipped in beside her and gathered her into my arms. It seemed as though the quarantine had never happened, and as if she had never been away from me.

"I think what you did was real brave," I whispered. "She shouldn't have licked you for it."

I felt her start to tremble, and tightened my arms around her, and then I heard, incredibly, her rich, glorious laugh.

"I wasn't gon' to save her from the polio, silly," she said. "I was gon' put her on that bus and send her off, and then I'd be the only one. Like I was in the beginning, with Daddy. It was her and Jamie that ran Daddy off, I know. If I was the only one, I know he'd come back. I know he would. He said he wasn't ever going to leave me, and he wouldn't have, if it hadn't been for those crybabies."

In the narrow white bed, in the white August moonlight, I felt very cold. She was asleep almost before she had murmured the last sentence, but it was a long time before I slept.

The next morning she did not come down to breakfast with the rest of us, and I did not like to remark on her absence, because I was afraid they would remember the quarantine and declare it back in effect. I knew that she was awake, and that she was not sulking, because she had talked cheerfully to me as I dressed.

We were almost through when she came into the breakfast room. She went straight to my father and climbed onto his lap, and put her hands on his shoulders and peered into his face. Her eyes were almost black with intensity, and her hair, which she had worn braided all summer, was unbound and stood in a just-brushed nimbus around her small, pointed face. The tea rose color came and went.

"I'm sorry I was a bad girl, Uncle Sheppard," she said. "I promise never to do it again. Please don't be so mad at me that you won't take care of me anymore."

My father looked at her silently for a space of time, delicate and rose-flushed in her thin white batiste nightgown. Then he gave her a hug, awkward but hard. I heard the breath go out of her in a little chuff.

"I'll take care of you until the cows come home, Puddin'," he said, and I thought that there was a trace, a minute and incredible gleam of wetness in his pale blue eyes.

"Thank you," Lucy said, and climbed down and pattered out of the room and back up the stairs.

I followed her in a few moments.

"Boy, that was some act you put on with Daddy," I said admiringly. "You had him eating out of your hand. I could never get away with that."

"It wasn't an act," she said. "I meant it."

"But you didn't have to do that. He'll take care of you. He has to. You're his niece."

"Well, I had to make sure," Lucy said.

"I'll take care of you, Lucy," I said. "I swore on my blood to do that. You don't have to worry about that."

"You aren't big enough yet," she said, and there was an entirely unchildlike, workman's practicality in her voice. "I have to make sure he does until you can."

That night a great storm, the grandfather of all summer thunderstorms, broke over the house on Peachtree Road, and even before the lightning and thunder swept cursing off to the east, a great breath of fresh, cool air out of the green-lit west came ghosting in to tell us that the heat—the monstrous, torpid Big Heat—had gone, and with it the sneaking, murdering polio, and for that year, at least, we were done with the shadow of that summer death.

CHAPTER
SIX

SOME PEOPLE SAY that the great change began then, in the years just after World War II; that the wartime economy which lifted Atlanta out of the doldrums of Depression never really faltered, and that a great trajectory which would span fifty years and literally bridge worlds was launched with the planes and ships of that war.

My friend Barry Gresham, who would later found the city's first pure research institute, holds that Atlanta's future was virtually assured when the young men who were our fathers returned from war or from wartime preoccupations and looked around them to scan the lay of the land. Those years were, Barry thinks, like a held breath, the preliminary gathering of muscles for a great leap of growth and progress that would never stop. Not, he says, overtly; the young men who would guide the progress and shape its direction were not yet themselves fully aware of their inherent power and their looming roles. They simply came home to tend to business and raise families, expand fortunes, carve niches, build lives.

But one day, toward the end of the 1950s, they would look up and see that a slow stagnation had set in; that the last tall building of the city's skyline had gone up nearly a decade before, and that Atlanta's engine choked and stuttered on idle. Their own fortunes had increased dramatically, but the city's had not. They would look around them and at one another in the clubs and libraries and patios of the Northwest, and, almost as if by prior design, would move together to ponder and plan, and the power of them would leap in the very air, almost as palpable as lightning, and wheels rusted for a decade would begin to grind.

But we children did not see the fateful change beginning, of course; to us, these golden men were just our fathers. We might have been dimly aware, though I doubt it, that we were entering another stage of growth, emerging from small childhood into a kind of *mittelkinder* principality, but this was just that: a stage, a phase, an extension of the same privileged and insular existence we had led for the first few years of our lives. We were almost laughably, stereotypically boyish and girlish. Hollywood of that era would have loved us: princely little Disney piglets. Pretty little Shirleys and Deannas. What was the cloying movie so popular at that time? *Angels with Dirty Faces?* That was us. *Our Gang,* only with money.

For we were the small heirs of Atlanta's social and financial elite, and on some level we knew it, and were secure, even offhand, within the impenetrable shell it cast around us. We knew, most of us, that we would inherit more than personal fortunes, but we were remarkably unaffected by the knowledge. Looking back, I can see that most of our parents labored mightily to keep us what they considered "natural," untouched and unspoiled by this legacy of substance and style. I never knew until after my father's death the extent of my family's wealth. Sarah and Ben Cameron, both with formidable trusts set up by grandparents, were required to earn their spending and Sunday school money. Most of us, Lucy and I included, had allowances that were smaller than those of many children across Peachtree Road in Garden Hills, and almost all of us did some sort of work to earn them. Virtually all the boys had a job at some time or other during high school. Virtually all the girls baby-sat and did chores. None of us knew anything of our fathers' businesses and professions; far less, perhaps, than the children of wealth and privilege in other cities. Sarah and Ben, Tom Goodwin, Carter Rawson, Snake Cheatham, Pres Hubbard, Charlie Gentry, me, Freddie Slaton, Lelia Blackburn, Julia Randolph . . . these small spawn of the big houses and others like us were sublimely unaware, even as it was beginning to happen, that our fathers would be mayor, bank presidents, heads of multistate utilities, editors and publishers and broadcasters, builders of cities and empires, chiefs of great altruistic foundations.

And we remained unaware for a very long time. We were, simply, the wiry, skinned-kneed players of playground baseball and football, divers and swimmers in club and backyard pools, racers of soapbox cars, builders of model ships and airplanes, fliers of kites, artists of marbles and mumblety-peg and sharpshooters of Daisy air rifles, captives at small, creamy dancing schools, attenders of Saturday matinees and readers of comic books, mothers of dolls and guests at tea parties, tireless riders of Schwinns, rovers in woods and dabblers in creeks, wrestlers and brawlers and trick-or-treaters and fledgling flirts and belles of an era that, in its innocence and insularity, will likely never be seen or equaled again.

Because our fathers were the most conservative of men personally, and because they idealized their wives and young children—most of them, at any rate—they strove to give us the childhoods of their own conventional dreams: carefree, sunny, simply and straightforwardly masculine for their sons, simply and sweetly feminine for their daughters, without stress or menace or the specter of premature and undue ambition. Without world-knowledge. With small, prescribed risks but little real challenge. They demanded almost nothing of us except what some of us could not give—conformity and adaptability—and if the price of those childhoods was as nothing to most of us, to a few, like Lucy and me, it was everything.

No, we saw no change in the world around us. Not then. To me, the great change came in the inner landscape, not the outer, and it did not take place for some years, until a summer night when I was twelve and Lucy was ten. Before then I was a boy among other boys, running as free as I would ever run, in the company of boys almost ludicrously like myself, at least on the surface. And where we ran, freer and lighter of heart and fleeter of foot than any of us, Lucy ran, too.

It was a wonderful time in the world for both of us. Both of us were, for the moment, free. Aunt Willa was almost obsessively concerned with the cultivation of herself and her younger daughter and had little time or attention left for Lucy, and for perhaps the only time in my life, my mother and father could find no truly glaring faults with which to tax me. I was as nearly an outgoing, normal, Buckhead-approved boy as it was possible for me to be, and I came close to excelling in one or two things that had the Bondurant stamp of approval. I played promising singles tennis, and I could, I discovered, run like the very wind. Both these skills drew from my father the only real smiles of whole-souled pride I have ever had. I cultivated them assiduously.

In retrospect I can see that Lucy and I worked as hard at being acceptable pack members as many adults ever work at their careers, and for a far more valid reason: The acceptance bought us time for our real lives. Each foot race won, each victorious tennis match, each day spent without drawing down calamitous disapproval on our heads earned us commensurate time for reading and talking and dreaming in the summerhouse. My mother and father smiled at my modest athletic prowess and chose not to pursue their displeasure when I spent the whole of a bright summer day cooped up with books and Lucy. Aunt Willa was

obviously grateful not to have an inventive and troublesome
Lucy underfoot, and did not care how much time she spent away
from the house, or where. Lucy had concocted the elaborate fiction that her father was involved in a long-range, top secret mission for the government in occupied Europe, and so was free of
her crippling preoccupation with his whereabouts, though she
still had the devastating nightmares with some regularity. We
had then a very good life, and we were under no illusions as to
what it took to maintain it. In the age-old manner of born victims, we cooperated fully and cheerfully with both our captors
and our peers and kept our inner freedom a secret.

Lucy's position as pack leader was so unusual as to nearly defy
credibility: That a little girl two years younger than the boy pack
around her could, in the bone-simple Atlanta of the late 1940s
and early 1950s, come unknown, unpedigreed and unheralded
into its small masculine society and simply assume command
boggled truth. But that is what happened. From the first, she
shunned and scorned the small girls of the big houses, and knew
with an extraordinary intuitiveness what it would take to win
the boys.

"Would you like to come over and play with Sarah one afternoon this week?" I remember Dorothy Cameron asking Lucy
during her first summer at 2500 Peachtree Road.

"No'm," Lucy said promptly, and then remembering Aunt
Willa's edict, "Thank you. I'd like to come play with Ben,
though."

"Do you think you could keep up with him?" Dorothy asked,
amused. "He's pretty big, you know."

"Yes'm," Lucy said. "But I don't much think he could keep
up with me."

What it took to win the boys in our crowd was mastery. Lucy
seemed born with it. More than any one of us, male or female,
she had daring, physical prowess, imagination. There was no feat
of strength or agility she could not master, no flight of fancy or
fable she could not best. Her great, world-invalidating laugh and
matchless eyes mesmerized us all, and she could always gather
a crowd with her throaty "Hey, listen, I have something to tell
you!" But it was the boys who crowded closest and stayed longest. The girls of our crowd would, at the birthday parties and
after-school play sessions, gradually withdraw to the fringes of
the group, falling silent, looking large-eyed and speculatively at
Lucy Bondurant spinning her magic around their brothers and
playmates. It was a look I saw in the eyes of the women around
her all her life, a look of wariness, a slight flaring of nostrils, as
if scenting danger.

It was Lucy who handed to me my position as, if not leader,

then fully vested comember of that small, yelping golden pack. I learned to run simply trying to keep up with her; when I found that I had an entirely unearned gift for loping great distances as fleetly as a gazelle, I outran her and all the others in the group and gloried in the victories, and her joy and delight in them was as great as my own. When I beat Tom Goodwin in singles at the Driving Club's junior matches one fine spring—the first and only time, for Tom was as natural a tennis player as any I have ever seen—Lucy's cheers were as loud as my father's. Lucy was, over the years, many complex and disturbing things, but she was never in her incandescent life jealous or small-spirited. What she had she gave away freely and with both hands, and she had, in those brief and bright young days, everything it took to lead the Buckhead Boys.

What she had most of was courage of such a high and glinting-edged degree that it flirted with being, and often was, sheer fool-hardiness. The day she became our unacknowledged but unquestioned leader was also the day she secured for me an unshakable place in those small ranks, and none of us there has ever forgotten it. I know that to be true; it was that day down at Brookwood Station of which we spoke first, we diminished and old-young Buckhead Boys, on the day of her funeral.

The Southern Railway's Peachtree Station, a beautiful small Neel Reid building in red Flemish-bond brick with the trademark Palladian windows, still stands on a long curve in Peachtree Road about halfway between Buckhead and downtown, in the section of the city called Brookwood Hills. In my grandparents' and even my parents' day it was where all of Buckhead left on the first stage of their Grand Tours abroad, and during the war just past it had been thronged with young men in khaki. It was in my boyhood still an extremely active station, with freight and passenger trains arriving and leaving almost on the hour, for Atlanta was first and foremost a railroad town, and its iron tentacles once reached out to the entire world. It was not a long bicycle ride from Buckhead; we could toil up the short hills and swoop down the long ones to reach it in about fifteen minutes, and though none of us were permitted to take our bikes onto Peachtree Road, we did so with regularity, and in relative safety, for the unspeakable traffic that clots its meager lanes now was manageable then, and much slower. We were accustomed to going south at least as far as Peachtree Creek at Peachtree Battle Avenue, to run wild in the memorial park there and wade and slosh in the reedy, still-clean creek, and it was only about a mile farther, up a long, heart-shaking final hill and down another, to where the station sat, brooded over to the south by the graceful, white-columned old mansion that housed the Washington Seminary for girls.

The station was irresistible to Lucy. She could, and did whenever possible, spend hours down on the long concrete apron behind the station where the trains lay at berth like great black bison, and whenever she was taken there she would come home covered with cinders and with great distances shining in her eyes. When we all graduated to bicycles, it was there that she led us whenever we had time to get there and back without our parents' missing us.

We first went there on one of the early-spring Saturdays after we all, by some seemingly tacit agreement, got our bicycles for Christmas. I think it was the bane of Lucy's existence that she was given a girls' bicycle, without the proud bar from seat to handlebars, and from the very beginning she took enormous, careening risks, as if to exorcise by her very daring the hated void where the bar that spelled manhood was not.

We met in the cobbled courtyard of Ben and Sarah Cameron's house, and Lucy was already shimmering with her plan.

"I double-dog dare y'all to go down to Brookwood Station," she said, grinning.

No one spoke, and then Pres Hubbard said, "I'm not supposed to go any farther than Peachtree Battle."

Lucy's cool gaze took in his brace and dismissed him. He flushed. She did not mention his infirmity, but it palpitated in the air like a beating heart.

Charlie Gentry, who had always been protective of Pres, said, "That's stupid. None of us is supposed to go that far. We'll all be grounded. I ain't going."

Lucy did not even look at him.

"You afraid too, Ben?" she said.

"I'm not really supposed to go that far either," Ben Cameron said. "But if you think I'm afraid . . ."

She dismissed him with a gesture.

"Well, *I'm* not scared," she said. She kicked the stand away from her bicycle and pedaled out onto Muscogee. She did not look back.

She was almost up the hill to Peachtree when I said desperately, "I'm going, too."

In the blink of an eye we were all pedaling up Muscogee after Lucy.

It was the first time we had ventured out of our immediate neighborhood, and the first that we had ridden very far on Peachtree Road proper, and we were, though we never would have admitted it, nervous and apprehensive. If any one of us had said, "Let's go back," we all would have followed him with alacrity, but since it was small Lucy who was urging us on, retreat was unthinkable. By the time we got to the station and left our bikes and went down behind where the noon train to Charlotte and points north lay panting from its morning run, we were all shying like ponies in a cloud of horseflies. It would not have taken much to scatter us like wild things.

"See, it's not late. The train's still here," Lucy said.

"It's going to leave any time," Tom Goodwin said. "It's almost noon. We really ought to go back."

"Shoot," Lucy said. "It won't leave for hours."

We all knew the train was due to leave. The luggage and passengers were aboard, and the conductor was making his final sortie along the apron, headed away from us. The breath of the great black giant came strong and even and slow, but we knew that at any moment it would deepen and fall into the gathering rhythm of departure. We looked at each other and then at Lucy, long and white-limbed with winter and slender as a young birch in her outgrown summer shorts and T-shirt. She had been restless and almost aflame all morning; we knew that we were not going to be spared being, somehow or other, scared to death. She looked back at us, bluely.

"I double-dog dare any of you to crawl under that train," Lucy said.

To a boy, we gaped at her. High spirits were one thing; suicide was quite another.

"Is everybody scared?" Lucy said. In the still afternoon she fairly shimmered.

No one answered her.

"I bet you *are* scared, all of you. Scaredy, scaredy, scaredy," she sang. "Big old boys two years older'n me, all scaredy-cats!"

"You shut up, Lucy Bondurant," Snake Cheatham spat. He was the largest of us, and a bully, but he was not afraid. Snake on the long hill over on Northside Drive where the Soap Box Derbies were held was wonderful, heart-swelling to behold. There was no dare he would not take, no risk run, in his spidery, magically engineered vehicle.

"Snake's a coward," Lucy said evenly. We waited for him to hit her, but he did not. Snake knew he was not a coward.

"Shut up, Lucy," he said sullenly. But he did not move.

"Ben?" she looked at Ben Cameron. He flushed with the red-haired temper he had from his father, but he dropped his eyes.

"No," he said shortly.

"Tom?" Tom Goodwin hawked and spat into the cinder dust of the apron and looked away.

"You're plain crazy, Lucy Bondurant," he mumbled. He, too, stood still.

That left, besides me, only Pres Hubbard, whose polio-stiffened leg would not bend for train-scrambling, though he did manage to keep up with us on his bike, and Charlie Gentry, who had severe diabetes and did not often accompany us on our cycle forays. Lucy's eyes skipped over Pres; she had left her mark on him already. Her eyes lit on Charlie.

"You scared too, Charlie?" she said.

"Yeah," Charlie said, Charlie, who never in his life, to my knowledge, told a lie. "I sure am. And if you try to make any of us do it, I'll tell all our dads and your uncle Shep. He'll tan your hide good." Charlie wasn't a snitch either, but he would do what he deemed necessary to stop an injustice aborning, and he did not like Lucy. He never had, not from the first day they met. I knew that he would, indeed, tell my father if Lucy continued to egg us on to crawl under the train, and I knew that retribution would be swift and terrible. This went far beyond mischief.

"Hey, Lucy," I said. "You're late for your music lesson. Let's go home and come back another time."

"Okay, then, you scaredy-cats," she said, ignoring me as if I had not spoken. "I'll go first."

And she slipped to the apron and snaked herself beneath the engine before we could blink our dazzled eyes. A heart-hammering eternity seemed to pass. My ears roared as they had on the day in the woods when we had cut our wrists. Finally, from the other side of the train, obscured by its huge, bulking blackness, we heard her voice sing out, "Easy as pie! Nothing to it, you scaredies!"

And at the same time we heard the first deep, preliminary chuff of the engine, and felt and saw the great black body shiver with the beginnings of its forward motion.

"Bum, bum, bum, here I come!" Lucy yelled, and she wriggled beneath the engine and appeared again at our feet, covered with cinders and dust and flushed with a positive luminosity of triumph. The train began, almost imperceptibly, to move forward. A second huge, subterranean chuff issued from its belly, and a third.

"I'm flat going to tell your uncle Sheppard on you the minute I get home," Charlie said, glaring whitely at her. His freckles stood out against his face.

"Yeah," Ben and Snake echoed, shamed and angry at her daring, and badly frightened. It was Lucy's dark genius, always, to frighten with her flaunting of the limits of the possible.

Charlie turned away and started up the apron toward his bicycle, and I plunged forward desperately and threw myself under the engine. The day seemed to go impossibly bright, and then dark. I seemed enclosed in a bubble of soundlessness and unreality. The great back wheels were crawling toward me as I wriggled lizardlike in the cinders and dust underneath, and the tracks were hot and hard under my back. There was a powerful smell of oil and smoke and heated metal. The blackness stank, and was total. I closed my eyes in utter terror and gave a great sideways thrust like a sidewinder and rolled out into the sunlight on the other side just as the huge wheels ground past me, and the giant's deepening breath filled the world.

I lay still in the sun of that spring day, eyes closed, breath coming in wheezes and gasps, and it was not until the last car was rolling past me that I scrambled to my feet and brushed myself off and arranged my clothing and body into a semblance of casual repose, so that by the time their goggling faces reappeared after the caboose, I was able to smirk at them like a young god, and flipped them a maddening small salute. All my limbs were shaking with a fine, palsied tremor, and I could not have spoken if I had tried, but I did not have to. Leadership surged sweet and powerful in my veins; approbation, envy and awe, in equal measures, shone on their faces. I could tell by their eyes that they would not tell, not on me and not on Lucy. We had stepped up onto a plateau where they could not follow. One by one, in total silence, they turned and went back up the steps and got on their bicycles and pedaled away. Lucy and I followed alone, a good distance behind them.

We did not speak until we were nearly home.

"Don't you ever do anything like that again, Lucy," I said. My voice was still shaking.

"No, Gibby," she said meekly. "I won't ever have to."

From then on her world was woven, warp and woof, into ours. She had more than earned her place at our head, and no one thought to question it for four or five years at least. And in all that time, there was no one who could best her. Indeed, even when she was eventually cut out of the herd, as befalls all leaders, it was not any failure of nerve or achievement that unseated her, but simply and inevitably her irredeemable womanhood.

She not only did things better than we could, she knew more. She knew more about the things that did not count in that minimal and rigid little world—words, pain, loneliness; the heart, the mind, the spirit—and she knew more about the things that did. Like sports. Lucy was a small savant at sports. Those were the great days of radio and newspaper heroes, and we had a pantheon of them: Charlie Trippi and Frank Sinkwich at the University of Georgia, Choo-Choo Justice at North Carolina, Doc Blanchard and Glenn Davis at West Point. Joe DiMaggio and Bob Feller and Stan the Man Musial. Jack Kramer and Pancho

Gonzalez and, in Atlanta, Bobby Jones and Bitsy Grant. Joe
Louis. We worshiped at the Saturday shrines of the big Cape-
harts, and Lucy worshiped just as fervently and unfeignedly as
we did. And she went us, invariably, one better.

If I idolized Doc Blanchard, Lucy espoused Arnold Tucker.
If Charlie followed Feller, Lucy cheered for Snuffy Stirnweiss.
If Tom worshiped Pancho Gonzalez, Lucy was an acolyte of Ted
Schroeder. While Snake could speak knowledgeably of half a
dozen legendary North Georgia moonshine runners and stock
car drivers, Lucy had pasted on her mirror a newspaper photograph of Baron Taffy Von Tripps winning at Monza. It was Lucy
who introduced me to the career of that luminous Swede,
Gunder Haegg, whose 4:01.4 mile hung perfect and alone in my
mind for years, like the evening star. These were not affectations
with her, but genuine passions, as fierce, if as ephemeral, as all
Lucy's passions. We did not resent them and we did not aspire
to them. It was as if, in Lucy, we had for a leader, instead of
a thin, vivid, small girl, some sort of wondrous genetic superboy.
I used to watch their faces sometimes, Charlie's and Ben's and
Tom's and Pres's and occasionally Carter Rawson's; watch them
looking at Lucy. With the exception of Charlie, I am sure that
they looked upon her and saw another, if infinitely superior, boy.
Charlie, I think, saw what I saw, but unlike me, he did not see
it with love.

I saw, as I had from the very first moment, the powerful and
unconscious seductiveness of her, and the sheer, strange, burning
beauty, and I could not believe that they did not. But they never
did, not until much later, and when they did see it, it was all
at once, and by then too late for them and Lucy ever again to
be what they had once been to each other, or ever again even
to be friends.

I suppose it was inevitable that she would overreach herself,
push her power over us past its limits and into catastrophe. To
small Lucy Bondurant last from New Orleans, fatherless, poor,
without patrons and on sufferance in the house of her uncle, the
exhilaration of her hold on the small princes of the big houses
must have been irresistible. All her life Lucy was a creature of
careening excesses and impulse; that first great step beyond the
bounds was entirely understandable and probably forgivable.
But those who guided her star were the ones least equipped to
understand and forgive. The consequences to all of us were swift
and severe. To her they were disastrous.

It happened on a sullen afternoon in September when we were
eleven and Lucy nine. By then our afternoon forays on our bicycles were refined and sophisticated enough so that we ranged
quite incredible distances, in a sort of Lafayette Escadrille forma-

tion, spread out behind Lucy on our shining Schwinns and Atlantic Flyers, flying fast and trailing immortality like a bright
comet's tail. It was a still, thick afternoon, heavy on our prickling
skins, and the wildness of the past summer still ran in our veins,
unthinned by two weeks back at E. Rivers Elementary. Lucy had
shot up over the summer, and was as attenuated and stylized
as a young willow tree, or a good colt, and nearly as tall as she
would ever be. The blue of her eyes was deepening to violet, and
her hair had finally been liberated from its pigtails and shaped
at Rich's Beauty Salon, courtesy of Aunt Willa's employee discount, so that it fell clean and straight to her shoulders, a sheaf
of pure, ash-dark silk with a sheen on it like a grape. She no
longer looked like a midget ruler of a race of simpler giants, but
a tall young boy king. She had no breasts and hips, but her waist
was beginning to narrow into the handspan that would for years
be her pride, and her small hands and feet were lovely. Astride
her bicycle, one arm upflung to urge us on, her hair spindrift
and wild, she might, I thought, be Hippolyta leading her Amazons into battle, and once told her so.

"Yeah, but the Amazons were all girls," she said dismissively.
"Boys are better."

No one else in our crowd would have known Hippolyta from
Wonder Woman, but they responded instinctively to the patina
of leadership that she wore so securely by now. There was no
place that we would not have followed her.

On this day the wildness and perversity that shimmered
around Lucy Bondurant set me in mind of the day, two years
before, when we had rolled under the moving train at Brookwood Station, and I felt the beginning of dread in the cooling
hollow around my heart. I think we all did. Nobody would quite
look at Lucy, and someone—I think it was Tom Goodwin—said,
"I can't stay long. I told my mom I'd clean the gutters for her."

"Me, either," Ben Cameron said. "Ma wants me back by five.
Daddy's bringing some folks home to dinner."

"Well, my mother doesn't make me run home like a puppy,"
Lucy said waspishly. "We've got three whole hours before you
sissies have to run home to yours. That's plenty of time."

"Time for what?" I said reluctantly. I emphatically did not
want to hear what she was going to say.

"Time," Lucy said, a little smile curving her pink mouth, "to
ride out to the Pink Castle."

We were all silent, and then Pres said, completely spontaneously, "The Pink Castle! The shit you say, Lucy!"

The Pink Castle was a great, crenellated, bulbous pile of pink
stucco and red pantile that lay far out West Paces Ferry Road,
where the big houses were farther and farther apart and more

and more sheltered by the dense hardwood river forest. It had thirty rooms and countless porches and terraces and loggias, and had been built vaguely in the sixteenth-century Italian style in 1923 by a wild-haired, captive Italian brought over for the purpose by Mr. and Mrs. Chalmers French. Mr. French came to Atlanta from Macon with an enormous, unexplained fortune, built his huge, improbable fairy tale of a house, and then died, leaving his much older and pathologically shy, childless wife, Hester, to rattle around in his mad fantasy in the deep woods, alone and friendless.

Because they had been in the city for only two years when the house was finished and Mr. French shuffled off this mortal coil, and because they had not entertained and virtually no one had seen the great house going up, there was no one to call on Hester French, and it was assumed that she would go back to her people in Macon. But she did not, and neither did she show herself; well after the acceptable period of mourning had passed she was still sequestered in what had become known as the Pink Castle, and still no one ever saw her except what tradesmen she would allow to approach the house, a gardener and his minions and a succession of maids and household help generally held to be inferior, so that they could not get work at the other big houses of Buckhead.

Our parents were avidly curious to see her, and even more to see her great, rococo lair, about which a curious mixture of fact and legend had sprung up like virulent green kudzu. But because she kept an armed and truculent guard in a gatehouse guarding the long driveway, and because the heavy chain from one massive stone post to the other was always kept fastened unless a tradesman's vehicle required ingress, not a single credulous soul had been into the enormous tangle of half-finished formal gardens and outbuildings that surrounded the main house, much less seen the house itself.

The delivery boys and the Negroes talked, though, and what they said titillated Buckhead. No one really believed them, but still . . . There was a moat full of black water and great things that thrashed and splashed and roared. Dogs so huge that they dwarfed even mastiffs roamed free through the grounds, and were kept so starved that they instantly set upon any visitor who was not accompanied by the guard. A strange, iridescent light flitted from window to window in the upper turrets of the castle, whose staircases were always kept barred and locked. The boxwood parterres on the multileveled terraces behind the house were clipped and shaped to form religious symbols, and a long sculpture allée held many terrible and grotesque representations of Christ hanging crucified on a variety of crosses. Hester

French herself was, alternately, a raving madwoman who prowled the turret rooms, hair gone white with grief and loneliness, murderously bright cleaver in hand; or a strange, fierce, beautiful half-savage who swam naked in the indoor swimming pool and offered herself hungrily to all tradesmen and servants, black and white, male and female, who entered the premises. Dogs and cats and small wild animals vanished into the grounds—their entire fifteen acres surrounded by a great brick wall topped with barbed wire and broken glass—and were never seen again, at least not intact.

Over the years, tradespeople and servants gradually stopped being summoned to the Pink Castle, and mean necessities were purchased in Buckhead by a gnomelike little manservant thought to be an Indian from India, who proffered a written list and never once spoke to the various shopkeepers he visited, and so information and consequently most interest about the house gradually dwindled and died. By that September afternoon, all that was known about the Pink Castle was that it had been empty for some years—for the little Indian had not been seen in Buckhead for that length of time—and that it had never been put on the market for sale. No one knew whether Hester French had died or moved away. The Buckhead police patrolled its grounds once in a while, though they did not enter the locked and barred doors and windows, but they never reported seeing anything amiss. Our parents did not even forbid us to go there anymore, the house and its denizens and legends were so long out of mind. I had not thought of it for years, and I don't think any of us had, except Lucy. But I can imagine, thinking of it now, that the house must have lain as perfect and seductive in her mind as any Avalon.

"The shit I do say," Lucy said into the windless afternoon. "What's the matter, Pres, is it too far for you to ride?"

It was a measure of the perversity simmering in her that she referred to the brace aloud, even indirectly. Lucy was never knowingly cruel. I still do not, to this day, know what so gnawed at her on that afternoon, but I know that it was powerful enough for her to break with ease her code of honor about Pres, and powerful enough to suck us boys along in her wake on a voyage none of us wanted to make.

"No," Pres said, flaming red, "I can ride twice that far if I want to. I can outride you any day of the week, Lucy Bondurant. I just need to be back by five, is all."

"Well, you will be if we get started right now," Lucy said, grinning over her shoulder. "I know you've really got to get back, Pres. You too, Ben. All of you, I guess. Because big old eleven-year-old boys couldn't still be scared of ghosts and hants and things, could they? When a little ol' nine-year-old girl ain't?"

I knew by that that she was dead serious about riding out to the Pink Castle. Lucy never would have resorted to ridicule to get the Buckhead Boys to do something she wanted them to do unless she figured she had to. She had never, since the day of the train at Brookwood Station, had to.

"I'm not scared of ghosts or hants or you or anything else in shoe leather," Pres said tightly, and got on his bicycle and began to pedal furiously away. One by one, as if by mute accord, we followed him silently. It took Lucy until the corner of Peachtree Road and West Paces Ferry to catch up and sail past us to the head of the column.

We went so fast that the wind whipped words from our mouths, and so we were silent until we reached the point, farther out West Paces Ferry than we had ever been, where the long, curving, overgrown ribbon of asphalt that was the driveway to the Pink Castle lay dreaming silently and ominously in the sullen glow of the waning afternoon. Still wordless, we got off our bikes and stood with Lucy at the mouth of that chain-barred tunnel of green.

"Well," she said, finally, her voice loud in the thick silence. "What y'all waiting for? Christmas?"

I truly believe that she had started out only to finally see it for herself, this forbidden enchanted kingdom in the woods, but by the time we had slipped the rusted chain easily from its mooring and started in our Indian file down the tunnel of poison green, the danger and perversity in her was palpable in the hot, dense air, and leaped like heat lightning from her mind into ours. Our fingers fairly crackled and spat with undischarged trouble by the time we laid our bikes on their sides on the great, cracked marble loggia and looked up at the Pink Castle. The sheer excess and improbability of it kept us mute. We were accustomed to large houses, but we had never seen anything like this.

"Holy shit," Snake said. "That's the biggest house I ever saw."

"Naw, it ain't," Lucy said. "But it sure is the ugliest."

Still subdued, but jerking and shivering with nerves, we filed up the marble steps and around to the enormous, glassed enclosure on the castle's right flank, which housed the stagnant swimming pool. We stooped and picked up rocks, chunks of broken concrete, rusted iron railings, whatever litter lay at hand.

When we reached the margin of the vile opaque green water, Lucy stooped and caught up a chunk of broken concrete.

"Might be snakes," she said, grinning fiercely.

"Might be alligators," Tom said, picking up a section of rusted iron railing.

"Might be elephants," Snake said, hefting a huge piece of granite.

For the space of a minute we all stood in the blind air, our heads and veins thrumming with electricity, holding rocks and stones and litter. The day blazed with queerness and danger. We were not, in that moment, altogether human spawn.

I don't know what might have happened if Lucy had not spoken, for even then we all hesitated, trembling like young animals at the scene of a slaughter. But she looked at us, one by one, in turn, and said, "Break the glass." And when still we hesitated, she drew back her white arm and threw her crumbling concrete straight through the many-paned wall facing us. Before that first silvery tinkle had died away, all our rocks and bricks were flying.

"Kill the witch!" Lucy shrieked. "Tear down the castle!"

"Tear it down!" we howled, obedient echoes. "Tear it down!"

It took us two hours. We worked our way from the swimming pool enclosure into the first floor of the house and through all the dark, empty, filthy rooms, smashing and powdering glass. We climbed the littered and listing twin staircases and shattered the leaded glass windows on the landing, and brought down the great, gap-prismed chandelier with a broom we picked up in the kitchen. We laid a singing crystal waste to the second floor, and to the small windows on the third. Not a pane, not a mirror, not an abandoned bibelot remained intact. We did not laugh, and I doubt that we spoke more than a few words to each other. I remember none. Like the maenads who tore Dionysus apart with their bare, blood-dappled hands, I don't think we came to ourselves until we had finished the third floor and were standing at the bottom of the stairs leading up to the turret rooms, eyes blinded, chests heaving, and I don't know if we would have stopped then, the love song of smashing glass was so loud in our ears, except that the banshee moan of the Buckhead police cruiser coming down the driveway finally outsang it. I don't know to this day if they were on their regular rounds, or if someone saw us start into the driveway and called them.

We stood silent, rooted with doom and enormity, waiting for them.

"We are going to catch pure and tee hell," fastidious Ben Cameron whispered, his vivid, clever face blanched. "And we deserve to. This was—just awful."

It was Charlie who told. I knew this time that he would. Even before the siren stopped and the police car spun to a halt on the loggia outside, I saw dawning comprehension and horror replace the wild, inhuman glass-lust in his brown eyes, large and spaniel-like behind the thick glasses, and saw the opaque skim of self-loathing dull them. I saw the look he bent on Lucy, too. I knew that he would not spare her, any more than he would spare himself. She knew it too, knew, in that instant, more: that her days at the head of the Buckhead Boys were ended here, in all this bizarre emptiness, amid spilled crystal blood. I saw her smoke-blue eyes clear of their madness and widen, and then go white-ringed with panic. She turned to me.

"Gibby," she began, in a child's whimper. "Gibby, please . . ."

"Don't say a word, Shep," Charlie said in a voice I did not know. Tears swam, magnified, behind the bottle-glass lenses. He was very pale. I could see him trembling from where I stood. "Shut up, Lucy. I'm not going to let Shep take the blame for this."

He was as good as his word. He told Billy Trammel, who came crunching up the glass-littered stairs and found us there, that Lucy had instigated the vandalism, and he told first his prim and furious father, who came to the station house to get him, and then mine when he arrived to fetch Lucy and me. I knew that he did not tell in order to divert punishment from his own head; Charlie was so straitlaced and honorable that his nickname within our pack was Judge, and in any case, he knew that there was no hope of deliverance now. We had all gone irredeemably past that. He had felt the bloodlust and been blinded by it just as we all had; he had rampaged freely with us through the house, breaking, breaking, breaking. Even if he himself had by some miracle escaped notice, he would have confessed his own blame. And all through the blistering tongue-lashing we received from Shorty Farr, the chief of police, and the quieter and infinitely more wounding words spoken by his stricken, sanctimonious father; even through his own tears—for we all broke down under the parental onslaughts and the enormity of our deed—I could see in his mild brown eyes a profound relief that it was ended, and that he would no longer have to follow Lucy on her mad, spiraling rides. I saw that same relief, though not so clear, in the eyes of several of the others.

"It was Lucy who started it," Charlie said over and over. "But none of us tried to stop her. I threw the first rock."

It was, of course, a lie, but at the words my long love for Charlie was born.

And so once again Lucy and I were in virtual quarantine, though this time the sons of many other houses of Buckhead were also under house arrest, and while the punishment was longer and more severe, I minded it far less than the isolation that had followed little Jamie's death. It was the beginning of my brief time as pure boy in a boy's world, a time I doubt I would have had if it had not been for the punishment and its attendant separation from Lucy. I think if it had not been for that day,

I simply would have followed Lucy's erratic dance on into my teens and high school, and been the more sharply dashed against the rocks when she finally did open her hands and let me free. As it was, I moved into the last days of my childhood in the company of boys, and made of one of them—Charlie Gentry—the great male friend of my life. That incarceration, and the few years that followed it, contain all I know of the light, clear bonds of masculine friendship.

But for Lucy it was a deep and howling loneliness, and anguish, and worse than that: an end, for all time, to power pure and simple. She had power again, great power, but it was never again clean and whole.

CHAPTER
SEVEN

THIS TIME OUR SEPARATION WAS COMPLETE. Martha and
Shem Cater moved my bed and clothing and books out
to the summerhouse and a crew from Moncrief came and
installed an oil furnace, and my mother came out silent and red-
eyed bringing winter curtains and bedspread and pillows and
some Georgia Tech and University of Georgia pennants for the
stucco walls, and from that day until this, I have lived in the
summerhouse behind the house on Peachtree Road. Although
I felt keenly the shame and isolation of my banishment, something under them leaped like a flame at the prospect of this, my
own private kingdom in the sheltering garden, and something
even under that, dim and shameful, stirred in mean and smug
satisfaction that this perfect domain had come only to me, and
was now barred to Lucy. I had never before had any power that
had not, essentially, been borrowed from her.

Her isolation was almost total. She was forbidden by a furious,
screeching Aunt Willa to have anything more to do with me or
with any of the boys in her former band, except in unavoidable
and supervised public situations like church and, later, school.
Meals together with the family were allowed, after the first two
or three days of confinement and trays, and we were permitted
to ride together in the Chrysler to Sunday lunches at the club,
but even then she was made to sit in the backseat with her
mother and the pious Little Lady, while I was sandwiched between my parents in the front. We were not allowed to speak
to each other, and for a while did not attempt to do so. For a
time during that incarceration Lucy spoke virtually to no one,

122

and kept her blue eyes on her lap or fixed on some point in the middle distance.

Never in all that time did I hear her cry or plead for leniency or attempt to justify herself. I think if she had denied culpability I would have backed her up, maybe even claimed blame myself, but I think we both knew that no one would have believed us. What was possible to Lucy was not, even then, possible to me, and our families knew it. Lucy might be, and often was, stricken with terror at the outcome of her actions, but she had a fierce small personal code that forbade begging for mercy—though she would fight savagely against what she perceived as inequities to others.

I think it would have served her better if she had begged. Aunt Willa might then have ceased the grim battle of wills that marked her lifelong relationship with her older daughter, might have been appeased by Lucy's terrible vulnerability. But Lucy never offered her that, and I don't think Aunt Willa ever saw it. I truly think that what she saw when she looked at Lucy was merely a profoundly visible embarrassment and a threat to her position in the house and the city, a threat that might at any time banish her back to the chicken farm in South Georgia. Before the incident of the Pink Castle, Lucy had been to her a shackle and a stumbling block, but not without value simply because my father at times looked upon her with something resembling pity and fondness. Now both had gone out of his cold eyes, to be replaced by a remote and inexorable distaste, and Lucy became to her mother simply and forever the enemy. I never knew a woman so without maternal love.

Many years later a psychiatrist, a warm, caring woman who treated and loved and ultimately despaired of Lucy, told me that in any family group there is a natural scapegoat, a sort of tacitly designated bearer of blame and punishment. There is no doubt that Lucy became, after the afternoon at the Pink Castle, the scapegoat in my father's house, and I think that even if she had not done—and continued to do—things that shocked and outraged my parents and her mother, she still would have worn the wreath of the sacrificial goat. She was simply so visible. A few people, like me, saw the living fire in the air around her, and those who did not sensed the displacement and were troubled by it.

I think in total darkness you could have sensed that Lucy was in the room with you. The force in her was so strong as to threaten to break free, and that kind of vivid, roiling life inevitably disturbs. It is far easier to label it aberrant and punish it than to examine it. And of course, all her life, and with a sort of blinded innocence, Lucy went in harm's way. The need for res-

cue and protection lay so deep and burned so strong that it out-
weighed virtually any lesson she might have learned, any
punishment she might receive. I could not have understood that
then, but I did understand that punishment of Lucy achieved
nothing and harmed her cruelly. What was meant to break her
cleanly succeeded only in bending, and that permanently.

For she was almost literally banished from our sight. Even
when the incarceration was ended and we were free to go about
our routines once more and resume speaking to each other, Lucy
was effectively removed from all but minimal contact with her
mother and sister and my parents and me. She had none with
the children of Buckhead. I am sure that Aunt Willa would have
put her into a convent if there had been any such thing in Atlanta
and the stench of Rome had not been so taboo, or sent her to
a boarding school if there had been money available. As it was,
it must have burned her starved and stinging heart like fire to
accept my father's curt offer of tuition to a small, pretentious
and patently inferior private day school that purported to "finish" subdebs but was widely known to break high-spirited or
problem preadolescent girls with an iron snaffle. And my mother's tiny, knowing smile as she extended the offer, and the silky
fan of lashes that shuttered the contemptuous triumph in her
eyes, must have seared equally deep. But Aunt Willa accepted.

I think it was for that triumph, for that humiliation, that Willa
Bondurant declared her war on Lucy, not for the vandalizing
of the empty house. But she accepted the offer with as much of
her carefully cultivated, modest grace as she could salvage. Better to cast out the offending eye than risk having it cause irreme-
diable damage. Aunt Willa was smart enough to know that talk
about Lucy would inevitably turn back upon her.

After school Lucy was free for an hour or so to pursue her
own interests, but since those had always centered around me
and the summerhouse or the band of boys she led, and since she
was forbidden absolutely to have anything to do with any neighborhood children except a few girls of her age deemed suitable
companions, she was virtually without friends. Lucy simply
would not associate with the little girls selected to be her playmates, and they in turn refused to play with her, and so she spent
most of her time in the echoing upstairs rooms where we had
once slept and whispered and read and dreamed our gaudy and
unsuspected dreams.

She must have been hideously lonely and often afraid, for the
silence and isolation of that attic warren seemed inviolable and
complete if you were alone in it; there was no sense that below
you the life of a great house hummed on. I know that it was then,
in those cramped, silent little rooms, that she began to write, but

I never knew what she wrote. She showed that first work to no one. I would see her dark head sometimes at the third-floor window as I left the summerhouse and started toward Charlie's house on West Andrews, or Ben Cameron's on Muscogee.

At the beginning of those days apart, she would be looking out at me, and would sometimes wave, a stiff, formal little salute, and I could see the blue of her eyes burning in her white face even from the driveway. But she never motioned for me to come up to her, or opened the window and called out to me, and she did not attempt to leave her room and steal out to the summerhouse, as she had during the time of our imprisonment after Jamie's death. I thought she looked wonderfully beautiful and romantic, like a princess held captive in an enchanted tower, and my heart would literally leap in my chest like a gaffed fish with anguish for her. But my father had said after he brought us home from the police station, "If I catch you going anywhere near Lucy again I will send her and her mother and sister away that very day," and I knew that he meant it.

I have never known him to be so angry with me as he was that day. He did not bellow; he could not even speak, and his face, usually red and knotted with annoyance at me, was absolutely white and still. His small blue eyes were actually pale, as though bleached by the acid of his fury, and his breath came so hard and fast that I thought he would have some sort of attack and die. It was my mother, weeping and hovering and touching me—first my cheeks, and then my shoulders, and then my disheveled hair, until I thought I would literally knock her manicured fingers away—who delivered the terms of my punishment and the outline of my life in the house after it was ended. Mainly, both consisted of an avoidance of Lucy. I would be required to work after school and during the following summer to help pay for the damage to the windows of the Pink Castle, but I had expected that and did not mind. All the other boys would, I knew, be charged with the same task. And I would have to move to the summerhouse, but that was such joy to me that I shut my eyes in order to keep my parents from seeing it and rescinding the order. It was the absence of Lucy that they thought would bring me to my knees, and for a time it nearly did.

I really believe it was at that point that my father, simply and without too much regret, washed his hands of me, for it was then that the constant carping on my activities and interests and inadequacies ceased, and then that my mother's doting and fussing began in earnest. He stopped planning my college career at Georgia Tech, or, a poor second, the University of Georgia, and abandoned almost completely any talk of bringing me into the family real estate business. She escalated her campaign to make a proper princeling of me. I might have taken refuge in sneaking up the back stairs to Lucy in her tower, or smuggled notes and books to her, or at the very least engaged her in that deep and unspoken communion that we had always been able to carry on with our eyes, as we sat at meals and in church. But she would not look at me, or speak, and in any case, I knew that my father meant what he said about sending them away. The saintly knight still lived in my breast, but his shield was lost and his spear broken. After a while I laid them down and slipped gratefully into boy-hood.

My first friend was Ben Cameron, and though the friendship never deepened and smoothed into the mellow, nourishing thing I had with Charlie Gentry, still it showed me the sheer pleasure of a relationship that lay lightly and was fed without pain from shallow roots. I never really got to know Ben. Nobody did, I think, except his family, and as it turned out, they knew him, perhaps, least of all. Certainly Julia Randolph, whom he began to go steady with soon after his sixteenth birthday and married just out of Georgia Tech, never knew Ben, though she thought she did. I like to think the two little boys of that marriage, the sons he adored so openly and fully, and with whom he became again a boy himself, knew him as deeply as he could be known, but it would have been the father they perceived and loved, not the man.

In any case, it did not matter, for with Ben the abundance of his flamboyant charm and his dark, glinting, sardonic wit made up for those depths held back. His enthusiasms were many and mercurial; February's clicking aggies and taws gave way to March's exquisite homemade kites, dancing in the spring wind over the Bobby Jones Golf Course, before you could blink your eyes, and you scarcely would have mastered his floating racing dives into the Driving Club pool before he was out and onto the flying roller skates that were the autumn thing we did. He was generous with his skills, and a swift and gracious teacher, but his body was so lithe and stylized in its power and grace, and his movements so liquid and exaggerated and dancerlike, that none of us could follow where he led, and he would be on to another passion before we had become passable in the last one he taught us.

He was a born dancer; Sarah and Dorothy Cameron both used to say that it was a shame ballet dancers were thought to be sis-sies, because Ben would have been a star and made a million dol-lars at it. He would shrug that off, flushing up to his coppery hairline, and laugh, but it was true. Ben on a dance floor was a light and a flame that flickered over our high school years. Girls actually shoved and jostled to be asked to partner his jitterbug, and he was such a natural that Margaret Bryan, who flogged ballroom dancing into us in her musty little studio above Spencers, Ltd., downtown, asked him at age fourteen to be a student instructor. She had never asked another of us, boy or girl, and we were all deeply impressed, though of course we teased him unmercifully. But Ben hated ballroom dancing and went to her classes only because small, shy Sarah asked him to be her escort, and as soon as the offer to instruct came, he quit going entirely, and refused to go back. Dorothy urged him, and Sarah's great eyes filled with blinked-back tears at the prospect of bearding that ersatz little cotillion alone, but in this, as in few other matters, his father overrode his mother.

"For God's sake, let him be, Dottie," he said once, when I was over at the Muscogee Avenue house being tutored in math by Ben, and his mother was after him to take Sarah to dancing class that evening. "Dancing should be as much fun as you can have with your clothes on. If he doesn't like it, there's no sense in doing it."

"But every boy needs to know how to dance," Dorothy Cameron said. "It's one social skill that's absolutely indispensable."

"He knows how, better than anybody in Margaret's entire gang of little gigolos," Ben Cameron said, the gray eyes that were also his son's resting with such open and unabashed love on Ben that quick tears stung my eyes, startling me. "He just doesn't want to do it. Isn't football and baseball and tennis and swimming and music and his design work enough? Not to mention his grades. What more does he need?"

Ben reddened and ducked back out of the little den where his mother and father were sitting, and Dorothy Cameron's eyes lit on me. I did not follow Ben; I was then, as I have always been, as drawn to the Camerons in a group as a cold, starving wild animal is to a fire, and I stood warming myself at their light.

"Shep will take Sarah to dancing class, won't you, Shep?" Dorothy said, smiling at me. Her warm amber eyes saw me, every inch of me, inside and out, and liked what she saw. It was her gift, as it was always Sarah's, to see you plain and like, even love, you for just that; to ask nothing of you; instead, to give to you. I could dance, after a fashion, but was shy and did not like the close contact with the girls, and found every excuse that my mother would accept to miss the classes. But for Dorothy Cameron I would have gone down to the Fox Theatre and danced alone on the great bare stage before a packed house, and besides, I liked sunny, elfin little Sarah.

"Sure," I said. "Sarah will be my girl for tonight."

I grinned at Sarah, and she reddened and smiled her soft, three-cornered, kitten's smile.

"Thanks, Shep," she said, and ducked her chin and vanished up the stairs after Ben.

"She'll be walking on air for weeks," Dorothy Cameron said. "She's been in love with you all her life, you know."

For all his generosity and near-theatrical gregariousness, though, young Ben Cameron was moody, and sometimes he would, quite literally, go away from you, uncurling as softly and quietly as a cat and padding out of the room, leaving whatever you were doing together spread out on the desk or table. At other times he would merely retreat back into his own head; you could still talk to him and get an answer of sorts, but the essential Ben Cameron was contained somewhere behind those clear gray eyes. You could see the essence of him moving there. It was unsettling, and never failed to leave me with a small frisson, as if, we were fond of saying, a rabbit had just run over my grave.

He did not look like a boy then. It was possible, when that happened, to see what Ben Cameron the man would look like, and I did not think that that man was happy, though I could not have said why. "What more does he need?" Ben Cameron, Senior, had said of his son. Could he, if he had been another sort of man, have seen the awful import of those words? Would it have made a difference? I don't know. But at those times, it seemed very clear to me that there was something more that young Ben Cameron needed, something vital to life. But I had no idea, then, what it was.

In addition to the tutoring in mathematics, Ben gave me one of the great and enduring loves of my life, gave it to me as lightly and openhandedly as he shared with me his expertise at marbles and dancing and the flying of kites. He let me chomp and hoot around on his clarinet, at which he was as effortlessly proficient as he was at everything else he attempted, and though I never quite achieved his technical virtuosity on it, I was smitten with a passion far stronger than his the instant I picked it up and felt the sweet heft of that ebony cylinder in my hands, and tasted the smoky-persimmon taste of the slick, bitten reed. I was hooked before the first mallardlike honks and skirling shrieks came issuing forth from the instrument, and nagged my mother so desperately and tirelessly that within a week I had a shining new clarinet of my own, chosen by me from Rutan's on one totally glorious spring afternoon, and lessons three times a week from the resigned, fastidious little man who taught Ben. I was quick to learn, if not especially talented, and I practiced so prodigiously that the sheer effort and the pounding force of my passion produced music sufficient to feed my yearning heart before that summer was out.

I will never forget the day the clarinet came alive for me. I was lying on my back in the deep grass of the meadow that ringed the lake up at Tate, totally alone in the day, noodling idly, the reed vibrating smoothly and tinnily against my teeth, watching a red-tailed hawk riding the thermals over Burnt Mountain and thinking of nothing at all, emptied out, still. And then, all of a sudden, the molten honey of "Frenesi" came spilling out of the mouthpiece, abundant and silvery and perfect. I gave a great start, and looked around as if I were being observed, and then I put the clarinet down and laid my head on my arms and wept.

Mathematics and music. Two absolutely true things that I have and would not have except for Ben Cameron. Now, whenever I think of him, over the pain and the outrage, always comes the healing gratitude. Ben; Ben of the gray-lit eyes and the ardent heart. I will not forgive Atlanta for Ben.

The other friend of my boyhood, and indeed, of my life, was Charlie Gentry. I can't remember a time when I didn't know Charlie. Illness was the first tie that bound us; our mothers took us to the same pediatrician for treatment of his diabetes and my asthma. And as our families knew each other from the club and Saint Philip's Episcopal Church and shared a hundred other nearly imperceptible ties of the sort that bound the families of Buckhead, it was only natural that we would become regular playmates.

For one thing, our infirmities relegated us to the role of onlookers in the fiercely masculine little society in which we moved. For another, the invisible ties of the "different" child, the one set apart, reached out swiftly and went deeply into us. Charlie and I knew one another in our hearts when we first set toddlers' eyes on each other in Dr. Forrest Davenport's office on Ponce de Leon, and that ken lasted, with few breaks, well past boyhood. We did not become close friends until that summer after Lucy and I were separated, but I think we both knew early, somewhere down where such things lie, that we would do so. I know that sometimes in my early childhood, when the asthma that disappeared around my tenth birthday still kept me awkward and withdrawn, a hoverer at edges, I would look across a group of shrieking, milling children and meet the grave brown eyes of Charlie Gentry and feel a kind of obscure peace, an occult comfort, steal through me. "Later," our glances seemed to say to one another. "Later."

I think our friendship would have become fact a lot sooner if Lucy had not come to live with me in my house. For, as I have said, from the very beginning, Charlie did not like her, and it was plain that the feeling was mutual.

He was the first one of us to call her a name, a thing so unlike

Charlie that the spiteful little incident hung on the air quivering
with shock, and was remembered for a long time by all of us
who heard it. It was at the Easter egg hunt on the great hill in
front of Saint Philip's, overlooking the bend in Peachtree Road
just before it sweeps into Buckhead proper, and we were all
standing in a bemused and dazzled knot watching Lucy, her
fiercely frilled new organdy skirts over her head, hanging by her
knees from the branches of a low-spreading dowager oak, dangling in her hand the gold-painted, beribboned prize egg she had
found almost immediately.

The promissory enchantment I had seen early in her had rip-
ened into a full-fledged spell on this fey April day of strange
green light and running cloud shadow and warm little winds that
doubled back upon themselves. By now the knot of children
standing below her was silent in entirely proper respect mingled
with superstitious awe . . . for hadn't she known exactly where
the prize egg was; skipped, in fact, straight to it? And didn't she
look, upside down in the lambent, shivering air, like some elemental spirit newly come among us from a magical place called
New Orleans, a creature of light and vapors and quicksilver? I
remember that no one spoke for what seemed the longest time,
and then Charlie's gruff, matter-of-fact voice came clearly:
"Shoot, that ain't so hot. Anybody can hang from a stupid tree.
Even a woods colt. She ain't nothing but a woods colt from
country-hick New Orleans."

The effect on Lucy was astounding. In an eye-blink she had
skinned down from the tree and charged Charlie, small fists flail-
ing, eyes shut tight with fury, face mottled white and red, tears
strangling in her throat. She did not say a word until she had
knocked him backward onto the new-green grass and bloodied
his nose, and she only stopped then because I grabbed her from
behind and pinioned her arms. I was both awed and embarrassed. Awed because I had never seen a girl lick a boy, much
less one two years older than she was, and embarrassed because
it was strictly against our code to hit Charlie, who both wore
glasses and had something so badly wrong with him that he had
to take shots for it every day of his life. No one had told Lucy
this, of course, but it seemed to me she should have known it
anyway. It was an etiquette born of the blood. Besides, I wondered, what was so terrible about being called a woods colt? It
sounded lovely to me, fabled and magical, like a unicorn or a
griffin. And with her silky black mane of hair and long,
gossamer-slender arms and legs, she did look rather like a colt,
a crystal one.

She would never tell anyone what had led her to attack Charlie, and she would never again have anything substantial to do

with him. He did not seem to care; seemed, rather, to be relieved.
I have often thought that the years in which she rode at the head
of the Buckhead Boys on their invincible bikes must have been
rather bad years for him, but by that time they had come to a
sort of elaborately indifferent armed truce, and I suppose that
the inclusion in that streaking golden pack was too precious, to
a boy used to making his way alone, to forswear for a point of
honor no one else even recognized.

On that day, I remember, I sought him out just before we left
the party, and whispered, "What's a woods colt?"

"It means she doesn't have any daddy," he said.

"Well, shoot, sure she does," I said. "He's not here, but she
sure does have one. He's in New Orleans or someplace. She's
crazy about him. Talks about him all the time."

"Well, that's what I heard my mother tell Mrs. Goodwin,"
he said stubbornly. "And I don't guess she'd say that if it wasn't
so."

I knew he was wrong, but I did not argue with him. I could
understand why he was so sure. Charlie's mother would rather
go naked at noon in Five Points than lie.

Of all the so-called "good" people I have ever known in my
life, Ben and Dorothy Cameron included, Charlie's mother and
father were hands down the saintliest. The odor of piety stood
so strongly in the air around them that in their presence even
dirty bare feet seemed un-Christian. Marianne Gentry taught
Sunday school and sang in Saint Philip's choir and was chairman
of Saint Rhoda's altar guild, and ran the Episcopal thrift shop,
where the cast-off garments of the women of Buckhead were dispensed at greatly reduced prices to a singularly unappreciative
clientele of indigent women from "down there" in Atlanta
proper, and in her spare time she painted flamingo-pink faces
of Jesus on china plates. Every newlywed couple in Buckhead
had one by the time she abjured portraiture and moved on to
sacramental macramé. She was the first face one saw on one's
doorstep when a loved one died, and often, uncannily, seemed
to precede the event itself by appearing, casserole in hand, before
the death rattle had begun.

I once heard Ben Cameron say to Dorothy, "If you ever open
the door and see Marianne Gentry standing there with a chicken
pot pie, don't hesitate. Go straight down to the bank and open
the lockbox and get everything out before the IRS seals it. I'll
surely be dead by the time you get home."

Charlie's father, Thaddeus Gentry, was a major stockholder
in the Coca-Cola Company, and I always heard that he was "in
business," but I don't think I ever knew precisely what that business was, as close as Charlie and I became and as often as I was

in and out of the house on West Andrews. Mr. Gentry went to
an office downtown; he was driven by a wizened little blue-black
gnome of a Negro man who smelled perpetually of the White
Rose snuff that bulged his upper lip like a lipoma. I believe now
that Thad Gentry must have had a sort of rudimentary family
philanthropic foundation going, for he was widely known to give
away money to the poor, and wore the epithet "Christian busi-
nessman" with the same pride that he wore his Rotary button.
His ferocious cheerfulness smote the very air around him, and
he would set upon you and cry, "Smile! God loves you!" whenever his path crossed yours. He was a round, squat little man
with the same thick glasses that Charlie wore, and the great
fleshy, smacking lips of a fish, and he liked putting moist, avun-
cular hands on the flesh of young girls almost as much as he liked
to give away his sanctified money. When he did, the girls would
smile thinly, and Marianne Gentry would smile thinly, and he
would merrily quote a snippet from the Song of Solomon, though
never going so far as to get to the part about the breasts being
like twin roes.

I never knew what he was about, with his scuttling hands and
stalklike crab's eyes, but I feel sure Charlie, with his quick sensitivity, did. I think Charlie's younger sister, Caroline, did, too.
I would see the dull red creep up her neck and into her cheeks
when her father laid his hands on the arms and shoulders of one
of her playmates. Caroline had her revenge, though. She ran as
amok as she could as soon as she was able, starting with the legendary Boo Cutler of Buckhead and working her way up the
eastern seaboard to New York, where she had acquired her second husband by the time she was twenty-five. I saw her once,
years after our childhood, at the Village Gate, listening to Bird
Parker, very drunk and leaning on the shoulder of a still-faced
black man wreathed in smoke that was definitely not that of a
Pall Mall. She did not see me and I did not cross the room to
speak to her. Caroline had left us all behind by then. I think she
lives now in Barbados in a villa left to her by who knows what
husband. My aunt Willa always clicks her tongue and shakes
her head when she speaks of Caroline Gentry, but I think on
the whole that Caroline didn't do so badly for herself. Not at
all. Not in comparison to those of us whose venue she fled.

But for a while in my childhood, one of the smarmier little
witticisms went, "What's pink and white and turns into a motel
when you say the magic words?"

"Caroline Gentry!"

The Gentrys were quite rich when Charlie and I first became
friends, but when Charlie was in his first year at Emory Law,
Thad Gentry suddenly went ferociously and ebulliently mad and

gave all the family Coca-Cola stock to a black television evangelist called Reverend Buddy, and Charlie and his mother were left in severely straitened circumstances.

"You'd think the sonofabitch would have the sense to give it to Billy Graham, at least," Charlie said mildly, but I knew that the breakdown was a cataclysm for him.

He transferred to Atlanta Law School at night and went to work for the Coca-Cola Company by day to support his mother and keep the big old Italianate house up, and Marianne Gentry went into a long and gentle decline.

Dorothy Cameron, who was perhaps a bit too enamored of that much-prized quality called gumption and was wont to apply it like a poultice to every ill that the flesh was heir to, snapped, "Marianne Gentry hasn't got an ounce of gumption. I don't think faith is worth a plugged nickel if there isn't a little gumption to back it up."

I know, though, that it was she and Ben who paid the taxes on the Gentry house while Charlie got on his feet. She and Ben always did like Charlie.

By the time Charlie graduated and married, he was doing so well at Coca-Cola that the upkeep of his mother was no problem, and he was able to bring his father home from Central State and install him properly and permanently at Brawner's. "And that," Charlie said resignedly, "considering the number of Buckhead people who end up there, is like coming home."

It's a mystery to me how Charlie kept himself so whole, so steeped in the cheerful, pragmatic integrity that was always, to me, the thing about him that set him so apart from the rest of us. Not many people are genuinely good. It may be that the tremendous effort he had to expend to accommodate his diabetes made him early into invincible stuff. Or it may have simply been genetic. Charlie sprang from a good gene pool, his palely loitering mother and exuberantly mad father notwithstanding. His grandfather had a glorious stint as a Mississippi riverboat captain before he came to Atlanta and settled down to buying Coca-Cola stock, and his great-grandfather rode with that glittering rogue, Jubal Early, in northern Virginia. I always thought that Charlie got the best of all of it. He was gentle, and honest to a fault, and fiercely loyal, even as a small boy, and what had been, in Thaddeus and Marianne, cant and fanaticism was smoothed in Charlie into a genuine and appealing decency which shone out of his astigmatic eyes like love, like perennial joy. Not that he was pious; far from it. Charlie was, if anything, wry and taciturn, and in repose, his sweet-ugly frog's face unlit by his mordant black-Celt's wit, he seemed downright phlegmatic. And he had learned early on to shield his vulnerability with a kind of affable, shambling passivity that sat perfectly on his short, stocky frame. But I knew, and more than a few other people came to know, that under the dun-colored cloak of the artisan beat a great and passionate heart.

I first saw that passion, perhaps saw it born, on an afternoon in March, when Lucy was still under strict house arrest and Charlie and I had just begun to go around together. There had been a peevish late winter ice storm the evening before, and Marianne Gentry had forbidden Charlie, with his penchant for colds and susceptibility to any infection, to go outside. Instead, we ended up on the third floor in the dark warren of rooms so similar to the ones in my own house, poking boredly through old trunks. Like me, Charlie was an inveterate reader—though his own reading ran to popular science and the Hardy Boys and Big Little Books, of which he had stacks and stacks—and a great builder of model airplanes. They hung about his room like clumsy, desiccated insects, and his hands always smelled, in those years, of dope. He was not a great imaginer or a dreamer of dreams, and he was certainly not a rummager in attics. I don't know why we were at it that day. But we were, probably because it was just slightly more interesting than the Monopoly game that his mother was pressing us to play with restless little Caroline downstairs. Trunk after trunk yielded only fragile, brittle old clothes and hats and scrapbooks and linens; the totems of many lives, I suppose, and things that, as such, would move and involve me deeply now. But then they seemed to us just old. Old and dirty. And they made me cough so badly that I feared that one of the long-dormant asthma attacks was about to shake my throat and chest like a demon terrier.

"Let's go on downstairs," I said. "This stuff is making me choke."

"Just a minute," Charlie said, and something in his voice made me turn and look at him. His face, in the dirty stipple of ice-light on the attic ceiling, was as luminous and white as a votive candle.

I looked down at what he held in his hands. It was a gray woolen uniform, faded and stained and so stiffened by age that he could hardly unfold it, and even in the darkening afternoon you could tell that the bleached braid and the buttons, and the pitted buckle on the creaking old belt, had once been gilt. Below it in the trunk lay a flat-topped forage cap, and below that, wrapped in a length of yellow fringed silk that might have been a sash, was a dull, pitted saber.

Charlie squatted before the trunk, perfectly still, the saber lying across his two outstretched hands like a sacrificial offering, and I saw in his transformed brown eyes that he had truly and forever lost his soul.

"My great-grandfather's," he said in the kind of voice that should be kept for worship, or after love. "He died in the Wilderness. I've seen his picture. He didn't look like any of us. I'm named for him, Charles Beauchamp. I didn't know these were up here."

"Hey, let me see," I said, reaching out to take the saber from him. He jerked it back, away from me.

"Don't," he said, and his voice was so queer that I stared at him. His face burned wax-white in the attic gloom, and tears shone in his dark eyes. The thick lenses of the glasses magnified them into a manic radiance. I dropped my hands.

"It probably isn't even your great-whatever's," I said perversely, for his refusal had stung me and the strange radiance alarmed me. "If it had been, looks to me like you'd have known it was up here. I bet it's just some old uniform somebody left in the house before your folks bought it and they just never threw it out. I bet this old geezer died of dysentery or something somewhere like Macon."

Charlie turned his rapt, gilded face to me again, as if I were a bothersome gnat, his hands caressing the length of the saber, moving to stroke the corroded cloth of the folded coat, lightly tracing the bill of the ruined cap. He moved them as lovingly and delicately as a blind man tracing the face of his beloved.

"They're his," he said in the same strange, faraway voice. "I can feel him. I can feel his blood running in there with mine."

In the fading pearled light I felt the hair prickle on the back of my neck, and the same cold I felt in Boris Karloff movies start on the backs of my shoulders. I was exquisitely conscious of the vast, dark, empty attic behind me. The door to the warm-lit downstairs looked miles away.

"Jesus Christ, Charlie," I whispered. "That's not funny."

He did not answer. I don't think he heard me. Slowly he pulled the stiff gray coat out of the trunk and laid it open on his knees, and held it up against his small, thin shoulders. Even in the dying light I could see the great, dark, fatal flower that bloomed across the left breast of the coat. A star-shaped tear rent its center. My breath seemed to slow and stop in my chest. Charlie looked down slowly, and touched the spot with a tender forefinger.

"It's his blood," he said. "The shot went in here. It was a minié ball. It must have stayed in him, because there isn't a hole in the back."

All of a sudden he lifted the coat and buried his face in it, and his shoulders shook with silent sobs. The unearthly chill fled out of the air and I scuttled across the dusty floor on my buttocks and put my arms around him.

"Hey," I said. "Don't. It was a long time ago. Don't be sad."

"I'm not sad," Charlie said, lifting a wet, shining face to me. "I'm happy. This is . . . this is real glorious."

From that afternoon on, what Charlie and I did together was search for relics.

There is a small army of them across the country, these relickers, a ridiculous and burning and somehow enormously appealing band of fanatics who spend their lives and often their fortunes walking the battlefields of the Civil War with metal detectors in their hands and shells both live and dead in the trunks of their cars. They are Northerners and Southerners, Easterners and Midwesterners; they are anyone at all, as diverse and fragmented and unlikely a fraternity as can be imagined, held together only—but insolubly—by the grand and unquenchable passion that had leaped to life in Charlie Gentry's eyes. They will, and do, willingly go to jail for trespassing on national battlefields and digging on government and private land, and they often lose wives and families to their mania. Some have lost limbs and even their lives, when a shell fired one hundred and thirty years ago finally finds its mark. Charlie had just joined them. And though one day he would become the head of one of the country's great philanthropic foundations, administering literally millions of dollars and doing incalculable good, his first love save one would always be relics and relic hunting, and he would continue to do it until the day of his death.

Many battlefields ring the city of Atlanta, sites of the age-blurred conflicts that most of us native Atlantans know far more thoroughly than our regular school studies, and they would come alive for me in the days of my late childhood, as I followed at Charlie's muddy heels in the dreaming, sunstruck silence of Kennesaw Mountain or Ezra Church or the old park at Peachtree Battle Avenue. Excitement almost as white and absolute as his would jet up within me when we actually found a minié ball or a belt buckle.

"This stuff was from the Army of Tennessee," he would say, reverently laying a filthy canteen or a shell fragment in his sack in a steaming cotton field near Big Shanty. "They were falling back from Dalton to get Sherman away from his base. Joe Johnston could see just what we're seeing now."

His gestures took in the silent green back of Kennesaw Mountain behind us. Living fire consumed us then, the fire of battle and youth and glory, and of death in the sunlight.

But in me, the fire of exhilaration would die when we left the battlefield and went home to supper. Charlie, I knew, carried that flame with him always, just under his stolid surface, and if I could not truly share it, still I felt proud that of all the boys coming to adolescence in Buckhead then, he chose to let only me know the warmth of his. Me, and Sarah Cameron.

It was many years before Charlie, shy with the homely outsider's boil-tender self-consciousness and crippled by his parents' prudish Christian sanctions, would have anything to do with the diligent coquettes who made up our singular high school crowd, called the Pinks and the Jells. Dalliance and flirtation descended on them at puberty, these unprepossessing small girls we had known all our lives; popularity and conquest became their raisons d'être, and many of them never yielded up that priority all their lives. Consequently, a few of us—me, Pres Hubbard, and most of all, Charlie—had less to do with the fabled Pinks of Buckhead than any of the boys who came of age during that excessive and altogether hedonistic time. But to all of us, the single exception was Sarah Cameron.

She was, from our earliest memory, included as naturally in our group activities, except for the four or so years that we all rode behind Lucy with the Buckhead Boys, as another small boy. Later, when Charlie and I began to go about in our oblivious twosome, it was only Sarah who was allowed to make a third.

"Where's Sarah?" I would say, as we set out on a morning's jaunt to Peachtree Creek.

"Oh, wait, Sarah's not here yet," Charlie would say, as we started for the woods behind the summerhouse.

I think it was because nothing, not a single tendon, muscle or atom of small Sarah, threatened or puzzled us. She radiated simplicity and a kind of joyous empathy. She was as staunch and greathearted a companion as any boy could wish, and supremely comfortable to be with because there was nothing about her oblique or veiled or obscure. Her white grin was quick and open, her sherry eyes were warm and lit with absolute approval; her taut, supple brown body was even quicker than ours to master the thousand little athletic rituals in the dance of childhood, and her mind leaped along with and ahead of us like a dolphin in a warm sea.

Whatever we wanted to do at any given time, Sarah brimmed with enthusiasm and skill at it. She could keep up with us in any game or activity we might devise, and in some she so far excelled us that, toward anyone else so gifted, we would surely have felt disgruntled and envious. But Sarah had her mother's quick sensitivity, and never pressed her advantage or showcased her expertise. In the water she was more than half mermaid, beautiful to watch, and on the diving board, at the top of one of her peregrine arcs, she was heartbreaking, fashioned of the air in which she hung. But in all the times Charlie and I swam with her, at the club or in the Camerons' pool behind the Muscogee house, Sarah never went off the high dive. She did that only when she swam and dived alone or with other children.

"I think the high dive's show-offy," she would say, when a jostling seal-brown flock of children urged her and Charlie and me toward the looming tower at the Driving Club pool. "The high dive's for people who have to prove they're hot stuff."

She and Charlie Gentry were the only two people in the world, for a long time, who knew of my total and paralytic terror of heights. They and Lucy. Lucy always knew.

Sarah had a sort of light about her rather like Lucy's, a warmth that drew people to her all her life, to bask at her flame. All her family had it; still do, those who remain. But it was not a light that burned or devoured. I came to think later that she was, in those early days, much like Lucy, with her grace and dark vividness and her physical agility and quick, quirky mind. Sarah was, perhaps, Lucy without the hungers and shadows, Lucy glowing instead of burning. In those short and sunlit days before high school, Sarah, like Charlie, was an abundance in my life, and I was comfortable and somehow filled when she was about, on our bikes or skates or in the haunted fields of Charlie's lost, glorious war. I liked Sarah a lot.

Charlie loved her.

I don't know when I became aware of that, when it dawned upon me with the force of revelation that the light in Charlie's brown eyes on those afternoon forays into the battlefields around the city was not all for the memento mori that we found there. Once I saw, it was as if I had always known, and that he had always loved her. And I think he had, literally from babyhood, loved her through all the early years when I was lost in Lucy and the ones later when we followed in her wake on our bicycles, leaving Sarah and all the other little girls behind. I remember a day when we had ridden down to the memorial park at Peachtree Battle and sat in the showering greenness of late summer, dangling our bare feet in the exhausted September water of Peachtree Creek. Sarah was talking of her great-great-grandmother, who had been a bride of nineteen when the war broke out, and had stayed alone on her newly acquired plantation down in Bibb County with a hundred slaves, a thousand head of livestock and a baby due in three months while her young husband rode off at the head of the troop he had raised.

"Sarah Tolliver Cameron," Sarah said, her eyes alight. "I'm named for her. I hope I'll be as brave when I'm grown up as she was. Her husband—my great-great-grandfather Beau— could have stayed with her till after the baby was born. Everybody wanted him to. She was the one who made him go. She said, 'What would I tell your son when he asked me why his father had not gone with our brave General Lee, gone when the Confederacy needed the stout hearts of her men more than even their women did?' Isn't that beautiful? Don't you think she was brave? I could never do that. I'd be scared to death."

"No, you wouldn't," Charlie said, and tears of pure exaltation swam behind his glasses. "You'd do the very same thing. You're a true Southern lady, Sarah. There's a poem my mother knows that goes, 'I could not love thee, dear, so much, loved I not honor more.' That's what your great-great-grandmama was talking about. You'd say that, too."

His face was so aflame that I could not look at it, and dropped my head to study my feet, green-white and misshapen in the tepid water. Sarah's face flamed at the compliment, and she dropped her eyes, too. But before she did, I saw in them that she did not love Charlie, and that the love she could not feel pierced her like an arrow. I felt that I had trespassed on a scene of unbearable intimacy, embarrassed and somehow myself dishonorable.

"What happened to your great-great-grandfather?" I asked briskly.

"He died," she said, still not looking up. "He never did come home."

"What battle?" Charlie breathed, ready at that moment to ascend into Heaven.

Sarah paused, and then, in a small voice, said, "He didn't die in any battle. He died of dysentery in some camp outside of Gettysburg."

I felt a great rush of affection for her. She could so easily have lied. It would have meant the world, the moon and stars and planets, to Charlie. But she did not. Something in me knew at that moment, and filed the knowing away, that with Sarah Cameron there was, as well as easiness, safety.

Sarah would not come to the house on Peachtree Road. She would trot as easily into Charlie's house as I did, and she would accompany us anywhere around Buckhead that was in walking or bicycling range, but she would, when the suggestion was made to go to my house and read my comics, or play in the summerhouse, simply disappear. I was nearly thirteen before I asked her why. She was then eleven, the same age as Lucy.

"Because," she said, looking at me levelly out of her great amber eyes, "I am afraid of Lucy."

I knew that she was not afraid of anything in the world, at least that Charlie and I could discover, so for a moment I simply stared at her, taken aback. Presently she flushed.

"I can't help it if you think I'm silly. I told you the truth. I really am scared of her."

"Well, that's just dumb," I said finally. "Why on earth would you be scared of Lucy? You never even see her. She can't hurt you."

"That's not the kind of scared I mean," Sarah said, and she would say no more. It was years before she told me what she meant.

Oddly, Dorothy Cameron said something similar, not long after her daughter had. I was sitting on the sun-warmed ground in the Camerons' back garden on a deceptively mild day in February, the year before I began high school, watching her put in late daylily bulbs. She wore a big straw hat of Ben's and dungarees, and sang lustily from under the brim that entirely shadowed her face, "I hate to see that evenin' sun go down. . . ." Her voice was rich and low, like warmed syrup, like Sarah's would be one day.

She stopped and pushed the brim of the hat off her face and looked at me.

"I haven't seen Lucy in months and months," she said. "Your aunt Willa isn't still punishing her, is she? I hope not. It's far too long to keep a child like Lucy penned up. It'll break something in her."

"No," I said. Dorothy Cameron was the only grown woman in my entire experience to whom I did not say, "No, ma'am."

"That is, she's not locked in her room or anything. But she goes to Miss Beauchamp's every day until four, and then she just stays up in her room until dinnertime. She doesn't talk to any of us, either, not even to me. I haven't really seen her for any longer than it takes to eat for ages. I think it's just awful, what Aunt Willa's done to her."

Dorothy Cameron did not reply.

"You don't like her, do you?" I said, seeing it suddenly. The conversation was an extraordinary one for a woman of forty and a boy of twelve to be having, but it was a mark of my curious and nourishing relationship with Dorothy Cameron that it did not seem at all so to me.

"It's not that," she said, sitting back cross-legged on the grass and wiping her face on her sleeve. "It's more . . . that maybe I'm just a little afraid of her."

My ears pricked. What was this fear of small, ephemeral Lucy Bondurant that lay over the hearts of the Cameron women?

"What on earth for?" I said.

"Because she *needs* so much," Dorothy Cameron said. "The poor child seems to be absolutely ravenous. She's like . . . some kind of motor with the governor left off, like a little engine out of control. I think she could be dangerous."

I laughed aloud. Lucy dangerous? To whom? She was herself the most vulnerable human being I had ever known, or would know.

"Oh, Shep." She looked at me and there was pity in her eyes. "Listen to you. You're already in thrall. Dangerous to you, maybe. To anybody she thinks might help her, have something she needs. . . ."

I was suddenly and clearly angry, I who could not even own my own anger at my mother. Though Lucy had pulled away from me and was not a figure of consequence in my life now, except by the sheer force of her absence, I felt the familiar stirrings of the saint-protector in my meager breast.

"Well, she's out of luck, then, because nobody's going to help her," I said sharply. "Nobody can, or will. They've got her cut off from everybody on earth but the Negroes. And how are they going to help her?"

It was true. Lucy now spent all the time when she was not at school or in her room or eating her silent meals with ToTo in the kitchen or in the little rooms over the garage or, sometimes, over in the Camerons' back garden, in the little house that Glenn Pickens shared with his parents. When she was there she never came around to the house or the pool where Sarah and Charlie, and Ben and I played. And she virtually never set foot in the back garden of our house, much less the summerhouse that she had so loved. Except for the lingering aura of Lucyness that lay in the air of all places where she was, I might not have known that she was still alive.

It was an odd time for me, that time swung between the first great Lucy-drunk stretch of my young childhood and high school. I had already had, in Lucy, a strange, chaste love so strong and pure that this absence of it was almost restful. And I had now a friend; had two, really, in Charlie and Sarah. I was grateful for the latter, and largely content to live in the mindless, sensation-drowned nowness of the moment, of simply being young. But there was a prowling unease and a waiting under the peaceful stasis, an emptiness. The hole in my heart was shaped like Lucy. I missed her. I did not know why she would not have anything to do with me. And yet, something in me was, disgracefully and cravenly, grateful for the hiatus.

I am sure that I knew, on some level, that it could not last.

Lucy broke it herself, on a summer night later that year, when my parents and Aunt Willa gave the largest party I could remember in the Peachtree Road house. It was in all ways a night

I will not forget. It was a portentous night, and a terrible one. But if it had not happened, I might have lost her forever.

The party was, I heard my mother say, to pay back a number of social obligations that she and my father had incurred during the past season. But I knew that it was to market Little Lady and, grudgingly, Lucy, to the mother-brokers of the Buckhead Boys. Mothers of daughters just coming to flower had one like it every summer. The formal selling of familial flesh would begin much later, with the elaborate machinery of the debut year. This first testing of the waters was much like a match race for year-old fillies. Everyone would be there.

Except me.

"No," I said. "I'm sorry. I'm not coming. Y'all can lock me up till I'm fifty, if you want to, but I'm not coming."

They could not budge me. Try as my mother might, I simply refused to put on my lone, too-short summer suit and pass hors d'oeuvres and trays of drinks to the coiffed and curried and strange-eyed mothers of the boys who were my friends. I did not care if they put an apple in the beautiful and foolish Little Lady's mouth and plumped her down, naked and buffed, on a silver tray in the center of the dining room table, but I was prepared to be grounded until I was twenty-one before I watched them parade Lucy before the matrons of Buckhead. I knew that she would only be there on sufferance, and that she would know it; that the real prize of this house was Little Lady, and they were only dragging Lucy out to show because people would talk if they did not . . . and besides, someone might take a fancy to her when the time came to marry off a son; who knew? Stranger things had happened.

"No," I said. "I'm sorry."

In the end, my mother gave in. Better an absent son and heir than one made stupid by sullenness.

And so I was alone when Lucy came to me in the summerhouse, lying on my back on the daybed under the lone wall lamp, reading *Moby Dick,* drowned in the power and sheer, awful truth of it. She stood in the door, against the light from the radiant, reverberating house, without speaking, and when I sensed her presence and raised my head to look at her, I did not know who she was for a moment. In her new yellow princess dress from J. P. Allen's 219 Shop and her first Cuban heels, with a gardenia from the bush beside the lily pond in her cloudy hair, she was the most beautiful thing I had ever seen. Before my eyes fully cleared and some of the old Lucyness settled back around her, I saw a woman, and could not speak with the weight of it on my chest.

I saw also that she held a nearly full bottle of bourbon in one

hand, and that she was more than a little drunk. Her mouth was
loose and her eyes hilarious with liquor. In an instant she became
small Lucy Bondurant again, ten years old, gaudy trouble riding
her head like a Cuban dancer's hat.

"Hey, Gibby," she said, giggling. "I brought you a surprise."

I do not know what got into us that night. I had never tasted
liquor and so far as I knew, neither had she. My father would
be furious, I knew, if he caught us drinking his stolen bourbon
in the summerhouse, and my mother would come near to dying;
volubly so. I could not even imagine what Aunt Willa would do.
I knew only that the consequences would be far more imaginative, far-reaching and terrible than any we had suffered so far.
Maybe Lucy and her mother and sister really would have to
leave the house. Perhaps I would be sent to McCallie or Gordon
or Georgia Military Academy, those last resorts of the unman-
ageable Buckhead Boy. I did not, looking at her and feeling a
great plume of pure joy and lightness rising up from somewhere
behind my ribs, care in the least. Lucy was far too drunk for caring.

"Wait'll I get a glass," I said. And before another hour was
out, we had drunk it all.

It was not late, perhaps ten-thirty. The party was in full spate.
We could hear the steady, deep rhythm of it chugging along like
a well-tuned engine; it would not start to falter for another two
hours. The night was thick and dark and hot; moonless, almost
starless. Cicadas droned off in the woods, and bugs committed
small, ticking suicides against the yellow light over the summerhouse door. Honeysuckle smelled powerfully all around us. Full
summer flowed in the night, but winter crouched off in the distance beyond the house and woods, winter and high school and
a profound change, an ending. A deep, sweet sadness like an itch
lay just beneath everything we said and did, but riding atop that
was laughter, the endless, mindless, unstoppable, drowning
laughter of first intoxication. I felt that I could laugh forever
with the sheer gladness of having her back with me, flopped on
her back on the daybed beside me with her pretty shoes kicked
any which way on the floor and her skirts up, showing a ruffle
of crinoline and a gleam of smooth white leg. She laughed, too,
laughed and laughed, laughed the rich, bawdy, affirming laugh
that will forever be in my ears, essence of Lucy.

And then, all of a sudden, she was crying. Crying so fiercely
and terribly that I thought they would hear her in the house,
over their music and their laughter, and I put my clumsy,
bourbon-bumbling fingers over her mouth; but she shook them
away. The crying spiraled up and up. I knew that if she did not
stop she would go out of control, and one of those great, desper-

ate fits of her childhood would carry her away, and she would be, for a long time, beyond help. She had not had one for years.

I pulled her against me and buried her face in my chest and held her until the crying began to slow and the trembling abate, held her so hard that her ribs hurt my fingers.

Presently she whispered, still sobbing, but less violently, "Gibby, it was so awful! I missed you so much! I finally just couldn't stand it anymore; I thought I was going to die and they would just let me; they wouldn't care!"

"But you wouldn't even talk to me, Lucy," I said. "I thought maybe you were mad at me or something; I thought you didn't want me around you. Why didn't you say something? I would have come. . . ."

"I was waiting for you to come save me! You said you would; you said you always would! *Gibby, why didn't you come?*"

"I . . ." I began, and then fell silent. She was right. I had promised. And I had not come. Why hadn't I?

"OH, GIBBY, I WAS SO AFRAID!" It was a great, primal howl of pure aloneness, with nothing in it of childhood.

My own boyhood fled as if it had never been. I took her in my arms again and stopped her cries with my own blind mouth, and before I finally pulled myself back from the answering mouth and hands and body of my cousin Lucy, I was on top of her, and she was thrashing wildly beneath me on the daybed, and moaning words I still, to this day, blush to remember, and I was so near to entering her that only catastrophe saved me. Instead of making love to Lucy in the summerhouse in my twelfth year and her tenth, I leaned over her and vomited on the floor, from Jack Daniel's black label and terror, and the sheer awfulness of it wrenched me sober.

I think it did her, too. I sat up, clothing half off, rubbing the vile taste off my mouth, looking at her with eyes absolutely wild and appalled, and she looked back at me from her huddle of skirts, mouth bruised and bare, silvery young breasts gleaming white, and in that instant she was sober again, and the desperate tears were gone.

In a moment she, too, was straightening her clothes as she left, pattering back toward the house through the summer dark with her new yellow shoes swinging by their straps from her hand. She did not say good night, or wave, or turn to look back when she gained the back door, and I spent the first entirely sleepless night of my life on the hot, tangled daybed, writhing in bottomless shame and misery and short-circuited adolescent tumescence.

In the morning at breakfast Lucy the darting, glinting child was back again, prattling happily to me, eating her cereal matter-of-factly, talking of the party as any excited ten-year-old would. My parents smiled on her for the first time in months, and even Aunt Willa, if she did not smile, at least stopped frowning, and only I seemed to notice the tiny quiver in Lucy's hands and the red stigmata of what must have been as virulent a hangover as my own in her eyes. She never mentioned that night to me again.

So we were back in that old dance, she and I. Shep and Lucy, Lucy and Shep. But under it, now, a different music surged. That fall I entered the eighth grade at North Fulton High School, and the world widened just as I had thought that it would, to include a great many odd and marvelous things, but so deeply did the scent of danger and taboo cling in my mind to that night in the summerhouse that it was, literally, years before I kissed a girl again.

CHAPTER
EIGHT

W HEN I CROSSED PEACHTREE ROAD on a breathless, flaccid morning that September and entered for the first time the red brick pile of North Fulton High School, I quite literally walked into another world.

I had moved easily in and around Buckhead all my life, of course, and had traveled east across Peachtree Road countless times, but it was always as a voyager on a specific quest: to buy something, to see something, on the way to somewhere else. I always returned home to our side of Peachtree Road like Odysseus, bearing the treasures I had gone questing for, without being touched in any significant way by the natives of that pleasant but lesser continent. The only time I had ever been in a home east of Peachtree was with my mother, when I was quite small and she went to get a home permanent from a gifted and deferential little woman who worked out of the kitchen of her home on Pharr Road.

To me, that visit was official, service-oriented: I felt about my visit to that neat, tree-shaded frame bungalow as I did about the few times I went with Shem Cater in the Chrysler to pick up our laundry from Princess in Capitol Homes, or to fetch Amos from Pittsburgh, or Lottie, our cook, from Mechanicsville. I got no sense, from these visits, that people really lived in those places. They were, instead, destinations that provided the great houses of Buckhead with their provender.

But I went into North Fulton High School, in a sense, to live. And inside those tall, arched doors a world wider and deeper than any I had known before flowered: wider, deeper, denser, more eccentric, far more raffish, many times poorer, a hundred times more exotic, a thousand times more seductive. I first goggled at it in simple disbelief, and then dived into it like a warm and all-nourishing sea. High school came for me, and for many of the Buckhead Boys, I think, just in time.

Lucy would not be entering North Fulton for two more years, and so it must have seemed to her, still held fast in the bowery little prison of Miss Beauchamp's School, that I was deserting her once again. She never said so; Lucy first learned her lifelong habit of long, veiled silences and closed face during her years in that terrible little dotted swiss ghetto, and she never spoke of them after they were ended except once.

"What was it really like, Luce?" I said on the day her incarceration at Miss Beauchamp's finally ended.

"I will never in my life let anyone shut me up again. I will kill them first," she said. And that, for Miss Beauchamp, was that.

So I knew that the school was bad and that she hated it, but I was never to know how bad, and how much. And I knew that my entering high school was abandonment anew, but again, I could only suspect how deep the wound went. In those days, Lucy was letting no one know that what was done to her in my father's house was ongoing anguish. Already in general disfavor, she sensed, I think, that to roil the waters would be fatal. And there was always in her fierce little heart something that refused to give satisfaction to her tormentors, real or fancied.

It bothered me that she closed a part of herself to me, the saint-knight bound so long ago with her protection, but the aftertaste of that night in the summerhouse still scalded my mouth, and for a very long time I found it hard to be totally natural with her. Eventually most of the strangeness simply wore away, and we drifted into our old routine of talking and reading together in the summerhouse or the sun porch or the library after school and in the evenings—for Lucy and I could never be apart for long—and I shared the bounty of high school with her, and once again we spun out the web of ken and dreams that had always bound us close. She still ran to me for comfort and showed her wild heart and its fears and joys and rages to me as she always had, but there was underneath it now a constraint that had never been there before, and I did not know how—or was unwilling—to break it. I know she must have felt my holding back, but she made no effort to move past it. All in all, Lucy had not, in the house on Peachtree Road, gotten very much return on the enormous investment of her hungry spirit and waiting heart.

And so she tightened her hold on the blacks around her. Until I came home in the late afternoons, Lucy's custodial care was largely in the rough, pink-palmed hands of Martha Cater, and

she astonished all of us, Martha included, by loving that old
black martinet so deeply and unconditionally that Martha finally
capitulated and loved her back. Lucy was, always, the only white
child I know whom Martha could truly abide. During that time
she would say, whenever one of Little Lady's newly learned wiles
and graces drew special applause at the breakfast or dinner table,
"Good thang she learnin' how to act nice and please folks, 'cause
it gon' be all she be able to do when she git grown. Ain't nothin'
but wind behin' them big ol' blue eyes."

She would say it under her breath, coming in or going out with
platters and trays, but not so far under that it did not fall upon
the ears it was designed to reach, and at such times, Lucy would
give her such a smile of whole-souled gratitude that it was as
if the sun had come out in the room. Little Lady would pout
and Aunt Willa would mottle unbecomingly with bitten-back
anger, and my mother would sigh and roll her eyes at my father,
but no one reprimanded Martha. To do so was unseemly and
drew one down to her level, and besides, I suspect that all of us
recognized the unfortunate truth in the remark. Little Lady was
so abysmally unintelligent that her reading and spelling were,
in fourth grade, barely on a second-grade level, and she was completely incapable of abstract thought. No matter, though. It was
clear, even at age eight, that she was soon going to look just like
Jane Powell.

As for Lucy, her relationship with Martha Cater was the font
of a lifelong love for, and a marrow-deep kinship with, most of
the blacks with whom she ever came in contact. ToTo, young
Glenn Pickens over at the Camerons', Shem and Lottie and Princess and Amos, thin, yellow Johnnie Mae at the Gentrys', Lubie
at the Slatons' . . . by the time she was twelve, Lucy was spending
more time with the servants of the big houses around her, and
their children, than with anyone else but me, and transferred to
whatever new black came within her orbit, instantly and indiscriminately, all the adoration that her small heart held. By the
time she was in her teens, her predilection for Negroes was a
source of great embarrassment for her mother and mine, and to
a lesser extent, my father. Beginning in earnest in that, her elev-
enth year, they forbade and cajoled and punished, but Lucy
would not give up her beloved black companions.

"Yes'm," she would say to Aunt Willa, when she was taxed
yet again with spending an afternoon with Glenn Pickens or an
evening with Shem and Martha in their rooms over the garage.

"Yes'm, I understand."

And she would smile, the blue eyes melting with contrition.
But the next day she would be back with her cherished black
companions once more. There was simply no stopping her.

I think it was because she saw so clearly what most of us did not, or chose not to: that the Negroes in our world were underdogs, supplicants, victims. I alone knew that this was the role in which Lucy had clad herself. Underneath her public gaiety, sassiness, charm, intelligence, generosity, what Aunt Willa called her feistiness, I had long known she felt profoundly helpless in the world, uncherished, vulnerable and alone. I knew, too, that she had fair reason to feel so. And because she did, she became, in the end, just that: helpless and vulnerable, though seldom alone, and never uncherished. That helplessness was always her greatest strength.

At any rate, in those last lonely days between childhood and puberty, Lucy at least had her blacks, and I believe that bond saved her. I had high school.

North Fulton High School gave me everything I was to know of heterogeneity until Princeton. It gave me a gleeful taste for, and sanction of, eccentricity; it showed me madness and meanness and goodness and absurdity; it limned for me both the value of particularity and the use of conformity. It showed me goodness, in the person of Miss Reba Marks, a slat-thin, blond-marcelled, much-mimicked old maid who taught passionate chemistry and died instantly at the crosswalk in front of the school, shoving to safety the Garden Hills Elementary child who darted out in front of a yellow Fulton County school bus.

It showed me evil, in the person of the short-lived, hulking, loose-lipped assistant football coach who got retarded and homely Scarlett Mitchum, from the rural wilds of Sandy Springs, pregnant, and then jeered openly at her hard, basketball-round mound of belly as she tagged after him adoringly through the halls and into the locker room.

It showed me danger, in the cool-eyed blond person of the legendary Boo Cutler, he of the lightning Mercury and the thunderous midnight runs out of Cherokee County, loaded with shine; it showed me despair, in the bleached persons of those anonymous students doomed, it seemed from birth, to be library staffers, nutrition aides, infirmary assistants, science clubbers.

And it gave me heroes, a different kind of romance from that Lucy and I had known in our reading and dreaming: not dead, not unreal. The radiant, careless ranks of the football and basketball and track stars. The editors of the *Hi-Ways* and the *Scribbler*. The cheerleaders and the beauties and the senior superlatives and the ROTC officers and their demure and beatific sponsors.

It even gave me, totally unexpectedly, a tantalizing and heady dollop of popularity. Lucy had been right; going into high school I had lengthened and toughened, and my face had grown to fit

my features a bit better, and I did have something of the look
of that golden, hawk-faced knight she had envisioned for me so
long ago; it was my uncle Jim's face that I saw in my mirror
now, though far younger and less defined. A mute shyness underlay and belied the knight, and I was never so naive as to be
unaware that my family's money gave me a cachet I never would
have had otherwise, but I was a good enough dancer, and even
shone modestly as a miler and relay team member, and so the
scanty popularity—or rather, to be exact, recognition—was not
entirely unearned. But I never wore it comfortably.

High school did not give most of us from the big houses many
new or close friends. I suspect it was already too late for that
when we entered; Buckhead simply ran too deep in us. Like the
Catholic Church, Buckhead kept for itself those it had for the
first seven years of their lives. The boys from the other sections
of Atlanta who came to North Fulton—from Sandy Springs and
Brookhaven and Morningside and Peachtree Hills and Peachtree
Heights and Brookwood Hills and Ansley Park—were suspicious of the smell of money that lingered about us, no matter
how hard we tried to conceal or even eradicate it. Of all the boys
I met in those teenaged years—literally hundreds—only one,
A. J. Kemp, became close. A.J., from far out Cheshire Bridge
Road. Thin, agile, clever, smoothly pompadoured, fiercely ambitious and almost feminine in demeanor; or at least, not simply
and rudely masculine: always the best dancer, the lone male
cheerleader, the "dresser," the actor, the first smoker of cigarettes, the one with the most sweaters and 45 rpms. A.J., one
of the funniest men I have ever known, and in the end, one of
the most loyal. He attached himself to us, the moneyed ones,
instantly and immovably, and made us accept him with the sheer
force and wattage of his personality, and before eighth grade was
over, he was one of us to the bone. I suspect he thought he had
garnered great advantages for himself in the association, but it
was we who got the long end of that stick. A.J. enriched us.

Years later, when I had been literally flattened under the catastrophe that set me outside the company of the Pinks and the
Jells, A.J. showed up at the summerhouse at lunchtime bearing
sandwiches and éclairs from Henri's and a six-pack of beer. Few
of the others had come, and I was surprised and painfully embarrassed to see him standing in the winter sunlight at the door,
blinking in at my dim, musty lair.

I could not speak, and for a long moment he did not; I had
the insane fancy that he would toss the food inside and flee, like
a keeper at the cage of some wild and desperate animal. And
then he grinned, his old, clever wizard's grin.

"I'll probably find gnawed bones lying around, and turds piled up in the corner, but I'm coming in whether you like it or not," he said, doing just that and leaving the door ajar so that the clean, merciless crystal light of noon flooded in.

"And what's more," he added, "I'm coming back tomorrow at lunch, and the next day, and every one after that until you quit living in this cave with the wolves and act like a human being again."

Tears of sheer, weak humility and gratitude filled my eyes, and I turned away, mumbling, "It's good to see you, A.J."

He followed me into the summerhouse and put his arms around me and hugged me. It was so unlike A.J. to do such a thing that my faltering composure limped back, and I was able to look curiously into his face.

"Aren't you afraid I'll set your pants on fire?" I said.

"Nope," he said, sweeping litter off my coffee table and setting out the sandwiches and beer. "But I used to wish I could set yours on fire. I just want to say one thing, Shep, and then I won't say anything more about all this crap. We all know you couldn't have had anything to do with it; we *know* that. The others ought to come, but they probably won't, for a while; you'd know better than me why that is, but I do know it's true. The reason I can come is I was never really one of you, no matter what you thought, or I did. This Buckhead shit doesn't bind me. So consider me an emissary from us all, and let me tell you that we think it's all a load of horse manure and we . . . we love you."

He mumbled this last, and his thin monkey's face flamed, and he ducked his head and bit into his sandwich. I got up and went into the bathroom and wept. Only one other man—not my father, not Ben Cameron—had ever told me that he loved me. No man ever did again.

A.J. came for lunch at least three days a week for a month after that, leaving his job at the bank downtown and taking the 23 Oglethorpe bus to the stop at Peachtree and Lindbergh and walking straight through the front yard to the summerhouse, bypassing the big house and any chance encounter with my mother. We never spoke of the fire again, only of the more distant past— of high school at North Fulton, and what it had given us. I don't suppose I will ever be able to tell A.J. what he gave me during that dark month. But I believe that he knows.

What high school gave us all, the gift that the Atlanta of that time alone in all the world had to give, was the Pinks and the Jells. I don't think any high school experience anywhere could have been even remotely like it. I know nothing has ever been precisely like it since.

No one is quite sure what the terms meant. "Pinks" is at least moderately self-explanatory: Pink tulle. Pink angora. Pink Revlon and Tangee lipstick. Pink cashmere twin sets. Pinks, for the girls of that golden elect of an entire generation. "Jells," or "Jellies," is almost impossible to etymologize. Jelly beans, I suppose, give birth to the term: bright, sweet, foolish, frivolous, almost entirely without substance or nourishment, but long indeed on pleasure. A confection completely of the moment.

The Jells of Buckhead toiled not, neither did they spin. They did not, on the main, play football or any other team sport, though some of them excelled at the showier and more indolent individual sports, like tennis, swimming and diving. Some even rode horses with considerable flair and style. All could dance, though, and did, endlessly. Dancing, in one sense, is what the Pinks and the Jells were all about.

The high school athletes largely ignored the Jells, and spoke of them, if they did, with contempt, and they were never a part of that elite teenaged brotherhood of drag racers, contact sports players, booze runners, Saturday night brawlers, bar drinkers, tobacco spitters, and legendary cocksmen. The Jells might occasionally hang out where the jocks and the toughs did, at the Peachtree Hills Pub or the Blue Lantern or even, and much worse, the Cameo Lounge down near the Greyhound bus station, but they were never welcome or comfortable there, and did not make a habit of it.

Almost to a Jell they worshiped the draggers, those fleet young gods of speed and smoke, and their rococo souped-up chariots. I remember countless afternoons and Saturdays, hanging over the fence out at the weedy dirt strip near the Bell bomber plant— later Lockheed—in Marietta, watching Boo Cutler and Floyd Sutton and their hard-muscled, greasy-nailed, narrow-eyed ilk throttling their screaming Mercurys and Pontiacs. We wouldn't have risked our necks and our cashmeres in the cars and couldn't have driven them if we had dared, but we worshiped, nonetheless. Automobiles were our Baals, our golden calves. Not all of us had them, by any means; Jellhood was bestowed on the poor and the average as well as the rich, and many Jells simply could not afford them. But most of the Buckhead Jells did. I received a vicious-looking two-toned red and white Plymouth Fury trimmed with bronze for my sixteenth birthday, and was as surprised as anyone at the gift. Even I did not think I was the type for such a car. I suppose it might have been my father's last shot at making me into a fitting rich man's son, a creature of charisma and dash, and it succeeded, at least for a little while, for it bought me no end of attendant Jells and flocking, fluttering Pinks. In the end, though, I could not sustain the image, and increasingly during the last two years of high school, it was Lucy who drove the Fury. It was always far more suited to her.

The Jells existed because the Pinks did. We squired them, admired them, set them off like shadow boxes, and ultimately—the point, I suppose, of it all—many of us married them. To have been a Pink in Atlanta in those dreaming days between Depression and Camelot was to have known, briefly, a kind of lambent perfection that does not—cannot—come again to any given life. How could it? It had nothing whatsoever to do with reality; Pinkhood was a four-year carnival a million miles long and an inch deep. What it lacked in substance it made up for in sheer excessiveness and style. Total adulation was the order of the day, and the girl who knew how to command it led a sort of Grand Waltz so intricate, all-consuming and extravagant that everything else—college, the debut year, the Junior League, sometimes even marriage—tended to pale beside it.

Not all the high school girls of Atlanta knew how to command it, by any means. Those who did not were ciphers, nonentities, miserable; those who did were Pinks. It was that simple, and that brutal. The ones who could not never forgot it. The ones who could never did, either. Many Buckhead women of my acquaintance will tell you, over a fourth or fifth gin and tonic at the club, that being a Pink in Atlanta was the best time of their lives. God help them.

What a Pink had to do to attain and keep the title was to be popular. It meant a kind of sprightly flirtatiousness, a covertly sensual perkiness, which forbade even as it invited. A fresh-faced, ponytailed actress of stunningly professional naiveté and virginity named Millie Perkins was the role model for my generation of Pinks, who all learned to flip their ponytails and thrust out their Peter-Panned breasts even as they clamped their knees together. Beauty was not a necessity, but pertness was. "Cute" was the best thing you could call a Pink. "Peppy" was next best. Monumental self-assurance underlay everything, or its facsimile; a Pink would rather be caught at a Phi Pi dance without an orchid to her name or an unbooked no-break than be adjudged nervous. Wender & Roberts must have led the nation in sales of Mum and Odor-O-No in those days, for a Buckhead Pink never sweated, did not even mist; and though she might duck her head and blush a hundred times a day, and drop her Maybellined lashes, it was never from social embarrassment.

"She's a lovely girl; so poised," was the highest accolade our mothers could bestow on our steadies. It was tantamount to the Good Housekeeping Seal of Approval, and predated many of the Northwest's grandest weddings.

Somehow, by the time they reached high school, the small, nondescript girls we had known and tormented and ignored all our lives had flowered overnight into Pinks. I never knew personally a girl from Buckhead who failed, or eschewed, Pinkness. It came with the Cedar 7 telephone exchange. There must have been some, but I think they were sent away to schools where lives and futures did not ride on such fickle, flimsy steeds.

Lucy knew who they were. I put the question to her once, when she had been at North Fulton about a year, and had bloomed into the pinkest Pink of them all.

"The fleebs?" she said carelessly. "They go off somewhere up North and study. They get acne and A's. They're gone, poof; you never see 'em again after seventh grade."

"Don't people think they got P.G.?" I said. It was what my crowd whispered about girls who suddenly enrolled in out-of-state schools.

"Lord, no." Lucy laughed. "Nobody would screw a fleeb."

The Pinks and the Jells grew up within the armature of a high school fraternity and sorority system that for sheer baroqueness would have dimmed the court of Louis XIV. Other cities may have had such organizations, but ours was an arena of such Venetian excess that by the time we graduated and met the real world head-on, many of us were ruined forever for it, and wandered through our lives in a sort of bewildered and petulant fog of loss, like colored Easter chicks peeping away in a coal yard. There were about twenty quasi-Greek organizations all told, perhaps a dozen fraternities and seven or eight sororities. Within their ranks was a gilded subculture of the "best": Phi Pi, to which Lucy and Sarah and Little Lady and all the girls I knew belonged, and Rho Mu, which was mine simply because it was where the Buckhead Boys invariably landed. Most of the larger Atlanta high schools had chapters; we had brothers and sisters at North Fulton, Boys' and Girls' highs, Marist, Druid Hills, Northside, NAPS (North Avenue Presbyterian School) and Washington Seminary.

Well, of course, Washington Seminary. So interwoven in the fabric of Buckhead life was that stately, columned old white mansion on the wooded knoll where a Ramada Inn stands now that practically every young woman of sterling Atlanta lineage since 1878 had been through its massive doors. Of my set, only Sarah Cameron, whose parents did not approve of private secondary schools, and Lucy, whose mother could not afford it and who in any case would have died before she allowed herself to be sent into another girls' school, did not attend. Both went to North Fulton, and neither suffered for it, for the education dispensed in the white high schools of Atlanta in those days was thorough, workmanlike and broad. In truth, more good, budding minds probably had fires lit under them in these schools than at most of the surrounding private schools favored then by Atlanta families, Washington Seminary included.

It was not, really, for an education that the daughters of the big houses went to Seminary, but for the first-rate polishing and marketing offered there. Traditionally, the sixth and last class period was devoted to the rapt, serious grooming of hair, nails and faces, in preparation for the ritual after-school stroll from front door down the driveway to sidewalk on Peachtree Road, where the assembled ranks of Atlanta's Jells, gathered like the clans of Scotland from the surrounding high schools, jostled and lolled, watching the sweet-swaying Pinks come nonchalantly out.

I can still see us, laughing in my idling Fury or A.J.'s renegade Chevy, watching the vestal parade switching down the driveway. Known to us since birth, the parading Pinks were as strange and exotic then as Mayan princesses. It was as if we had never seen them before.

"Look at those boobies!" A.J. would squeal in exaltation, his face contorted in ecstasy. "*Look* at that pair!"

And we would hoot, groan, clutch our heads and fall against the seats in transports of rapture, as if we had never seen that particular pair of cashmere-sweatered breasts before in all our lives.

"Oh, Jesus, *look* at that can," Snake would bellow. "Backfield in motion!"

And we would beat upon the sides of the cars, baying excelsior. I do not know why Seminary's chatelaines did not chase us away with fire hoses, but they did not. The school always lived Louis Sullivan's great adage, "Form follows function."

Oh yes, Washington Seminary knew on which side its dainty bread was buttered. It took the combined ranks of the city's school officials close to two decades to stamp out the sororities and fraternities, and at the height of the campaign, in 1952, Seminary lifted its lovely head, gave an aristocratic sniff and announced that it would ignore the ban. As Washington Seminary went, so went the city. The Pinks and the Jells went dancing on.

Indeed, dancing was what we were about, we wellborn, time-lavished, cashmered and saddle-shod spawn of this small city on the make and on its way up. From December to June, each Friday night, one or another of the sororities or fraternities would hold its great formal dance of the season, to which all the other sororities and fraternities in Atlanta were invited, and in the fall, before the formality set in with the winter rains, we had citywide skirt-and-sweater dances. Thirty-odd glittering, jittering Fridays, stretching in a crackling silver skein from October until late May, and on each one of them, like a gemstone, a dance.

We danced at the Brookhaven Country Club and the Druid Hills Golf Club and the Ansley Golf Club and sometimes, if one of our parents would stand sponsor, at the Driving Club. We danced in high school gymnasiums and out at Robinson's Tropical Gardens on the Chattahoochee River and in each other's homes and on each other's porches and terraces and verandas, and around each other's pools. We slow-danced, noses buried in fragrant, Halo- and Prell-scented hair, fingers splayed against fiercely boned young waists, bare, dizzying white shoulders and cheeks pressed against us, lost and drowning in "Moonglow" or "Sentimental Journey" or "These Foolish Things," aching with love and grateful for the bobbling, swaying bells of crinoline that smothered our fierce erections.

We jitterbugged, skittering and popping at the end of one another's arms like drops of water on a griddle; our springy, nimble feet flew like gandy dancers' to the strains of "Pennsylvania 6-5000" and "In the Mood" and "String of Pearls" and "Chattanooga Choo Choo." Music washed over us and eddied around us as endlessly as the sea: tides of music lapped through our days and surged over our nights. Music poured out of record players and jukeboxes and radios all over Atlanta, connecting us one to another like a surf of blood in our veins; music spilled out of the horns and reeds and drums and pianos of fifty different combos and dance bands, from Bill Haley and the Emory Aces to the legendary likes of Ralph Marterie and Woody Herman, the latter secured through the good offices of a brother or cousin at Georgia Tech and our fathers' cash money.

We waltzed and tangoed and shagged and lindied; we bunny-hopped and boogied. Some of us even Charlestoned, and A. J. Kemp once drew a cheering, clapping crowd at Brookhaven with a twenty-minute exhibition of the Lambeth Walk, looking for all the world, in his rented tux and his boneless snake's elegance, like a lank-haired Fred Astaire. Stag lines ran out the doors into the May-sweet nights on half a dozen country club terraces, and we cut in methodically on the Pinks of our choice in a grand, ritualized pattern of advance and retreat. Some exceptional Pinks could not dance three steps before they were cut in on, and one girl—I think it was Little Lady, just after I went away to school—established the amateur record with thirty breaks during one chorus of "Stardust." That one still stands, I am told. All over Atlanta, on those luminous Fridays, in the velvet dark of winter and the tender new green lace of spring, to the music that beat like a pulse buried deep in the marrow of our youth, we danced. We danced.

"We'll remember this all our lives," Sarah Cameron said to me once, at one of the first sorority dances I took her to. She wore a cloud of yellow tulle over a bobbing hoop that belled up in back when I pressed her against me, swaying to the slow, sinuous strains of "Stardust," and a hypnotic river of honeysuckle poured into the open windows of Brookhaven from the fringes of the dark golf course.

"I'll remember that I flunked geometry because of this stupid dance," I said sourly. In the beginning I was distinctly ungracious to Sarah.

"You're an awful fool, Shep," little Sarah Cameron said. I remember that she was not smiling.

Dancing would have been enough to make those years memorable: thirty-five dances in as many weeks, and none to be missed, if you were a true Buckhead Pink or Jell. But in addition, there was always a formal, seated dinner beforehand, at one of the city's scant few "good" restaurants, like Hart's on Peachtree, or at the Paradise Room of the Henry Grady Hotel, or in some long-suffering parents' dining room, and a breakfast afterward that might last until 4:00 A.M. Sometimes, after the breakfast, we would skin into blue jeans and pile into whatever cars could be commandeered, and go out and climb the great, black bulk of Stone Mountain to the east of the city, lying winded and lipstick-smeared on the granite brow as the sun came sidling up. Or we would drop off our dates, after some obligatory skirmishing in the front or back seat—for no Pink would catch monk in earnest unless she was seriously pinned, and though some of us did go steady in the early years of high school, most played the field until lust and attrition parted us from our pins in exchange for heavy, expert petting in our later years—and go out and race, ineptly, our cars on the Marietta Highway, old U.S. 41, until dawn. I don't remember why our parents let us stay out so late weekend after weekend, or how we survived the sheer fatigue of it. I do remember being as tired toward the end of each spring term as if I had mononucleosis. Tired and broke.

Because each event on any given dance evening—dinner, the dance itself and breakfast afterward—meant, for a Pink, a date with a different boy, and each date meant an orchid. Not just any orchid, either; purple was so far beyond the pale that a fat vocational student at Southwest DeKalb High wouldn't have worn one to a DeMolay formal at the Veterans of Foreign Wars post. Pure, waxen, pristine white, nestled in net and tied with satin: we bought forests of them. I can see them now, on the bosoms and wrists and at the waists of the girls of Buckhead, usually three and as many as six, if the Pink was an officer of the sorority giving the dance.

I remember a dress that Lucy had, in her sixteenth year and my last one at North Fulton; it was the deep, jeweled navy of

a Christmas night sky; silk velvet, and scalloped up at the hem
to show the clouds of snowy crinolines underneath. Lucy had
chosen it as a background for her white orchids; Red Chastain
was taking her to the Phi Pi winter formal, and she was the social
chairman that year. She had other dates for dinner and breakfast;
I don't remember who—and all in all, eight orchids were pinned
and tied and taped about her. There were three on the strapless
bodice of the dress, one on each wrist, one at her waist, one at
the front scallop of the skirt, and one in her hair, worn loose
on her shoulders, as cloudy and drifting as a squid's ink in a clear
sea.

"You look like a florist shop," I said, as she stood looking at
herself in the ormolu mirror in the foyer, waiting for whoever
was taking her to the dinner.

"I look wonderful," she said, smiling dreamily. "Nobody has
ever had this many orchids. Seven is as many as there's been,
ever. I'm going to keep them all in my scrapbook, to remember
the night I had more orchids than any girl ever in this town."

"Well, it's going to smell like a funeral parlor," I said meanly,
stung because I could afford only one orchid for Sarah Cameron,
who had asked me to be her escort, and my father would not
spring for a second. Stung by that, and by something else that
I did not care, then, to examine.

"The only reason you've got that many is because Red's father
is stinking rich."

"Exactly," Lucy said, the smile deepening. "Red's daddy likes
me. He wants Red to bring me by before we go to the club so
he can see me in my dress." She turned from the mirror to look
at me, her face incandescent.

"Oh, Gibby, you know who I wish could see me tonight? With
all these flowers?"

"Yes," I said, smiling back at her, the meanness gone from
my heart to be replaced by a great wrench. "I know who. He'd
be so proud of you he'd pop his buttons, Luce. You'd knock his
eyes out."

"Would I?" she breathed, looking at me with eyes that saw,
not me, but that first long love. "Would I?"

"Yes," I said. "You bet your fanny you would."

Orchids, orchestras, satin and velvet and tulle dresses over
drifts of crinoline, rented tuxedos; dinners and dances and breakfasts. No wonder we all worked summers and often weekends,
even we sons of millionaires and near-millionaires. Wonder only
that the Jells who were not rich could afford it at all, even with
their jobs. I know that A.J. worked much harder during high
school to finance the seasons of the Pinks and the Jells than he
did to maintain himself later at the University of Georgia, clerk-

ing after school and on Saturdays at Bates Camera on East Paces
Ferry, and running the projector weeknights at the Buckhead
Theatre. I cannot imagine what the parents of those resourceless
Jells felt when another autumn of dancing and spending came
wheeling around. Despair, probably. But a kind of fierce unspoken pride, too, I'd be willing to bet. To be the progenitors of an
Atlanta Jell, to have sired one of the elect of a generation . . .
it must have made up for a great many skimpinesses and mean-
nesses and omissions. I hope so. I know that Melba Kemp, A.J.'s
widowed mother, who saw him through high school on her earnings from the Jolly Tot Shop, told me just before she died, when
A.J. and Lana brought her by to see me, that those years when
he ran with the Buckhead Jells were, in spite of the privation,
the happiest of her life.

"Why?" I said, thinking of her days in the shop on aching feet,
and her nights alone in the tiny house at the far end of Cheshire
Bridge while A.J. was out at the dances in the country clubs and
great houses that she would never enter.

"Because it was something, that crowd you all ran around
with," she said, smiling. "All those dances and parties, and a
different pretty girl for every one . . . You boys were really something. I never saw A.J. have such a good time since."

A.J. gave Lana and me a little mock shrug of demurral and
rolled his brown eyes heavenward behind his mother's back. But
despite the gesture, I knew that she was right. A.J. was born to
be an Atlanta Jell, and nobody I ever knew did it better.

Pink-and-Jellhood was not limited to the splendid preenings
of the sororities and fraternities, by any means. For its initiates,
it reached out to define, consume and finally become the whole
of life. After school, after the ritual viewings and pairings on the
sidewalk in front of Washington Seminary and the concrete circle in front of North Fulton High, we stuffed ourselves into the
available automobiles and fanned out to take the city.

There was, in the full-blown years of Jellhood, my Fury; there
was Snake Cheatham's 1939 Mercury convertible, the Black
Booger; there was Ben Cameron's souped-up Chevy, which he
bought with his entire life's savings on his sixteenth birthday,
and A. J. Kemp's disreputable and fiercely admired 1935 Chevy
without top or fenders, which Buckshot Jones at Northside Auto
Service on Howell Mill finally gave him, just to keep him from
mooning around the premises anymore. We careened all over
the city in that naked, shivering wreck. We would stop at the
last filling station before we crossed the Atlanta city limits hur-
tling toward downtown, and A.J. would leap over the door and
lie on his back underneath and insert the muffler. Coming home,
he would repeat the performance and remove the ineffectual de-

vice. Otherwise, around Buckhead, he simply drove it flat out and braying. None of the Buckhead constabulary particularly cared. A.J. was something of a local hero to auto aficionados for getting the Chevy running at all.

Some of the girls had cars, too. Freddie Slaton's father gave her a little red Triumph for her sixteenth birthday, probably and rightly figuring that hornet-mean little Freddie was going to need all the advantages she could get. Most of the Washington Seminary Pinks had cars. One way or another, after school and on Saturdays, we took to the streets like flocks of migratory birds, and our flyways were fully as stylized and inviolable.

Around Buckhead, we favored Wender & Roberts Drugstore for afternoon milkshakes and Cokes, and afterward the Buckhead and the Garden Hills theaters. Farther afield, we might alight at Rusty's or the Pig 'n Whistle or Peacock Alley or Harry's or Moe's & Joe's or the fabled Varsity, down at North Avenue and Spring, near Georgia Tech. Dr. Brewer's Wagon Wheel at the intersection of Piedmont, Roswell and Old Ivy was popular for barbecue, and Tyree's Pool Hall, where the one-eyed hustler would take on all comers, was forbidden and thus irresistible. In the summers, we steeped in the chlorine-smitten, azure pools in Garden Hills and Moseley Park, or at our parents' clubs, or in one or another of our backyards.

Bowling alleys with lurid pinball machines and jukeboxes, the covered bridge out at Sope Creek, the fatally alluring Chattahoochee River which was the dividing line between Fulton and Cobb counties, the ball field down behind Peacock Alley, Minor and Carter's Drugstore downtown—they all knew our imprint, held the ghosts of our restless and bedazzled spirits. Oh, the magic, the eldritch, spindrift glamour of streetlights through the new April green of the trees spilling over Rusty's or Harry's parking lot, honeysuckle and mimosa as thick in our nostrils as the Emeraude and Tigress rising steamily from the unimaginable cleavages beneath the Peter Pan collars and sleeveless, V-necked blouses. Blood and Miller High Life pounded so forcefully through our veins then that we sometimes felt that we would simply burst apart with the sheer being of young.

Inevitably, with all those hormones rampaging and all the beer and illicitly bought gin and bourbon flowing and all that forbidden white flesh flashing, there were fist fights. Most occurred during the dances, though usually outside during intermissions. I remember one, in my senior year, at Druid Hills Country Club, when Red Chastain knocked a marauding Jell from Boys' High clear through the French doors onto the terrace after he tried repeatedly to cut in and capture a shimmering Lucy during a no-break. In those days, it was not unknown for a popular Pink to have her no-breaks booked years in advance, and by that time everyone knew that the third no-break at each formal belonged, on Lucy's card, to Red. The Boys' High Jell could not plead ignorance. It was a short fight, and a brutal one, and though no one particularly liked Red, we all thought the mangled Boys' High Jell got what he deserved. No one, in those days, broke the rules of Pink-and-Jellhood with impunity.

Our fathers tolerated these fights with remarkable humor and resignation, though our mothers usually wept or scolded. We might be dutifully admonished, and sometimes desultorily punished or grounded, but our fathers knew, as we sensed, that it was important for us to learn to do our fighting in a controlled and gentlemanly manner. I am sure that my father suffered keenly because I never ventured to test my antlers in combat. It may have been a time dominated by females, by the pursuit and courting of them, but it was, nonetheless, rankly masculine in tone.

"How'd you get that shiner, kiddo?" Ben Cameron asked me once after Sunday lunch at the Driving Club, pointing to the black eye I had gotten from Snake's elbow during a particularly exuberant boob-spotting session outside Seminary. "What does the other guy look like?"

"Shep doesn't fight," my father said dryly. "He's a lover. Didn't you know?"

Since I was sixteen and had never had a formal date except for Sarah, I reddened.

Oh yes, my father suffered.

And so in this way, through our glittering citywide networks and borne on our immortal wheels, we became true princes of the city, ranging all over it, tasting it in all its moods and hours and seasons, stretching in its sunlight, exulting in its warm darkness. It was no wonder that none of us wanted to go away to school, except, perhaps, those, like me, on whom Jellhood always sat askew. It was a ridiculously hedonistic, totally self-absorbed existence. In those cloud-borne, pell-mell days, we were our own first great obsession.

Our second was sex.

When I think of the sexual tenor of those times, what flashes back to me is a cold well of fear in the stomach and a constantly aching crotch, covered with a thin veneer of goatish, biceps-knuckling bravado. From puberty on through graduation, and often beyond and into college, we were so obsessed with sex that I wonder how we hid our perpetual erections, or dragged them through the endless days and nights. We awoke to wet sheets; talked of sex on the way to school; stared and fantasized and discussed the Pinks through six entire periods; nudged as close

as we could in the cars and booths and movie seats after school
in order to brush, with elaborate casualness, a breast or thigh;
necked desperately with whoever would let us in the long evenings after dates, in front of darkened houses and at such designated lovers' lanes as Sope Creek, Oakland Cemetery, the public
parks and the drive-ins (on the last rows, out of the lights); petted
to the limits of sanity and Pinkhood if we were pinned or about
to be; and then went home and jerked off guiltily and in vast relief before falling asleep, awaking damply and beginning the routine once again. Like an army of Onans, we spilled our seed
mightily upon the ground, but almost never in the patch for
which it was designed.

In pairs or in groups we lied elaborately about what we did
to whom, and how she moaned and begged for more, and where
she learned how to do the things she knew, and we tried to appear cool with each other even as we pulled sweaters and magazines over our laps to conceal the craven tents leaping in our blue
jeans. We ranged as far away as the infamous Plaza Pharmacy
on Ponce de Leon to buy rubbers that soon desiccated in our
wallets, and the Jell who did not have on the surface of his Bux-
ton an imprinted circle from a condom was no Jell at all. Even
I had one, given to me by Snake Cheatham, who was our official
Trojan and Ramses distributor, but needless to say the occasion
for it never arose, and I'm not sure I would have known how
to put it on if it had. And despite our preening and crowing and
posturing, I don't think many of us did. We all said we fucked.
I think I could count on the fingers of one hand the Jells in high
school who actually did. If you didn't, you talked about it. If
you did, you didn't. It was just that simple. The quiet ones of
us were the ones that, in our secret hearts, we revered. But we
simply could not manage to keep quiet about the Great American Nooky Quest that drove us like a generation of lemmings.

"Did she? Did she?" we would all snigger fiercely in homeroom, to the one of us who had announced, the day before, that
scoring that night was all but accomplished.

"Fucking A," the scorer would say carelessly, making a jaunty
circle with thumb and forefinger.

"What was it like?" Breaths held, hearts pounding.

"Like bombs away, man."

"Jesus!"

The key, of course, was the Pinks. It was a tenet of Pinkhood
that a Pink knew how to promise worlds, galaxies, universes with
her eyes and smile and voice, but knew, too, how to deliver virtually nothing and still keep the Jells circling. Most of the Pinks
I knew could do it. I don't know how they managed; it must
have been more difficult than quantum physics, given the length

and frequency of the monk sessions in the automobiles of the Jells.

Even the girls who were pinned were presumed chaste until proven otherwise, and since there was literally no way to do that except by an obvious pregnancy, the presumption held even when the couple's automobile was seen to be rocking in the last row of the drive-in like a dory in a high gale. Virgins or not, the Pinks of Atlanta twitched through their high school years wearing chastity like armor, and the girl who screwed and liked it, or even worse, told, was out of the pack faster than a spavined yearling in a migratory caribou herd. I never knew a Buckhead Pink who had sex and admitted it except Lucy, and somehow, all rules were off when it came to her. The prices she paid were higher, and had been paid earlier, than any we could exact.

It was an era of incredible double standards and witless innuendo, fueled by unrequited lust and made both piquant and terrifying by the absolute taboo of pregnancy. "P.G." or "preggers" or "knocked up" were punch lines to locker room jokes and also the words a Jell dreaded most to hear from a white-faced, tearful steady. For a Pink, pregnancy was pure and simple social suicide. I'm sure many more Buckhead girls than I knew about made predawn visits to the sinister clinic in Copper Hill, Tennessee, whose address every prudent Jell secreted in his wallet along with the Trojans, and I am equally sure a number of quiet visits to respectable Northside physicians, who just happened to be family friends, ended in more than an invoice. Snake Cheatham, who went through Emory Med and interned at Grady before he snared a residency at Piedmont, told me much later that during our college years some people whose names were most vividly and fondly inscribed in our *Hi-Ways* came to him asking how to terminate a pregnancy . . . but that was when we were, mostly, at Tech and Georgia, in the wider and looser days of fraternity parties in earnest and far more open drinking.

I knew of no illicit pregnancies though there was always talk going around. I don't know how the Jells of my high school days coped when they got caught, if they did. Not one of the Pinks dropped abruptly out of school like one or two anonymous non-Pinks did each year. Maybe some of those summers abroad, or at relatives' cottages at the more remote resorts, had dual purposes; I wouldn't have known a pregnancy in those days if the water had burst at my feet. And no matter what lies and half-truths we told each other, no matter what female functions and phenomena we tittered about—breasts, buttocks, menstruation, masturbation, aphrodisiacs, sexual techniques, the dark convolvulus of the female genitalia—we would not have talked about pregnancy and abortion. It was far too terrifying and too near.

But the quest for tail went on unabated through our high school years and into and through college. Some Jells got their first experience with sex from Frances Spurling, a cheerful nymphomaniac of fifteen who lived with her parents behind a seedy white frame grocery store on Roswell Road, who would call up the boy of her choice and say, "Your bananas are ready. You can pick them up at three." Or four, or whenever her parents were not about. And the boy would go, trembling and swaggering, over to the store and park behind the stock shed out back and steal into the filthy, black, cobwebby interior, and Frances, her underpants down around her meaty ankles, would be awaiting him on a pile of gunnysacks, and would grab him and stuff him inside her with no more ado than if she were manning the grocery cash register, and buck wildly for a moment, until he spilled his nervous seed more in bewilderment and haste than passion, and then dry herself off with the gunnysack and push him, still zipping up, out the door, saying, "Bananas are a dollar a pound this week."

My own inevitable encounter with Frances came the Hallowe'en I was fourteen, a good year after everyone else I knew claimed to have been ushered through the gates of Heaven by her. For sheer ignominy, little in my life has ever matched it.

The year before that, Snake Cheatham had organized a small and highly elect club, a sort of secret society among the Buckhead Jells, called the Touchdown Club, and membership was based solely upon one's having scored with a woman. Since there was no conceivable way to prove this with any Pink in her right mind, the initiation rite agreed upon was a visit to Frances Spurling, the successful completion of which she rewarded with an X made with red ballpoint ink on the wrist of the new initiate. It was diabolically clever and simple: Frances proved to be incorruptible in this matter, and would not award the coveted red X unless the deed was, indeed, accomplished. Since she received from each initiate the sum of two dollars cash money for each rite of passage, the temptation to accept the occasional discreet bribe must have been great, but Frances hung tough. Once on the path to the storage shed behind the grocery, one knew one had no recourse but to perform.

Charlie Gentry and I were the last of the Buckhead Boys to join the Touchdown Club, and finally let ourselves be goaded and humiliated into this Allhallows foray simply because there was no other even faintly honorable alternative.

"Tonight or never, Bondurant and Gentry," Snake jeered that afternoon. "And if it's never, the whole school's going to know about it in the morning. Frances awaits you at nine. X marks the spot."

Charlie and I set out that night with the spirits of the Atlanta dead and the hoots and jeers of the all-too-live Buckhead Boys in our ears, desperation and utter despair stopping our voices.

"I'll probably get asthma and die," Charlie said finally, pedaling woefully along beside me out black Roswell Road on his bicycle. "I'll probably choke to death right there on top of old Frances, or wherever you're supposed to get. I hope I do."

"Listen," I said, shame nearly strangling me. "I've got a red ballpoint pen and twenty-five dollars. It's all I've saved for the past two years. I'm going to offer to buy her off, and if she says no, we can just make an *X* on our wrists and say we did, and she's lying."

"No," said Charlie, who would rather face Torquemada than lie. "We can't do that, Shep."

"Well, I can," I flared. "You and your principles can fuck old Frances Spurling till midnight, if you can't bear to lie about her. Thank goodness I'm not as pure as you."

"I'm not pure," Charlie said miserably. "I've got seventeen dollars in my pocket myself. But if she won't take our money we're dead, because Snake says she has her own secret way of making the *X*, and nobody but her knows what it is. It won't do us any good to lie."

We pedaled on in silence, doomed.

But the great god Pan was kind to us that night. When we reached the stygian storage shed behind the dark grocery and knocked timidly on the door, and at the muffled "Come in," pushed it open and went inside, it was to see Frances Spurling, by the light of a khaki plastic Girl Scout flashlight, sprawled out on her gunnysacks looking distinctly unseductive in flannel pajamas, a big, bulky wool bathrobe and huge fleecy slippers. Even Charlie and I could tell it was no costume for deflowering youths. Our hearts leaped up in our racketing breasts.

"You can just forget it for tonight," Frances said sullenly. "I fell off the roof just before you came."

"Jesus," I said, wincing. "You shouldn't be out here, Frances. Did it . . . is it real bad?"

"Well, it ain't a lot of fun, I'll tell you," she said. "But there ain't going to be any bananas tonight, you bet."

"Lord, I guess not," Charlie said vehemently, real horror in his eyes. "You want us to call your folks? They probably ought to take you to the doctor. . . ."

"I don't need no doctor, I just need to get in bed with a heating pad," she said. "I been out there in the cold waiting for y'all since eight. I reckon that's worth two dollars."

"Well, sure," I said, reaching for my wallet, deliverance spinning lightly in my ringing ears.

"No," Charlie said stubbornly. "I'm sorry about your . . . accident, Frances, but it's not our fault. We didn't know . . . and we came all the way out here on our bicycles. I don't see how you can ask for two dollars for that."

"Charlie . . . " I began desperately.

"We'll give it to you if you'll do the *X*'s, though," he said.

She glared at him balkily. Then she said crossly, "Oh, shit, all right, stick your wrists out here."

We did. She made quick, sharp crisscrosses on them, and then held her fat pink palm out for the money. I got mine out. Charlie did too, and then paused.

"Are they the right *X*'s?" he said.

"They're the right *X*'s, you little sonofabitch," she said. "Now get on out of here. My daddy would shoot you in the head if he caught you out here."

We went. We went pedaling back down Roswell Road toward the three-way intersection where Snake and the others were waiting for us with flags flying and hearts high, shouting and singing, "We're off to see the Wizard" and "I've been working on the railroad."

"I've been working on old Frances," we bellowed.

But as we neared the intersection Charlie began to go quiet, and when we got off our bikes and went up to Snake and held out our anointed wrists, Charlie suddenly blurted, "Wait a minute. It's all a lie. We didn't. We couldn't. I mean, Frances couldn't. She fell off the top of her house tonight and hurt herself. She really couldn't. We did try, Snake."

Snake just stared at us for a moment, and then he began to laugh. He hugged himself and staggered around on the freezing sidewalk; he bent double and yelled and wept and howled with laughter; he beat the wall of Wender & Roberts, and covered his face with his hands, and bayed his hideous mirth to the sky. All the others laughed, too. Ben, and Tom Goodwin, and Pres, and A.J.—they laughed and laughed, and it seemed to me that I would hear the sound of that laughter eternities later, safe at last under the quiet earth of Oakland.

"You silly shits," Snake roared. " 'She fell off the top of her house and hurt herself'! Oh, Jesus! Don't you know anything? She fell off the roof! She got the curse! She was riding the rag! She was flying Baker flag! Oh, Jesus!"

He did not, after all, tell the entire school that Charlie and I failed in our attempt to screw Frances Spurling. He simply and for four years after that awful night called us, in front of everyone we knew, the Roofing Brothers. I do not know to this day if anyone outside our crowd knew what it meant. Probably everyone did.

It was a high price to pay for not buying Frances's bananas.

Others like Frances did a brisk trade in the various neighborhoods adjacent to Buckhead, and I suppose it's a good thing, or the Jells would have, to a man, gone to their marriage beds virgins. But I can't think there was a lot of romance in it, and we lived, then, for romance. Other boys—rogue males like Boo Cutler and Floyd Sutton—were commonly known to screw nearly constantly, anyone who caught their fancy, and this proficiency was as much a part of their lustrous legends as their expertise with drag racing and shine running. We admired it enormously, but, like the dragging, few of us sought to emulate it. No Pink would have dated twice a Jell who put a serious move on her, and Jellhood was more to be cherished, in those days, even than nooky.

No. We necked and petted and lied and leered and ached and cursed and jerked off, but fuck we did not, most of us, until the altar was virtually in sight. I am sure that's why so many of us married on the very day we graduated from college, and a few even before. I am equally sure that the high mortality among my crowd's marriages was due to that long enforced abstinence. By the time we got out of college, we simply couldn't wait any longer to get laid. Whatever compatibility and commonality of interest we had with our girls was centered below our waists.

It was a strange time in the world, and in Atlanta too, so far as sex went. Lucy and I talked about it once, late in the sixties when both of us had been burned by passion and its aftermath and knew, at least a bit better, of what we spoke.

"You know," she said, looking across at me in the gloom of the summerhouse veranda in a spring twilight. "It's funny when you think about our parents' lives while we were growing up. There wasn't any scandal. I can't remember any great, glamorous sexual scandals like you hear about among the filthy rich in other places, like Palm Beach or Long Island or Los Angeles, places like that. We had some divorces, and lots of nervous breakdowns and alcoholics, and suicides and all that stuff, but do you ever remember a single soul running off with somebody else's wife or husband, or getting caught in bed, or breaking up marriages, or any of the good stuff? Can you remember even one crime of passion? I can't. Lord, look at Mama; if ever there was a woman made to stay on her back and fuck her way through the Northside, it was her; still is, the way she looks. And the way she was before she married Daddy. But never since she set foot in this house has she had a date; I can't even remember her looking sideways at a man, not to mention flirting a little, or wearing something sexy. She might as well be a nun. And Mama is no saint, believe me. It's this town. What is there in this town?"

I thought about it. She was right. Sexual scandal had no part in the lives of anyone of my parents' generation; not that I knew of, anyway.

"I guess it's because most of us haven't had our money very long," I said. "And we're not all that grounded in our status, if we have any. If you're new rich, you're not too likely to risk your social status with scandal. Not that kind, anyway. I guess that comes later, in the older places like Charleston and New Orleans and Savannah, or the really big ones like New York, where nobody gives a damn. It was the early fifties then, after all. Now, when anything goes and everybody's doing everything with everybody, nobody cares anymore. That generation sinned, of course, but it seems like they were more sins of omission than commission. And the wages were the wages of repression. I think maybe everybody was too busy making money."

Lucy stretched her long legs out in front of her and lit a cigarette. "Mayor Hartsfield had it all wrong," she said. "We weren't a city too busy to hate. We were a city too busy to fuck. What a waste. Money is only money, but a good fuck is a fuck."

I speak of the Pinks and the Jells as "we," but it is largely an editorial we. I attended the endless dances, but usually as a nonparticipatory member of the stag line, one denizen of the ant-hill that gave the butterfly Pinks such vivid life. I almost never went to the dinners beforehand, or the breakfasts afterward. When I absolutely had to have a date, I took Sarah Cameron, with whom I had been at ease from the beginning of our lives. I sometimes joined the swooping flocks after school, but only because the Fury was such a powerful seductress, and I usually ended up dropping clunking, iron-weighted Pres Hubbard off at his house and going relicking with Charlie, or going home to study and then slip fathoms back into the old, nourishing, ongoing communion with Lucy.

I liked the aimless, bright wheeling and admired the glorious mating plumage of the flock, and I knew the drill, thanks to family money and the herculean efforts of Margaret Bryan and sheer proximity to my generation of anointed. It was just that it all felt queer and stilted to me; remote and uninvolving, as if I was engaged in some sort of elaborate charade that no one recognized as such but me. I always felt, watching a ballroom full of pretty girls swaying like a bright, precious garden in the soft little wind of music, that they were not, somehow, real, not truly present; and that I alone breathed and moved and spoke.

But at other times, in the cheerful, antiseptic cacophony of Wender & Roberts, or in mindless, pell-mell midrush down the last long hill on Peachtree before the city limits of Atlanta loomed up, it seemed as if everything and everyone around me was real, superreal, hyperreal, and only I did not truly exist. Only with Lucy did actuality flow both ways. I had a sliding perception of reality in those days, but I knew absolutely and without knowing how that for me it lay somewhere else than the Buckhead and Atlanta of the Pinks and the Jells.

"Where will you go?" Sarah Cameron asked me once, when I spoke of leaving Atlanta when I was able.

"To New York," I said, not knowing why I said it, only that it was true.

"How long have you wanted to do that? I never heard you talk about it," she said, surprised.

"Always," I said, as surprised as she to find that it was true.

Unlike virtually anyone else in my immediate crowd of Jells except Charlie Gentry, I liked to study, especially history and English literature, and I made impressive grades. The grades were never the point; I could lose myself for hours in the dreaming, sunny flower fields of the school and public libraries, and only after I came blinking and stretching up for air and awareness did I realize how totally happy I had been. It was the beginning of my lifelong passion for pure research, the only love save one that never left or betrayed me. It has been what I have lived with and one of the very few things I have lived for, these many years in the summerhouse.

The resultant grades, though, made my mother smile, and even my father would occasionally nod approval at the pristine string of A's, though he seldom failed to remark that with my height, I ought to be a first-string guard by now. Lucy, however, applauded them with her whole heart, and Lucy was still, in those days, the sun that warmed me, even though, since that night in the summerhouse, a sun that I knew could also sear me mortally.

It never occurred to me to ask her to any of the dances and parties; I honestly did not, at least consciously, think of her in that way, and she did not seem to consider me romantically. She was still, to my eyes and senses, utterly and powerfully seductive, but she did not yet seem to be conscious of it, and I had, in those few charring moments on that spinning daybed, distanced myself so completely from her as a woman that I could observe her almost as thoroughly and clinically as a sociologist.

And in every other respect, we had not changed for each other; even though I had moved into a world that was far closer to adulthood than hers, we were still safe havens for each other. I think we both sensed that a romantic alliance would have spoiled that, and we still, and always, needed each other in that way more than in any other. So I took Sarah Cameron to the few dances I attended and then came home and spun them out for Lucy's delectation like a parent bird with a ravenous chick, and she gave me back the great lift and leap of her rich laugh, and her boundless, soaring approval. In those days, as I have said, I was her heart, and she, conversely, was my wings.

I did not see, never saw, really, the look of adoration on Sarah's small face when she lifted it to me. I can still scarcely credit that it was there. Charlie would tell me occasionally, "Sarah has a crush on you," and I simply did not believe him. I suppose I thought he was transferring his long, aching, silent love for Sarah onto me, and I hastened, each time he said it, to hand that love back to him.

I could not believe that any girl could look at me with adoration. I had long since, on some tender and carefully submerged level, accepted my mother's dictum that I was too immature and sensitive for what she termed "that silly teenaged boy-girl business," and also my father's that I was simply not the man for it. Neither, now, was true, but I did not know that. The real truth was that I was not, by now, a sissy, and there had never been anything effeminate about me. I had simply, on that night with Lucy, buried desire deep.

And so we went, I wading aimlessly in the shallows of Jellhood, a great waiting for something I could not name filling what crannies of my being were not occupied by Lucy, she stoically doing her time in the sunless prison of the terrible little girls' school, both of us still caught, and content with the captivity, in the roles of heroine-victim and savior-saint. I don't know how long it would have gone on thus, but it seems to me now, from the vantage point of the passed years, that it was doomed to end exactly the way it did.

Lucy graduated from Miss Beauchamp's with just enough credits to secure her freedom and virtually no academic honors the spring when she was twelve, and that fall entered the eighth grade at North Fulton High. Busy with my long hours in the library and the autumn flurry of Jellhood, and still savoring with her the old, cell-deep kinship at home after school, I noticed no appreciable change in her. She still looked to me as she had for a long, suspended time: a silvery willow sapling, a fine colt frozen at the apogee of its childhood. I had long stopped wondering why no one but me noticed the air-charging impact of her. She seemed to slip into the stream of North Fulton without so much as a ripple. I scarcely saw her at all during those first days.

In the third week after school started, I went down onto the burning athletic field to meet the three other members of the 880 relay team for the second practice of the season. Ben Cameron and A. J. Kemp were both on the team; oddly, for few Jells participated in high school sports. But the 880 was perfect for Ben's whiplike speed and grace, and A.J. in motion of any kind was wonderful to watch. The fourth member was Fraser Tilly, a small, rabbity, stone-silent junior from out beyond Sandy Springs, who could lope forever like a timber wolf and sprint like the jackrabbit he resembled, and was better at the 880 than the three of us Buckhead Jells put together.

It was the sixth and last period of the day, and several knots of boys and girls dotted the bleached grass of the field, preparing to stumble with loathing through the last physical education classes of the day. It was so hot that the figures on the far end of the field seemed to shimmer like mirages in a desert, and sweat soaked the hideous blue and white shorts and shirts that North Fulton required for P.E. Even A.J., even elegant Ben Cameron, looked awful in them, swaddled and storklike. The girls looked, simply, unspeakable. The Pinks at North Fulton hated being seen in their P.E. uniforms even more than being caught in home-permanent curlers and papers, with Noxzema on their acne.

I was late, and the track coach was a new one, a beetling, cliff-like Teuton with a no-color burr of a crew cut and cold, Baltic eyes. He had tongue-lashed A.J. so badly for missing the first practice that A.J., the irrepressible one, the golden-tongued smart mouth, had had tears in his eyes before he was done. I ran silently down the stone steps of the stadium, my cleated shoes in my hand, in dread of the coach's coiled tongue.

But they were not looking at me. They were standing close together in a huddle, backs to me, heads close together, obviously staring at something across the field that I could not see. They were laughing, and though I could not hear what they said, I knew the tenor of that laughter. I had heard it a hundred times in locker rooms and dark booths, when the talk of fucking and genitalia began; had even tried, clumsily, to join in myself. It was the laughter of the Buckhead Jells for a girl considered to be little better than a whore. I heard the huge coach say something that ended in " . . . little pussy right out there on a stick. Bet we could all get a lick of that without even asking for it."

I reached the group and looked beyond it to see who they were talking about, and it was Lucy. She was standing with her sixth-period soccer class, doing absolutely nothing but standing stock-still in the sun on the edge of the group of girls, dressed, as they all were, in the hated blue bloomers and white shirt. But all of a blinding sudden I could see what Ben and A.J. and Fraser Tilly and the coach saw: the white flesh of Lucy Bondurant looking so totally naked in the merciless sunlight of September that the shorts and shirt might as well not have been there; small, sharp breasts that appeared absolutely bared even under the starched

white; long legs joined in so obvious a cupping of tender genitalia
that the blue bloomers could have been made of transparent netting. Lucy's clothing was not tight, and she did not flaunt her
body; did not even move it. She simply stood straight and still,
looking back across the field at them, and I could both feel and
see the molten blueness of her eyes in an empty sunlit silence
that rang like a bell, over and under the sly, fetid laughter of
the 880 team.

They turned and saw me then, and fell abruptly silent, and
the laughter stopped. Ben reddened, and A.J. looked away. *Ben,
A.J. . . .*

Fraser Tilly and the Prussian coach busied themselves knocking dried mud off their cleats. The afternoon swung around me;
the air swarmed like bees. Lucy stood before my friends and
teammates and the hulking, alien betrayer utterly exposed, and
now everyone knew what it was that, in the dark center of me,
I had always known: Lucy Bondurant went naked in the world.
Lucy could be taken. I had, once again and now irrevocably,
failed to shield and protect her, and in that moment, the power
of my sainthood fled for the last time, and only the hunger for
it remained.

CHAPTER
NINE

WHEN I TURNED SIXTEEN and got the red and white Fury, the last rational barrier to full participation in Jellhood fell, and I could think of no good reason to avoid the dinners and dances and breakfasts, and so, borne by the daunting splendor of my wheels and urged on by my mother, I began to attend the bulk of them.

"You simply cannot think of missing another one, Sheppie," my mother would say, coming out to beard me in my den in the summerhouse when a determined inquisition at dinner unearthed the fact that I had not gone to the last two or three and had no plans for the one upcoming. "These little parties are where the debutante lists are drawn from; you know that as well as I do. Do you want to go through five or six entire seasons without being on a single list? Your future is being built right now. Of course you're going. Now come on in the house and call one of your pretty girlfriends. Little Sarah Cameron would just love to go with you. Do you want me to call Dorothy for you?"

And, face flaming with the sheer awfulness of my mother calling the mother of a girl, even Sarah, I would stalk into the big house and slink sullenly into the telephone niche under the foyer staircase, and dial the Camerons' number.

"Sarah," I would say without identifying myself, "I've got to go to that stupid Alpha Nu thing Friday night, and my mother won't get off my back until I get a date. I don't guess you want to go, do you?"

"Thanks, Shep," Sarah would say. "I'd love to go. It sounds like fun."

Even at fourteen, she had a woman's full-throated and warming voice, with the rich little hill of laughter under it that always drew people to her, and her simple, glad-hearted acceptance was so much more gracious than my mean, muttered invitation that I blush even now, all these years later, to think of it. It didn't occur to me then that I was being rude to Sarah. It was many years before I fully stopped taking that bounty of approval and affection for granted.

Those Friday evenings when I departed in the Fury, white orchid in hand, pleased my parents almost more than anything I had ever done, and the fact of that made me obscurely truculent and melancholy. I went to the dances gracelessly and morosely, but I went correctly. My father took me down to John Jarrell's and had me fitted for a magnificent tuxedo, the only one I have ever owned; it was a lustrous, penguin-black single-breasted suit of fine wool, with a rich satin shawl collar, and with it I wore a blinding white pleat-front shirt with a soft collar and French cuffs. A black satin cummerbund and tie completed the outfit, and my grandfather Redwine's onyx and gold cuff links and smoked pearl studs were grace notes.

These my mother brought me on the night of the first Friday evening dance of that season, insisting on inserting and fastening them herself. As she bent in front of me, I could smell the smoky, bittersweet breath of Hermès' Calèche that was her signature that autumn, and the clean, light floral odor of the shampoo that her hairdresser at J. P. Allen's used. I was not used to being so close to my mother, and felt a powerful, nervous urge to push her away and run. She half turned, and I closed my eyes so as not to see the pearly cleft of her breasts in the keyhole cutout of her neckline. She straightened and pushed me away to arms' length, her hands hard on my shoulders, and looked up at me with a sheen of tears in her dark sloe eyes.

"My handsome man," she said. "My little blond boy, all grown up now and going off into the world, leaving his mama behind all alone. It cuts me to the heart to have you leave me, Sheppie."

Since I wasn't going anywhere but around the corner to the Camerons' to pick up Sarah and then perhaps three miles farther away at best, out to the Brookhaven Country Club, I felt that the tears were gratuitous and false, a bit of arcana staged for my benefit, and was embarrassed.

"I'm not going anywhere, Mama," I said.

"Yes you are, Sheppie," she said, smiling her closed, odalisque smile at me. "You're going very, very far in your life. I've always known that. Your father can't see it, but I can. You're a very special boy, and you're going to be a very special man. A sensi-

tive, talented, gentle man. And so handsome; well, just look at
you. You look as handsome as Leslie Howard tonight, in your
new tuxedo. Oh, I *am* jealous, Sheppie. All the girls are going
to be crazy about you. I'll bet half of them are in love with you
now. You'll make somebody a wonderful husband, and then
you'll forget all about your poor old mother. But one day you'll
see that nobody, not one of them, ever loved you like your
mother did."

She leaned forward to kiss me, and her eyes were half-shut,
and she smiled a smile of something I had never seen before,
something slow and secret and out-curling like a tentacle, and
in pure panic I jerked away and turned to my image in the mirror. A blank-eyed, wavering blond man looked back at me, tall
and badly frightened. Both the woman and the image were so
totally alien that I felt, for a moment, completely without a context, utterly awry in my own skin. Then my mother laughed, her
old, indulgent laugh, and the world came spinning back into
focus.

"Don't worry, I'm not going to embarrass you to death by
kissing you," she said. "Go on now, and pick up little Sarah.
I have to tell you, Sheppie, that we're so glad it's her you're taking and not Lucy. Time you had some other little friends besides
Lucy. You're just too old for that cousin business now. People
are already talking about it."

I fled blindly, hot to the roots of my hair, and did not take
a deep, easing breath until I gained the seclusion of the Fury,
which stood gleaming and ready for me on the circular drive in
front of the house, shined to a lacquer polish earlier in the day
by Shem Cater. Increasingly, in those latter days of high school,
my encounters with my mother left me shying with nerves and
near to staggering under an oppressive weight whose name I did
not know. It was pure, clear, light relief to walk into the little
sitting room at the Camerons' house where Sarah, Dorothy and
Ben waited for me. Ben Junior had already left, to pick up pretty,
pug-nosed Julia Randolph over on Arden.

Even in her freshman year, Sarah was already well known and
popular at North Fulton, destined to be, as her mother had been
before her, the one who ran, with sunny willingness and no vain-
glorious aspirations at all, the "serious," service-oriented organizations and activities of high school. Not that she was a
goody-goody or a grind; she was a varsity cheerleader, and
known throughout the city for her swimming and painting skills,
and she never once in four years, that I know of, sat out a Friday
night dance. With her perfect, supple little body and her clear,
deep amber eyes and instant dimpling smile and cap of dark,
glossy hair—cut short so that she did not have to wear a cap

in the water when she dived and swam—she was as appealing
and good to the eye as a pet squirrel, and as captivating. It has
never been possible to look upon Sarah Cameron without a smile
of pure response starting on your mouth. From her birth, she
has had Dorothy's enormous energy and purpose without her
austerity, and Ben's easy charisma without his pure, focused ego.
The best—or at least, the most livable—of both.

When Sarah graduated from North Fulton, the list of honors
and organizations under her photograph was the longest in the
Hi-Ways. It read, "Sarah Tolliver Cameron. We predict, the first
Mrs. President. Student Council, Annual Representative, P.T.A.
Representative, Y-Teens, Secretary and Treasurer, Junior Class,
President, Senior Class, Swimming Team, Gold Medal, All-City
Swimming and Diving Competition, Cheerleader, Nominating
Committee, Rabun Gap Guild, Home Economics Fashion
Show, Le Circle Française, R.O.T.C. Sponsor, Honor Roll 10
Quarters, National Honor Society, Who's Who, Student Court,
Senior Superlatives, Senior Play, Southeastern Outstanding
Young Artist of the Year, Atlanta *Journal-Constitution* Best All-
Round Cup, Graduation Speaker."

"Just look at the list of honors little Sarah has under her
name," my mother said at the breakfast table the morning after
Lucy brought her senior annual home. My mother never ceased
in her campaign to ally the houses of Bondurant and Cameron,
and she never managed to refer to Sarah as anything but "little
Sarah." I looked at the *Hi-Ways,* smelling new leatherette and
fresh, sour ink, and saw Sarah's familiar chipmunk face smiling
out at me over a vast sea of type. On the opposite page, Lucy's
face, dimmed to mere piquancy as always by a camera, looked
obliquely out over a naked line or two.

"Yeah, isn't that something?" Lucy said, yawning and scrubbing swollen, smudged eyes with her fists. She had been out with
Red Chastain the night before, and I had heard the MG come
burring up the driveway at nearly 5:00 A.M. By now, no one even
bothered to admonish Lucy about it. She looked like a petal from
an exotic flower that had lain out all night in a driving rain, damp
and bruised and used up.

"I imagine they charged her the standard ad rate," Lucy
drawled, draining black coffee. I scowled at her, and Aunt Willa
frowned, but did not bother to say anything. My mother smiled
her secret smile. She knew her point was well taken; the contrast
between Sarah's bountiful accolades and Lucy's meager two
lines hung vibrating in the air of the breakfast room. Lucy's said,
"Lucy James Bondurant. Hold the presses! Men overboard!
Scribbler Staff Four Years, Editor in Chief, Senior Year. Rabun
Gap, Tallulah Falls, Who's Who."

Four years of Lucy Bondurant, and in summary, all one could know of that complex stroke of pure flame was that she belonged to two organizations that were bestowed upon the elect of the Buckhead Pinks as automatically as their smallpox vaccinations and their birth certificates; that she labored only for the student newspaper and only there left a spoor of herself; and that she had as her middle name that of her early-lost and long-adored father. It was Sarah Cameron who shone from the pages of that world.

But at age fourteen, when I first began to squire her to dances and a few other *de rigueur* social occasions, Sarah was still, to me, endearing little Sarah Cameron, who was comfortable to be with for hours on end, who could swim like a minnow and dive like an otter and keep up with me on any weed-choked battlefield or any dance floor, and toward whom I felt absolutely no compelling obligation. She did not, therefore, weigh heavy on my heart, but sat lightly as thistledown in my mind. It was still, then, for me, Lucy who bore down, who burned, who clung, who shone.

Going into her teens, there was not a girl or woman in Atlanta from twelve to thirty who could touch Lucy Bondurant for sheer impact. She was an absolute, essential flame; everyone who knew her in that time would remember her all their lives. At thirteen, she was as tall and fully developed as she would ever be, her blue eyes unclouded and black-lashed and extraordinary, her waist spannable by two masculine hands, her dark wings of hair, not cut into the flips and later the ducktails of the day, but falling softly against her cheeks in the sleek, loose pageboy of the preceding decade. Until they cut it in the hospital, many years later, Lucy wore her hair that way.

Her impact was not that of classical beauty, but a matter of what she called her engine and I thought of as her aura: a vivacity, a sheen, an electricity that ran at full throttle and, except when she slept, continuously. Even her bad habits had charm, a cachet, which many were, all her life, to imitate unsuccessfully. From somewhere—I suppose her beloved Negroes—she had learned to swear like a sailor, but she did it in such a pure, honeyed drawl and with such a vulnerable innocence in her blue eyes that the effect was entrancing. A whole generation of Atlanta Pinks learned to say "shit" and "fuck" from Lucy Bondurant, but it became none of them but her.

She also adopted smoking two or three years before the other girls in her crowd took it up—for almost everyone in our day smoked, Pall Malls and Viceroys and Parliaments, in blue and white crushproof boxes—and she adored liquor from that first stolen swallow of my father's Jack Daniel's. But she did not

drink as a matter of course until considerably later. Lucy in her
early and middle teens ran largely on spirit. Her galvanic physical presence assured her a constant swarming circle of boys, Jells
and otherwise, but it did nothing to endear her to a generation
of Atlanta women. I don't think she even noticed, and I know
she never cared. From the moment she walked into North Fulton High School, from the moment she lifted her head and stared
across a bleached and blinding athletic field into the hungry, betraying eyes of the 880 relay team, it was men for Lucy, men
all the way.

Despite the portent of that day on the athletic field, it began
slowly, that consuming, lifelong passion and refuge of Lucy's.
For the entirety of her freshman year, Aunt Willa did not allow
her to date, despite the fact that other freshman girls, especially
the Pinks, went regularly on double, if not single, dates to the
dinners and dances and even breakfasts afterward, and were allowed to go in groups to early movie dates, or for sodas after
school. I don't know why Aunt Willa was so strict with Lucy
that year. There had never been any trouble with boys up to then,
and I am sure she did not know about the night in the summerhouse. Perhaps she, too, saw in her daughter that naked, hungry,
infinitely vulnerable and powerfully sexual creature the relay
team had seen on that hot September afternoon. Perhaps she
knew that unlike the repressed and biddable Little Lady, Lucy
was not going to go sweetly and conventionally through her adolescence to an early and stable marriage. Perhaps she remembered her own sexual abandon, and its consequences—though
I doubt that. I don't believe that concern for Lucy motivated
the prohibition. I think, as I thought then, and as Lucy knew
absolutely, that forbidding her daughter to date when everyone
else did was Willa Bondurant's way of punishing her, of saying,
in effect, you are cheap and trashy and cannot be trusted, so you
must be curbed. It must have planted the idea of promiscuity
deep. And as any captivity always had, the ban made Lucy furious and desperate. I truly believe that if Aunt Willa had been
reasonable about her dating in that first year of high school,
Lucy's life might have taken a different course. But it may be
that, even then, the die was too decisively cast for malleability.

She did not rail and storm and protest, as she would have once.
She had learned well the consequences of that. She simply set
out, efficiently and methodically, to attract every male who came
within range, and she did it without lifting a finger. Lucy unaware was as seductive, in those early days, as a prepubescent
nymph. Lucy aware and plying all her weapons was in another
league altogether. By the end of the school year, there was not
a male student at North Fulton High, and not many among the

Jells of all Atlanta, who did not know that Lucy Bondurant was hot to trot, and loaded for bear—though it was not generally thought that she would, as yet, put out. The consensus on that was that it was just a matter of time, and the stampede to be first geared up then, and did not cease, so far as I knew, until Red Chastain came along and put the competition on ice.

Lucy made her move rather elegantly, even I had to admit, if not particularly subtly. She left home ahead of me in the mornings, claiming an early homeroom, and promptly upon arrival at North Fulton went into the ground-floor girls' rest room and made her face up. Since Aunt Willa had also forbidden makeup, Lucy had simply stolen what she needed from Wender & Roberts, and when she emerged from the rest room it was under a vivid, expertly applied frosting of Maybelline and Revlon. She needed no mascara or eyeliner, but I seldom saw her during those days at school without a hectic slash of "Cherries in the Snow" on her soft mouth, and she smelled exotically of a scent called Tabu, which she loved and wore all through high school and beyond, until her bluestocking classmates at Agnes Scott College told her she smelled like a *cocotte*.

"They meant French whore, of course," she told me that year, "but God forbid that word should cross a Scottie's lips. You should see their faces when I say 'fuck' and 'shit.' They call fuck 'the F word.' And they say 'the Black Act' or 'the Dirty Deed' when they mean fucking. I don't know what they're going to tell their children: 'Daddy and I got you the night we did the Black Act,' do you think?"

Lucy did not have to steal the Tabu. I bought it for her the Christmas of her freshman year, and gave it to her in the summerhouse, so my parents and Aunt Willa wouldn't know she had it. She only dabbed it on after she left for school, and solved the problem of its lingering ghost by telling Aunt Willa that her sixth-period teacher sprayed it lavishly on herself just before the final bell rang, and invariably got some on Lucy and those other students who sat in the front rows.

"I'd move, Mama, but Miss Cleckler puts the best students right up front. It's an honor. I don't want to hurt her feelings," she said earnestly.

Silky, facile lying was another social skill she picked up in that supremely formative year at North Fulton. On the main, it served her better than the business with men.

She wore the same skirts and pullovers and cardigans and Bass Weejuns with a penny in them as the other budding Pinks did, but she tucked her sweaters into the band of her skirts and pulled them tight, and unbuttoned the cardigans one or even two buttons lower than anyone else did. Nothing showed; the North

Fulton faculty could find no reason to tell demure little Lucy
Bondurant to pull out her sweaters and button up, but they
smelled the trouble in the air around her, and watched her with
a scrutiny nearly as hawklike as that bent upon her by the boys.
Lucy smiled her full, angelic smile and crinkled her Madonna-
blue eyes at one and all, and never put a foot wrong. It was a
bravura performance, and left to her own devices, she could have
sustained the delicate sexual shadow play, I am sure, for as long
as she had wished. Once again, it was Aunt Willa who pushed
her over the line from covert to overt.

For a long time that year, I had been aware that there was
a kind of tension, a high, humming sexual energy, running
through any group around Lucy. Several times clustered boys
would redden and fall silent when I approached, as they had that
day on the athletic field, and I knew at once that it was Lucy
they had been talking about. Once or twice I heard her rich, free
laugh before I saw her, and there was in it such an alien note
of promise and lushness that before I recognized it, I would
think, "God, who is *that?*" I really thought, once, that some new
young woman teacher had come to the school and stood, incredibly, in the middle of a crowd of panting, sniffing male students,
promising things that most of us only dreamed about with her
laugh. And then the group would part and I would see that it
was Lucy, and the laughter of the boys would stop at my appearance, but Lucy's did not.

As she could not date, and had to be at home within thirty
minutes of the last class at North Fulton, she took to skipping
classes and going off the school premises with one boy or another. I know that nothing happened during these occasional
fifty-minute forays, because I would have heard about it instantly. As it was, the whole student body knew when Lucy
began to vanish quietly from one class or another. She did not
do it often, but she made no secret of these absences, and the
boy in question inevitably crowed about it like a bursting little
bantam cock, so the Pinks and the Jells knew to nearly the second how long she spent with Floyd Sutton down in Moseley
Park, smoking cigarettes, or when she went down to Rusty's at
lunchtime with Snake Cheatham in the Black Booger and drank
a hot beer he had brought along in a paper sack. I suppose it
was just a matter of time until she connected with Boo Cutler.

In addition to his monstrous, pulsing Merc, Boo had an enormous Harley-Davidson motorcycle that he said he had won in
a crap game up in Floyd County one weekend, and though he
was forbidden by the school authorities to bring it onto the
school grounds, he kept it stashed at Winton Gladney's Shell station just around the corner on Peachtree Road, and sauntered

to and from there and school. Jell or not, there was not a boy at North Fulton who would not have sold a small shard of his soul to the devil to ride with Boo Cutler on the mammoth, growling Harley, but no North Fulton boy but Floyd Sutton ever did. Instead, Boo would ride out during lunch hours, and just about whenever else he chose, with one young Atlanta woman after another, half-terrified and half-proud and near to choking with nonchalance, riding pillion. The girls of his choice were always the bright, hard, thinly pretty ones who belonged to no club or group at all, the sorority of Pinkhood most especially; perhaps they figured they had nothing to lose by a ride with Boo, and much in the way of panache to gain. They were almost invariably apprehended and punished by the faculty, and never rode again behind Boo on the Harley, but the knowledge that they had once done so put real color in their cheeks over the Tangee, and a lift beyond elastic in their shoulders. Boo himself never observed the punishments meted out to him; he simply continued to come and go in classes and on and off the campus as he pleased, and no one ever managed to separate him from the Harley. We learned early on that the rules by which we lived our lives were not the ones Boo Cutler observed. For some reason, the knowledge did not rankle.

Boo broke his moratorium on Pinks when Lucy started at North Fulton, and even though he was a junior to her freshman, he paid his own brand of cool, lounging court to her from the very beginning. He would appear beside her in the cafeteria line, silent and heavy-faced, and the jostling pack of boys who had been bent on sitting at her table at lunch melted away like April snow, and she and Boo would eat alone, talking of who knows what . . . for no one had ever heard Boo say more than a mumbled word or two.

He would walk down the long central hall between classes with his gold-pelted arm draped heavily around her shoulders, their heads, one dark, one blond and cut in so short a crew cut that the burned pink scalp showed through, close together. He would simply saunter along, a cigarette behind one ear and the pack rolled into the cuff of his white T-shirt, saying nothing, and Lucy would match him stride for stride, looking up at him with those eyes like Caribbean water, laughing her dark, fudgy laugh.

Once, for the space of a week, she wore his letter jacket, and then, as abruptly as she had accepted it, gave it back. No one had ever given Boo's jacket back to him without being commanded to do so. Lucy's legend waxed. My whole crowd was waiting for me when I got to homeroom the next morning, pressing me for details, but I had none to give. Lucy would not talk about Boo Cutler with me, or about much else that happened during the day at school. At home with me she was as she had always been: fierce, funny, direct, candid, imaginative and wholeheartedly approving. Lucy the flamboyant little temptress became Lucy the enchanted changeling child again when the walls of Peachtree Road closed around her. I ignored the temptress and welcomed the changeling. I hated her new public role, and the direction in which it was taking her, but she did not speak of it and so I did not, either. That had always been the unspoken contract between us.

On an April afternoon of sudden showers and swelling earth, Lucy left her fifth-period American history class and rode with Boo Cutler on the Harley out Peachtree Road to Brookhaven, where they drank beer and smoked a cigarette or two on the front lawn of Oglethorpe University. She had always had an uncanny sense of timing about her cuts, so that no faculty member had ever seen her leave, and even if she was missed in class, could produce a better-than-good forgery of Aunt Willa's signature on a brief, typed note of excuse. It was sheer accident that on this day, Mr. Bovis Hardin, the cadaverous and ardently Calvinistic assistant principal, was leaving a lunchtime seminar on distributive education at Oglethorpe, and saw them there together on the grass. Everyone knew Boo Cutler, faculty included, and by this time there was no mistaking Lucy Bondurant, either. Bovis Hardin did not even pause to Brylcreem his hair before he was in the principal's office with news of the sighting, and they wasted no time calling Aunt Willa in her little assistant buyer's cubicle in the back of the lingerie department of Rich's. By the time Lucy got back to the school and was walking nonchalantly into her sixth and last period class, Armageddon was at hand.

"That old letch said that Boo and I were kissing on the grass, and that he had my skirt up around my neck," Lucy said later.

"Did he?" I asked.

"No. I hiked it up to keep from getting motorcycle grease on it. We weren't even kissing, he was telling me a dirty joke, whispering in my ear," she said. "Old man Hardin saw what he wanted to see. Don't think for a minute he wouldn't like to get my skirt over my head himself. I've seen the way he looks at me in the halls."

I believed her when I heard the story. It wasn't that she did not lie, it was just that I always knew when she did. In any case, it did not matter. She was given a staggering number of demerits, and Boo Cutler was suspended for the remainder of the year— which undoubtedly suited him just fine. The dirt track out at Lakewood was just getting ripe for racing, and in any case, he had gone as far with Lucy as she would allow. He promptly transferred his attentions to Caroline Gentry, an alliance that was more fruitful in every way than the one with Lucy had promised to be. Lucy, he told Floyd Sutton and his cadre of cronies at the Peachtree Hills Pub, was a cockteaser. It was an epithet that doomed her with the hood element at North Fulton, but only served to send the Jells into fresh transports of anticipation. Someone, they reasoned, had to be first.

Lucy was taken home in white, crackling silence by Aunt Willa in the taxi in which she had arrived, but the inevitable battle was joined just inside the door, in the foyer, and I walked straight into it when I got home from school. Five different students had rushed to tell me of the showdown in the principal's office, and I had hurried. I knew that Willa Bondurant would not take this new blot on her escutcheon with grace.

She didn't. I could hear her screaming from the street, through the heavy, closed front door. By the time I gained the foyer, she had just about spent herself; her voice had a winding-down quality to it, and her breath came so fast and hard that her breasts hove like buoys in a heavy swell under the seemly challis of her little Wood Valley shirtwaist. Lucy stood opposite her, very straight, back against the newel post of the staircase, face white as a new gardenia, but still and expressionless. Her hands were behind her back.

" . . . common as gully dirt, nothing but white trash!" Aunt Willa yowled, nothing of Old Atlanta in her voice now. Wire grass and chicken wire fairly sang in it. "You'll be pregnant as a yard dog before you're sixteen, and then what in God's name do you think is going to happen to you? Because you pure-and-tee can't stay in this house if you get yourself knocked up, sister. I won't have a streetwalker for a daughter!"

There was a ringing silence.

"Like you were, Mama?" Lucy drawled sweetly. She smiled.

Aunt Willa slapped her daughter so hard that Lucy's head rocked back, revealing a tender and somehow heartbreaking crescent of white neck. Her mother wheeled on her stiletto heels and clattered up the stairs to her room. We heard her door slam. No other sound came from the top of the house. My father must have been out; the Chrysler was gone. I don't know to this day if my mother was in her room and heard the exchange. She usually was at this time of day, napping or reading. But she never mentioned the scene, and needless to say, I did not either. She did not even inquire, this time, why Lucy was once again confined to her tiny third-floor room and was sent her meals on trays for nearly two weeks before she came back downstairs to join us. During those high school years, my mother was enigmatically silent on the subject of Lucy, though her finely arched eyebrows stayed near her lustrous hairline most of the time. Indeed, she managed so completely to disassociate herself from Willa Bondurant and her errant daughter that she was able to murmur scurrilous and wickedly funny things about them to her friends with perfect composure, as if they were nothing to do, really, with her. I heard her do it quite often. She gained something of a reputation as a wit for these sallies, as well as for being "a saint for putting up with those two under your roof all these years," as Madge Slaton said to her during bridge in the drawing room toward the end of that year. Mother had a way of turning even the grimmest situations to her own advantage. It was a matter of superb, impenetrable detachment. She became, in time, a past master at it.

I was left alone with Lucy in the foyer for a moment that afternoon, and we stood silent, watching flying cloud shadow dappling the black and white harlequin tiles of the floor.

"But she *was* a streetwalker, or worse," Lucy said too gaily to me, the red imprint of her mother's hand still bloodlike on her cheek. "Anybody who can count knows that. Why on earth would Daddy have married her if she hadn't been pregnant with me? Poor white trash like she was? At least *he* was a gentleman."

And she went upstairs to begin again her exile.

By the time she finally came down, Aunt Willa had retreated into some impregnable inner citadel of imagined Atlanta ladyhood, and had withdrawn, emotionally and actually, as far as possible from her wayward daughter. There had been a wall of cool near-dislike, a kind of critical distance, between Lucy and her mother ever since little Jamie had died and Aunt Willa had begun to lavish her expectations and affection so openly on Little Lady. Now the wall thickened and grew taller, until she barely spoke to Lucy when they met at meals.

By some tacit washing of her fleshy, well-tended little hands, she had withdrawn the ban on dating and Lucy began to go about openly with the boys she had met and teased in secrecy all that year. In a way it seemed to slow her down some. We heard no more talk, for a little while, of openly sexual activities centering around Lucy, though there was always innuendo. At least she made her dates pick her up at the house on Peachtree Road. My parents or her mother were seldom around to meet them, but I made it a point to be somewhere in the vicinity of the front door whenever Lucy was going out. I already knew all the boys who dated her, of course; I simply thought it dishonorable that nobody from the family was about to see to the small, important social ritual of leave-taking. I was, by that time, irredeemably a creature of a thousand immutable, iron tenets and rules, whether I liked it or not. My mother had done her early work well.

I knew there was talk among the Jells about my hovering, and a good bit of avid speculation about the nature of my attachment to my cousin Lucy. I hated the idea of the talk, but I hated even more the lack of interest that the absence of parents and relatives when her dates called implied. It seemed to me tawdry and lax, a disgrace on the family and the house. I knew the neglect and its implication could mark Lucy as "easy" faster than almost anything she might do herself. And so, like Anias, I watched at the gate.

Aunt Willa watched, too, though not openly and publicly. She hovered when Lucy got a telephone call from a boy, and always seemed to be outside the little downstairs sun-room that had become Lucy's teenaged haunt when boys were in the house. They almost always were that year. She openly forbade her the summerhouse with anyone other than me, and early on in Lucy's dating career there were hushed, hissing tirades behind the closed door of Lucy's room when she came home late, which she did increasingly. After a while Aunt Willa stopped sitting up, and the futile tongue-lashings ceased, and no one waited up for Lucy anymore. I knew that the lack of supervision was common knowledge at school, and that the early-morning necking and petting sessions in the shadows of our porte cochere lengthened accordingly, because I heard the cars as they drove in, and I usually heard them much later as they ghosted guiltily away. I would wait until I saw the flush of yellow from the portico light go out, and then, finally, I would sleep. After that first year, I did not lie awake listening for Lucy.

When I was fully grown and well away from there, I came to see that Lucy's powerful and burgeoning seductiveness was not only a reminder to Aunt Willa of her own teen persona, but a threat to the flimsy respectability and social acceptability she had managed to draw around herself. Willa Bondurant's presence in the drawing rooms and clubs and at the luncheons and fashion shows and charity balls of Atlanta was too hard won and tenuous for her to allow talk about Lucy to jeopardize it. But not even I could control Lucy, much less her mother, and so Willa simply withdrew, hoping, ostrichlike, that she would draw down upon herself no guilt by association.

For her part, Lucy, who had begun employing her natural seductiveness to keep herself comfortingly surrounded by and, more often, in the arms of the various highborn young men who were copies, albeit pale ones, of her father, began then to use her sexuality as a weapon of defiance against her mother. She dated more and more frequently, often having an engagement with one young man for an afternoon movie, another for a milkshake afterward and a third that evening. She pulled her belts tight and

thrust her breasts forward and rolled her hips. She went to every
dinner and dance and breakfast given by every high school sorority and fraternity in Atlanta for the next four years, and came
in from each of them smeared and crumpled and heavy-eyed and
hickeyed and irrepressible. Her smile grew steadily more brilliant and promissory, and her laugh richer, and her eyes bluer
and more intense, and her whole flamelike ethos more glittering.
The talk began in earnest in her sophomore year and never
ceased, and I heard every bit of it, and suffered. The only thing
I did not hear was that she had finally done the Dirty Deed with
one of the groaning Jells, and so I knew that technically she was
still a virgin, although that technicality hung by the thinnest of
filaments imaginable. Lucy in those years left a trail of tumescence behind her as thick as the Great Wall of China.

I don't think Aunt Willa heard any of the talk. Her preoccupation with Little Lady had deepened into obsession, and by then
even my mother had to admit that this little gilt ace in our familial hole had become as malleable and chiming and lovely and
essentially brainless a little Atlanta belle as one could wish. Little
Lady was a virgin of the highest and most marketable order. She
could not remember her father, but she did remember, vividly,
her mother's histrionic descriptions, when they first came to our
house, of the times James Bondurant had come home drunk and
beat her and little Lucy, and of how he had once threatened to
kill all of them with a claw hammer. Consequently, she was so
terrified of the men she had been trained to please that she allowed no one to touch her beyond the obligatory dance holds,
and those lightly, and so went through her immaculate debut
a few years later and her dainty provisional year of Junior
League, and finally to her early and brilliant wedding to bull-
necked, blue-blooded Carter Rawson a virgin of vestal purity.

That she began, ever so discreetly, to sip bourbon steadily
through the days and evenings soon after that grand affair did
not necessarily have anything to do with any trauma from her
wedding night; might, indeed, have been Jim Bondurant's genetic legacy to her. However, as Lucy said after the first time
Little Lady fell on her pretty Pekingese face during dinner at
the Driving Club, "Oh, bullshit, of course it was fuck-shock.
Lady always thought, until her wedding night, that you did it
with pistils and stamens. Lord, I can't abide a fool."

Only with me was Lucy her old, flickering, will-o'-the-wisp
self; me and the Negroes in her orbit. With them, especially with
moody, brilliant Glenn Pickens over at the Camerons' and
dumpy, stolid ToTo at our house, who were near her own age,
she was, perhaps, even more essentially herself, because she
loved to give, to please, to teach, to impart information and

watch it sink home, and there was little by then that she could tell me that we had not already shared. ToTo was hopeless; her response to Lucy contained, only and ever, a one-celled, doglike devotion. But Glenn Pickens's mind leaped and flashed like a rainbow trout in sunstruck spray, and he spent hours listening to Lucy's free-flowing fancies and odd, glinting insights.

The only times I ever saw Glenn really smile in my life, then or later, was at some notion of Lucy's, and I think that the only tendrils of humor and whimsy he has in his complex, darkling soul today were planted there in those days by her. With him the seductress simply took herself off and the open, sunny changeling came out of hiding, and the two odd and good young minds, so far apart in the countries of birth and environment, met in a shower of sparks. Even Ben and Dorothy Cameron stopped sometimes to listen to them spar and banter, and though Glenn and Lucy would temper their talk to the adult ears, in the sun of that easy approval they would go on.

"She's good for him," Ben said once, walking with me and Dorothy back to their house while Lucy gathered up her books and Glenn got ready for his late-afternoon sessions with the English tutor the Camerons had found for him. "I can't quite grab hold of it, but she does something for him all the studying we can buy for him doesn't do."

"It's that she shows him a white person's world with no holds barred and no strings attached," Dorothy said. "She gives him all of herself and no matter how hard we try, most of us white folks just can't do that with the Negroes. But how can we expect them to move into our world if we don't show them what it's really like? Or what we are? That's what Lucy does for Glenn. She shows him what is possible."

"Lord God," Ben Cameron said, ruffling Dorothy's dark hair. "Don't ever let anybody outside us and Shep hear you say that. The Klan will start knocking crosses together before you can say 'Jim Crow.' You're right, though, of course. That's just what it is. The possible. It could open more doors than any law we could manage to get on the books."

"Now who's Klan bait?" Dorothy Cameron said.

"Well, let's hope she doesn't get bored with Glenn and stop coming," Ben said. "I often wonder why she does. Pretty as she is, I wonder that every little thug in Buckhead isn't camped on your doorstep, Shep."

"They are," I said, and though that's all I did say, Dorothy Cameron shot me a swift look of pure compassion. She knew, of course, what Ben Cameron or any of our fathers would not have: that Lucy Bondurant was the talk of Buckhead, and why. And she knew more; knew, somehow, that the fact was a kind of obscure agony to me. I was grateful for the knowing, but it embarrassed me, and I did not go to the Camerons' after school again when I knew Lucy was there with Glenn Pickens.

In any case, it did not matter, for Aunt Willa somehow got wind of the afternoons that Lucy spent with Glenn in the Pickenses' little house behind Merrivale House and forbade her to go there ever again, or even to speak to Glenn, and made it so plain that if she disobeyed she would be sent away to whatever out-of-state boarding school could be found for her—"and with what I can afford you won't like it, sister"—that Lucy capitulated without a word. She simply drew in a little closer upon herself, and clung more tightly to Martha and ToTo and me, and escalated her sexual warfare against Willa to include open smoking and covert drinking. Nobody knew about the drinking yet but me, for no one else heard her hectic giggle when she came in at night, or the clumsy stumblings at the front door, but I thought it was only a matter of time for that, too, and my silent Lucy-anguish bored deeper.

I do not remember seeing Glenn Pickens smile ever again, though, of course, he must have.

We saw the Negroes in our world, in those last tranquil days before May 17, 1954, when *Brown* v. *Board of Education* fissured the dike, in a kind of simplistic pentimento. On the surface, they filled two roles for us: furniture and court jesters. The Pinks and the Jells of Buckhead had grown up in a sea of black faces, but those faces invariably loomed over hands at work in our service: nurses, cooks, maids, chauffeurs, gardeners, washwomen, even wet nurses. They might be infinitely and boundlessly loving and patient with us, and we might revel in their warmth, but it was the warmth and comfort of old, well-padded furniture that we took from them, anonymous and belonging inalterably to our houses. Most of us were aware, on some deep and never-probed level, that we had power over them, even as small children; too many shrieks and tears and complaints from us, and the nurses and tenders would be gone back to the projects before our pink little mouths had closed. I don't think any of us ever examined the basic horror of that power then, for children—especially the children of that time and place, and even its teenagers and young men and women—do not question the anatomy of their worlds. It is as it is. For most of us, introspection and awareness came much later, if at all, when the fire storms raging over the South could not be ignored even by us out in our Buckhead fastnesses. By then, of course, it was all academic.

When they were not providing us with comfort, the Negroes we knew entertained us. The Pinks and the Jells had a ready stable of Negroes who could be counted on to amuse and charm us endlessly with their antics, antics so redolent, in our blind young eyes, of the only kind of blackness we knew. They were those most prized pieces in our furniture collections, "characters," and we loved and laughed at all of them, and knew none of them.

There was Blind Willie, who played wildly infectious, raunchy rhythm and blues guitar at Peacock Alley, and Snake-Eyes the carhop, who named several of his countless children after favored Jells, and mincing, transvestite Sister, who wore a Carmen Miranda turban and high heels and dispensed languid curb service at Rusty's until a committee of indignant Northside mothers descended upon Rusty or whoever his factotum was and demanded Sister's banishment on moral grounds. There were the incredible carhops at the Varsity, monarch among them the outrageous, androgynous Flossie May, whose singsong litanies and lightning feet provided diversion nearly as enthralling as the celebrated and utterly taboo jig shows down at the Municipal Auditorium on Saturday nights. We attended these latter affairs regularly, lying to our parents, and stationed ourselves in the upstairs balcony, where we danced and drank beer and shouted and laughed, and rained trash and bottles down upon the dancers, and rocked our bodies to the blasting, insinuating rhythm of the Negro music that was unlike any we had ever heard before, pounding and insistently sexual. Why we were not simply set upon and murdered afterward for our insolence is a tribute to both the good nature of those dancers and the smug and muffled tenor of the times. Ten years later, we would have been.

It was one of the real dichotomies of Lucy's character that she so openly and truly loved many individual Negroes, and yet participated with such obvious relish in the mimicking and debasing of the race itself in those awful dancing balconies, pointing and laughing with the best of us at the dancing Negroes out on the floor. And yet I knew that even while she did, she was the only one of us who would have cheerfully and naturally gone right on home after the show with any one of them who had asked her and danced and talked away the remaining hours of the night, and thought absolutely nothing of it. As Yul Brynner said in *The King and I,* "is a puzzlement," and one of the many about her I never solved.

We were, most of us, openly and casually racist, and told and laughed at our share of nigger jokes, but I think it was largely a cultural thing and had nothing in it of personal heat, like our laughing rudely at Yankees while knowing virtually none of them, or our parents' denying stoutly that they were archconservatives, even as their chauffeurs drove them to the polls to vote for Franklin Roosevelt. But a few of the boys I knew at North

Fulton were venomously and very personally bigoted, and acted—or were said to act—upon it. Boo Cutler and Floyd Sutton come to mind; both were said to have stalked and shot Negroes from their streaking cars in the black nights on nameless South Georgia farm roads, and I have seen Boo, once at the Blue Lantern and once at Moe's & Joe's, knock a weary and smart-mouthed Negro carhop to the ground and kick him nearly unconscious.

When Martin Luther King was shot in Memphis, the story was all over Buckhead, in the weeks following, that Boo Cutler was actively and intimately involved in the plot, was perhaps even the finger behind the one on the trigger. There may have been some credence to it; the story still has currency today, though Boo himself is long dead of a brain tumor. I remember that I thought of that story when I heard of his death, lingering and lonely in the dreary VA hospital out on Briarcliff Road, and then thought how strange it was that so many of those eerie loners who alter history in violent and terrible ways turn out to have had blooming in their brains that hideous, silent flower. Perhaps Boo always had it. None of us were surprised when we heard.

But under the smiling, primary-painted facades of child-tenders and tap dancers, the Negroes in Atlanta were, as they were all over that America, bringing themselves to a slow and inexorable boil. Not much of it showed then. In the very early fifties, Atlanta Negroes lived, as they had for decades, along a blighted east-west axis in the southern quadrant of the city, in peeling, rat-infested housing projects and sweltering neighborhoods so wasted by poverty, unemployment, ill health and crime that no Northsider who had not actually driven through them would believe they existed. Many of my crowd never did.

On the east and west fringes of the black belt a few affluent neighborhoods of quite grand homes clustered in cloistered solitude, and on Auburn Avenue downtown, to the south of the central business district, a handful of black-owned office buildings and factories and warehouses stood. But the rest of Sweet Auburn, which served as a Main Street for the black community, was given over to infinitesimal, struggling businesses and services in appalling disrepair. In the downtown proper, and indeed, all over the city and cities like it in and out of the South, "White Only" and "Colored Only" signs flourished like skin cancers on everything from churches to train stations to restaurants to drinking fountains to rest rooms. The Negroes of Atlanta were still, going into the second half of the century, as disenfranchised and disaffected as serfs in a medieval city-state.

A few recognizable black leaders emerged, in those days, to

stand for their communities and petition the white power structure for the human solutions so desperately needed, but they approached, when they did, in private and in secret, after hours and with, metaphorically at least, their hats in their hands. No wonder that deep in those black waters a great tide was rising; wonder only that it did not burst free sooner and with far greater force, and that we favored white children by all that black bounty and largesse could not, in that most transparent of pentimenti, see it building. But we did not.

Our fathers saw it, though.

"When do you think your father first realized what Glenn would be to this town?" I asked Sarah Cameron once, at the top of Glenn Pickens's incredible trajectory.

"Probably the day Glenn was born," she said.

She didn't miss it far.

The great golden age of their full potency, when as the celebrated downtown white power structure the fathers of the Buckhead boys and girls would literally alter the face and persona of the city and pull it with sheer, concerted force into the mainstream of America, was still a few years away when Sarah and Lucy and I were teenagers. But the generators were beginning to hum, and the gears to be oiled and readied.

They were still young men then, in their late thirties and early forties, and for the bulk of their adult lives they had been occupied with tending family fortunes and extending personal arenas. But they knew fully, even before the city and the nation perceived them as anything more than an extraordinarily close group of wealthy men living in a northern suburb of Atlanta, that their roles would be those of catalysts, pragmatists and, most of all, alchemists. They would be required to, and would, transmute base metal into gold. I think the only thing they did not know yet, in those days, was the sheer, dizzying scope of their spheres of influence.

Literally since their births they had known each other, and moved as easily in one another's homes and clubs as they did in their own. It was always that proximity, that mutual pool of kinship, which gave them their unique power. Its basis was always the remarkable psychological similarity of class attitudes that made them comfortable together. They were ready, but they were not yet fully mobilized. In those last quiet days before both civic growth and civil turmoil, they were largely concerned with looking around to see what they could see. Their concerted social antennae were awesome.

They saw a city stagnant since the flurry of building directly after World War II, crying out for office space and air facilities to catch the faltering torch that the railroads had dropped. At-

lanta had always been a service city, a mover of goods, a branch
office town, but now they saw business and money turning away
in impatience, going elsewhere, because the wheels at home were
not numerous or sturdy enough to take the weight. They saw
business after business come South, sniff around, find little to
their liking in the way of facilities or quality of life, and head
for New Jersey or Texas. And they saw a formless black population, large and growing, with, as yet, no real political muscle,
but with an enormous potential for it.

They were not stupid men, or shortsighted; they knew, even
as they espoused it personally, that segregation could not and
would not prevail, and that when it crumbled, they could either
profit from it or be crushed beneath its fall—but fall it would.
Being good businessmen, if indifferent humanitarians, they
began to put their feelers out to the simmering black community.
Far better to have the Negroes of Atlanta buying from their businesses than burning them. Far better to lure Northeastern business South with the promise of open, peaceful schools than put
their burgeoning strength behind a last romantic schoolhouse-
door stand doomed to fail before the first federal marshal appeared.

They were well-connected men, even in those early days; they
knew what the tenor of the nation's highest courts was, and knew
that bullheaded defiance of a federal ruling on school integration
would tip Atlanta squarely back into the somnolent quagmire
from which it had so painfully struggled after the war. Mayor
Hartsfield had the right idea, but the wrong syntax: It was not
so much that Atlanta was a city too busy to hate as that in Atlanta, organized, official hate was bad for business. These twenty
or thirty men who were, to us Pinks and Jells, still only our fathers put aside their menus and began, from their tables at the
Capital City Club, to reel in the lines all of them had into the
blasted streets and housing projects of South Atlanta.

The lines were myriad, and went deep. Many were those of
master-servant; every Buckhead family had its own coterie of
black familiars among the men and women who came out on
the 23 Oglethorpe buses every day to serve them, and they knew,
also, families of those people. And then there was the network
of blacks in service at the clubs and the restaurants they fre-
quented, and at the labor levels of their businesses and those of
their friends. Being leaders themselves, they knew personally the
scattering of black leaders who were visible in those days and
the still fewer ones who were not, and they were on first-name
basis with the administrations of the six black schools in the lustrous, Rockefeller-funded Atlanta University complex in the
southwest quadrant of the city. This may have been the most

important and the most fortuitous tie of all; it was the educated young blacks who administered, as well as participated in, the civil rights movement when it came, and when it did, our fathers had their contacts, if never their agents, in place.

And they kept the contacts fresh and immediate. Even during the heart of that anguished struggle, when the White Citizens' Council and the flaming, colorful segregationists were the most vocal and the news out of Birmingham and Little Rock and Selma came smoking in over the wires, and every blinding-hot summer day dawned on another threatened riot in one embattled black community or another, the men of the Club and the black leadership of Atlanta talked. They talked daily and for hours, in black homes as well as white, and even though they met in secret, still they met. When action came—when the public schools were kept open in defiance of the state's law and in compliance with the country's; when Ben Cameron, then mayor, stood on top of an automobile in Mechanicsville for hours in the fierce heat of an incipient riot, talking, talking; when one by one the "White Only" signs began to come down, and even that innermost of sanctums, the Commerce Club, seated Negroes for lunch—it was usually because one specific and powerful white man said the necessary words into the necessary ears, and because many of those ears were black.

It wasn't, despite what the Chamber of Commerce did and does tell everyone who will listen, particularly exemplary handling of the matter of race; often it was not even decent handling. The motives behind it were never pure. Most of it came reluctantly and at least ten years too late. But it came, and it came without clubs and dogs and fire hoses and blood in the streets of the city. I think it came because the men who would soon make up the Club had their ears open in the early 1950s, and heard the soft mutter of the drums almost before they began.

"Remember them all together at somebody's party, back when we were at North Fulton?" Lucy said once during one of our nightly telephone calls. "God, they were gorgeous. Not physically, so much; but powerful. Lord! Power is just so goddamned *sexy!*"

She was right. They were an impressive group, sitting all together at one of their luncheons or in one of their bank board meetings, or even gathered at a party in Buckhead. Young, attractive, tanned from golf and tennis, easy with one another, purposeful. They were still cadets, but they knew they would have the power of which she spoke, and they knew where it would come from: Their own fathers and mentors, for many years before them the official Club, would pass the batons on to them at the appointed time in an almost formal transfer of power.

Even before they came into their real and final strength, they were formidable. To sit at lunch in the Capital City Club downtown on Peachtree Street, a symmetrical and mellow old cream-brick mansion rimmed about with leaning office buildings, was to see pure power in repose, drinking its ritual two prelunch bourbon and branch waters and eating its London broil. It was almost palpable in the air; you could get physically dizzy from it.

Toward the end of March in my senior year at North Fulton, my father asked me to come downtown and meet him for lunch at the Capital City Club. I was as profoundly surprised as if he had asked me to attend a burlesque show with him. And I was distinctly apprehensive. I had been to the club, of course, many times; it and the Atlanta Athletic Club were my father's downtown clubs, and he took us all there occasionally, for lunch or dinner after football games at Georgia Tech, or for the New Year's Day buffet in the Mirador Room. But I had never been there alone with him. I had not been anywhere alone with my father, by that time, in several years. The last time I could remember was to see the Lone Ranger in a one-man show at Grant Field, on his great, shining horse, Silver. I think I was eleven then.

I went down on a Friday noon, parking the Fury in the lot beside the club on Harris Street and tossing the keys to ancient liveried James, who had been fielding keys ever since I could remember. I ran lightly and in ear-ringing dread up the shallow stone steps and into the marble lobby.

"Morning, Mr. Sheppard," fat Charles, who commanded the door, said to me, smiling as if I were his favorite nephew. With Charles's memory and what he must have seen of white people's foibles over the years, he could have been a very powerful and dangerous man, if it had occurred to him. Perhaps it had. Perhaps even then, Charles had, in some dark closet back at his home in Southwest Atlanta, a burgeoning file marked "Indiscretions, White." I liked the idea then, and I like it even more now.

I went along the short, thick-carpeted corridor under the mural of ecstatic darkies sitting on cotton bales on an idyllic, never-seen riverfront dock, past the glowering bust of some dour, anonymous Confederate general or other and the lined portraits of past presidents, and up the mahogany stairs to the Mirador Room on the second floor. My heart was hammering so hard under my new blue lightweight wool blazer that I thought I would hyperventilate and faint at the feet of Edgar, who opened the door into the holy of holies with the same "Good morning, Mr. Sheppard," only minus the smile. Dignity was the order of the day in the Mirador Room.

I could not imagine why my father wanted to have lunch with me, but I sensed that there was no hope of its being casual or even pleasant. It had about it the air of an appointment in Samarra. On the way across the gleaming parquet floor, which became, in the evenings, a little dance floor, I imagined that he would tell me that we had lost all our money, and I would have to drop out of Princeton, where I had applied and been accepted, and go to work. Or that he had cancer and was dying, and I would have to do the same. Or that Lucy was being sent away somewhere irrevocable and distant, and I would never see her again, and he was preparing me. Even as I smiled at him, sitting at his accustomed table in the corner of the second tier, his face red under the thinning thatch of blond hair, and registered that the smile he gave me back was as ghastly as a death rictus, I was marshaling my defenses and lining up my arguments. The last weapon in my arsenal, outright refusal, seemed, in his actual presence, simply unimaginable. I did not think I was going to come out of this encounter unchanged.

To my surprise, Ben Cameron unfolded his lean length from the chair opposite my father and rose to greet me, and my thrashing heart gave a mad buck of relief and subsided. Whatever it was, I had an ally. I reached the table and put out my hand like the confident young man I was not and had never been.

"Hello, Mr. Cameron," I said. "Daddy."

"Hello, Shep," Ben Cameron said, giving me his warm grin that had nothing in it but pleasure at seeing me. "Good to see you."

"Son," my father said formally. The fierce wolf's smile never left his red face. He gestured at the chair next to Ben and I slid into it.

"Sorry I'm late," I said, frowning purposefully, like a man who has set aside important affairs to keep a date. "Traffic on Peachtree was awful all the way in."

"Get used to it," Ben Cameron said, smiling ruefully. "It's not going to get any better in your lifetime. Although it's a fond, if perhaps premature, hope of mine that one day we'll have some kind of fast rail system that will bring people right through all that mess and downtown in a few minutes. But I'm afraid you'll have to muck it out along with the rest of us until we can part the city from enough money to do it."

I looked at him blankly, and then at my father. I had not made any secret of the fact that I had been accepted at Princeton and then hoped to go to New York to work for a year or two afterward, before I decided what I would do with the history or political science degree I planned to acquire. My father certainly knew all that, though he had long since ceased to comment on my

plans when I talked of them. I had thought he had lost interest,
and I had been glad of the fact, if left with a surprisingly sharp
taste of loss in my mouth.

Ben Cameron knew, too. I had talked about Princeton with
him more than once; his father had gone there, and Ben had gone
with him to reunions once or twice as a child. Why, then, was
he talking as though I would soon be driving down Peachtree
Road to the office downtown where my father had recently
moved his real estate affairs? Was this something to do with
Princeton? Had my acceptance been a mistake, and were they
trying to break it to me gently?

Ben lifted a lazy hand and smiled genially at me. All of a sudden I did not know him; it was as if I had never seen him before.
My father continued to smile, too.

"I know, I know," Ben said. His voice was slow and thick and
hearty, not his at all. "Princeton and all that. But look here,
Shep, I got to talking with your daddy at the Athletic Club last
week, me and Tom Rawson and Frank Hubbard, and it just
seemed to us, all of a sudden, that your going all the way up there
and then on to that overgrown Yankee town is a terrible loss,
both to your mama and daddy and to this town of ours. Your
dad here told me your mind was made up and there was no use
trying to change it, but hell, you know me, I'll try anything once.
So I invited myself to lunch with you and your pa and I'm going
to give you my best shot."

The waiter came and put an amber glass with ice in it down
in front of me, and said, "Mr. Shep," just as he did to my father,
and I stared as stupidly at the glass as I had at Ben Cameron.
Then I looked at my father. His face was redder than usual, and
his small blue eyes were fierce with something I could not name,
but he kept on grinning, and gestured at the glass.

"House bourbon," he said. "Good stuff. Thought you might
as well have one with Ben and your old man. You're old enough
now. Practically a man; shot up before I noticed, somehow."

"They'll do it, won't they?" Ben Cameron said, still in a voice
that sounded as if he were in a not very good play. "Ben Junior's
practically into Tech now, and taller than I am, and my little
old Sarah-puss is a grown woman. Pretty one too, huh, Shep?"

"Sure is," I said, sounding as banal as he did, and knowing
it. What was wrong with him? He did not sound even marginally
intelligent, and yet the far-ranging, high-soaring conversations
I sometimes had with Ben and Dorothy Cameron were among
the most prized hours in my life.

I took a large swallow of the bourbon, to cover the silence that
was worse, even, than Ben Cameron's false bravado and my father's fierce, gnarled smile. I choked into the silence, and spit

bourbon onto my blazer and the table, and felt the fire run from my collar to the roots of my hair. I had not tasted bourbon since that night with Lucy so long ago in the summerhouse, when trouble had hung thick and deadly around us. I felt it here too, now, in this dim, grand room of mirrors and damask and polished dark wood.

"That's sippin' whiskey," Ben Cameron said. "Fry your eyeballs. Better take it slow. You don't want to go out of here on your hands and knees . . . though I've seen your pa do just that in his time."

He poked my father on the arm, and my father gave a great, jolly bray of laughter. I realized that they were talking, or attempting to talk, to me as they did among themselves, in the rough, simplistic, ritualized jargon of the wellborn Atlanta man among his peers. Instead of pleasing me, it made me want to jump up from the table and run.

"Well." Ben put his hands flat on the table and looked at me, and the amiable, red-faced jester was gone and a taut, contained, commanding stranger looked out of the clear gray eyes. I had never seen this Ben Cameron either, but knew instinctively that I was seeing the man who counted in clubs and boardrooms, who moved matters and men and would one day lead them.

"What do you say to rethinking this Princeton business, Shep?" he said. "The university's got a good history department if that's what you want, or Tech's got a first-rate industrial management or even political science department. Don't worry about getting in; we can take care of that. Get you into Chi Phi, too, if you want to, or SAE, or God help us, even KA; I think Alex Cheatham was one of those sorry hounds over at Athens. Or track; you ought to do real well in the 880 at either Tech or Georgia. Coach Kress is a good friend of mine. You ought not have any trouble running a little varsity track if you want to."

I was still silent, and I suppose he mistook my silence for refusal, but in truth, I could not have said anything if I had wanted to. What was going on here? Why was this conversation happening?

"If it's real estate you're worried about, I don't think your daddy would be too heartbroken if you tried your hand at something else for a little while," Ben went on, cocking a sandy eyebrow at my father, who nodded solemnly, not looking at either one of us. "It's a rewarding career for a man, Shep, real estate; an honorable way to make a living, and done right, a way to give something back to the community. And your dad's holdings are considerable indeed. You surely know that. Managed well, they would do a lot both for your family and your town. But if, you know, you just aren't interested, well, I don't think your dad would mind if you went into another field, as long as you stayed around home. That right, Shep?"

He looked at my father again, and my father nodded once more, looking now, intently, at the little shaded lamp on the table, as if he had never seen one before. I continued to gape.

"So I took the liberty of calling a few of your daddy's and my old friends," Ben Cameron went on. "You know, Snake's daddy, and Carter's, and Pres's. One or two others. Good men, that you've known all your life. And all of them said they'd be proud to have a boy like you in their business. What do you think, Shep? Construction? Banking? One of the utilities? Television? The market? Hell, I'd even let you give selling my little old snake oil a shot, if you think you'd like that. Point is"—and he pointed his fork at me, and looked intently into my eyes with an expression in his own that was as oblique, and yet as freighted with import, as any I have ever seen in a man's—"we need you here. In Atlanta. Not only us, but a whole new generation of people coming on behind us. Your generation, and even the one after you. You have talents—a weight, if you will—that you may not even know you have, and you surely will have substantial family assets one day, and both should be kept in your own city. Do you read me, Shep?"

"Yessir," I said. "I guess I do."

"Well? Will you think about it?"

I looked at my father again, and this time he was looking at me, and I saw in his face a kind of enormous, guarded flatness that covered something I could not fathom. And then suddenly, I will never know how, I did know it. It was a great, formless, all-pervading indifference, to me and to this conversation, and beneath even that was a simple dislike that I knew had its genesis not in me—for you do not dislike that which you have put out of your mind—but in Ben Cameron. My father did not want to be here with me and Ben Cameron having this conversation, and he did not want me to stay in Atlanta and manage his real estate holdings one day, and he could barely veil the resentment at the man opposite him, who was trying so hard to persuade me.

It was a moment of perfect, ringing epiphany, and through the shock of it I wondered, mildly and mindlessly, at what precise moment my father had given up on me as the son he had so long intended to inherit his kingdom.

And then I wondered what power Ben Cameron had over him, that he sat here with the skull's smile on his heavy face, and listened while his oldest acquaintance tried to keep me where he himself no longer wanted me: in the house on Peachtree Road.

I don't know where I found the clarity or the courage. I have never been noted, in my dealings with my father, for either.

"Thanks, sir, but there's really no use thinking about it," I said briskly. "I really do want to go to Princeton and on to New York like I'd planned, and that's what I'm going to do, if my father will still agree to it."

My father made a gesture of concurrence and dismissal, and raised his finger for the waiter with the check, and excused himself.

"I've got a man waiting in my office about the Summerhill property, Ben," he said. "By all means have coffee and dessert and put it on my tab. Thanks for coming over. I didn't think it would do any good, but I wanted you to see that for yourself. Shep." And he nodded again at me without looking at me, and walked across the shining lake of the floor and out of the Mirador Room.

"Want anything more?" Ben Cameron said to me, and I shook my head, misery falling down over me like a thick, dark curtain. I had made my point and gained for once and all that freedom I had longed for, but the pain in my heart told me that it was at a price I could not yet even calculate. It was one thing to suspect that your father simply did not consider your existence significant. It was another to have it demonstrated to you.

"Let's get out of here, then," Ben said. We were silent as we walked down the stairs and out to the parking lot, and then, as we waited for James to bring our cars around, he said, "You're smarter than I gave you credit for, Shep. Princeton's the place for you, and after that . . . well, we'll see. I had no business putting the arm on you like that. I hope you'll forgive me for any pain it caused you. Will you shake on it?"

I took his hand, and he grinned his slow, magical grin, which had fired so many of my small childhood darknesses into healing light, and I felt a very small curl of hope and easiness trickling back into my frozen heart. I grinned back.

He got into his big new Lincoln, and shut the door, and then put his red head out the window and squinted up at me in the bright sunlight. The pure, thin light of early spring touched his head with fire.

"You know, I've always thought you were pretty special, Shep," he said. "I'd have been proud to have you as a son; still would, much as I think of that son of mine. I was wrong to pressure you. But one day when you're back from school and have some time, I want you to come over and talk to me about your family's business. I promise I won't try to sell you on it, if by that time you truly believe it's not for you. But there are some things about it you need to know, and I don't think your father is ever going to tell you. Will you do that?"

"Sure," I said, tears of love and gratitude prickling behind my eyes. I squinted as if in the sun, so he would not see. "But can't you tell me now?"

"Nope. Not the right time for it. But before too long. Don't let me forget. It's important."

"I won't," I said, and he eased the car into gear and flipped me a small wave and slid out into the stream of traffic on Harris Street.

I drove back to North Fulton in the Fury, filled, if I had not been before, with the absolute, still certainty that whatever there was for me in the world lay far away from Atlanta and all its sucking resonances. I had forgotten the last thing he said to me before I got as far as Palisades Road, where Peachtree Street becomes Peachtree Road.

CHAPTER
TEN

T HAT AFTERNOON I had a tentative date with Charlie Gentry to try out a new World War II metal detector he had gotten for his birthday, in the vast, echoing battlefield out at Kennesaw Mountain, but I did not keep it. I did not even remember it until I was eating dinner that evening. I drove instead straight from North Fulton over to Muscogee and went looking for whichever Cameron was around. I was, by that time, so drowned in confusion and self-doubt and the delayed pain of my father's dismissal that I knew I would have to talk with someone about it or founder under the misery, and I headed for Merrivale like a pigeon homing toward its cote.

As I left the Fury in the cobbled front courtyard and headed around the side of the house toward the little den where the Camerons were usually to be found at that hour, it struck me that this was literally the first time in my life when I did not, swiftly and instinctively, bear my hurts home to Lucy. It was such a jolting perception that I stumbled in midlope, feeling somehow traitorous and skulking, as if I were actually betraying her. And then the thought came whole and clear into my mind: Don't talk to her about Princeton until you've lined up your allies. I knew then on some hidden level what my conscious mind had not admitted before, that Lucy was the most powerful obstacle my flight from Atlanta would ever have. I had not gone home because I was afraid to.

She had never said much of anything about my plans to go away to school after graduation because I had not talked much of them myself. I did not speak of them to my parents, beyond the necessary self-conscious exchanges about applications and fees and such, because I feared that my mother's possessiveness and my father's angry contempt would break down my resolve. As it happened, neither had made much fuss about it when the application had gone off, or even when the acceptance had come. It had been in the late spring of my junior year, and I suppose that both of them thought I might see the folly of my ways in the intervening year if they simply left me alone. Why Lucy had not responded more fervently, one way or another, I could not even guess, except that she was, in those days, sunk in her own alienation, and perhaps did not really register the import of the acceptance letter.

I had put it away in my desk out in the summerhouse the day after it had come and showed it to no one else, but I could sense it there all through the next year, glowing steadily like a talisman. It had been Dorothy and Sarah Cameron who had seemed the happiest for me, and so I knew that if succor and resolve were going to be available to me, it would come from them. Lucy, I sensed, was not going to take the actuality of my leaving at all well, and I could not, bruised as I was by the luncheon at the Capital City Club, have stood up to her.

I found Sarah in the little glass-walled studio that Ben had had built for her just off the pool house in the back garden when the extent of her talent had become obvious. She was there most afternoons when she was not at swim team practice or one of her extracurricular activities, I knew; she loved the white-walled, light-washed haven in the wooded garden, and I liked to see her in it. To watch Sarah in her studio, silky dark hair tumbled and amber eyes intent, moving back and forth from her easel to her palette, was like watching some wild creature function perfectly in its habitat, at ease and unobserved. I had the same sense of rightness when I watched her in the water. She was absolutely, totally unself-conscious and natural in those two milieus, and I felt soothed and suspended watching her in them, like Pippa in my knowing that just then, all was right with the world.

Even now, at sixteen, Sarah did not go in the swooping, shouting caravans of the Pinks and the Jells on their after-school expeditions. She never had. It was not that she was not asked; by her sophomore year, there was not a Jell in Atlanta who would not have been pleased to have Sarah Cameron beside him at Wender & Roberts or in the Buckhead Theatre, and Charlie would have died for it. It was simply that the world Ben and Dorothy Cameron spun out on Muscogee Avenue was still so all-encompassing and enriching that Sarah, if not young Ben, had no desire yet to leave it.

She said something about that once, many years later, on a New Year's Eve that must have been the most painful of her life, and I was surprised at the depth and clarity of her perception. I don't know why I should have been, by that time. The fruit of my unawareness had become bitterly ripe then.

"You could have been really good. Maybe great," I said on that night. "You could have been one of the ones they know in New York and Europe, if you'd kept on with your painting. You're just as much a casualty of all that Cameron wonderfulness as Ben was."

"No," Sarah said. "I'm a casualty of my own nature. I'm like Browning's last duchess. I 'liked whate'er I looked on, and my looks went everywhere.' I loved my art, but I didn't have any real focus, Shep. If my family ever did me any harm, maybe it was that. All that virtue, all that happiness and balance and energy . . . it flattens peaks and fills up valleys."

On this March day, Sarah was working on a still life of flowers and the family's battle-scarred old black tomcat, Moggy. The flowers were daffodils, a great, rowdy whoop of them so crammed into a blue pottery pitcher that they seemed a solid, shimmering sun of pure yellow, and I thought that she had just picked them from the wooded back garden, because moisture still clung to their frilled cups and leaves, and the fresh-rain smell of them was powerful in the air. Moggy had already been painted in, and lay black and glowering and wonderful on the canvas, with the ebony presence of a panther, on the scarlet wool shawl that Sarah had posed him on. The daffodils were just coming alive under her brush, strokes of captive, teeming light. The painting shouted and leaped and quivered with life, all primary bursts: red, blue, yellow, black, green. It was as primal and fierce as a Gauguin, but with a dancing, linear delicacy that was pure Sarah. The painting was massively adult, joyously sensual. It was hard to believe it was the work of a sixteen-year-old girl. But Sarah at work, slight as she was and childlike in an enveloping old paint-smeared shirt of her father's, had nothing of girlishness about her. Before she saw me I watched her for a moment through the open studio door. The sense of power and focus about her smote through the silence.

She saw me then, and grinned and waved her brush, and I came through the door and flopped down on the rump-sprung sofa against the fireplace wall. She was lightly tanned from the first of the spring sun, and the little crinkles of white that radiated out from her eyes were already etched in faintly. Under the shirt she wore blue jeans and sneakers and a striped T-shirt, and in them she looked more than ever like a taut, golden little boy. But the deep swell of her breasts under the shirt was all Dorothy's and all woman. Sarah and her mother had the most perfect bodies I have ever seen without, for some reason, ever being in the least overtly sexual. Sarah today has a waist that I could wrap my hands around, and not a hint of blurring under her chin, and a spine as straight as a hollyhock. In the pure, underwater light of the studio she was as clean and light and good to look at as a fish in clear water. Some of the heaviness on my heart lifted.

She looked at me.

"Is it the Princeton thing?" she asked.

I gaped at her. It had been months since we had talked of Princeton.

"Daddy called Mother when he got back from lunch with you and your father," she said. "He said it was pretty awful for you. He feels really bad about being a part of it. He thinks you're doing the right thing by going. I don't think he'd have done it except your father asked him to."

"I know," I said, grateful that I did not have to explain the whole thing to her. "He told me when we were leaving the club. I don't blame him. He and Dad have known each other practically all their lives. And he loves this town. I can understand why he'd think I ought to stay here. I just don't think he understands why I need to go . . . or he didn't, until today. He said some things that make me think he does now."

"He does," Sarah said. "And he's right. Why are you so upset? You're not changing your mind, are you?"

"I'm not upset," I said.

"Come on, Shep," Sarah said quietly.

"It was just that . . . God, Sarah, I wish you could have seen my father's face. Or his eyes. He didn't even hate me. He just didn't see me anymore. You could feel him washing his hands of me right there at the table. I thought we'd settled the business about Princeton; I thought he'd at least accepted it, even if he didn't like it. It's not like he still thought I was going to stay here and go into the business with him. I didn't know he was still thinking that I might. . . ."

"Something in your voice does sound like you're changing your mind," Sarah said.

"Not really," I said, not wanting to look at her intent cola-brown eyes, but not able to look away, either. They held mine like a cobra's held a mongoose.

"It's just that all of a sudden I wondered . . . what difference it was all going to make, in the long run. I can go to New York from Georgia or Tech or Emory as well as I could from Princeton."

"You'd never do it," Sarah said. "Never in this world."

"Well, I would," I said, annoyed.

"Even if you did," Sarah said, "you need Princeton before you do it. You need to meet some people who aren't like us before you actually get out in the middle of them. You don't know any people who aren't like us. You don't know any artists, or any . . . Jews, or any milkmen."

"I know you. I can meet Jews and milkmen here."

"No," she said. "It's not the same."

"Well, there sure as hell aren't any milkmen at Princeton," I said flippantly. I didn't like the tenor of the conversation. Sarah was supposed to comfort, not challenge, me.

"Oh, don't be thick," she said impatiently. "If you back out now you'll be sorry the rest of your life. Where's your gumption?"

I blew up at Sarah for the first time in my life. I had come to loathe that word, that uniquely Atlanta epithet, that flattener and oversimplifier and homogenizer of souls, and I absolutely refused to hear it from her soft, sunny mouth.

"Goddamn it, Sarah, if there's one word in the English language that stinks to me, it's 'gumption,' " I shouted. "It's a word for Babbitts and bullies and boneheads. It's synonymous with a *total* lack of imagination and empathy. It's simplistic and it's . . . sentimental. God, it's not possible to have gumption and be realistic at the same time! It's an arrogant word, and it's a tyrant's word. Look at my father, or your grandma Millie. She beat people over the head with gumption till the day she died. Hell, I think she actually *hated* any woman who wasn't fighting off Indians while she was dropping her baby in a cornfield during a tornado. Don't use that stupid word on me because it doesn't mean *shit!*"

"I know," Sarah said, grinning. "Wrong word. I'm sorry. You're right. And you're right about Granny. You could never have told Granny that it's courage that's the real prize, not gumption. The two don't have a thing to do with each other."

"I don't know anybody with courage, either," I said sulkily.

"I do," she said. "You have it."

"Sarah, what on earth are you talking about? You know I never did have any courage," I said. I was honestly surprised.

"You endure, Shep," she said, looking down at her little brown, paint-smeared hands. "You carry that family of yours on your back like Atlas did the world, and Lucy too—yes, her too—and you go right on doing what you need to do. You've refused to go into your father's business, you've refused to go to Georgia, or Tech, or Emory—Lord, I'd be terrified to do that. What is all that if it isn't courage?"

I looked at her and smiled, and she smiled back, the full, healing smile that had first made me easy with her.

"I wasn't really going to back out," I said. "I just needed to talk to somebody before I went home. I'm sure Mother knows about the famous lunch today, and the whole thing is going to come up again at dinner. Thanks for the ammunition."

"Anytime," Sarah said, equably, turning back to her easel. I went out of the studio and back around the house to the Fury, and I could feel rather than see the amber eyes on my back as I walked. Under their weight I strutted just a little.

I was wrong about dinner. Aside from saying mildly, "Shep has decided he'll be going on to Princeton this fall after all," my father did not mention our luncheon at the Capital City Club, either during the meal or, essentially, ever again. The handwashing had been complete. My mother did not seem too displeased, either. I came later to see the reason: Many of the best families of the South had sent sons to Princeton over the years. With its classically beautiful campus and its reputation for bestowing with some frequency the gentleman's C, it was the only Ivy League school deemed proper for an Atlanta boy who intended to come back home and ply the family trade. And it did, admittedly, add a certain cachet.

"They don't seem to come back changed, somehow," my mother told Dorothy Cameron one day not long after that, and Sarah reported the comment to me with glee. I laughed with her and let it lie. I intended with all my heart not only not to come back, but to be changed as completely as possible. New York still shone like a grail for me, safely away up there beyond the dreaming spires of Princeton.

But over its pristine, shimmering image now there hung, like some bright scrim in a dream, Lucy's face, wretched and importuning.

For I had been right in that flash of insight I had had about Lucy directly after the lunch with my father and Ben. She had reacted instantaneously and violently to my father's dry, small comment at dinner. I had not seen her behave so at a meal since we were both children. Everyone at the table simply looked at her openmouthed.

"*You can't!*" she cried, standing up so suddenly that her chair nearly toppled behind her. "Gibby, you can't! You promised! I won't let you! Uncle Sheppard, don't let him! Make him stay here, make him go to Emory and live at home—"

"*LUCY!*" Aunt Willa's voice cut Lucy's anguished tirade short, and she stopped in midsentence. Her blue eyes lost their wild white ring and their mad colt's light and went abruptly dead, and then tears welled and spilled over. They ran silently down her face, which had gone as white as long-bleached bone. She looked at me silently, the tears running, running.

"Oh, Gibby, how could you?" her lips said, but no sound came out with the words. She turned and knocked the chair the rest of the way over, and ran out of the dining room and up the stairs. No one spoke until the thud of her feet vanished behind the slamming of her door.

"I'll just see about this," Aunt Willa said in a tight, high, furious voice, slamming her napkin down beside her plate and then catching herself and folding it elegantly and replacing it. She made as if to rise, but my mother laid a hand on her arm.

"Better let her compose herself, Willa," she murmured, her curved little smile showing nothing but a calm, Madonna-like sweetness, her lashes veiling her eyes. "You know how undone she's been lately. Sheppie can go talk to her later and fix things right up. We don't want her doing anything she might . . . regret later."

I felt, at that moment, the same hate for my mother that blazed out of Aunt Willa's eyes before she flattened them back into civility. Lucy's midnight petting sessions had gone no more unnoticed in our house than they had in the other houses of Buckhead, only unremarked. I knew it was to these that my mother referred.

Lucy was still crying hard when I went up to her room at ten that night, and she would not let me come in.

"Go away," she sobbed. "I don't want to see your face. I hate you! You promised, and you broke your promise!"

"Come on, Lucy, let me in," I called softly, rapping on the door. "What did I promise? Not to stay here and go to school, I didn't. You knew about Princeton; I told you a long time ago. You saw the letter last year. . . ."

"I didn't think you'd really do it," she said, in a voice thick and hopeless with abandonment. "I thought you were just fooling around about it. I never thought you really meant to leave."

"But you said—"

"I DON'T CARE WHAT I SAID! YOU PROMISED ME YOU WOULD TAKE CARE OF ME FOREVER AND YOU'RE BREAKING YOUR PROMISE!" she shrieked, and there followed a loud thud, where she had thrown something heavy against the door. I was suddenly infinitely weary and sad, and I simply did not think I could cope with Lucy any longer on this night.

"Good night," I said dully. "I'll see you in the morning. We'll talk about it then."

She did not answer, and I heard the crying start again.

But in the morning she was calm, if red-eyed and pale, and she did not mention my going to Princeton. She left for school early, and I can't remember if we talked of it again at any length before I left, because it was that very afternoon she came home

enveloped smugly in the yellow MG and the goatish golden aura
of Red Chastain.

She had met him at one of the Friday night dances the past
winter, at the same time we all did, and he had been hanging
around her at the various dances and dinners and breakfasts ever
since like a randy hound, but she had never shown even the
slightest interest in him, and he had never been in the Peachtree
Road house. I often wondered why. By any standard I could
imagine, Nunnally "Red" Chastain should have been a prize infinitely worthy of Lucy's steel. There was scarcely a Pink in Atlanta who would not have given up her no-breaks to go steady
with him, but though many of them managed to capture his attention long enough for one or two dates, no one but Lucy
seemed to hold his interest very long. Small wonder. I honestly
think, even in those unformed high school days, Red Chastain
could have had any woman over twelve and under thirty he set
his sights on.

He was the son of a vastly wealthy fertilizer manufacturer in
Southeast Georgia, and had been shipped around the South from
one military school to another since he was seven years old, seldom lasting more than a year before being expelled for some fla-
grant, lazy and mocking infraction of the rules. They usually
involved fighting or drinking, or both. He was a tall boy about
my age, but because of his predilection for trouble, he was a year
behind me at North Fulton, where he had transferred at midyear
after his latest ouster, this one from the Georgia Military Academy in College Park to the southeast. He was living temporarily
and conditionally with his aunt and uncle on Northside Drive
and attending North Fulton as a last resort before his father gave
up totally on his education and cut him off without a penny.

Red had not altered his habits one iota, but North Fulton,
being a public school, was more lenient than the military fastnesses in which he had previously been held captive, and the aunt
and uncle were classically poor relations and frightened to death
of Red's smiling, murderous father. No one reported his indiscretions, and it was not likely that anyone would. They only
served to add luster to his legend, except in Lucy's eyes.

"He thinks he's God's gift to women," she said dryly. "I've
got news for him."

Red was silver-blond and had hooded, drowsy blue eyes and
his father's slow, insinuating grin and blind white temper. He
was purported to have three or four aborted pregnancies to his
credit in small cities and towns around the South, and was a
wonderful dancer, a whiplash athlete, and possessed of the kind
of quick, spurting rage that many Southern men mask behind
affability and slow, sweet smiles. He was called Red because of

the lightning flush of fury that flooded his face when he was provoked, which was often. He was not dull-witted; far from it. Red was as quick and cunning as a cobra. Indeed, despite his abysmal academic record (and because of his father's alumnus status and potential for endowment) he planned confidently to go on to Princeton when he graduated from wherever he finally prevailed. This was the first thing Lucy ever told me about him, smiling sweetly at him as she spoke: "Red, this is my cousin Gibby Bondurant, who looks after me like a big old brother whenever he can. Be nice to him, because he's going to Princeton just like you. Maybe you-all can room together."

And she slid the smile from Red over to me in one smooth, rich pour, like molasses.

Red Chastain looked so much like the faded photographs of a young Jim Bondurant Lucy kept in a scrapbook in her room that I started when I met him, as if he had actually been that gilded ghost.

After that first day, there was hardly a moment that spring when Lucy was not in his company. He picked her up in the mornings and drove her to school, and ate his lunch with her, and walked down the halls at school with his long arm about her waist as Boo Cutler used to do, and carried her books to the open MG afterward and tossed them into the back and drove her away, and brought her home in the long green twilights in time to eat dinner, change her clothes and climb again into the MG. The burr of the car was the first thing I heard before leaving the summerhouse for school in the mornings, and the last I heard in the evenings before falling asleep. Lucy still necked and petted long into the nights of that last honeysuckled spring, but the mouth and arms and auto now were those of Red Chastain and Red alone, and the only reason I knew that she was not going all the way with him was, as with all the others before him, that no one was talking about it, and they would have been, instantly, if it had been accomplished. No one talked of anything else that spring but Lucy and Red Chastain.

My parents said nothing about her alliance with him but smiled pleasantly at Red when he ground up the driveway in the MG, and he was always the soul of punctilious courtesy with them. He was charm itself with Aunt Willa, and she was as cordial to him as I ever saw her with any of Lucy's boyfriends; almost, though not quite, coquettish. Red had that effect on most women. And of course, he was powerfully, spectacularly rich. Aunt Willa was a shade warmer to Lucy that spring, or at least, not so noticeably cool. Her bread was always fresh and ready for buttering.

Even in her near-total absorption with Red, Lucy was behaving oddly with me. She was alternately sharp and contentious and wistful and almost seductive, constantly in an emotional flux, and I put it down to the fact that she still did not want me to go away and leave her alone in that unloving house. But Sarah had her own ideas about Lucy's mercurial moods.

"She's so jealous that you take me places she could kill us both," she said once, and then blushed furiously. But I dismissed that with such unfeigned ridicule that she did not mention it again. And the days spun on toward June and the end of school, and through them all, Lucy burned like a white candle on the arm and in the yellow MG of Red Chastain.

In the last week of May, a scant week before I graduated from North Fulton, we went in a flock of snorting cars on a still, hot afternoon out to the Chattahoochee River, where it ran under the tall old abandoned steel bridge beside Robinson's Tropical Gardens.

We were all there, my immediate crowd, the small set of Buckhead Boys that predated even the Jells; many of us in the pairs in which we would move into our adult lives. Ben Cameron came with dark, gentle Julia Randolph; Tom Goodwin with tiny, venomous Freddie Slaton; Snake Cheatham with Lelia Blackburn; Pres Hubbard with plain, aristocratic Sarton Foy who had just moved to Atlanta from Savannah with a royal-blue genealogy that left ours in her dust. A. J. Kemp brought Little Lady, who was allowed to tag along even at fourteen because A.J. was poor, polite, and adjudged harmless by Aunt Willa. I was with Sarah Cameron; even Sarah seemed afflicted by the restlessness that rode under the flat surface of the day, and abandoned her studio. Charlie Gentry was alone, but he rode with Sarah and me, in the backseat of the Fury, cracking smart-ass jokes and glancing at Sarah to see how she would respond to them. I saw him in the rearview mirror.

Lucy came with Red Chastain.

We had not planned to come to the river; we had just left Wender & Roberts, bored with the stale chill of the air-conditioning and the hanging hiatus in our lives, and drifted in a jostling flock out to the water as if sung there by a water witch. We went there three or four times during the springs and summers; vaguely, as if to check in.

We could not have said why. There was better swimming than the Chattahoochee available to us in a dozen pools, and better necking at Sope Creek and a dozen other spots. Drinking was best done in the parking lots of a handful of drive-ins around town, under cover of darkness and pulsing neon. There was no place on the river in those days to put a boat in; and in any case, river rafting did not become a craze until two decades later.

None of us would be caught dead fishing; it was, to us, the social equivalent of bowling. The river was not even a very scenic one, as rivers go. It ran flat and opaque and rusty with the slick mud of the foothills from which it sprang, and there were not, this far south, any appreciable shoals or rapids or waterfalls.

The river was deceptively deep and fast-moving under its sluggish snake's hide, and was, even on hot days, still cold in its depths in May. But it looked, simply, like a brown, slow, overgrown creek heaving itself along between flat, weedy banks. There were some fine stands of great old willows and hardwoods along its banks, and graceful bamboo forests, and in a few places the land soared high into granite palisades, and the pastures and forests bordering it were still largely innocent of the beetling, overpriced, shabbily built chalets and châteaux and villas that shouldered greedily down to its fringes a decade later. But still, there wasn't much in the way of natural splendor to lure us there. It was simply that where there is living water, the young near it will—must—eventually come.

"I swear," Lelia Blackburn said, holding her hair up off her sweating neck. "If it doesn't go on and rain I'm going to jump out of my skin."

"How about your clothes?" Snake said, and she slapped him lightly.

We were all about to pop out of our skins like ripe grapes that day. There was thunder in the thick, wet air, and our arms and necks crawled with it. The heat was intense for May, and had gone on too long. The end-of-school social season for the sororities and fraternities was at its fever pitch, and we were all worn and sated and heavy-eyed. Several of the girls were angry with their boyfriends and each other, a normal state that intensified at this time of year, and sniped and jabbed with sweet, sucking accuracy.

"Sarton, I can see smack through that skirt when you stand against the sun," Freddie Slaton chirped. "Tom would kill me if I showed off my panties to everybody in the world like that."

"You're probably the safest girl in America," patrician Sarton drawled. "The sight of your panties would probably put the world into a coma."

Undischarged sexual tension hummed like electricity prowling a live wire; most of us had necked and petted ourselves near crazy in the long, hot nights after the dances. Exams loomed. And over us all, especially those of us who were seventeen and eighteen and seniors, there drifted the freighted miasma that overhangs each of the great divisions of life and time. Graduation loomed; could not be held back, no matter how many raw young hearts cried out for it to halt; would, inevitably, come.

For most of us, there was the certainty that whatever else it held, life would never again be, for us, so sweet and seamless and golden. It was our first taste of loss and inexorability, and we quivered with that promissory loss like violins tuned to infinity.

Restless Ben Cameron was the only one of us who came close to articulating what we all felt: "We won't ever come back to this bridge," he said, his gray eyes far away and somehow drowned.

"Oh, we will too," Julia chimed. "Of course we will."

"It won't be us who comes," he said.

No one asked him what he meant.

There was no traffic on the old bridge—the new bridge just downriver had siphoned it off—and the smooth, flat water ran silent in the sun toward Apalachicola and the sea, mesmerizing us. Not even cicadas buzzed in the stillness, though there came, cool and rippling, the small splashes far below of snakes or turtles or other water creatures entering the river. It was three-thirty in the afternoon when we got out onto the bridge and stood there, our forearms resting on the pitted old railing, looking down into the dull mirror of the water. Its surface this day was not brown but the rich gray of pewter, and the entire May sky and the great, silver-edged galleons of the thunderheads were caught in it. It was like looking down into the mirror-twin sky of a heretofore unimagined world. There was not even a breeze; the wind had died at noon.

Sarah is adamant in her contention that it was Lucy who began it. She is probably right. I was too far away to hear her, but it was in all ways Lucy's sort of thing, and on this day she was primed for it like a pulsing pump. She fairly glittered there in the still, silent sunlight, with energy and restlessness and the strange, skittering tides that had been driving her since she met Red. I knew when they got out of the MG that they had been drinking, and not just beer. I could smell whiskey sweet and heavy on Red's breath, and Lucy's cheeks burned with the two hectic red circles that liquor always painted there. Her eyes stabbed back light from the sun.

"The last one in that river is a—a Bovis Hardin," Sarah says Lucy cried. And was out of her skirt and sleeveless blouse and black Capezio shoes before the words were out of her mouth.

My head was turned away from the water when I heard Snake's cry, "Hey, you idiot, you want to kill yourself?" but even as I swiveled to face them I knew that I would see Lucy. And there she was, standing poised on the railing with white-gripping toes, stripped down to her nylon panties and bra, naked on every silvery-white inch of her save a few, giving a strange, long, wordless, jubilant cry and diving like a polished knife out and down

into the sky-smitten water, fully twenty feet below. Red
Chastain, stripped also to his undershorts, followed her in a lazy,
panther's racing dive. We all stared in absolute, dream-snared
silence. For a heart-stoppingly long time there was nothing on
the steely water but the concentric stigmata of their dives, and
then their sleek, wet heads broke the surface like seals, and their
strong, slim arms brought them to a little sandy beach some
yards downstream, fringed with showering willows.

We were wrapped for another long moment in sun and singing
air and river silence. And then Snake cupped his mouth with
his hands and gave the great, hideous Tarzan cry out of all the
Saturday matinees of our childhood and went off the bridge.

"Kowa Bunga!" yelled Ben, and followed him.

"Oh, God, I'm going to get *killed* for this!" Julia shrieked, but
she slid out of her pedal pushers and blouse and squeezed her
eyes shut and jumped in feet first, after Ben.

Julia would have leaped into hell after Ben; in a sense, she did.

The long tension of the day was broken then. One by one,
shouting, the Pinks and Jells of Buckhead skinned out of their
clothes and dived into the river. Before I could even get a strong
breath, there were only four of us left on the bridge. Pres could
not swim in his heavy metal brace; he grinned and yelped from
beside us. Charlie risked a diabetic's death from cold and infection if he swam in any but summer-warmed water. I still stood
there, on the pitted macadam. And Sarah Cameron, by far the
best swimmer and diver of us all, stood indolently at the railing,
smiling coolly down at them while they shouted at us to strip
and dive, dive, dive!

"It's the worst kind of showing off," she said to me in a low,
urgent voice. "It's gumption and not courage. Be really brave
and don't do it."

Of them all, only she and one other person knew that my fear
of heights went beyond mere terror into mindlessness.

Lucy had always known.

They thrashed out of the water and stood on the little beach,
gasping at the audacity of their own act, wet, laughing. Even the
girls laughed. Even Freddie Slaton, looking like a water snake;
even Little Lady, looking like a soaked Easter chick. Even Sarton
Foy, looking like what she was—a sopping, near-naked aristo-
crat.

"Dive, y'all! Dive! Dive! Come *on!*" she shrieked. "You're
chickenshits if you don't dive!"

Sarton is the only woman I ever knew besides Lucy on whose
lips profanity sounded like an Ave Maria.

Everyone was laughing except Lucy. Lucy did not laugh, did
not even smile. She stood a little apart, dripping and slender as

a water reed, head thrown back, body gleaming through the sucking nylon, blue eyes blazing straight into mine, hands cupping her mouth, and called up, "Come on, Gibby, jump, or we'll think you're a North Fulton fruitcake! Come on! Mark my trai-i-i-l!"

And at that shared, blood-and-heart-deep summons out of our childhood, I ripped off my pants and shirt, scrambled desperately up onto the hot steel railing, steadied myself on the struts and poised blindly for a dive. I opened my eyes then, for one despairing moment, and looked down into the water so sickeningly far below, and saw there instead only the endless, wheeling sky. I toppled backward onto the bridge, pulled myself up on my hands and knees, and vomited.

From below, Lucy's laughter soared above a scrambled chorus of hard, bright jubilation. It seemed to go on forever. By the time I had gotten numbly into my clothes and walked back to the Fury where I had parked it on the verge of the bridge, stiff and silent with Sarah in my wake, Lucy had come sleek and dripping and incandescent up the bank, shimmering like a young otter. Red Chastain grinned insolently beside her.

"What's the matter, Gibby?" she said lightly and merrily. "Eat something that didn't agree with you?"

Red laughed.

Sarah Cameron drew her slender brown arm back and slapped Lucy so hard that her neck snapped back and her wet hair lashed across her face. Someone is always slapping Lucy, I thought stupidly.

"I will never forgive you for that, Lucy Bondurant," Sarah said in a voice I did not know and never heard again. "Shep will, because he's a fool. But I won't."

We walked on past them, and were in the airless front seat of the Fury before we heard any of them speak, and I could not tell what it was they said. I turned the key and eased the car onto the sunlit emptiness of Paces Ferry Road. Neither of us looked back.

We drove home without a word, but when I let her out at the bottom of the long Cameron driveway, I leaned over and kissed Sarah briefly on her soft mouth, which tasted, surprisingly, of tears.

"Thank you, Sarah," I said.

"You're welcome, Shep," she replied.

From that day until the summer morning I left for Princeton, I went few places without Sarah at my side.

Lucy's tears of remorse that evening were fierce and real enough, and she was so wildly and desperately penitent that I forgave her as I always had and would; as Sarah had said I would. But the slight remove between us now was impenetrable. I had found to my great pain and profound surprise that the true legacy she had bestowed upon me was not, as I had thought, the power of savior and near-sainthood, but the open wound of vulnerability. An invisible and invincible shield, one that we had forged together on nearly the first day we had known each other, had been breached, and blood had been let. Neither of us, I know, ever forgot that day, though no one in our crowd spoke of it again, at least in my presence.

Almost immediately after the incident on the river the word got around that Lucy was doing the Black Act with Red Chastain almost every night, sometimes two and three times, and that they had vague plans to get engaged when he finally graduated, if he did. She wore no fraternity pin, for Red had refused to join one, so I had no way of knowing if the latter rumor was true.

I knew the former one was. Lucy walked in ripeness and moved in a new thick, sweet slowness that spelled, even to my wildly untutored eyes, completion. I seemed to feel about it, simply, no way at all.

I never spoke of those speculations to her, and she did not to me. We spoke of little in those last days; I kept away from the house as often and as long as I could, taking refuge at the Camerons' until they good-naturedly ran me home each evening, and she kept to her room when she was not with Red. She did not even eat her meals with us in that last week. I don't know where she ate, or if she did. Once she stayed out all night and there was a flaming row with Aunt Willa in the foyer when she came in after sunrise, still adjusting her clothing. But I don't think she was punished, or abided by it if she was, for she was not around the Peachtree Road house that week, and I felt, mainly, an obscure and guilty gratitude that I would not have to ride out another exile with her. I wanted, then, two things only: I wanted to be near the ease and lightness and safety that was Sarah, and I wanted to get away from Atlanta and into Princeton.

It did not occur to me until much later that both Sarah and Princeton might want something in return.

I left a full quarter earlier than I had planned, on a day in late June when rain and coolness had come back to town, and the air smelled of honeysuckle and newly mown grass and grateful, sucking earth. I took the train from Brookwood station, for cars were not allowed on the Princeton campus until junior year, and my weeping mother and the smiling Camerons and Sarah came in the sweet, cool early morning to see me off. My father was at The Cloister on Sea Island at a realtors' meeting; he had said his cold red good-byes earlier. Lucy was off somewhere with Red Chastain. We had, somehow, said no good-byes at all.

Sarah came regularly to Princeton for football games and, later, Colonial dances, and my mother and father came, rarely, for formal, constrained, parental visits, but except for brief and obligatory trips South for Christmas and Easter and a few unavoidable vacations, I did not come home again for a long time, and then through no choice of my own.

By that time, Lucy had gone.

PART
TWO

CHAPTER
ELEVEN

ON A MISTED SUNDAY MORNING in late October, in the beginning of my junior year at Princeton, I sat with Sarah Cameron in the window seat of one of the big, grand suites high up in Blair Arch and kissed her, and put a trembling hand on the sweet heaviness of her breast.

She lifted her face to me from the hollow of my shoulder and smiled.

"Please don't, Shep," she said softly. "I don't know how to handle it. And we said we wouldn't, yet."

"I know," I said, my voice splintering in my throat. "But just think. You could tell people when you're an old lady that you lost your virginity in Dub Vanderkellen's room at Princeton when you were eighteen. It's too good an opportunity to pass up."

"Nevertheless, I think I will," she said, sitting erect on the old tapestry pillows and pulling her shoulders sharply back, as she did when she was hurt or offended. I knew my attempt to be sophisticated and devil-may-care, as I felt befitted a visitor, even on sufferance, to the lair of one of the country's richest scions and the school's most accomplished womanizers, had instead sounded only crude and insulting. I reddened fiercely. Sarah, even half-lying on the window seat of Dub Vanderkellen's legendary room, where uncounted indigo-blooded society girls had allegedly yielded up their family jewels, was still Sarah. What I had said was beneath both of us.

"I'm sorry," I said, looking at the rich mahogany tangle of her curls and the slim, shapely shoulders and winging little shoulder blades under the burgundy cashmere. I felt, besides

219

shame and embarrassment, a powerful urge to shield Sarah which had nothing in it of the fierce, otherworldly protectiveness I had so often felt for Lucy. This was a practical and tender kind of feeling, and warmed instead of pierced. Sarah was only eighteen, and still very much Dorothy Cameron's daughter, but she was also mine. Both of us had, over the space of this last year, come tacitly to acknowledge that.

"I know," she said, in her light, rich voice, and turned her face, still sun-browned with summer and lit with her whole-souled smile, back to mine. "It was too good to pass up. I might have said it if you hadn't. But to make it a good story it would have to be Dub Vanderkellen in the flesh that I lost it to, and I'd just as soon do it with a frog. When I do, it's going to be with Shep Bondurant, and I'll be fifty times prouder, even though I don't know where or when it will be."

I kissed her again, lightly, on the forehead just under the curls and felt expiation and a fine well-being flow through me. Sarah may not, in her entire life, have stopped hearts, but she certainly did start a lot of warm, steadfast engines.

"Dub would not be exactly thrilled to hear you called him a frog," I said, tossing the luminous name off my tongue with a familiarity that two short months of shared membership in Colonial Club did not warrant. I might not be able to admit it to myself, but I was mightily impressed with belonging to the same eating club as one of the mighty Vanderkellens of Pittsburgh, Palm Beach, Antigua and London. I had known wealth all my life back in Atlanta, but I had never even conceived of wealth on a scale such as I encountered at Princeton, in the persons of three or four, in the main, rather nondescript undergraduates, of whom Dub Vanderkellen was hands down the crown prince. Vanderkellen steel undergirt, it seemed, the entire free world. Still, it was the romance of the great family name, and not its money and power, that so intrigued me. I have always known pretty much where my weaknesses lie.

When I had seen Dub leave the Sunday morning milk punch party at Colonial in the savage little racing automobile of a whippetlike Bryn Mawr girl in a camel hair cape, I had made bold to ask him if I could take Sarah up to his room to see his fabled view. Dub had one of the few truly grand suites, vast and sumptuously furnished with old family pieces and commanding a spectacular 180-degree vista of the campus over Cannon Green toward Nassau Street, at the very top of Blair Arch, a crenellated and cloistered and mullioned Tudor Gothic pile of brick and pale stone which established for good and all the trend toward Gothic architecture on American college campuses. My own freshman and sophomore suite in Holder, before I had moved into Colonial, had reeked picturesquely of antiquity and genteel dust, but it did not hold a candle to the big suites in Blair.

"Sure," Dub had flung back over his shoulder, intent on the flash of pearly thigh the Bryn Mawr girl was showing as she slid into the Jaguar. "Go on up. Lay off Sarah, though. She's too nice a girl for what you're thinking. Leave that to the pros."

His laughter, even that froggy, followed him insinuatingly out onto Prospect Street as the Jaguar growled off, and the group around us laughed, as Sarah and I did, though I was the only one who flushed. Dub knew, of course, that it wasn't the view, but the wondrous room itself and the spoor of its storied occupant, that I had wanted to flaunt in front of Sarah. Everyone else knew it, too, and chafed me good-naturedly. Sarah had only visited Colonial this one time, for the Yale game, but she was an instant hit with the members, as she had been with my smaller and earlier crowd when I lived in the fourth entry of Holder Hall. I knew that already there were Colonial members who would have drubbed me with workmanlike thoroughness if they had thought I might dishonor her. Sarah inspired that feeling of little-sister, daughter-of-the-regiment closeness wherever she went, and it spilled over into stronger stuff here as well as in Atlanta. I had seen the same look on the face of Mac Thornton, my melancholy Warrenton, Virginia, roommate in Holder, and on the face of Chalmers Stringfellow just this weekend, that I had seen so often on the blunt, spectacled face of Charlie Gentry. Real caring, it was. And tenderness. It made me proud of Sarah on many counts, not least among them that it was on my arm that she came into this endlessly beguiling, infinitely wider world of Princeton.

Now Sarah butted me under the chin with the silky top of her head, her hair smelling clean and dry and somehow like trapped sun, and said, "Dub Vanderkellen looks like a frog and he *is* a frog. Nobody in their right mind would get near him, in this room or anywhere else, if his name was Smith or Jones. Or," she added gravely, "Bondurant."

I gave her a mock crack on the chin with my balled fist and turned and looked out into the wet late morning, and sighed a great sigh of pure happiness. For the moment, everything was so perfect in my world that I could almost hear the great minor, interior music of the planet. This small treasure, this perfect, compact being that was Sarah, that was my own, sat beside me in the very rooms of one of the great names in American society and industry, who was now incredibly my own clubmate; and spread out below us in the last of a light autumn rain was this place that had so quickly and totally claimed my heart and soul and imagination, this Princeton.

I had felt the spell of it the moment I had gotten off the dinkey from Penn Station at Princeton Junction two autumns before and looked around me into a gray-greenness that was as timeless and rich with myths and shades as Arthur's England. It was a different feeling altogether from the fierce pull of 2500 Peachtree Road, and the sheltering arms of the summerhouse. Those enclosed. Princeton enlarged. From that moment, something in my heart flew free and soared up to meet it, singing. I feel it still, whenever I think about Princeton in those years, and the years in New York that came later.

This had been an autumn of mists and mellowness, warm and as yet without real bite, and so even in the last weekend in October, some of the living wildfire of the centuries-old hardwoods on Cannon Green still flamed. There had come, in the night, a brief, soft little rain which had lingered through the morning, and though it was ending now, puddles still lay on the walks crisscrossing the green and the many quadrangles, and gleamed on the gray and rose and blue slate roofs, and dripped from the black iron posts and chain links that bordered the grassy areas. All of Princeton that we could see—the great, grim Romanesque bulk of Alexander, the mellowed bricks of Nassau, the white gleam of Whig and Clio, the arches and spires of Witherspoon and Holder and Dodd and Murray Dodge; the spires of the University Chapel and the Firestone Library, the Sunday quiet of Nassau Street and Palmer Square—shimmered with wetness. The campus seemed as it did so often to me, especially in winter: underwater. It is the image that I still see, these many years later.

"I think I like it best when it rains. Gray seems right for it," I said to Sarah, taking a deep breath of thick air. There had been a bonfire on the green the night before, after we had beaten Yale, and the smell of the wet fire still curled upward, sour and alien and faintly dangerous, and yet somehow good.

"I can see a hundred colors in the gray," Sarah said, leaning out alongside me. I rested my chin on the top of her head. "Rose and blue and green and violet and black and even yellow. Chrome yellow. Can't you? Princeton could never be just plain gray."

It had been the kind of weekend that I had envisioned whenever I thought "college" in my childhood. Disney might have created it, or rather, James Hilton, along with Mr. Chips. Sarah had flown in from Atlanta on Friday evening, on a big Delta DC-7, and I had borrowed Mac's Plymouth, so like my own Fury, and driven over and picked her up. As a junior, I was entitled to have the Fury with me now, but of course Lucy had taken care of that and so I was without wheels, and would remain so until I graduated, and even after. It did not particularly inconve-

nience me. I seldom left the campus except to go into New York
with Alan Greenfeld, my third suitemate from Holder, and we
took the PJ&B for that, and I almost never went home. An automobile could be borrowed from a Colonial member when necessary, as it had been today. I suppose my father would have
replaced the Fury for me if I had asked, and I am sure my mother
would have, but I did not. It did not seem important. As I have
said, the Fury always seemed more a part of Lucy than of me,
and I did not miss it.

I had dressed carefully for the trip to the airport in Philadelphia. We would be coming back for a cocktail party at Colonial,
and then I planned to take Sarah to Lahiere's for dinner, and
then we would come back again to the club and dance. The "big"
dance was Saturday night, with a jazz group from Eddie Condon's that someone's father had arranged for, and drinks and
a buffet for the alumni, but Friday would be in some ways better:
the living room darkened, the records long on slow, smoky ballads and short on rock 'n' roll, the members and their dates
locked together in the ritual swaying that had run through and
under and over so many of our diverse teens, a glinting common
thread.

I wore a light Harris Tweed jacket and a new white oxford
button-down from Langrock's, and white bucks, and gray flannel trousers. I knotted and reknotted a new Colonial tie until
I had it just right, and turned my head this way and that in the
dim, watery little mirror in my cubicle in the club, to see if Harold at the barbershop had taken too much off the top. It was
the era of crew cuts, but with my long fledgling hawk's face I
looked ridiculously like a molting bird in them, pink scalp shining through the blond, so I settled for a kind of short, smooth
helmet, as created for me by the resigned Harold. I was as close,
in those years, as I would ever come to being vain about my
looks.

I walked out of Colonial into the soft bronze sunlight of late
afternoon, jingling the keys to Mac's Plymouth and whistling
"Darktown Strutters' Ball," not at all unaware of the picture I
made on the veranda of the old columned clubhouse, on this old,
leaf-lit street of clubs and privilege and influence. The best so
far of young America, I thought mistily and insufferably smugly,
at play in the spring of youth after a week of preparing for the
service of the nation.

It was Princeton's primary skeletal bone, that notion of service; I had heard it since my first chapel service, and I bought
it instantly and openheartedly. Most of us then, I think, did.
There at that service I heard first the great prayer for Princeton:
" . . . And to all who work here and to all its graduates the world

wide give your guiding Spirit of sacrificial courage and loving service." Service. I loved it. I felt, on that October evening, that I could dedicate my life to it gladly. But first, I would go and pick up Sarah.

The old street was alive with young men like me, taking a breather from their sacrificial labors to slide into the drumbeat of the Yale weekend. On the verandas and steps of every club we stood, wellborn, well dowered, well dressed, well connected, well primed for our worlds, present and future. A few early-arriving girls stood with us, vivid in suits and twin sets against all the muted tweed and gray flannel, laughing the fruited laughs of youth and confidence and mastery.

All the clubs were out in force. They varied subtly in ethos and rank, these creamy bastions of casual privilege, but not a man on those verandas this autumn night felt himself completely untouched by the finger of God. Whether the others, the great submerged iceberg of Princeton, the independents, the grinds, the meatballs, felt that validating finger was a matter of the idlest speculation, because none of us on Prospect knew many of them. The eating clubs of Princeton are not and never pretended to be long on democracy and compassion; indeed, when Woodrow Wilson, who was then president of the university, outlawed fraternities, the clubs were what sprang up to replace them, and were essentially different only in name and degree.

But those of us who dwelled in the Eden of Prospect Street did not often consider the dichotomy between sacrificial service and the organized exclusion of outsiders. Even I, essentially an outsider from birth, was too warmed at the life-giving fire of exclusivity to let that worm emerge often from the golden apple. I had, after all, a bright heritage of privilege and exclusivity of my own. We all did. Consistent awareness would at that point have been asking, I think, a great deal.

Sarah got off the plane in Philadelphia looking every inch grown-up and wonderful in a dark red suit with a mouton collar, her swift smile and the red wool lighting her face like a candle. I kissed her on the cheek before speaking, trying to buy myself some time to assimilate the sheer strangeness of her. It was a thing that happened for the first few moments every time I saw Sarah in Princeton: Such a strangeness, an utter lack of context, surrounded her that I literally could not think who this small, radiant woman—for she was that, obviously—trotting on slender high heels to meet me might be. Sarah in the limbo of airports or railroad stations was not a part of the world I had left behind in Atlanta and not a part of the world of Princeton either, but an exquisitely carved small denizen of nowhere and everywhere.

I felt the satiny sheen of her cheek and smelled the clean,

soapy smell of her, and heard her hesitant "Hey, Shep," and all of a sudden she was Sarah, and a humming, sweet-fitting part of this new world, and I felt a surge of something near love that she could do that: be at once a part of both. I did not think anyone else from Buckhead could have managed it. Sometimes, when a fresh wonder emerged from the soil of this new Eastern world and caught me in surprise and delight, I instinctively turned to the shadow figures of Charlie or Lucy to tell them about it, and then realized, with a small sinking that was keenly physical, that they would not—could not—have understood. That they could not in any sense come into Princeton, as Sarah could, and share it with me. Charlie was too sunk in Atlanta and the South; Lucy in her own complex needs and soaring fancies, and her new insistence that the only Shep Bondurant she would acknowledge was the one of Peachtree Road and the great house on it.

But Sarah . . . Sarah walked regularly and effortlessly out of that world to go with me wherever I went, and the joy I took in her whenever she did it was, indeed, very near to a kind of love.

"Hey, Sarah," I said. And then, laughing, "Hey, Sarah Tolliver Cameron!"

At the dance that night she shimmered in her red and her joyful, unaffected Southernness, and the exotic dark birds from Radcliffe and Bryn Mawr and Sarah Lawrence and even Wellesley and Vassar paled in annoyed comparison. Everyone in Colonial, indeed everyone in all the clubs, could dance, but that night Sarah and I showed them what the dancing of the Atlanta Pinks and Jells could be, and it was something else entirely. I have never danced so long and so well and so effortlessly, and she matched me step for step, beat for beat, down to the smallest pause and pat and sway. We might have been hatched from a double-yolked egg; we held the floor for nearly an hour, ringed with clapping Colonials and scowling Seven Sisters. Margaret Bryan would have counted her life well spent if she could have seen us.

I have never known such exhilaration; I remember thinking, swinging Sarah into another endless chorus of "In the Mood," that A. J. Kemp had nothing on me. Vernon Castle didn't, Gene Kelly didn't, Fred Astaire didn't. As for Sarah, she might have been liquid poured from a golden ladle by a celestial hand: When we finished our exhibition, laughing and sweating, the entire club lined up to dance with her. She was still high on the night and the music and the approbation when I took her back to her room on the quiet street just off University Place, where the genteel old widow of a much-loved Romance languages professor let chaste rooms to visiting girls of good birth. I had found the old lady early in my freshman year, on Mac's recommendation, and had presented her for, and received, the approval of Ben and Dorothy Cameron, so that Sarah might visit as she liked. They placed no restrictions on her trips to Princeton; they had always trusted her, and did so completely, I think, with me. It was she herself who limited the visits to two or three a year.

"I don't want you to get tired of me," she said matter-of-factly, after her first visit, when I was a freshman and she was only sixteen. "And you will, if I'm up there every time you turn around. And then I need to keep my grades as high as I can, because I want to go to Paris to study at the Sorbonne for a year after college, and Mother and Daddy said I could if I kept up an A average through North Fulton and Scott. It would mean everything to my painting, Shep."

Now I lifted her small hands there in the shadows of the widow's front porch, and looked at them, and saw the faint lines of Prussian blue and alizarin crimson under her short nails, where no amount of turpentine and scrubbing could reach. Her hands were rough and warm and capable. Sarah would never have the slender, elegant fingers that were Lucy's, or the polished, perfect ovals that gleamed at the tips of the Radcliffe and Bryn Mawr fingers. I kissed first one hand and then the other.

"See you for breakfast, or do you want to sleep?"

"Are you kidding?" she said, beaming up in the dark. "Breakfast! And then . . . what? Is there some place here you can dance at nine o'clock in the morning?"

"No," I said, and kissed her mouth, feeling the shape of her laughter on it. "You can put some of that energy into a softball game. We've got a game with Ivy and their girls at ten."

"Watch out then, because I have a fast ball that's never been hit in recorded history," she said, turning and walking to the door. And then she ran back and flung her arms around me and hugged me hard, and when I looked down into her face, tears glinted in her shadowed eyes, even though she was smiling.

"Oh, Shep," she said, "I'm just so happy."

And before I could reply, she was gone into the house of the widow. I watched until the dim downstairs light went out and one went on in an upstairs window, and then I walked back up University and picked up McCosh Walk and went across the sleeping campus under a high, white-sailing moon to Washington Road, turning onto Prospect across from the dark bulk of 1879. This time I whistled a tune that shivered with resonances out of Atlanta and the endless, Byzantine dances of the Pinks and the Jells: "It must have been moonglow . . . way up in the blue . . . it must have been moonglow . . . that moonglow gave me you."

I was asleep the instant my head hit the thin inherited pillow in my cubbyhole at Colonial.

We dived into Saturday and whirled through it as we had the dancing on Friday night. The day was a glory, perfect in itself. The sun rose gentle and stayed so. A small wind redolent of the faraway ocean and the nearer, sun-warmed pine forests blew upon us until sunset. We won the softball game with Ivy and the football game with Yale, and the night air at the bonfire afterward, on Cannon Green, had been balmy enough for beer jackets and shirtsleeves and cardigans. We whooped and yelled before the leaping flames and shadows, and then walked around the campus in the moonlight, dimming by then with the fast-scudding clouds from the west that came in freighted with rain. Someone, some group—not the Nasoons, I know, but almost as good—was singing under Blair Arch, and a crowd had gathered to listen. We paused for a moment.

" . . . situated and saturated in New Jer*see*," they sang. And then, "Going back, going back, going back to Nassau Hall. Going back, going back . . ."

The crowd joined in, Sarah and I with them. She had learned the Princeton songs early.

"We'll clear the track as we go back," we sang, our voices spiraling up into the far shadows of the old stone arch. "Going back to Nassau Hall. . . ."

I sensed rather than saw Sarah's tears, and turned.

"If you say one word to me," she whispered fiercely, moonlit tracks on her wet face, "I'm going back to my room and stay there until time to go home tomorrow."

I did not. I merely squeezed her hand and bellowed my way into the next offering, thinking, but only very dimly, how fortunate I was to be standing here in this place, on this night, with, beside me, a small, greathearted girl who would weep for the beauty of Princeton.

I wish that I had thought it more clearly.

We went on then, back to Colonial for cocktails and the alumni buffet, and danced again, far into the evening, to the trio from Eddie Condon's, and I kissed Sarah again before the widow's dark house, a longer and deeper kiss this time, and this time it was not she but I who disengaged us and gently steered her up the steps and into the house. I think I could have known all there was to know of Sarah's small body and vivid heart that night, but something in me wanted almost desperately to keep the surface and the tenor of the night as the day had been: all of a piece, evenly weighted, perfect. I remember thinking as I hurried back across McCosh Walk, this time jogging to beat the beginning rain, that Sarah and I had all the time in the world.

Now, in two hours at best, it would be time to take her back to the Philadelphia airport. I thought that we would go and have some lunch at Lahiere's again, and then maybe drift down and watch the 150-pound boats practicing for the Ivy League regattas on Lake Carnegie, but I stayed where I was, forearms on the thick stone sill of Dub Vanderkellen's window, looking out over the campus. A small break in the scudding clouds spilled a ray of pale sun onto the spires of the chapel and the library. A black, sideways-loping campus dog larruped maniacally into a pile of yellow leaves and scattered them, a miniature golden tornado in the gray morning, and then loped away toward who knows what doggy destination. I was not even aware that I was smiling until Sarah's finger traced my mouth.

"I can see why you love it so," she said. "It's like a movie, isn't it? Not completely real. Like a book."

She was right on both counts. There was, for me, a powerful and seductive storybook perfection about Princeton that nothing—not the gray sludge of February or the endless cold rains of March or the suffocating damp heat of late May and early September; not the real inequities of the caste system or the imagined vengefulness of some of the Irish and Italian proctors; not the endless mashed potatoes in Commons or the anxiety of Bicker or the aching humiliation of not being asked to be part of an ironbound or getting the bid to Cottage or Ivy that you wanted; not even the two suicides in anonymous, below-the-salt dorm rooms over the Christmas holidays that happened while I was there—ever spoiled for me. I think I was one of the few people to graduate from Princeton fully as smitten as the day I entered. It seemed the first thing in my life that was just as it should have been; that fulfilled its promises, that was mine alone. Even 2500 Peachtree Road, even the summerhouse, had been partly Lucy's. Princeton was the one great love in my life that I never had to share.

And I loved the world around it. New York, of course: visiting Alan Greenfeld's family in their cavernous, dark old apartment on the Upper West Side, with the severe Bauhaus furniture, listening to the first real intellectual and liberal political talk I had ever heard at a family table, then going on with Alan to meet our blind dates (Sarah Lawrence and Jewish, pale and interesting) under the clock at the Biltmore, and then out into that peculiarly Manhattan blue-purple that always, to me, seemed to be a November twilight. The Taft Grill, Peacock Alley, Café Society Downtown, Eddie Condon's Basin Street East, the Village

Vanguard, the Five Note, the Village Gate. Jazz pouring wild and free, honey and smoke, seemingly endless Manhattans. Perhaps, after we had seen the girls to their train, Roseland, where a dime-a-dance girl, beautiful in every way to my eager-to-be-jaded eyes, once asked me, "What's your tie? That's Cap, isn't it? I bet you were Lawrenceville."

"How'd you know?" I asked, blushing at the lie.

And back again the next weekend, on the early train from the PJ&B to Penn Station, or to Philadelphia's Thirtieth Street Station for the Penn game, or Bryn Mawr. . . .

Or, sometimes, to some age-blurred, fortresslike house in Bronxville or Old Saybrook or Short Hills or Bucks County, for more intoxicating talk about books and music and art and theater and national politics (this time, conservative) with the parents of friends, parents who seemed to perceive me as an equal, parents who had so little in common with any I knew in Atlanta save, perhaps, Ben and Dorothy Cameron that they might have been from another planet.

And always, New York. It lay there just out of reach, physically and chronologically just beyond Princeton, a promise in itself, a continuum. It meant that the new enchantment would not end with graduation, but would only enlarge, expand, ripen and bloom. After Princeton, this.

I found the Firestone Library early on. Besides Lucy and Sarah, there was one other meeting in my life that changed the shape and direction of it, and it was with that great, spired eminence, not two decades old but with the look of ages about its splendid bulk, even then the largest open-stack research library in the world. There was never any doubt in my dazzled mind, when I first set foot in it, that it was mine alone. After my initial visit to Firestone, when I was not eating or sleeping or in classes or at Colonial or spending a weekend in New York or, far more rarely, with Sarah, I was immersed in it.

I took to independent study and research like a long-landlocked duck to water, and immediately changed my major from political science to history, with a minor in English literature, as the discipline that allowed the most time for submerging myself in Firestone. I would, I thought, when I did think, get myself some sort of job in New York after graduation that allowed pure, cloistered research—a museum, a historical foundation of some sort, not more than an hour's drive from Firestone—and after that, perhaps I might teach, at some fine, small New England school or college that had its own first-rate library. I did not in the least mind the reality of low pay and obscurity for the rest of my life. My heart had found its watershed, my mind its manna.

Now I looked over at Sarah. The weak sun sidled repentantly in through the infamous Vanderkellen window and caught her face and hair and the deep, rich cranberry of her cashmere sweater. She had pinned on the orange chrysanthemum with the little gold football and the orange and black ribbons I had given her yesterday for the game, and it should have looked awful with the deep red, but it didn't. Sarah in the new sunlight looked made of light and fire and flowers. She grinned.

"I expect Mickey Mouse to lead a locomotive right down Nassau in one minute," she said. "Or to see a unicorn grazing on the green."

"I know," I said. "I feel the same way about it. It's wonderful, it's idyllic, but what does it have to do with the real world? Will it even work in the real world?"

"Who cares if it's make-believe, so long as it works for you?" she said.

"Not me," I said. "So far it's working just fine. Maybe I'm not real myself, and that's why it fits so well."

"None of you are," she said, the grin deepening. "Not anybody I've met at Princeton is . . . oh, I don't know; totally real. You're all alike somehow, as different as you all are. Such innocents."

"Dub Vanderkellen is an innocent? Grunt Grady is an innocent?"

"I mean . . . it's like Peter Pan. You're like the legion of lost boys up here, all hidden away up here in this wonderful boys' world."

"I'm not sure that's so good," I said, frowning. I wasn't. Innocent? Lost boys? "Besides, who's calling who innocent?"

"Whatever else it is, it's awfully attractive," she said, ignoring that last. "It makes me wish I could be part of it, a real part."

"You are," I said.

She was . . . and not, perhaps, in a way she would have liked. I was aware, as dimly as I was about everything in that time, that Sarah herself was a part of the seduction, the sorcery of Princeton, and as such, was a part of the make-believe. I knew that our relationship was a light, shadowless, Technicolor college love, without anguish or anger or pain or sweat, and certainly without much physical fulfillment. Oh, we necked a great deal: kissed, petted, even, and we found it very good indeed. But somehow I did not, then, need to take it any further. Not in those pregnancy-haunted years. Not with Sarah. When she pulled herself away, saying, as she always did, "We really shouldn't, Shep. Not yet," I did not press her. I could have had her at almost any time; I know that now. But: Time, I thought, we have all the time we want.

Sometimes, though rarely, I thought past the shadowy museum in New York and would envision, as if through a scrim of peace and pleasure, a small house somewhere on an Eastern campus and myself, in dilapidated slippers and elbow-patched cardigan, reading in a book-strewn library while a slim, sweatered woman poured amber sherry into delicate old glasses on a silver tray beside a fire, humming Vivaldi as she did so. She looked a great deal as I thought Sarah would in some years, and though I did not pursue this, still it gave me the same obscure and warming comfort the entire vision did. The whole scene seemed welcoming, comfortable, dense and rich; it fit like a perfect skin. Once or twice it crossed my mind that that was what the life I had left back home on Peachtree Road should have offered me, as heir of that house, but the thought was without pain or bitterness, and I did not harbor it long.

For now, and here in this wondrous place, I had Sarah. When she was not with me, days and sometimes a week would pass without my thinking of her, and that did not seem to me strange, either. Our closeness was born of Princeton, not Atlanta, and when she *was* here she occupied me totally. There was no real conclusion in sight for us, and none was needed—for me. That there was for her I could not see; she demanded nothing of me, then or ever. I wish she had. My Princeton fugue drowned out, then, the rare and beautiful melody that had been given to me long ago.

We went out into the brightening day and walked across Nassau Street to lunch. She did not want to go to Lahiere's, but instead to the Nassau Tavern, so we sat in the cool, subterranean dimness with the carved lives thick around us and ate cheeseburgers and drank coffee. Norman Rockwell's Yankee Doodle mural and Dick Kazmaier and Hobey Baker stared down at us. Somebody punched Bing Crosby on the jukebox—"I give to you, and you give to me . . . true love, true love"—and we held hands across the table.

"Will I see you anytime soon?" I said.

"How should I know?" she said. "You don't ever come home."

"I'll come for the Harvest Ball and for a day or two at Christmas," I said. "Mac wants me to go skiing at Stowe with him and Brad over New Year's. They're taking dates; want to come?"

"I can't," she said. "You know there's all that stuff, all those parties. I was hoping you'd be home to take me."

It was the year of her debut, and after the great June ball at the Piedmont Driving Club there was all the furor of the Little Season in the summer, and the Harvest Ball at Thanksgiving, and parties again at Christmas. There would, I knew, be parties every night through December, and often in the afternoons as well.

"You know why I don't come home, Sarah," I said. "You know what it's like with my father now. I'll be home for the Harvest Ball; I said I would. Let Charlie take you to the others. He'd carry you on his back barefoot in a snowstorm to every one of them, if you wanted him to."

"Don't make fun of Charlie," she said crisply. "He's very dear, and he's constant. Charlie is *there*, Shep."

"I wasn't making fun of him," I said. "And I'm there, too, when it counts. I'm there when it's you. I came for your senior prom."

"Yes," she said. Her eyes were on the furry old carvings in the tabletop. "But you didn't come for graduation. And you said you would."

We were both silent, and then she lifted her head.

"I'm sorry," she said. "I'm nagging, and I swore I never would. Lord, I sound like Freddie Slaton. It didn't matter about graduation. Not to me. I don't know about Lucy."

So here it was.

It burst over me then, the surging, deep-buried sense of the absent one, she who was not here and yet was most powerfully here; she about whom our elaborate silences had rung loudly: Lucy.

Lucy.

Yes, I had gone to Sarah's senior prom, which was also Lucy's, the previous spring but not, as I had promised, to their graduation.

And yes, I think it had, for a little while, mattered a great deal to Lucy that I had not. But only for a little while.

After that night, even I could see why Sarah did not mention Lucy to me in any of the letters she wrote me at Princeton, and why she had not during this autumn weekend. If the incident on the Chattahoochee River bridge had not drawn the battle lines between them clearly, those last moments on the dance floor at Brookhaven did—and for all the assembled Pinks and Jells of a generation to witness.

It was Sarah's way to go to earth with her deepest emotions; Dorothy had taught her that trick early and well. I knew that she would not speak of that night, or of Lucy, again unless forced to. I was less clear as to why I could not do it. There was a real and acknowledged alienation between Lucy and me now, and part of my silence was anger and grief. That much I could own. The part that felt so like fear I could not, and so, like Sarah, I thrust that deep.

"You couldn't be like Freddie Slaton if you tried," I said. "But what you could be is late for your plane, if we don't get going. You ready?"

"Yes," she said. "Shep?"

"Hmmm?"

"I don't think there's ever been a more perfect weekend in the history of the world."

"I don't either," I said. "Never better. First of many. First of very many."

"Yes," Sarah said.

CHAPTER
TWELVE

WHEN I CAME INTO THE PEACHTREE ROAD HOUSE on that Friday afternoon the previous May, for Sarah and Lucy's senior prom, only my mother had come running downstairs to greet me, and for a moment the strangeness of coming out of Princeton and into this echoing world of my childhood kept me off-balance, so that I was not completely sure who this dark, lissome woman whose arms bound me so tightly might be, and stepped back a fraction.

It was a near-infinitesimal drawing away, but enough to make her tighten her arms and bury her face in my neck, and begin to weep. My mother did not often weep, and her tears appalled me then as they always had. I patted her awkwardly and hugged her as hard as I could will my muscles to do.

"I've lost you, just like I knew I would," she wept into my new Brooks oxford cloth. "I knew if you left you'd never really come back to me. Oh, Sheppie, you pulled away from me!"

"No, I didn't, Mother," I said, still patting industriously. I thought she had lost weight; I could feel the ribs under the silk of her blouse, and the hammering of her heart. She had changed her scent; a muskier and more assertive one rose out of her inky hair to assail me.

"It's just that you looked so young in this light; I thought you were Lucy running down the stairs."

"Oh . . . Lucy!" she said in exasperation, but I could tell she was pleased. She pulled away from me and tilted her head as she looked at me, preening. "Lucy doesn't run down these stairs, she sneaks up them—at four in the morning. She as good as lives

234

with that Chastain creature now; God knows where they go. We never see her."

I felt the faintest stab of something; the old Lucy-thrust. I don't know why my mother's words surprised me. I knew that Lucy was as deeply involved with Red Chastain as ever; my few brief visits home over the past two years and my mother's letters confirmed that. Lucy herself, during the rare moments we had been together, had been airy and chattering and almost completely withdrawn from me. I thought that she was still angry and hurt with me for going away to Princeton; her behavior was almost exactly as it had been in the last days after my own graduation from North Fulton, when she had let me leave without saying good-bye.

All right, I had thought then, I'll play it her way. I don't owe her an apology for going away to school. She can come to me or we can just go on this way forever, I don't care. I did, of course, but could not admit it. Lucy's defection into the arms of all those Jells, and finally into Red's, had gone deep with me.

I had thought, though, that Princeton and my new closeness to Sarah had healed the wound. And they had, or nearly. This stab was just that: a knife flick, tiny and delicate, and then gone.

"Let me look at you," my mother said, and did. I had not seen her since the previous summer; I had spent holidays with Mac or Alan, and had gone with Haynes Potter and his family to their place in the Berkshires for Christmas.

Her eyes misted again, and there was something in them—a tiny point of light—that looked oddly like triumph.

"There's nothing left of my boy," she said. "It's all man now. All man and all Bondurant. It's almost uncanny. Your father will be livid."

"I should think it might please him that I look like him," I said, surprised at the hurt that her words engendered. My father had lost the power to hurt me while I was safely ensconced in Firestone and Colonial, but pain bit at me now, tiny and snakelike, under his roof.

"Oh no," she said, smiling silkily. "Wrong Bondurant, you see."

I did.

"Where is Dad?" I said, too casually. "Where's Lucy? And Aunt Willa?"

"Your father is playing golf up at Highlands," she said neutrally, as if we both did not know that my father kept as far away from the house on Peachtree Road as he could when I was in it.

"He'll be back Sunday before you go. He wants to see you.

Lucy is out with Red Chastain, of course, doing whatever it is that they do. And Willa is on a buying trip to New York, believe it or not. They actually made the creature head buyer for the lingerie department, and she's gone up to load Rich's up with Yankee underwear. Come have a glass of iced tea with me and tell me all your news."

"Well, I thought I'd run over and see Sarah a minute . . . " I said.

"Oh, of course, Sarah," said my mother. She did not say it as icily as she might. My strengthened alliance with the house of Cameron pleased her mightily, I knew. Besides, she liked Sarah. All the women in her crowd did. Sarah had a manner with older women that was respectful but not deferential, and she was genuinely knowledgeable about the things that mattered to them: porcelains, English antiques, genealogy, who was who in and around Atlanta. "Nothing but refeened ass kissing," Lucy called it. Sarah herself called it her "biddy routine."

I moved toward the telephone under the stairwell, and at that moment Lucy burst into the house and threw her arms around me with such force that we both stumbled. My mother sniffed and retreated upstairs. Outside on the circular driveway I heard Red Chastain's MG burring away, out into the traffic on Peachtree Road.

As remote as she had been before, she was immediate now, hugging me enormously with arms that I remembered and yet did not, laughing and crying at the same time, her face buried in the hollow of my neck where it just fit, smelling of the heart-tuggingly familiar Tabu, feeling marrow-stirringly like . . . Lucy. I felt the constraint of the past two years drain away as if it had never been, and was instantly and in every way home. I held her away by her shoulders, and looked into her face, and knew that I had Lucy—the Lucy of my childhood, the gay and brave companion, the radiant enabler, the Scheherazade, the magical Elaine to my Lancelot—back again. I kissed her on the cheek and swung her around, and set her down on the tiles of the foyer. I had forgotten how tall she was, and how slim: Her dark blue eyes were almost level with mine, and I could have lifted her with one arm. And I had forgotten the sheer, electric impact of her. The same invisible but palpable implosion that I always felt on seeing her after an absence radiated out in the air around her. At eighteen, Lucy Bondurant was quite simply splendid.

"You look great," I said ineffectually.

"So do you," she said. "You've changed. I like it. You remind me of somebody, but I can't put my finger on it. . . . Tab Hunter, maybe, but with a hawk's nose. . . . Oh well, it'll come to me."

I was astounded that she could not put a name to the likeness she saw in me, but she could not, not then or ever. I think she was unable to in many more ways than one.

"You'll stop traffic tomorrow night," I said. "Are you going with Red, or is that a silly question?"

"Who else?" she said. "I won't have much more time with him. His dad got him into Princeton, *finally,* after making him spend this whole last year at North Georgia, and says he can kiss the family loot good-bye unless he toes the line up there. Translated, that means I can't go up and visit him until at least his junior year, and he can't come home except at Christmas and for a week in the summers. Mr. Chastain likes me, but he knows me pretty well, and Red too. He's already talked to Mama about it. She says she'll jerk me out of Scott the instant I get off the plane if I sneak off and go. They both mean it, I'm afraid."

"You mean he won't be here for your debut?" I said.

"I'm not making my debut," she said, grinning at me.

"The shit you say!" I exclaimed, aghast. "You *have* to, Lucy!"

It was the reflexive Buckhead Jell talking, through and through. My reversion had been almost instantaneous. For Lucy to miss that gilded autumn rite of passage was as unthinkable as her bowing to Old Atlanta buck naked. It was the beginning of everything for the Buckhead girls and their boys, that one grand November night at the Piedmont Driving Club, the Harvest Ball. From there the girls would move on as inexorably as figures on a Swiss clock through the prescribed stations of the Atlanta social cross: Christmas dance, Bal de Salut, Rabun Gap–Nacoochee Guild, Tallulah Falls Circle, Cotillion, Music Club, Piedmont Ball, and on into the endless pantheon of charities and auxiliaries, each with its crowded and glittering social calendar, and its ceaseless volunteer labor.

It would launch us, too, the brothers and suitors and husbands-to-be of those carefully tended blossoms, into our own fixed trajectories: From the escort lists of half a hundred mothers in and out of the South, we would go on into the Nine O'Clocks and the German Club and the Benedicts and the Racket Club and so on and so forth, ending up in the Driving Club and Capital City and Brookhaven and at the heads of those myriad charities and committees whose balls our wives chaired, and from there on into the service of the city. It was the one true way and the one true path. Nobody of substance did it any other way.

A thought sandbagged me. Would they dare, even to Lucy Bondurant?

"You don't mean to tell me you didn't get into the club?" I goggled. Saint Shep the Defender leaped out of his moldy cave, snatched his rusty armor and scrambled to buckle it on. I would have a full complement of carefully waved, blue-rinsed heads for this.

"Oh, don't be dumb, of course I got into the club," Lucy said. "They wouldn't dare not ask me, while I'm living in Uncle Sheppard's house, anyway. I didn't join, that's all. Holy shit, Gibby, you should have seen Mother's face when I told her. And your father's, for that matter. You'd have thought I'd said I was going to marry a nigger at Saint Philip's on Easter Sunday. Mama still isn't speaking to me, and I don't think your daddy is, either. I haven't really seen him since then. The only reason I'm walking around free is that your mother told them to lay off me. She said she thought I'd made the right decision, under the circumstances. Trust Aunt Olivia to do the right thing."

Her smile had nothing in it of mirth.

"What circumstances?" I said dimly.

"Jesus, Gibby, are they giving you stupid pills along with the saltpeter up there in Boys' Town? The Red Chastain circumstances, of course. Why should I come out? I've been about as out as a girl can get for two years now. Aunt Olivia wasn't born yesterday."

"You mean, because you're . . ."

"Sleeping with him," she said sweetly. Her smile burned almost through me to the bone. The radiance in the air around her was, all of a sudden, too bright. Her eyes glittered with more than high spirits and joy at seeing me. I felt, then, the million little knife edges that hedged her in.

"The Dirty Deed, the Black Act. Fucking. You have, I trust, heard of fucking? Though I don't suppose for a minute that you and the Divine Sarah have—"

"Well, God, you surely aren't the only girl in Atlanta who ever made her debut as anything less than a virgin," I said hastily.

"No, but I'm probably the only girl in Atlanta who got caught in the act on the pool table in the men's grill at Brookhaven by the greens committee," she said.

"Christ, you don't mean . . ."

"Yes, I do. In midhump, as it were. Doing it like a mink. It's the only time I've ever known Red not to be able to finish what he started."

I knew that she was trying, for some reason, to shock me, but I also knew that she was telling the truth. I had an infallible radar when it came to Lucy's lying. This was no lie. I was silent.

"Don't worry, Gibby," she said. "You don't have to save me

from this one. I would have absolutely *hated* all that charity and volunteer shit. And I've saved your folks a ton of money. Little Lady's coming right along behind me, you know, and it's going to take a mint to bring her out. No, tomorrow night is my debut. Wait'll you see my dress. I'm flat going to scald some eyeballs."

She was right. Traditionally, the girls at North Fulton wore flounced and ruffled pastel hoopskirts to their senior proms, but when she came down the beautiful old staircase the next evening, before Red came to pick her up, Lucy was in white silk, as fluid and sweetly poured over her luminous slenderness as a column of cream, and her shoulders gleamed absolutely naked and pearled with youth and powder. She wore no jewelry, but had brushed her shoulder-length pageboy until it flew like dark thistledown around her narrow head, and in her hair she had fastened three perfect white gardenias from the bush in the garden outside the summerhouse. The dress was slit up to midthigh on one side, and one impossibly long leg, a pale satin-brown from the spring sun, glimmered in and out. She wore white high-heeled sandals and carried a little silver envelope. The only color in all that incandescent black and white was the red of her soft mouth, a translucent scarlet stain, as if she had been eating berries, or drinking blood. She gave off her own light, there in the dim foyer. I turned from adjusting my black tie in the ormolu hall mirror and stared at her. I could not have spoken. There wasn't, on this night, anything else to be said about Lucy James Bondurant. No other girl at the prom would even be noticed.

She smiled. And then she came a few little running steps down the last of the stairs and into my arms, and I swung her around again, and she was laughing, laughing with a kind of fierce joy.

"Oh, Gibby," she said. "I thought you never *would* come home again!"

"I thought you didn't want me to," I said, setting her down.

"Well, I was being silly; I thought you'd know that. You always did. But anyway, here you are, and now everything's going to be all right."

"What's going to be all right? What's wrong?" I said, my ears pricking.

"Nothing, now that you're here. Absolutely nothing at all. Here, fasten these for me, will you? Aren't they sweet?"

She handed me a string of pearls, still warm from the cup of her hand, and turned to face the mirror and lifted her heavy dark hair with both hands. I fastened the strand. They were beautiful, small and perfectly matched.

"From your daddy," she said. "Before, I might add, he knew that I wouldn't be coming out. I offered to give them back, but he said no, of course to keep them. So I did. I ain't no fool."

I heard the deep, powerful purr of a great engine on the driveway, and cocked an eyebrow at her.

"Red's got his daddy's Rolls tonight," she said. "I told him I wasn't going a step out of this house if he came in that fucking MG."

She looked into the mirror at our heads, one fair, one ebony, close together.

"Aren't we a matched pair, though?" she said. "We look like an ad for . . . oh, I don't know, something rich and wonderful. Like we couldn't possibly have anything but the most perfect life in the world. It should be you taking me to this thing tonight, you know, Gibby."

"I'm no match for Prince Charming Chastain, Luce," I said. "You'd make me miserable flirting your head off and going outside to neck or worse with everybody under ninety. But he knows how to control you."

"Yes, he does," she said, and her smile was gone. "That's why I hang on to him, you know. He's a mean bastard, really, but he wrote the book on control."

Shem brought the Fury, waxed and humming, around to the front of the house and I drove around the corner to Muscogee to pick up Sarah. She was still upstairs dressing, but Amos showed me into the little den at the back of the house, where Dorothy Cameron was watching television alone. It had been a day of thunderstorms and high winds, and another storm was grinding through, peppering the black window glass with driving rain, splitting the lashing trees with lightning.

Dorothy kissed me and indicated the chair where Ben usually sat.

"You'll have to get up when he comes, because he won't sit anywhere else, but right now he's out in the kitchen toasting some cheese sandwiches," she said. "Would you like a drink?"

"I guess not," I said. "It's going to be a long night."

"Then come and tell me all about Lucy," she said. There was more than prurient interest in her severe, beautiful face: I knew she had always been genuinely concerned about Lucy.

"Well, it's just that she didn't want to make her debut, and I can't say that I blame her," I said defensively. "What kind of a life is that for a woman, really, all that volunteering and do-gooding? There's so much more an intelligent woman could be doing—"

And then I remembered that she had been voted Woman of the Year by the American Red Cross for her volunteer work at

Grady Hospital, and I flushed a dull, hot red. "I didn't mean you. . . ."

She laughed. "I know you didn't. But tell me. If we volunteers didn't do the things we do, who do you think would do them?"

"Maybe somebody with fewer talents," I said. "Somebody who didn't have so much else to give somewhere else. Look at you. You could have been a great chief operating officer, a chairman of the board, or a doctor, or . . . whatever you wanted to be. Anything. You didn't have to *give* it away."

"And how many lifetimes would all that have taken?" she said, smiling affectionately at me, as she had when I was an outspoken little boy. "No, Shep, it's the only decent thing to do with prestige and privilege, with money. People without those things don't have the resources or the drive to get done what needs doing. It's poverty that corrupts the will and energy, not wealth."

"Well," I said, "but what about all those women who don't want to do the charity bit? The ones like Lucy, who want to be something else, something more, and have the gifts for it?"

She nodded. "They're the casualties in this particular time and place," she said. "Ambition and difference—they're the two things the rest of us women won't tolerate. We punish them. Maybe it reminds us of what we didn't do. Lucy is going to be punished for this free-spirited little decision of hers, if not now, then later. She's a casualty, whether she knows it or not. Now ambition for a man, for her husband, that's a different matter."

"If you're so wise, why don't I feel better about this whole thing?" I said.

"I suspect it's because you see a truth that's under the truth I'm talking about. I think you always could do that, Shep. Be careful with it—we'll probably try to punish you for it, too."

"Who's going to punish who for what?" Ben Cameron said, coming into the room with a tray bearing two melted cheese sandwiches and two tall glasses of pale beer. "Hi, stranger. Good to see you."

"I am you, if you spill that beer," Dorothy Cameron said, rising to take the tray from him, and he came to me and put his arms around me and hugged me as naturally as if I had been young Ben. I felt a powerful tide of warmth toward him. He was, as Sarah said later of Charlie, constant. He had always been all I had known of fatherly affection.

"It's a real change to see your ugly face around here," he said, one arm still around my shoulders. "All we ever see is Charlie Gentry. I asked Dottie the other night if he'd moved in with us."

I laughed. I knew and Ben knew that Sarah dated Charlie when I was not at home largely because he and Dorothy insisted that she see other boys, feeling that she was far too young for an exclusive relationship. Charlie knew it, too; he had said to me the last time I was home, "She'd drop me in a minute if you'd crook your little finger." He said it matter-of-factly and without a trace of rancor on his sweet, freckled face. "But hell, I don't care. You aren't going to do that, apparently, fool that you are. And a little of Sarah is better than none."

I believe that Ben and Dorothy always knew where their daughter's heart lay, long before I did, and they approved, if only tacitly, our relationship. Dorothy as much as said so that night.

"I'm eternally grateful that I'm past all that social folderol and can stay home and watch *Gunsmoke,*" she said, smiling at me. "It's a foul night. I'm glad it's you taking Sarah. I don't worry about her when she's with you."

"That may not be all that flattering to Shep," Ben said, the gray eyes twinkling. There were new lines etched in the thin skin under them, and the hints of pouches, as if he were very tired, and I thought he looked much older, and somehow extremely formidable. I remember that Sarah had said he was becoming active in Atlanta politics—not a normal thing for a man of his station—and I could see, suddenly, that he would make a leader to be reckoned with, for all his boneless ease and Celtic whimsy.

"Shep knows what I mean," Dorothy Cameron said. "He isn't like the others, nice boys that they are. You say the same thing yourself, so don't leer at me, Ben Cameron."

"I think I'd better get out of here before you turn my head," I said, grinning back at her. I was very flattered, and tried not to show it.

"I wish I could," she said. "I'll bet nobody has ever really tried. You deserve to have your head turned a little, Shep."

Sarah came into the room then, vivid as a zinnia in warm coral tulle, and I smiled involuntarily at the goodness of the way she looked. We hugged, stiffly and self-consciously, and said our good nights to Dorothy and Ben, and by eight o'clock we were bowling out Peachtree Road in the last of the evening rain toward Brookhaven and the North Fulton senior prom. I was eager, excited, even. I had seen few of the Pinks and the Jells in two years.

They were all there, drifting and settling and eddying away again like migratory swallows. The old ballroom shimmered with crepe paper and lanterns and a spinning colored spotlight, and the band—a second-echelon but well-regarded rock 'n' roll group out of Nashville—was thumping and gyrating into its first number. A few couples were on the floor, and others were detaching themselves from small groups and sliding out into the music. It was steady and insinuating, but not frenzied, as it would be later in the evening, and I swung Sarah into an easy jitterbug, hoping to get in a respectable quota of dancing before the real madness started. I never learned to do the aggressive, sensual, pelvis-snapping rock steps of that time, and was grateful that Sarah's bursting dance card would keep her on the floor as long as she wanted. I knew that she would be content to sit out most of the howling, insistent numbers—or go outside to the terrace with me. Sarah could do the beach-bop business of the fifties as faultlessly as she could do anything with her elegant little body, but her soul, like mine, shied away from it.

It might have been my own senior prom, not Sarah and Lucy's, there was, on the surface, so little sense of time passed and change happened. The original core group of us was there in the familiar formations: Sarah and me, Ben and Julia, Snake and Lelia, Pres and Sarton Foy, looking even plainer and more aristocratic than ever, Tom and Freddie Slaton. A.J. had brought a stunningly pretty pink and white-blond senior from Washington Seminary, who looked all evening like a white baroness captured by Amazonian pygmies, and Charlie was, as usual, stag.

On closer examination, there were a few surface transmutations, many of them merely a deepening of the small stigmata already laid down: Ben Cameron was now so brilliantly animated that his old, quick grace seemed flamboyant and theatrical; Charlie's sweet, shambling pragmatism had deepened almost into phlegm; the anxious discontent in Freddie's sharp little eyes had atrophied into darting malice. And despite the first-glance sameness of the setting and the dress and the players in this stylized masque, there hung about it, for me, a profound strangeness which lay just below the surface of the night. It was not the old sense of unreality I remembered from my earliest days at the dances of the Pinks and the Jells, but a keen aura of impermanence, so that I almost expected the entire scene to slide away into the wings, like a lavish set from an opera, and some other, utterly unimaginable set to come grinding out. Two years had altered me irrevocably, if not the others.

Lucy and Red Chastain were nowhere to be seen.

By intermission the evening was in full, sweating cry, and we Buckhead Boys drifted out into the parking lot with our dates and sat on the bumper and fenders of A.J.'s newest vehicle, a 1938 Cadillac hearse so vast and shining and massive that it resembled a lava rock atoll. A.J. had brought grape juice and a bag of ice and Ben Cameron had vodka, and we sat drinking Purple Passion in the still-wet parking lot under a slim silver moon, the piercing fragrance of honeysuckle and mimosa from the lawns of the big houses on West Brookhaven washing across to us on the still air. I hated the thick, cloying taste of the drink, and I think most of us did, but we drank from the thermos top that A.J. passed around as deeply and solemnly as if it had been a communion chalice. I think we all knew, that night, that it was just that, and that this was in all likelihood our last communion.

Out here in the dark, change, endings, little dyings quivered in the air around us like a silent detonation, even more powerfully than in the last few days of my senior year at North Fulton, for now, after this upcoming graduation, the girls—the glue that had held us together since birth—would be dispersing, too. We boys had, two years before, moved out into our own arenas: I to Princeton; Ben into the architectural school at Georgia Tech; Snake into premed at Emory; A.J. downtown to the Atlanta Division of the University of Georgia; Pres Hubbard to the university itself, over at Athens; Tom Goodwin to his father's school, Sewanee; Charlie into prelaw at Emory. But, except for me, we had stayed close to Atlanta, or at least within a couple of hours' driving distance.

The girls were different. Only two of them—Sarah and Lucy, who would enter Agnes Scott College in Decatur—would be staying in Atlanta after this summer. Julia Randolph planned to go to Auburn with three of her Washington Seminary classmates, Lelia Blackburn was slated for Sweet Briar, Sarton Foy would follow her female ancestors into Wellesley and Freddie Slaton was being shipped off to Pine Manor Junior College in the dim parental hope that separation from Tom would dull some of her gnawing hungers and proximity to Boston would burnish some of her razor edges. We would come back together again, of course, at holidays and summer vacations, and in the endless formal patterns of the great Atlanta social quadrille that we were entering, but after tonight a flawless surface would be ruptured, a perfect wholeness opened and corrupted, and we knew it. The Purple Passion made several more rounds than it might have ordinarily.

A tootling fusillade of rock music from the old stone clubhouse signaled the band's return, and we slid down off the hearse and began to move toward it, walking slowly and in pairs, arm in arm. I remember that the moonlight lay so dense and shadowless over the surging hills of the golf course that it looked bathed in some ancient, awful silver sun, and the smell of mimosa was heartbreaking. Just as Sarah and I gained the door, a scream of

engine and tires broke the thick night behind us, and we turned
to see Red Chastain's father's black Rolls careen into the parking
lot, rocking viciously on two tires. We all stood still, waiting for
Red and Lucy to get out of the car and come toward us, but they
did not. Rock music louder than that inside the club blared out
of the Rolls's open windows, and over it we could hear the sound
of Red's voice, and then Lucy's, raised in a furious quarrel.

"Trouble in paradise," A.J. said.

"Oh, just a little lovers' spat, probably." Snake grinned.
"Maybe we ought to go throw cold water on them."

"Are they fussing, Shep?" Freddie asked, sweetly and avidly.
"I heard they've been fussing all spring over Lucy running
around with Mr. Cameron's Negro houseboy, or whatever he
is. Poor thing. I heard Red told her he'd take his pin back if she
didn't stop. And she didn't, because I saw them out in the Camerons' side yard the other day when I drove by there."

She looked brightly at me, her red head cocked like a mali-
cious little bird's, and in that moment I truly hated her. Freddie
Slaton would always peck delicately at pain and trouble like a
vulture in offal.

"I don't have the slightest idea, Freddie," I said. "I've barely
seen her since Christmas."

"Well, what about it, Sarah? Ben?" Freddie pressed. "You
have to admit she's around your place with that Glenn What's-
his-name an awful lot, whenever she's not with Red. What's
going on there, anyway? Tell!"

Sarah drew a sharp breath preparatory to answering her, but
Ben Cameron cut in with his smooth, dry voice which managed
somehow to glitter.

"You probably see a lot more of Glenn Pickens and Lucy than
Sarah and me, Freddie," he said. "As much as you seem to ride
by our house. Daddy said at breakfast the other day that if he
didn't know better, he'd think the little Slaton girl was thinking
of buying the house."

Freddie looked affronted, as she always did when one of her
intrusions provoked the response it deserved, and huffed herself
up like a bantam chicken, but whatever she might have said to
Ben was lost in an explosion of sound from the far end of the
parking lot. We saw a glass come spinning through the window
of the Rolls and shatter on the asphalt, followed by something
larger that might have been a bottle, and a shriek from Lucy.
Even at this distance I could tell that it was rage and not pain
or fear. I was embarrassed and angry with her, and with Red
and Freddie, and ready to be angry with whoever spoke, but no

one did. After a moment we went back into the club and the
dance bowled on.

For the rest of the evening I kept an uneasy eye on the door,
waiting for them to come in, but by the time the band finished
the last throbbing, shouting chorus of "I Got a Woman" and
segued into "Goodnight, Sweetheart," they still had not appeared, and I figured that the quarrel had been serious enough
so that he had taken Lucy home—or that they were coupled in
furious atonement in the velvety backseat of the Rolls. The
thought repelled and disturbed me as the image of Lucy copulat-
ing with Red always did, and I pulled Sarah closer to me and
buried my face in the springy silk of her hair. She nuzzled her
face into my shoulder, and we swayed together wordlessly and
dreamily, abandoning ourselves to the myriad endings that were
now upon us, drowning, at last, in them. All around us, couples
were doing the same thing. As loud and explosive as the entire
evening had been, these last few minutes of it were quiet, quiet.

So that when Lucy came pelting into the ballroom and across
the floor, her breath sobbing in her throat, her sandals clattering
on the waxed old boards, everyone stopped and looked at her.
In truth, it was not possible to look anywhere else.

Lucy looked utterly wild, mad, almost dangerous. Her face
was nearly as white as the silk dress. Her blue eyes had that eldritch white ring around them that I had rarely seen since the
terrible nightmares and fits of hysteria of her childhood. Her
dress was pulled askew so that one breast trembled nearly out
of it. The gardenias were gone from her hair, and it flew wild
around her head; strands of it whipped across her forehead and
her mouth. Her lips were reddened and puffed and bare of lipstick.

She stopped at the edge of the dance floor and looked around
in intense concentration, seemingly oblivious that nearly three
hundred people were staring silently at her. Her eyes scanned
and scanned, and then found me, and she smiled. I had never
seen such a smile on her face before, and could only stare. If it
had not been for the dress and the indefinable Lucyness of her
slender body and her lithe, free stride, I would not have known
who she was.

She walked straight across the dance floor to where Sarah and
I stood, and put her hand on my arm, ignoring Sarah as totally
as if she did not stand there beside me. At this distance I could
see the magenta prints of fingers on her upper arms and shoulders and throat, and smell a strong gust of bourbon. I did not
doubt that she and Red had been drinking all evening. I knew
that they did to some extent whenever they were out together
now, but I had never seen Lucy drunk in public before. I would

have known that she was tonight, though, even if I had not seen the hot, opaque, unfocused glitter in her eyes.

"Hey, Gibby," she said merrily and clearly. She did not slur. "I came to claim my dance. You know, you promised me the last dance."

I did not reply for a moment, and Sarah did not either. She stood quietly beside me, her hand still on my shoulder, looking gravely at Lucy. She knew I had not promised Lucy the last dance; this was historically reserved for the girl you came with. All of us knew that; had for years. It was a tacit rule none of us would have thought of breaking.

Lucy seemed to see Sarah for the first time, and smiled again, a great, broad, incandescent smile.

"Sarah won't mind, Gibby," she said, and this time she did slur just a little, and rocked on her high heels so that she had to put out one hand to steady herself against my arm. "Sarah'll wait for us to finish. Good old Sarah. Sarah'll just sit all quiet like a little old puppy dog and wait for us . . ."

"Where's Red, Lucy?" I said, steadying her and trying not to see the avid, embarrassed faces of my friends and classmates around me. I damned her silently. "Let's go find Red—"

"No! I want you to dance with me!" she said. Her voice rose. "Put your arms around me, Gibby, and dance with me . . . dance with me . . ." She locked her arms around my neck and sagged against me, so that I was forced to hold her to prevent her from slipping to the floor. I looked at Sarah desperately over Lucy's head; her face was scarlet, but it was still and composed.

"Why don't you take her outside for some air?" she said to me, in a low, even voice. "I'll be fine; I can get a lift home with Ben and Julia."

"That's right," Lucy said in a singsong voice, her eyes closed, smiling, swaying. "You're a nice girl, Sarah; go on home with your big brother and let me dance with Shep—"

Rage flooded me coldly and fully then. I took Lucy by her upper arms and thrust her away from me so suddenly and sharply that her head bounced on her neck, and she opened her eyes and looked at me in the old simple, lost, Lucy bewilderment. I felt the traitorous twist begin in my heart, but the rage was stronger.

"Stand up, Lucy," I said. "I have this dance with Sarah, and I'm going to dance with her, and then I'm going to take her home. If you need some help getting back out to the car, I'm sure somebody will help you"—I looked around and found Charlie's calm white face, and our eyes met, and he nodded slightly. I thought there was a tiny flicker of triumph behind his thick glasses—"Charlie will help you. But I am going to dance this dance with Sarah."

Lucy stared back at me, and her face blanched even whiter than I had thought possible, and a quick wash of tears filmed her eyes, and then vanished, to be replaced with a pure and silver glitter of something I could not name.

"You do that, Gibby," she said. It was a drawl, low and controlled, all drunkenness gone as if it had never been. It rang in the huge room like a bell. "You dance with little Sarah, and then you take her home, and when you get there you roll her over and fuck her brains out, why don't you? Oh, but of course . . . you can't do that. She doesn't have anything to fuck. Red tried, he told me all about it; tried all one night while you were at Princeton, and you know what? She didn't have a hole! Got no hole at all, because Sarah isn't really Sarah, you know; she's one of those cute little plaster elf things that grin at you in miniature golf courses, and everybody knows elves don't have holes. . . ."

Sarah turned and walked off the dance floor and I followed her. It was very quiet in the big ballroom; Lucy had stopped talking and no one else spoke. It was a truly terrible moment, and the worst and longest walk I have ever taken, or ever will again. I could not imagine how Sarah could keep her head erect and her shoulders even and her step firm and steady after those killing words, but she did.

It had been a uniquely dreadful thing for Lucy to say, a terrible analogy; it had always been her gift to find the kernel of unalterable truth in everything, and there was, in the analogy of those awful, grotesque, painted elf-parodies, grinning from among the little bridges and white, puffy toadstools of every miniature golf course we had ever seen, a tiny, caricatured core of Sarah. It was there in her carved, miniature body, her generous red mouth nearly always smiling, her high color and her huge sherry eyes under straight black brows. I knew that everyone in that room would, whenever they saw one of those ghastly homunculi, think fleetingly and guiltily of Sarah Cameron, no matter how much they might love her. I knew that I would, and Sarah would. At that moment I could have killed Lucy for that diminishment.

Sarah did not speak when I handed her into the car. I reached out to take her in my arms, but she gave me a look of such desperate control and entreaty that I did not. I knew she was fighting tears, and that any gentleness would break her. It upset Sarah so badly to cry in front of people that it almost made her sick, and so I just said, softly and helplessly, "Sorry"; she nodded, and I nosed the car out onto West Brookhaven, and then onto

Peachtree Road. As we came into Buckhead, deserted and lunar, she reached over and switched on the radio, and I knew she had won for the moment her battle with the tears, but I still did not touch her.

"Don't come in, please, Shep," she said, when I pulled into the cobbled courtyard of the Muscogee Avenue house. "I know I'm going to go upstairs and cry, and then I'll feel better and I'll be okay in the morning. Come talk to me then, and have some lunch. And don't worry. You aren't responsible for Lucy. I know that."

"Sarah," I said, tasting the words on my tongue in the darkness. "Sarah, I love you."

"I know that, too," she said, and let herself out of the car, and vanished into the door to the little sun-room.

I went home determined to wait up for Lucy no matter how late she came in, and confront her with her behavior. I did not know what I would say to her, but I did know that what she had done to Sarah Cameron was beyond any pale I could imagine, and that I must not let her get away with it. It seemed the most important thing I would ever do; it seemed to me, that night, that great, profound things, things of deep and everlasting import, rode on my forcing some accounting from Lucy. But I had no idea what those things might be, and in any case, I did not do it, for she had not come in by full light the next morning, and I finally fell asleep in the hot, ashy dawn of a new spring day.

When I awoke, at eleven o'clock, she was sitting on the end of my bed in the summerhouse wearing black Capri pants and a fresh yellow blouse and smoking a Viceroy. I squinted stupidly at her through the smoke, and then the previous night came sliding back into my mind, and I sat up and took a deep breath and said, "Look, Lucy . . ."

She smiled. She looked as if she'd had ten hours of sweet, untroubled sleep, and only the faintest ghost fingerprints on her forearms and another set at the base of her throat remained of all the anger and ugliness.

"If it's about last night, I'm sorry, Gibby, and I know I was horrible, and I'll go over later and tell Sarah how sorry I am. I had a good reason for acting so awful, though, and I wanted to tell you about it."

I could not imagine how she could look so untouched and young and somehow clean and whole there in the dimness of the summerhouse, and I simply stared at her for a moment, and then I said, "Lucy, there can't be any reason in the world good enough to justify how you acted last night, and whatever it is, I don't want to hear it."

"Well," she said equably, blowing smoke out in twin plumes through her nose, "you have to hear it, want to or not. You have to help me fix it. I'm three and a half months pregnant, and we've got to make some plans. I thought I better catch you before you went in for breakfast so we can figure out the best way to go about this."

My ears rang. I simply could not answer her.

"I want to have an abortion," she said, when I did not speak, "and I don't have any money. I know a place in Copper Hill, Tennessee, I can go to, a real doctor in a real clinic, and perfectly safe, but it costs six hundred dollars and I can't get that much. And I know you have that trust money from your granddaddy. . . ."

"It's Red's, of course," I said. My mouth felt stiff and clumsy, numb. My tongue was enormous.

"Of course," Lucy said. "Whose else would it be? What do you think I am, Gibby?"

"Then get the goddamned money from him!" I shouted. I was surprised at the depth of my anger and shock. Given Lucy's behavior with Red, this was almost to be expected.

Lucy's reasonable aplomb vanished.

"I can't tell him! I could never tell him!" she cried.

"Why the hell not?" I hissed furiously. "He who dances must pay the piper. Or he who fucks must pay the abortionist, to be exact. God almighty, Lucy, he's got money coming out of his ass! Why can't he take responsibility for his own baby? Come to that, why can't he marry you? Wasn't he going to, anyway? What difference does it make if it's now rather than later? His old man can support all of you; that's what you ought to be thinking about, not a damned abortion—"

"He can't marry me!" She burst into tears. I saw that they were the old, old tears of real pain and fear and desperation, and my heart contracted. This was Lucy, this was still Lucy. . . .

"Why the hell not?" I said again, my voice softening in spite of myself.

"Because his father says he'll cut him off without a cent if he either knocks anybody up or marries anybody till he's out of Princeton, and Red knows he'll do it. He told me if I got pregnant it was the last I'd see of him, and he meant it!"

"Christ, what a bastard," I exploded. "Then good riddance to him. No, Lucy, I'm not going to pay for any abortionist. You could *die*. . . ."

"This man is good, Shep; everybody goes to him."

"What do you mean, everybody?"

"God, do you think I'm the only girl in Atlanta this has ever happened to?" She laughed bitterly. "You don't see any shotgun weddings or unwed mothers in this crowd, do you? You bet your ass you don't. This is the guy they go to. The families always pay. He . . . he's fashionable, like the hairdresser all the Buckhead girls go to, or the right fitter. Only, can you see your mother or father paying for my abortion? Or Mr. Chastain, for Christ's sake? And Red's not going to."

"Lucy," I said, "you could have the baby."

"I WILL NOT HAVE A BABY WITHOUT BEING MARRIED!" Lucy shrieked. "I CAN'T TAKE CARE OF A BABY! I CAN'T EVEN TAKE CARE OF MYSELF!"

She began to cry then, and she cried so hard that I went to her and put my arms around her, as I had first on that day so long ago when she had run away and been punished, and gradually she stopped the terrible sobbing. We sat in silence for a time.

"You said you'd always look after me, Gibby," she whispered against my bare chest. "You promised, the day we cut our wrists."

Here it was again, that peculiar litany, the maiden supplicant to the knight, that she reverted to whenever she was pushed to the brink of terror and impotence. Those narrow childhood wounds, that thin young blood that ran so deep . . .

"Luce, I don't have any six hundred dollars," I said. "I don't have anywhere near that, until I graduate. That'll be way too late."

"You could marry me," my cousin Lucy said. She raised her face to mine, and it was radiant with more than tears. Deliverance shone there, simple and joyous. "You could marry me, Gibby. We could drive to Maryland today, this morning, and I could come live in Princeton and we could get a place somewhere, and I could get a job, and you could go right on studying. . . ."

"I can't do that," I said numbly. "You can't do that. You know you can't. Lucy, I can't always take care of you. I'm not able to. You just can't expect me to do that."

"That's just what I do expect," she exploded again, tears jetting anew from her eyes. "Because you promised me on your blood that you would!"

"Lucy," I said again desperately, "I wasn't even nine years old when I said that! You weren't even seven! You always keep coming back to that day, and you must know that we were just children playing a game. . . ."

My voice dwindled and stopped. I sat still and slumped. She

did not speak. She stared intently into my face. Presently, I suppose, she read my answer there, because she stiffened and sat up, and pushed my arms away.

"I have to go back to school this afternoon," I said. "I tell you what. You go see a doctor and find out for sure, and then call me. I'll think about it, and we'll work something out that will maybe let you go away and have the baby, and you can say you're visiting . . . oh, somebody. . . ."

She gave me a brilliant and truly terrible smile.

"Never mind, Gibby," she said. "With any luck, maybe we'll find out it's only cancer, and you'll be off the hook. You can be the one crying the loudest at my funeral, and everybody will say what a devoted cousin you were."

"Lucy," I whispered, but she turned and walked out of the summerhouse.

I started after her.

"If you come one step further I'll tell everybody it's yours, Gibby," she said without looking back. "And you'd better believe I mean that. Go on back to your precious Princeton. I don't ever want to see you again."

And I did. I did not even go over to see Sarah; just called and said I'd overslept and needed to go on to the airport, and that I'd see her for graduation in a couple of weeks, and took the noon plane to Philadelphia and the dinkey to the PJ&B. All that week I waited for Lucy's call, sick with misery, worry for her and an anger that I still could not name.

The call from Atlanta came five days later, but it was from my mother, not Lucy. As calmly as if she were discussing my laundry, she told me that Lucy had taken the Fury out in a great afternoon rainstorm and had lost control of it and slammed into a bridge abutment on the new interstate highway up near Gainesville. She was in Piedmont Hospital with a concussion and a deep laceration on her temple, and internal injuries, but she was expected to heal routinely, even though she had lost a great deal of blood. But the Fury was a total wreck. I thought there was a certain measure of satisfaction in my mother's voice, though whether it was in relation to the damaged niece or the wrecked car, neither of which she had ever liked, I could not tell.

I called Lucy in her private room at Piedmont after supper that night.

"What about the baby?" I said without preamble.

"What baby?" she said, and her voice was gay. "There isn't any baby, Gibby. Not anymore, there isn't."

Lucy graduated with her and Sarah's class a week later, looking, according to the photographs that Aunt Willa took, like an

El Greco angel, in a white cap and gown, with a small white bandage like a beauty spot on her delicately hollowed temple. Aunt Willa and my mother and father were there to see her, and Red Chastain, looking handsome and supercilious in his blue blazer and gray flannels and white bucks, and even Red's father, grinning enormously and ferally.

But I wasn't.

CHAPTER
THIRTEEN

"I NEVER GET OVER THE FEELING that I'm going to see Frank Sinatra scrooched up under your steps, screaming for heroin," Sarah said, pressing closer to me as I fumbled for the key to my apartment. She had never quite gotten over *The Man with the Golden Arm* when I had taken her to see it at the Playhouse on one of the Princeton weekends, and she never failed to evoke Sinatra's tortured wraith when we climbed the marble steps to my place on West Twenty-first Street.

I could see her point. That area of lower Manhattan, from about Eighth Avenue over to the Hudson River, is called Chelsea now, and is, I understand, thoroughly gentrified. But in the late fifties, when I moved there, it was a dim and, in places, downright eerie slice of the city, decaying and sullen, with all manner of funny stuff in the air and in the blood, including heroin. I routinely found supine bodies amid the trash cans and more unspeakable jetsam in the basement stairwells of my block, between Eighth and Ninth, and after the first two or three encounters, stopped automatically calling the police. In all but two cases, the bodies turned out to be derelicts sleeping off the night's load of muscatel out of the wind. Of the other two, one was comatose from heroin, and the other, a livid and terrified-looking old woman, was dead. After nearly a year, I prided myself on being able to distinguish the quick from the dead at a glance.

The bodies did not bother me. My apartment was the entire first floor of a once-grand old brownstone with a rear view into a ruined garden—I literally looked into a low, sturdy ginkgo from my rudimentary kitchen—and it was cheap enough so that I did not have to have a roommate. That it was airless, dark, scurrilously shabby and probably deserving of condemnation hardly even registered with me two days after I had moved in. It was now as clean as a week of scrubbing and chipping and mopping and painting could get it, it was comfortable enough if you did not insist upon aesthetics and it was close via foot, bus and subway to both my job at the New York Public Library and the jazz clubs in the Village. I stepped over the human refuse of the Lower West Side and walked on the lambent air of pure joy.

I heated water for coffee on the stained old gas stove in the tiny kitchen, and Sarah and I took our cups and sat out on the fire escape. It was April, and the ginkgo was lacy with transparent new green. From the dark garden below, the smell of the tough urban honeysuckle rose up, battling the general miasma of the West Side. It had been an early, warm spring, and the night was almost as balmy as an April night in Atlanta. The clash and snarl of traffic on Ninth had tapered off in the small hours of Sunday morning so that we could hear human sounds: footfalls on Twenty-first, and a radio from an apartment down the block, and a dissonant mewling that might have been feline or human, but certainly meant climactic passion, from the unseen garden floor. Sarah giggled at the sound, which told me that she was still tipsy from the gin and tonics we had drunk. Ordinarily, she would have ignored the sounds of love.

"Sounds like fun," she said, burrowing her curly head into my shoulder in its accustomed niche. I pulled her close against me.

"Want to try it?" I said.

"Uh-uh," she mumbled. "I'm too comfortable. Another time, thanks."

I grinned into the night, over the tangled curls. We both knew by now that we weren't going to make love, not, at least, at present; knew it well enough and were comfortable enough with it to tease each other about it. I think she enjoyed the teasing, and I know I did. It lent a titillating saltiness to what would otherwise have been almost too deep and sweet a relationship. Not now, the teasing said, but soon. Maybe tomorrow. You never can tell. In any case, there wouldn't have been time tonight. Sarah's spring break from Agnes Scott College ended on Sunday, and she would have to go back to Atlanta on an afternoon plane. I glanced at my watch. Only hours away now. It was very late.

It had been a weekend as idyllic in its way as the ones at Princeton. As she had there, Sarah slipped without a ripple into the world I had staked out for myself in New York, and if the things we did and the places we went and the way we were with each other did not delight her totally, I never knew it. She merged into the all-consuming fugue I had created as seamlessly

as vapor or air, became a part of the wholeness and flow and
lilt and pulse of my life in Manhattan as she had in Princeton,
as if she were flesh and bone of both me and it. It was such an
androgynous thing, this fitting of Sarah to me, that it seemed
a part of the larger legerdemain that the city wrought on me,
and I often could not—or did not stop to—observe where Sarah
left off and New York began. It was wonderful for me; I gloried
in all of it, but it struck me later that perhaps Sarah would have
welcomed a kingdom of the heart that was all her own. She did
not, on those weekends, get that exclusive focus from me, but
she did share down to the last cell of her the kingdom wherein
I dwelled. It spelled such a total absorption to me that I never
once wondered if, for her, it was enough.

On Friday, when she got in, we had dropped her luggage off
at the Barbizon Hotel for Women, where Ben and Dorothy insisted that she stay and where indeed she did, and had gone to
dinner at Alan Greenfeld's family's apartment near Columbus
Circle. Alan was there with a fair, straight-haired Bennington
graduate named Gerta Neumann who was an intern at *The New
Republic,* where Alan had worked for the past year as a junior
political editor. It was the first time Sarah had been with me to
Alan's, and I did not know how she would fare; she was as alien
to this world of liberal Eastern Jewish families and activist leftist
politics as they were to our cloistered banal Buckhead one. But
she did fine; her quirky wit and unaffected openness won them,
as did her soft accent and beautiful manners. Ben and Dorothy
had left a great many doors open for Sarah.

On Saturday—yesterday, now—we had nearly worn ourselves
and the city out. One thing about Sarah that especially endeared
her to me was her stamina; her little athlete's body and shapely
steel-muscled legs ate up New York as effortlessly as even my
loping attenuation did, and we walked what must have been ten
miles before the tender green sunset. By 6:00 P.M. I was waiting
in the primly collegiate lounge of the Barbizon while Sarah
changed, feeling as though I were back at a mixer at Bryn Mawr
or Sarah Lawrence, and then we went to dinner at Mama
Leone's, Sarah glowing beside me in polished peach cotton, and
ate garlic-smitten pasta with white beans, the cheapest thing
Mama was proffering that night. We drank a great deal of
equally cheap Chianti and laughed a lot and held hands under
the table, aching pleasantly with the day's walking, and then I
took her down to hear Brubeck at the Village Vanguard.

I was always aware of feeling the most deeply about Sarah
when we were listening to jazz together. She soaked it in through
every pore and assimilated it in every cell and gave off its deliri-
ous fruits from her very skin, like body heat. She knew what it

meant to me, and so she would have put all her heart and soul into listening in any event, but her childhood years in the Muscogee Avenue house with young Ben had given her an early start; she had been brought up on the elegant intricacies of Artie Shaw and the arid crystal syncopation of Charlie Parker. Her wonderfully orchestrated body swayed as naturally to the aggressive, hard-driving bop of the forties and early fifties as to the slightly later drifting, pastel atonalities of the so-called "cool" jazz that so spoke to me. Sarah loved and listened to a lot of music—symphonies, opera and even the yowling country ballads that besieged Atlanta from all sides—but I have never seen her so lost in anything as jazz, except her own painting.

I know that she was not merely attempting to please and impress me, because she played the prized records from her own extensive jazz library almost daily, throughout her life. But I did like to think that I showed her new dimensions and depth to something she already loved. She told me once that if it had not been for those New York nights at the Blue Note or Birdland or the Village Gate or Nick's or Basin Street East or the venerable old Vanguard she would still be snapping her fingers to Count Basie and Woody Herman. I fed on the remark: Sarah's gratitude made wonderful nourishment.

When we came up out of the smoky dark onto the street, we were sweating and still dazzled and full to our hairlines with the boundless exuberance of the quartet. Their odd-metered time signatures and skittering improvisations were mesmerizing, but the thing that set the room rocking and clapping and shouting aloud was the sheer joy in the music and the unfeigned and open delight in each other that flashed like heat lightning between Brubeck, Morello, Wright and Desmond. Their eyes were constantly on one another; they could sense when one or the other was going to seize a riff before it happened, and would slide back to accommodate it; their heads nodded and grins widened until finally they were nodding and laughing aloud with the wonder of the never-to-be-repeated flight of sound, which careened around the room like a captured bird. When you heard Brubeck and his group, even then, you heard love as well as artistry in action, love for the sound and for each other, and it was impossible not to drown in it and then burst up dripping and shouting.

We were quite drunk when we reached the sidewalk, and only half the intoxication was from the seemingly endless stream of gin and tonics that I had signaled for. The dent the evening had made in my grandfather's legacy would have popped his dry old eyes, but I think he could have been persuaded of its necessity if he could have sat in the smoke-blued dark of the Vanguard that night and heard Brubeck take off. Sarah and I both were on our feet with the rest of the crowd at the evening's end, when the quartet swung out of "Time Out" at a hundred miles an hour and came crashing down the last stretch into "Take the A Train."

It was the third time Sarah had visited me in New York. I had not been home since the weekend of her and Lucy's senior prom, except for two or three visits, each lasting hardly more than a day. I did not go home to take Sarah to the Harvest Ball that Thanksgiving, as I had promised; I called and told her—the only lie I have ever told Sarah, and one I am quite sure she did not believe, though she accepted it with her customary cheerful grace—that I thought I was coming down with the flu, and wished she would ask Charlie to step in for me. She did, simply and sweetly, I'm sure, and he accepted, and I think that they both had a wonderful time. Sarah always loved Charlie; loved being with him, loved the ease and staunchness of him, and his wonderful sweetness. Charlie, for his part, loved Sarah, of course, in quite another way, and would, I knew, gladly give up his scholarship to Emory Law to be a part of that ball, one of the great formal rituals of her life.

I did not go home that Christmas or Easter, either, and I did not go between my junior and senior years at Princeton, and I never told Sarah why, hoping she would assume that the tension between me and my father was behind my absences. But I know that she knew of the alienation between Lucy and me, though probably not what had caused it, or how deeply it went. I know because she did not speak of Lucy even when it would have been natural to do so. Sarah and I spent most of my last two years at Princeton and my first in New York speaking of everything in the world but Lucy Bondurant.

A week before I graduated satisfactorily *cum laude,* in June of 1958, a letter came from Bud Houston in the trust department of the Trust Company of Georgia, telling me that my grandfather Redwine's trust for me was operable effective the date of my graduation, and what the terms were. They were liberal: a small yearly set amount for the rest of my life, which I could spend any way I chose, without restriction or penalty. I went into New York and opened an account at Manufacturer's Trust, and asked Bud to transfer the entire sum into it, and to do the same each year on the anniversary of the trust's becoming active. He did not like that at all, and spoke of investments and instruments and whatever bankers use to keep your money working for them, but in the end he only grumbled mildly and complied. He said nothing about consulting my father; I would have taken his head off if he had.

I had heard nothing from my father for more than a year, ex-

cept for the careful, neutral mealtime pleasantries we exchanged
the very few times I did go home, and I knew that with the acti-
vation of my trust fund, he had in fact as well as in spirit at last
washed his hands of me, and that I would get no more of the
Bondurant largesse from him, either then or, probably, ever.

And though this bothered my mother greatly and caused her
to weep on my shirtfront for nearly a half-hour the last time I
was home, and to sob, "It would all be yours, Sheppie, all of it,
if you'd just come home," the defection of my father and his
money lay weightless on my heart. What I had on my own was
enough. My ties to him, and consequently, to my mother, were
broken with the receipt of my grandfather's money. The great
primary artery connecting me to Atlanta, that of Lucy, was cut.
I left Princeton on the Saturday afternoon of my graduation and
went straight into Manhattan and slid into it like a liner into the
sea.

Through the doubtless annoyed but supremely effective offices
of Dub Vanderkellen's father, who was a major benefactor and
president of the New York Friends of the Library, I found almost immediately a job as an assistant to an assistant curator
in the rare manuscripts department of the New York Public Library, which consisted mainly, that first year, of pushing carts
laden with desiccated seventeenth-century Flemish illuminated
sacred parchments, bound in gnawed and stinking, perpetually
damp leather, from the dank bowels of the library to the new
temperature-controlled manuscript hospital. It was undemand-
ing work and mildly absorbing, as ferrying mummies might be,
and ended at two o'clock in the afternoon, and it paid me just
slightly above starvation wages. They were sufficient to procure
the apartment, and the trust fund bought a small amount of unhealthy food and a larger amount of good liquor, and most important, opened the museum and theater and gallery and concert
hall and restaurant and jazz club doors through which I dived
like a fox into its earth. I rather liked the job, and had no immediate plans to look for something more challenging, spending most
of my free afternoons upstairs in the library's open stacks reading. I loved the city with every fiber of my being. Princeton had
been, I found, the preliminary round; Manhattan was the main
event.

Nights I spent at the small jazz clubs both uptown and in the
Village, and once in a while even up in Harlem, listening trans-
ported to the cold, wailing or hot, skittering dissonance of a new
kind of jazz that seemed to fry the very roots of the hair on my
scalp. I heard them all: Ellington, Hines, Krupa, Hampton, Ken-
ton, Rich, Gillespie, Blakey. And best of all, the legendary reed
men who followed Bird Parker out into the world: Coleman

Hawkins, Paul Desmond, Zoot Sims, John Coltrane, Stan Getz, Gerry Mulligan, Sonny Rollins, Ornette Coleman. I would go home after the last set and noodle far into the clanking dawn on my clarinet and the secondhand saxophone I had bought at a pawnshop my first week in the city. When I was not listening or playing or working, I was talking, endlessly talking, of the immortal profundities and never-ending possibilities that seemed to glitter in the thick air of New York, and bounce sunstruck off the very pavement like the flecks of mica in it. My companions were New York Princeton classmates and the friends of friends I collected in the city; not many, but enough to give me the warm-wrapped feeling of a set to belong to. We were all of similar swathed and privileged backgrounds and education and all bound with the common cord of music and youth and endless promise and the deep, constant kiss of the great city itself. I lived on almost nothing, grew thinner and nervier each day, read and worked and played and explored, and in general stretched and used every fiber and sinew and nerve and drop of blood and vapor of spirit within me.

And always, the music, and always, Sarah.

I could not imagine that I would ever want anything else.

But if I could not, it seemed to me that everyone else could. Throughout that first year, my mother kept up a steady barrage of telephone calls and then, when I simply stopped answering the phone, switched to letters. The gist of them was always the same: "You are throwing away your life. All we have given and could give you will count for nothing if you stay up there playing at that ignominious little job and frittering away your grandpapa's money on that awful music and liquor. You are an Atlanta Bondurant. People are talking about you. Come home. I don't care if you don't want to go into the business; do anything you want, but just come home. I'll see to it that your father is reasonable about everything."

By "everything" I knew she meant the Bondurant money, and I thought she probably could make my father see reason, as she put it, simply because at least half of it was hers. After a while I did not answer the letters, either. But she kept them coming. "Come home, Sheppie. Oh, come home, my baby. Come home."

Letters came from Dorothy Cameron, too, and they said essentially the same thing, though in gentler tones, and for different, loftier reasons: "You are very special to Ben and me, Shep, and you have gifts and talents you have not dreamed of yet. You should put them to work. There's nothing in the world so satisfying as giving back to the world some of what it has given you. It's a sacred trust. We flout it at our own risk. And Shep, New

York doesn't need those gifts. But Atlanta . . . oh, how we need our rare Shep Bondurants."

Dorothy, the eternal altruist, the inexorable, if gentle, conscience to a generation. I knew she meant what she said about giving back to Atlanta, and I also knew that she and Ben would grieve deeply, if silently, should Sarah leave home and cast her lot with me, a thousand miles away. I did answer Dorothy's letters, cheerfully and promptly, but I suspect she was not satisfied with the noncommittal tone or content of them. But unlike my mother, she did not plead or chide.

Even Charlie wrote me: "Enough is enough. The big city is all well and good, but Buckhead's a dump without you. Come on home, boy. There's a little curlyheaded Scottie who misses you something awful. And I warn you, I've taken her to five dances this year, and I'm taking her to another one Saturday night."

I called him after that letter, at home where he was still living, resignedly I knew, with his mother. I just wanted to hear his froggy, familiar voice.

"You don't have to report to me or ask my permission to take Sarah around," I said. "She's free to date anybody she wants to, and you're it, apparently. I'm glad you are."

"You ought to be," Charlie said, and I could see the wide grin on his square face. "Nobody else would look after your interests like I do."

The letters disturbed me, though, and finally I asked Sarah if she felt the same way everyone else seemed to about the way I was leading my life.

"Well," she said practically, "you're not ever going to have much money, you know, and you grew up used to a lot of that. But I don't think that matters much to you, and it certainly doesn't to me. I'm only glad to see you so happy. You're like somebody turned a light on inside you. I never saw that at home. I only wonder if it's always going to be enough for you . . . if one day you're not going to want more from life. I don't mean materially. I mean . . . oh, I guess I mean experientially. If the way you're living now ever loses its intensity, it might seem awfully minimal to you, I'm afraid. And by that time, you may have lost the best chances you'll have to make other moves, and your contacts, and your momentum."

"It sounds like it wouldn't be enough for you," I said, looking at her sharply. "I thought you loved the way I lived, and the city, and the things we do. . . ."

"I do. Right now, I think being here in New York with you is about the most perfect thing I can imagine in the world. But I don't know that I always will."

"Would you want more money, or a better place to live?" I asked. This *was* disturbing.

"No, I thought you understood that. What I'd want more of is achievement. Mine, mainly. There it is, Shep. It's what I was raised for. It's all I know. I can't do all that much, but I need to take what I can do as far as it will go. And I need to give something to the world; I'm my mother's daughter there. It's why I want that year in Paris for my painting, and why I don't just chuck most of that ridiculous Junior League charity stuff."

"You could certainly achieve almost anything you wanted to in New York," I said. I was aware that I sounded more than a bit sullen. "You could take your painting further here than you ever could in Atlanta."

"I know it," she said, and smiled. "That's why I don't get on you about coming home. It's not me I worry about needing more. It's you."

She had said it as she got on a plane to go home after her previous visit, and so I could not pursue it with her. Sarah had a penchant for dropping provocative bones into the conversation just as she was leaving me; I thought perhaps that it was because she so hated confrontation and knew I could best her verbally in most arguments.

She dropped one on this Sunday night, as we were walking through the grubby, dun-colored concourse at La Guardia toward the Delta flight that would take her back for the spring quarter of her junior year at Agnes Scott.

"We have to talk about Lucy sometime, you know," she said, apropos of nothing at all, and I looked at her in surprise. She smiled at me and continued walking. "I know y'all have had some kind of falling out, and that it must have been a bad one, because you haven't seen her, and you haven't said a word about her since you were home for our prom, and that's three years, Shep."

"We did have an argument," I said. "I guess you could say it was a bad one. She doesn't want to see me, and I can't say that I mind. I don't see why we have to talk about her. It really doesn't amount to anything."

"You must think about it, though," she persisted. There was a troubled frown between her level black brows. "You must think about her *sometimes.*"

"I don't," I said slowly, tasting the words and finding them to be essentially true. "I really almost never do. It's funny."

Sarah said nothing, but her smile widened.

"What are you grinning at?"

"I just plain don't believe you," she said. "There is some corner of your heart that is forever Lucy Bondurant." Sarah was reading Rupert Brooke that year.

"Well, you're wrong," I said impatiently. "This time you're wrong."

We talked no more about it, and in due time Sarah's flight was called, and I kissed her and she walked away from me toward the gate. And then she turned, and I saw that her eyes were wet.

"Oh, Shep," she said, "don't come home! I don't care what any of them say. You're right; stay here. If you come home, it will be to her."

And she was gone out onto the twilit tarmac and up the spidery steps into the DC-7 before I could answer her.

On the way back to West Twenty-first in the cab, I thought how very rarely Sarah was wrong about me, and how strange that she should be this time, and about this. For I was sure of it: I thought of Lucy very rarely, and then only fleetingly, and when I did, I felt, simply, nothing at all. It was as if all those years under the vivid, all-consuming, head-spinning, life-giving spell of my cousin Lucy had never been. Had that last meeting with her in the summerhouse burned me so that I had simply buried it beyond reach? Or could it be that she was so totally and supernormally of that place that she could not be of this one?

Sarah was right about one thing, though. It had been almost a year since I had even heard about Lucy, and that information had come not from her, but from, of all people, her mother. My aunt Willa. She had called me one raw Friday evening and said that she was in New York on a buying trip, and would love to have lunch and a nice catch-up chat the next day. She was, she said, staying at the Royalton on West Forty-fourth Street, and thought we might run over to the Schrafft's at Forty-third and Broadway. I hated the teahouse fussiness and the appalling food at all the Schrafft's but she took me by surprise, and besides, I knew we could eat cheaply there and was fairly sure that I would be expected to pay. In Aunt Willa's world the man, no matter how impecunious, always did. We made a date for noon the next day, and I went to sleep that night with the thought lying fullblown in my mind: There's something about Lucy that she wants me to do, and I'm going to hate it.

I saw Aunt Willa immediately; she had snared a corner table by the window and sat there looking out into the flow of traffic on Forty-third Street like an incognito queen spying on her subjects. The past few years had deepened her beauty; I knew that she must be about forty now, but all that showed of the passing of time was a sort of sheen that lay on her like the bloom of a grape. She still wore a great deal of pale, opaque foundation and

hectic scarlet lip and nail polish, and her eyes were made up into
the slanted doe eyes of that period, but she was so slender now
that the lush breasts and hips no longer literally leapt out at you,
only beckoned, and the clothes she wore were obviously expensive, though plain to the point of severity. Lucy had always had
so much of the Bondurants about her, despite the startling Slagle
coloring, that I had never seen even a vestige of Aunt Willa in
her, but now, in her full and splendid maturity, I saw in Willa
Slagle Bondurant's dark grace and stillness something of what
Lucy the woman might one day become. Both women took the
eye, Willa with her utter femaleness, Lucy with both that and
the exuberant life that literally leaped off her.

I sat down warily, with a sense of walking clear-eyed and of
my own volition into a trap. It could not be interest in my welfare
that prompted this luncheon; Aunt Willa had never so much as
held a conversation with me alone since she had brought her
family to the Peachtree Road house. In fact, I had never seen
her engaged in a one-on-one conversation with anyone in all my
memory. She participated in conversations in whatever group
she found herself in, turning from this person to that like a sly,
clever child mimicking adult behavior, but she seldom seemed
to initiate conversation, and she virtually never talked with the
children of the big houses of Buckhead. I think that in her mind
we had no power to either hurt or help her in her obsessive quest
for Ladyhood, and so did not, for her, exist. Except, of course,
her own daughters, the one who was boon, and the other who
was bane. I could not imagine simply talking with her as I did
with Dorothy Cameron, or even my mother, and I had a moment
of panic as I walked across the floor to her table, and wanted
to turn and run.

I need not have worried. Aunt Willa did all the talking. From
the moment she pecked me on the cheek, engulfing me in a powerful musk of something dark and sophisticated, to the moment
she put down her coffee cup and lighted a Parliament, icing its
pristine white tip with a virulent berry stain, she did not stop
her lilting, witless chatter. I did not need to say anything, and
did not, beyond an occasional "umm-hmmm" and "oh yes."
Between the shrimp cocktail and the ladyfinger something-or-
other, Aunt Willa talked incessantly about her career as a full-
fledged buyer for Rich's of Atlanta (soon to be head buyer), and
what my "little crowd" was about (weddings and engagements
popping like firecrackers), and what her set was up to (hitting
every tea and fashion show and charitable ball that could possibly have been held in the past year, with herself, as well as my
parents, as virtual mainstays of them), and what was happening
to Atlanta (growing like a weed; skyscrapers and shopping malls

shooting up everywhere, and the town absolutely full of tackpots nobody knew. "Everyone says Ben Cameron will be the next mayor, but why he wants to is beyond me"). It was more than I had heard her say in any given five years at home.

Finally she slowed and stopped, and gave me the full battery of her languid red smile.

"Well, I've really let myself run on, haven't I?" she said archly. "And not a word about you. How are you, Shep? One reason I wanted to see you was that Lucy misses you so much, and I want to tell her all about you."

"In a pig's eye you do, Aunt Willa," I thought, and said, "I'm just fine. How is Lucy?"

This was what she had come for; I had, of course, been right. You could literally see her marshal her weapons and take aim. She dropped her lids so that the impossible lashes feathered on her cheeks, and let her pretty white hands turn palm up, helplessly, on the table, and paused a beat. Her voice, when it came, was low and freighted with a mother's sorrow.

"I am deeply worried about my daughter, Shep. She is headed for heartache, and I wanted to ask your advice. You always did seem to be able to get through to her when no one else could, and what daughter listens to her mama nowadays?"

She looked up with a rueful little smile. Mischief and forbearance danced in it. "Nice bit of business, Aunt Willa," I said silently. Aloud I said, with such reluctance that my voice dragged with it, "What's the matter with Lucy?"

"Lucy is about to get herself kicked out of Agnes Scott," Aunt Willa said, "and if she does, she can forget all about marrying Nunnally Chastain, because his father will cut him off without a red cent when it comes out why she did. And it will come out, Shep. You know how Lucy always manages to get herself talked about by the very people she ought to be cultivating."

I grinned in spite of myself, hiding it behind a swallow of coffee. I did indeed know how Lucy drew talk as easily as she did eyes, and how little she cared about either, except as they might be used as weapons in the long guerrilla war with her mother. I knew, too, that whatever Lucy was up to at Agnes Scott that might get her expelled was of virtually no import to Aunt Willa, compared to its consequences: the loss of the inestimable social gloss that the name Chastain shed over everything and everyone it brushed. If it weren't for the jeopardy in which it put that gloss and the money that spawned it, Willa Bondurant wouldn't care if Lucy was mainlining heroin on the steps of Presser Hall.

"What's she up to?" I said.

"Well, among other things, among *many* other things," Aunt Willa said, drawing a great vermilion mouth with a slim gold lipstick and deftly flicking a glob off a canine tooth, "she has written an editorial in the little campus paper she edits about that horrible Martin Luther King and how he's a new American saint, and several newspapers around the South have printed it. The *Constitution* had a headline that said, 'Deb Defends Sit-Ins: An Atlanta Princess Takes up the Flag of Freedom.' Can you imagine? The *idea!* All over the South! And she's not even a deb, strictly speaking, much less a princess. I tell you, I've heard nothing since the story ran but that; everybody's laughing about it. Well, not everybody. Babs Rawson didn't think it was a bit funny. She literally cut us dead at the Driving Club last week, and Little Lady was sitting right there *with Carter!*"

Well, I thought, of course, Lucy and the Negroes again. It was the only thing left that raised Willa's ire, and the only one likely, in these days, to inflame Buckhead enough to seriously threaten her clawed-out niche in its society. But surely . . .

"Surely they can't be serious about expelling her from Scott for *that,*" I said. "My God, she's been editor of that paper for both years she's been there, and that's unheard of for a freshman and sophomore. They must know what they have in Lucy. I thought her journalism and English grades were right at the top. . . ."

"Oh yes, they are, but they're the only ones that are," Aunt Willa said. "She's so close to flunking everything else she's taking that I've had letters from every one of her teachers. And then of course she's broken every rule they've got in the book, and when they call her up before that what-do-you-call-it, judiciary thing, and punish her she just laughs and goes right on doing whatever she likes. Why, I got a letter only two days ago from the dean of women, and it said that Lucy could be one of the most vital voices—that's what she said, vital voices—to speak out of the South in her time, she's got such a gift for writing. But first, she said, she's got to graduate, and the way she's going, she's not going to make it. I know what she means, of course. Lucy never studies. She spends all her time with that Negro boy Ben Cameron is raising over there, that Glenn Pickens person. Now Ben's sending him to college, no less, down at that Negro school on the Southside, More-something—"

"Morehouse," I said automatically.

"—Morehouse," she went on, "and half the time Lucy's down there with him, in meetings about civil rights and sit-ins and all that vulgar stuff. Why, last week there was some kind of sit-in over in South Carolina, and there was your cousin Lucy right in the middle of it, the only white face in all those black ones. Of course both papers got ahold of it and ran it!"

"Is Agnes Scott upset about that?" I asked doubtfully. I knew

Scott to be conservative in the extreme when it came to its educational policies and the rules by which it bound its girls, but I did not think it could afford to take an official stance on such matters as the incendiary new civil rights movement. Scott shunned publicity of any sort. And then Sarah had said nothing about it, and I knew that Ben and Dorothy would have her out of there in a moment if the school spoke out against desegregation.

"They say not. They say it's her grades, and her attitude about the rules she breaks," Aunt Willa said. "But of course that's it. And Farrell Chastain is plenty mad about it, let me tell you, and so are Babs and Bill Rawson."

"What about Red?" I asked curiously. I knew that Red Chastain was an indolent and merciless bigot, but I also knew that he was about as politically aware as a dung beetle. "Is Red mad at her, too?"

"Oh no, I don't think so," Aunt Willa said. "I gave in and let her start going up to visit him at Princeton, hoping it would keep her too busy to run around with the niggers"—her voice had slid up gradually into its wire-grass whine, and several heads turned toward her, but she did not notice. I felt myself redden, and wanted to disappear under the table—"but it doesn't matter whether he is or not, because if Farrell Chastain lays the law down to him, you can bet he'll drop Miss Lucy faster than a rattlesnake, rather than lose all that money."

"Well, and has she stopped?" I asked, genuinely curious. I had never known Lucy to be either intimidated into dropping something she wished to do, or diverted from it.

"Well, she hasn't been out with that colored boy for the past week, but then he's over in Mississippi stirring up the niggers over there about registering to vote, so she hasn't had the opportunity. She'd be over there too, except he told her she couldn't go. Said it was too dangerous. Listen, Shep, I want you to talk to her. Surely you can see she's about to ruin her life, much less all our good names. Will you call her and talk to her? She'll listen to you; she always would."

"Aunt Willa," I said as forcefully as I could, "I can't do that. The last time I really talked to Lucy was two years ago, and at the end of that conversation, she told me she never wanted to see me again. She'd hang up on me before I said hello."

To my utter horror, she put her face down in her hands and began to cry. I knew she was not faking. The sobs were harsh and ugly and racking. More eyes fastened on us. They seemed to leave smoking craters in my flesh. She did not appear to notice.

"She's going to ruin everything for me," she sobbed, and her voice was that of the chicken farmer's daughter again, fifteen years of careful, relentless cultivation gone from it. "She's not going to stop until she's done it. Oh, I wish she'd just died when she was born. . . ."

Anger flooded me, over the embarrassment. "All right, I'll call her, but I don't want to hear you say that about her ever again," I said, the iron and ice in my voice surprising me. Her, too, apparently; she stopped crying and looked up at me. Despite the tears, her mascara had not run.

"Thank you, Shep," she said meekly. "She's over at Princeton this weekend, but she'll be back tomorrow night. Sunday. Could you call her then?"

I agreed to do it, not at all sure that I would, but so eager to get out of the terrible ruffled restaurant and into the cold, bright Saturday sunlight that I would have promised her anything. Restored, she kissed me airily on the cheek and clicked off on her four-inch heels, unable to keep the waggle entirely out of her shapely, taupe-swathed behind. I saw heads turn after her as she sailed down Forty-third Street, heading east toward Fifth. And then she was gone.

I might not have called Lucy after all, but I met Alan Greenfeld for dinner that night and we went down to hear Horace Silver at Nick's, and he told me that he had been over to Princeton that day, to pick up some things he had left in his old suite in Holder, and had seen Lucy with Red Chastain on the veranda of Tiger, and that both had been falling-down drunk at high noon, and all over each other. The old Lucy-worry, which had been dormant so long, flooded back over me like cold salt water, and I hardly slept at all that night. I knew then that I would call her, and would probably regret doing it, but that it couldn't be helped. The old ties had held after all; the old bond still ran deep. "We be of one blood, thou and I . . . ."

Red was a junior at Princeton then, and I had not seen him for two years, and had seen him very little even in the year we had been there together. But I had heard enough about him to know that he was trouble pure and simple, if I had not known it before. He had lived his first two years in a suite with three other Southern boys whom I had not known, Southerners of a certain type that used to turn up at Princeton with some regularity. They were, like Red, cool and smilingly murderous of temper, lazily athletic and prowlingly indolent, and entered Princeton wilder and more jaded than most of us left it. Red and his roommates were the centerpiece of an entire set of these attractive and decadent Southerners, most of whom eventually found their way into Tiger, and all of whom spent their spare time drinking in their rooms and whoring in New York. Red and his roommates had moved all the beds in their suite into one room and fitted the other up as an elegant working bar, and the endless cocktail party and worse that prevailed there was the stuff of legend far beyond the Ivy League. I did not care a whit about Lucy and her involvement with her beloved Negroes, nor, really, if she flunked out of Agnes Scott, but I cared about her association with a whole crowd of Red Chastains. I made the call.

After I said hello, there was a long silence, and then Lucy said neutrally, "Hello, Gibby," and her rich voice might have been in the very room with me. In my mind I saw her slouched on the Chinese Chippendale chair in the telephone alcove under the front stairs, feet up on the risers, a cigarette dangling from her long fingers. I had seen her that way a hundred times before.

It was not a good call. I stumbled and hemmed and hawed and stopped and started, and through it all she was silent, not helping me at all. Finally, in desperation, I blurted out that I had seen her mother in New York and that everyone was very worried about her, and I wanted to talk to her about it.

"About what?" Lucy said pleasantly.

"About . . . oh, shit, Lucy, about school, and the poor stupid Negroes, and mostly that bunch of corrupt fools Red runs around with at Tiger," I said in a rush. "You've got no business messing around with that gang. You're going to get yourself talked about all over the East Coast."

There was another pause, and then her creamy, winy belly laugh curled out at me over the wire. Despite my annoyance, the corners of my mouth quirked at the sound.

"What else is new?" she said. And then she stopped laughing. "You've turned into a real prick, Gibby," she said coolly, and the words stung me more sharply than I thought was possible. "You've got no business telling me who I can and cannot hang around with. You lost that right two years ago. Remember?"

And she slammed down the telephone. A blast of the old desolation in which absence from her had once drowned me swept over me again. For one anguished moment, the empty space between us where once so much had spun and sung back and forth bruised and lacerated me. And then both feelings were gone as if they had never been, and Lucy faded out of my mind like smoke, and what I had told Sarah tonight became again true. I had seldom thought of her since.

So I was as shocked as if I had seen a literal apparition when, at three o'clock on a Sunday morning the following November, I floundered out of sleep to answer a pounding on my door and opened it to find Lucy, distinctly drunk and looking lost and lovely in a man's filthy London Fog, leaning against the doorsill, smoking and smiling at me.

"Hey, Gibby," she said. Her voice was loose with liquor, but as rich and warm as I remembered. It seemed as if I had heard it only hours before, instead of months. I felt stupid and thick with sleep and confusion, and could not, for a moment, make my voice work.

"Lucy?" I said finally, hoarsely.

"Can I come in?" she said.

I cleared my throat. "Yeah. Sure. Come on in," I said, and held the door for her. She turned and waved toward the street, and I saw an idling cab slide away into a fine, opalescent mist that had not been there when I went to bed. There was a chill under the rain, and Lucy's breath, as she turned back to me, was frosted white. The misting rain was caught in her tangled, silky dark hair and haloed her head like the streetlights below. She came into my apartment and glanced around my tiny living room carelessly, as if she was not registering what she was seeing. She probably was not; her eyes had the flat glitter they got when she had had too much to drink. She sat down on my thrift store sofa and crossed her long legs and stuffed her hands into the coat pockets and looked up at me, still smiling, still glittering. Then she laughed aloud, the deep, plummy laugh that she had had since her earliest childhood, and I grinned in return, a completely involuntary twitch. Few people failed to respond to Lucy's laugh.

"Aren't you going to ask me what I'm doing here?" she said gaily, and I thought then that there was something more than alcohol burning inside her. For the first time, it occurred to me that her presence here might mean trouble of some sort. I had not thought to ask her if there was anything wrong, despite the hour and the fact that she had said she did not want to see me again, and that I had not known she was anywhere within a thousand miles of me. She appeared, was here; that was all. Lucy in my apartment at three o'clock on an autumn morning was an absolute, and needed nothing else. She filled it as naturally and totally as she had our childhood nursery, or the summerhouse.

"What *are* you doing here?" I said. I was suddenly and uncomfortably aware that I wore only the pair of chinos I had pulled on hastily when the knocking had begun. I was not cold; the rattling old radiator kept the apartment almost tropically warm—when it worked—but I felt vulnerably naked.

"I was in the neighborhood," she said, giggling, "and thought I'd drop in."

I sat down in a rump-sprung butterfly chair opposite her.

"I assume you're up for a weekend with Red and the gang at Old Nassau," I said.

"Right you are," she said. The hectic laughter bubbled just under her voice and burned in her cheeks. "It's the Yale game. Red never misses it. Only he did this year. He's been passed out in his room since eleven o'clock this morning. Well, who gives a shit? There were seventy-four others to party with."

"Lucy," I said, stung with annoyance and distaste and something else I could not name, "you're heading for more trouble than you knew there was in the world."

I could hear the fussiness in my own voice, and expected her to throw it back at me, but she didn't. She got up from the sofa and paced around the little room, still wrapped in the raincoat, looking at the few photographs and posters I had tacked up, and the one drawing—a vivid, darkling pastel of Satchmo blowing it out at the Vanguard, done by someone named Pierce I had never heard of before—and picking up and putting down my few bibelots.

"You don't have to worry about me, Gibby," she said over her shoulder. "When couldn't I handle Red?"

"Well, light somewhere," I said grumpily, "and I'll make us some coffee. From the looks of things you can use some. It's a wonder you made it all the way in from Princeton on the train."

"I didn't. I caught a ride with somebody," she said.

"Who?"

"Oh, God, I don't know, Gibby, I didn't get his name. What difference does it make? I don't want any coffee. Don't you have anything to drink? And maybe an old abandoned cigarette?"

"There are some cigarettes in the desk drawer," I said. "They've been there since summer, so they're probably unsmokable. And it's coffee or nothing. Sit down and take your coat off. You make me nervous pacing around like that."

She turned to me, smiling a strange, closemouthed smile, and then suddenly threw the coat off and dropped it on the floor, and stood there wearing only a white nylon slip. She was naked underneath it. I could see the dark shadows of her nipples, and the patch of smoky hair at the V of her thighs. I dropped my eyes.

"The rest of my pretties are hanging on the wall in the living room at Tiger," she said. "I'm their fair lady of choice this weekend, and I gave them my favors. Instead of one knight, I've got seventy-four. Not counting Red, of course. See what you could have had, Gibby?"

For some reason, I flushed as if this were not Lucy, whose narrow, white whippet body I had known almost as well as my own since childhood. I turned away and walked back to the kitchen, which lay at the end of the pullmanlike row of rooms that made up the apartment. I could hear her unsteady steps behind me. I filled the kettle and set it on the tiny stove and turned around to face her. I was not going to let a drunk, contentious Lucy throw me. I decided to ignore her nakedness.

"Well, how do you like my place?" I said. "Is it anything like you thought it would be?"

"To tell you the truth, I hadn't thought about it," she said. "But I do like it. It's like a little train. It's like . . . oh, Gibby, you know what it's like? It's like Dumboozletown, Florida! Do you remember Dumboozletown?"

She began to laugh again, and the laughter spiraled up and up, until I was afraid that it would go off into one of her old fits of hysteria, but it didn't. It was simply laughter. She threw her head back with it, and laughed and laughed.

I was about to join in, seduced into mirth against my will, when I saw the marks on her throat. They were ugly and unmistakable, the vermilion prints of ten fingers there at the base, where the slender white column joined the elegant, ridged collarbone. An older, purple bruise spread up the side of her neck into her hairline.

"Who choked you, Lucy?" I said. "Was it Red? It was Red, wasn't it? Did it happen this weekend? Is that why you came?"

She stopped laughing abruptly, and put her hand up to her neck, tentatively, as if the marks still hurt her.

"He didn't choke me," she said. Her face closed. "He just kind of shook me a little. He didn't know he was being so rough. He was awfully sorry. No, it's not at all why I came. I told you. I just—"

"Lucy, this is me. Cut the shit," I said. "I know a choke hold when I see one. What was he, drunk, or just mean as hell?"

She didn't answer. I saw that her eyes had found my lone bottle of bourbon, which I kept mainly for visitors; besides the obligatory drinks at the jazz clubs, to make up the cover, I rarely drank then. I could not afford it, for one thing. She reached out for the bourbon, staring at me defiantly. I shrugged. I knew when I was beaten. She unscrewed the top and took a long pull from the bottle, and then put it down and wiped her mouth with the back of her hand.

After a long moment of silence, she said, "He doesn't mean anything by it, you know. Red doesn't. I was being sort of loud and silly, and he couldn't get me to stop, that was all. It's just his way of showing me that he loves me."

I just looked at her.

"Daddy used to do it," she went on, her voice getting louder. "It's not uncommon. Daddy did it because he loved me, too. I'd be bad, and he'd kind of hit me, and then he'd cry because he'd had to . . ."

I suddenly remembered a twilight in the foyer of the house on Peachtree Road, long ago, after small Lucy had run away for the first time and had been spanked by Aunt Willa, and had said then, "Will you hug me now, Mama?" and Aunt Willa had snapped at her, and Lucy had retorted that her father had hugged her all the time, and Aunt Willa had said, "No, he didn't. He never did hug you. You always were a bad girl, and he never did hug you one single time. He hit you, that's what he did. You were so bad he hit you every time you turned around."

And Lucy's great cry of anguish and betrayal, and her sobs diminishing up the great curved stair . . .

"Your mother was telling the truth," I said softly.

She knew what I meant; of course she did. She had always known what I meant.

"Well, maybe. A little, I guess," she said. "But it was only because he loved me, Gibby. That was all it was."

I was silent under the great surge of pain I felt, and the hopelessness. Of course Red Chastain hit her; of course she allowed it; courted it, even. The smiting father, Red's quick fist . . .

After a little space of time she said, matter-of-factly, "I think he's dead, Gibby. In fact, I'm sure of it. I know now that he died in the war, and they didn't know how to let us know."

I did not have to ask who she was talking about. Jim Bondurant stood there in the room with us, whole and living and radiant with remoteness.

"How do you know?"

"Because he would have come for me otherwise," she said simply.

There was nothing to say to that either, so I didn't reply. I just leaned against the counter sipping coffee and watching her. She took a couple more sips from the bottle and lit one of the brittle cigarettes I had found for her, and then she looked up at me and smiled. It was her old smile once more, free and lighthearted.

"Do you remember when we cut our wrists and mixed our blood, Gibby?" she said.

"Sure," I said. "I thought I was going to faint for about five hours afterward."

"I still have my scar," she said, holding up her slim wrist. A thin white line crossed the little delta of blue veins beating there, like half a delicate bracelet. "Do you have yours?"

I held my wrist up to the kitchen light. I had not thought of that day for a long time, not since the day in the summerhouse after her senior prom, when she had evoked the promise that we made then. The scar was there, smaller and fainter than hers, a tiny bleached tributary in the faded tan on my wrist. I held my arm out beside hers and we looked at the scars.

"Poor Luce," I said. "Some knight I made you. I haven't managed to save you from a single dragon so far, have I?"

She looked at me intently, as though by sheer force of will she could extract something from me. Her pupils were black and huge.

"You could save me from one now," she said.

"Red?" I said, dread starting cold in my veins.

"No," she said. Her face looked, abruptly, as if it was starting to crumble, and suddenly she was crying silently, tears sliding down from her light-struck eyes to her chin, dripping off it and pearling down onto her slim, bare shoulders. "No, not Red."

I put my hands on her shoulders, feeling the fine bird's bones through the silky, taut skin, and walked her to the bed and sat her down on the side of it. She did not lift her head, and the tears fell, hot and light, on my hands.

"What, then?" I said.

"Oh, Gibby, I'm so afraid," she whispered, turning into my shoulder, burying her face in the hollow of my neck. I put my arms around her and stroked her back. How many times had I sat like this, holding Lucy while her dreams shook her like a malevolent terrier?

"Tell me what you're afraid of, Lucy," I said.

"Of everything in the world," she sobbed, her voice muffled in my neck. "Of everything that I can't control."

I tried to laugh hearteningly, and did not succeed.

"Then you'll be afraid most of your life, baby," I said.

She turned her face up to me, and it was fierce, savage, half-blind.

"Then I won't live, because I can't stand that—to be afraid for the next sixty or seventy years! I can't even stand it for one more! I'd rather die!"

"Lucy, nobody can control their lives, not really," I said, as reasonably as I could. "But it doesn't mean you have to be afraid all the time. You just . . . sort of forget about it and go on and live your life. You cope. You hang on. And nothing much happens to you, really, in the long run."

"Well, other people are stronger than I am, then," she said, hiccuping. "Or they have something I don't, something that was left out of me. Because I can't stand not being . . . safe. Not knowing what's going to happen to me next. It's like waiting to fall off the world. I feel that way all the time, Gibby, all the *time!*" Her voice rose. "I have to *know* I'm safe. I have to *know* somebody's taking care of me. . . ."

"Lucy . . ."

The crying became wilder, spiraled up, up.

"Promise!" She sobbed. "Promise me! Promise me you'll take care of me!"

"I promise," I said automatically, stroking her back and her hair, feeling the force of the fear and grief out of her deepest childhood under my hands.

She rested there against me for a moment, taking great, deep breaths, and I thought, my own breath held, that perhaps this time one of the terrible spells had, after all, been averted. Then she said, "Do you mean it?"

"Sure I do," I said.

"Then marry me."

I was silent, the shock stopping my breath in earnest for a moment, cursing myself for not seeing where she was heading. Then I said, my mouth still against her hair, "Lucy, the surest way I know to wreck both our lives is to marry you. Understand right now that that isn't going to happen. Not now, not ever. It wouldn't be right. It would ruin us both. Cousins don't. Cousins *can't.*"

Her movement was almost that of some great snake, one of the constrictors, a boa or an anaconda. She turned in my arms as swiftly and with such a smooth slide of muscle that before I could even flex my own she was all over me, and against me, wrapping her legs around my waist, squirming herself beneath me, wriggling out of the slip. She did not speak; her breath came in short, sharp snorts through her nostrils, and she made little high, keening sounds, like an animal. Her hands were at my fly and then inside, and then I felt her warm nakedness against mine, and a great deep, primal thrust and surge, a monstrous great stiffening, and knew that I was about one beat away from losing this fury inside her. My erection felt as massive and volatile and inexorable as a volcano. She found it frantically and was guiding it into herself at the same moment that I tore myself free of her and rolled off the bed. Under the pounding desire was a white anger, and under that, even more powerful, a blind fear.

I turned to the wall and zipped up my pants, fighting for breath and control. I did not hear her move. I pulled on a T-shirt and stuffed it into my pants, and buckled my belt.

"Get up and put on your coat," I said levelly around the breath laboring in my chest. "I'm going to take you back to Princeton."

Incredibly, I heard her laugh, and turned. She was lying naked on her back, hands under her head, legs asprawl. I turned my head away.

"You did want it, didn't you, Gibby?" she said, and her voice

was light and sweet and young. "I know you did. I could feel
it. I can see it now, down there in your pants. Lordy, it must
be something fantastic by now, because I know you've been saving it all this time for Sarah, and we both know she wouldn't
know a hump from a hula hoop, don't we? So what do you do?
Jerk off? Get it down in Times Square? What a waste! You better
think again, Gibby. I could give you a hundred times better before breakfast than little Sarahpoo Cameron ever could in her
entire life."

I picked up the raincoat and jerked her up off the bed and
pulled it around her. She stared at me, smiling and wild-eyed,
and then the subterranean something that had burned deep
within her all evening, like a fire in the earth under a peat bog,
died abruptly out and her face was empty and tired and slack.

"I'm sorry, Gibby," she said, and her voice was so nearly normal that I blinked at her. Nearly normal, but not quite. The life
had gone from it. "I get really sloppy when I drink too much.
Red was right to belt me. Look, I don't want you to take me
back. I've made enough mess of your life tonight. Just call me
a cab and lend me some money, will you? I'll send it to you when
I get home. I can be back in Princeton before my hero even
misses me."

"You sure?" I said, looking at her intently. She smiled briefly
and pulled the belt of the trench coat tight, and raked her long
hands through her wild hair.

"I'm sure. I'd apologize, but it's too late for that. Besides, you
know me. Incorrigible. Oh, Gibby, sweetie, I do love you. I do.
Don't look so worried. I'm okay, truly. I'm going back to Tiger
and rout Red out and make him buy me breakfast at the Tavern.
I'm going to eat until he doesn't have a red cent left."

Reassured, if only slightly, I walked her out into the silent,
wet predawn street and over to Ninth, where I flagged a late-
cruising cab. Ninth looked, in the iridescent mist, like a movie
set, neon-slicked and ribboned with the opalescent snail's track
of a few just-vanished tires, empty and yellow and black and
white. I half expected to see Gene Kelly dancing his way home
through the gutters of Chelsea.

I put all the money I had into Lucy's hand and closed her fingers over it, and put her into the cab.

"Penn Station," I said to the driver. I put my head into the
window and kissed Lucy's cheek, feeling the wetness of the mist
and of her still-fresh tears there. She looked, in spite of the liquor
and the long night and the dirty raincoat, utterly beautiful, and
at her answering wide, world-healing smile I wondered, briefly
and wildly, what it might be like, after all, being married to Lucy

Bondurant and custodian of that slender, lovely body and all its urgent hungers.

"Be good," I said. "Maybe I'll see you Christmas. Take care of yourself, Luce."

She reached up and touched my mouth very lightly with the tips of her fingers.

"That's just what I'm going to do, Gibby," she said.

That night, just past nine, when the night rates came into effect, my mother called me and told me that Lucy and Red Chastain had left Princeton early that morning and driven straight through to Elkton, Maryland, and had been married there by a justice of the peace.

A great stillness settled over me then, which might have been emptiness, or might have been peace.

CHAPTER
FOURTEEN

SARAH GRADUATED *magna cum laude* from Agnes Scott College in June of 1960, and then all the Buckhead Boys and their girls were, to all practical purposes, launched into a wider world. For most of us, that simply meant leaving our nearby Southern college cocoons and moving back into our old rooms in the big houses of Buckhead, or to apartments no more than three miles at most from them, and taking jobs in our fathers' businesses or in those of their friends, none of which were located more than five miles from the pedimented and porticoed doorways we had grown up behind.

But close to home as these new establishments were, they were important rites of passage, not to be skipped, and gave all of us a heady sense of having left the nest. The few of us who actually had left, in the literal sense of the word, like me and Lucy and Red Chastain, were not spoken of so often as mavericks and loners, now that all of us were, in effect, scattered to the winds of fate. The leaving of home was the thing, whether it meant three blocks away or two thousand miles. We turned, in that year, from the sons and daughters of the big houses to young adults with our own venues.

It was the year that the marriages began, and so those venues of our own tended to be, if not the traditional minuscule brick and cinder-block garden apartments in Colonial Homes and East Wesley Court, or the red-brick tenements behind WSB Broadcasting on its high hill overlooking Peachtree Road, then small, neat Colonial "starter" houses in Collier Hills or the area west of Bobby Jones Golf Course just off Northside Drive. Even in the vastly reduced circumstances that Buckhead's young marrieds found themselves, it never occurred to any of us to move east of Peachtree Road. On our own, we had precious little money, but everyone knew that we would have, and we had had from birth our territorial imperatives.

Ben Cameron and Julia Randolph were the first of us to marry, and I went home for the ceremony at All Saints, at four o'clock on the Saturday afternoon Sarah graduated, six hours earlier, from Scott. Despite the blazing hot June sun outside, the old red stone church was dim and cool, and so many white tapers glowed at the altar that the sanctuary looked like the Christmas court of Henry II. There must have been five hundred people there that day, the majority of them unknown to the bride and groom.

Ben Cameron was fifty years old and just coming into his legendary power in Atlanta, and for the past few years had been chairman of every successful fund-raising effort from the Community Chest to the March of Dimes. He was, that year, vice president of the Chamber of Commerce, to become its president the next, and was already, Sarah said, formulating a formal plan of growth and progress for the city that he felt would literally transform it into one of the country's great urban centers. He seemed to know literally everyone who might conceivably wield muscle and influence in that pursuit, and they were all in the church that day, to share the marriage pageant of his firstborn child and only son. Young Ben had had a full complement of friends at North Fulton and Tech, and Julia and her own prominent family were suitably endowed with friends and relatives, but on that day the sanctuary of All Saints fairly teemed with the dark-suited, unassuming, imperial power brokers of a city poised to make its move. Charlie Gentry would reflect later that the feeling that crackled silently in the air of the hushed and radiant church was just what it had seemed to be—electricity.

I was an attendant, as were the entirety of our set and a spill-over of Cameron and Randolph cousins and a couple of fraternity brothers and sorority sisters. There were twenty-four of us in all, a double phalanx of massed black and white and drifted, banked pink organdy at the altar. Sarah was Julia's maid of honor, and so came down the aisle last of the attendants, on the arm of A. J. Kemp, who looked dapper and almost feral in the flickering dimness, like a clever monkey dressed in a tuxedo. I was at the altar in place when they started down the aisle, and Sarah's great eyes flew to mine the length of that vast, shadowy oblong, and she winked. I winked back. Ben and young Ben stood at the foot of the altar, facing the back of the church, where Julia would appear, and in the soft candlelight Ben Senior looked almost as young as his son, humorous and slender and seeming somehow to lounge, even though he stood erect and poised. As for young Ben, I thought at first that he had been drinking, such hectic circles of color burned in his cheeks, and such a tinsel glitter filmed his gray Cameron eyes. But I knew that he would not do that on his wedding day, and put it down to nerves. Ben had always been nervy and volatile.

The organ segued into Purcell's "Trumpet Voluntary" then, and the crowd stirred and murmured softly and turned to watch as Dorothy Cameron came down the aisle alone, on the arm of the young Cameron cousin who was her usher. She was out of place in the traditional Atlanta formal wedding structure; she should have preceded the attendants, after the mother of the bride. But Augusta Randolph had died when Julia was eleven, and Ben had wanted his mother to have this singular place of honor, and Julia agreed. Dorothy Cameron walked the aisle with the same easy grace with which she might have crossed her front lawn.

She smiled as naturally at her son far down at the foot of the great altar as if they had been alone in the Cameron sun-room, and he smiled back, a wide, vivid white smile, and then he moved his eyes and smiled to Sarah, and then to me. I felt a sudden and consuming rush of love for her. She was giving her son to another woman as openhandedly and full-heartedly as she had given everything to him all of his life, and taking joy from the giving. There was nothing in her of my mother's dark, sucking love. Dorothy Cameron at that moment, in her soft French blue and her little corsage of white lilacs, was all light and warmth.

In the choir loft, partially hidden by the great altar itself, a trumpet quartet stood, brass blazing golden, and tossed the shining, pure notes of the voluntary out into the cathedral air, and the murmur that had started with Dorothy's appearance swelled as Julia came into view, on the arm of her father. Angular and snub-nosed and among the nimblest of the Washington Seminary varsity basketball team, Julia on that day, in a cloud of her grandmother's candlelight lace, seemed to hover above the aisle like a feather, or a snowdrop, and glided like a young queen. Her plain, freckled face flamed with the day and her adoration for Ben, and I thought it was true, that old saw, that all brides were beautiful on their wedding day. Lucy's white face leaped unbidden into my mind for a split second, bleached by fatigue and the fluorescent light in the bare little office of a Maryland justice of the peace, the marks of her new husband's hands on her throat hidden by the heavy fall of hair. I banished her image into air, and turned my eyes to Sarah. Her own eyes welled with tears as Julia reached the foot of the altar and gave Ben a tremulous

smile, and she glanced at me, made a tiny, disgusted moue and
blushed, but the tears did not stop. They slid silently down her
cheeks and into the bouquet of stephanotis she held, as her beloved older brother became a married man and leaned over and
lifted his wife's veil and kissed her gaily.

"That ought to be us," I thought. "What's the matter with
me? She's lovely and whole and strong and good inside and out.
I don't think I can love her any more than I do now. I know
she loves me. Why don't I just marry her? When she comes back
from Paris . . ."

Ben went straight from his Sea Island honeymoon to a job
with a promising new firm of rather controversial young architects, two of whom had studied with the radical Bruce Goff at
the University of Oklahoma, and he and Julia moved into the
obligatory small clapboard saltbox on Greystone Road in Collier
Hills, which had been John Randolph's wedding present to his
daughter.

Soon after that, Tom Goodwin married small, sharp-edged
Alfreda Slaton, along with all her hungers and wiles, and they
moved into a one-bedroom apartment in Colonial Homes. Tom's
father had lost the agency and the house and most of his savings
the year before, and for the first time in his life, Tom faced a
future that would be fueled by his earnings alone. A.J. told me
that they had taken bets among themselves on whether or not
Freddie would go through with the marriage, knowing that the
Habersham Road property was beyond her nimble little talons
for good and all now, but she had—probably, A.J. said, because
she had spent the best years of youth pursuing Tom, and knew
that to take the field after new quarry now, her few skimpy
bridges long since burned, would be folly amounting to perpetual
maidenhood. Another theory was that Colby Slaton had said he
would put his daughter out of the house if she did not marry
Tom; no one, it seems, was eager to harbor Freddie. It would
have been as uneasy a menage as a house with a small cobra in
it.

Freddie Slaton Goodwin hated Colonial Homes, and suffered
while she lived there. She was bitten raw with ambition for Tom,
her jealous resentment of the new houses and cars and parties
and vacations and family heirlooms the others were taking for
granted only slightly concealed by a saccharine winsomeness. It
was generally agreed among the Buckhead Boys that Tom was
a good guy, if not overly endowed in the brains department, and
would probably do middling well in his job as an account executive for a novelty advertising firm for a while, but that Freddie
was going to ruin him in the end.

"Dealing with Freddie Goodwin is like being strangled to

death by a climbing rose," Charlie wrote me later that year. Just out of Atlanta Law, where he had transferred when his father had his breakdown, Charlie had moved out of his mother's house and into an apartment in Colonial Homes with a friend from Emory, and had an active social life among the young lawyers and bankers and corporate executives who were beginning to flock to the city. Everyone liked Charlie, both in his social circle and in his job as a fledgling corporate attorney with the Coca-Cola Company, whose stock had made his family's now-dissipated fortune. Of us all, Charlie was the only one who was not seeing anyone in particular—except, of course, Sarah, and everyone, including Charlie, knew that for the sweetly futile exercise it was.

Before that year was out, Snake Cheatham married Lelia Blackburn, Pres Hubbard married Sarton Foy and Little Lady Bondurant made the match of the season and possibly the decade by marrying, in her sophomore year at Brenau, the baroquely wealthy Carter Rawson. We had not really known Carter well; he was a couple of years older than most of us, and had spent most of his time away at Phillips Exeter and then Yale and Wharton. But none of us doubted that Carter was a genius at business, as his father was and his grandfather before him, and that he would make of his family's vast land development company a name that shone on other shores than America's. Nobody questioned, either, what a man of his vision and worldliness saw in the essentially turkey-brained Little Lady. She was so exquisitely beautiful and well and specifically trained for a pivotal position in society that she could have walked into any city in the country and run its foremost charity balls without turning a honey-blond hair.

Adelaide Bondurant Rawson was possibly the most valuable property that Carter Rawson would ever acquire, and her long, arduous cultivation paid off in spades and diamonds for my aunt Willa. On the day she gave over Little Lady into Carter's pirate-dark hands, she was asked to serve on the hospitality committee of the Piedmont Ball and to join both the Friday Femmes and the Every Thursday Study Club. Not even my mother belonged to the Every Thursday. Mother went to bed for an entire weekend with one of her migraines, and did not get up until Monday. Aunt Willa went, for the first time in twenty years, to lunch at the Driving Club alone with my father. Not a blue-rinsed head turned; she had known they would not. People might talk about Willa Slagle Bondurant, lingerie buyer, lunching alone with her brother-in-law; they would not talk about Willa Slagle Bondurant, mother-in-law of Carter Rawson III.

A. J. Kemp, like Charlie, was unmarried, laughing that he

could not afford a wife until he had made his fortune in the large and conservative bank of which Snake Cheatham's father was president. But he was said to be serious about an agreeable, intelligent, awesomely plain and warmhearted girl of no background at all from Hogansville, Georgia, named Lana Bates. None of us except Freddie Goodwin had met Lana or knew anything about her, except that she was a teller at the bank, and was starting into the bank's junior executive training program, where A.J. had met her. Freddie knew her only because when she had learned of her existence, she had gone straight downtown and into the bank and up to Lana's window and introduced herself, and asked her to have coffee at her break, and had spent the entire fifteen minutes sweetly catechizing her.

"Her father is a livestock farmer," Freddie said afterward, her little eyes glinting with the satisfaction of one who has found, at last, someone impossible to be envious of. "And it ain't white Angus, either, if you know what I mean. He raises Poland China *hogs.* Lana had a prize hog herself when she was a 4-H girl. Some of it must have rubbed off. She could definitely lose a tad of lard, and her nose turns right up like a little old pink snout."

Somebody told her to shut up, causing her to huff and sputter, but when our crowd did meet Lana, no one was impressed, and we treated her with such remote, exquisite courtesy that A.J. didn't bring her around anymore, and didn't come himself; he married her that Christmas in the little white frame church in Hogansville with no one from Atlanta in attendance but his mother, Melba, who must have bitterly, if silently, mourned the phantom Buckhead princess bride she had labored so long to make possible for A.J.

"The right wife could have really made something of A.J." was the common word among the aging Buckhead Boys a few years later, when A.J. and Lana left Atlanta and went back to Hogansville, where A.J., to everyone's astonishment, ran the farm that Lana's father had left her.

"And it's no bigger now than it was when he met her," a renewed Freddie murmured. "It's still just a little old thing with pigs and chickens and cows and not but one or two tenants. A.J. does his own plowing. She helps him in the field."

But I thought by then that A.J. had known early something we did not, and had precisely the right wife, and that she had, indeed, made something of him. Loyal A.J., his hunger finally fed. . . .

It was, everyone who lived it has said, a particularly good time to be young and hopeful and possessed of limitless bright prospects, and a good city to be all that in. After the smug, uneasy years of the Silent Generation, where archconservative eyes saw a wild-eyed Communist behind every tree ("and a wild-eyed nigger behind every Communist," Lucy said later), a new decade was blowing in on the freshening salt wind off the coattails of the vivid young presidential candidate from Massachusetts, who spoke of new commitments and unimaginable horizons and selfless service, that old seductress of the young, and who left the graphite-jowled Richard Nixon in his silvery dust on the nation's television screens. In Atlanta, as in the rest of the South, racial unrest stirred like the great dragon at the base of the Norse earth tree Yggdrasil, but the city's penultimate pragmatism bid fair to tame the serpent, in the name of good business. After years of stagnation, Ben Cameron and his tough, aristocratic new power structure were training their sights on a six-point program designed to keep the public schools open, build a vast new network of local freeways, implement a new program of urban renewal, erect a world-class auditorium-coliseum and stadium, get a rapid-transit system rolling and tell the country about it in an ambitious, if chauvinistic, public relations effort called Forward Atlanta. An attractive and high-spirited spate of bright young men and women from small towns and cities and universities all over the South were pouring into the city to work and live and play, and were staying to marry and settle down and become themselves Atlantans. Many of them became, in time, our crowd's friends, and remained so all their lives. Our parents wouldn't have given them house or club room, though they would, of course, have been courteous, but we would and did; by the end of that decade, about half the memberships in the social and civic clubs around the city were in the names of the out-of-towners, and even the Driving Club had a few on its rosters. These were not the tackpots of whom Old Atlanta still speaks; those tend to be Yankees and Arabs and Texans, or whoever is perceived to have enormous push and money and no commonality at all of ancestry. These new youngsters were, to our astonishment, as presentable as we were. They just hadn't had the good fortune to have been born in Buckhead. No one but the oldest of the Old Guard held it against them.

What we had, I think, in those first hopeful days of that incredible decade, was a town that was fast becoming a real city, in every sense of the word: a young upland city whose beauty was still untrivialized by asphalt and concrete, whose youth had not yet become arrogance, whose ambition had not become venality, whose energy had not become uproar. It was beginning to be a city of uncountable intriguing parts, yet it was, then, still small enough to be perceived all at once. If I am sorry for anything about my absence in those years, I am sorry about missing Atlanta as it spun into the orbit of Camelot.

It was about the time of Ben and Julia's wedding that the calls from Lucy began. When the first one came, the week after I had gotten back to New York from Sarah's graduation and Ben's wedding, I thought at first that something calamitous had happened. It was five o'clock in the morning, past the hour even the most dedicated drinkers of my circle would call to cajole me into going somewhere or providing a last one for the road, and I was fully awake and focused in every fiber when I picked up the receiver.

"Hello?" I said warily.

There was a rushing silence like you get on long distance, and then a deep inhalation of breath, and then Lucy's voice came, familiar and strange at once, borne out on the little sigh that I knew was exhaled smoke.

"Hey, Gibby," she said. "It's Lucy, honey." From then on until her death, almost every telephone conversation we had began with that deep drag from the cigarette, and her throaty little "Hey, Gibby."

"Lucy? What's the matter?"

"Nothing's the matter," she said. Her rich, lazy drawl did not sound as though anything was. "What would be the matter?"

"Lucy, it's five o'clock in the morning!"

"Oh, that's right. You're three hours ahead. I never will get used to that. It's just two here. Did I wake you up?"

"Oh, no," I said sarcastically, annoyance at her flooding in after the relief of finding that she was all right. "I had to get up to answer the phone anyway."

She laughed, and that dark silk banner rolled across three thousand miles to me, and brought her into the room. I could see her boneless slouch, and the precariously lengthening ash on her cigarette, and the long legs propped up on whatever was at hand. California seemed as close as the next apartment.

"What's going on with you, Gibby?" she said. "Tell me your news. Tell me about graduation, and Ben and Julia's wedding."

"Lucy, I could tell you all that at eight o'clock at night, or in broad daylight, just as well as dawn. What are you doing still up? I know you didn't just get up, so you must not have gone to bed yet."

She laughed again, and I heard the slight edge of unstable brilliance that liquor always gave her laugh.

"I've been to a party," she said, "and everybody else has pooped out, and I'm not sleepy yet. Just bored. And all of a sudden I thought I'd like to hear your voice. It's been a long time, Gibby."

"Only eight months, two weeks and four days," I said. I might have been, on some level, relieved to have Lucy in other hands than mine, but I was still nettled by her long silence.

Word of her and Red had come fairly frequently from my mother, who got it from Aunt Willa, who in turn got it from Red's meek, woebegone mother. His father had not spoken to him since he had left Princeton and married Lucy. I was exasperated by my mother's calls, and at the creaminess of the ill-concealed satisfaction in her voice when she related the latest of Red and Lucy's decidedly unmeteor-like odyssey, but I always listened. I had, I found, a deep and simple need to know where Lucy was.

On the morning after their wedding, after waking in an Ocean City motel room with a monstrous crimson hangover and a ravening thirst, Red had telephoned his father in Atlanta and, with a fine show of bravado, told him about the wedding and announced that he was bringing Lucy home for a visit before returning to Princeton, and that he thought a small celebratory party at the Driving Club might not be amiss.

"The next party you have is apt to be at the V.F.W. in wherever you are," Farrell Chastain said, "because you aren't getting one more red cent from me while I'm alive or after that, either. Whether or not you keep on at Princeton depends on how bad you want to wait tables or jerk sodas."

Red did not think these were viable options. He asked to speak to his mother. He could hear her weeping in the background, and pleading to be allowed to talk to her son, but Farrell Chastain would not permit it. He hung up. When Lucy awoke, as badly incapacitated as her new husband, it was to learn that he had been turned away from his father's door like her own father before him at *his* marriage, and that her bridge to the cloistered world of Peachtree Road and its great houses—the only one she had ever known—was blazing away merrily. Whether she met it with fear or panache I do not know, but it must have been a very bad moment for her. She was, she must have realized, as neatly trapped as a rat in a cage, and that knowledge had always sent Lucy wild.

Red had then announced that he had always wanted to be a marine and enlisted within the hour at an Ocean City recruiting office, and they left at noon for Parris Island, South Carolina, in the white Jaguar that had been Farrell's high school graduation present to his son. Between them, they had fifty-five dollars and fourteen cents. When he wired his bank in Princeton for funds, Red discovered that his father had closed his account, and a furtive phone call home at an hour when he knew his father would be at work yielded only the two hundred-odd dollars that his mother had in her household account. She promised, still

sobbing, to wire it as soon as they let her know where they would
be living, or Lucy would be. Red would live on base in conditions
he had not known existed. Given their combined assets, Lucy's
first married home was the Flamingo Motel, located two miles
outside the base on a pitted two-lane blacktop road, backed by
a savage, mosquito-spawning low-country marsh. The Flamingo
did not have a pool. It did not even have air-conditioning. By
the time Red's first paycheck came and she found a tiny cinder-
block efficiency apartment in nearby Beaufort, she was welted
all over with festering bites, and had dropped six pounds from
her elegant greyhound's body.

There had followed, for Red, boot camp, officer candidate
school at Quantico, Virginia, an invitation to the elite and dangerous Army Ranger School at Fort Benning, and finally, a tour
of duty as a second lieutenant at Camp Pendleton, California.
For the spoiled and indolent son of a very rich man, Red took
to it all like a pintail to water. Whatever recessive outlaw genes
underlay his smiling, sleepy rages and scarlet lapses into brutal-
ity came surging to the fore during the grueling hours of basic
training and the stylized savagery of ranger training, and Red
at last found his level. It was not nearly so refined as the one
he had occupied for the first twenty-one years of his life, but the
constant adrenaline high of danger and mastery and the small,
select society of his murderous peers more than made up for the
loss of creature comforts and privilege his father's money had
bought him.

Red found that he was as good at being a golden killing machine as he had been at being a rich boy. And he liked it a great
deal more. It gave him a focus and a license that all the civilian
years of his life had not. By the time he was twenty-four years
old he was as totally assimilated into his new persona and world
as if he had been born to it, and Lucy hung there with him, a
silver and ebony fly in an elite and lethal amber.

I don't know precisely how her new life was for her, or what
she thought about it. As she had done with the hated little girls'
school when she was small, she refused to talk to me about those
first months as a marine bride, traipsing from South Carolina
swamp to sun-blasted Georgia plain and finally to that barren
Quonset hut on the high ocean plains of southern California,
scoured by the merciless sun and punished by the Santa Ana
winds. She never did, to my knowledge, tell anyone about them
and her silence spoke for itself. To sensitive, imaginative Lucy
Bondurant, quivering with life and terror and bravado and vulnerability like a tuning fork, uprooted from the only refuge she
had ever known and the few friends and family who were all she
had; no longer the devil-may-care, supremely desirable will-o'-

the-wisp who tormented and titillated a generation of sweating
Jells, but now merely a thin, mosquito-bitten second lieutenant's
wife at the rock bottom of the Marine Corps social pecking
order, it must have truly been what her silence proclaimed it to
be—unspeakable. But there was nothing of that in her voice during that first telephone call, and it was only much later that I
began to think what indeed her first year as Mrs. Nunnally
Chastain must have been like.

"Why don't you wake up Red and party with him?" I said
on that June night in 1960, when the first call came. "As I recall,
he was always in the forefront of the better parties of our generation."

"Red's been out for two weeks slithering through the swamps
with a knife between his teeth, garroting rattlesnakes and blowing up yuccas," she said, giggling, and the liquor flashed in the
giggle, too. "He's in training to overthrow Cleveland."

"Then who were you partying with?" I asked.

"His C.O.," she chortled. "Perfectly adorable little old Texas
boy named Rafer Hodges. Captain Rafer Hodges, U.S.M.C.
Seven feet tall and towheaded as a yard dog, and with a tattoo
that says 'Semper Fi.' I'm not going to tell you where it is. Only
his platoon and his wife and I know that."

"And where was this wife?" I asked carefully. This sounded
like more trouble. I did not know why I was surprised.

"At home polishing his saber, I guess, or sleeping the sleep
of the just. Where she said she was going when she stormed out
of the officers' club after old Rafer danced with me for the fourth
time straight. She really pulls rank, Gibby. Six other senior wives
toddled right out behind her. What the hell, it just left that many
more marines to party with. And I outdrank them all. Think
of it, Gibby, I drank seven marines under the table in one night!"

"Lucy, you are going to absolutely fry yourself with those
women if you don't watch it," I said despairingly. "You can't
behave in the service like you did at home. You'll be an outcast
and Red's career will be down the drain. You must know that.
Is that what you're trying to do, wreck him with the marines?"

"Oh, shit, Gibby, you're still a prick, aren't you?" she said,
sullen now. "Those women were squiffed to the eyeballs themselves. I'll be good from now on, and charm their pants off them,
and they'll forget it in no time."

"Tell me something," I said. "Why are you drinking so
much?"

"Because," she said, "it makes everything special."

"Luce, you haven't even been married a year. You shouldn't
have to drink for things to be special. Even if you hate the life

out there, there's Red; you don't hate Red. My God, you went with him for five years before you married. You must love him."

"Red's changed," she said briefly.

"How?" I asked, not wanting to hear it. Those dark fingerprints . . .

"Oh . . . I don't know. No way and every way, really. He's . . . totally absorbed in the rangers; sometimes he doesn't even come home when he could. He and some of the other guys will go out for days at a time into the desert, with just knives and a couple of matches, and come back stinking and filthy and drunk and happy as larks. And he doesn't much want to party and dance at the club anymore, and you know how he used to love that . . . but mainly, Gibby, it's just that he doesn't understand me. I know now that he never did."

I could have told you that five years ago, I did not say.

"You're not the easiest gal in the world to understand," I said instead.

"You understand me, Gibby," she said softly. "You always did."

Presently she hung up, and I lay there in the bleached, clamorous New York dawn, troubled, trying to imagine the truth of Lucy. Later, I put it together: The absences from the meager base housing, more and more frequent, longer and longer, while Red slipped into that literal country of lost boys, the U.S. Rangers. Later, the tours of sea duty, long months on end. Lucy left behind, knowing no one but marine wives, who disliked and distrusted her for her beauty, her high spirits, her Southern exoticism and the dangerous shoals of mischief and more than mischief they sensed just below her vibrant surface. Their husbands and their husbands' superiors, much taken with her reckless dash and splendid looks, and in some cases downright smitten, but sensing in Lucy Bondurant Chastain the stuff of reprimands and toppled careers. A few disastrous evenings at the officers' club in which she drank too much, flirted too brazenly, slipped outside with too many crew-cut young officers. A few equally disastrous teas and receptions in which she wore outrageously provocative clothing and said "shit" in the hearing of wives much her senior. And so she found herself a literal pariah, on that hot and unimaginable coast, alone both in her home and away from it. And the phone calls to New York, over the course of that hot summer, began in earnest.

The pattern was always the same: the late-night burr of the telephone, the deep, indrawn breath as she dragged comfortingly on her cigarette, and then her voice spinning across the country to me, rich and low and thick with all our shared history: "Hey, Gibby. It's Lucy, honey."

And there would follow the gleeful recounting of her latest escapade, and what she had said to whom in the commissary, and how she had that fool of a captain lifting bumpers out in the officers' club parking lot, and how she had shocked that old trout, the rear admiral's wife. She was usually drunk, and always, under the glee and high spirits, there ran a litany, a near-frantic dirge, of loneliness and something more, something high and silvery and skewed. The calls came closer and closer together, and by the end of the summer they were coming almost every night.

About the middle of August the tales of Red Chastain's drunken and abusive behavior toward her began, and she would sometimes sob plaintively over the telephone, frankly drunk herself more often than not, and began to beg me to come out to Pendleton and rescue her.

After each of the first of these calls I had called her back the next morning, when she was clearheaded and sober, and each time she laughed her warm, infectious laugh and told me not to pay any attention to her, she couldn't hold her liquor worth a damn anymore. So I did not, after a while, worry quite so frantically about her, and listened to the next call with a reasonable amount of skepticism. But the calls continued, and each time she sounded so genuinely frightened, and so desperate, that fear for her and rage at Red would come flooding back, and I would find myself in the same old stew of Lucy-begotten agitation I had simmered in for much of my life.

Sarah visited me several times that summer, and each time she was witness to one of Lucy's late-night calls. She would fall silent when they came, and her lashes would slip down over her great amber eyes, and her mobile mouth would tighten, but she never said anything about them.

On one such evening, something I said—or did not say—must have alerted Lucy to the fact that Sarah was in the room with me, because she said, "Oh, am I interrupting anything, Gibby? Like coitus interruptus, I mean? I can always call you back. But no, I guess not. Sarah no coito, does she? I swear, Gibby, if you marry that girl, you're going to have to get you one of those rubber dollies from Japan with the hole that the guys take on sea duty, because you sure aren't going to get any from little Miss—"

I hung up on her, hot-faced and furious, and Sarah looked at me curiously, but I did not, of course, tell her what Lucy had said. It was insulting and outrageous, and Sarah had already suffered enough from Lucy Bondurant's capricious tongue. And besides, Lucy was right. Despite the closeness we felt for each other, and the hours and days we spent alone in my apartment, and the real, aching sweetness and passion of our kissing and petting, Sarah and I had not made love. We almost had, many times, both of us wet with sweat and fairly shaking with need for each other. But we had not.

I think we were both a little ashamed that we hadn't. Our times together seemed made for physical love. The grand scope and boundless largesse of the city itself fairly shouted for a grand passion to match it. New York in that last golden time before the sixties began to corrode was made for lovers. All around us, both in Manhattan and in Atlanta, the marriages and beginning pregnancies of our peers spoke of what Sarah's fierce grandmother, old Milliment, called sanctified joy. I think the bottom line, for Sarah and me, was that our joy was not sanctified. Absurd as it seems now, in my set at that time you did not casually sleep with, and risk impregnation of, the girl you planned to bring into your ordered and strictured world as your wife. And whole and fully passioned adults as Sarah and I were, we were denizens of that world first. Though we had not talked of marriage with any formality, we both assumed that we would take that step only after Sarah had her year at the Sorbonne. In that suspended and time-stopped summer of 1960, marriage seemed far more than a year and an ocean away.

We did try. Once or twice Sarah simply did not pull away from me, and we lay naked and joined but for a last crucial inch or two of scalding space. And once I actually entered her. But her little gasps and moans turned abruptly to cries of real pain, and I withdrew, cursing myself and her and our parents and the South and all the generations of women from out of both our histories who hovered over us on my narrow iron bed, crying "Stop! Shame! Wrong!"

Afterward, Sarah sat up amid the coiled covers and wept in shame and frustration.

"Oh, Shep," she cried, "who the hell *am* I? Am I a lady or an artist or a cockteaser, or what? I'm not a complete anything! I'm not even a good wanton!"

After that, I did not let things get so close again. I was often the one to pull away. For us, we agreed, waiting was the right, if not the comfortable, thing. We agreed on everything in those days, shared all that we had. All we seemed to lack was a grand enough passion to get us properly fucked, but I guess that lack was in its way a lethal one. For myself, I despised my status as a virgin, feeling that it made of me both an emotional and an actual neuter. But a deep well of fear stopped me from seriously considering sex with anyone but Sarah. I had not, perhaps, actually had a woman, but I had had that desire and lost it to my cousin Lucy all those years before in the summerhouse behind the house on Peachtree Road.

The week before she was to leave for Paris, in early September, Sarah spent a final weekend with me. Still blamelessly based at the Barbizon, she nevertheless spent all but a scant six hours of sleeping time with me that Friday night and Saturday, and at ten o'clock on Saturday night, after a day of soaking up enough galleries and museums and walking and looking and munching and hand holding and furtive kissing to last us the nine months until she came home again, we were just sitting down to a take-out pizza and a bottle of Chianti when the telephone rang. We both knew, with radars sharpened by impending separation, that it was Lucy. Sarah did not speak.

"I'll cut this short," I said, reaching for the telephone. Sarah still said nothing. She nodded.

But I did not cut it short. Lucy was calling from the apartment of one of the other marine wives at Pendleton, and between her incoherent sobs and the other girl's indignant breaking in, it took me nearly an hour to get from Lucy that Red had blackened her eyes and cut her lip and locked her out of their apartment, and had threatened to split her skull if she came back in.

"Oh, Gibby, what should I do? He's awfully drunk; he could kill me," she wept. Her voice was slurred with liquor and the damaged mouth.

"Call the MPs, Lucy," I said, fear and outrage at Red swamping and drowning my anger at her call. "Don't mess around with him. Just call the MPs right now."

"I can't," she wailed. "They don't bother the rangers. Everybody knows that. It's like a club, or some kind of conspiracy. Nobody bothers the goddamned almighty rangers! They'd put me in jail instead!"

"They don't have any jurisdiction over you, Luce," I said. "Listen, are you drunk, too?"

"Maybe a little," she sniffed. "But that doesn't give him the right to beat me up. Listen, Gibby, you've just got to come. You've got to get me out of here. . . ."

At last I soothed her, and extracted a promise from the other wife that she would call me in the morning and tell me how things stood then. I knew that my concern for Lucy was audible; I could feel it thickening my voice like river silt. I put the phone down and turned to Sarah, who had not stirred from her chair. Her face was very white, and the high color in her cheeks burned even brighter, but her expression was mild and questioning.

"She's in awful trouble," I said. "He's beating her regularly. He's hurt her pretty badly this time. She wants me to come. I really ought to go."

And Sarah exploded.

"If you go out there, Shep," she said between clenched teeth, the sherry eyes all pupil and spilling angry tears, "you'll have her for the rest of your life. It's what she wants. She always has. You're a fool if you can't see that. And maybe it's what you want, too, no matter what you think or say. But it's not what I want. And I won't have it. I'm not going to share you anymore with Lucy Bondurant! I'm *not!*"

And she frightened herself so thoroughly with her outburst, and her hurt was so deep, that Sarah, whose mannerly tears I had seen perhaps three times in our entire lives, burst into a storm of weeping. She ducked her chin down and crossed her arms over her chest and rocked back and forth on the spavined sofa, crying the square-mouthed, heartbreaking sobs of a suffering child. I had never in my life seen Sarah so abandoned, or heard her make such sounds.

The sight of her pain burst inside me like a rocket, purging me of Lucy and her three-thousand-mile tendrils of woe, and I moved over and took Sarah into my arms and pressed her so hard against me that I literally stifled the sound of her crying. But the great, racking, silent sobs continued, and a hard, continuous trembling, and I laid her back on the sofa and put my long body over hers, trying with every pound and inch of me to stop the terrible trembling and the cries, to scourge the anguish out of her.

"Don't, Sarah, don't, don't," I whispered into the drenched and matted hair, into her ear. "Please don't . . ."

"Oh, Shep, do it now!" she cried out into my own ear—and I did. Without thought, without qualm, without regret, without consideration for the pain she must feel, or the fear, I shucked her out of her clothes and went into her and plunged there, back and forth, back and forth, and felt her settle around me and find my rhythm and ride with it, and felt her hips rise and fall and quicken and her legs clench my back, and heard her great, hoarse cry as we came together and my own cry escaped me—a cry of gratitude and simple relief and a joy as old and deep as the world.

When my breathing slowed and I moved off her and propped myself up on one elbow and looked down into her face, she smiled a smile of utter luminosity and reached up and traced a track down my cheek. I realized then that the wetness on my face was partly from my own tears.

"We did it," she said, grinning. I thought that I had never seen anything so beautiful as Sarah Cameron was at that moment, lying stained and red-faced and slack on my sofa, wet curls matted black around her face, crimson flooding her still-tanned skin. She looked to me then like a ripe and perfect plum.

"We did it," I echoed. "And I'm going out and hire a cannon

and give a twenty-one-gun salute. God! I had no idea! You know,
I guess, that I never have before . . ."

"I know," she said.

"Has that ever bothered you? It's not exactly normal."

"What's normal?" she said, stretching luxuriously. I watched
the play of swimming muscles in her elegant little body, and the
sheen of sweat on her. "It was the first time for me, too."

"Well, God, of *course* it was," I said. I had never considered
that Sarah was not a virgin.

A thought struck me then, and wiped the goatish satisfaction
clear out of me.

"Sarah, listen, do you think you could get pregnant? I mean,
when's your next . . . period?" And I appalled myself by reddening to my hairline.

"In a couple of weeks," she said, blushing herself. Intercourse
did not make the Pinks and the Jells of Atlanta blush, but menstruation did, and so far as I am concerned, still does.

"But it's okay. I won't get pregnant."

"How do you know?" I said. "I didn't . . . use anything."

Sarah's face flamed even redder, and she dropped her eyes.

"I did," she said.

I simply stared at her.

"I have a diaphragm," she went on rapidly in a voice so low
that I could hardly hear her words. "I put it on right after we
came in. I got it from Snake a year ago, and I've worn it since
then every night we've been together when I came to New York.
You may think I'm trashy, but you don't have to worry about
me getting pregnant."

"Sarah . . ." I couldn't think of anything to say. I thought of
what it must have cost her to go to Snake and ask for a diaphragm; would he have had to examine and fit her for it? I did
not know. The idea was too appalling to entertain. Had she so
mistrusted me, then?

"Were you afraid I was going to force you?" I said.

"Oh, Shep, *no!*" She was truly aghast. "I wasn't *afraid* you
would, I *hoped* you would! I just couldn't get myself past the . . .
the point of no return . . . but I always hoped that one night you'd
just go on and . . . do what I couldn't . . ."

I took her back into my arms and held her close, not speaking,
rocking with her a little, consumed with love and gratitude.

"It's a good thing you're leaving for Paris," I said finally, "because I don't think I'd ever let you out of bed if you weren't
across an entire ocean."

"Am I worth waiting for?" She grinned.

"You bet your ass you are," I said. "Your little perfect pink
and white ass. But, Sarah—no longer than it takes you to get

off the boat and get here. And then, just think . . . all those days and nights and months and years of sack time ahead of us . . ."

"Yes," she said. "All the time in the world."

It wasn't until she was getting on the plane at La Guardia the next evening that, typically, she turned to me and said, her amber eyes crinkled with mischief, "You know who we have to thank for everything, don't you?"

"Who?"

"Lucy, of course. You ought to send her a dozen roses. Or I ought. Or on second thought, forget it. It would make her crazy. She'd be back here in three hours, sobbing on your door-step, and I won't be here to tell her hands off."

"Then I'll tell her myself," I said, kissing her a last long time.

"Don't forget," she said, turning to leave me for Atlanta and then Paris, and taking what felt to be the bulk of my soul with her. "If I ever catch you in Lucy Bondurant's clutches, it's going to be curtains for us. I am a woman of few words and strong mind."

And she was gone into a dazzle of late September sun.

I went back to the apartment on West Twenty-first and sat down to wait for her to come home.

Three weeks after Sarah sailed for France on the *United States,* Red Chastain went out on his first long tour of sea duty, and Lucy was alone at Camp Pendleton for nearly eight months. She called me the night he left, the familiar liquor slur in her voice, the tears just under it.

"Gibby, can you come out here and see me? I'm going to die of loneliness by myself all that time."

It was three-thirty in the morning, and it suddenly struck me with the clarity of revelation that there was no earthly reason why Lucy had to call me at that hour to tell me she was lonely for Red Chastain. I took a deep breath.

"Lucy," I said, "no. I can't come out there to see you. I can't and I won't. You're a grown, married woman. You've got eight months to be safe from Red, if that's what you want, and nothing you have to do and nobody to be accountable to, and I don't want you to call me again unless it's a certifiable, life-threatening emergency, and then it better be in the daylight, my time. If you're lonesome, make some friends. Take a course. Plant a gar-den. Plant a tree. Write a book. But don't tell me about it."

"What would I write about, Gibby?"

"Anything, Luce," I said. "Anything at all that comes into your head. I'm sure you'll think of something."

And I hung up the phone and turned off the light. The tele-phone rang twice after that, at thirty-minute intervals, but I ground my teeth and did not answer. It rang again the next night at eleven, and the next at eight, and both times I sat staring at it while it rang, fists clenched, teeth gritted, and after that it did not ring again. Whatever Lucy elected to do to pass the days and weeks and months until her husband came back to catch her up in their dreadful red waltz, I did not hear of it.

Fall passed, Christmas came and went, the spring was born and grew old. Sarah wrote vibrant, brimming letters and I answered with yearning ones. I saw friends or did not, ate or did not, listened to and played jazz or stayed home, buried myself in my underground tunnels and vaults and the cloistered aboveground stacks, slept, awoke, did it all again; and the emptiness where Sarah was not gradually filled, as the days passed and the time of her return approached, with a great, slumbering anticipation that was born in my groin as well as my heart. I did not think I could wait to see and touch and smell and taste her again.

She was due in at midmorning on the fifth of June, 1961. Ben and Dorothy Cameron came up from Atlanta to meet her, and I went up to the Plaza the night before she landed to meet them for dinner in the Oak Room. In all my years in New York, I had never been into the dark, graceful old room, with its air of age and privilege and substance. Ben and Dorothy always stayed at the Plaza; it had been Ben's father's accustomed lair when he visited New York, and as Ben said, the Camerons didn't play around with tradition.

I looked at him closely that night, as if for the first time seeing the man the entire country would know, within a few years, as the aristocratic mayor of the Southern city that somehow managed to keep, in the fire storms of the mid-1960s, a kind of furious peace with its black citizens. Against the mellow old paneling of the Oak Room, I watched him toying with the silver and taking the level gray measure of the moneyed men and women around him, most of whom instinctively lifted their heads to stare at him, and I saw too that much of the laughter had gone out of his light Celt's eyes, and been replaced with a kind of narrow measuring. His pupils were contracted to pinpoints in the dim light; that, and the web of white weather lines in the thin, tanned skin around his eyes, gave him the look of a man accustomed to gazing great distances. For the first time in my life, I felt just a little uneasy with him, not quite so effortlessly comfortable as I had with the lounging, laughing young father of Ben and Sarah. Dorothy, beside him, did not seem changed. In simple cream silk, which set off her vivid coloring and cameo features and enriched the dark hair and brows that were Sarah's, she glowed like an Advent candle. I thought she looked very beautiful. Sarah would be a beautiful older woman.

Ben talked a little, after the dessert plates had been taken away and the old five-star cognac that he loved brought, about the six-point program for the city's growth that Sarah had told me about earlier, and about the public relations effort he hoped would bring Atlanta into national focus.

"It's called Forward Atlanta," he said, and I laughed before I thought.

"God," I said. "Talk about horn blowing and flag waving. It ain't exactly subtle, is it?"

He grinned. "Nope," he said. "Downright gauche. But I don't knock it. In fact, I'm the one who thought of it. Atlanta is gauche, Shep. Always has been. But that gaucherie is going to set us on fire in the next ten years."

"What about the race business?" I said. "That could literally burn you up."

"That's the kicker, of course," he said, his grin fading. "That could sink us. But I don't think it will. It's not good for business. And I've got some agents in place who can do a lot to defuse it. But you're right; it could be bad. We can't let it happen, that's all. We need the Negroes with us, not against us. We need their cooperation and we need their money. We can't do everything that needs doing without them."

"Can you do it even with them? It's a radical proposal, Ben, to completely remake a city. . . ."

"Yes. We can do it," he said. "We can *just* do it. They call us the power structure, you know; sometimes, the Club. And we are those things, and that's why we can get it done—we have a lot of money and we can finance the big stuff at home. And we're in absolute accord on what needs to be done. That's eighty percent of the battle. We can make the big push alone, by ourselves. But after that, to sustain it, we'll have to have more than momentum. We'll have to have outside money. And with that, of course, will come outsiders. And the Club, or we Buckhead guys, if you will, will be doomed. We know that; there it is. There just aren't enough of you hometown Young Turks coming up behind us."

"Are you still pushing for me to come back to Atlanta?" I asked.

"I guess so," he said.

"Why? The city you're talking about doesn't need another librarian."

"The city I'm talking about needs another smart, thoughtful young man with money," Ben Cameron said.

"I don't have any money, Ben. I'm not apt to have any," I said honestly. Surely he knew about the estrangement between me and my father.

"You don't know what you have, Shep," he said. "Your father never *let* you know, and never let your mother tell you. Do you even know where your family's holdings are?"

"Not really," I said. "Down in the southeast part of town somewhere around the old cotton mill, I think. . . ."

"Well, I'll show you exactly where when you get home."

"Ben . . ."

"Goddamn it, Shep, you'll have to come home eventually to marry Sarah, even if you leave the next day," he said crisply. "I'm not going to let you get out of town without taking you by the hand and marching you down to Cabbagetown and showing you just where the Bondurant dough comes from."

I lifted my hands and let them fall. I did not feel like arguing that my family's real estate holdings were as unlikely to become mine as the Brooklyn Bridge was. My head was too full of tomorrow and the coming of Sarah.

They arranged to pick me up the next morning on the way over to the West Side docks, and I waved aside Ben's offer of a cab and walked the forty blocks home. I walked slowly in the soft air, letting the slackening rhythm of the city night suck and swirl around me. I thought of nothing, and was happy. It was nearly midnight when I got back to my apartment, and the shrilling telephone had almost stopped ringing when I got the door unlocked and picked up the receiver.

I was fully expecting to hear Ben's voice, or Dorothy's, but the voice that came on the line in the little hollow of air that meant long distance was that of a crisp, businesslike young doctor in the base hospital at Camp Pendleton, California, and for a moment I could not take in what he was saying. And then I could: Lucy was in the hospital, five of her teeth knocked out and her broken jaw wired shut, with an additional broken collarbone and fractured forearm. And there was, in her scalp, a shallow, trenchlike laceration where the bullet from Red Chastain's service revolver had grazed her.

I did not say anything, and the voice went on. The Pendleton MPs were looking for Lieutenant Chastain, it said, and Mrs. Chastain would be well enough to be released on the following Monday morning, but since she could not be alone, and since no one at the Atlanta number she had given them would speak with her doctors or her husband's superiors, all of whom were very concerned for her precarious emotional state as well as her injuries, there seemed to be nowhere for her to go. She had said that her cousin, Mr. Bondurant, would come and take her to her home in Atlanta, and if it was possible, they hoped I would do so immediately. She was so frantic for me to come that they could not restrain her, and had twice had to snip the wires that held her shattered jaw so that she could breathe. They could not, the doctor said, be responsible for her condition if I did not come.

I sat on the edge of my bed for a long time, looking blindly at my feet in their smudged white bucks, sitting squarely together on the floor like good poodles commanded to stay. Then I lifted the receiver and called the Plaza.

I have never known Ben Cameron to be so coldly angry before or since. He said, "I see," a couple of times while I talked, in a voice that was as flat and arctic as a tundra, and when I was done he said, "Shep, you are a complete and miserable goddamned fool if you go out to California after that poor little piece, and if you do, I can't imagine how long it's going to take before I can talk to you reasonably again." And he left the line and handed the phone to Dorothy.

I really believe she understood. She indicated that she did. But she was greatly hurt and disappointed; I knew that, though she did not say so. Instead, in her lovely, low, patrician voice, she said, "What is it about Lucy, do you suppose, Shep? What do you see there, what do you sense?"

"I . . . it's just that she's so vulnerable, Dorothy," I said, endlessly and utterly tired. "And she's totally alone now, and helpless. And in spite of what you think and the way she acts sometimes, there's something innately good and simple in her. . . ."

"No," Dorothy Cameron said. "There's no such thing as innate goodness. Goodness is learned, hard. It presupposes kindness. And Lucy is not kind; she is too afraid and hungry for that. Innocence; that's another matter. That's what's under Lucy, that's what you sense. A terrible, ruthless, implacable innocence. But kindness is a corrupt angel, and it is learned, and Lucy has not learned it and never will learn it."

She paused, and I heard her sigh, and heard a world of fatigue and defeat in the sigh.

"Of course you'll have to go, Shep," she said. "You can't live your life, nor Sarah with you, under the shadow of a refusal to do so. I only ask that you be very, very careful with her. She is a danger to herself and a worse one to you. I'll explain to Sarah. She'll understand."

But Sarah did not understand. By the time I came home from California almost a week later, with a pale, shrunken, nearly unrecognizable Lucy and installed her in her old room in the house on Peachtree Road, after having extracted from my mother and hers a reluctant promise of no I-told-you-so, and rushed to the downstairs telephone niche to call Sarah, it was to hear, from a muted and old-voiced Dorothy Cameron, that Sarah had, just two nights before, announced her engagement to Charlie Gentry. The announcement had been sent to both newspapers, Dorothy said, and would appear in the combined edition on Sunday. That was, of course, tomorrow. She hoped that I would come by and speak to Sarah and to Charlie, who would be there with the family for the congratulatory calls that would follow the announcement as inevitably as the morning sun followed the dawn. Both were anxious to talk with me.

"I hope you will, Shep," she said. "This has been a very, very hard thing for Sarah. It will be a kindness to her if you'll come. She said to tell you that she'll wait for you tomorrow afternoon in the studio."

But I left Atlanta later that day and went back to New York without seeing her.

CHAPTER
FIFTEEN

W HEN I WOULD NOT GO TO THEM, they came to me. I had not been back in New York a week before the phone rang in my apartment, on a Friday evening, and I lifted it to hear Charlie Gentry's voice. Even without the absence of the small hollowness that meant long distance I would have known that he was in the city with me. His voice had such an immediacy that I instinctively held the receiver away from my ear.

"Sarah and I are at the Plaza, and we want to see you," he said without preamble. "None of us can live decently until we've talked. We're not going to go home until we have. When have you got some time?"

He had not said "Hello," or "How are you," or identified himself. Despite his phlegm, Charlie had delicacy and empathy, and he knew that there was no need and no way to frame this conversation in convention. And he knew very well how I was. He had been that way for years: stricken and without Sarah.

Pain and a child's simple, consuming fury at the unfairness of it all surged into the cold, whistling hollow that had filled my chest ever since I had heard Dorothy Cameron's words the Saturday before, and washed back out, tidelike. I saw rather than felt that my knuckles around the black plastic telephone receiver were blue-white, and my whole body was clenched, as one does just after a sudden injury to brace for the pain that will inevitably come boiling in. I hated them both in that moment, weakly and hopelessly, and I felt tears prickle in my eyes. But I willed the pain to stay back.

"I haven't got any time for you, now or ever," I said. My

words sounded childish and impotent even to me, though my voice was level. "I don't have anything to say to either of you. I don't know what you can possibly think you have to say to me. Go on home and go to some parties, or get married, or do good works, or all three."

He sighed.

"Sarah said you wouldn't want to. I didn't believe her. I thought we were more to each other than all this. We're not going home, Shep. We can outwait you, if we have to, but we're going to talk to you. Can we come down?"

"No," I said instantly, in something close to abhorrence. "I'll come up there." I thought I would die, would kill them both, before I let them come here, to these rooms that were my own, that were where Sarah and I had made love and the beginnings of a life. If they came here, every place and everything I had would be contaminated with the pain of them, and I would literally have no refuge. I already sensed the poison of their pairing in the warm air of the city outside, as if it had drifted out from the hotel uptown and curled down into the Lower West Side to find me. When I hung up the telephone I went to the windows, mindlessly, and closed them. Then I put on a gray seersucker suit and a black knit tie and went over to Eighth and hailed a cab. When I got out in front of the Plaza, it was almost nine, the hot, pearled gray of a Manhattan summer twilight, and the white globes of lights were just blooming on Fifth Avenue along the perimeter of the park.

I thought it was sly and meanspirited of them to go to earth in the Plaza, that impenetrable, unassailable fortress of privilege and grace, that spiritual *pied-à-terre* of all the Camerons back to Ben's grandfather. They might as well have been receiving an enemy at an ancestral castle. Power bulked dark against the lucent west, over the hotel. A small part of me, clear and somehow divorced from the clenched deadness, knew that there was not one fiber of Sarah Cameron that was sly or meanspirited, or of Charlie either, and that Sarah had instinctively taken refuge in the Plaza simply because it represented safety and comfort to her. That lucid fraction quivered for an instant with Sarah's pain, as well as my own; actually felt it. But the cold nothingness in me froze it out. Let them do their worst, say their piece, be gone from my city. I would keep a noble silence; they would feel their own cravenness and deceit. Sarah would weep; she would change her mind as they spoke, beg to have me back; it had happened. I ran lightly up the stone steps into the lobby, heart hammering under its glacier.

I had thought they would be waiting for me there, but they

were not, and they were not in the Oak Bar or the Palm Court.
I asked at the desk, not for Charlie, but for Miss Sarah Cameron.
It never occurred to me that they would not have separate
rooms, and they did.

"Miss Cameron asks that you join her in her suite," the desk
clerk said. "Mr. Gentry is with her. Please go up."

I went into the paneled elevator, smelling of good carpet and
lemon wax, and pressed seven. I had never been in an elevator
or a room at the Plaza, and did not think that I would again.
The thought came, unbidden and riding on a dart of promissory
pain, that for the rest of their lives Sarah and Charlie Gentry
could, if they wished, enter this elevator together and be borne
swiftly up to rooms overlooking the park—perhaps the same
ones that the Camerons always had here—and close the door
upon the rest of the world, and that until a week ago, it would
have been me beside Sarah, instead of Charlie. My presence beside Sarah in elevators and hotel rooms seemed as fantastic now,
as unreal, as Charlie's did. Unreality settled over me like a thick
cape, and I burrowed gratefully into it, wrapped away from the
pain.

As soon as Charlie opened the door I knew that coming here
had been a mistake. He stood silently aside for me to enter, and
he looked square and sober and substantial in an olive summer
suit that did nothing for his sallow skin and dark freckles, or
his great brimming, magnified brown eyes. He looked years
older. Only the eyes were the same, mild and bottomless with
Charlie's own mischief and goodness. He did not speak, but
touched my shoulder lightly. I went into the lamplit room.

Sarah sat on a small flowered sofa in front of a great window
that did, indeed, overlook the darkening park, and she rose when
I entered the room and started toward me, then stood still on
the blue carpet, hands clasped loosely in front of her, feet in polished pumps set squarely together. She wore a yellow linen dress,
and her curly crop of hair was smoothed down and back in some
way I had never seen, and her smile was small and seemed to
fight to stay on her mobile mouth. She, too, looked older, suddenly years removed from the ardent, laughing, sweat-sheened
girl who had lain in my arms on West Twenty-first Street a scant
nine months before; and I remembered, dimly and witlessly, that
of course, she had had a season in Paris since we had last met,
and wondered at the change that those months had wrought.

But then I knew that it was not Paris that had changed Sarah,
or the passage of time that had touched Charlie. They looked,
in that warm-lit, gracious room hanging in the midair of Manhattan, irrevocably and every inch and for all time married. The

wedding that was yet to be seemed already years past. There seemed to be no space between them, even though they stood a room apart, and I felt with a plummeting finality verging on physical nausea that somehow, if I had not seen them here, if they had come instead to me, there might have been some possibility of averting the thing ahead, some hope for me. Now, here, there was none. It was done, even though it still lay before us, and the great pain that had been scratching and whining at my door now entered, roaring. I could not speak for it, could not get a breath around it, and so I simply stood in that night-floated frigate of a room looking at them, first at Charlie, and then at Sarah.

"Hello, Shep," Sarah said, and her voice went into and through my heart like a rapier.

"Hello, Sarah," I said. My own voice seemed to come from a source quite apart from me—the overhead light fixture, or the little flowered china clock on the dressing table. I was profoundly surprised that it sounded normal.

"I've called down for some drinks," Charlie said. "I thought we'd have them here and talk a little, and then we hoped you'd let us take you to dinner. You pick the place."

It was that "we" that did it; that "we" which included, now, nothing of me. Rage came riding cold and red and rescuing over the pain.

"I don't think I want to drink with you, Charlie, old boy," I said. "And I believe I'll pass on that dinner. Victory dinner, is it, or a little prenuptial chowdown? You don't have to feed me. I could stay, though, and watch, just to make sure things get done right, you know, like they did in imperial Russia on the royal wedding night, to be sure everybody's parts were working okay."

I heard Sarah's swift indrawn breath of pure hurt, and saw Charlie's face flame dark and ugly. A furtive tongue of shame fed the fire of my anger and it leaped even higher. I knew I would regret my words to the day I died, but I wanted, suddenly, only to wound them, to hurt.

"I can set your mind to rest about Sarah's parts," I said. "They work just fine. I've always wondered about yours, though. We all have."

"God*damn* it, Shep—" Charlie began in a high, shaking voice, but Sarah overrode him.

"Don't take it out on him," she said, and though I was still looking at Charlie, could not look at her, I knew from her voice that she was crying.

"Be mad at me, if you have to be mad at anybody. It was me

who asked him. It was all my idea. He'd never betray you; he never would. . . . Don't take it out on him, please, Shep. At least listen."

I turned to her then. Sure enough, she was crying; she stood in the lamplight against the dark sky, beautiful in yellow and lost to me, and cried, now, for Charlie Gentry. Or at least, I thought that she did. I willed the rage to drown the pain again, and it did.

"What can you possibly say to me, Sarah, that you haven't already said?" I said. "I thought we'd said it all. I know I did. I thought you had. You sure said a lot, the last time we were together. I can't imagine that you have much to add to that."

She turned and ran from the room into the bedroom and shut the door behind her, and I stood looking at where she had been, where now there was only glass, and beyond it, the spangled night. In it I saw, reflected, Charlie lift his shoulders and let them drop again, as if under the weight of great fatigue, and saw him reach a hand out to me, and turned to him. I looked at the hand that he held out. It was square and rough, with blunt-tipped fingers and numerous little scratches and half-healed nicks; Charlie would go through his entire life with the stigmata of his beloved relics on his hands, and the stains of the red Georgia earth that entombed them. It was the same brown hand that had reached for mine through all our shared childhood, that had steadied and supported and applauded and sometimes rescued me, and I saw it in that alien room through a sting of sudden tears. My own shoulders slumped and I lowered my head, but I did not take his hand.

He sat down on the edge of the sofa and looked up at me, motioning me into a wing chair opposite, but I did not sit.

"I know you think I've betrayed you, Shep," he said heavily, "and maybe I have. Maybe I did. But I would have taken her any way I could get her. And it didn't seem to me that you wanted her bad enough. Somebody ought to want Sarah more than anything in the world, and I always did, and I always will. She needs to be cherished. You never cherished her, Shep. I'm going to devote my entire life to making her happy. And maybe, between me and Atlanta, she will be. She needs to be in Atlanta. She was born for it—"

"No!" I shouted. "She was not! No! She was born for me; you know that! She knows it! You're such a poor second choice you're not even close, Charlie! She was just trying to get back at me for going after Lucy; we would have worked that out, but there you were, sniffing around like a dog in heat, and all of a sudden she couldn't even wait one week. . . ."

The color drained entirely from Charlie's face, so that I knew in a ghastly instant what he would look like dead, and he stood up and took a breath so deep that I could hear it tremble and shake in his throat.

"I want you to leave," he said. "I thought we might talk this out with you. I thought we might be able to keep this friendship. I even thought you might give us your blessing; she wanted that, badly. We love you. I did, I do; she does, too. But not like this, and not ever again until you apologize to Sarah. . . ."

The bedroom door opened again, and Sarah came out and stood in front of me and looked so searchingly into my face that I thought I would drown under the endless amber look, or faint from it. The little white lines that fanned out into the faintly tanned skin at the corners of her eyes were deeper, as if she had been squinting, or laughing into the sun, but I knew that Sarah had not, lately, been laughing. Her eyes, and the skin around them, and her short, tilted Cameron nose, were red, but her voice was low and composed. She leaned a little toward me, but she did not touch me. I don't think I could have borne that.

"I have to matter to somebody as much as he does to me, Shep, or I'm . . . totally devalued," she said. "I have to matter that much, or I simply don't exist, somehow. It's silly, maybe, but there it is. I saw when you went out there to get Lucy that I didn't, to you, and that I never would. It would mean everything to me if you could understand how I feel."

I abandoned myself to the rage. It was a feeling, almost, of luxury, of satiation; orgasmic. I had never felt it before, not with my mother or father, not even with Lucy. There was in it, under the sure and certain knowledge of unredeemable, irreparable damage, a kind of savage absolution. I laughed. It was an obscenity even in my own ears.

"You are wrong," I said to Sarah. "You are wrong about me, and you are wrong about that, and you are wrong about everything. You lied. It wasn't me you wanted. You wanted a pet dog, not a husband, and you got one. Enjoy it."

And I slammed out, nearly toppling the room service waiter in the hall outside the door, and rode in a muscle-quivering silence down on the elevator with a flat-voiced man and woman wearing plastic name tags, and left, in the same instant, the hotel and the life of Sarah Tolliver Cameron. I knew that if I should ever meet her again—and I did not plan to do so—it would be Sarah Cameron Gentry I met, and that the meeting would be utterly insupportable.

There should be a body of literature for the male rejected in love. There is one for women. Women stricken by love, or pierced by the loss of it, are strewn through the world's literature like broken roses, and thus is the word made suffering flesh, if not actually ennobled. There are maps for women, blueprints, handbooks, as it were. Emma Bovary lived in that country of pain, Anna Karenina did, Antigone, Mary Magdalene, thousands of their punished kinswomen. The world's tears are their tribute.

But the rejected male is a joke, an embarrassment, a wimp. Worst of all, he does not know how to go about the business of mourning a lost love; who is there to tell him? His discomforted friends will tell him to get going, get drunk, get laid, get another love. And above all, keep quiet about it. Literature and precedent tell him nothing at all. And so he blunders through pain as I did, inept and unconsoled and suspecting, rightly, that he is a figure as ridiculous as he is unwelcome. Ultimately he, like me, withdraws.

After that unspeakable night at the Plaza, my world grayed out. The city that had so charmed and energized me seemed to have become, in some subtle way, almost my enemy. It was, all of a sudden, difficult to get around, to move through traffic, to thread my way through a day. My job and my small society no longer engaged me as they had done when I had the solidarity of Sarah beside me to give them resonance. Even the rush and pour of jazz, which had run through my veins intermingled with my very blood, seemed flat and tepid. I sometimes played my clarinet and saxophone late at night, desultorily, noodling dispiritedly on the fire escape into the hot predawns until fatigue or a maddened neighbor drove me inside again, but I no longer went to Basin Street East or the Vanguard or the Half Note in the evenings. It seemed, not tragic to revisit those places where Sarah, at my side, had flamed with life and joy, but merely pointless. The only thing that did not lose its luster was the glimmering lure of antiquity deep in the stacks of the library, flashing like the golden carp in the pool at Versailles. I was soon spending almost every waking moment that I was not down in the basement working there, reading, reading. I drowned myself in Attica, Thrace, Mycenae, Crete. Long hours might slide by thus, without pain. I stayed until the night crew tossed me out and closed up. A long retreat, I think, began then.

It would not be true to say that every waking moment was filled with pain, but it is fair to say that those which were not were packed in numbness like ice. I learned in those days to will parts of my consciousness dead and cold and calm, and became proficient enough at it so that respectable parts of each day were spent out of the pain's crushing path. Work was the anodyne

all the truisms held it to be, and I became a tireless and awesomely focused worker. If my efforts had been bent on something
more substantial and enriching than trundling rotting paper
from one subterranean chamber of the library to another, I
might have quickly made a lustrous name for myself in some
worthy field. But I did not even think of changing my work; the
labyrinths were as friendly and shielding to me as the poor, mutant Minotaur's to him, and they performed the same function:
they hid me. I burrowed underground by day and into miles and
tons of leather and paper by night, and when both of those ref-
uges were closed to me, I drifted home and tried to hide behind
fast-tarnishing brass and wailing dissonance. That was not so effective as the maze and the stacks. That was when the pain came.

It was sharp and particular and mappable: pure loss, pure loss.
Sometimes, when I had been hidden and deadened away from
it for a few hours, it would waylay me afresh, and the force of
it would fold me over like stomach cramps. Its worst component
was the scalding memory of my behavior toward Sarah and
Charlie, and the sheer treachery of my reaction to their engagement. I had never before so completely lost control of myself,
never before so completely hated and hurt. I had not known that
such excess was in me. I had not known that I could behave so
badly, and exult in it in the bargain. Shame burned its own separate path alongside the other, larger pain's trajectory, and
pure fright at finding such alien corn in my own level field
compounded both. It was a vicious potion. I could not seem to
summon the strength to fight it, even as I recognized the
ludicrousness of languishing in it. Even my own absurdity was
clear to me; I was spared, that terrible summer, nothing at all.

Sometimes, when I could not sleep in the thick, hot nights,
I would try, doggedly, to understand this thing that had my en-
trails in its talons and would not let me go. I had, after all, had
plenty of experience with loss, starting with my father and ending up, over and over again, with Lucy. I was not, had never
been, so naive as to think one did not ever lose what one valued.

But somehow my father and Lucy were things that belonged
to me by birthright, things that I came into the world already
in some way attached to. The first was not so much mine as I
was his; that rejection might be explained simply and brutally
by the fact that I did not measure up to his criteria. In the case
of Lucy, we were mutually and synergistically fashioned to meet
and feed each other's needs, and did so for a long time before
she, too, was—or seemed to be—lost to me. And whatever else
she was to me, Lucy was, and always had been, my responsibility.

But Sarah . . . Sarah was a gift. Sarah Cameron had been my

gift from life, the only one I was ever given until Princeton came to me. That I had not cherished her enough, had in my blind fashion taken her sadly for granted, did not change the fact that Sarah came to me fully and wholly and without condition. Every time the loss of her surfaced anew, the anguish was as red and wet as the day it had been born, and underneath it lay, each time, incredulity. I had not thought that life took its gifts back. But then, as I said, I had never really had any gifts except Sarah and Princeton.

I fled back to Princeton and Firestone Library a few times that summer, but the small, persistent shade of Sarah Cameron was so palpable on that leaf-drowned campus that I kept half turning to her, and finding only vivid, shimmering air where she had just been, and I could not go back again. Obscure anger flared at those times; anger at life for stripping me of both Sarah and Princeton; anger at Sarah for purloining even Princeton from me; and most painful of all, anger at myself for letting her go. I could taste the validity of this last, and it smote me so that I buried it deep, and in time the fresh, blistering pain dulled from searing agony to visceral ache, and I knew, gratefully, that if I walked gingerly and held myself lightly, I could manage, in some fashion, to live with that.

I did not hear from Sarah and Charlie again, of course. I believe I would have, if I had reached out a hand, apologized, made the first move, but I could not. It would not have brought her back, and any lesser payoff was not worth the enormous effort. I heard, in July, that they had moved the Thanksgiving wedding back to September, and that it would be very small, families and a few old friends only, in the little walled garden of the Muscogee Avenue house. I heard this from my mother, who seemed as aggrieved at being deprived of the season's undisputed social event as she was furious at my defection from the house of Cameron.

"I thought you'd want to know, and I don't guess anybody else from here will bother to tell you," she said on the telephone. She did not say that everyone there thought I was a bounder of the first water, and wondered avidly if Sarah was pregnant by me and Charlie was rescuing her, but the words shrilled and trembled on the wires between us, and I hung up as soon as I decently could. No wedding invitation came; I was grateful for that.

My mother was right. I had heard from almost no one in Atlanta since I had brought Lucy home from California in June—not that that was unusual. With the exception of her and Sarah and Dorothy Cameron, I had seldom heard from home. Lucy called, a few days after Sarah and Charlie had returned to Atlanta, and when I hung up the telephone at the sound of her voice, called again. This time I let the phone ring, and she did not call a third time. Letters came from her, though, and kept up for some weeks, but I tore them up unopened, and finally they dwindled and stopped. I could not think of Lucy in those days without a red-fired blackness flooding my brain, a blind, implacable rage that frightened me badly. But it, too, abated after the letters stopped. By and large, the deadness held, and when it did not, the ache could, after all, be borne.

And then, in early August, Dorothy Cameron called.

"Shep, dear, it's Dorothy," she said, and in that split instant the anesthetized ache fled and a pure, silver and terrible new grief like a piano wire stabbed my heart. I wanted to weep, to keen like an Irishman at a wake, to wail like a banshee; I wanted to crawl through the eight hundred-odd miles of wire between West Twenty-first Street and Muscogee Avenue and lay my head in her lap and sob like a child, brokenhearted and inconsolable, until I fell asleep there, finally spent. I literally could not speak around the knot of anguish in my throat. It was not only Sarah who was lost to me now.

I managed some sort of strictured croak that did not fool Dorothy Cameron.

"Oh, my dear," she said. "I *am* sorry. I haven't called until now because I knew it would be as awful for you as it is for me; I haven't been able to pick up the phone to call you without crying. It's ridiculous. Neither of us has died. Ben is really quite annoyed with me. But it's time to stop this foolishness now."

And magically, the lethal knot loosened and I was able to speak. It has always been Dorothy Cameron's greatest gift, that of healing.

"I've missed you," I said. "And I didn't even know how much till I heard your voice just now. I would have called, but I've acted like such a horse's ass I didn't think you'd want to talk to me. God, Dorothy, I've made such a mess of everything. . . ."

"Yes, you have," she said, but she said it so matter-of-factly that even in the admission there was healing. "But you're the one who's been hurt the most by it, by far. We're pretty much all right down here. Sad to say, the world has a nasty way of stepping over our prostrate bodies and going right on. Hiding away up there and not answering letters or the telephone is not necessary and really not very smart. I'm calling to ask you to reconsider coming home. Just for a visit, of course."

"Dorothy," I said, "I can't do that. I agree with you that hiding out is stupid as hell, but one thing I can't do is come home yet. Did . . . did Sarah ask you to call?" A starved and craven hope slunk up from somewhere out of the ice-packed depths of me, skulking like a coyote through my heart.

"Sarah? No," Dorothy said. "You were awfully rough on her, Shep. I don't think Sarah's going to call you, or Charlie either, and in any case, I wouldn't intercede for either of them. They're fully capable of handling their own affairs, no matter how badly I might think they're doing it. No, Sarah didn't ask me to call you, but Lucy did. She says you won't answer her calls and letters, and she needs very badly to see you and talk to you. I believe she does, Shep."

"Lucy? My cousin Lucy?" Simple astonishment made me stupid. I had packed Lucy at the very bottom of the ice crevasse, lower even than the pain of Sarah and Charlie. Lucy was the last name I had ever expected to hear on Dorothy Cameron's lips, and to hear it couched in a request for help was as alien to my ears as if she had begun speaking Senegalese.

"Lucy, yes," Dorothy said briskly, and I could tell she was losing patience with my obtuseness. I shook my head like a dog coming out of water.

"Okay," I said. "What kind of trouble has Lucy gotten herself into now? And I warn you, Dorothy, I don't much want to hear it, whatever it is. Lucy has wrecked things for me the last time she's going to. She's a grown-up woman, a divorcée, and she's got enough sense and skills to look after herself now. Let her do it, or let her find somebody else to hang on to. I can't afford to talk to Lucy right now, much less come down there and grub around trying to clean up whatever mess she's made."

"As a matter of fact, she hasn't made any kind of mess that I can see," Dorothy said equably. From childhood she had been used to my outbursts; I had felt safe in letting her field them when I had trusted no one else but Lucy with them. "Rather the opposite, in fact. She has a job that she seems to love, and she's paying what she can toward her room and board to your parents, and I've never seen her quite like this. She seems . . . happy. Just happy. Not excited, or keyed up, or manic; there's a sort of inner glow to her, and a quietness that I never saw before, and that I frankly find most appealing. I think she may have a new young man, though she won't say, but in any case she's been coming over and talking with me in the evenings for the past few weeks, and I've simply never seen such a change in a young woman. She says you're responsible; I can't imagine what you said to her. I don't think it's a pose, either; I'd spot that in Lucy in a minute. Sarah thinks it's genuine, too. Lucy has spent a good bit of time with Sarah, going shopping with her and helping with wedding details. Sarah says she apologized very genuinely for all the trouble she caused for everybody, and with real tears in her eyes. Sarah was quite touched. Charlie's still holding out, but you know Charlie. . . ."

I did, indeed, and knew that Charlie had what Hemingway called an infallible shit detector when it came to Lucy Bondurant. I did, too.

"Well, I'm glad to hear she's not in trouble, but if I were you I'd walk softly around the new Lucy," I said. "She's capable of being whoever she needs to be. This makes me nervous as hell."

"I know," she said. "That's why I think you should come home and see for yourself. She wants you to so badly that you can tell she's nearly bursting with it. She says she really needs to try and make things right for you, that she can't get on with her life until she does, and that she doesn't know how to reach you. Shep, I'm convinced that that's just what she means to do— get on with her life on her own. The work she's doing is really quite valuable, and she's done some writing, too, that she says something might come of one day or another. It's as though she knows a lovely secret; as though there's a candle lit within her. Luminous . . ."

Well, I thought. Luminous is the word for Lucy. Always was. What is it really? I wonder. Aloud I said, "I'm not going to come home, Dorothy; I just can't do that yet. But I'll talk to her if she still wants me to. Tell her to call me. I'll take it this time. And . . . Dorothy . . . how is Sarah? How is she, really? Is she . . . you know . . . happy?"

"Happy?" She tasted the word as if she did not know what it meant. "No, I don't think Sarah is particularly happy right now, Shep, but she's very much all right. She will be very useful in her marriage and here in Atlanta, and I believe that in time that will make her happy. She could not be useful in New York. No matter what you think, she could not be. And for girls like Sarah, being useful is far more important in the long run than being merely happy."

My heart hurt, briefly and profoundly. Sarah was not happy. Three weeks away from her marriage and she was not happy. Useful . . . useful Sarah. In that instant I saw her life.

"Damn your high-minded crap, Dorothy," I said, not loudly, but with trembling vehemence in my voice.

"Shep, don't," she said. "We love you. We feel your pain. All of us do. Don't lash out at us like this."

"I'm sorry," I said.

That night I wrote Sarah and Charlie, a letter apiece, short but as warm and penitent as I could make them, benedictory. I apologized for my behavior and gave my blessing, feeling like a Borgia pope as I did so, false and corrupted. I love you, I signed off to both of them. I wept a little, tired, shamed tears in the hot, thick darkness as I dropped the letters into the mailbox on the corner of Twenty-first and Ninth, but I felt somehow ennobled too, exalted. I imagined Sarah opening hers in her studio and reading it, saw the blessing of the autumn light from the window wall on her face, saw her close her glowing eyes and droop her dark head over the letter. I could not see where Charlie would open his, for his apartment in Colonial Homes was not a part of the country of our youth, and it seemed that I could really see Charlie Gentry only there. He seemed caught in our mutual boyhood as in amber, and I could no more imagine him at the altar with Sarah, or in a new white bed with her, than I could at his executive's desk at the Coca-Cola Company's new headquarters on North Avenue. I was glad for that.

Two days later a telegram came from them, signed, all our love, Sarah and Charlie. Please, please, it said, come home for the wedding.

But I could not do that.

During the next three weeks I managed quite well not to think of them, but I did think a lot about Lucy.

"She says you're responsible for the change in her," Dorothy Cameron had said. "I can't imagine what you said to her."

For a long time I could not remember, either, and then I thought perhaps I did. It had been on the plane that lumbered interminably toward Atlanta from Los Angeles, somewhere over Utah, I thought, or at least early in the trip, before fatigue and the afterwash of pain and drugs took her down into sleep. I had been trying to have a serious talk with her, but it had turned out to be pretty much a monologue, for she would not talk about Red Chastain or her marriage, except to say that it was, of course, over.

The Pendleton MPs had finally tracked Red to a flyspecked cantina back room on an unimaginable side street in Tijuana, and had brought him back to base in handcuffs on the day before we left for home; two of his superior officers had come to see Lucy in the hospital, to ask what action she thought she might want taken, but she had begun to tremble and cry again and so the doctor and I had asked them to leave, and they had, and we quit that high, sun-punished plain without seeing her husband again, and to my knowledge she never saw him again while she lived. I knew that she planned to file for divorce as soon as she got back to Atlanta, but beyond that, she had no plans at all, and so I switched my attack to her work, and what she hoped to do with the rest of her life. My own seemed, then, firmly set in its own incandescent orbit, and I wanted to get back to it and on with it, and to see her set onto some path that was least likely to disturb mine. I was wild, at that time, to be home with Sarah.

"You could be a really good writer," I said to her. "You could be published nationally right now, that's how good you are. All your professors said so. I know from reading your stuff—what little there's been of it. You know so, too. But instead you've wasted all those good years screwing around with people like Red Chastain. God, you Southern women. You're content with so damned *little.*"

"Lord, Gibby, are you one of those feminists?" Lucy said, gingerly tasting with her broken mouth the term that had just begun to creep into the vernacular.

"I guess I am," I said, after thinking about it. "Aren't you? I thought all women with half a brain would be."

"No," she said. "I hate women. You know that. Men are all you can trust."

"Lucy, just look at your men," I said in despair.

"Yes, Gibby, but they're predictable, all of them. I know what they're going to do. I can handle that. Women are mysterious. You can't read them. And that makes them automatic enemies. It's better to have a man on your side, as well as by it."

"That's bullshit," I said. "It's an excuse you women use for not doing anything of your own with your lives."

"Well, we've raised a damned lot of you Southern boys' children," she said sharply, stung.

"No you haven't," I said. "Black women do that."

She was silent for a long time, and then she fell asleep and slept the rest of the way home. Could that small snippet of talk, words spoken in a sealed metal cylinder hung somewhere over the fabled red West, really have changed Lucy Bondurant? I could not imagine that it had, but I could recall no other. . . .

Charlie and Sarah were married on the Saturday after Labor Day, and I did not mark the occasion in any special way at all. I had saved a lot of chores for that Saturday, and at the particular moment that I estimated Sarah Cameron became Sarah Gentry, I was midway between Gristede's and my laundry with a package of Kraft macaroni and cheese dinner and a sack full of soiled clothing. I passed the kosher deli on the corner of Ninth and Twenty-third, and muttered aloud, *"Mazel tov,* Sarah," and on impulse went into the dark, garlicky shop and bought a carton of chopped liver, which Sarah had loved with an absolutely Hebraic avidity. I went on home in the still-hot September twilight and put the liver into the refrigerator, and the telephone rang as I closed the scabrous door.

It was Lucy.

"Hey, Gibby," she said, and all of a sudden joy and sadness

and pain and glee and simple one-celled nostalgia swept me, so
that my voice, as I said, "Hey, Luce," sounded like that of someone else entirely in my own ears.

"What's happening?" I said.

"I've just come back from the wedding," she said, and her
voice, around the small exhalations of the inevitable cigarette,
sounded soft and full of something that I did not associate with
her. Tenderness? Pity?

"Yeah?" I said. "And how was the wedding?"

"Well, it was very sweet. Very small and simple, and over in
almost no time, and not really so awful at all. Nobody cried or
carried on, and both of them seemed okay happy but not deliri-
ous. Already settled, somehow. Sarah hugged me before they left
and told me to call you up and tell you about it before some old
battle-ax did, and that they missed you and hoped you'd come
see them when they got back from their honeymoon, and that
was that. I was the only one of our family to go; not many outside
people were there at all. I just wanted to tell you before anybody
else did, or sent you some stupid clipping, that it was okay. It
really was. You wouldn't have minded it at all."

There *was* something different; it was there in her voice, like
a quality of light. I kept listening for the bright sharpness, the
wild-honey irony, the little tongues of captivating malice that
I knew so well, but they were not there. Nothing was but gentleness and a most un-Lucylike succor.

"I . . . well, thanks, Luce," I said lamely. "I appreciate that.
I'm glad you went. Dorothy said you'd really been a help to her
and Sarah since you got back."

"I hope so," she said simply. "I've been awful to Sarah all my
life, and I hope I can begin to make it up to her. I wish I thought
I could to you."

"No need," I said. For the first time in my life I was uncomfortable talking to Lucy. I could not think of anything to say.
I felt none of the red rage toward her that I had earlier in the
summer, but this quiet-voiced stranger called up no other emotion to take its place. It was like trying to make telephone conversation to the most casual of acquaintances.

"So where are they going on their honeymoon?" I said, merely
for something to say, and then was horrified at myself. I did not
want to know, did not want Lucy to think that I did, and shrank
from the images that the word evoked as from a pit of fire and
vipers.

"I think just up to Tate," Lucy said, and I smiled involuntarily. Of course. Tate. The big old family cottage up on Burnt
Mountain, which Sarah loved so much. I could see her there,

diving like a brown otter into the dark blue, freezing little mountain lake, riding her bicycle around the little dirt road that ringed it, tossing lichen-furred logs from the woodpile beside the back door onto the fire booming in the great stone fireplace, standing hipshot at the old stove deftly handling a cast-iron skillet. I could see square, dark Charlie stumping along behind her, standing beside her, looking up at her from the disreputable easy chair beside the fire with his whole soul in his eyes. But I could not see them climb the old pine staircase together, toward the bedrooms off the gallery upstairs; I closed my eyes against that. . . .

Of course Sarah would take Charlie up to Tate. It was where we would have gone, she and I. I had not thought of it before, but I knew that it was. Sea Island would have come later.

"Gibby," Lucy said into my silence, "please come home. They'll be gone for a couple of weeks at least. You won't run into them. And I need to see you. I need to try and make some of this up to you. I think I can, if you'll let me. But I can't stand being . . . alienated from you like this. I want to go on with my life and try to make something out of it—by myself, I mean— and I don't think I can do that until I know you've forgiven me. I have to know that."

"I do, Luce," I said, and meant it. "I don't have to come home to do that. I do—not that there's anything to forgive you for, really. Why don't you come see me instead? If you're short, I can send you a plane ticket—"

"Gibby . . ." She took a very deep breath. "I want you to come home because I've written a book and Scribners is publishing it and it comes out next week, and there are some parties and things here for me, and I want you to come and take me to them. I don't want to go by myself, Gibby, and I don't think Mama and Lady much want to go with me."

"Lucy!" I shouted over the phone, as if she could hear me only that way. "That's . . . Goddamn! That's wonderful! That's . . . Why didn't you say something? When did you do that?"

"I wrote it way last summer and fall, after Red went on that eight-month tour. Remember? I called you up and whined for you to come out and keep me company, and you said to write a book or plant a tree or something? Well, I did—I wrote a book. And when it was finished I called Professor Dunne at Scott and she knew an agent in New York, and I sent it to him and he sent it around, and Scribners took it—and here it is. I didn't say anything about it because I didn't think you wanted to hear about that or anything else from me—and you didn't, right then—and it seemed so far away, anyway . . . but, oh God, Gibby, it got closer and closer to publication day, and Rich's is going to give me this autograph party, and Mr. and Mrs. Cam-

eron want to give me this little cocktail party at the Driving
Club, and even Mama thought she might manage a little tea with
your mother, here at the house . . . and I just realized that I didn't
think I could get through any of it without you. So I went and
talked to Mrs. Cameron about it, and she said—she called you,
didn't she?—she said she'd try and get you to come home, and
so I thought maybe if I called you after she had . . ."

"When are these parties?" I said, my heart pounding with
pride in her.

"Next weekend. Next Saturday and Sunday."

"I'll be in Friday night. Can you meet me at the airport?"

"Oh, Gibby, of course I can! Oh, bless you! I'll pick you up
at your gate; I've got a little car of my own now, a Volkswagen.
I got the loan myself, and Mr. Cameron cosigned it, it's blue—
oh, shit, Gibby, I've missed you so! And I'm so scared!"

"What are you scared of? Don't be scared. You've got the
world by the tail now," I said. "Nothing ahead but roses and
clover."

"Because," she said, "I'm just so happy. And I don't know
how to handle that. And nobody ever gave me a party of my
own before."

And she was right. Nobody ever had.

I sat up all that night, noodling around on my clarinet and
playing and replaying my Brubeck records, softly so the meno-
pausal Puerto Rican widow upstairs would not call the police
again, and I thought about the two of them: Sarah and Lucy.
Lucy and Sarah. Or, rather, I did not so much think as let the
lifelong tapes of the two of them stored in my memory run. I
did not want, on that evening, to think. Through the long darkness two women shimmered and played behind my eyes, both
of them vivid, both of them ardent, both of them beautiful, both
of them in some way mine and then not mine. Neither easily de-
finable, neither easily given over. Both of them in essential ways
shapers of lives—mine and others—yet so different one from the
other that it seemed incongruous that they could be the major
bones in the armature of a single life. But they were. My life without them was unimaginable. And yet from this night forth I
would be required to try to lead it without at least one of them.

Lucy and Sarah, Sarah and Lucy. It seemed to me, in that still
predawn hushed even stiller by the beginning of a silent, soft autumn rain, that they were like the figures on a Swiss clock, moving in and out and back and forth in my life in a formal, stylized
dance, the one now advancing while the other retreated, and
then changing to slow, measured order and beginning again. I
could imagine nothing, should the clock stop, but emptiness. So

I ceased the imagining and let the tapes run again. Lucy and Sarah, Sarah and Lucy . . .

Toward daylight I slid finally and irrevocably toward sleep, and the thought that the music and the tapes in my mind had kept at bay through the dark hours surfaced and struck, and I finally let the desolation of it take me down: Tonight was the wedding night of Sarah Cameron Gentry, but it was not mine.

CHAPTER
SIXTEEN

T HE NEXT FRIDAY NIGHT I SLEPT, for the first time in my
life, in the big back bedroom that was the guest room of
the house on Peachtree Road.

It was a strange night, and largely sleepless; full of sounds and
shadows and shiftings that I had heard all my life, but alien to
me now because I heard and saw them from a different angle.
When I did sleep, it was lightly and poised on the surface of unconsciousness, as a soldier will sleep in a battle zone where ambush is possible.

I was acutely conscious of, could almost feel on my skin, the
presence of my aunt Willa in the other back bedroom across the
hall, and even more so of the bodies of my mother and father,
which presumably lay side by side in the great front bedroom
where they had, to the best of my knowledge, slept since before
my birth. I lay very still in unaccustomed new pajamas under
the thin white linen sheets, listening despite the ridiculousness
of it for the joyless noise of their unimaginable coupling, as I
had lain listening in the hated small dressing room in my infancy
and early childhood. Lucy, who had put an end to that torture,
did not sleep tonight under this roof, but in the summerhouse
which had for so long been mine. I did not precisely begrudge
it to her, but I missed the refuge of it keenly. This cold white
bed in this austere dark room did not beget ease.

We had sat late in the summerhouse, she and I, after the sorry
little ritual of homecoming between me and my parents and
Aunt Willa had been played out. My mother, looking glossier
and more sinuous and whiter of skin than ever, had clung to me
and fussed and patted and chirred, and Aunt Willa, every spec-

tacular inch the Atlanta society matron now, smiled and smoked quietly in the warm darkness of the side porch where we gathered, looking, looking. My father, somehow redder and more furious of face even as he bared his yellowing teeth in what passed between us for greeting, had a couple of quick bourbons and nodded and grinned ferally and said yes, the Rolls-Royce in the driveway was new; I'd have to take it for a little spin sometime while I was home. I grinned back, feeling my mouth stretch with it, and said I'd sure like to do that, knowing that I would not, and that he would not offer again.

Soon after that he took the bourbon decanter and went back inside to the library, saying that he had a good bit of paper work to get cleaned up if the ladies planned on having a tea party that weekend, and I did not see him again until just before I left for New York on Sunday night. He was not at Lucy's autograph party at Rich's the next day, or at the cocktail party Ben and Dorothy gave for her at the Driving Club; my mother told me that he had an out-of-town business appointment, but I do not remember where she said it was, and in any case I did not believe her. I did not know where he went, but I knew why. Lucy and I escaped to the summerhouse as soon as we decently could, with relief that was probably as obvious as it was profound.

"I hope you don't mind," she said, snapping on a single lamp beside the deep, sagging old blue sofa and sinking into its cushions. "I moved out here a week or two after I got home, in June. Nobody seemed to know what to say to me, and I could tell that the cast and the bruises bothered everybody, and it just seemed easier all the way around. Martha brought me trays and I slept, mostly, and after I felt better I got the job, and then it was better to be out here because I didn't wake anybody leaving or coming home. I work pretty late sometimes. And then, I didn't think you were coming back; but if you mind, I'll move my things out of here in a second. I didn't change anything at all. . . ."

She had not. The summerhouse looked almost exactly as it had the day I had left it to enter Princeton. My books and records were in the same untidy rows I had left, and even the Georgia Tech and University of Georgia pennants on the walls were undisturbed. A hanging whatnot that my mother had put up still held my 880 trophies and a lone, blackened junior tennis trophy from the club, and a small glass case of perfect minié balls that Charlie had given me one long-ago Christmas still sat, thick-felted with dust, on my old desk. Only the desk showed evidence of Lucy; it was piled with books and notebooks and yellow legal pads, and a battered old Smith-Corona portable sat squarely in its middle, neatly covered. I'd have known that Lucy Bondurant lived in these rooms, though, if I had been led into them blindfolded. Over everything, over the drying musk of grass and the yellowing September woods out back, and the breath of the dank-scummed lily pool just beyond the veranda, and the cool-sour stucco smell of the summerhouse itself, rode the silky-teasing scent of her Tabu.

"I don't mind," I said. "I like to see you out here with your typewriter and your brand-new life; I'll like thinking of you here when I'm back in New York. It's a good hideout for an author. And I think it must suit you. You look wonderful."

She did. Lucy had always looked wonderful, of course, but there was something totally new about her this weekend; Dorothy Cameron had been right. I had noticed it the moment I stepped off the plane, and the sense of it had grown with each passing hour that we spent together. There wasn't any physical difference; I had looked for that when I hugged her and held her away from me and studied her, because the sense of otherness had smitten me so powerfully the moment I saw her tall figure in the crowd around the airline gate. Her black-satin hair still fell in its blue-sheened pageboy against her slanted white cheekbones, and her rose and cream color was the same, if a bit heightened with excitement. She wore no lipstick and no makeup on her light-drowned eyes, and that was, for Lucy, unusual, but I had seen her without makeup many times before. And if she had been slender before, she was downright thin now, a thinness of sinew and taut-stretched flesh that vein and bone, here and there, gleamed through. But on Lucy, thinness still meant only whippet elegance, and a refining of her extraordinary grace.

No, the difference was born inside her, and it shone out of her blue eyes and in the soft curve of her mouth like mist from morning water. I thought of the trick we used to do with a flashlight when we were small; we would hold it, lit, in our mouths or shine it behind our hands, and were in those moments illumined from the inside out, glowing creatures of light and bone. If Lucy had done the same with a pure white candle, the effect would have been what I saw now. There was a word that fit her but I could not think of it.

We stopped at Rusty's on the way to the Peachtree Road house, "to shore you up before the onslaught," she said. "Once the weekend gets into gear, we won't have any time together at all. *Après moi le déluge.* I hope you aren't going to hate all this folderol about the book."

"Are you kidding?" I said. "I couldn't be any prouder of you if you'd won the Nobel Prize for literature. I'll happily go through this with every book you write. Are you working on another one? And when are you going to tell me about this one?"

"Oh . . . later. Soon. Tonight, maybe," she said.

She finished her Coke and made a rude childhood noise against the bottom of the glass with the straw. I was drinking beer, and had asked if she wanted one, too, but she had shaken her head and asked for Coke instead.

"No more booze," she said. "I'm strictly a Cokaholic now."

"Well, good," I said. "I was getting a little worried about you there for a while, to tell you the truth."

"With good reason," she said. "I'm not the nicest person in the world when I drink. Or when I don't, for that matter. Listen, Gibby," and she turned to me quickly, so that the bell of hair swung against her cheek. "I want to say this before you shush me. I'll be sorry until the day I die for what I did to you and Sarah. You should be up there at Tate with her, not Charlie Gentry, and you would be if it hadn't been for me, and I know that. No"—for I had started to protest—"let me finish. I can't undo that, but I can keep from making anybody else unhappy ever again with my selfishness and my neuroses, and I'm going to. My heart will hurt me every time I see Sarah Gentry or you again as long as I live, and if it helps at all, I want you to know that I've changed. I really have. That may be small comfort, but it's all I can give you. That and just to love you always and wish you everything that's good in the world for the rest of your life."

It was an extraordinary speech by any standards, and for Lucy it was astounding. I literally did not know what to say, so I said, for a moment, nothing at all. And then: "I liked the old model pretty well. I hope she's not in mothballs for good."

Her glorious, throaty laugh rang out, and relief flooded me. Somewhere under this—the word I wanted danced maddeningly just out of reach—this paragon my old adored and enthralling Lucy lay. It was enough, for now, and I switched on the radio of her little VW bug, and leaned my head back against the seat and inhaled deeply, eyes closed. The smell of the dusty honeysuckle foliage that fell over Rusty's parking lot fence swam into the car on the sharp-cutting strains of "Moonglow," and the ash from Lucy's cigarette reddened in the darkness as she dragged deeply on it, and sudden young laughter spilled from the open window of the car next to us, and just for that moment it was 1953 again, and the summer moon shone on us, and I was truly home. It was not until hours later, when we sat in the semidarkness of the summerhouse and Lucy, her face carved pure and cleanly in lamplight and shadow like a young Joan of Orléans, spoke of moving out here to avoid giving bother to the household, that the word I had wanted at the airport flashed into my mind: saintly.

"There's another reason I'm out here, too," she said as if reading my thoughts.

"And that is?" I said.

"Mother and your folks don't want me in the house. In fact, they want me to move all the way out of it and get a place of my own. They've given me a month to look around, and I thought it would be better to lie low while I did, so I wouldn't keep everybody upset. They're really pretty angry with me. I can't say that I blame them."

"Here we go," I thought. "There *is* trouble, then; I should have known. Why else would she want me to come home? But I can see why she pulled the wool over Dorothy's and Sarah's eyes. This new-Lucy business is so good it's eerie. . . ."

I felt deeply, endlessly tired. Worse, I felt near-sick with disappointment.

Aloud I said, "Let's have it, Luce."

She looked at me quickly, and I could swear that the bewilderment in her eyes was genuine. And then she laughed again, the healing, full Lucy-laugh.

"Oh, poor Gibby! No, it's nothing you have to do anything about. It's nothing you could do anything about even if I wanted you to. Only I can, and I have."

"Then what?"

She did not answer at once. It was as hot as a midsummer night in the room, and she twisted her heavy hair up off her neck and held it atop her head. Her plain white oxford shirt fell away from her thin neck, and I could see clearly the notch where Red Chastain's gun butt had smashed her fragile collarbone, and the little white tracks in her hairline from the stitches in the scalp laceration his bullet had made. Sweat pearled her neck and upper lip. I wanted to cry, suddenly, she looked so punished and vulnerable and young. The armor her insouciance had given her was gone.

Then she said, "It's my job. They really hate what I'm doing, and they think I took it to spite them, like I . . . guess I did those editorials I wrote at Scott, and the marches and sit-ins and things I went on. You know. I don't blame them for thinking that; why shouldn't they? But I can't give it up, Gibby. I love it with every little shred and scrap of me. I don't think I ever really knew what it was to love work, or to love people in the way I love these—"

"For God's sake," I said, "what are you doing? Nursing lepers? Hooking? What?"

"I'm working with the civil rights movement," she said, her face literally aflame with a kind of joy. "I'm working downtown at a place called Damascus House, in an old church in the black section down below the capitol. Right next to Capitol Homes, you know; where we used to go to get the laundry from Princess? It's an inner-city mission, really, run by Father Claiborne Cantrell. I know you've heard of him, or read about him—he's been in *Time* and *Newsweek* both. I guess he's pretty radical for a Southern Episcopalian. Anyway, he had to give up his ministry at Saint Martin's after he'd gotten arrested for the fourth time sitting in, so he just went down to Capitol Homes and found this old empty church and outbuildings and set up Damascus House, and it's been the model for literally dozens of inner-city missions all over the South. I met Clay—Father Cantrell—at a rally in early July, and was just spellbound by him like everybody is, and literally begged him with tears running down my face to let me come and work for him, and he finally did. . . . Oh, God, I just never knew until now, but this is my real niche, the thing I was meant to do with my life!"

I had to smile, even as the import of her incandescence and the new, uncritical affection for the human race dawned. Lucy and the Negroes again. No wonder her mother and my parents were furious. An amusing little feature about the Defiant Deb taking up the cause of equality in the Atlanta *Constitution* was one thing; *Time* and *Newsweek* were quite another. When would they learn that trying to separate Lucy from her beloved Negroes was as futile as parting the moon from its tides?

But the implications of her passion were, to me, ominous.

"Lucy, what you're meant to do with your life is write," I said. I said it as neutrally as possible, so as not to echo the other furious voices in this house. "What is it you do at this Damascus House?"

"I'm registering voters," she said. "I'm matching government resources to individual needs. I'm working in the soup kitchen and driving the bus and getting bail bond money for the sit-ins, and . . . oh, Gibby, there's so much to do."

Her blue eyes spilled out a light very near that of madness, and I was almost afraid of the otherworldliness about her.

"Can't you do as much for the movement by writing about it as by dishing up soup?" I said. "You must see what kind of career you could have as a novelist; you told me about your reviews. My God, the whole town is turning out to honor you tomorrow, practically. You have great power; couldn't you reach more people that way?"

"I love them, Gibby," she said simply. "I love the black people. I need to be close to them. They're better friends than any I ever had. I want to be right in this with them; Clay says we have to walk among them and with them to have any credibility."

"Ah, I see," I said, thinking that I did. "Clay. The good father. Lucy, don't you see that you're doing nothing in the world but chasing off after another man, doing what your latest savior tells you to? Don't you see that?"

She smiled at me. It was a very sweet smile, and a gentle one. "I don't blame you for thinking that, but you're wrong, Gibby," she said. "I told you I've changed, and I meant that. You'll see what I mean about Clay when you meet him. The sheer goodness of him is just . . . consuming."

I was silent, looking at her in the lamplight. She seemed content to sit under my gaze without talking, curled up bonelessly in the depth of the sofa, smoking. At least she had not forsworn that. It struck me that Lucy, who had never been able to assure her safety by finding a trustworthy protector in any of her men, had decided to assure it now by being a very good girl indeed. The bad girl had, after all, come to endless grief. And who was, after all, more assured of society's approbation and benison than its saints? I knew that this premise was as false as any she had lived by before, and that she would eventually come to fresh grief from adherence to it. I thought, also, that whether she knew it or not, there was a good measure of the child spiting its parents here.

For indeed, from what she had told me, Aunt Willa and my mother and father were, for once, totally united in their disapproval of Lucy's association with "that crazy radical and the niggers down there." Quit that awful business, they had said, and get a decent job somewhere on the Northside—like the society section of the newspaper, or perhaps teaching in a little private academy in Buckhead, or even helping out in the gift shop at Piedmont Hospital as so many of the Leaguers do—or move out of the house. I could only marvel at her tranquility in the face of the ultimatum. Heretofore, she would have been stricken to blind white terror at the prospect of being ousted from the only security she had ever known.

"I take it you're not going to quit, then," I said. It was not a question.

"Of course not."

"Well, then, have you got an apartment or something?"

"Or something, I guess. I've got better than an apartment, Gibby," she said. "I've got, or I'm going to have, a husband."

This time I could only stare at her, as dumb as the proverbial ox there in the living room of the summerhouse, which had been since childhood shelter and haven to both of us. The air between us seemed to shimmer just as her eyes and face did, and I felt dizzy and disoriented. I remembered that I had had no dinner, and had last eaten a hasty sandwich in the library employees' cafeteria at noon. It seemed a thousand years ago, and in another country.

She reached over and put her hands over mine, and looked intently into my face. I could see her features with stark, winter-light clarity: the extraordinary blue eyes, on fire; the igh, straight-bridged nose; the kid-leather texture of her skin; the tender pink pulp of her mouth. But I could not make them come together into a face.

"Be happy for me, Gibby," she said, her voice little more than a whisper. "I love him. I respect him. He's brave and committed and strong, and he adores the ground I walk on. He's older—he's thirty-eight—and he's an accountant who's been with Damascus House since Clay started it, and he's solid and quiet and wry and cynical and he has a wonderful smile and the strength of the earth, of the world. . . ."

"An accountant. Lord, Lucy. Does he have a name?" I said.

She laughed. "Jack. Jack Venable. John Creighton Venable, of the Chattanooga Venables. He's an accountant mainly because his family has money. It's even older money than your folks', and his folks won't speak to him, either; we have an awful lot in common. He moved here about two years ago; he's had a terrible time in his life, Gibby, and he needs me as much as I do him. His wife—Kitty, they called her—ran off with another woman and left him with two little boys. Toby and Thomas; they're nine and eleven now. The boys found her note and read it before Jack did. . . . She was always unstable, but nobody suspected she was a lesbian. Those poor children! Toby, the littlest one, didn't talk for almost a year after that. I'm going to take such good care of those children, Gibby, you just won't believe it's me. And Jack . . . he's just the most wonderful father."

"Yes, but . . . an *accountant?* Audits and P and Ls amid the great unwashed masses?" I grinned. I could no more conceive of Lucy married to an accountant than to a Bantu chieftain. Less, as a matter of fact.

"Don't knock it, Gibby," she said evenly, and her eyes snapped fire. "Those great unwashed masses, as you so charmingly put it, need a few little minor things like household budgets and help with welfare and social security. Frivolous stuff like that. Jack does it for them twenty hours a day for money you'd drop in five minutes at John Jarrell's. What are *you* doing?"

I reddened, and was quiet.

When I met Jack Venable later that night, I saw immediately that this plain, pale man, with his stark white hair and his air of deep stillness that verged on stolidity and his patience and obvious quiet enchantment with the burning, leaping flame that was Lucy was, indeed, just what she had said he was—a wonderful father. For her. The perception was unavoidable. I wondered if he saw it. I did not think that she did.

"Well, why not?" I thought, around the ghostly old desolation, the old, old Lucy-loss that the news of her impending marriage had resurrected in my heart. "Maybe what she needs is somebody older and settled, who'll take care of her and cherish her. God knows, she's had little enough of that."

Jack Venable and his motherless children lived in a century-old farmhouse, she said that evening in the summerhouse, outside the little town of Lithonia, twenty miles to the east of the city. The boys attended public school while Jack commuted to his job, and were cared for after school by an old black woman, who also cooked and cleaned and did the family laundry. Lucy was enchanted with the prospect of living in the country, on a real farm.

"Later on we'll raise chickens and pigs and . . . stuff," she bubbled. "And I'll have vegetables and flowers, and the children will have a pony, and Jack can watch his birds and things. . . . It's perfect. And meanwhile he and I can ride to and from Damascus House together. Oh, Gibby, it's what I always needed and didn't even know it—this commitment to something really important, and a truly good, quiet man, and simplicity . . . nature, the seasons, the earth. . . ."

Remembering the firefly who so thrived and shimmered in the insular, urban air of Buckhead, my heart shrank at the thought of Lucy on a farm in rural DeKalb County. But I did not, of course, voice my apprehension.

"Well, Lucy, sweetie," I said, "it all sounds . . . as nearly perfect as this earth gets. When is the wedding? Can I come be best man?"

Her face flamed, and she dropped her eyes. "Well, you see, Gibby," she said, "it's going to be right soon, maybe like in a couple of weeks, and Glenn—Glenn Pickens, you know, the Camerons' Glenn—wants to be our best man, and of course Clay will perform the ceremony. It's going to be at Damascus House, really a tiny affair, and only the . . . the Negroes who live there, the residents . . . are going to be guests. Nobody here even knows it yet. I thought with the way my mother and your folks felt about everything, and the way some of the Negroes feel about rich white people . . ."

"I'm as poor as Job's turkey, you know that," I said, stung. Even her discomfort did not compensate for the obvious fact that I would not be welcome at my cousin Lucy's wedding. "Come on. This is me, Luce."

"I know, Gibby, and if it were just me and Jack, I wouldn't think of having a wedding without you. But your daddy—your family—owns an awful lot of land down around Damascus House, and people down there know it. Some of the folks there are tenants of y'all's. White absentee landlords are not exactly popular down there."

"I don't own any of it," I said stubbornly. "It's my father's, not mine. And nobody knows who I am, anyway."

"Yes," she said in a subdued voice, "they do."

I let it go at that. I did not, really, want to give her pain. And she would, as she said, be cared for, be safe. . . . Atlanta was, after all, nothing to me anymore.

"Well," I said, as cheerfully as I could, "when do I get to meet this paragon of virtue, this Jack Venable?"

"Later tonight, I hope. He's been out of town all week," she said. "But he's going to meet us down at Paschal's La Carrousel tonight at ten. One of your high muckety-muck jazz guys is playing down there, and I thought you might like to go with us. Glenn Pickens is going to be there; you know Glenn. You know where it is; we've been before, remember? Senior year at North Fulton? Lord, you don't care that it's a black club, do you?"

"You know I don't," I said. "But isn't Jack going to be at the autograph party? Or the cocktail thing?"

"No," she smiled ruefully. "He hates the Driving Club and everything it stands for, though with his family's background I'm sure he could get in if he wanted to . . . or had the money. His family has cut him off that, too. And he isn't very high on my writing, so I'm not going to make him come to the thing at Rich's. He hates all that publishing stuff."

"He sure seems to hate a lot of things, for a licensed professional peacemaker," I said. "Don't tell me he doesn't think your writing is any good."

"Oh, no, it's just that he thinks I'm so much more valuable to . . . society, I guess, at Damascus House. And he's right, Gibby. Writing seems awfully self-indulgent in times like these. Later, when the movement has accomplished what it means to, and I've quit work and we're home in the country . . . he says he won't mind me writing some then."

"Good of him," I muttered. I did not like the sound of this.

But I did like Jack Venable when I met him later that night, on the weedy sidewalk down in Southwest Atlanta in front of Paschal's Motor Hotel. It was nearly ten-thirty, and there was no one else on the street in front of the unprepossessing two-story motel and restaurant that was the unofficial epicenter of the fledgling civil rights movement. I felt as if I were in another Atlanta, one I had not really known existed, for this was a street of shadows and banal shabbiness and thin, dreary light from the few streetlights left unbroken, and I was distinctly glad when the stocky figure that stepped out of the doorway proved to be

Lucy's future husband. I had, as Lucy had said, been to La Car-rousel before, but it was with a jeering, jostling group of Pinks and Jells, and in another time altogether, and we had gone in the same spirit in which we went to jig shows at the auditorium and to Peacock Alley to laugh at Blind Willie. This lunar street was not a place in which to laugh. I was acutely conscious that an aura of Buckhead and the Driving Club hung about me as powerfully as an actual scent. Lucy seemed untouched by the sense of strangeness and incipient peril; we had left her VW in a parking place a block and a half down the street toward Atlanta University, and she had walked the prickling no-man's-land beside me with the same slouching ease that she walked the waxed floors of the Driving Club. Once she had glanced at me.

"Relax." She grinned. "You'd think we were going into the heart of darkness. Got your blowgun on you? The group we're going to hear, incidentally, is called the Mau Maus."

"God, really?" I said.

"Christ. No. It's called the Ramsey Lewis Trio," she said. "They're terrific; I've got one of their albums. Jack got to know them when he was doing some work in Washington. They're more civilized than we are."

"I know who Ramsey Lewis is," I said shortly. "I have every album he ever made." It irritated me that she had so quickly scented the slight, sour fear coming off me like heat. Physical bravery has always been hard-won for me, but Lucy was born with an abundance of it.

I knew, in the way that a native will know things about his city without knowing how he became aware of them, that some of the greatest jazz names in the world had for decades come to La Carrousel, the motel's club, on a regular basis. Basie, Hampton, Don Shirley, Red Norvo, and the entire pantheon before and after them, ducked in and out of town to play their incomparable sets in that elaborately ordinary, even dingy, cinder-block motel and restaurant and club, and very few whites ever heard them, or even knew that they were there. The Paschal brothers did not advertise. They did not have to. People in the large black community who knew jazz, and a few favored whites, always seemed to know who was in town when, and the club was always jammed.

We stood on the sidewalk for a moment, blinking in the light from Paschal's sign, and when Jack Venable came out to meet us, Lucy's smile lit her face with an intensity that paled the neon.

"Hi, sweetie," she said, going to him with both hands out. "Have you been waiting long? Come over here and meet Gibby."

"Hi," he said, kissing her on the cheek. "No, I've just been walking around softly and carrying a big banjo. Hello, Shep. I

damned sure ain't going to call you Gibby. I don't think I'll kiss
you, either."

"God forbid," I said, grinning in response to his sweet white
smile. Except for that, and the white hair, he looked so astoundingly anonymous that he might have been sent from Central
Casting to play a middle-aged man in a crowd. He was pale all
over, from his thinning hair to his small blue eyes, webbed and
pouched in fine wrinkles, to his face and hands and arms. He
wore transparent plastic-rimmed glasses and a beige golf shirt
and tan gabardine trousers and old desert boots, and his stomach
was soft and mounded over the belt of the slacks. His jowls and
the underside of his arms were loose. He did not miss being short
by far.

But the smile was wonderful, wrapping you in celebration, and
his voice was deep and good, and I liked the way he looked at
Lucy. I had seen Charlie Gentry look at Sarah that way, and
I knew that all of this man, flesh, spirit and sinew, was extended
as votive offering to the slender girl-woman whose hands he held.

"You all ready?" he said. "Glenn's waiting for us inside. He
went ahead to get a table. I don't know who else will be around.
The word is that the man himself is coming, a little later."

Lucy said, softly, "Oh . . ."

"The man?" I asked.

"King," he said over his shoulder. "MLK. He's here a lot.
The guy could teach a course in jazz at any university in the
country, if he wasn't otherwise engaged."

A little frisson played on my backbone, vertebra by vertebra.
The night became, suddenly, very real. I was not slumming in
a Negro jive joint where I might take my ease and watch the
jolly blacks disport themselves for my amusement. I was walking
into the nerve center of a movement whose purpose and passion
paled with its simple human significance anything my privileged
and pallid life had known, and I would be, for a few hours,
among the awesome young men and women who had made and
were making it happen. I might even be in the presence of one
of the great and luminous legends of my time or any other. Nonchalance fled.

Threading my way through the close-crowding small tables,
pushing through the near-palpable planes of smoke lying motionless in the air, I was keenly aware of eyes on us. Jack and
Lucy walked ahead. I followed them erectly, my head held high,
a silly-feeling, unbanishable smile on my mouth. I had never before been one of the few whites in the midst of an all-black crowd,
and I was aware that a part of me was searching the room for
hostility as a wolf would sniff the wind.

But there was no hostility and there was very little curiosity, that I could feel. It was a quiet crowd, with only the sinuous, seminal flow of the music winding through it like a great, joyous heartbeat. I had time to think, stumbling after Lucy and Jack, that Sarah would have loved the sound of the Ramsey Lewis Trio, and would have walked in the prickling darkness of La Carrousel as naturally and fluidly as she walked into, or out of, water. But I could not. I was rigid to my eyebrows with the desire not to appear as if I were slumming. In truth, I had never felt less like Lord Bountiful in my life. I was consumed with a simple desire to let everyone see how grateful I was to be there. I caught myself smiling right and left, and felt my face go hot in the darkness.

"Jesus, will you stop nodding like somebody in a bad play, Gibby?" Lucy whispered over her shoulder, amused. "You look like Lord Mountbatten reviewing the troops."

They stopped at a table against a far wall and lowered themselves into chairs, and I dropped into one at the end of the table. Glenn Pickens sat across from me, not smiling but not frowning either, and when he had kissed Lucy lightly on her proffered cheek and hit Jack's shoulder softly with his lightly balled fist, he said pleasantly and neutrally, "Hello, Shep. It's been a long time."

"Hello, Glenn," I said. "It has. How are you? You're looking good."

He was. I remembered him as a thin, intense, reedy-necked boy, a jug-eared, caramel-colored stripling eternally polishing one or another of Ben Cameron's succession of black Lincolns or passing a tray with tongue-clamping concentration at some soiree or other of Dorothy's. But he had filled out since then, and seemed to have grown considerably taller, so that he bulked large in the semidark of the room. His head was long and narrow and well shaped, and either the jug ears had receded or his skull had grown to accommodate them, and the glasses that now sat on his oddly Indian nose were horn-rimmed, giving him a scholarly, prosperous air. I remembered Lucy saying that his grades at Morehouse had been extraordinary, and that he planned to get a law degree at Howard when he felt that he was no longer needed in the movement, but that he had become so valuable to Dr. King, along with a few other young lieutenants like Julian Bond and Andrew Young and John Lewis, that she could not foresee a time when he could do so. I knew, too, that he had served considerable time in exceedingly inhospitable jails around the South, and that those young shoulders had felt the bite of more than one truncheon and fire hose. I was stricken suddenly mute in his presence. I had thought, when I heard those things about him, how odd it was for a figure that had been almost part of the furniture of my childhood to be transmuted, willy-nilly, into a warrior on the ramparts of history. Interesting, I had thought.

Now, in his presence, I could not seem to speak. I caught myself about to say, "Tell me what you've been doing," and reddened again, thinking that saying it to him would be as incongruous as saying it to Martin Luther King himself. The music swelled up then, and I was grateful for the din.

Across the table, Lucy leaned over to talk to the young woman at Glenn Pickens's side, and Jack held up two fingers for the waitress. The girl with Glenn was very pretty, almost as striking as Lucy in the dark room. She looked smart and finished and composed, and there was about her an air of crisp authority. I thought that she seemed vaguely familiar, but I could not find the association. She wore a simple beige linen skirt and silk shirt, but they were so perfectly cut and so fluidly poured over her small, ripe body that they might have been cut and hand sewn for her. I thought that she was built like Sarah, and she had Sarah's ease and elegance and presence, except that she was a rich, shining chocolate brown. My own whiteness seemed to wink rottenly in the gloom beside all the rich shades of dark flesh around me.

"They're light-years ahead of me," I thought, lumping Lucy and Jack into the world of the young woman and Glenn Pickens. "My world is practically second nature to them, but I can't be at ease for five minutes in theirs. It was probably a mistake to come here."

Lucy touched my hand. "This is Gwen Caffrey," she said, her hand laid lightly on the dark girl's arm. "She's the new six o'clock anchor at Channel Seven. She's very, very good at what she does and she's mean as a snake, so watch your step and your mouth."

She smiled, and the girl smiled, and held out her hand. I took it. It was warm and surprisingly rough, as if she did hard work with her hands. Perhaps she did. Or had.

"I'm glad to meet you," I said. "I've never met an anchor before, much less a lady anchor."

"Nor a black one either, I'll be bound," she said, and it was so nearly what I had been thinking that I felt the traitorous blood rush up my neck into my face yet again. Shit, I thought, I've blushed more tonight than I did in grammar and high school put together. She laughed, but it was a friendly laugh. I smiled uncertainly.

"Relax," she said. "Nobody else has, either. There haven't been but a handful of us, and none before me in Atlanta. I've never met a Princeton man before, so we're even."

"Lucy's been talking again," I said, just to have something to say. I was not exactly coming off as a raconteur this evening.

"No, actually it was Glenn who told me about you," Gwen Caffrey said. "He said he knew you when you were all growing up in Buckhead."

"That's right," I said. "But I'm surprised he remembered me. There were such a lot of us around the Camerons' all the time—"

"And all little white kids look alike," Glenn Pickens said from across the table. I could not tell if he was teasing or not; his impassive face did not change, or his eyes behind the thick glasses. Somehow I did not think he was. I remembered that Lucy had said earlier, of the blacks at Damascus House, "They know who you are," and I felt naked and uneasy. I had not ever considered that I might exist as a person to Glenn Pickens, son of Benjamin Cameron's chauffeur, any more than he had existed, as a person, to me.

Lucy and Jack Venable laughed, easily and naturally, and I thought that Glenn Pickens was smiling, though it was more a very small grimace and looked as though it might split his carved taffy face. So I grinned too, feeling like a blundering albatross in a flock of lustrous crows. A willowy young waitress came by, and hugged Glenn Pickens briefly, and we ordered a round of drinks. The music, a playful piano weaving in and out around a bass and drums, swarmed through the room like a loosened hive of bees; the very walls throbbed with it, a teasing rhythm now bright as a school of minnows in sun-dappled shallows, now as glistening-dark as viscera, with a heavy blues beat and a witty, self-mocking counterpoint. I swam into it instinctively, my feet tapping with it, my face turning to it of its own volition. The pianist, a crew-cut young man with glasses who might have been, like Jack, an accountant, raised a cheerful hand to us, and Jack and Glenn Pickens saluted back. Lucy looked young and at ease and very happy; I knew that she was loving the night and the lounge and the sound and the evening. I began to relax, very slightly.

Lucy leaned over and touched my shoulder.

"Okay?" she said. "Do you like it?"

The trio slid into Ellington's "Come Sunday," and I smiled at Lucy. "It's wonderful. They're terrific. It's a treat to hear them in person; I never have. Thanks for letting me come, Luce."

She gave a little wiggle of pure happiness. "If Martin Luther King should come in I think I'd ascend straight to Heaven," she said.

Jack Venable smiled and tightened his arm around her shoulders and gave her a little squeeze. "I'm not going to let you leave me even for him," he said.

"King might be here," Glenn Pickens said. "He's in here a lot. Some of his crowd are over there at that table by the bandstand; I see a couple of kids from my old neighborhood who are good lieutenants of his now. Want to meet them?" He did not wait for Lucy's assent, but raised his pale hand and beckoned toward a large table in the opposite corner of the room.

Two very young men materialized out of the gloom at Glenn's elbow and stood looking down at us. One was round and short, almost fat, with skin lighter than Glenn's, and startling ghost-gray eyes. The other was slender and very handsome, and as dark as Gwen Caffrey. Both were a good bit younger than any of us; I did not think they could be much past their teens. But it's a young man's crusade, I reminded myself. Dr. King himself is only in his thirties.

They greeted Glenn cheerfully, and he clapped each on the back and introduced them. The short, pudgy one was Tony Sellers and the taller, blacker one Rosser Willingham; I vaguely recognized their names from news accounts of the student sit-ins last year, and the freedom rides earlier this summer. Both had demonstrated and marched with King, and both had gone quietly and matter-of-factly to Alabama jails with him. Both had been beaten, bitten, kicked, gassed, shot at. Rosser Willingham had, I knew, been hit. Self-consciousness thickened my tongue when Glenn introduced me, which was, I thought, just as well. Lucy smiled her incomparable smile and held up her hand to be shaken. As always, at Lucy's smile, there were quick and genuine answering smiles.

"It's good to meet you, Lucy Bondurant Chastain," Tony Sellers said. "I hear about you. How do you like Ramsey Lewis?"

"I think he's fantastic," Lucy said. "I like him better than Don Shirley, even, and Shep here will tell you that for me that's going some."

"Ramsey will be pleased to hear that," Sellers said.

"We missed you in Washington this summer," Willingham said to Glenn Pickens. "You'd have loved it. If I remember correctly, you always did love a crowd. You'd have been in your element."

"I was busy this summer," Glenn said. He was not smiling now. I thought I heard something very near defensiveness in his voice. "I figure we're going to need a master's degree or two somewhere in all this horsepower. There'll be other marches. I'll be there for those."

He looked hard at Rosser Willingham, and then he smiled his minimal smile.

"Gwen almost got to go, though," he said, touching her arm lightly. "Her station was going to send her up there, but at the last minute they decided she was too little, and sent a guy instead. She promised them she'd grow five inches if they'd let her play with the big kids, but nothing doing."

"Station?" Tony Sellers said, looking across the table at Gwen.

"She's just been made six o'clock anchor at Seven," Glenn said. "And she has a talk show on WCAT three nights a week."

"Terrific, we can use you," said Rosser Willingham. He was not smiling.

"Not unless I can interest you in coming on the show with a new recipe for three-bean salad or a spray for rose blight, you can't," Gwen said.

"Roses. Who*oeee!*" said Willingham.

"That's right," Gwen said. "Roses."

Eyes held.

"What's going on here?" I thought. "She's just told both of them to flake off, in so many words. And Glenn's acting funny as hell toward them. Aren't they all in the movement together? Why are they trying to one-up each other?" I felt acutely uncomfortable. My earlier awe fled before the discomfort.

"I was with you in the sit-ins when I could get loose," Jack Venable said suddenly, with such unaccustomed solemnity that I thought he must be speaking satirically, but the moist, messianic gleam behind the plain, serviceable glasses told me that he was not. "I wanted to go on the freedom rides, but my time wasn't my own then. I have more, now. Is . . . are you . . . is there anything coming up that could use some willing bodies?" His soft body, leaning very slightly toward the two young black men, radiated a nearly bizarre middle-aged willingness.

My face burned for him. I was glad of the darkness. I had not dreamed that a romantic boy lived in that phlegmatic CPA's flesh. Is that what had so called out to Lucy?

"There's some good action coming up in Mississippi this fall, if you're really interested," Tony Sellers drawled. "Real knife-in-the-teeth guerrilla stuff. Might be just up your alley."

I saw Jack's face darken, and felt my sympathetic flush mount. Lucy leaned forward.

"I loved your sit-in at Rich's," she said. "I was there. It was wonderful. God!"

The young men looked at her expressionlessly, politely.

"I'm glad you liked it, Miss Bondurant," Willingham said. "It was strictly an amateur job, of course, but we thought it had a certain energy and freshness."

I felt the heat spring out at my hairline in drops of perspiration. Glenn looked down into the depths of his drink, and Gwen Caffrey attended brightly and determinedly to the jazz trio, which was swinging into "The In Crowd," pulling herself almost physically away from the rest of us. I could not look at anyone. "They think we're utter fools," I thought.

Lucy grinned.

"Don't patronize me, sonny," she said. "My maiden name is Feldstein. My grandma is a lampshade in some fat burgher's house in Argentina as we speak. I know your act. I have style. Spurn me at your own loss."

Rosser Willingham grinned back at her, suddenly. He raised two fingers in salute. The group slipped into ease once more.

"Those were some kind of days," he said, laughing. "There must have been close to fifteen hundred folks on that picket line downtown at one time. It circled all downtown Atlanta. God, there were shuttle buses to take people down there and back, and we had two-way radios and special signs that rain and spit and worse wouldn't wash off, and we had special coats for the girls so they wouldn't get spit on—and worse again. Man, we thought we were big stuff. Hot shit. And we were, we were."

Glenn Pickens alone did not laugh with them.

"Is the Lord here?" he said.

"The Lord?" said Lucy.

"King. I heard he might be."

Willingham and Sellers looked narrowly at him.

"He's in the dining room," Tony Sellers said.

"God," Jack said reverently. "It really is headquarters, isn't it?" He looked as if he might weep with the wonder of it.

"Yeah, well, at least we know we can get served here," Willingham said. "We can't say that about every place, you know. It's like John Lewis said about Nashville. Somebody said, 'Well, we don't serve niggers here,' and somebody else said, 'Well, that's okay because we don't eat 'em.' "

There was more laughter. I felt an inadequacy that bordered on shame, and a dark fascination. These young men were dangerous; they were total, they were whole. Behind the banter and the cool laughter and the dismissing eyes were marches; beatings in dark, hot country nights and squalling, mean urban noons; terror and imprisonment and bombs and fire hoses and dogs and guns in darkness. In those eyes ambushed black men spun forever in their doorways, frozen; children flew into pieces in the roaring air of churches.

I dropped my own eyes.

"It's not the only way," Glenn Pickens said suddenly. Everyone looked at him.

"Malcolm X said just the other day at the militant labor forum that the day of nonviolent resistance will soon be over," he said evenly, pleasantly.

Still, they looked at him. No one spoke. Gwen rolled her eyes to the ceiling and tossed her sleek head; I thought I had never seen anyone who wished so sincerely not to be present. The silence spun out.

Finally Rosser Willingham said, "Oh, hell, Glenn, Brother Malcolm's nothing but an uppity nigger who didn't make the cut." He laughed, but no one laughed with him.

"He's a born rabble-rouser," Tony Sellers said.

"Isn't that what we're all trying to do?" Glenn said. "All of us? Rouse the rabble?"

Jack Venable laughed, a rasping, nervous sound. No one else did. The music wove its separate strands around us. The tension held. My skin crawled with it, and I knew Lucy's did, too. I wondered how soon we might leave, and where the bathroom was, and if I could ever cross the staring room to find it. I could not see Lucy's face, and I did not really know Jack Venable and Glenn Pickens, and Gwen Caffrey seemed to have gone as far away from us all as was possible without getting up and leaving the table. I felt primally, abysmally alone. It was as bad a moment as I could remember.

Another figure was beside us suddenly.

"Do your mothers know you boys are out?" said a voice that would have a dream, had stirred a nation, preached love and gentleness from a hundred besieged pulpits and a score of jails. My breath seemed to stop. I heard Lucy give a little soft gasp. I looked up. He stood there wearing a cardigan sweater against the chill of the air-conditioning, and a white shirt with an open collar, and slacks, looking as inevitable as a mountain, larger than any of us, preternaturally solid and focused, *there*.

We were on our feet in an instant. Lucy almost upset her chair as she scrambled out of it, and Jack reached out to steady her. So did Martin Luther King. At his touch she stopped still and looked up at him, her old, special radiance in her face, not speaking, staring at the dark moon of his face, the thick lips smiling, the slanted, faintly Mongolian eyes, the solid set of the shoulders, the good hands. He smiled back. Of course he did.

There were introductions all around. He did not linger. He said a few words to Sellers and Willingham and told Glenn Pickens he was proud of his new master's degree. He shook Jack Venable's hand, and gently disengaged it when Jack could not seem to stop pumping it. As he turned to leave, he paused beside Lucy. "I hear you're going to be married soon, Mrs. Chastain," he said. "I wish you every joy. It's a wonderful, hopeful time in your life. A wedding is always a fine thing."

Lucy looked into his eyes and smiled with her whole being, and he touched her arm, softly, and then he was gone into the crowd, and the trio broke gleefully into "You Been Talkin' 'Bout

Me, Baby," and Jack Venable pushed back his chair and said, "We've got to get going, Lucy. Tomorrow's a school day." I could hear the exaltation under the prosaic words.

We all dispersed then, Tony Sellers and Rosser Willingham into the sacrosanct back room of the club after King, Glenn Pickens and Gwen Caffrey to another and presumably more agreeable table, Lucy and Jack and I outside into the just-cooling night air. We were silent for a moment on the pitted pavement under the pallid neon, still caught in the currents of the evening. Lucy stood with her arms linked through mine and Jack's, her head drooping onto Jack's shoulder. Still we said nothing. All of us, I think, had a sense of import greater than the evening's events warranted. Nothing, after all, had transpired in the dimness of La Carrousel that might not have been expected to take place between young Atlanta Negroes and liberal whites on a September night in 1961. But I, for one, had a powerful sense of something ending, and something else beginning, and more: a powerful sense of Lucy's having stepped away from me and irrevocably into another country, one where I could not follow.

I thought, looking at the two of them there on the sidewalk—Jack and Lucy, one known to me, the other not—that they were initiates into some kind of mystery as exalted and profound as those of Eleusis, and as such were a unit now, a singleness, that I could never penetrate. A sorrow as old and dark as the earth washed me briefly, a kind of September *Weltschmerz.* I have lost Lucy too now, I said in my heart, and knew it to be true. It had never been, before: not to physical separation, not to anger, not to marriage. I had lost her, now, to a dream and an army of arrogant young martyrs and a pragmatic urban saint who would not live out the decade. I did not think she would return.

Finally she reached up and kissed Jack Venable on the cheek and he kissed her in return, and said, "I hope it's the first of a million good nights, Shep," and I said, "I hope so, too. I don't have to tell you to take good care of her," and he said, "No, you don't," and raised a pale, freckled hand in salute and turned and shambled away toward his car. I wondered, irrelevantly, what sort of car he would have; his retreating figure looked as though it should fold itself into a road-worn Chevrolet with its backseat piled high with sample goods. He looked almost grotesquely, in the warm darkness, like Willy Loman.

Lucy looked up at me.

"Do you see now?" she said.

"See?" I said. I thought I did, but perversely did not want to give her that small gift.

"See what I mean about the Negroes, and Dr. King, and the movement and Jack . . . oh, the whole thing. Can't you see how

wonderful, how special . . . it all is? Oh, come on, Gibby, I know
you can."

But I could see only that from this night on I would walk
through the world without my cousin Lucy. I do not know why
the knowledge gave me such desolation. Until this weekend I
had been profoundly angry with her, through with her, done
with her; I had not had any thought of letting Lucy Bondurant
back into my life.

It was not until we were back on the Northside of Atlanta,
bowling along under the yellowing trees that fell over Peachtree
Street in front of the old brown stone pile of the High Museum,
that I finally was able to give her what I knew she wanted.

"He's a good guy, Luce, and it was a good night," I said.
"You're going to be okay now."

"Thank you, Gibby," she said in a child's small, drowsy voice,
and put her dark head on my shoulder, and was asleep before
we reached the green-hung intersection at Palisades where
Peachtree Street becomes Peachtree Road.

Her parties and the tea went off without a hitch, and were just
what I had thought they would be: the occasion for a small flutter of congratulations to the author, more for the fact that she
had finally and against all considered opinions made something
of herself than for the slender little novel which all of them
bought and few would read; and for much drinking and considerable eating; and for catching up on news after the hiatus of
vacation and before the autumn social season began. Lucy, looking somehow diminished and muted in the unaccustomed public
approbation, shook hands and kissed cheeks and smiled her new
sweet smile, and signed her dashing black, back-slanted Lucy
J. Bondurant on perhaps thirty books, and thanked everyone for
coming, and behaved in general so like the biddable and charming debutante and Junior Leaguer she had refused to be that
older Buckheaders were mollified and smiling and our own
crowd was frankly puzzled. I saw eyes cut toward Lucy all weekend and heads go together, and heard whispers exchanged, and
I felt rather than saw the same eyes on me. I knew that I was
being scrutinized for evidence of trauma from Sarah and Charlie's marriage, and so smiled more and wider and kissed more
cheeks and clapped more backs than I would have ordinarily.
My mother and Aunt Willa were at all the parties, elegant and
cool, not showing by so much as a muscle tremor the outrage
Lucy's new preoccupation had engendered. I wondered how
they would take the news, and the circumstances, of her new
marriage. I thought I could imagine, and grinned involuntarily
at the prospect.

My father was not in attendance at any of the parties, and Ben Cameron was not at the cocktail party he and Dorothy gave at the Driving Club. Dorothy, whose welcoming kiss to me was as warm and natural as if great gulfs of pain did not lie between us, whispered in my ear in the receiving line, "Please don't think Ben's avoiding you. He's down at the Walahauga at a rally, but he's going to try to get back before the party's over. Lester Maddox is giving us a hard time, and the election is only two months away. Ben absolutely must have the Negro vote to win or he'd be here."

It was only then that I remembered that Ben Cameron was running for mayor. I could not remember who Lester Maddox was.

"Is he still mad at me, Dorothy?" I said.

"Yes," she said, "but not in the way he was. He'll get over it, Shep. And he's never stopped loving you."

"He should have," I said. "He ought to just wash his hands of me."

"He'll never do that, and neither will I," she said and kissed me on the cheek, and passed me on to Lucy, slender and oddly prim in dark blue fall cotton and Ben Cameron's snowdrift of white orchids.

"Are you the lady who wrote the dirty book?" I said, hugging her. "How about letting me take you away from all this? Your place or mine?"

She giggled, but it was a subdued and mannerly giggle. "I wish we could just go somewhere and talk," she said. "I know you're going back tomorrow right after the tea, and I don't know when in the world we'll really talk again. But I'm meeting Jack at Camellia Gardens after this, and we're going to the eleven o'clock service at Damascus House in the morning. . . ."

"Don't worry about it," I said. "I think I'll go out and get some dinner with Snake and Lelia and maybe A.J. and Lana. I'll see you in the morning. By the way, you look wonderful. I remember when you had eight of those things stuck on you at one time."

She looked down at the orchids, and her blue eyes filled with tears.

"I was the prettiest girl in town then, wasn't I?" she said.

"What do you mean, was? You still are," I said. "You talk like you're fifty years old."

"Part of me is," she said softly. She was not smiling.

"Well, the part I can see is still the girl every Jell in Atlanta had the twenty-year hots for," I said, squeezing her hands, and was dismayed to see the tears spill over the black fringe of her lower lashes and run silently down her cheeks to her chin. Her mouth trembled and broke. She put her arms around me and fitted her face into the side of my neck, as Sarah had done so often, and whispered something into my ear. I could feel the heat of her tears, but I could not hear what she said, and I raised her chin with one hand and looked questioningly at her.

"I said, 'I love you, Gibby,' " she said. One of the tears fell from her chin and trembled, crystal and perfect, on the waxy white petal of her corsage. "And I said, 'Good-bye and God-speed.' "

"I'm just going back to work," I said in a too-jolly voice. "I'm not going away forever and ever."

"Yes, you are," she said.

After the tea my mother and my aunt Willa gave for Lucy at the Peachtree Road house the next afternoon, I did not see her again, and I did not wait for my father to come back from wherever he had been, to say good-bye to him. I hugged my mother longer and harder than was my custom when I left Atlanta to go back to New York, for the thought was in my mind that I probably would not come back to the house on Peachtree Road, or to the city, for a very long time, if ever. There was no reason, now, to do so. Two of the three women who had claimed my heart were gone from me, and so was the man who should have, and most of the other ties that I had to the city were light and ephemeral. My mother, as if reading my thoughts, began to cry again, and I pulled myself gently out of her grasp and patted her shoulder, and said, "Tell Dad good-bye for me," and took a cab to the airport. I got a seven o'clock Delta flight back to La Guardia. By the time I unlocked my door on West Twenty-first Street, the Sunday night traffic was thinning, and only a stream of lights over on Ninth spoke of any life, or the forward momentum of time. The air in my apartment was as old and arid as the breath of tombs.

Sometime in the small hours of the morning I came awake with the heavy, marrow-deep certainty that my time in New York was over. I knew, utterly and passionlessly, as an old man knows, that there was behind me in Atlanta no one who needed me, and there was, now, in New York nothing more that I needed. That afternoon I wrote my Colonial Club friend Corey Appleby, who was teaching French at Haddonfield Academy, in Vermont, asking if there were any faculty positions open, and when his affirmative reply came by return mail I borrowed Alan Greenfeld's Corvette and drove up the following weekend. Within another two weeks I had been accepted as an instructor in medieval history, with additional classes in freshman English, to start when the new term did, on January 5, 1962. I did not feel any way at all about this change in my life except very tired, and endlessly, stupidly sleepy. For the remainder of that autumn and early winter, when I was not at work, I came home to West Twenty-first Street and slept.

Four days before Christmas, just as the first snowstorm of the season came howling in from New Jersey unfurling its battle banners of blowing snow, my telephone rang at 6:30 P.M., burring over the television newscast to which I had fallen asleep on my sofa. When I picked it up, it was to hear the voice of Lucy Bondurant Venable, which I had not thought to hear then or perhaps at any other time, thick with her familiar long-distanced tears, telling me that my father had had a massive stroke on the golf course at Brookhaven that afternoon and was completely paralyzed and not expected to live the night, and that my mother was prostrated and in seclusion, and could not be comforted until I promised to come home.

And so, I left New York at dawn the next day in a rented U-Haul and drove, instead of to Vermont, back to Atlanta and the house on Peachtree Road. I planned to bury my father, comfort my mother, stash my meager belongings and fly to Vermont as soon as I decently could. With luck I could still make the first day of classes.

If anyone had told me, when I saw the Atlanta city limits sign rise up out of a fast-failing December twilight on the highway in from Gainesville, that I would never leave it again, I would have laughed in his face.

CHAPTER
SEVENTEEN

MY FATHER DID NOT DIE, THOUGH. All through the cold, gray day and night that followed, I parked the U-Haul at truck stops and drive-ins and called home, and the message, relayed by my aunt Willa, was the same: "There's been no change. He's still in intensive care and is unconscious most of the time, and when he's awake we can't tell if he knows anybody. There's been a little movement in one hand and in one side of his face, and maybe just the tiniest bit in one of his toes. But basically there isn't any change. It's a miracle he's still alive. Hub Dorsey doesn't think he can last another day."

But he did last, through the gray miles that I hacked out of New Jersey and Pennsylvania and Virginia in the bumping, unwieldy truck, my few belongings rattling and shifting behind me with the vagaries of the monotonous four-lane federal highways. That first day I made North Carolina by full dark, and pulled up to a dingy little cinder-block motel outside Kannapolis when fatigue and a spitting sleetfall made driving any further impossible. I picked up a hamburger and french fries and a carton of coffee at the dirty, white-lit little motel diner and stumbled back to my room with them, and wolfed them down cold while Aunt Willa's low "Atlanta" voice told me what it had all day: "No change. No, there's been no change." I turned on the flickering old Philco television set across from my bed and stared stupidly at *Peter Gunn* until it melted and slid into blackness behind my stinging eyes, and when I opened them again, it was midmorning and a dispirited maid was rattling my door and an amazonian North Carolina lady was showing an ecstatic, adenoidal morning

343

show host how to make corn bread dressing for turkey. I pulled on last night's weary clothing and trotted to the diner, and drank coffee as I received Aunt Willa's morning message, "No change."

Because of my late start, it was nearly dark when I followed Highway 23 into North Atlanta, through ugly, meager Doraville and Chamblee; past Oglethorpe University, where Lucy had once been apprehended necking with Boo Cutler by the almost forgotten Mr. Bovis Hardin; past Brookhaven Drive, where, out of sight to my right, the Atlanta Pinks and Jells had danced away so many nights at the Brookhaven Country Club, and where, two days earlier, my father had dropped, stricken, to the frozen earth; past the beginning of the big old houses that would line Peachtree Road, now, until they reached the bridge over Peachtree Creek at Peachtree Battle Avenue. On my left, where for many years Mr. John Ottley's great farm, Joyeuse, had lain along a sweet-curved, deep-wooded sweep of Peachtree Road, a low white jumble of buildings in a sea of automobiles gleamed eerily in the icy mist, and I scrubbed at my reddened eyes with my fist, for a moment utterly lost, until I remembered that a shopping mall called Lenox Square had been built there a year or so before, a worldly Xanadu said to be, at present, the largest such mall in the country.

I could believe it. There seemed to be thousands upon thousands of cars bellied up to the mall like voraciously suckling piglets at the teats of a gleaming, corpulent white sow. White lights danced and twinkled on spindly evergreens fringing the parking lots. Of course: Christmas shopping. I felt, for a moment, such a nostalgia for the old, warm-lit, Evening in Paris–smelling confines of Wender & Roberts on Christmas Eve that my heart flopped in my chest, and then Lenox Square vanished and I was into and through Buckhead, bright-lit and traffic-choked now, and coming into the last great curve of Peachtree Road before I reached 2500.

And then even it was past, dark-bulked and beautiful behind its iron fence, only one light burning upstairs in my parents' room, no automobiles waiting on the graceful half-moon front drive. I drove on down Peachtree Road past Peachtree Battle shopping center and up the long hill to Piedmont Hospital where my aunt Willa had said she would be waiting. When I had last talked to her, at noon, she said my mother had wakened from the deep, drugged sleep Dr. Dorsey's needle had given her, and was bathing and dressing to receive visitors. Hub Dorsey had forbidden the hospital to her until tomorrow—if indeed, there was one for my father. Dorothy Cameron had been with Mother most of the time since she heard the news about my father, and was coming back after lunch to see to the flow of traffic in the house. Shem, Aunt Willa said, would drive me down to Piedmont if I wanted to stop by the house first, but I said I would come straight there. I wanted to see for myself how the land lay before I encountered my mother. I wanted to be informed, crisp, authoritative and very, very clear about what must be done and who would do it; I wanted to have a long-range plan of action formulated and ready for presentation. The plan did not include any possibility of my staying at home. My mother must see that from the very beginning.

When I got off the elevator in the scaldingly bright intensive care waiting room at the hospital it seemed for a moment that my entire life lay in ambush for me. The knot of people who sat about on plastic chairs and sofas or stood looking out at the lights of the traffic streaming past on Peachtree Road were all there for my father; old Buckhead had, like great elephants, come to encircle one of their own fallen tribe. Dorothy Cameron sat, small, erect and calm-faced, on a sofa beside Lucy, patting her clenched hands. Jack Venable stood at the windows, back to the room, hands in pockets, looking out into the night. Ben Cameron, almost totally iron-gray now, and looking tired and grim, sat on another sofa beside Aunt Willa, who was pale and still and perfectly turned out in severe black jersey, smoking a filter-tipped cigarette. On a molded plastic chair a little apart from the others Sarah Gentry sat, as straight-spined and composed as her mother in the pink and white stripes of a Piedmont volunteer, her dark, curly head slightly bowed, her small hands clasped in her lap. I saw the modest fire of Charlie's diamond on her finger. At the sound of the elevator bell she lifted her head and looked straight into my eyes and I saw the smudges of fatigue under her own, and the spark of recognition and then the old joy that leaped in them. Her wide mouth, bare of lipstick, slid into its warm, bone-remembered smile.

"Shep," she said soundlessly, her lips forming my name. In the merciless light of the waiting room, my own fatigue dragging at my limbs, I felt the renewing joy of the sight of her run into my arms and legs, followed by a near-physical blow to my heart.

Lucy saw Sarah's smile and turned her head and saw me, and jumped up and ran to me, her face stained with recent tears, her eyes red and swollen. She looked blue-white and terribly thin, and nearly shabby in a wrinkled plaid skirt and sweater I thought I recognized from our North Fulton days, and her glossy hair was tied back in an untidy ponytail. Even in her obvious anxiety and dishevelment she looked beautiful, but suddenly, years older. The hands she thrust into mine were icy cold and chapped nearly raw.

"I thought you'd never get here," she said, and the tears welled into her eyes afresh, and I hugged her distractedly.

"What's the news?" I said.

"Still no change," she said, her voice strangled. "He's on a lung machine, Gibby, and Dr. Dorsey still says he doesn't see how he can live . . . oh, he just looks so awful! White and all twisted and shrunken, and hooked up to about a million tubes . . . I can't stand to see him like that!"

I wondered, holding her loosely and getting my bearings, why she was so upset. My father had never been close to Lucy; even she must have acknowledged that years ago. I remembered the morning in childhood after she had run away with Little Lady, after Jamie had died, and been so terribly punished, her coming in her thin nightgown and climbing into his lap and making her little speech about being sorry, and being a good girl if only he would not send her away, and his arms going reluctantly around her, and his voice promising that he would look after her always. Puddin', he had called her; I remembered it vividly. And afterward, she had said to me, "I have to make sure he takes care of me until you're old enough to do it."

But he had not, and I never had been.

That was the key, of course; my father represented to Lucy the only security and safety she had had in all her childhood, and his stroke must have called up that old black terror, the stuff of her nightmares. But she was grown and married now, and had moreover married, almost literally, a father. I looked across at Jack Venable, still staring out into the December night. His rigid shoulders and back told me that he wanted no part of this insular, privileged group, and was here only for sufferance of Lucy. I wondered if the harbor Lucy had thought to enter with her marriage had been, after all, closed to her.

I started over to speak to Aunt Willa and Dorothy and Ben and Sarah; and then Hubbard Dorsey, my family's physician since old Dr. Ballentine had died and my father's occasional golfing partner, came out of the swinging doors from the intensive care unit. He, too, looked tired and rumpled in his white coat, a stethoscope swinging around his neck, but when he saw me he smiled and came toward me, and I knew, somehow, from the set of his shoulders and the quickness of his step that my father had turned some sort of corner and was not going to die.

He put his arm around my shoulder and drew me to the group in the sitting area, and said, "Well, I don't think we're going to lose him for a while after all. His vitals are much more stable all of a sudden, and he's breathing on his own, and his EKG is nearly normal again. He's still profoundly paralyzed; I don't think that's going to change, though I can't say for sure at this point. He could fool us; he sure has me, tonight. But unless he has another massive stroke—and that's always possible, of course, especially now—I think he's going to make it. This time."

Lucy began to cry in earnest, and I handed her over to Jack, who put his arm around her and drew her over to the window with him, away from the group. Dorothy and Ben Cameron smiled and stood and stretched, and Dorothy kissed me and Ben gave me a small, stiff, wordless hug, and my aunt Willa rose and came over to me and kissed my cheek as if we did that sort of thing routinely, and said, in the candied voice that had long since replaced her wire-grass cat's squall, "Hello, Shep dear. What good news, isn't it? You brought him luck. I'll go call Olivia right now, and then you must go on home and see her. She's wanted nobody but you since this happened."

"I'll go home in a little while, Aunt Willa," I said. "I want to see Dad first, if I can." I looked questioningly at Hub Dorsey, and he nodded.

"For a minute. I'll go back in with you."

I walked over to Sarah then, and stood before her with absolutely no idea what I was going to say. I had not seen her since her marriage, indeed, not since that terrible night at the beginning of the summer, at the Plaza, and no words formed in my brain or on my lips. I simply looked at her. It seemed to me that she was much thinner than when I had last seen her; a thinness that seemed more an atrophy of her fine, taut swimmer's muscles than any loss of flesh. Her faint year-round tan had faded to a sallowness I had never seen before, and the circles under her amber eyes were a deep saffron. Her thick, dark brows were untidy. I wondered if she had been ill. She put her hand up, tentatively, and touched my cheek, and I noticed, over the trip-hammering of my heart, that it was as cold as Lucy's, and that for the first time since I had known her, there were no faint half-moons of paint under her nails. I covered her hand with my own and said, "Hello, Sarah. It was good of you to come."

"Oh, Shep," she said, and the rich voice was the same, warming my heart even as it smote it, "of course I came. How could I not? This is my day for the mail cart, and I stayed on till you came. I wanted to see you before I went home."

"I'm glad you did," I said. "Is Charlie around?"

She laughed, and the laugh was the same, too, simply Sarah's and no other.

"No, he's at the office again for the third time this week. Mr. Woodruff has a new project going, and everybody's hopping to over there. He says to give you his love and he'll see you tomor-

row, and he especially says to get you over to the house for dinner as soon as you can come."

"Where do you live?" I said. It seemed an insane thing to ask,
but I realized that I did not know.

"We have a little house on Greystone, about a block down
from Ben and Julia," she said. "I think Ben hates having his little
sister right under his nose, but he can't say so. They're having
a baby just any minute now—did anybody tell you? Everybody
you know lives in Collier Hills, Shep, or nearby. Snake and Lelia
are one street over on Meredith, and Pres and Sarton are looking
at a house on Walthall, and Tom and Freddie are in Colonial
Homes, just a minute away. When Christmas is over and things
have calmed down for you a little, I want to get us all together
at a little party for you. . . ."

"I'd like that," I said, knowing that I could not bear it, but
secure in the knowledge that I would be two thousand miles
away in Vermont before she could possibly put a party together.
"You look fine, Sarah. . . ."

"I look like twelve miles of bad road, and you know it," she
said, grinning. "But it's temporary. Well. Go on in and see your
dad. I don't have to tell you how glad we are that he's getting
better."

"Me, too," I said, and kissed her cheek, which was as cold
as her hands. The light, lemony Ma Griffe that she loved met
and enfolded me. I turned to Hub Dorsey.

"Let's go," he said.

We walked through the swinging doors and down the hall toward the nurses' station, the smell of illness and its electronic
heartbeat filling my nose and ears. Mortality winked on overhead screens; death dodged somewhere just out of my sight,
starched and antisepticized almost into respectability, but still
there, and stinking.

"You said you think he's going to make it," I said. "Is that
the lowdown, or was that for Lucy and Aunt Willa's sake?"

"No," he said. "I think he probably *will* make it. I also think
he'll probably be sorry he did . . . if he's able to think anything
at all. There's no way of telling now what kind of brain damage
we're talking about, and there won't be, for some time. He could
be relatively clear, or simply a vegetable. And as I said, the physical trauma is massive. He can move one hand and the toes of
one foot, and he can turn his head from side to side. He can't,
of course, speak, and I very much doubt that he ever will be able
to. But as I say, he could fool us all. He must have the constitution of a mastodon."

My father looked so much like a wax dummy hooked up, for
teaching purposes, to an astonishing array of machines and mon-

itors that his plight simply did not seem real to me, and so, standing at the side of his criblike bed and staring down at him, I felt nothing at all except a kind of mild wonder that he looked so small. In the ghastly green half-light from the dials and screens, shrouded in his white hospital gown, wires snaking off and out of him, I thought that he looked like nothing so much as one of the hapless insects who blunder into the webs of the beautiful big autumn writing spiders we have in the South, the Argiope, and are immediately mummified in white silk and sucked to papery husks. He was breathing on his own, a thin, peevish wheezing that moved his chest up and down, and one eye was open, blue and furious, focused on the ceiling. The other was closed, and his half-closed mouth was twisted as if in suppressed laughter, or the beginnings of tears. His arms were pinioned to his sides with straps, and he was strapped into the bed, too.

"Why is he strapped in like that if he can't move?" I said. "I don't see how he could get over those side rails even if he could."

"Another stroke could convulse him so it would pitch him right out of there," Hub Dorsey said. "I heard the one he had almost doubled him up in a backward somersault on the golf course."

The image of my father flopping gymnastically on the velvety green at Brookhaven was both terrible and funny, and I swallowed hard to suppress the crazy, forbidden laughter that bubbled in my chest.

"Another stroke . . . could he have another one?"

"He almost certainly will have another one," Hub said. "If not now, sooner or later. It's what will kill him, most likely, if he doesn't go into pneumonia from this one. It could be tonight or ten years from now, or even twenty. Most likely he'll have a series of small strokes, so tiny that you may not be aware he's having them; transient ischemic attacks, we call them. They can go on for a very long time. Or as I say, another big one could come along and that will be it."

"Ten years," I said, looking at the intubated corpus of my father but seeing the red and blond giant who bulked over my childhood. "Or twenty . . ."

"That's right," he said. "That's why I said he'll probably be sorry if he makes it, and you all will come to be sorry, too. It's no kind of life, Shep. I vote for the pneumonia, myself. Any doctor would. We don't call it the old man's friend for nothing. All things considered, it's a good way to go out."

"Christ," I said under my breath. How could he stand here beside this wrecked man, clinging so hideously and wonderfully to his ruined life, and speak of good ways to go out?

He put his arm around me again. "No doctor is reconciled

to death, Shep, but we're even less reconciled to what can be its alternative. That is not your father and my friend there, strapped in that crib like a deformed old baby. That's a mutant and an embarrassment. An accident. That was meant to die. The man did die, two days ago on the golf course. You're going to have no joy in what's left, I can assure you. Olivia is going to have even less. I ask you now, if pneumonia does set in, to let me leave orders that no life-sustaining measures be taken. And I advise you now that if he does linger on to put him in a nursing home as soon as he leaves the hospital. If he can be rehabilitated, they can do it better than we or anybody else can. If he can't, at least there will be a chance of a life for Olivia and you."

"I don't know what Mother will want to do . . ." I began.

"She wants to do what you want. She's already told me that you will make whatever decisions have to be made. I think she just wants to have it over, Shep, and believe me, the best thing is to let him go if he possibly can, and to put him in a home if he can't."

An endless white fatigue washed over me, so powerful that I almost buckled under it. My knees shook, and my head began a long, slow spin. He saw it, and took me by the arm and steered me out of the room.

"Let's go get some coffee and maybe a bite to eat," he said. "The cafeteria's open, or the drugstore across the street. Or we can run on up to Biuso's. I bet you drove straight through. When did you last eat?"

"No, I had a lot of sleep last night, and a good lunch," I said. The dizziness was ebbing. "I think I'll go on home now. Is my mother all right? Aunt Willa said she wasn't able to come to the hospital."

"She's all right now, I think," he said. "She was pretty hysterical when it first happened. I've kept her fairly well sedated. But right at first . . . I don't know. Crying, and laughing . . . I've never seen her like that. I didn't think it of her, somehow. It must have been a closer relationship than I thought it was, if you'll forgive me for saying so. . . ."

I raised my hand. I didn't blame him for thinking it. I was surprised at my mother's reaction, too. I would have said that practically nothing but proximity and long habit and the complex family real estate holdings were left of whatever ties had originally bound them. But then, I thought, I was the last person in the world to qualify as an expert on the relationships of others. I did not think that I would ever again be surprised at another man's love. Or another woman's.

"I'll think about the nursing home," I said. "Meanwhile, if it should come to that, no machines and no respirators, okay?"

"Okay," he said. "Good boy. Good man. I'm really sorry about this, Shep. It's tough on an only son when he stands to lose his dad."

"Thanks, Hub," I said. "I'll be okay. It's Mother I'm worried about." I turned away so he could not see my face, read there the traitorous absence of grief.

"She'll be all right now that you're home," he said. "She's asked for you constantly for the past two days. You're going to be just what she needs to get her through this."

I thought of the white hills of Vermont, the old pile of brown Gothic bricks waiting for me at Haddonfield, the slow, deep, sweet new measure of time and days that would be mine to slip into. I was more determined than ever not to miss the beginning of the new term. I had already decided what I would do: I would find a good nursing home for my father, instruct Tom Carmichael, my father's corporate attorney, to find a good business manager as soon as possible, break the news of these decisions to my mother and leave again before the new year dawned on the city. I knew it could all be done, even on the shortest of notice, even at Christmas, simply because I knew what the sort of money my father commanded could do. If necessary, I knew that Ben Cameron would help me. All the newly powerful men of Buckhead would. If my mother objected, I realized that I was quite capable of stealing silently out of the summerhouse with my bags in the dawn before she was awake. I would do what had to be done, and I would do it fast, and then I would be gone. I had known at the first sight of Sarah's pinched white face that I could not stay here.

I got the U-Haul out of the parking lot and drove back north on Peachtree Road. It was nearly ten o'clock in the evening now, but the river of automobile lights and the glare of neon on the road limned the landscape as clearly as at sunset. I realized, suddenly, that those lights had not been here when I left Atlanta for Princeton. This stretch of Peachtree Road had been dark then, except for streetlights and a few pale smears of neon where an occasional unprepossessing restaurant, Johnny Escoe's or Rusty's or Vittorio's, crouched among the big old houses and dense trees. Now many of the small forests were gone, and raw, square new two- and three-story commercial buildings shouldered in among the offended houses, and many of the houses themselves wore the discreet signage of businesses: insurance companies, law and dentist's offices, regional or branch or sales offices of national concerns. Filling stations and dry cleaners and liquor stores winked their availability at this holiday season, and a madly improbable Polynesian restaurant with a thatched roof and a listing, enormous outrigger canoe occupied the curve across from the hospital. Its sign proclaimed it the Kon Tiki, and someone had—whimsically, I hoped—set up a manger scene and crèche on its minuscule lawn, beside the outrigger. One great, yawing plastic camel seemed in the act of planting a splayed foot in the canoe. Once again I bit back the madman's urge to laugh aloud. I thought that once I got started, there was no power on earth that could stop me, and I knew that it would never do to walk into the beautiful house at 2500 Peachtree Road, now a house of sorrow, braying my laughter like an infidel.

Always, as long as I could remember, the great, fanlighted white front door of 2500 had worn, at Christmas, a simple green boxwood wreath with a red velvet bow, fashioned at my mother's direction by Weinstock's Florist over on Roswell Road. Shem Cater put up the spotlight that showcased it the week before each Christmas, and with the austere grace of the Federal door itself and the fan- and sidelights and the slender Ionic columns of the portico, it was as dignified and lovely a Christmas door as there was in Atlanta, far more so than the cheerful, rococo and more approachable excesses of Ansley Park and Garden Hills and the Governor's Mansion. It suited the simple American Georgian lines of the house and the ornate, symmetrical iron fence surrounding it, as exquisitely as everything else my mother set her hand to. The sight of it now, gleaming out of the cold mist, touched my heart with a jet of warmth and peace, and I instinctively pulled the U-Haul around back to the stable-garages, rather than leave it, blotlike, on the semicircular front drive. Shem Cater must have been looking out for me, because he was at the back door of the little latticed summer porch before I could reach for the knob. For once, Martha was beside him. He pumped my hand and said, "Glad you's home, Mr. Shep, glad to see you," and old Martha gave me a fierce, brief hug and said, "It about time, Shep. Git in here out'n the cold fo' you freezes us out." Martha never had, in all her life or mine, called me Mr. Shep. The dark, intricate, clean-ash smell of them enfolded me and I was, vividly and inalterably, home.

My mother was waiting for me, not in the little glassed sun porch that was our winter sitting room, or in her and my father's upstairs bedroom, but in the living room. I could not ever remember my parents' sitting there when there was not company in the house, and I felt, walking into the vast room with its apricot-washed plaster walls and its distinctive ivory wood moldings, like an intruder, a Vandal or a Visigoth come to sack and plunder. I was very conscious, all of a sudden, of my travel-stained clothing and the fact that I had not had a bath since I left New York. My beard stubble was blond and invisible, but in that cold, beautiful blue, apricot and cream room, it felt as though it brushed my knees, rank and Hasidic.

My mother sat on one of the pair of satin brocade sofas flanking the great gray Italian marble fireplace and mantel. The enormous baroque wood overmantel and chimney piece gave the room its focus, and my mother, in a dark red velvet robe which echoed the darkest of the faded colors in the old Oriental rugs, looked like a medieval duchess, or like Guinevere receiving the prisoners her husband's knights brought back from their quests for her dispensation. The enormous decorated Fraser fir that shone before the curtained Palladian windows, a twin to the one in the hall rotunda, and the light from the leaping fire were the sole sources of illumination in the room, and she needed only a small Italian greyhound curled at her feet to complete the picture of somber medieval splendor. The smell of the fire's heat on the drying needles of the tree, and the fragrant pine and smilax garlands on the mantel and the stair in the rotunda, and my mother's bittersweet perfume seemed somehow heavier and more piercing in the vast, warm, fire-leaping semidarkness.

"Shep, darling," she said softly, not rising, but holding out both hands to me. I went and sat beside her on the sofa and took them, and she laid her forehead lightly on my shoulder and sat there, still and quiet, so that I finally had no recourse but to put my arm around her shoulders and hold her. For what seemed a very long time, we sat so, not moving, neither of us speaking, I because I could not think of anything to say and her musk and nearness dried my mouth, she because of whatever obscure mother-son game she was playing. On the whole, I did not mind the silence and stillness so much. It was better than the hysterical laughter and tears Hub Dorsey had spoken of.

She raised her head and looked at me, and I saw that her dark sloe eyes were perfectly made up, and had the flat, high glitter of fever in them. Two hectic spots of color burned in her white face, and she had put on lipstick that matched perfectly the supple fall of silk velvet that she wore. Her lightless black hair was pulled back into a severe bun on her neck; she had worn it so since the war, and in a world gone bulbous with Jackie Kennedy bouffants and beehives, she looked sinuous and Art Deco–ish, an elegant thirties blacksnake in a flock of peeping golden biddies. The look suited her; it always had. Creamy freshwater pearl buttons gleamed at her fleshy little ears, but other than those and her wedding rings, she wore no jewelry.

"This is a terrible time, darling," she said. "Worse than terrible. Tragic. I've been so frightened and worried I thought I would die; and there's been no one close to me to comfort me. Only that eternal Willa, hovering and whispering. But now that you're home, everything will be all right. I can lean on my strong, brave boy. Oh, I thought the time would never pass until you got here, Sheppie!"

"I went by the hospital before I came," I said, "and Hub tells me he's almost positive Dad will pull through. I guess Aunt Willa called you. Ben and Dorothy Cameron are there with her, and Lucy and Jack, and Sarah. You mustn't worry too much, Mother. He seems to have rallied pretty well."

I saw no reason to tell her what Hub Dorsey had said about my father's ultimate chances, and his prospects of having any sort of life. I knew I would never speak of his appearance.

"I should be there with him, but I just wanted you so badly that I couldn't seem to leave the house until you got here," she said in a frail, tired little voice. "I've kept in touch constantly, though; Hub and Willa have called every half hour, and now that you're here and Dad's on the mend, I'm going to spend every waking hour at his side. I'll go first thing in the morning, and stay all day. But now I want you to sit down here with me and get your breath and tell me your news, and have a real visit. Just like the Christmases when you were a little boy. Remember when you thought the living room was Rich's, because the tree was so big? You were scared to come into the room. I think you were three then, but maybe it was four or five, and so adorable in your little pajamas with the feet . . ."

The used, hurt little voice had gained strength and intensity as she spoke, until, incredibly, it was a freshet of glittering, girlish chatter, and I looked at her in simple disbelief. Could she have been drinking? Or was she slipping back into the hysteria Hub had described?

"I don't have any news that won't keep," I said, thinking of the looming haven of Haddonfield. It would be suicidal to speak of it now. "What I'd really like to do is have a bite to eat and a shower and go to bed. I haven't eaten since noon. And you ought to get some sleep, too; you're wound up like a clock. Did Hub leave you something to help you sleep?"

"Oh, my poor baby," she cried, pressing her white hands to her mouth as though she had been given appalling news. "Of course you must have something to eat! We'll have Shem bring us sandwiches and drinks here in front of the fire, wouldn't that be festive and Christmasy? Oh, do forgive your selfish old mother; I should have known you'd be hungry! Maybe we'll open some of the Christmas champagne and have a real little party—"

"Mother," I said, holding up one hand, "no champagne, really. A sandwich and a glass of milk or a cup of coffee will be fine. Let's just go raid the kitchen, okay? I don't want to keep

Shem and Martha up when they must have gotten as little sleep as anybody else."

She looked puzzled for a moment, as if she could not think why Shem and Martha Cater would be missing sleep, and then smiled ruefully.

"My thoughtful boy," she said. "Of course. They've been almost as worried about poor Dad as I have. Come on into the kitchen, then, and I'll make you a sandwich with my own hands. It will be a pleasure to cook for my boy again."

Since I could not remember that she ever had, I said nothing. We went out of the dim living room, she preceding me, her slender body fairly dancing along on narrow feet in high-heeled gold pumps. I saw the gleam of sheer stocking on her instep, and also that she had fastened the knot of hair at her nape with a circlet of glittering stones—rhinestones? diamonds? She might have been walking into a charity ball at the Driving Club. She moved as if to music.

The kitchen was warm and bright-lit, and there was a plate of turkey and ham sandwiches on a cloth-covered tray, and fresh coffee in the electric pot. Shem and Martha had apparently gone back to their rooms over the garage. The kitchen radio was tuned to WSB, and the score from *Camelot* swam into the room, that ersatz anthem for an entire generation: "Don't let it be forgot, that once there was a spot . . . for one brief, shining moment that was known as Camelot . . ."

My mother perched herself on a kitchen stool and crossed her elegant legs, and sipped the coffee I poured out for her. I wolfed sandwiches until a restoring satiety bloomed in my stomach, and poured coffee for myself. It was hot and heartening. We might have been an illustration in one of my mother's glossy women's magazines, by Norman Rockwell or even worse, Jon Whitcomb: mother and son, smiling over a late-night snack in a warm, bright kitchen in Anywhere, U.S.A., in that most benedictory of times, the opening years of the 1960s. Pain and stenches, death and tubes, frozen snarls on silent lips and deadly flowers blooming in ruined brains—these did not, in our four-color, dot-matrix world, exist. My mother had not just this evening risen from a sleep of drugs and anguish; my father did not lie, wired and spasmed, in a hospital two miles away; Sarah Cameron did not wear the gold ring of Charlie Gentry on her slim finger; my heart was not wizened and gray because of it. I put down my coffee cup and grinned fatuously at my mother, once again aware that I had nothing at all to say to her, no words of wisdom or comfort, none of fealty. I wanted nothing so much as the old, peaceful oblivion of my darkened bedroom out in the summerhouse. I could not think how to get there without getting up from the kitchen and bolting out into the cold night, and my mother's bright, waiting smile said plainly that there was more expected of this night, and of me. The dolorous medieval lady of the sorrows had fled midway in her little speech about Christmas when I was a child, and had not returned. This woman was a creature of wiles and pleasures, waiting and wanting only to ply them for her son.

"Well," I said, finally. "That really hit the spot. Would you like to go back in by the fire?"

"Oh no, it's really too stiff and formal in there, isn't it?" she said. "Let's sit here for a little while and talk, and then I have a surprise for you upstairs. Tell me, how was Sarah? Was she glad to see you? Is she pregnant yet?"

It was such a completely unexpected turn of conversation that I actually choked on my coffee, and spit a little onto the table in front of me. She laughed, a silvery little giggle.

"You've still got a tiny little bit of a crush on her, haven't you, Sheppie?" she said, almost gaily. "I thought you did. Well, it doesn't matter. There are a million pretty girls in Atlanta, and we're going to see that you get reacquainted with every one of them, now that you're home. There are some of the cutest new girls in town you ever saw, too; I see them all the time at League meetings and at lunch. Career girls, lots of them. Pretty *and* smart. You don't need Sarah. You'll cut such a swath you just won't believe it. You're really a handsome boy, Sheppie, I always thought you were, no matter what Daddy said, and now that you're all grown up—"

"Mother," I said in a kind of disbelieving desperation, "we probably need to talk some about Dad. We'll wait until you've seen him tomorrow and had a chance to talk to Hub before we settle anything, but I think you ought to be aware that things aren't . . . very good with him. . . ."

"Well, of course, I know that," she said. Her face did not change. "He's had a bad stroke. How could things be good with him? But Willa and you both said he wasn't going to die. . . ."

"Not die, maybe, but there's a very good chance he won't ever be himself again, and he might not . . . might not . . . be able to take care of himself, or maybe even move. . . . I just don't want you to think that everything is going to be like it was," I said. "I don't want you to think that and be hurt when it isn't. Mother, he could live for years without ever moving again. We really are going to have to make some plans. . . ."

She gave me a smile of such brilliance that it was nearly feral, and I felt the skin on my neck and the backs of my hands crawl.

"I have already made what plans need to be made," she said. She might have been discussing a speech school luncheon. "I did that yesterday and today while everybody was at the hospital. Of course nothing is going to be the same. I know it's likely he'll be paralyzed. At least he won't be dead—that's something. I'll have a husband; you'll have a father. There'll still be a man in the house. Two, now that you're home."

"Mother," I said, "you can't mean that you're going to bring him home! Do you know what it means to be totally paralyzed, to have somebody in the house who's totally paralyzed? Who would look after him? You'd never in the world manage, not even with Shem and Martha and Aunt Willa. When I said make some plans, I meant find a good nursing home, get him into it when he leaves the hospital, find somebody to look after the business—"

Her red-tipped hand dismissed me.

"Oh, pooh on the business. Tom Carmichael can run the silly business until you learn your way around it. He can tell you all you need to know about it, and you can turn your father's library into your own office, or go downtown a few times a week, if you want to—it's all he ever did. And of course I'm going to bring him home. I'm moving him into Willa's room, and making a sitting room out of Little Lady's bedroom, and turning the little dressing room into a nurse's bedroom, and we'll have them around the clock, and later I'll hire him a live-in companion-nurse. And I'll help look after him myself. Who else did you think would do it? He's my husband. In my family, we look after our own. . . ."

This time I simply looked at her. Her face seemed to shine with plans and busyness and a kind of crazy saintliness, and with something else too. Power played there like heat lightning. Of course she would keep him near her, of course she would tend him herself. She would have it all, then: the power of this house, power over him; she would have both the power and the man at her fingertips. And she would have the added luster of this new saintliness: Olivia Bondurant, caring for the helpless husband, sitting patiently by the bedside, laying cool hands on the silent, raging face. The mantle of small-town selflessness, long laid aside in little Griffin when she left it to marry and come with my father to this worldly city, slipped as easily onto her shoulders as if it had been tailored for her.

"Where will Aunt Willa sleep?" It was all I could think to say.

"Willa is going out to the summerhouse, and if you don't think she's furious about that, you can think again," my mother said in obvious satisfaction. "But what can she say? She can't dictate where she'll sleep in her sister-in-law's house; she's been lucky all these years even to have a roof over her head. And Little Lady

and Carter surely haven't knocked the doors down setting her
up over there. No, the summerhouse is perfectly fine for her, and
that way she won't be underfoot upstairs with a sick man in the
house. Though I know she'd love to nurse him herself, thinking
she could get him to leave her a little something in his will. Willa!
Lord! She's lucky I don't put her out in the street altogether!"

My throat and tongue dried to dust, and my heart knocked
sickly. The summerhouse—my cool, beautiful haven; the one
place where Lucy and I had hidden from the world and felt, at
last, perfectly safe. It made me literally sick to think of Aunt
Willa in it, her chic, insinuating head buyer's clothes, her carefully chosen little bric-a-brac, as like the ones in the Peachtree
Road house as she could find, the clinging female scent of her. . . .
I swallowed hard, and felt salt bile flooding the back of my
throat. Even if I was not going to be here, was not, for all practical purposes, ever coming home again, I could not bear the
thought of Willa Slagle Bondurant in the summerhouse.

"When . . . when is she moving out there?" I said around my
thickened tongue. The thought hit me, sudden and terrible, that
perhaps she had already moved, and that I would have to spend
these necessary Christmas nights in the cold, cheerless guest
room, or even worse, in Aunt Willa's cast-off lair. I was ready
to run howling into the night and take hold of her alien possessions with my bare hands and fling them out of the summerhouse
into the cold, dead garden.

"She's moving as soon as I can get that dreadful little fairy
from Rich's in here to redo her room for Daddy, and to make
a few other changes," my mother said. "He's already brought
some sketches and fabric over; he did that the same day I called.
Let's see. Was it day before yesterday? I guess it was. It seems
like a million years ago. Oh yes, he was dancing on the doorstep
not four hours after I called the decorating service. The name
Bondurant still means something at Rich's, even with all the
tackpots in town."

She smiled in obvious satisfaction at the thought of the poor
Rich's decorator, rushing through the festive debris of Christmas
to her doorstep clutching his swatches and samples and sketches,
and I thought, "She means the same afternoon Dad had his
stroke. He was in the hospital and they didn't know whether he
was going to live or die, and she was shut up in her room with
everybody thinking she was hysterical and prostrate, and what
she was doing was planning to redecorate the house. She's refea-
thering the nest and he's not even out of it yet." I could not
speak.

"And now," she caroled, "the big surprise. The best part of
my plan. Come on, Sheppie. It's for you. And it's upstairs."

I got up and followed her out of the kitchen. The two grinding, interminable days on the road in the U-Haul and the meeting at the hospital and the sheer awfulness of my twisted and intubated father and the cold weight of Sarah in my heart washed over me like a great, freezing surf, and I stumbled silently along behind my mother up the beautiful freestanding staircase simply because I was too tired to do anything else.

She paused at the door to her and my father's bedroom, at the left end of the upstairs corridor, and looked back over her shoulder at me, and the smile she gave me was tight-stretched and glittering, like everything else about her on this strangest of nights.

"Are you ready?" she said. Her voice had a child's lilt.

"I guess so," I said numbly. I could not think of anything in the world I was less ready for on this night than a Christmas surprise. Sleep was what I wanted, sleep and sleep only.

"Voilà!" cried my mother, and flung open the door.

I had not been in this room a dozen times since I left the hateful little cubbyhole off it, where I had slept my captive voyeur's sleep from infancy to the coming of Lucy. I frankly hated it, even though it was by far the best bedroom in the house. It seemed to me that the very walls had captured and held the force of my infant rage and fear and disgust. I avoided it even when expressly invited by my mother to enter, which had been seldom. My father had never bade me in. I stood behind my mother in the doorway, as reluctant to enter as if the room were a cobra farm.

It was an enormous room occupying most of the top left wing and running the depth of the house, with great floor-to-ceiling Palladian windows facing Peachtree Road and the back garden and the summerhouse. I remembered that when you looked out the back windows in summer, you could see the deep forests of Buckhead rolling away toward the river, with small, weblike tributaries of streets, and islands that were the rooftops of other great houses thrusting up out of the rolling green. It was like being on the bridge of a great ship, and was the one thing about the room that I had always loved. There was a vast, shining sea of polished oak floor, scattered with thin, glowing old Orientals in the soft pastel tints of Kirman and Bokhara, and in front of the rose marble fireplace, set into another Palladian-arched niche in the ivory paneled walls, two pale rose brocade sofas faced each other across a pretty tea table.

My mother's little French writing desk sat before the windows looking onto Peachtree Road, and two great mahogany armoires flanked the fireplace. On the wall across from it, floating in luminous ivory space, sat the bed she had shared all the years of her marriage with my father, a chaste, spare Hepplewhite tester with a starched lace canopy and a coverlet of faded, rose-strewn satin. The roses, I remembered her telling Aunt Willa when she first came to the house, had been embroidered by her maternal grandmother for her hope chest. The coverlet was always carefully folded back at night upon the blanket chest that sat at the foot of the bed; I knew that it concealed a dual-control electric blanket. My father might share in silence that white battlefield, but he would do it in comfort. Everything in the room had always been rich, elegant, serene, orderly, conventional. Like, in all respects, my mother.

Off the bedroom proper were, back to back, a glassed sleeping porch, also facing the garden, where my father sometimes read or napped on a sagging daybed, and the villainous little dressing room that had been my earliest Coventry. The doors giving onto them from the bedroom were shut now, and the big room was dim-lit. At first, my tired eyes could not accommodate the dimness.

"Well?" my mother chirped. "What do you think?"

Leaning around her, I nearly gasped aloud. I reached automatically for the doorjamb to steady myself. I was looking into the sanctum of a mad white hunter.

The entire room shimmered and swam, now, in a kind of demented pentimento. Underneath, the skin and bones, the wood and silks and velvets and plaster of the room as it had always been, shone in gracious harmony. But the overpainting, the surface—it was as if Ernest Hemingway at his bloated, monomaniacal worst had battled to the death with Aubrey Beardsley, each determined to leave his imprint on the room. The bed, the chairs, the sofas and tables and chaise, even the floors and the tall windows were draped with samples of fabric, piled with pillows and paint samples and primitive bibelots, feverish with great, virulent, billowing and trailing green plants. The bed had been shrouded in a coarse, gauzy material resembling cheesecloth, and over its delicate coverlet lay a throw fashioned from the hide of some animal that had never set hoof to American soil. The old Orientals were covered with zebra hides, and in front of the fireplace a leopard-skin rug with the snarling head still attached had been laid down. Bedside and end tables had been pushed to the corners of the room, and great standing oblong drums replaced them. On the ivory walls, spears and javelins were crossed and grouped artfully, and over the twin sofas the heads of more great, snarling beasts howled their choler into the dimness. There was a stifling, jumbled impression of bamboo, vines and earth-toned batik. In the corner by the sun porch door, a brilliant macaw sat on a perch in a tall standing cage.

When I still said nothing, my mother took my arm and drew

me into the room and over to one of the sofas, where she more or less pushed me down, to sit on a stiff fur pillow. Even as my head whirled and my eyes spun wildly around the room, my fingertips registered the fact that the fur was not real. I looked from my mother's white, magenta-cheeked face, its crimson lips smiling, smiling, to the leopard's head at my feet, and saw that it was not real, either. Neither, on closer examination, were the heads on the wall over the sofas. I was grateful for that. I did not know about the fur throw and the plants and the macaw. The javelin and spears looked real enough to gut you if you put them to the test. In the middle of all of it, my smiling, thrumming mother looked as crazily, plastically beautiful as a comic-strip drawing of Sheena, Queen of the Jungle.

"Say something," she ordered me, standing hipshot in her blood-red velvet, a jungle priestess about to order me staked out for the soldier ants.

"Holy shit," I breathed, entirely spontaneously. "Are you going to bring Dad home and put him in the middle of all this?"

"Don't be silly," she said impatiently, flinging herself down on the sofa opposite me and taking a cigarette from a painted clay bowl I had never seen before. I felt simple gratitude that it was not a skull. "This is for you."

"Me?" It must have been an outright squeal, because she laughed and reached over and patted my knee, leaving her hand there.

"You. You're the man of this house now, and you need a man's room. Time to get you out of that silly summerhouse and up here, in the big house and the big bedroom, where you belong. The little man from Rich's—Ronnie, and he *is* good, darling, even if he's terribly light on the rug—says that the safari look is just everywhere nowadays, what with the good new fur synthetics and all the inexpensive brass and copper imports, and everything. He says practically every important house in the East has at least one safari room. All this is just for effect, of course; these are samples for you to pick from, and you can . . . tone it down a little, if you like. Or you can even go a totally different way. The nautical look is good, too, he thinks, because of Jack Kennedy, you know, but we thought this was best for the scale of the room, and I knew you'd always liked adventure stories, and animals, and that book about the jungle that Kipling wrote. I told him about that—he wanted to know what you were like, of course, and when he heard it, he said this would be just the thing. It's not my cup of tea, of course, but I have to admit it's really very clever. Look, the drapery on the bed is supposed to simulate mosquito netting, and the drums are quite authentic, though I forget where he said they came from. I will say that the parrot may be a bit much. . . ."

She ran down then, and cocked her head to one side, and peered into my face. Her smile, as she waited for my reaction, was the full, creamy half-moon of a woman very sure that she has done a good thing.

"Do you like your Christmas present, darling?" she said.

"Mother," I said, and my voice cracked in my throat like an adolescent's. "Where are you going to sleep?"

"Oh, sweetie, don't worry about me," she said merrily. "I'll be in with Daddy a lot of the time. And I thought I'd just have a little nest made in the sleeping porch there, just a bed and a built-in closet and my dressing table. I don't need much room. Ronnie says we can easily cut a separate entrance in from the hall, so I don't have to go through your room to get to it. You can keep the little dressing room for your things. Isn't it all fun, Sheppie?"

I looked at her, there in her red and her power, in this terrible room where the frustrated little decorator from Rich's had exorcised all his angry, skewed eroticism. Who was she? Medea, Gertrude, Jocasta? I did not know her. Whoever she was, she would, if I moved into this room, truly have it all: money, power, the fallen husband down the hall, the son in her bedroom again. I felt physical nausea, and swallowed hard against it. I rose from the couch on rubbery legs and walked toward the door. Behind me I heard the swish of her legs in their sheer nylon as she jumped up from the other sofa, and the soft pattering of her heels as she followed me.

"Sheppie," she said. "Sheppie . . ."

I turned. She was standing by the bed.

"I don't care who you put in this room," I said. "You can put H. Rider Haggard and Frank Buck and Mr. Ronnie from Rich's in here all at once, if you want to. I wouldn't sleep one night in it if it was the last room in the continental United States. Not like this, and not in a goddamned nautical decor, for Christ's sake, and not—I repeat *not*—with you in the little room right under my elbow. Not any way at all. Mother, I'm not going to stay in Atlanta, get used to that idea now; I only came home to see about Dad and get things squared away for you—"

"NOO-O-O-O-O!" It was a long, terrible wail; I thought of wakes and deaths and banshees. She sagged down onto the bed, and sat there, half-sunk in fur, her hands clenched in her lap, her little feet in gold shoes neatly together, her mouth squared off in a child's rictus of grief and outrage.

"You can't leave me!" she howled. Tears spurted from her closed eyes and tracked mascara down her white face. "You can't leave me now! Not after him, not after that—I won't have anything, if you leave me! I won't have anything, then. . . ."

I looked at her in silence. On the huge bed she looked very small, no larger than a child, a prim, good and very simple child, bewildered and foundering in a grief she could not comprehend. And I knew that at this moment she was not Jocasta, but only little Olivia Redwine from Griffin, Georgia, invalidated in her soul, like her foremothers and sisters and heirs, without a man. Even with everything around her—the money, the position in the city, the great house and its furnishings, the clothes and cars and clubs and charities and balls and luncheons—even with all this, she was nothing without a man of her own, be he husband or son, paralyzed, emasculated, dead. Everything in her life told her this. She believed it in her shrinking soul. And I knew she was right. I thought of Lucy, and of Little Lady, sold into marriage with Carter Rawson, and of my flayed and driven Aunt Willa, and of the fingernails of Sarah Cameron, innocent now of paint. I suddenly hated the South, hated it fully and redly, this beautiful land of woman-killers, this country of soul-breakers. I would not stay here. I would not.

But I would not press that matter until after Christmas. I could not do that to the sobbing child-woman in the terrible fur bed. Let her think that I would stay; if need be, I would sneak away in a near-distant cold red dawn, as I had thought I might. I had, by now, no compunctions at all about that, or about lying to my mother.

I went to her and sat down beside her, and put my arms around her.

"Hush," I said. "Hush, now. I didn't mean it. If you really need me, of course I'll stay. I just . . . it's just that I can't stay here in this room. This is your room. This is Dad's room. The summerhouse is my place; I love it out there. I always have. If you want me to stay, you're going to have to let me have my way about that."

She gave in without a whimper. I think that the threatened loss of me wiped out any disappointment she might have felt at my reception of Mr. Ronnie's handiwork. The ghastly bedroom was not mentioned again; I do not know when, in the span of days that followed, Mr. Ronnie of Rich's and his minions came and took away the unwanted artifacts of the heart of darkness. I held my mother until she stopped her sobbing and nodded in my arms, and I pressed her back gently on the fur pillows and drew Mr. Ronnie's impossible fur throw up over her, and turned off the lamps, and escaped through the icy-breathed night to the summerhouse. The day seemed, by now, forty-eight hours old.

I was just slipping into sleep myself when I turned over and saw, on the bedside table, a copy of Lucy's book. I had one in New York, but I had not read it; had meant to start it in the new year at Haddonfield. She had not pressed me for comment. Indeed, oddly, she had scarcely mentioned her novel the entire time I had been home for its publication, and had not talked of it since, either in her letters or her phone calls to me. These latter had been full of Jack and the movement and the day-to-day routine at Damascus House, of her adventures in the bus and the government agencies and the soup kitchen and, less frequently, at La Carrousel; but of this book and any others she might one day write, Lucy said nothing. I wondered who had put it here, beside the bed. Not, I was sure, my mother. I reached out and picked up the little volume. It was the story of a small white girl raised by a black family in New Orleans during the Depression, I knew, and its title was *Darkness and Old Trees*. I smiled. Lucy had always loved Frost.

I propped myself up on one elbow, shivering in the cold, switched on the bedside lamp and opened the book. On the dedication page, I read, "To my father, James Clay Bondurant. We be of one blood, thou and I." And on the title page, in Lucy's slanting backhand, "Dear, darling Gibby: Mark my Trail!"

I laid the book back down on the table and turned the light off again, and rolled over, and scrubbed my face into the crook of my arm, and wept—for the diminished and doomed woman in the mountebank's bed in the big house, and for the unwritten and unmourned books of Lucy Venable, and for the clean fingernails of Sarah Cameron Gentry.

CHAPTER
EIGHTEEN

IN BUCKHEAD, when a titan falls, the rest of his kind draw close around, to shield the fallen one from predatory, alien eyes and claws and to succor the stricken family. Or at least that was so in the Buckhead of my father's time. Nowadays a felled member of the Old Guard would probably be lucky if three people of public consequence know his name. Today's power brokers are several generations newer and often many shades darker than those of that whirlwind decade, and they tend to meet, lunch and network at places like Morton's, Mary Mac's and the Peasant Restaurant chain. Old Atlanta still does not lunch at these spots. Hardly anyone cares that they do not, except, perhaps, a few of them.

And so it was that beginning the next morning, on Christmas Eve, the house on Peachtree Road was filled with the familiar faces and voices that had been the foundation of my entire childhood. From about eleven o'clock on they came, the men and women who had been my parents' contemporaries and the fathers and mothers of the Pinks and the Jells, and, in smaller numbers, the Pinks and the Jells themselves.

All morning and afternoon Shem Cater answered the door and took hats and topcoats and parked and brought around cars, smiling decorously and wearing a white jacket I had never seen, and Martha, in the kitchen, kept coffee and cookies and little sandwiches and cheese straws coming, and at about four that afternoon, set out the sherry and bourbon and gin decanters on the tea cart in the living room. I don't know where the food came from, or when they prepared it; I could only think that the black people of Buckhead had as keen a sense of ritual and propriety in these cases as did the white, and probably keener. I know it had not once occurred to me to see to the basting of hams and the stocking of the liquor cabinet, and I did not think that my mother, embroiled as she had been with Ronnie of Rich's in transforming her bedroom into an African veldt, had done so. My father's wake—for I thought of it as such, even though he clung on and on to his blipping and blasted life in Piedmont Hospital—was entirely, and most properly, the province of Shem and Martha Cater.

My mother spent the day at the hospital, so I hovered uncomfortably in the living room in a coat and tie and received the stream of visitors. Across Peachtree Road in Garden Hills, they would have come bearing cakes and casseroles; on this side, they brought armfuls of forced blooms from greenhouses or great, showy, foil-ruffed poinsettias, and cards to be laid on the silver tray in the hall rotunda. From somewhere a chaste leather book for addresses had been produced, and sat on the table next to the card tray, and everyone signed their name as matter-of-factly as if it had been a funeral at Patterson's. I suppose the Buckhead equivalent of the jungle drums had done their work, and all his contemporaries knew that when Sheppard Bondurant had collapsed on the golf course at Brookhaven, he had entered his own covenant with death, even if the fact of it had not yet occurred. Hub Dorsey was one of them. His prognosis would be known. It was, indeed, a death they came to mark.

I kissed the cold, sweet-smelling cheeks of the women, and shook the gray-gloved hands of the men, and looked at all of them with eyes sensitized by fatigue and circumstance. The women seemed to me much the same, pretty and warm and elegant in their furs, smiling and moving easily in this house that they knew, as they did all the other great houses of Buckhead, nearly as well as their own. None of them called me Sheppie, but the nickname was implicit in their hugs and soft "Sweetie, I *am* so sorry"'s. There was not one of them who had not known me from infancy.

But the men were different. I could see and feel it vividly, I suppose because I had not seen many of them in literally years, and my eyes were fresh. These twenty or thirty men, the young fathers I remembered from Little League and high school football games and country club locker rooms and backyard swimming pools and gardens and verandas; these indulgent and paternal men who smiled knowingly when their wives fussed over their sons' late hours and slipping grades and general hellraising—they had come into their power, and banded together, and were poised to make their move, and something looked out of their eyes that I had never seen. They were the Club now, and they knew it, and soon the city and the Southeast would know it, and the young princelings who were their sons finally knew it, and knew, consequently, where their own power would one day lie.

All this I could sense as clearly as an animal senses the nearness of water in a dry month, though I could not have articulated it. I could read it in their faces and bearings, and in the manner of their sons, my friends, the Buckhead Boys. I felt as alien from it all, as conspicuously alone and profoundly different, as if I were another species entirely. Something altogether new and heady seemed to crackle in the firelit room, and seep outside into the cold air of the dying year, to reach out and pervade all Atlanta. Ben Cameron, coming in at midafternoon with young Ben behind him, was the newly elected mayor of the city and would take office in the new year, and underneath the grace and courtliness and seeming indolence which had always been his hallmark, I seemed to see and hear and taste the force that would resculpt the city's skyline and rewrite its future. He was, in that room, fulcrum and focus and funnel of the concentrated power of a generation. When he took my hand I half expected to see sparks fly between our flesh, and feel the bite of him.

Ben did not stay long. He greeted the small crowd in the living room, exchanged Merry Christmases, ducked into the kitchen to speak to Shem and Martha, as he always did, clapped me perfunctorily on the shoulder again and said, "Anything we can do, Shep, of course. Don't be a stranger."

I knew that he meant the former. I was not sure about the latter. Ben and I had not spoken at any length since that night the previous June at the Plaza, just before Sarah came home from Paris. I knew that he was furious at me, but he had not betrayed that anger to me in the few brief meetings we had had since, and I wondered if it had abated. On the whole, I thought perhaps it had. Dorothy was as warm as she had ever been, though she did not discuss Sarah and Charlie, and Sarah herself seemed settled into her role as young Buckhead wife and volunteer worker. With his election and the revolutionary plans he and his set had for the city, I thought that Ben Cameron surely had more on his mind than the bumblings of Shep Bondurant. All the same, I caught his eyes on me several times during his visit, and they were as measuring and speculative as if I were a newcomer to the group. I felt obscurely uncomfortable under that sharp gray gaze, like a child or a dog who knows something is expected of it, but not what.

"Come by the house when you have a leg up on things," he said as he shrugged into his camel hair coat and took his felt hat from Shem. "We need to have a real talk."

"I'll do that," I said, knowing that I probably would not. I could not imagine what we might have, now, to talk about, except Sarah, and I did not think either of us wanted to venture into that closed country. I would go and see Dorothy Cameron, but I would do it during a morning or afternoon when Ben was at work. The week after Christmas, before I left for Haddonfield, would be fine for that. Somehow it was important to me that Dorothy know why I was not staying in Atlanta.

Young Ben lingered behind his father, and stayed in the living room drinking bourbon by the fire until the last visitors had gone home to their Christmas Eve dinners. When I came into the room after seeing the last caller off, he was standing at the drinks tray mixing another, and he lifted it in salute and dipped his narrow head, the dark red hair, cut longer than was in fashion, slipping down over his gray eyes. He retreated to one of the apricot sofas and sank into it and stretched his long legs out before him, crossed at the ankles. He wore a pale blue cashmere sweater over an open-necked white oxford cloth shirt, and gray slacks precisely tailored to his long legs and slender hips, and his narrow dancer's feet were shod in rich, buffed loafers. Except for the web of thin lines around his eyes and the incipient crepiness on the backs of his hands and his neck, he literally did not look a day older than he had in high school. I knew he had accomplished much, however; he was becoming known for the soaring, gull-winged single-family houses he was building in the wild hills and river bluffs of the city's northwest suburbs, and was, my mother had told me, the chic young architect of the moment among the new money that was pouring into town.

Ben loved residential architecture, and had so far held out for that, but Snake Cheatham's father was so taken with his design sense that he had talked Ben into designing one of his suburban branch banks, and the beautiful, winged stone and glass structure caused so much comment that Ben was at work now on preliminary designs for two more. The first had been featured in *Architectural Digest,* and the calls were beginning to come in now from around the country. He was, my mother said, thinking of leaving the firm and going out on his own, but would make no decision about that until Julia had her baby. Even with his obvious prospects and Ben Senior's money behind him, Julia was, Mother reported, extremely nervous about Ben's leaving an established firm to fly solo.

"I understand from Dorothy that they had a real row about it," Mother had said, with some relish. I suppose that since her own son had little of note that she might boast of, it pleased her when the crown prince of the house of Cameron came a modest cropper in his marriage.

Ben and I sat in companionable silence for a little while, the dying fire snickering behind its screen, the tree beginning to glow in the unlit room. He finished his bourbon and put the glass down on the table beside the sofa.

"I have to get on home," he said. "Julia's folks are expecting us for supper. Her stepmother makes oyster stew every Christmas Eve, out of library paste and sheep's milk, I think. It's a tradition." But he made no move to get up.

Then he said, "You're not going to stay, are you?" and I was so taken by surprise that I said, simply, "No. I'm not."

"Good boy," he said, and I looked at him more closely. It seemed to me then that he burned with the same kind of fever-shimmer I had seen on the day of his wedding, and that his gray eyes were so bright with it that if I had not been so close to him I would have mistaken their glitter for tears. But he was not crying.

"How did you know?" I asked. I had not spoken of leaving Atlanta to Dorothy, or to anyone else for that matter.

"Because you're like me now," he said, closing his eyes and resting his head against the dull sheen of the brocade. His coppery hair against the apricot, the firelight leaping on both, was beautiful. "You're different. You walk on the outside. You wear the mark of Cain. There's nothing for you here."

"What mark of Cain?" I said, puzzled. Why did he speak of being an outsider, of being different? I could think of few human beings more fitted for the life of Buckhead than Ben Cameron, Junior.

"I don't know. It sounded good." He grinned, his eyes still closed. "But I'm right, aren't I? Whatever there is for you is out there, isn't it?"

He did not speak of Sarah, never had, but I knew what he meant.

"Yes," I said. "I'm leaving the first of the year. But please don't say anything about it. I'm going to have to climb out the window in the dead of night as it is. God, my mother . . ."

"I know," he said. "They wrap you around and suck your life and pull you right down to the bottom, don't they?" Aside from the bitterness of the words, there was something old and dead in his voice that made me sit slightly forward at the same time I shrank back. I hated the sound of it. What was happening here?

"Go soon, Shep. And go fast and far," he said, the gray eyes still shuttered with thick, coppery lashes. "Zigzag while you run and don't look back. Bomb the bridge behind you."

"Ben . . . " I began, and he grinned and heaved himself upright and rubbed his long, slender fingers through his hair.

"Sorry," he said. "I'm just feeling elegiac tonight. I don't like

Christmas, and it makes me nervous to see my friends' fathers start to die, and the baby's late and everybody's jumpy as hell. Christ, I think one minute I can't stand it until that kid gets here, and then I think I'd just as soon it never did. I don't mean that, of course, but a baby . . . it's so final, Shep. Nothing is ever the same after a baby comes. The . . . possibilities shrink so."

"I guess it comes with the territory," I said lamely. I could not imagine how it would feel to be going home on a Christmas Eve to a wife and a soon-to-be-born, life-changing child.

"That it does," he said. He laughed. "That it does. Well. This time I'm really out the door. Julia will be fit to be tied. She can't get out of her chair and into her clothes without help now, and it makes her mean as hell. I'll have to get home and dress her."

"How is Julia?" I said automatically. I thought of the small, wiry athlete's body, and the adoring brown eyes and snub nose and tiny monkey hands of Julia Randolph Cameron. I could not imagine her foundering in a chair, unable to dress herself.

"As big as a beached whale and twice as unaesthetic," he said, and he was not smiling. "Whoever said that pregnant women are glowing and beautiful sure as hell didn't know Julia."

It was such a meanspirited thing to say that I could not reply. I did not even know the voice in which he spoke. In the firelight the planes of his face were sharpened into near-caricature, a jack-o'-lantern's face. I thought suddenly of his grandmother, old Milliment, and what a terrible tongue she had had. There must be a dominant gene there somewhere. There was nothing in Ben now of his father or his gentle mother, or of Sarah.

At the front door he paused, and suddenly put his arms around me and hugged me hard, and then was gone out into the dusk. Last night's icy mist was coming down again, and the streetlights beyond the iron fence along Peachtree Road wore opalescent collars. Headlights wore aureoles, and tire tracks left a snail's nacre on the black asphalt.

"Merry Christmas, Shep," his voice floated back. "God-speed!" I did not hear a car door slam, and thought he must have left his car around the corner and down Muscogee, at his parents' house. I wondered if Sarah and Charlie would be there tonight, for the Welsh rarebit that was Dorothy Cameron's Christmas Eve tradition.

My mother was still at the hospital, and Shem and Martha had said good night and left. They were going to visit ToTo and her husband, Shem had told me earlier in the day; ToTo had married a line mechanic at the Ford plant out in Hapeville, and lived in Forest Park, and had two little girls. I thought of calling Lucy, then realized that I did not know her number in Lithonia, and in any case, she would be having her first family Christmas

Eve with Jack and the boys in the old farmhouse. Even Aunt
Willa was absent; she had, I knew, gone to Little Lady and Carter's new brick Georgian in Wyngate, and would be spending
Christmas Day with them at Carter's parents' great stone pile
on Dellwood. The house around me was dark, and I was very
much alone.

I went out into the kitchen and fixed a plate of leftover party
sandwiches and poured myself a cup of coffee, and retreated into
the little sun porch off the living room and put an old Charlie
Parker album on the phonograph. I settled, self-consciously, into
the big, rump-sprung chair that was my father's, found it surprisingly comfortable, leaned my head back and let the Bird's liquid
silver skitter over and around me like mercury spilled from a
thermometer. I was drifting far away, sitting with Sarah at the
Vanguard, when I heard a voice say, "Shep? You asleep?" and
looked up. Charlie Gentry stood in the doorway to the living
room, his topcoat pearled with droplets, his wood-colored hair
plastered to his square skull. The old smile of extraordinary,
heartbreaking sweetness curved his mouth.

"I knocked and hollered, and I could hear the music, so I
came on in," he said. "The door was unlocked. I figured you
were here; nobody else listens to the Bird."

"Charlie!" I cried out, sleep washing away constraint so that
only the old joy at seeing him prevailed. "God, I'm glad to see
you! Come on in. I was sitting here feeling like Little Nell."

"I thought you probably were. I was just by the hospital and
saw your mother, and she said you were here by yourself. I'm
on my way over to the . . . to Dorothy and Ben's, but I wanted
to check in here first. Sarah's still at the children's party at the
speech school."

I stood before him, stiffly and awkwardly, love and anger and
hurt and the sheer span of years thick in the air between us, and
then, as if some common restraint had broken, we both laughed
and moved into each other's arms and hugged.

"I've missed you," I said, into his clean-smelling mouse's fur.
The top of his head came just under my chin. I noticed that his
hair was beginning to thin on top, like a tonsure.

"Me, too," he said. "Asshole though you are."

I poured us a couple of bourbons and threw another log on
the living room fire and we sat in the tree-lit darkness. Outside,
full night had fallen, and the mist had thickened until it only
missed becoming sleet by a hair. I thought we would probably
have ice before morning. The branches that scratched against
the windows and the ornate black iron scrolls of the fence
gleamed with more than wetness, and the great furnace in the
subterranean depths of the basement kicked on, and I heard the

carolers from Covenant Presbyterian Church, across the street, begin their traditional Christmas Eve rounds of Buckhead.

"Hark the herald angels sing, glory to the newborn king . . ."

Their voices were thin and silvery in the tender hush of the night. Traffic on Peachtree Road had thinned almost to a trickle.

"This is the first time it's seemed like Christmas," I said.

"I know. Tough Christmas for you folks," Charlie said. "Hub Dorsey says he thinks your dad will pull through, though. That's good news."

"No, it isn't, Charlie," I said. I had just gotten Charlie back. I was not going to start talking platitudes to him now.

"No, I guess it isn't, at that," he said. "As bad as it is for him, it's going to be worse for you. It's hard, trying to be the man of the house when nobody's prepared you for it."

I thought of Thad Gentry, radiantly maniacal, a permanent fixture at Brawner's now, and of the hard years when Charlie was trying to put himself through law school, and work, and take care of his mother. Now he was the man of two houses. I wondered if he found it an extra strain. I did not think so, not with Sarah in one of them.

He did not ask me if I would be staying in Atlanta; I was sure he just assumed that I would. We did not, that night, speak much of our personal futures. But Charlie did talk of his present, and with such unfeigned and humble joy that I found myself grinning broadly as he talked. Even though Sarah was the principal component of his happiness, he was so sweetly fitted into his world, so obviously and perfectly a creature of it, that it was impossible not to smile at the sheer rightness of it all, as you would at a woodland creature in total harmony with its environment. In his dark blue suit and polished oxfords he looked years older, as he had on the awful night at the Plaza, but his face, now, was smooth and pink with contentment and enthusiasm. He had put on a few pounds, and I could see that in a few years Charlie would be, instead of a small square man, a small round one. He would, I thought, be the archetypal Jaycee and Rotarian, the one the others all depended on, the one who chaired the less visible and glamorous committees, the one who stayed latest and got in soonest, the one who would forever be secretary-treasurer. I did not think this pejoratively. Charlie was an innocent and a believer, and that kind of goodness is only scorned by small, stupid men. And under the stolid decency and the burgher's happiness, the fierce, holy passion of the small boy with the new relic still burned.

"Things are going good for you," I said. It was not a question. He looked at me shyly, as though the awareness that his happiness had been bought, in large part, with my pain made him ashamed.

"To paraphrase Max Shulman, Charlie, God never told nobody to be stupid," I said, and he grinned, and I knew that it was exorcism enough.

"So good it scares me sometimes," he said. "You know, Shep, I never thought I would be any kind of star, and I never even wanted to be. Just a good lawyer and to have a family, and to be able to make Atlanta better in some small way—shit, even I can hear how holy that sounds—but it really was all I ever wanted. But now . . . I don't know, something nice is happening at Coke. I can't explain it, except that . . . well, some of the higher-ups have kind of noticed me, and are smoothing the way for me, and the word on the top floor is that they've got big things planned for me."

He looked so pleased and embarrassed at the same time that I laughed aloud.

"Wait till they find out you never got your knot-tying merit badge," I said. "Who is they? How high is up?"

"Well . . . Mr. Woodruff."

"Jesus," I said sincerely. "You really have caught a comet's tail."

It was true. Robert W. Woodruff, longtime chief executive of the Coca-Cola Company and one of the country's great philanthropists, whose several family foundations had reshaped the city: hospitals, libraries, museums, theaters, university centers, parks, schools of engineering and liberal arts, endowments, public buildings and private charities; disburser of hundreds of millions of dollars to the benefit of Atlanta; fiercely anonymous power behind literally every throne in the metropolitan area, a man whose will was, without its being known, the city's command—not an insignificant patron for a twenty-five-year-old attorney with a new degree on whose pristine whiteness the ink was barely dry.

"What did you do, catch him in the barn with the bottler's daughter? Save his setter from a runaway train?" I said.

"I don't know what I did," Charlie said. "I've been in Legal over there all along. And by no means on the top of the heap, either, and then one day Mac Draper came by and said Mr. Woodruff wondered if I'd join him and a few others in the executive dining room for lunch, and I did—we didn't even talk business, really; just about Atlanta, and how I feel about it, and what I thought—and a few days after that he calls me in and says he wonders if somewhere down the road apiece I'd consider leaving the company and coming to work for him at one of the foundations."

"Is that good?" I said. I realized that I honestly did not know, and that a true Buckhead Boy would have. The gulf between me and the city yawned even further.

"Are you kidding? It's like being pulled out of the orchestra and given the baton. Or it is to me, anyway. It's not likely to be a job with much pizzazz attached to it, but I think I could do a lot of good there in the long run. For the city, I mean. What I can't figure out is why me?"

"Why not you?" I said, feeling the old warmth his diffidence had always called out in me. "You're bound to be a good lawyer, Charlie, or you wouldn't have finished first in your class. You've got terrific prospects. Ben Cameron's son-in-law ain't chopped liver. And I don't know anybody who loves this benighted town like you do. If I had six hundred million dollars you're just the guy I'd ask to give it away for me. Besides everything else, you're the most incorruptible guy I know."

He reddened with pleasure, and actually ducked his head. I laughed again.

"So what's going on right now?" I asked.

His face lit up. "God, Shep, everything. Just everything. You're not going to believe this town in ten or fifteen years; I can't even begin to tell you what's on the drawing board. Everything's coming together for Atlanta: Ben as mayor, these men we've known all our lives behind him, money and muscle and intellect and passion—and Mr. Woodruff at the nerve center, with his lines out everywhere, like a . . . like a spider in the center of a gigantic web. Awful analogy, but he's in touch with literally everything and everybody; nobody makes a move in town without his okay. You'll never hear about it, but it's true. The best thing we've got going for us—or they've got going for them—is that there's enough money in the power structure to finance the growth. We don't have to go out of town for it. Lord God, listen to what's on tap for the next ten years or so: a major league sports stadium and teams to go in it? We can do that at home. No need to go borrowing outside. A new arts center? A rapid transit system, a new freeway system, a new airport? Let us make a few calls. We can work something out. Direct flights to the capitals of Europe, offices and consulates of every major country in the world on Peachtree Street? More new skyscrapers in the next decade than almost any other American city has ever put up in fifty, branch offices of virtually every Fortune 500 company, office parks stretching for hundreds of square miles in the five counties around us, shopping centers in every community in the same radius, apartments and housing? Give us a year or two. . . ."

He paused for breath, his face messianic.

"What about the race thing?" I said to him, as I had said to
Ben Cameron during a similar conversation not a year earlier.

His face cooled, and a troubled frown crept between his clear,
magnified brown eyes.

"Race is everything, of course," he said. "The schools have
to be desegregated next September by law, and if we can't cope
with that none of this will get off the ground. The city just won't
survive it. But Mr. Woodruff wants them kept open, and so,
somehow, they will be."

"Just like that?" I said.

"Just like that." He was not smiling.

"You think the schools' being kept open will be enough? It
seems to me that even here, in the very war room of the civil
rights movement, there's not enough integration to fill a gnat's
drawers," I said. "I don't notice any black tide creeping out
Peachtree Road."

He frowned, then.

"It's not all that bad," he said. "The buses are integrated. Negroes can play on the public golf courses. They can stay at a few
hotels and some of the restaurants, and go to the movies most
places. They just don't do those things yet."

"So when does Martin Luther King join the Capital City
Club?" I said. Charlie was not complacent, but his innocence
suddenly made me want to poke him a little. How could he live
in Atlanta, profess to love it as he did and not see that, essentially, the barriers were still in place, that no load-bearing walls
had come tumbling down?

"You're right, we need to do something about the clubs, and
I'm afraid that's going to be the toughest, though it's by far the
least important," he said. "But we'll do it eventually. We're not
stupid. The white leadership is not stupid. Ben Cameron has
been meeting unofficially with some of the black leadership at
the Commerce Club all during this sit-in business."

"And what did they have for lunch?" I said. I could not seem
to stop baiting him.

"Don't be an ass, Shep," he said. "It was after hours, and they
met in a back room. As I said, Ben isn't stupid, and neither are
the Negroes. Manhattans and London broil would blow the
whole thing out of the water. We'll work it out because we have
to work it out. Because Mr. Woodruff and a few other men like
him want very much to work it out. Atlanta has two things going
for it that most Southern cities don't: an established black community with a gracious lot of money behind it, and a politically
savvy and wealthy white power structure who are committed to
making the race thing work. You watch Ben in the next few
years. Hell, you'll see results sooner than that; Forward Atlanta

has already begun, and the six-point program goes into effect about the time he takes office. I'm prouder than hell to be part of it, no matter how small and how far behind the scenes I am. Or will be."

"And I'm prouder than hell of you," I said, and meant it. "You're a good man, Charlie. You deserve everything that's happening to you. Don't ever sell yourself short."

The ormolu clock out in the hall rotunda chimed eight, and he got up to leave. I got his coat off the chair where he'd dropped it, and helped him into it, and walked him to the door.

"Young Ben was here this afternoon," I said. "I'm not at all easy about him. Something seems to be eating at him. Have you noticed?"

He looked at me, perplexed. "No," he said. "I thought things were coming up roses for him. The jobs and recognition, and the new baby and all . . . what could be wrong? You sound like Sarah."

"What does Sarah think?" I said. I had to consciously form the sound of her name on my mouth, to consciously push it out into the air toward this small, staunch man who was now her husband.

"Just that something is wrong. She can't put her finger on it, and she has to admit that she has no real reason for thinking so. But she's mentioned it several times. I know it worries her."

"It worries me, too," I said.

"It's probably just the baby coming," he said. "It's a . . . an extraordinary time. Shep . . ." and he paused.

"Yeah?" I said.

He turned his face up to mine, and it was absolutely luminous. "I wanted you to know before anybody except Ben and Dorothy. It's really why I came by. Sarah wanted me to tell you. She's . . . we're going to have a baby. She's almost three months pregnant. It's due in June."

I felt stillness come down over me like a cast net. I thought of Sarah's thinness, and the circles under her amber eyes, and of her words at the hospital: "I look like twelve miles of bad road. . . . But it's temporary."

"Congratulations, Papa," I said, and the tears that swam in my eyes, obscuring him for a moment, were for his joy as much as for the great, vast, windy emptiness that was the middle of me.

"Thank you," he said. "I don't guess I have to tell you that next to Sarah herself, this makes me the happiest man on the face of the earth."

"No," I said. "You don't have to tell me that."

When the great white door shut behind him, there was a twin

to it, an echo, inside me, somewhere in the vicinity of my arid heart.

Somehow we got through that travesty of a Christmas Day, my mother and I. It seemed that half of Buckhead asked us to share their family dinners, but my mother demurred, reluctant, perhaps, to surrender the picturesque pathos of the brave, beautiful wife alone beside her husband's hospital bed on Christmas, and I was grateful. I don't think I could have sat making conversation in some gracious dining room or beside an ancestral fire, awash in privileged celebration, while every fiber of my being shrieked to be away and gone. My mother suggested that we go to the Driving Club for midday dinner, but I vetoed that quickly. It was too much my father's place, too fraught with the flotsam and jetsam of my childhood. I did not want to suffer the courtly sympathies of dignified old black Frost, at the door, or of Chilton, in the bar, or of any of the stewards and waitresses, most of whom had known me by name and temperament since I could toddle. I wanted, from now on out, as few tendrils reaching out from that vanished Atlanta as possible. I wanted to leave here light and free, without the burning red marks of their suckers on my flesh.

So we went to Hart's on Peachtree Road, that lovely old stone bastion of mediocre food and quintessential Buckheadness, one of the few approved places besides two or three clubs where Old Atlanta dined with regularity. When I was small it had been a private home, and its new owners had wisely left the beautiful, high-ceilinged rooms and the great, arching oaks outside nearly intact, so that you felt, sitting there, that you had entered still another dining room like those you had visited all your life in Buckhead. I think perhaps that accounted for its popularity with my parents' set. "Oh, we're not really going out," they would say to one another. "We're just running up to Hart's." And indeed, the elderly Negro staff knew most of them by name, and would ask after their health and their children, and so the sense of being among their own prevailed there. I think that perhaps the most virulently regarded consequence of the civil rights movement, among old Buckhead, was when its proprietors closed Hart's rather than allow Negroes to dine there.

My father continued his clawing, imperceptible ascent out of the stroke's mortal grip, though the paralysis did not improve, and except for his foot, which gained mobility every day, he lay rigid and ruined, turning his furious face back and forth from my mother and me to the window, making no sound. But each day another tube or so was removed, and by the end of that week he was able to swallow some of the viscous mess a nurse spooned into his blasted mouth, though most of it dribbled down his chin.

Hub Dorsey thought that once the catheter could be removed, and he was able to swallow medication easily, we might begin to think of taking him out of the hospital. He simply shook his head despairingly when I told him of my mother's plan to bring my father home and install him upstairs, and said he would talk to her himself. I don't know whether he did or not. If he did, it was in vain. Mr. Ronnie of Rich's, wall-eyed with silent reproach at me and trailed by a flying wedge of minions, came with wallpaper and fabric and paints and pillows, and the suite of rooms in the right wing that had been the province of Aunt Willa and Little Lady and, so briefly, little Jamie Bondurant began to be fitted out for an invalid Eastern emperor. I lay low in the summerhouse or the downstairs sun porch, out of the way of his bustling malevolence and the paisleys and velvets and silks and gilt that streamed up the staircase like the spoils of Cathay. I did not like Mr. Ronnie's idea of an imperial sickroom any better than I had his safari bedroom. It might have succored a dying Philip of Macedon, but I thought it was likely to hasten my father, whose idea of decorative frivolity was the murkier clan tartans of the Scottish Highlands, right off across the Styx.

My aunt Willa, faced with the loss of both her long-occupied bower and the summerhouse, had no recourse but to accept my mother's lilting proposal that she make "a darling, private little apartment of your very own" up on the third floor, in the little warren of rooms that had been mine and Lucy's in early childhood. She was momentarily bested, and knew it, but to her credit, she put a good face on it, and immediately set out to charm the fickle Mr. Ronnie until he was spending most of his time up there with her, happily spreading out his samples and stapling fabric and poufing pillows. My mother seethed at his defection, but said nothing. She knew as well as Willa, as well as Lucy and I before her, that the attic was Coventry, even done up to resemble a seraglio. So it was an impasse. With both women in the house thrumming with subterranean anger and masking it with sweet smiles and drawled pleasantries, I took to burrowing into my father's hallowed library, where the huge oak doors shut out sight and sound, and beginning to thumb, tentatively, through the files and papers that were the visible hieroglyphics of his business affairs. They made absolutely no sense to me. I had fared far better with my Babylonian antiquities.

I visited a few of the Buckhead Boys and their wives that week, largely because it would have looked odd if I had not, though I did not go to see Charlie and Sarah. And I spent one evening with Lucy and Jack, in the farmhouse at the end of an unspeakable dirt road miles outside Lithonia. I had never been that far east in DeKalb County, and got lost, lurching along black, sodden country roads where the undergrowth leaned so close that I could hear the squeals of its furrows in the hand-rubbed lacquer of my father's great, wallowing Rolls. When I finally arrived, an hour late, it was to find Lucy flushed and disheveled from the heat of the old gas stove in the vast, dingy kitchen, and the two sallow, thin-faced boys querulous with hunger and their hated "good" clothes, and dinner drying in the oven, and Jack Venable pinched and dry-voiced with exasperation. The house itself was a shambles, sadly in need of paint inside and out and without central heating, so that you dashed from one small, overheated room to another through dark, arctic wastes of plasterboard and canted linoleum. Jack had wanted a "real" farm; he had gotten a bargain in this one.

We ate a horrendously bad chicken fricassee in the large front room that obviously served as Lucy and Jack's bed-sitting-room, on card tables which had been covered with the exquisite old damask that my mother had given Lucy for a wedding present. My own Georg Jensen crystal candlesticks sat on the grown-ups' table, and I recognized the rose-sprigged china and the thin goblets as my family's Royal Doulton and Baccarat "second set," which had been my paternal grandmother's and which my mother had never liked. An enormous space heater glowered furiously in front of the closed-off fireplace, and the great bed in the corner, as dark and tall and massive as a Viking ship, was obviously an old piece from Jack's family. It was covered with a thin, faded chenille spread, but at its bottom a cloudlike peach drift of goose-down comforter lay.

The whole house was a schizophrenic amalgam of spavined, dismal authentic North Georgia country and satiny Buckhead wedding largesse. On the whole, I thought that the stubborn, dreary country was winning the battle. Lucy's brave bits of china and crystal and damask and silver were poignant to me, instead of stylish and go-to-hell, as she no doubt intended them to be. I wondered how she felt about the reality of her bucolic new kingdom. When I left the room after dinner to go to the bathroom, at the other end of the house, I hurried through what seemed endless wastes of glacial darkness and found, in the dim, stained bathroom, along with a bulbous, claw-footed tub and tall, skinny, rusting old fixtures, another roaring space heater and a Dewar's scotch carton in which a rangy, suspicious mother cat lay on an old flannel bathrobe and nursed lank, striped kittens. When I reached over to pet her, she spat and hissed expertly.

It was not a good evening. My lateness and the ruined dinner undoubtedly contributed, but the strangeness went deeper than that. The children were, I thought, unusually unattractive even given the trauma of their mother's defection and their father's redefection to this much younger interloper. They eyed me and Lucy out of the corners of small, pale eyes, and picked their noses, and pointedly refused to respond to her questions and comments, speaking elaborately and only to their father. They would not even look at me.

Jack himself was silent, eating methodically, nodding and saying "yes" and "no" to direct questions, but little else. He drank gin martinis steadily before dinner, and scotch after, and sat in a great, sagging morris chair beside the space heater and watched television in silence while Lucy served coffee and cognac and made conversation that was so animated it bordered on the febrile. She was drinking a good bit herself, sipping steadily on a never-dwindling glass of orange juice that smote the air around it with vodka, and though she was dressed in black velvet Capri pants and a silk shirt, and wore her graduation pearls around her slender throat, I did not think she looked well. Her creamy, rose-flushed skin was raw around her mouth and on her knuckles, as if she washed only in hard, cold water, and her suede flats were scuffed and slick and stretched on her slender feet. Her heavy, silky blue-black hair had been drawn back into a ponytail as it had when I saw her at the hospital. The ends straggled at her nape, and I felt a sudden surge of anger. Lucy's regular haircuts at Rich's were one of the precise, immutable rituals of her life, and her glorious hair was the only one of her splendid physical assets of which she had ever seemed vain. Were they so poor that she had given up haircuts along with nearly every other luxury she had been casually accustomed to? Why did Jack not get her shoes fixed for her, or buy her new ones? Was she so absorbed in the drama and momentum of their work with the movement that she had simply abjured all worldly trappings, or were they now beyond her reach? I hated the way she looked and the way she obviously lived. The house, besides being dilapidated, was not clean. In it, she was like an Arabian mare in a muck-wet draft horses' barn. If this was the haven Jack Venable had offered her, I wanted to shove it back down his fleshy throat. And why was he so silent and so rude? Had they had a fight, or was this his customary demeanor, now that they were married and she was no longer an elusive flame, but struggled to burn on his hearth?

Despite Lucy's chatter and gaiety, and her rich laugh and her bawdy gossip, invariably prefaced with her breathy, rushed little "Oh, listen, Gibby," the evening rolled over and lay lumpen and dead at our feet, and I rose to leave only a couple of hours after I arrived, pleading the freezing wind and the bad roads and the distance back to Peachtree Road. Jack heaved himself reluctantly out of his chair and walked with me and Lucy to the door, and gave me only a perfunctory handshake and a "Come again, Shep. And watch the drive there. You don't want to knock the bloom off that Rolls."

I was so angry with him, and his coldness toward Lucy, and the mean-spirited lack of cherishing, that I turned back halfway to the Rolls, meaning to say something light but significant like, "Take care of her, Jack, I'm taking names," but the words died in my throat. He stood with his arms around her in the dark doorway of the farmhouse, his head bent to hers, and there was such tenderness in the angle of his face, and in his hands on her shoulders, that I felt a lump rise in my throat. Whatever ate at Jack Venable and had caused him to freeze Lucy out tonight, it was not lack of love for her. I navigated the lurching miles back to Atlanta troubled in my soul for my cousin Lucy, but not on that score.

The day after that, Tom Carmichael and Marshall Haynes, my father's man at the Trust Company, came by to see me. Shem Cater brought them into the library, where I had given up for the morning on the ledgers and statements and files and taken refuge in an old volume of Bulfinch that had been my grandfather Redwine's. They got right down to business.

"We need to set up a series of meetings, Shep, either here or at my office or down at the bank," Tom said, and Marshall nodded his sandy, crew-cut head. It was said by my crowd, who undoubtedly got it from their fathers, that he was a wizard with corporate accounts, and very much the young man to watch during the next couple of decades. To me, he looked about thirteen, an anemic thirteen at that, and I remembered that when my father had first been passed along to him, after old Claude Maddox had retired, that he had been furious at the seeming slight of being handed over to a mere child. But after the first month or two, he had stopped his grumbling, and had after that begun to speak of "Haynes" in the same tone that he did "Carmichael" and "Cheatham" and "Cameron." Marshall Haynes and I looked at each other with the instinctive dislike of the young, competent hireling for the young, incompetent princeling, and vice versa, and smiled brilliantly. Each of us knew the other had something that he would never have, and that he envied.

"I figure we can get you in shape to operate autonomously in about six weeks," Haynes began pleasantly, and Tom Carmichael picked it up: "The day-to-day operating procedure is really quite simple; your dad handled it in a couple or three hours each day, and there wasn't any reason for him to go down to the office every day, except to have lunch at the Capital City or Commerce Club," he said. "You know the staff; they're as fine people as you'll find for their sort of thing, and your dad trained them the way he wanted them. They can, essentially, carry on day to day by themselves. But you need to be able to function as manager and decision-maker, and between us, Marshall and I can fill you in on assets and portfolios and such, and broad-brush a picture of the structure and legalities of things."

Marshall Haynes nodded this time, and I thought they resembled nothing so much as a second-rate father-and-son comic routine.

"You're going to need some brushing up, even if you've been familiar with the business all your life," he said. "Though Tom tells me your field is classics, not real estate. The real estate picture has changed almost entirely since you left for school, and there's just no telling which way it's going to take off in the next year or so. Foreign capital, REITs—there are a lot of new wrinkles we can teach you. Better get it out of the way right in the beginning, so you can pick up the reins before too much time has elapsed. Then it'll be pretty much your show, with us in the wings to back you up, of course. We'll be there whenever you need us."

He grinned, an attractive replica of Tom Carmichael's grin— the official Old Boy grin of the men who were now the Club— and I leaned back and gave the grin back to him and said, perversely, "Sorry, but no dice. I'm glad you came by; it'll save me a phone call. But I'm not going to be brushing up and picking up reins and running shows. I'm leaving the next week for Vermont to teach classics to fat little rich kids, and what I really need for you guys to do is find me a good business manager who can brush up and pick up and run shows, and find him fast, and turn the whole shooting match over to him. Like tomorrow or the next day. You can do that, Tom, can't you?" I purposely did not include Marshall Haynes in the question.

They were silent for a moment, looking at each other, and then Tom said, "I can do that, yes. But I'd hate to. Listen, Shep, don't do anything ill-considered or hasty. I know things haven't always been . . . roses and clover with you and your dad, but everything's changed now. You just can't up and walk away from this."

"This isn't hasty, Tom, and it's been considered every way it can be," I said. "And I can indeed just up and walk away from it. In fact, I can run. All this stuff is nothing to me, and that's the way it's going to stay."

His face was wintry and disapproving. "I'd say it was everything to you, on the face of it," he said. "Of course, it's your business."

"Yes," I said. "It is. And this is what I choose to do with it. I want you to go ahead and do it for me right away, Tom, or I'll do it myself, and it will undoubtedly be done wrong if I do. Okay?"

"I . . . okay," he said. "All right. I ask only that you think it over for a day or two, talk with your mother—"

"That's the last thing I'm going to do, and if I hear that you've breathed a word of it to her, I'll have your hide," I said. I did not know why I was being so hard on him; he was a man of dignity and substance, and had served my father well for a long time. It felt wonderful, though. Marshall Haynes's eyes on me were watchful and held a glint of grudging respect, and that felt even better.

"Surely you mean to tell her what you've told us," Tom Carmichael said frostily. "You can't just flit out of here without telling her. Her own holdings are substantial, to say the least—"

"Of course I'll tell her," I said. "I may be a classicist, but I'm not an ogre. But I'm not going to tell her until later. Next week, just before I flit out of here, I think. She's got too much else on her mind now. I don't want to upset her before I have to."

Seeing that I could not be swayed, they went away, undoubtedly to the Capital City Club to lick their wounds and plan, over the Catch of the Day and a nice little Chardonnay, how best to circumvent me. They need not have bothered.

I was back in the library the next morning, deep in Bulfinch, when Shem Cater put his head into the door, grinning like a bad imitation of Rochester, and said, "Comp'ny to see you, Mr. Shep," and Ben Cameron walked into the room behind him.

He stood in a patch of pale midmorning sunlight on the faded old Oriental, hands in the pockets of a beautiful dark blue cashmere topcoat, his ruddy hair like rusted iron in the weak morning light. He was not smiling.

"Morning, Ben," I said, getting up from the morris chair I had been slumped in. "Sit down. Can I offer you some coffee?"

"No," he said. "I've got a thermos in the car. Get your coat and a muffler and gloves, Shep, and come with me, if you've got a little time to spare. I want to show you something."

"What is it?" I asked.

"I'd rather show you," he said. "Indulge me if you will. I'll have you back in a couple of hours. We can get some lunch downtown, or at Brookhaven, if you'd rather. You're not in the middle of something that can't wait, are you?" He looked pointedly at the Bulfinch, and I laughed.

"No," I said. "Nothing that won't wait. Let me get my stuff."

When I came back from the summerhouse in my coat and an old Princeton muffler, he was already waiting in the big black

Lincoln on the front drive. He was sitting in the backseat, and I was profoundly surprised to see Glenn Pickens sitting at the wheel in a neat, dark suit and tie, gray driving gloves on his hands. The Lincoln's powerful motor was idling, and Glenn eased it into motion as soon as I closed the door on my side behind me. He, too, was unsmiling, and said nothing beyond his neutral "Good morning, Shep" in response to my greeting. Looking at his impassive yellow face, I found it impossible to believe that not four months before we had shared a night of unease and transcendence at La Carrousel. I did not know he still drove for Ben Cameron; somehow I thought that chore had ended when he had graduated from Morehouse and law school. But then, remembering that it was Ben who had put him through both, I figured that he was probably grateful enough to oblige Ben whenever he could. His greeting was the last time he spoke until nearly the end of the drive.

"Am I being kidnapped?" I asked, accepting a cup of coffee from Ben's thermos, and grinning as he added a dollop of brandy from a silver flask in his pocket.

"As a matter of fact, you are," he said. "This is in the nature of a command performance. And there's a condition. No questions—not until we've seen what I have to show you. Agreed?"

"Sure," I said. "Just keep that brandy coming and you won't hear a peep out of me."

He was silent and preoccupied, and I stole an occasional quick glance at the clean, sharp profile I had known all my life and yet did not know, feeling oddly constrained to be bowling down Peachtree Road toward the downtown section beside the mayor-to-be of the city, drinking his brandy and being driven by a lifelong acquaintance. I wondered if he did not feel strange himself sometimes, out of context and ambushed by his own life. He hardly spoke as we floated along, the big Lincoln, a new one, eating up the familiar miles into the city's heart. Once, as we gained Five Points, the epicenter of the business and financial district, he turned to me and said, "You knew that Sarah is pregnant, didn't you?"

"Yes," I said. "Charlie told me Christmas Eve. Is she all right?"

"No," Ben Cameron said somberly. "She's not. She looks like hell, and she's sicker than a dog. Dorothy tells me that's temporary, but it bothers the hell out of me. Sarah's never sick."

"I'm really sorry," I said lamely. For some reason his tone made me feel as guilty as if I had caused Sarah's morning nausea.

"You ought to be," he said. He withdrew again into abstracted silence, whistling soundlessly between his teeth and drumming his fingers on his knee, and I fell silent too, affronted. Whatever his daughter suffered, I was sure my pain was the greater.

Glenn Pickens slid the Lincoln through Five Points and east on Mitchell Street, past the courthouse, the beautiful Art Deco spire of City Hall and the dirty granite and marble pile of the state capitol. In this hiatus between Christmas and the New Year, the streets were nearly bare of traffic, and only a few pedestrians, Negroes mainly, scurried up the long hill beside the capitol building, thin coats and jackets pulled close against the icy wind that had come booming in with the long-hidden sun. The dead, brown mats of lawn and bare peach tree saplings around the government buildings looked desolate and forsaken, and the big Christmas tree on the Capitol lawn, beside the statue of Tom Watson, whipped in the gusts from the west. Occasionally, in the wide, clear spaces around the government buildings, the Lincoln rocked softly from side to side in the wind's unbroken force. I closed my eyes against the glare arrowing off the hood of the Lincoln, and Ben put black sunglasses on his narrow brown face. With his clear gray eyes shielded, he looked dangerous and foreign, like a Sicilian bandit.

Glenn Pickens turned behind the Capitol onto Capitol Avenue and we slid down into the great, and to me featureless, wasteland to the south and east, where much of Atlanta's Negro population lived. I had been down into the Southeast before, usually with Shem Cater in the Chrysler, to fetch or return one or another of my family's servants, but to my blind white eyes, the streets on which the Negroes lived were much like the Negroes themselves: they all looked alike. I looked questioningly at Ben, and he gave me back the look, but he did not speak. Glenn Pickens did not, either. I felt a very faint tremor of uneasiness, like a foreshock to an earthquake that only a bird or an animal might sense. What could there be, in this bleak landscape, that Ben Cameron wanted to show me?

One by one, we ghosted through the black communities to the south of the city's heart: Summerhill, Peoplestown, Joyland. The desolation and poverty of these small communities seemed to me as unredeemed as they were uniform; I could not tell where one left off and the other picked up. But Ben knew; he pointed them out by name as we passed through, and in the same conversational tone as he had spoken earlier of Sarah and the weather, talked of their distinct characters, their particularities. Every now and then he'd say, "Am I right, Glenn?" and Glenn Pickens would say, "That's right, Ben," or, "Not exactly. That's Mule Coggins's poolroom, not Morley's." How in the world, I wondered, in the course of his crowded juggernaut life, had Ben Cameron had time to learn the geography and ethnology of these dismal little black habitats in the bowels of the city? Were there, in his quicksilver mind, faces to go with the names? Another man entirely might have been sitting beside me, and I felt shy and stupid and young. In point of fact, I was all those things.

The Negro communities were comprised of warrens of small, narrow streets, many unpaved, with wooden and cinder-block and brick one- and, infrequently, two-story houses crowded so close together that often not even a driveway separated them— which did not seem to matter so much. I saw few automobiles. Most sat squarely on the streets, or sidewalks where there were such, with only a few feet of dirt or concrete for yard space, these littered with broken toys and bottles and trash. Most of the houses had long since lost their paint and some had lost their windowpanes, and had blind eyes of cardboard or newspaper. Steps up to sagging porches were piled bricks or cinder blocks, and outhouses leaned crazily in some of the weed-choked back-yards. I knew there was city water—I saw fire hydrants, and open sewage stood frozen in gutters—but still the outhouses pre-vailed. Occasional vacant lots choked with the brown skeletons of kudzu vines broke the monotonous rows of shacks and tene-ments; I knew that in the summer whole blocks here would wear the virulent, poison green mantles of the kudzu, and would be the better for it. Smoke billowed from many crazed and tumbled chimneys, and I wondered if those houses did not have any other sources of heat. The wind down here, unbroken by any of the tall buildings that shielded the city's heart, was truly brutal. All of the puddles I saw were solid with dun-colored ice. I saw few people in the residential neighborhoods, but the ones I did see were thin, underdressed children and old women.

Through each neighborhood ran a larger cross street with a shabby grocery store, a drugstore, liquor stores, pawnshops, and a café or two. There were more people here, men mainly, teen-aged and young and middle-aged, lounging in and out of stores and cafés, standing in frozen-breathed groups on street corners beneath shattered streetlights, shoulders raised against the cold, prowling eyes following us in the Lincoln as Glenn idled it past. I felt like ducking my head against the dead inexorability of those eyes, but Ben met them squarely and measuringly, and Glenn Pickens lifted a hand occasionally to someone he knew, and re-ceived in return a languid salute. I wondered if any of them knew who Ben Cameron was, riding by in the Christmas cold in his great black Lincoln. I had a feeling many of them did.

"Where are all the women?" I said, forgetting that I was not supposed to ask questions. I had not seen a single woman who appeared to be under the age of seventy since we had entered the Southeast.

It was Glenn Pickens who answered me.

"They're all back where we came from, Shep," he said, not turning his head. "They're working in the kitchens in Buckhead."

My face burned. I should have known that. I had walked into it. Beside me, Ben Cameron smiled, a half-smile.

Once, driving through Summerhill, he gestured toward a nest of streets to the right. More of the miserable little houses, as lunar and unpeopled as the others, huddled there.

"That's where the new freeway will go through, and where the stadium will go, we hope," he said. "It's the best site we've got, and the plans are complete for it."

"Where will those people go?" I said. "The ones who live there?"

He laughed. There was no mirth in it.

"Good question. I'm sure they'd like to know the answer," he said. "Holy Christ. We can raise eighteen million for a new stadium, and the housing authority can pledge fifty million to wipe out the slums in a decade, but they can't seem to relocate a single black family whose home they knock down, or spend a penny on communities like Vine City or Buttermilk Bottom. We've got to do better than this. We've got to do a lot better."

"I thought there was some public housing," I said, despite the fact that I was pretty sure it was not to me that he spoke.

"Oh, God. Four. Exactly four public housing projects since 1936. We're going to be mighty lucky if we get through this next summer without somebody literally lighting the fires under us."

Glenn drove us through Mechanicsville and Pittsburgh, where I remembered calling for Amos and Lottie, and then over to Boulevard and up through Chosewood Park and Grant Park, with its prim green middle-class haven of the zoo and cyclorama, and across Memorial Drive and past the oasis of Oakland Cemetery. I took an involuntary deep breath of pure relief, back now on familiar and hallowed ground, and then we were heading east on DeKalb. We skirted the odd, half-familiar little linear enclave of Cabbagetown, which, though desperately poor as the other neighborhoods, was relentlessly all white, and the great, crouching jumble of Fulton Bag and Cotton that brooded over it, and then, just beyond it, Glenn Pickens turned down into another little neighborhood and stopped the Lincoln.

"We'll walk from here," Ben said. "Better wrap that scarf around your head, and take a gulp of this brandy. We've got a ways to go, and the wind's picking up."

"Where are we?" I said. I had never been this far east before, never ventured beyond the part of Cabbagetown that I could see from our family plot on its myrtle-shaded hill in Oakland Cemetery. This was literally the back of the moon to me.

"It's called Pumphouse Hill," Ben said. "The only water up in here used to be an old public hand pump on the top of that hill yonder. If you wanted to wash or drink or flush or douse your fire, you toted water from that pump."

"Most people up here still do," Glenn Pickens said. He had gotten silently out of the car and come up beside us, a covert-gray cloth overcoat pulled up around his ears. "City ran some water up here in the fifties, but not many families can afford it. I don't think two thirds of the fire hydrants up here have worked for ten years."

Ben frowned. "That's the city's bailiwick, not the citizens'," he said. "There's no excuse for that. I'm going to get on Dan Roberts's ass when I get back."

"We stay on Dan Roberts's ass," Glenn said. "To be fair, it's not all his fault. Kids pound the mains open the minute the crews leave in the summer, to get cool in the spray, and then he's just got to get a crew back up here and fix them all over again. He does the best he can. He hasn't got that many crews."

"Well, I'll get on his ass anyway, just to set a precedent," Ben said. "No sense waiting till January second for that."

We walked down the first street in Pumphouse Hill. We had not gone three houses in before I began to wonder if I was going to be able to bear this. As wretched as the other neighborhoods had been, Pumphouse Hill made them look nearly palatial in comparison. I had never seen anything like it. The tiny houses were all decades older and in far worse repair than in the other neighborhoods, some without whole roofs, most without one or more windowpanes, all made of unpainted, rotting, green-scummed wood. Virtually no electric lights burned here, though light poles and power lines yawned and drooped, and few of the chimneys had smoke coming from them. In Pumphouse Hill I saw no people, not even the old.

The unpaved street was thick with filth and unspeakable things. I was, for the first time that day, glad of the subfreezing temperatures; the stench would have been unbearable if the excrement that lay clotted in ditches and under windows had not been frozen. At front and side doors, frozen garbage and refuse and piles of frozen, rotted vegetables lay where they had been tossed. I saw several newly dead dogs and cats, not crushed by automobiles, but simply lying stiff and banal and hopeless, as if they had fallen and frozen to death in the night. Once I stumbled, and caught on to Ben Cameron's arm, and looked down to see what I had stepped on. It was the crushed and frozen carcass of a rat the size of a small fox terrier. I felt the gorge rise, thick and sour, in my throat.

There were no more than six or seven streets in Pumphouse Hill; it occupied an area of perhaps no more than four city blocks. But the human misery and degradation on them was enormous, immense; it filled the world; smote my heart and my tongue to silence. I remembered a letter Sarah had written me last spring, about a trip she had taken to Naples and the literal communities she had seen dug out of the bomb rubble, left when Mark Clark took his troops up Monte Cassino. Pitiful, terrible, heartbreaking burrows dug in rubble, each with a family living in it like some mutant, subterranean species, wild and wretched, she had said. Screaming their hate at whoever passed. Pumphouse Hill reminded me of that letter. We walked up and down each street, only the sound of our footsteps scrunching on the ice-bristles in the red clay, and the whistling wind, and the occasional thin yelp of a dog breaking the radiant, terrible, sun-frozen silence.

Only once did I bring myself to speak.

"Is there anyone down here? Does anybody live here?" I said. I had seen no one, literally, since we started out from the Lincoln. I realized that I had spoken hopefully.

"Oh yeah," Glenn Pickens said. "Lots of folks live here. They're all inside in bed."

"Bed?" I said stupidly. Did he mean they were making love, or sleeping? Ill? What?

"Yeah, bed," he said. "You've heard of bed. It's where the folks up here go to keep warm, when they can't pay the electric or gas bill and they can't find firewood. You can always pile on another dog or young'un."

Once again I reddened. We walked the rest of the terrible, blasted frozen neighborhood in silence. When we got back to the Lincoln and climbed into it, I was shaking with cold and shock. Under the shock, far down, was a profound anger.

"Why did you take me up there?" I said to Ben Cameron.

He poured brandy into coffee and handed it to me. He looked for a long time into my face, his gray eyes opaque.

"I thought you ought to see it firsthand," he said. "Your family owns it."

The wave of revulsion and rage that swept me then knocked me, literally, against the backseat of the car.

"I don't believe you," I said through stiff lips, my ears ringing as if someone had fired an elk gun hard by them. "My parents . . . they couldn't . . . they couldn't possibly know it was like this. They can't . . . they wouldn't . . ."

"They can, and they do," Ben said, and I knew that he was

telling me the truth. It was as if I had always known, or rather, that the blood and bone of me had known about Pumphouse Hill, even though my brain had not.

"Or your father does, anyway," Ben Cameron went on. "He has for years, because I've been after him that long to clean it up, and so have the others. I can only assume Olivia doesn't know. I don't believe she would permit it. Shep, I've known your father half my life; his backing made my campaign possible, and I owe him in ways you'll probably never know about. But I swear I'd have him in court over this if it weren't for Miss Olivia. I grew up playing with her when we visited in Griffin. Our families have been friends for decades. We've led our entire adult lives together. So I really haven't pushed this, and I've persuaded . . . some of the others . . . not to, either. Now, though, your dad is out of the picture, and you're here, and it's a different ball game. It can't wait any longer. I'd have given you some time, because I know you're unfamiliar with your father's business, and everything's in an uproar, but we're out of time now. Glenn says there's really bad feeling down here, and it's getting worse, and with things shaping up the way they are around the South between the races, this has got to be remedied and remedied quick. It could go up just anytime. I thought the quickest way to get it started was to show you."

I said nothing, and then I looked at Glenn Pickens.

"I really didn't know," I said.

"I didn't figure you did, Shep," he said. His face was closed. "But you do now."

"I do now," I said.

We did not speak on the way home, and we did not have lunch downtown or at the club, and the Lincoln had not stopped completely on the half-moon drive at 2500 Peachtree Road before I was out of it and running up the staircase to my mother's room. I could hear myself shouting in my own ears, a crazy and faraway sound, as though, two blocks over, a madman raved, close to tears. I must have screamed at her for a long time. When I stopped, my voice was so hoarse that I could hardly whisper.

My mother looked up from the hand of solitaire she had laid out on her writing desk; she did not speak, but watched me attentively while I shouted and screamed, there in a pool of honeyed afternoon sunlight.

"It has never been your father's property," she said calmly. "It is mine, and always has been. My daddy left it all to me, every bit, and said it would be my . . . my annuity, and I should just sit and let the money pour in, and never put a penny of my capital into it, and that's just what I've done. Your father would have sunk half our assets into it long ago, but I've always remembered what Daddy said, and I would never sign it over to him, or let him pour the money that will soon be yours down that awful rathole. And don't get haughty with me, my dear son. I don't have any complaints from my tenants. God knows where they'd find lower rents in the entire city."

I had to turn my back on her. I thought of the way she had lived all her life, and what the hopeless misery of those silent, invisible wretches in the cold beds of Pumphouse Hill had bought her, and how little of that misery would ever penetrate these creamy white walls, or her creamy white skin. I thought of what it had bought me. I thought of my gentle, patrician grandfather Redwine, and of the trust he had left me, and of what financed it. My head swam with shame, my ears rang with it, my veins ran with it.

Without turning back to her, I said, "You will let me authorize Tom and Marshall Haynes to get started tomorrow cleaning that place up and getting some decent housing in there, or I will be on a plane out of here before nightfall. I mean it, Mother. As much as it takes, for as long as it takes. Or I'm gone, and before God, I'll never set foot in this house or look at your face again."

"Sheppie . . ."

"Take your pick, Mother," I said.

We fought it savagely back and forth like two wild animals all that afternoon and into the night, but finally she agreed. I knew she would. For once I was glad of the sickly power over her that she herself had invested me with: that of the sovereign man, he alone able to validate her. I used it efficiently and with a ruthlessness born of horror at her and contempt for myself. Before we retired, she to her restored bedroom and I to the summerhouse, she had agreed to let me redeem, as best I could, Pumphouse Hill. I fell into a hollowed-out sleep thinking that I would call Ben Cameron first thing in the morning and tell him. With any luck, it could be livable by summer.

But it was not a day for luck, or for mercy. In the small hours of that morning, while my mother and I slept our separate sleeps of depletion, an arsonist's fire howled through Pumphouse Hill, and the fire department, hampered by sixteen-degree temperatures and high winds and inoperable fireplugs, could do little. In the morning some hundred-odd homes were burned to the frozen ground, and eleven people were dead, seven of them children.

Afterward, I heard, the police came to believe that someone who knew that my family owned the property had set the fire and then alerted the newspapers virtually when the first match was struck, because a reporter was on the telephone to my mother almost before the first fire truck screamed into the inferno, and only minutes later a cadre of reporters and photographers was on the doorstep of 2500. I was wakened by a wild-eyed Shem and stumbled, blinded with sleep and still struggling into my bathrobe, up the path to the house and into the foyer, but it was too late. In this, too, mercy had abdicated us entirely.

My mother, bone-white and idiot-faced with terror, stood at bay in her own foyer, her satin and lace robe askew and her black hair wild and witchlike on her shoulders. I was just in time to hear her shriek, "It's not my property! I don't know anything about it! I've never even seen it! It . . . my son owns it! I deeded it to him years ago! He's the one who always looked after it! He's the one, he's the one you ought to be talking to. . . ."

Her words, and my photograph, gaping and blank-eyed in the beautiful foyer of the house on Peachtree Road, were on the front page of every newspaper in the state the next morning, and in many out-of-state ones. In the Atlanta *Constitution,* the headline read: "Fire Destroys Holdings of Buckhead Slum Lord." And a subhead under it: "Heir to Buckhead fortune called responsible for slum death trap."

I did not speak to my mother again while she lived.

Ben came again that night, late, and brought a bottle of Wild Turkey with him. I was in the library, where I had been since the reporters and photographers had left in the cold red dawn. I had been there all day. No one had come into the room, not even Shem Cater, who had, without my instructing him, left trays of food at intervals on the console outside the door and rapped softly on it and gone away again. I had not eaten any of it. I did not think many people had come to the house; though I could not hear the front-door bell from the library, I could, through some trick of acoustics, hear tires on the front drive. I had heard them only twice. Buckhead encircles its own when death or sorrow strikes, but when disgrace visits, they circle the wagons and the offender is left naked outside on the howling plain. On this day, I was glad of that.

I had lit the fire that Shem kept laid in the fireplace early that morning, and kept it roaring with wood from the brass chest beside it. But I had not turned on any lights, and when Ben came into the room, he seemed to leap and swell with shadow and firelight. I had not heard his car, and my first thought was that he must have cut diagonally through the woods that linked the back of Muscogee to Peachtree Road. He wore a thick Scandinavian ski sweater under an old down hunting parka and ancient rubber hunting boots from L. L. Bean. The heavy outdoor clothes made him look much younger, more like the Ben Cameron I had always known. I was not surprised to see him. I had, I realized, been sitting in the dark room like a child at the end of its resources, waiting for Ben to come and tell me what to do now. I had not been able to think or feel since my mother's voice had died away in the foyer.

He sat down on the deep sofa across from my chair and opened the Wild Turkey and poured us both a tumblerful. We drank it silently in the firelight, looking at each other.

"Where is your mother?" he said finally.

"She went up to her room early this morning and locked the door," I said. My voice was rusty with disuse. "I don't think anybody has seen her but Hub Dorsey and Tom Carmichael. They've both been here. And Martha takes food up. She'd probably see you if you went up."

His hand dismissed my mother.

"You've been in here all day," he said. "Shem told me. I stopped by the summerhouse, but you weren't there, and I came on to the back door."

"It's better in here," I said briefly. I was so endlessly and profoundly tired that it was an effort to frame the words. Tired, and disinclined entirely to tell him that I had felt too vulnerable and unguarded in the summerhouse, too open to intrusion and prying eyes and voices and cameras. The big house, at least, was as tight as the fortress my mother and I had turned it into. And too, I was obscurely reluctant to sully my perfect refuge with the poison of this treachery.

"Better stay here in the house for a day or two, just to be on the safe side," Ben said. "I've got some unofficial guards posted out front and back to keep the press and the gawkers away, and with any luck at all—which you haven't exactly been long on lately—all the hooraw will die down in a few days. I'm going to cut through the woods and come in the back door for a spell for the same reason. I don't want it to get out that there's any collusion between us. Besides, it's kind of fun."

"Collusion?" I said thickly. I did not understand.

Ben put his drink down and leaned forward, his forearms resting on his knees and his slender brown hands dangling loosely. He looked into the blue-spitting fire. Then he began to speak. He talked for quite a long time, while the graying log fell in a shower of red sparks and I tossed a new one on, and it too began to dull into ashen gray.

By the time he was done, he had told me that, in essence, he and the Club were going to let my mother throw me to the wolves. They were all aware of my blamelessness, he said, and were unanimously outraged by her betrayal. I would have the best legal counsel in the South, if matters came to that; several of their own lawyers were at that moment in conference back at the house on Muscogee Avenue, and a direct line to Mr. Woodruff was open and in use. They could with some assurance promise me that though there would likely be an investigation, there would be no grand jury, no more press coverage, and of course, no criminal charges.

But no one was going to come forward and refute my mother's charges.

I knew that they could do what they promised. Physically, I would be safe. I knew, too, that they would do the rest of it. His grim face told me that. There did not seem anything to say, so I said nothing.

"Do you know why we're letting you hang, Shep?" he said presently, when I continued to stare out into the star-chipped night and did not respond to him.

"To save my mother, I guess," I said dully.

"No," he said. "To save us all. You included. All of us out here in Buckhead. To save Buckhead itself, and the way of life that's all we know. These are dangerous times, and a false step from any one of us now could lose us that way of life in an eye-blink. Just up in smoke. It almost went last night. It's going to go soon enough anyway, but if we play things just right, we can hold that day off until you—all of you boys, the next wave, so to speak—are ready to take up the reins, and our families are safely provided for. It can't get out that one of us right here in Buckhead, one of our women especially, sat by and knowingly permitted this awful thing. I can't let that happen. This god-damned race thing is just too volatile. Better you, an outsider of sorts, someone who just might have had the excuse of not being on the spot. It's the worst thing I'll ever do, letting this fiction go on, and it's probably the worst thing this city will ever deal you. But I'm going to do it. I'm going to have to save my people. I'm going to have to spare my city the consequences of this. I'm not just going to be saying words next week when I put my hand on that Bible."

I still did not say anything. He reached over and laid his hand on my hair, and brushed it lightly back from my forehead. I felt warm, weak tears in my throat.

"In every sense but the biological one, you've been my son," he said. "God, I wanted you for a son-in-law, as good a man as Charlie is. But I'll take you any way I can get you. Nothing's going to change between us. Not on my part, anyway; I wouldn't blame you if it did on yours. There's something I want you to remember, though, and think about. Your day is still to come, Shep. In twenty years or so, when it's your time, there'll be an entirely new and different set of folks in power in Atlanta, new people who'll never have heard of this fire, and couldn't care less if they had. You're not going to lose your . . . place in the sun, not in the long run. But we *are* asking you to defer it. *I'm* asking. We'll be eternally in your debt; the whole city will, though sadly, they'll never know it. We'll try to make this up to you, somehow.

"But if you feel you just can't go along with us, if you really think you have to bring your mother into it . . . well, I'll have to let the courts and the press have their way. The stakes are just too high."

He said nothing more. In a minute or two he got up and padded out of the room on his rubber soles and closed the door softly behind him. He left the Wild Turkey on the table between our chairs.

It was a measure of Ben Cameron's power and grace that, sitting in my father's library in the ruins of my life, I saw his point.

CHAPTER
NINETEEN

T HE POLICE NEVER FOUND the Pumphouse Hill arsonist. In truth, I am not sure how hard they looked. Clem Coffee, the first of an entirely new breed of college-educated cop and as alien to Atlanta's blue ranks as a ballerina in a split T formation, was Ben Cameron's man, and though he put his men through the correct motions, he did so quietly, and with virtually nothing leaked to the press. Apprehending the arsonist would have opened an enormous can of worms, a squirming feast for the press, and I can imagine that Clem was as relieved as Ben and the Club and, I suppose, my mother when the one slender lead—the anonymous call to the newspaper at 4:50 that morning—remained anonymous.

There was almost nothing to go on. The reporter who took the call could say only that the voice sounded as if it came through fabric of some kind, and was educated and precise, and gave the location of the fire and suggested that the newspaper contact Sheppard Gibbs Bondurant of Buckhead for further information. Clem Coffee, who came once to the house with Ben to talk with me and look upon me with some small compassion (though he carefully and quite correctly said nothing that was not routine), believed that someone who knew of Pumphouse Hill's ownership saw Ben and Glenn Pickens and me walking through it that afternoon, or was told about our visit by someone who did, and seized the moment, as it were. I thought that that must surely narrow the field enormously. How many residents of the Southeast could possibly know who held the titles to their purgatories? How many would care?

"You'd be surprised," Ben said, and Clem laughed sourly.

"There's an information network down there that would put USIA to shame," he said. "I'd be surprised if it wasn't common knowledge that the property was . . . not yours."

"Then why won't somebody come forward?" I said.

"Shit, Shep, they don't care who hangs, as long as one of us does," Clem said. "But there's not a lot anybody can do if the arsonist can't be found, and you can bet your ass nobody down there is going to blow the whistle on a brother. They won't even talk to my boys."

"Not even for murder? That's what it was," I said.

"Especially not for murder. Better that you carry that load, whether or not you deserve it. Whoever set it was pretty sure there wouldn't be any reprisals to you or your family or to anybody in the Southeast; at least that's my theory. It's not one I'm making public, needless to say. Besides, it worked, didn't it? Pumphouse Hill is being cleaned up."

It was, tentatively and excruciatingly slowly. My mother had conveyed to me through Tom Carmichael her belated eagerness to divert some family money toward the rehabilitation of the existing property there, and I had authorized him to hire a general contractor and get started. Ben was looking for some loan money, to see what could be done about rebuilding the burned blocks. He thought there might be some federal assistance available. As Ben had predicted, in the absence of a suspect and no criminal investigation, the uproar over Pumphouse Hill soon died away in that first month of the new year.

It was of no particular comfort to me to find that the world did indeed go on, but, of course, it did. Ben Cameron was inaugurated on January 2, looking like a slender, steel-crowned king in the winter sunlight as he stood on the steps of City Hall afterward, Dorothy and Sarah and Charlie and Ben and Julia, holding tiny Ben Cameron III in her arms, around him. An indefinable something, the sense of gears moving forward and a great, interior motor purring softly into life, permeated the hard crystal air of 1962. Ben immediately rammed through legislation to wipe out all restrictions on duties of black policemen; it was his first act as mayor, and prophetic of the tenor of his entire administration. A new $50 million municipal auditorium was announced, and an urban residential development for blacks opened in Thomasville, down in the Southeast. In Washington, John Kennedy was at the apogee of his trajectory, and Jacqueline Kennedy had quite simply conquered the world. Late in February, Colonel John Glenn rode a ridiculous, flame-farting little comet around the earth and Camelot moved into the heavens. And in the Peachtree Road house, my mother came out of her self-imposed exile and took up again, with scarcely a ripple, the silken tapestry of her life.

I do not really know how she fared during the month in her tower. I still do not know why she immured herself there. If it was to avoid censure and consequence, she must have seen within a week that there would, for her, be none. If it was to avoid me, it must have been apparent almost that quickly that she need not bother. When I went into the summerhouse on the second night after the fire, it was, so far as she was concerned, for good. I doubt very much that she felt shame or remorse about Pumphouse Hill or the fire, though she undoubtedly did suffer honestly and deeply over my withdrawal from her. For the first week or so after the event, she sent almost hourly messages by Shem or Martha importuning me to come out and talk to her, and when they did not prevail, sent Tom Carmichael to see me. I would not open the door to him, either. Finally Hub Dorsey pounded on the door one evening until I let him in, and he pleaded with me to end this foolishness and go and see my mother.

"She's in terrible shape, Shep," he said. "She isn't sleeping, and I don't think she's eaten for nearly a week; she must have lost ten pounds. She cries all the time. Look, I know the score on things. Ben talked to me. It's a heavy load for you; we all know that, even if we can't talk about it. But I really can't be responsible for her welfare if you won't let her try to square things with you, or at least talk to her. It's punishment enough for her, to have to live with what she's done. If she loses you on top of your dad, I don't think she'll come out of it. This is killing her."

"No it isn't, Hub," I said, and he soon went away, shaking his head. I did not blame him. Two generations of physicians had had very little joy of the Bondurants.

After that, for a day or two, my mother herself came and wept at my door, and rapped on it, and called and called and called, promising all manner of things which I managed to effectively drown out with Beethoven and Brubeck. She sent reams of notes in on the trays that Shem Cater brought me from the kitchen, but I burned them in the fireplace in the living room of the summerhouse, and scattered the ashes. I was profoundly thankful that she had never gotten around to having a telephone installed. She tried once to send a message to me by Ben Cameron, who was the only visitor I permitted during that time, but he told me matter-of-factly that he had advised her to back off. Apparently she listened to him. Her sorties and entreaties stopped, and she pulled herself together and bathed and dressed and had her

hair and nails done and stepped back into the careening winter
social orbit that was her day-to-day life, paler and thinner and
more beautiful than ever, and no doubt much admired for her
bravery in the face of the disgrace her son had brought on the
house of Bondurant. Except for Ben and the Club, I did not think
that many of Old Buckhead knew the truth of that.

I quickly learned her schedule, and fashioned a life around
it. When she was out of the house, I would go up and bring back
books and papers and whatever furnishings I wanted from my
father's library, and a few paintings and trinkets. Shem told me
that my mother never went into the library, and that they had
not seen her in the kitchen since before Christmas. It was from
the Caters that I learned that Aunt Willa had finally moved her
belongings up into the newly refurbished attic rooms, and that
my mother was bringing my father home, with a full complement of round-the-clock nurses, the second week in February.
After he was installed there, they told me, Aunt Willa took to
sitting serenely beside him for hours at a time in the evenings,
knitting or reading or doing her nails, while the night nurse
drank coffee in the kitchen or watched television in her tiny bedroom. My mother, they said, came in to visit him once in the
morning and again late in the afternoon, after she returned home
from whatever luncheon or committee meeting or shopping trip
was on her agenda, and stayed a half hour or so each time. It
was Willa Slagle Bondurant who was constant.

I would have loved to know how my mother felt about that,
but somehow I could not ask the Caters, and they did not volunteer the information. Mother would have kept her composure
in front of them, in any case. It must have been a bad time for
them, these two black custodians of whatever family life there
had been in the house on Peachtree Road, with my mother and
me at such odds and a wire-grass outlander ensconced at the bedside of their fallen employer. But they never betrayed by so much
as an eye-blink that they felt grief or unease. Perhaps they did
not. Shem fetched trays for me and helped me move furniture
and volunteered, occasionally, to drive me somewhere, and Martha cooked and cleaned for me and washed my clothes and
grumbled and fussed and muttered just as she always had, and
I thought more than once how much we all owed to their con-
stancy, and how excruciatingly little we deserved it.

Once, when Shem had driven my mother away in the Rolls,
I went up to the big house and climbed the stairs to where my
father lay in the unspeakable seraglio that had been created for
him by the triumphant Mr. Ronnie, and sat for an hour in the
chair by his bed. He looked at me with the one fierce, membraned

old eagle's eye that was open, and the skewed mouth moved a few times and a sound like a maddened beehive came from it, and the fingers of one wasted hand scrabbled at the bed covers, but he could do or say no more than that, and was so sapped and bleached and twisted that I could recognize literally nothing of the fierce blond Visigoth who had loomed over my childhood except the enraged, blue-white eye, and did not mind when the nurse came and drove me away. It was months before I went back. On the whole I saw little reason, for a long time, to leave the summerhouse.

I could not, now, leave Atlanta for Vermont or New York or anywhere else. I was free enough to go of course, but it was somehow unthinkable. I suppose it was an obscure and savage kind of pride that kept me captive in a small house behind my own great one, in hiding from the woman who had betrayed me before her and my entire world. Or perhaps it was depression; the real, clinical kind, which saps will and freezes limbs and thickens thought and reaction. Lucy told me later that she thought so; she was no stranger, by then, to the deeper malaises of the human spirit.

But I did not feel sad or anxious or even discomfited in those diamond-bright early days of my first winter at home. I felt, in the bowered fastness of the little white Georgian summerhouse, as clear and still and neutral and somehow *fitted* as mountain water in a pool. Later, I thought, I would decide what course I would set my life upon; later I would make calls, write letters, see people, think of leaving the summerhouse and the city and the South once more, find a direction and a momentum. Later I would explore how I felt about my father, and perhaps even begin to touch, very gently and infinitely slowly, the interior crypt where I had buried the enormity of Pumphouse Hill and the fire and my mother's words. Later . . .

I did not even think of seeing my mother.

I have said that Buckhead circled the wagons and cast me out on the plain, but that is not entirely true. From the beginning Lucy came, almost every night at first, and always with Jack in tow because the Volkswagen had finally died in its tracks and they had, now, only the little Ford station wagon that had been the one thing he brought away from his first marriage, and they rode to and from Damascus House in it. The first night she came, after about a week of trying to reach me on the telephone, she said, "I don't care what the papers say and I don't care what you're not saying. I know that you had nothing to do with that horrible slum or the fire or any of it, and I think somebody is hanging you out to dry. I don't know for sure, but I suppose it's

Aunt Olivia. It makes me madder than shit that you won't talk
to me about it, but if you won't, and if you want to bury yourself
out here for a million years, that's okay with me. You can't stop
me from coming by here, and you can't fire me, and I won't quit.
Now. I'm not going to talk about it anymore until you bring it
up yourself. I just want you to know that I love you and you
can't fool me."

"I know it," I said. "I love you too. Tell me what's happening
at Damascus House."

And she launched into her newest tale of sit-ins and marches
and Martin Luther King sightings, while Jack Venable sprawled
before my fire, drinking scotch and eating peanuts and smiling
at her with his whole good, gray heart.

It seemed outwardly more a badge of Lucy's newly espoused
high-mindedness than of any essential poverty that she wore her
pilled and shapeless high school sweaters and skirts, and that
her shoes were thin-soled and scuffed and her only winter coat
the one Aunt Willa had bought her at the Wood Valley Shop
the year of her aborted debut. She wore them all with her usual
dash and slouching elegance, so that, on her long, thin-to-bone
body, they seemed rakish and perversely attractive. But I knew
that between them she and Jack must scarcely make enough at
Damascus House to keep food on their table and gas in the Ford.
Jack's Harris Tweed jacket was good, but so old that its cuffs
and collar were frayed, and his pants were shiny and stretched
taut over his ample rump. I wished, that winter, that I could just
go out and charge an entire new wardrobe for Lucy at Rich's
or at Frohsin's or J. P. Allen's. And I probably could have done
so. I have an idea my mother would have paid, silently and
swiftly, any bills I might have incurred. It was part of the enslav-
ing pride that I incurred, that winter and spring, almost no expenses at all.

Sarah and Charlie came, too. The first time, they sat side by
side on the sofa in the summerhouse living room, dressed almost
alike in gray flannel slacks and loafers and oxford shirts under
crewneck sweaters, and I was struck, as I never had been before,
how similar physically they were, now that Sarah's pregnancy
had squared her off and puffed her vivid cheeks slightly. Both
were small and dark and solid, there in the low lamp- and firelight, and both wore the same expression of determined cheerfulness. Strain showed itself in every line of their bodies, though,
and twice they spoke together and stopped, and began again, and
broke off, laughing uncomfortably. They talked of everything except the one thing on all our minds: the charring of children in
the glacial predawn of Pumphouse Hill. I don't think it would

have been so bad if they had come alone to see me, but together
Sarah and Charlie Gentry had a newly acquired gloss of genteel
conventionality that neither had ever worn separately. It was as
if the only map they had for marriage was the elaborate and
banal one that had circulated for half a century in Buckhead.

Finally, Sarah knit her dark brows together and said, "Listen,
Shep, something feels queer to me and I want to get it out in
the open," and I saw Charlie, behind her, shake his head quickly
at me, no. So I knew then, if I had not before, that Charlie knew
the truth of Pumphouse Hill, but that he and Ben and the Club
had deemed that their women not be told, not even Sarah. Of
course. The old code would be brought into service now, in the
face of unpleasantness and disgrace: Let us protect our impres-
sionable, frail women, even at the cost of trivializing them. To
me the cost was much higher; it was dishonor. Sarah Cameron
Gentry would have been better able to deal with Pumphouse
Hill, as she was with all reality, than any of them.

But I said, lightly, "Everything feels queer to you, probably.
It's called pregnant. You look great, Sarah. How do you feel?
You weren't too pert there for a while."

She stared at me out of the black-fringed sherry eyes for a moment, and then said, "Oh, all right, Shep. I'll play this stupid
game, whatever it is, that you and Daddy and Charlie have
thought up. But you simply have no idea how childish it is. Yes,
I feel terrific, thanks. No more morning sickness, no nothing.
But 'great' is, I think, the wrong term. What I look like is an
illustration for a story on unwed teenage mothers in some damn
woman's magazine."

I laughed aloud and Charlie did, too—more out of relief that
the taboo had not been broken, I think, than at the aptness of
Sarah's description of herself. But she was right. With her
scrubbed face and huge, clear eyes and glossy red cheeks and
tousled cap of curls, the small shelf of pregnancy that showed
under the crewneck sweater made her look like a waif on the
way to the Florence Crittenton home for wayward girls. Her athlete's muscles had kept the rest of her slender body taut, and her
deep breasts were hidden under the oversized sweater, and she
looked entirely as young as she had that long-ago day out at the
Chattahoochee River, when I had first become aware of her as
a woman. It seemed, all at once, incredible that so much time
and change and pain had passed between us.

A week later, on a warm night in February, she came again
to the summerhouse. This time she was alone.

"Something is wrong. I want you to tell me what it is," she
said without preamble, sitting down beside me on the sofa and
peering into my face.

"Nothing is wrong in the way you mean," I said, knowing that she knew I was lying. "Plenty is wrong, of course, but you know about that. It's going to take me a long time to get over the fire."

"I hate this," she said, leaning back and jamming her hands into the pockets of her maternity top. "I absolutely hate this stupid . . . code of silence, or whatever it is. It dishonors all of us, but it dishonors me the worst. For God's sake, Shep, this is me. Can you possibly think so little of me that you won't trust me with the truth? Don't you know by now that I would never tell anyone else, if you asked me not to? Having this between us is . . . a wall. A wall we can't get around or over."

"Please don't ask me, Sarah," I said, in a tight, low voice.

"I don't have to ask you," she said. "I know. It wasn't you, was it? It wasn't you, and everybody is letting you take the blame for it. Oh, Shep, I hate them all, and I almost hate you for letting them do it—"

"Sarah!" My eyes were shut tight with pain and despair. Her words and her rich, low voice were red-hot iron spears in my heart.

"Okay," she said softly. "All right. I'm sorry. I won't put you through any more of this. Will you give me some coffee, or a cup of tea? I'd absolutely love a bourbon and water, but that's out until the baby comes."

I heated water and poured it into an old Quimper cup with a tea bag and brought it, with one teaspoon of sugar as she took it, and put it on the table beside her.

"Thanks," she said, but she did not drink the tea. She sat, arms around her knees, staring into the ashes of last week's dead fire, which I had not yet cleaned out of the fireplace.

Out of nowhere, I heard myself say, "Sarah, are you happy?" and then wished I could bite off my tongue. We had been so careful, both of us, when we met, to steer our conversations extravagantly wide of these rapids.

She looked at me without surprise.

"Yes," she said. "Yes, I am happy. Not in the way you mean, I don't think, but in another and very good way I *am* happy. How could I not be? Charlie is maybe the best man I've ever known, in the real sense of the word, and he's wonderful to me, and this baby has made me happier than I ever dreamed it would. I really didn't know I was going to feel this way about having a baby. I'll probably have seven thousand of them."

She paused, and then she said, "I won't ever be happy the way we could have been happy together, but this is another thing entirely, and it was a total surprise to me. I did marry Charlie on the rebound, Shep, and he knew I did, and I don't deserve what I got in return for that. But you don't have to worry about me."

"I won't, then," I said, my eyes stinging. "Are you painting now?"

She laughed, uncomfortably, I thought. "Where in the world would I paint in that doll's house?" she said. "And then Dr. Farmer doesn't want me to fool around with all that lead until the baby's here. There'll be plenty of time for painting."

"Don't stop too long," I said. "You're too good. It's too much a part of you."

"It was a part of something else," she said. Her voice sounded as though she was talking to herself. "It just doesn't seem to have anything to do with now. It's . . . not real, somehow."

I was silent, and so was she. She drank off her tea, and looked at me obliquely, and I was aware that there had sprung up in the air between us a strain so intense and uncomfortable that it was almost palpable. We were out of things that could safely be spoken of, and neither of us dared enter that other country.

Finally she rose and I walked to the door with her, and she reached up and kissed me on the cheek and said, "Is this as hard on you as it is on me?"

"Yes," I said.

"I thought it was," she said, grinning her old light-up-the-world grin. My heart did its now-accustomed, aching fish flop.

"I don't think I'll come again, Shep," she said. "Maybe sometime with Charlie, but not often. You understand why, I know. And I think you know that we . . . that I love you. I'll be here in two seconds flat if you need me. But we can't be . . . just friends."

"No," I said. It was true. Sarah and I could be perfectly amiable acquaintances, and we had, at least once, been truly glorious lovers, but simple friendship was now forever lost to us.

For the first time since that night so long ago in the same room with Lucy, I drank until the bourbon tide took me completely under and when I awoke it was morning, and the sun was high.

On a day in March of booming wind and high sun, when the first of the great spring skies had begun, a man from Southern Bell came in his panel truck with instructions to install a telephone in the summerhouse. When I asked him who had authorized it, he jerked a thumb backward and said, "Lady in the big house yonder."

"Well, you can tell the lady in the big house yonder that I don't want a telephone, thanks just the same," I said. "Wait a minute, let me get you something for your trouble, though."

"You Mr. Bondurant?" he said.

"Yes."

"Lady said to tell you not to be an ass, that she was tired of waiting for you to come to her, and she couldn't very well come to you. Said to call her the minute this thing was in. Said you'd know who she was."

I did, too. The "ass" had tipped me off. It was not my mother's style.

When the phone was installed, I sat down and dialed Merrivale House. Dorothy Cameron answered on the second ring.

"Well," she said. "The corpse that speaks like a man. Can you walk, too, or is it just the voice that works?"

"Dorothy, you ought to know me well enough to know I don't want this goddamned thing," I said. "Appreciate the gesture though I do. My mother will be on it fourteen times a day."

"She won't if you don't tell her you have it," she said. "I told them to bill me for it. It's not charity. I fully intend you to pay me back. Listen, Shep, I want to see you. Enough of this foolishness is enough. I'd come over there, but somebody would be sure to see me—I'm not about to crawl through the brush with a knife in my teeth like Ben does—and it would get back to Olivia that I was sneaking over there to see you, when I won't even speak to her, and the fat really would be in the fire. I want to be able to talk to you when I want to, and for starters I want you to come over here."

"Over there?" I said. "Now?"

"Well, now would be wonderful, but I don't think I can expect that from Buckhead's only authentic hermit, can I? No, come after dark, if you don't want to see anybody, and let yourself in the sun porch door. Ben will be downtown at a meeting tonight."

"I don't know, Dorothy," I began. The thought of leaving the summerhouse suddenly panicked me.

"Get over here, Shep, before you freeze up entirely and really aren't able to leave that pretty little prison of yours," she said curtly, and I said I would. I knew that I would have to leave the summerhouse sometime and venture out into the world, and that what she said was true. I was indeed in danger, as each day went by, of never leaving it at all.

I started out after dark that night, thinking to go through the woods, but suddenly the close-pressing undergrowth and trees felt suffocating and fetid, and the night wind was dense and heavy with swelling buds and sweetness and the promise of spring. On impulse I turned toward the big house and began to trot, and jogged past it down the drive to the sidewalk, and soon was loping flat out up Peachtree Road toward Muscogee. I wore tennis shoes and my old high school warm-up sweats, and the sidewalk felt wonderful under my feet, almost springy, and the tight muscles in my calves and thighs worked and throbbed and loosened. There was no one on the sidewalk, though cars went by steadily on Peachtree Road, and except for the pale pools of the streetlights, I ran in cool, sweet darkness. My heart labored in my chest, and a stitch started, flamelike, under my ribs, but the singing, free-ranging wind ran behind me, propelling me along, and by the time I turned the corner onto Muscogee and began the long pound down its first dark hill, I felt that I was naked as a newborn and swimming, drowning in air and space. It was a wonderful feeling, glorious. When I came crunching up to the side door to the Camerons' sun porch I was soaked through and blowing like a dolphin, but I felt light as a hollowed reed, and clean.

I hugged Dorothy Cameron in an excess of euphoria, aware all at once how very much I had missed her. In her long cherry velvet robe she looked, in the lamplight, so much like Sarah that I had to laugh. Only the streaks of silver in her coarse curls gave her age away, those and the fine little lines that radiated out from the corners of her eyes. Her strong chin and cheekbones were just as clean and chiseled as Sarah's, and her step as light. She laughed back at me, and hugged me, and held her nose lightly.

"To quote Leroy," she said, "you smells tired. Is you been working?"

"No," I said. "I's been running."

She poured me a bourbon without asking if I wanted it, and one for herself, and we sat in the little sun porch that was almost as familiar to me as the one at 2500 Peachtree Road, and talked. On shelves and on the paneling of the fireplace wall the lares and penates of that great house rested: Ben's civic awards and honorary degrees and diplomas, young Ben's trophies and plaques, Sarah's swimming and diving ribbons and medals and her wonderful, incandescent paintings. I felt a keen physical pang looking at the paintings; they were like the left-behind clothing of someone who had died. Ben's trophies troubled me, too, though the import of the feeling eluded me. I kept my eyes, for the rest of the evening, on Dorothy.

She did not speak of the fire and its aftermath except to say, "It's time you began to come out of the summerhouse now," and, when I asked her if she really hadn't spoken to my mother since, "I really haven't and I probably won't. She's beyond my forgiveness or lack of it, but she shan't have it, anyway."

And so I knew that she, unlike her daughter, had been told of my mother's part in the thing, and was, like the men of the Club, a member of the conspiracy of silence. I did not think she was a willing one. I knew that Ben had always told her everything and would not hold this from her, but I knew, too, that he would swear her to silence, and that she would honor it, even while hating her pledge. I suspected that she was the only woman in Atlanta except my mother and probably a number of black women who knew the entire truth. Something smoothed and eased deep within me, and a vestigial kind of peace breathed itself across my heart.

We talked, instead, of the comings and goings of Buckhead, and of its gossip and eccentricities, and of Ben's hopeful young term in the fast-changing city, and of the red-haired young president with his fingers in the sky as well as the earth, and of the accelerating civil rights movement and Lucy's deepening involvement in it. We talked of gardening and music, and the litter of kittens out in the garage, and the greening trees and the newly built beaver dam in the cold, deep little lake up at Tate, and of art and drama and travel. She said, ruefully, that she and Ben had had to give up a long-dreamed-of trip to Europe that May with more than a hundred members of the Atlanta Art Association, because Ben felt that a newly elected mayor shouldn't spend a month during the first year of his administration away from his city.

"I see his point," she said. "It would look awful. But Lord, I hate to miss that trip. Practically everybody on it is a lifelong friend of ours. It would be like a monthlong house party. It's been a long time since Ben and I have just cut loose and done anything silly. This would have been the perfect excuse. I tried to give the trip to Sarah and Charlie, but of course she's due in early June, and they don't get back until then. You don't want to go and take a friend, do you?"

"Not on your life," I said. "My mother's going. I don't think Europe's big enough for both of us."

She reached over and squeezed my hand. "If you can joke about it, you're going to be all right," she said.

"Of course I am," I said. "Did you think I wasn't?"

"I didn't know. It's been as bad a thing as you're likely to have in your life."

"Well, then," I said, "maybe it's good to get it over with early. From here on out will be gravy."

When I was 'set to leave, Dorothy Cameron did a wonderful thing for me. She probably did not even know how wonderful, though I think she had some idea that it would be useful. She took me into their library and showed me five large wooden crates sitting there on the old stone floor, and said that they were the diaries and journals her father, grandfather and great-grandfather had kept from childhood on. Three complete, lovingly and faithfully detailed patrician lives, bridging more than two hundred years and reaching from a Dorsetshire manor house to the warm red earth of Virginia, and then down through the Carolinas to, finally, Atlanta. The Chase men of Merrivale House, Dorset, and points far west and south, alive now in fine, spidery writing in volume after volume of yellowed vellum.

"It's an idea I had," she said, when I stood staring at the crates, uncomprehending. "I know how you love pure research, and I know what a gifted writer you are. And I know, too, that to save your soul and sanity you need some real work to do, something valuable. So I'm going to give you my family, instead of dumping them on the historical society where nobody will ever even read them, much less really see what's there. I'm not just being conceited, Shep. It strikes me that my family is almost laughably, prototypically Georgian—the compleat Georgians, sort of—from England via Virginia and the Carolinas and on down into Georgia and here. We didn't come over with the debtors just out of prison to Savannah, with Oglethorpe; there's been lots written about them. We were one of the few relatively educated and wellborn families to migrate to the colonies. I don't recall ever reading anything comprehensive about that sort of settler. But the South's bones rest on them. You have a huge work of history and sociology here, all bound together by blood ties, and in the words of the men who lived it. I think you ought to write it. I think you could do a splendid job of it. Altogether, it would take you about twenty years, but I suspect you've got the time. And it would be an enormously valuable thing to do. Would you like to try? I'd rather you did this with your life than take to drink or buggery or pedophilia."

The Compleat Georgian was born that night, and Dorothy was right. I fell in love with the gifted, ornery, eccentric men who were clamoring and jostling to get off those crumbling pages, and the liberation of them did indeed, many times over, save my sanity and my soul. Perhaps it may again. I would very much like to see the *Georgian* go out into the world, fully fleshed and breathing. If it should happen, it will be because Dorothy Cameron knew on that night, as perhaps no one else alive could know then, what it would take to redeem me. And she gave me, that evening, the next quarter century of my life. When I went home it was with Leroy in Ben's Lincoln, the five crates of Chases shimmering in their life and richness on the backseat and in the trunk.

I unloaded them that very evening, and the next morning, even before I could get a carpenter in to measure for the bookcases that would be needed to house them, I sat down on the floor in a pool of spring sunlight and began.

I had a sense that spring that I was, slowly and imperceptibly, fashioning a life for myself as well as an order for those other lives. Before, in the bowels of the New York Public Library, I had been merely passing through antiquity, biding time in the parchment lives of others. Now I was beginning to map a universe wherein I, as well as those captive Southerners, might honorably live. The thought was deeply satisfying, and fed, in part, the insatiable mouth of the pain that the fire and its aftermath, and my mother's terrified treachery, had unleashed.

It was a good thing. Almost no one from my previous life in Buckhead came near me that spring. I don't think it was censure so much as embarrassment, a kind of tribal reticence for which I myself had set the standard with my withdrawal, that kept the Buckhead Boys away from me. A.J. came, of course. And Charlie looked in occasionally, and Ben, and I talked with Dorothy Cameron regularly, but Sarah did not come again, and in midspring, even Lucy stopped her nearly nightly visits to the summerhouse with Jack. She called me one night, tears thick in her throaty voice, and told me that Jack had balked at coming by the house that evening, and that they had had a fight about it, and he had ended by refusing to visit anymore and forbidding her to come alone on the rare occasions when she had the Ford to herself.

"It's not you, Gibby," she said, around drags from her cigarette. She was drinking, too; I could hear the chink of ice against glass over the wire. "He's truly fond of you. It's me. He says I'm a bad example to the children, and that I'm neglecting them and spending all my free time with you. He says from now on we're coming straight home from work and doing things with the boys, like a normal family. It's bullshit, of course. We never were a normal family. They're not normal kids. They never liked me worth a damn, and it's worse now than it ever was, and they hate every minute I spend with them. These evenings together around the goddamned family hearth are as much an ordeal for them as they are for me. But Jack eats them up. All of a sudden he wants us to be Ozzie and Harriet, or the fucking Cleavers, or somebody. He knew I wasn't like that when he married me. He knew what I was; he knew where my real commitment was. This is a total switch. I can't be that kind of stupid, smirking little wife and mother."

All her saintliness seemed, in that moment, to have fled, and I was vaguely relieved.

"Maybe the kids will come around when they're a little more used to you," I said. "Nights at home with them for a while can't be all that bad."

"With those two they're hideous," she said. "Unless you're into advanced nose picking. There's no way they're ever going to accept me, Gibby. To their little minds now it was I who ran off their sainted mother. And to make it worse, Jack wants us to have a baby of our own. He's thrown away my diaphragm. We try every night—God, how we try. Wouldn't that be a fine mess, me pregnant as a yard dog trying to march and drive a bus and register voters?"

"Don't you want children?" I asked. "Somehow I just took it for granted that you'd have them."

"Not everybody is as maternal as your precious Sarah," she said waspishly, and then, "Oh Lord, I'm sorry. It's the liquor talking. I guess I'm jealous because I suspect that she'll be a better mother than I could in a million years. And then I have to be honest with you, I hate this business of your rooting around over there in Sarah's family tree."

"Why on earth would you hate that?" I said, honestly surprised. She had professed herself overjoyed that I had found significant and absorbing work to do. It would, she had said, make her feel much better to think that I was not withering with loneliness and isolation.

"I don't really know," she said. "It's illogical and totally unworthy. I guess . . . I just feel like it's one more tie to Sarah Cameron, and one that will last practically all your life. I don't know why that bothers me, but it does."

"Sarah is out of my life now, Luce," I said. "You know that as well as anybody."

"No I don't," she said in a low voice. But she dropped the subject, and thereafter, every night, her throaty "Hey, Gibby?" (Pause. Long, indrawn breath of cigarette smoke.) "It's Lucy, honey," prefaced my daily dose of life outside the summerhouse walls. I came to depend on it, and miss it keenly when, on rare occasions, it did not come. During those first long months of isolation, Lucy was my window on the world.

In early May my mother left with a hundred-odd members of the Atlanta Art Association for her monthlong tour of the galleries and museums of Europe, and I felt free to wander, in the late afternoons, into the big house. Sometimes I visited with Shem and Martha Cater in the kitchen, and sometimes I went upstairs and sat for a few silent minutes beside my father, mute and captive still in his warped flesh, and sometimes I simply sat on the little sun porch off the living room, with the afternoon light falling on the black and white tiled floor and the deep green walls and the airy white wicker furniture, deep-cushioned in what my mother always called "Dorothy Draper red." The cush-

ion in the big armchair that had been my father's was gradually
springing back without the ongoing burden of his heavy frame,
and the indentation there now fit my own thinner and lighter
body. It was the only place in my mother's house where I felt
that I had some small territorial imperative. By this time, I no
longer thought of it as my father's house. Even an ocean away,
my mother dominated it now.

On the first Sunday morning in June, I was hovering between
sleep and an elusive wakefulness that promised breakfast in the
sun-room of the big house, where I had taken it for the past four
Sunday mornings of my mother's absence, with a pot of coffee
and the Sunday papers. She was due home from Paris late that
evening, and then my tenure as master of the manor at 2500
Peachtree Road would end. I did not mind, except for the loss
of those tranquil Sunday mornings, and was considering abandoning sleep for waffles and sausage when I heard the bedroom
door open and a soft voice call, "Shep?"

Even with my eyes closed, even half-submerged in sleep, I
knew the voice was Sarah's, but I was not surprised. In that half-
lit world where all ambiguities can be rationalized and all dis-
crepancies justified, I felt only a deep, sweet contentment at the
rightness of Sarah's voice calling me out of sleep, and I felt myself smile even before I opened my eyes. I kept them closed for
a moment, knowing that the perfect contentment would flee with
the falling of the light upon them.

I felt her weight as she sat down on the edge of my bed, and
was reaching out for her, eyes still closed, when she said again,
"Shep," and this time something in her voice snapped my lids
up as if they were attached to wires. I sat up in the tumbled bed
and blinked against the fierce white June light streaming in from
the door through which she had just entered, and looked at her.

At first I thought she had come to tell me of some terrible
thing that had happened to Charlie, or her soon-to-be-born baby,
for her face was so swollen and distorted from crying that I could
scarcely recognize her, and I could hear the sobs caught in her
throat and see its strong column trying to work around the strangling brine. Fresh tears ran from her reddened eyes and dripped
from her chin onto her maternity smock, and I stared stupidly
at the splotches they made against the blue chambray. It was
only then that I realized that nothing could be wrong with the
baby, because it was still there, a great, elastic mound under the
smock. I lifted my eyes in dread from the front of her to her face.

"Has something happened to Charlie?" I said. I could scarcely
form the words.

"No. Not Charlie. It's . . . Shep, Daddy just got a call from

Carter Stephenson at WSB. The . . . the . . . your mother's
plane . . . it crashed, Shep. It crashed on takeoff at Orly, and
I'm afraid they're all gone. It's just now coming in over the radio,
and there aren't any details yet, but Daddy made sure there's
been no mistake, and . . . I'm sorry." She dropped her face into
her hands and wept aloud. "I'm sorry. I came over here to tell
you because I didn't want you to hear it by yourself on the radio
or when some reporter calls, and now I can't . . ."

"All gone," I said, stupidly. "That's absurd, Sarah. It has to
be a mistake. There were too many of them . . ."

The pit of my stomach was icy cold, and the coldness was
seeping up and out and into my arms and legs, turning them flaccid and useless. I remember thinking very clearly that if I got
up out of the bed I would crumple to the floor, or worse, wet
my pants. But beyond that I could not seem to think, and I did
not feel anything at all. Despite what I had said, I knew, somehow, that Sarah was right. She would never come here to bring
me such news unless she was absolutely sure that there could
be no possibility of mistake. My ponderous mind, struggling to
get into some kind of forward gear, embraced another tidbit of
information like a jellyfish settling down over a minnow, and set
about assimilating it.

"More than a hundred," I said. "More than a hundred, and
I . . . you . . . we knew all of them. That was Buckhead, Sarah.
Those were the people we've known all our lives."

"One hundred and six of them," she said, as if she were recit-
ing sums in school. "One hundred and six members of the Art
Association. One hundred and fourteen people from Georgia.
A hundred and twenty-nine in all . . ."

"Survivors," I said thickly. "Were there any survivors? You
can't be sure about that yet. . . ."

"Two or three people, when part of the plane broke off," she
said.

"Maybe . . . " I began.

"No. They were all crew. Nobody else. Nobody, Shep. All
gone."

"Jesus," I said, utterly crazily. "Aunt Willa can move out of
the attic."

"Oh, my poor darling Shep," Sarah cried, and put her arms
around me and buried her face in my shoulder, in the hollow
where it had always fit so neatly, and I held her as she cried,
thinking only that holding Sarah now was like holding a basketball between us. The glacier that had crept down over my mind
was snowy and seamless, perfect.

Presently she lifted her head and wiped her eyes and looked
at me.

"I told Charlie I'd be right back," she said. "He's over at the house with Mother. Daddy's gone down to City Hall. He's going to Paris tonight. Mother is in pretty bad shape; everybody on that plane was her and Daddy's close friend from babyhood, practically. I wanted to come and tell you, and Charlie said I should. . . . Shep, I'd like to stay with you today, if you'll let me. I don't want you to be by yourself. Or maybe you'd come back with me to Mother and Daddy's . . ."

"No. Thank you, Sarah, but I think I'll go out to Lucy's," I said, surprising myself. I could think of little with my rational mind that would be as comfortless as that meager little farmhouse in the company of a taciturn Jack Venable and the two sullen changelings. But something in me, powerful and visceral, wanted my cousin Lucy. We had both lost the great anchor of our childhoods, cold iron though it was, and I did not think that Sarah, with her constant legacy of Ben and Dorothy's clear, sunlit love, could begin to understand the clutching complexities of that loss. I was perfectly numb now, but I knew that the numbness would not last, and when it lifted, I wanted to be with the one person who would understand my canted grief—if grief, indeed, there was.

"I understand," Sarah said in a small voice, and I thought my old radar, once so alive to all of Sarah's tides and nuances, detected a tiny edge of hurt.

She got up to go, ponderous and bowed under the weight of the low-hanging baby and the grief, and said, "We're only a few steps away, and we want you to come or call any time of the night or day. Mother said to tell you the guest room is made up and ready, if you'd like to spend the night, and in any case she'll call in an hour or two."

"Thank you. Thank you both," I said. "Tell her for me. And thank you for coming, Sarah. It must have been hard for you. . . ."

"Of course I would come," she said, beginning to cry again. "Of course I would come. Nothing on earth would have kept me away. . . ."

"I know that," I said. "Go on home now. Your mother will need you. I'll be all right. I've got to talk to Aunt Willa and see about telling my father."

"Oh God," she said, and went out of the summerhouse, sobbing.

After she left, I simply sat there in the June morning, trying to keep the cold silence white and perfect in my mind. But the edges of it now were beginning to be licked with flame.

The telephone rang, and I lifted it and laid the receiver on the table, where it burred hopelessly for what seemed an eternity be-

fore stopping. I got up and walked on reedy, wavering legs over
to the radio, and switched it on.

The reports were fuller now, and clearer. At a little after noon,
6:29 A.M. Atlanta time, the chartered Air France Boeing 707,
carrying a full crew and complement of passengers, skidded off
a runway on takeoff at Orly Field, Paris, killing all passengers
and all but two of its crew in a fireball of yellow JP4 fuel when
it exploded in a gully at the end of the strip. Among the victims
were 106 members of the Atlanta Art Association returning
from a month's vacation via the chartered jet. It was the worst
single-plane disaster in aviation history. Most of the charred
bodies, still strapped into their seats, had not yet been recovered,
but those that had were being taken to temporary morgues in
an old part of Orly Airport. Later they would be taken to the
morgues of Paris. . . .

I sat there for a long time, mindless, floating, while the news
from France swelled and grew like a monstrous lily. An entire
family of six: the Carters . . . I had known them all. Sister Carter
had been one of the prettiest Pinks of my generation. Freddy had
run track two years ahead of me at North Fulton. Twenty-seven
married couples, many of them with children back in Atlanta.
Doctors, lawyers, brokers, businessmen, bankers, ministers, artists, patrons, philanthropists—the civic, cultural and business
leadership of a city of a million people, their names familiar to
anyone who read the newspapers of that city, in stories concern-
ing the Capital City Club, the Driving Club, business development, hospital aid, opera, symphony, drama, art shows. . . .
Thirteen Junior Leaguers. Thirty members of the Driving Club.
Twenty-one of the Capital City Club. Old Atlanta. Buckhead.
"In the City of Light," a eulogy later that week read, "all that
bright light gone."

And Olivia Redwine Bondurant. She, too. Gone. Burned up
in a radiant mushroom three thousand miles away from
Peachtree Road. I was, I thought in dull surprise, in all but
name, an orphan. The thought was as alien as if someone had
suddenly assigned to me the appellation "assassin" or "revolutionary," and had as little relevance. I could not rid myself of
the image of my mother's long, lustrous, black hair, loose from
its elegant twist and aflame. For a long time it was the only image
in all that silent, hissing whiteness in my mind. Around me, the
silence hammered and rang, and the light grew very bright, then
dimmed.

After a while I picked up the telephone and dialed Lucy and
Jack's number. Jack answered on the second ring, in an angry
whisper.

"She's been trying to get you for an hour," he said. "She was hysterical; she needed you, and she couldn't get you."

"I'll come now," I said. I was surprised to hear that my voice was steady.

"No. I've given her two tranquilizers and she's finally asleep. Don't come. It will only upset her now. Later, maybe, when she's had some rest—"

I hung up on him.

"What about me, you asshole?" I said aloud, but without heat. "It's my mother who was sizzled down to a cinder, not Lucy's." I could not seem to stop yawning. I sat for a moment, not knowing what to do with myself, and then got up and walked up to the big house. Aunt Willa would, I knew, be at church at Saint Philip's, but I did not want a nurse blurting out the news to my father.

Someone had obviously just called Shem and Martha Cater, looking for me, for Shem was on his way out the back door, his dark face actually ashen.

"Mr. Shep . . . " he began, and I saw that there were tears in his brown eyes, and that the yellowed whites of them were red with veins. I could not imagine that he had in any sense of the word loved my mother, but she and my father had given shape and definition to his and Martha's lives for the past thirty years or so. The simple shock must have been profound. They would feel as lost and rudderless as I did.

"Has my father heard?" I said.

"No, suh. He asleep. I tol' the nurse to give him two of them pills, an' hush up that cryin' when he wake up. He gon' sleep for a spell now."

"Good work, Shem," I said.

I put my hand on his shoulder, and he covered it with his rough brown one. We stood silent for a moment, and then he said, simply, "What we gon' do now?"

"Bring the Rolls around," I said, again enormously surprised at my own words, but knowing instantly that they were the right ones. "I'm going down to City Hall."

"Yessuh," he said, straightening his shoulders, and I thought that his step, as he turned away toward the garage, was stronger and more purposeful. When I had changed clothes and come out into the portico, he was standing beside the ridiculous, shining cliff of a car almost at attention, wearing a severe, dark livery that I had never seen.

"What's with the uniform, Shem?" I said, getting into the backseat.

"You goin' to see about bringing Miss Olivia home, ain't you?" he said.

"I guess so," I said, knowing only then that I was.

"Well, then," Shem Cater said.

He said nothing else on the drive down the empty, sunny Sunday waste of Peachtree Road, a black man of Buckhead on the first leg of a long, long journey to bring his mistress home again. His silence, and the livery, pierced me like nothing else did the whole of that endless and terrible day.

It felt strange to be out, after the weeks of seclusion in the summerhouse. The very air and space around me pressed on my back and shoulders, as if I were stark naked, and terribly vulnerable. The feeling intensified the overbright queerness of the day.

The street in front of City Hall was deserted, but the flags already hung at half-staff, and when I climbed the curving, shallow marble stairs to Ben Cameron's office on the second floor, the crowd spilled out into the corridor. I recognized several people I knew, and stared, puzzled, until I remembered that of course, the crash in France was a Buckhead tragedy; almost everyone who had died in that ditch outside Paris had lived within two or three square miles of one another. These familiar faces, white and blank with the same shock that must have been mirrored on mine, were here on the same mission I was: to learn from our elected chieftain what we must do next. We nodded to one another, but did not speak. The tears, the comfortings, the mutual embraces, would come later, with the pain.

Most of the crowd were reporters, though, and I was scarcely on the top step before I saw recognition dawn on the first face, and then two or three of them detached themselves from the rest and began to move toward me. I could read "human interest" all over their pale, avid faces; here was the very fallen princeling slum lord whose mother had so recently condemned him for all the world's delectation, come to lay claim to her charred flesh. Cameras swung into position and sweat broke out on my forehead. My heart began a sick trip-hammering, and nausea rose into my throat. I turned my head from side to side in panic; there was no retreat from them, and I knew that I could not face them.

I saw them lower the cameras and step back before I felt the hands on my shoulders from behind, and then they parted and made a path for me, and I was steered through them and into the outer office and beyond it, into Ben's own private office. The door closed firmly, and I turned around to see Glenn Pickens, massive and looming in his dark suit and tie, his long yellow face hard and still and something looking out of his obsidian eyes that would have scattered far more than a band of reporters.

"Thanks, Glenn," I said weakly.

"I'm sorry, Shep," he said in his flat voice. "About all of it."

We looked at each other for a moment, and then he turned and went out of the office without speaking again and closed the door behind him, and I looked through the small knot of silent people to where Ben Cameron leaned against his desk, a telephone to his ear and one in his hand. He looked up and saw me and paused a moment in his conversation, and then lifted the idle receiver and motioned me into a chair and went on talking. I sat down and watched him.

He was dressed in the tennis clothes he had obviously been wearing when the first call came, and there were streaks of red dust on his shoes and shorts. I knew from those that he had been playing at the Rawsons'; they had the only dirt court in Buckhead. His face was bone-white beneath the permanent tan and the scattering of dark freckles across his cheekbones, and the flesh of it looked stretched and flayed, almost hanging from his thin, good bones. He looked older by years than I had ever seen him, and his gray eyes were almost as red and swollen as his daughter's had been that morning. For the first time I thought what exquisite anguish he must be living. Not only had he lost nearly a hundred of the people who were the mainstays of his life, but he must bury his own grief deep and act with coolness, grace and authority for their families and the city at large; swallow his own pain that theirs might be the more quickly assuaged. Most of us could retreat into the comfort of our substantial caves, dragging our sorrow in behind us like bones, and press close among the pack of our peers for warmth, but he must go now, his own agony deep and silent, to a foreign land and sift those burned bones and see them home again, the eyes of the world upon him, and then come home himself and start his city forward once more. It would be a long time before Ben Cameron could weep, or even sleep. I felt a great rush of pure love for him. I had no doubt at all that he could and would do it, and do it well.

Despite the pandemonium in the outside office, which had been set up as a sort of nerve center for the press, the inner one was quiet. Ben's assistant, Peg Hartley, ample and tearstained and capable, manned another telephone. Two or three aides came in and out with telegrams and lists and statements to be read and signed. A shrunken, silent Air France representative slumped in a chair by a window. Snake Cheatham's father and Doug Fowler, Mr. Woodruff's right-hand man at Coca-Cola, stood together at another window, backs to the room, talking in low voices. Carter Stephenson from WSB and Gordy Farr from the *Constitution* sat facing each other across a small table, writing furiously. On Ben's desk I saw a yellow telegram, atop a steadily mounting pile, that read, "Mrs. Kennedy and I are terribly distressed to learn of the plane crash in France which cost your community and the country so heavily. Please convey our very deepest sympathy to the families who experienced this tragedy." A note in Dorothy's handwriting said, "I've sent Leroy over to get Alice and Bax's children and their clothes until Tully can get herself together. If anyone calls about them, tell them they're with us, and I don't think they know anything yet."

Alice and Baxter Fuller, young Ben's age, the latter Ben Senior's godchild, among the youngest of the couples to die in the crash. Married their freshman year at the university, they had had their family immediately, and the two little boys were now five and three. This had been the first time Alice and Bax had ever left them; I remembered that Dorothy had said she and Ben had practically browbeat them into taking the vacation and leaving the children with their grandmother and nurse. I could only imagine how they must feel about that. Besides being personally beloved of them, Bax Fuller was obviously going to be one of the most luminous of the next generation, a prime contender to take up the torch of the Club. A rising young lawyer, church elder, former president of the Legal Aid Society, Atlanta's Outstanding Young Man a few years earlier, a director of the state YMCA and member of the Driving Club and Commerce Club, a nearly lone young voice lifted against segregation—and a Buckhead Jell without peer. The flames in my white mind, which had engulfed only the hair of my mother, reached out now to frame another known and living face, this one nearly my own age.

Ben put the phone down and came around the desk and hugged me.

"Bad news, partner," he said. "Bad day. The worst. I'm sorrier than I can say about your mother."

"Thanks," I said. "I'm . . . me, too. It's just not possible to believe it, is it?"

"Ah, God, no," he said, and his voice broke. "Christ, Shep, this was . . . my entire generation. I grew up with most of these folks. Laura Rainey was the first date I ever had; we went to a swimming party at Sibley French's house, and she had a two-piece bathing suit. We all talked about that for weeks. And if I hadn't met Dorothy I probably would have married Jane Ellen Alexander. And the first time I ever got drunk—and practically the last—was with Tommy Burns, up at Tate one Fourth of July, on sloe gin. Whit Turner and Howard Shelton and Marjorie Callahan . . . dear God, it's like a small city was just wiped out, or a little country. And in a way it was. . . ."

He stopped and rubbed his eyes, and looked at me.

"Is there anything special I can do for you?" he said. "You know I'm going over tonight. I promise you I'll . . . see that she gets home safely."

"I want to go with you, Ben," I said.

He shook his head back and forth quickly, no, and opened his mouth to speak, and then stopped.

"There's no way it's going to be anything but grim," he said. "And there's nothing you can do—there's probably not much even I can do. This is the time for official people, the medical and government boys, and they're not going to take too kindly to me, much less you . . ."

"I won't get in the way," I said. "You won't even know I'm there. But I've got to go, Ben. And I really want it to be with you."

"All right," he said finally. "I guess this is one trip you've earned. Got a passport?"

"Oh God—no," I said.

"Doug," Ben called across the room to Doug Fowler. "Can the Man pull one more string and get us another passport by tonight?"

Doug Fowler looked dubiously at me. "I guess he can, if it's absolutely necessary," he said.

"It is," Ben Cameron said. "See about another seat on the five-fifty-five Delta flight to New York while you're at it, too."

To me he said, "You're calling in an awful lot of chips at one time, Shep."

"I know," I said. "There isn't any way I can thank you."

"Yes there is, but that can come later," he said, and went back to the telephone. I went out to the curb, where Shem Cater was idling the Rolls, and he drove me home to change. On the way, I heard Ben's voice, deep and quiet and measured, begin an official statement over the radio: "Atlanta has suffered her greatest tragedy and loss. Our deepest sympathy is extended . . ."

"Turn it off, Shem," I said, and he did. We rode on home in silence.

An hour later, as I walked into the big house with a small bag, dressed for my flight and dreading with all my cold, still heart going up to tell my father, Aunt Willa came tapping down to meet me, still in the white linen suit she had worn to church. Her face was colorless and blank, and her eyes looked somehow bleached, giving her the unfocused, witless look of a trapped rabbit. Her hands shook slightly, and she kept wetting her red lips with her tongue. I stared at her. What I read on her exquisitely enameled face was not grief, but fear, pure and simple. I could have imagined several reactions from my aunt Willa in the face of losing by violence her sister-in-law and captor, but fear was not one of them.

"Is my father awake?" I said.

"He's just stirring. I came down to see if you wanted me to tell him. I know it isn't my place, but he sometimes seems to accept things from me that he won't from the nurse, and I know how terrible this is for you. . . ." Her voice actually cracked, high and crystalline, with the weight of the fear.

All at once I knew what she was afraid of, and a powerful surge of sympathy stirred me. It was gone quickly, but in its aftermath I felt closer to Willa Slagle Bondurant than I ever had, or ever would again. As awful as her servitude to my mother had been, and as odious her position of sufferance in this house must have felt to her, there was still a sort of warped symbiosis between them, a twisted but unbreakable bond which held her secure even as it bound her fast. Now that her smiling jailer was dead, that tie was gone, and I, the presumed successor, had no reason at all to honor or even tolerate her presence here. Both her dependent daughters were in the care of husbands, and she herself, as she well knew, was, in her tricked-up little attic suite, only one step away from the actual street. I knew, in that instant, so completely how she felt that my own mouth went dry. My own tenure here had often felt precisely that fragile.

I set down my bag and put my arm around her shoulders and sat her down on the bottom stair in the foyer.

"I'd be very grateful if you'd tell him," I said. "He's been more your responsibility than anybody's since we brought him home, and nobody has a better right than you. It's just something I don't think I can do. I'll see about him when I get back, but for the time being, I wish you'd take charge of him."

She simply looked at me, her huge eyes filling, incredibly, with tears. She did not speak.

"And, Aunt Willa, for God's sake, get your things out of that damned attic and move them down to Mother's room," I said. "There's no sense in it just sitting there empty, and I'm not about to move from where I am. I want to see you settled in there when I get back, okay?"

She only nodded, tears tracking mascara down her satiny cheeks, the red mouth trembling. She leaned forward and gave me a little hug, and I heard her whisper, "Thank you, Shep." As I closed the great white door behind me and got into the Rolls, I reached up and touched the wetness her tears had left on my face.

I never saw her cry again.

When I got to the Delta gate that afternoon, Lucy Venable

was waiting for me. She sat with a small suitcase beside her, feet firmly together, hands folded in her lap like a good child waiting for her train back to school. Her head was bowed and I could see that her eyes and nose were red, but her face was calm and still, and she showed no signs of the hysteria against which Jack had sedated her that morning. She looked surprisingly well, even rather wonderful, considering both her alleged prostration and her recent appearance. Her blue-black hair was back in its old glossy, raven's-wing pageboy, falling forward against her high cheekbones, and she wore a red linen sheath and a red lacquered straw pillbox hat and low-heeled alligator pumps, none of which I had ever seen before. Several eyes in the crowd at the gate were on her, and coming upon her like this, unexpectedly and without context, I could see why. Lucy looked entirely herself again, awash, somehow, in the invisible fire that used to cling about her.

She lifted her head and saw me, and jumped up and ran to me, throwing her arms around me, and by now all the eyes swung to us. Her face was devoid of makeup and very pale, but her extraordinary eyes danced with the old October flame, and she smelled of her signature Tabu. She kissed me on the cheek, and I felt her heart hammering against my chest, and she whispered into my ear, "We're not going to talk about Aunt Olivia, not right now, so don't worry. I'm going to help you, not make things harder for you."

"You look really wonderful," I said. "Did you come to see me off? Where's Jack?"

"Thanks," she said, smiling her great, affirming old Lucy-smile. "I borrowed it all, lock, stock and barrel, from Little Lady not two hours ago. And no, I didn't come to see you off. I came to see you on. And Jack's at home, sulking in his tent."

"To see me on . . ."

"I'm going with you. I borrowed the fare from Carter. I have a seat and a passport—it's all arranged. There's nothing at all for you to bother about."

Before I could reply Ben Cameron came up with Hinton Drexel, the city attorney, and Carter Stephenson from WSB.

"Hello, sugar," he said, kissing Lucy. "Shep. You've got the prettiest bon voyage committee in the place, I see. We about ready? They're holding a block of seats for us."

I opened my mouth, not knowing at all what I was going to say, but Lucy spoke before I could.

"I'm coming with you, Mr. Cameron," she said. "You can put me off this plane if you want to, but I'll just get on another one if you do. There is no way Shep is going over there to see about his mama without me."

Ben Cameron looked from her to me in silence, and then shrugged. "It's a free country," he said, with a faint grin. "And a free airline. I'm sure Shep will be glad of your company, Lucy."

And so it was that Lucy Bondurant Venable sat beside me, those long hours into and out of New York, and later, over the limitless black Atlantic, as I flew to Paris, France, to attend to the mortal remains of the mother who had so loved and injured me, and who had never loved her niece at all. It was, I reflected somewhere in midflight over all that wild, heaving blackness, an awesome show of power, even though posthumous.

Ben and Hinton Drexel and Carter Stephenson slept very little. I saw them, heads together in the seats in front of me, talking in low voices, whenever I lurched up out of the thin, sporadic sleep that swirled foglike about me in the darkened plane. Lucy did not talk much. After eating her dinner, during which she told me matter-of-factly that Jack was blackly furious with her for coming and had refused to drive her to the airport, and so she had simply taken a taxi from the farm to Little Lady Rawson's house on Dellwood and put the arm on Carter for the enormous fare, she said, "I'm going to sleep if I can, and you should, too. Tomorrow is going to be a god-awful day," and huddled up into the corner by the window and slept, her hand in mine. After an hour or so I had the stewardess bring us a couple of blankets and pillows, and tucked Lucy into them and put my own head back, and to my surprise, did sleep a little. The first time I awoke, she had thrashed around in her seat so that her head drooped onto my shoulder, and I laid my cheek on her sleek crown and drifted back under, the clean, warm smell of her hair and her Tabu curling down into sleep with me. Whenever I awoke after that, the soft weight of her, and her scent, told me where I was, and why. When I came fully awake the last time, sweating and struggling up out of dreams of flames and endless running, she was yawning and stretching, and the early sun was touching the blazing silver wings of the big TWA jet, and below us, still blue with darkness, the lights of Paris were going out, one by one.

As we began the long circle for our approach into Orly, Ben came and sat down on the arm of my seat. He had straightened his tie and put his jacket back on and combed the iron-threaded red hair, and looked, incredibly, controlled and immaculate, every inch the mayor of a great city. Only his gray eyes, pouched and dull with fatigue and pain, betrayed the long night's anguish.

"I want to tell you what I know about the crash," he said. "There's probably not going to be time later, and I don't even know who, if anybody, will be meeting us, and how much English will be spoken. This is everything I have; it's all the Air France people could give me just before we left New York."

He took a deep breath, and so did I. Beside me, Lucy shifted in her seat and took my hand. The Air France flight, borne by the chartered Boeing 707 *Château de Sully,* was about to become alive at last, and I don't think any of us was sure we could bear the reality.

"They started down the runway on time, at about twelve-thirty," Ben said. "From what the witnesses say, they never lifted off the ground. The pilot must have realized immediately that something was wrong—apparently he locked the wheels and tried to abort. The tires wore off on the runway, and then the rims; they say you can see the skid marks for about eleven hundred feet. It clipped a couple of telephone poles and jumped an access road and slid another thousand feet on its belly and went into a maintenance shed. That's what broke it up and probably what caused the explosion—that and all those tons of fuel that flooded through the fuselage. It stopped within a hundred yards of some little town near the airport; they think the pilot was trying to avoid it. It flew apart in several pieces, and they all burned except the tail section. That's where the crew that survived were. They were thrown clear. Practically the whole village heard and saw it, as well as a crowd at the airport, but nobody has any idea what went wrong, or why the pilot tried to abort. It's not likely anyone ever will. Fire trucks were there almost immediately, and people from the village, but they couldn't get close enough to pull anybody out, and in any case it would have been too late. It was . . . very, very quick."

Nobody spoke, and then I said, "So they were . . . blown up."

"No," Ben Cameron said. "They were incinerated. The fuel was a fire storm. It burned itself out pretty quickly, but there's no question of any identification."

Lucy made a small sound beside me, and her nails dug deep into my palm. I did not feel them; it was only later that I saw the red crescents where they had bitten into the flesh. But she did not cry out.

"I'm sorry, Lucy," Ben said. "But you need to know what to expect, both of you. I imagine there'll be some international press there, and we may—you may, Shep—have to try and identify . . . any personal effects. I don't want you to be sandbagged in front of reporters and cameras. I'm here to represent the whole city, and you'll be doing that too, like it or not, just because you're with me. If you think you can't handle it, I'll get somebody to take you to a private lounge in the airport till we get done there. I surely wouldn't blame you. I don't know if I can handle it myself, and I don't have anybody kin to me down there. Lucy, I'm afraid I'm going to have to ask you to stay behind when we go . . . to the morgues. It's just no place for you."

"All right, Mr. Cameron," Lucy said meekly, and I shot a sideways look at her. I knew with my old, infallible Lucy-radar that she had no intention of staying behind while I combed the scene of the sunlit slaughter for evidence of my mother. I knew too, with the same antennae, that she would be all right. I could not say the same for myself. I still felt no emotion, but a fine, delicate trembling had taken possession of my arms and legs, and my veins felt as though they crawled with swarming bees. I did not think I could stand or walk.

After Ben went back to his seat and we began our descent, Lucy took my hand into both of hers and turned it over so that my wrist was exposed. She put her cheek down and pressed it against the thin white bracelet of the scar the kitchen knife had made so long ago, out behind the summerhouse.

"You didn't faint or get sick or anything that time," she said. "Remember? You went right ahead and did it, and in the end you were fine. It must have hurt you like hell, because it did me, and I'm not even funny about blood. But you did it. And you can do this. There won't be any blood, Gibby, and there wasn't ever any pain. There couldn't have been time for that. Not even time to be afraid. Just . . . light. Remember that. Clean, radiant light. That's all. I know I can do it, and I know you can, too, because we be of one blood, thou and I."

And even though I knew that she was wrong about the fear, that there would have been time for that, and that one day, sooner or later, the awful speculation about what the last moments before impact must have been like for those hundred of my friends and acquaintances and my mother would come to haunt my days and nights—even though I knew all that as well as I knew that Lucy sat beside me in an airline seat—I knew, too, that I could indeed do what I had come to do. Clean, radiant light . . .

I could do it.

"I love you, Lucy," I said.

We stepped out into the hot morning light of Paris and into a controlled frenzy of official sympathy. There must have been thirty or forty people in all, many of them members of the French official family, in frock coats and striped trousers, others representatives of government agencies and private concerns with connections to the airline. The American ambassador, a short, solid man who looked as though he should be walking an I beam high above a city somewhere, was on hand with members of his staff, and behind them all, held at bay by a cordon of blue-coated gendarmes, a couple of hundred reporters waited quietly. I remember virtually nothing of those first minutes except being handed from one pumping hand and working mouth to another, nodding and smiling inanely, with Lucy behind me murmuring softly, over and over, *"Merci, monsieur. Merci, bien sûr."*

The only clear thought I carried away with me from that morning was surprise that she knew French—I had not known that she studied it at Scott. Once I looked back and saw that a small throng of the dignified and formidable Frenchmen in their grand, ritual morning costumes were clustered about her, bowing deeply over her outstretched hand and kissing it, and I thought how typical of Lucy that she should come, uninvited and without status, in her sister's borrowed red, and steal the entire show from the newly prestigious dead of Atlanta. My mother, I thought, would be furious with her. I suppressed a horrifying desire to giggle, and remembered what John Kennedy had said about his wife's thunderous French conquest: "I am the man who accompanied Jacqueline Kennedy to Paris." In that moment, Ben Cameron and Hinton Drexel and Carter Stephenson and I were the men who had accompanied Lucy Bondurant Venable to Paris. The thought stiffened my spine and legs, and I clung to it as to a buoy in a wild sea.

After the greetings, which seemed to stretch into sunny infinity, we were taken into the airport to an Air France lounge, where the reporters followed us, and Ben held a press conference. The reporters of half a dozen nations were surprisingly deferential and considerate, and Ben fielded their questions with the same dignity and composure with which he had handled the greetings, even though he knew no French, and once even grinned, when a third or fourth reporter inquired politely who the beautiful lady in red was. Lucy was introduced as a niece of one of the victims and I was presented as the bereaved son, and we both nodded and blinked into a hundred exploding flashbulbs, most of which were trained on Lucy, and then, finally, the press conference was ended and we were taken, by limousine, out to the end of runway 26 where the *Château de Sully* had burrowed into the unforgiving earth like a great, ungainly phoenix missing its appointment with the air, but failing, this time, to rise from its deadly birth flames.

The crash site had not been visible from the air; either we had come in from a different angle, or the dying night had shrouded it. Now, in the clear sun of Monday, June 4, there was no avoiding that blasted moonscape, no leaving that black country of the dead. Desolation spread for hundreds of yards, ashen and silent, and the only thought that ran through my mind as I walked into it behind Ben, Lucy at my side, was a refrain made of her words that morning: "Light. Clean, radiant light . . ." But there was no light here.

Firemen and police had been at work for twenty-four hours, and the wreckage had been raked over and over again after the bodies had been loaded into mortuary vans and taken away; sifted for the burned memento mori that would aid in identification. The huge tail section, towering four stories into the air, stood intact, a great, ungainly space-age stele. Below it, strewn over the burned earth, chunks of twisted and fused metal were the plane's unidentifiable vitals, molten and bright as viscera in spots where the soot and char had been knocked off. The four engines were recognizable, but they had been blown so far apart that they were without context on that silent, black plain. Beyond the blackness the little town of Villeneuve le Roi, which the pilot had managed to spare, lay dreaming in the sun. Birds chirped and the knots of people behind the guards' cordons talked in low voices, staring at the first of the clansmen come from America to bear home their dead, but sound seemed to stop and fall to earth at the edge of the blackness. It was as if that great scar was inimical to any offering from the living. Beside me, her feet scrunching in ashes, Lucy whispered over and over, "We be of one blood, thou and I." Her hand was cold and tight in mine, and I do not think that she knew what she whispered; it was like a child's mindless and comforting little incantation. Ahead of me, Ben and Hinton Drexel said nothing at all as they walked. Carter Stephenson scribbled in a small notebook.

We were ankle-deep in those hundred-odd lives. Personal objects were as thick in the rubble and ashes as hailstones after a storm. Most were half-burned and so blackened that it was useless to probe them, but many were recognizable, piercing, incongruous, icons not of death, but of stubborn, unquenchable life. Guidebooks, menus, ashtrays, wallets, traveler's checks, a French doll bought for a child who would never hold it, an incredibly unbroken bottle of fine champagne, an Athens, Georgia, Rotary Club flag, a silver-knobbed cane, a gold evening slipper, scraps of tulle and velvet, an intact brocade shawl. Ben reached over and picked up the cane and the shawl. I could see that tears ran down his face, but it was still.

"This is Wynn Farrell's cane," he said, in a thin, old voice. He was not speaking to anyone in particular. "It was his father's, and his grandfather's before that, I think. Wynn didn't need the damned thing, but he took it everywhere with him. Said it made him feel like Maurice Chevalier. And this is Elizabeth Carling's shawl. I've seen her in it a hundred times, on cool nights, at the club or at parties. Dear Jesus, none of us are going to get over this."

"Light," I said to myself, half-aloud. "Clean, radiant light . . ."

After a while the objects stopped making any sense to me and might have been clods of earth, or stones, and I was no more affected by them than I might have been by anonymous outcroppings in some ancient lava field. I had been far more moved by the crumbling manuscripts that I ferried in my cart in the tunnels beneath the New York Public Library. When at last we left that sunstruck, silent charnel field and headed in the limousines into Paris for lunch, I found that I was quite hungry.

Lucy did not go with us to the morgues to look at the dead. In the end, she did not even ask to go. Ben had our driver drop her, along with Carter Stephenson and the obviously smitten young man from the American embassy, at the excellent and anonymous small hotel near the embassy where rooms were held for us, and she said only, getting out of the car on the arm of the young man, "Remember, Gibby. We be of one blood. . . ."

Even when I met her in the dark little hotel bar afterward, and we drank steadily through the dinner hour and into the evening, and there was ample time and opportunity for her to do so, she did not ask about that afternoon, and she never did in her life. By that time, after so many hours in my company and the invisible company of the dead, I am sure that she simply, as she always had, knew. It was, that full and silent knowing, almost her best gift to me.

Ben and Hinton Drexel and their party went to all five morgues that afternoon. After the first one, I waited in the limousine. It was not that I was shocked or sickened or near collapse; it was that after the first one I knew that any more searching of the dead faces was futile. It would not be by sight that they were identified, and it would not be that day or that week, or even, probably, for many weeks. My presence seemed, suddenly, an unbearably boorish and brutal intrusion. If my mother lay in the morgue that I visited, I did not know it, and if she lay in one of the others, no one of us could have told. The bodies, severe and formal in proper white sheeting and chilled into antiseptic stasis in the cold rooms, were hardly defaced. In most cases the hair had not even been burned off. The skin had simply been browned a taut, shellacked yellow-brown, almost the precise shade of centuries-old mummies, so that identification was impossible.

I walked with Ben among the smiling brown dead of Atlanta in that first morgue and saw nothing that had to do with life and living; life had been closer out on that silent, terrible plain, under the new summer sun. Ben stayed behind to look over the per-

sonal effects that had been taken from the bodies while I went
back out to the limousine and sat down in the backseat. The
middle-aged driver asked me something in rapid, nasal French,
and when I simply shook my head, handed me a small aluminum
glass of brandy, and I drank it, thinking with an insane peevish-
ness that I would have to surrender the now-familiar image that
my mind had kept, of my mother with her hair in flames, and
in its place try to fix a new one of my mother with the hard ocher
face of a millenniums-dead Egyptian princess.

Ben and Hinton Drexel went back to their rooms to begin the
long, awful business of telephoning the families back in Atlanta,
and Carter Stephenson went to file his stories, and Lucy and I
drank through the fabled *l'heure bleu* of Paris and into its cool,
late-falling night. We held hands but we did not talk much. We
did not get drunk. Neither of us mentioned dinner, nor did we
speak of what we both knew: that there was nothing more for
us in Paris, and that we would arrange the next day to go home.
I do not think that either of us felt the trip had been useless. I
know that I felt, obscurely but deeply, that some unnamed and
unknowable but essential thing had been accomplished, and I
have been grateful all the years since that I went, and that Lucy
went with me.

But I felt just as strongly that we must not linger in Paris. By
tacit agreement, we both rose from our table at about nine
o'clock and went upstairs in the little scrolled, iron-caged lift to
our adjoining rooms. She did not ask me if I wanted to talk for
a while, or needed company; she simply kissed me on the cheek
and said, " 'Night, Gibby," and unlocked her door and went in,
closing it behind her. I undressed and got into bed, tired beyond
thought and nearly beyond feeling, and waited for sleep.

But it did not come. Nothing did. For what seemed like an
eternity I lay in the dark, aware of everything and nothing, the
very air seeming textured and heavy against my naked flesh, as
empty and cool as a grape skin.

Around midnight, Ben Cameron rapped softly on the door
and then pushed it open, and I realized that I had forgotten to
lock it. He came in and sat down on the edge of my bed as Sarah
had done, incredibly, only thirty-six hours before.

"Are you asleep?" he said, and when I said no, he reached
out and turned on the little bedside lamp. He was so drawn that
the skin of his face looked like crumpled tissue paper, but he was
smiling.

"I just had a call from home," he said. "Sarah had a little girl
this afternoon at four-seventeen. She and the baby are just fine.
She wanted me to tell you. And she wanted me to tell you that

they're naming her Olivia Redwine Gentry . . . because she wants your mother's name to go on. She asked me to tell you that."

"Thank you, Ben," I said.

"I brought this back for you, too," he said. "They had it in storage at the third . . . place we went. I'm pretty sure it's your mother's, and I thought you might want to keep it. We know where she is, now, Shep, and we can bring her home for you. She wasn't . . . she was unmarked."

He put a small object onto the bedside table and got up and left the room, closing the door behind him. I reached over to the table. He had put a shoe there, a narrow, stiletto-heeled evening pump of the sort that I had seen a hundred times before, in my mother's closet or on her narrow feet as she left for a party. She had them custom made in New York and sent to her, and they had her monogram embroidered in gold thread in the inside lining. This one was blackened on the outside, but the satin-lined inside was unsullied, and I saw it there, in intricate script: ORB. Olivia Redwine Bondurant.

I turned off the light and sat holding my mother's shoe in my hand, and then, finally, in the heavy darkness, I wept, aloud and hard and painfully, like an utterly inconsolable child, not for what lay in the third morgue of Paris, but for what had laughed and danced in the beautiful, foolish shoe and for the hopeful best that would live on, now, in the name of Sarah's firstborn. I cried until I thought my chest would burst with the anguish; I could not stop; the tears poured and pounded on. I remember thinking, for the first time in my life, that it was possible to simply die of tears.

Sometime that night—I do not know when—Lucy came into the room and slipped into the bed with me. She was naked, and her body was long and light and silken and cool, and she pressed it around and against and under and over me, and her warm, sweet open mouth was against my face and hair and cheeks and eyelids and nose, and finally over my mouth, so that I sobbed directly into the breath of her, and then, simply and with a deep, deep flowering, she took me inside her, and rocked with me to a beat as old and deep and primal as the world, and was Lucy was Sarah was Lucy was Sarah was Lucy was my mother was Sarah was Lucy, was the world, was the universe . . . and all that I had not felt budded and bloomed and swelled and burst loose and roared through me and she took it into herself, and I was freed.

We flew home to Atlanta the next day, and we did not speak of that night directly, then or ever. When she told me three months later on a day of high honey sun up at Tate, where she and Jack and I had gone for the weekend, that she was pregnant, and I said, "Lucy, is it . . . ?" she only shook her head.

"I don't know," she said. "I honestly and truly don't know and never will, Gibby. It could just as easily be Jack's, and if it isn't he'll never know it."

And I had to be content with that, because she seemed so.

But when, in March of 1963, her daughter was born in Piedmont Hospital, in the middle of a three-day ice storm, and I asked the baby's name, there was something more than pride and love for that tiny, perfect girl child in her luminous blue eyes when she said, "Malory. Her name is Malory Bondurant Venable."

PART THREE

CHAPTER
TWENTY

F ROM THE VERY BEGINNING, Lucy's bond with her daughter was an extraordinary thing. I did not imagine it; everyone spoke of it. Aunt Willa, every inch the doting Buckhead grandmother, said, "I swear, that child is listening to Lucy. Look at those eyes following her." And Jack, leaning back exultantly in his chair in the summerhouse living room on the night of Malory's birth, said, "It's like looking at two mirror images facing each other. Or twins of some kind. Those identical blue eyes staring at each other with such intensity you can almost see the sparks jumping between them. And the sounds the baby makes when Lucy talks to her. Like she understands, and talks back. Lucy says she does. I swear to God, Shep, I love my boys, of course I do, but I never felt anything quite like the feeling I have for that little girl. It's almost out of the same piece of what I feel for Lucy. Tell me, really . . . did you ever see such a beautiful baby?"

"No," I said. "I never did. Of course, you could count the babies I've seen on the fingers of one hand. But she does seem prettier than it's right for a baby to be."

"Thank God she takes after Lucy," he said, swallowing his scotch. His doughy face was flushed, and softer than I had seen it since the first days of his marriage to Lucy; somehow boylike, despite the thinning white hair and fine-etched lines. "I'd hate to pass the Venable puss on to a little girl. But Malory is pure Bondurant."

I kept my face still over the queer pang in my chest. I would have to get used to that momentary sweet-sick heaviness, I thought, for Malory Venable was indeed pure Bondurant,

433

though it was more the Bondurant-ness that looked out of Lucy's eyes and the eyes in her treasured old photographs of her father, than mine. I thanked God for that, even though an infinitesimal part of me felt an obscure disappointment. After all, I decided, what did it matter? Malory Venable was blood of my blood, to one degree or another, and I had the license, at least, of doting cousin to excuse my enthrallment. For like everyone else who saw her in her first days of life, I fell to tiny Malory Venable without a shot's being fired.

I saw her on the afternoon of her birth, before anyone besides Jack and Aunt Willa did. Lucy had left instructions that I was to be admitted as family, and so, when I came into her hospital room on that brilliant afternoon of crystal ice-chaos, she was alone with the baby, banked and bowered in flowers and bathed in the first of the returning sun, Malory sucking sleepily at her blue-veined breast. I felt my face go hot at the sight of her translucent, remembered flesh, but I am sure she did not notice. Lucy, that day, was afire with rapture.

We looked at each other over the baby's silky dark head for a long moment, and then she said softly, "Oh, Gibby, look. Just look at her."

I walked over and kissed Lucy on the cheek, and smelled the fresh, milky smell of new baby over her Tabu, and my eyes prickled. I could not, for some reason, look full at the baby.

"She's gorgeous, Luce," I said. "She looks just like her mama."

"More like her granddaddy, don't you think? Or at least like the male Bondurants. I thought at first she had something of Mama around her mouth, but I don't think so anymore. And there's nothing there at all of poor Jack. No, it's all Bondurant. Look at that little blade of a nose—you all have it."

There was nothing of portent in her words, nothing but enchantment with her baby. I relaxed and looked fully at Malory Venable for the first time. She turned her head from Lucy's breast as if she had felt my look, and gave me a wide, fully focused smile. It was such a deep and direct look, and her lambent, light-spilling blue eyes, so like Lucy's, had in them such a sheer sense of ken, that I felt a physical shock in my stomach. I moved my head and her eyes followed, and the smile widened. She made a soft, liquid little sound very near an adult chuckle of charm and joy. A great, helpless, foolish love flowered thickly in my heart and reached its tendrils out toward her. There was nothing in it of nuance and complexity; it was, and has remained, the purest and simplest emotion I have ever owned, all light and air and certitude.

Lucy was almost vibrating with joy and love that day, talking

soft nonsense to the baby, whose eyes followed her face with a
focus and concentration that were indeed adult in intensity. Her
face as she looked down at tiny Malory was so incandescent that
I wanted to turn my own away from it; outside eyes seemed, in
the face of that hungry love, intrusive. I felt a kind of superstitious fear for her, an apprehension that had nothing to do with
any practical future. That kind of perfect, leaping, shimmering
love surely tempted fates and gods. I felt the old, fierce desire
to protect, to enfold, to cloister both of them away, and then remembered that that task now lay with Jack Venable.

"You'd better do it right, buddy," I said inside my head, and
meant the words.

To Lucy, I said, "Is there anything I can get you? Besides
flowers? You won't need any more of those for about ten years."

"No," she said. "I have everything I'll ever want in the world,
Gibby. Right here in this room. Oh . . . but you know what you
could bring me? That old copy of Malory. *Morte d'Arthur.* Is
it still around the summerhouse, do you think? And *The Jungle
Book.* I want to read them to her right now, before we go home.
I want her to know where she comes from, and what will be important to her."

"I guess they're still in the bookcase," I said. "If they're not
I'll buy them for her, my first present."

"Oh, please find them, Gibby," she cried. "I want her to hear
'We be of one blood' from the book we heard it from. I want
our books."

"I'll look," I said. "And I'll bring them tomorrow, if I can.
But it isn't going to make any difference to her for about six
years, you know."

"No," she said, perfectly seriously, her smile gone, the blue
eyes burning, burning. "She'll know. She knows now. She knows
what I say to her, and I know what she says to me. You can
think I'm crazy if you like, but it's true. Malory is me and she
is mine, and she will hear me calling her all her life, no matter
where she is in the world. And she'll come."

I left her then and went in the fast-falling dusk back to the
haven of the summerhouse, a kind of dread hammering at my
ribs that did not ease with firelight and bourbon and Martha
Cater's hot vegetable soup. I knew what the unchanneled force
of Lucy's love could do, and the fear was as much for her as for
the infant on whom it focused. I found the Malory and the Kipling, and sat reading them late into that January night, and my
dreams, when I fell asleep on the sofa before the dying fire, were
full of kaleidoscopic images of great bears and black panthers
and wolves and caparisoned chargers and fire: the endless, unquenchable fire of Pumphouse Hill and Paris.

Lucy's feverish happiness shimmered on unabated until the day that Jack was to come and take her and Malory home, and on that morning she awoke already in the grip of a full-blown depression that bordered on catatonia. She lay with her white face turned to the window, looking at the bare trees lashing in the wind along Peachtree Road, not moving, not speaking, hardly breathing, and she would respond to nothing and no one. When the nurse laid Malory on her chest she did not put up her arms to cradle her, and the child would have slipped off the bed if the nurse had not snatched her up. They took the baby away to be rocked and given her first bottle in the nursery, and she did not cry until the door closed between her and her mother. But then her screams could be heard all the way down the hall and into the closed and glassed nursery, and the nurses there reported later that they did not stop until she literally fell asleep from fatigue, hours later.

Jack and Aunt Willa came and sat beside Lucy and chafed her hands and talked to her, but she did not answer. Jack, his hair and hands still bearing smudges of the fresh white paint with which he had prepared the farmhouse for Lucy and Malory's arrival, was near frantic. It was obvious that the old black woman back in Lithonia could not cope with both the baby and Lucy in this condition, and he could not stay away from his job more than a few days. Without Lucy's salary, tiny as it was, he could ill afford to miss even the few days he had planned to take to bring them home. When, by noon, Lucy had not responded to either of them or her obstetrician, and a psychiatrist had been summoned, Jack called me, and I came and sat down beside her and took her hand and called her name softly.

"Luce," I said. "Come on, Luce. It's Gibby. Talk to me."

This time she turned her head and looked at me, and I almost gasped aloud. The change in her since the day before was profound. Her vivid blue eyes were so devoid of light and life that they looked like a watercolor that had been left out in the rain. Her entire face was flattened and somehow thickened, without planes, and paper-white. Her cracked lips made the shape of my name: Gibby. And then she said, in a dry whisper, "I never saw the trees so pretty. October really is the best month, isn't it?"

I felt ice form along my spine.

"It's March 1963, and you have a new little girl, and it's time now to cut this out and take her home with Jack," I said, too loudly. She closed her eyes and turned her face back to the window.

"I don't know any Jack," she said in a frail, fretful child's whimper. "I don't have any stupid little girl. Gibby, take me home. I want my daddy. I want to go home."

Jack Venable gave a soft grunt of pain, and Aunt Willa snorted in delicate outrage. I shut my eyes in despair. Lucy said no more that day. The psychiatrist closeted himself with her for an hour or so, and the results of the tests her obstetrician had ordered came back, and at dusk both came out to the waiting room and sat down with us amid the magazines and coffee cups and over-flowing ashtrays.

"It's a classic postpartum psychosis," the psychiatrist said. He had pure silver hair over a face as satin-pink and unlined as an infant's. A baby-butt face, Lucy would have called it.

"I know it looks bizarre, but it's not uncommon, and this is by no means the worst case I've ever seen. I think she'll pull out of it fairly quickly with medication and some good nursing care, but both will have to be constant. I understand Mr. Venable can't manage that at home. Is there somewhere we can take her where she'll be able to have total rest and quiet, and the baby can be looked after?" He looked at Aunt Willa and me; I knew that there was no other choice, and nodded. Aunt Willa followed my lead, lips compressed.

"We'll be glad to have her," I said. "Martha Cater can look after her, and I'm sure she can find us a baby nurse. Maybe her daughter can come. She looked after Lucy when she was little herself. We're close to the hospital and not all that far from your office, Jack, and you can come by before and after work—or stay over yourself, if you like. We've got plenty of room."

I looked at him questioningly. For some reason, my heart was lifting, and wings beat in my chest.

"I . . . well, okay. Sure," Jack said. I knew that he hated the idea of Lucy back in that house of wealth and privilege and cold-ness. I also knew that he knew he had no choice. "I'll be much obliged. But just till she can get on her feet again. And I'll pass on staying over, thanks. I'll look in when I can."

"Fine," the psychiatrist and Lucy's obstetrician said heartily, in concert, clearly relieved to be rid of the embarrassment of a messily skewed ending to a routine case of seemly Buckhead childbirth.

"Sounds like the best solution," the psychiatrist said.

"Well." Aunt Willa got up smartly and smoothed the gray wool sheath that cupped her elegant hips and buttocks. "I'd bet-ter go get things changed around so we can fit a baby in. Let's see . . . hmmm . . . no, there's no other way but for Lucy and the baby to have my room, and the little dressing room, and I'll move up to the attic. We can't very well move poor Big Shep, or his nurse. My goodness, so many sick people and nurses . . ." Her voice trailed away as she clicked down the hall toward the elevator, a path of poisoned honey spreading behind her. I knew, and Jack probably guessed, that beneath the honey and the martyred mother's words, Willa Slagle was raging anew at this troublesome daughter who would not leave her in peace in the gracious bower where she had, finally, gone to earth.

And so Lucy came home again to 2500 Peachtree Road, with a nurse and Malory, and was installed in the big bedroom upstairs, and old Martha brought ToTo in from Forest Park and found a wet nurse from one of the projects, and Aunt Willa went back to work, and I went back to the summerhouse and the clamoring ancestors of Sarah Gentry. And all the time, as I worked, the knowledge of tiny Malory Bondurant Venable, shimmering there in the little dressing room that had been my own first nursery, lay whole and still and perfect in my heart.

For a week or so Lucy simply lay still, staring out her window into the tops of the trees that had sheltered her summers until she married Red Chastain. She was allowed no visitors, but occasionally I stole in from the summerhouse to stare down at Malory, sleeping in her pearly perfection as ToTo rocked and napped, and then I sat for a while beside Lucy's bed. I would hold her hand and talk to her of small things and nonsense, and sometimes she would press my hand, and once or twice she smiled. One afternoon, toward the end of the first week, she said, abruptly and weakly, "I get so tired when I think about having to take care of her always, Gibby. I can't even take good care of myself. I don't know what's going to happen to us."

They were the first words she had said to me since she left the hospital, and I started visibly.

"Jack will take care of both of you, of course, Luce," I said, but she only shook her head weakly and fretfully on the pillow.

"He'll try, but in the end he won't be able to," she said.

"Sure he will. But I'll help," I said. "If you and Malory ever need any extra taking care of, I'll always be here."

"Will you, Gibby?" she said, turning her thin, white face to me.

"Of course. Always."

She was silent for a bit, and then she smiled. It was a fuller smile, stronger.

"Yes," she said. "I think you will, now."

Soon after that she began to improve, and in another week Aunt Willa took her to Sea Island for ten days in the early spring sun, and when she came home, lightly tanned and with some of the sunken hollows in her face and body filled in, she was gay to near-ferocity again, and seized Malory and hugged her until the baby screamed.

"You didn't cry for Mommy, did you, precious angel?" she said into Malory's satiny cheek. "I know you didn't. I felt you every minute, and I sent you messages a thousand times a day, and I know you were a good girl. She was, wasn't she, Martha? Wasn't she, Shep?"

"Yes'm," Martha Cater growled. "She ain't cry after you gone. I ain't never seen no new baby as good as this one."

I knew that old Martha hated making the admission; she had glowered and stomped around the house when Lucy told her she was going away, and predicted havoc and sleepless nights and the ruin of Malory. But it had not happened. The baby had cried bitterly and inconsolably for an hour or so after Aunt Willa and Lucy had driven away, and then, as if indeed receiving some interior signal, had looked about her, startled, and stopped the crying, and gone promptly to sleep. I know, because I was holding her at the time. Her cries had reached me even in the summerhouse, and I had not been able to let her cry on and on, without solace. She knew me, I thought, and relaxed the tiny, knotted muscles when I picked her up, but the crying did not stop until nearly an hour later. I told Lucy this, and she smiled her thousand-watt smile.

"I know," she said. "We stopped for breakfast at the New Perry Hotel and I heard her, all of a sudden. Just in midbite. I can't explain it. And I . . . just talked to her. I went back in my head and sent her a message, not to cry, that I was with her and it was all right. That you were there and would take care of her. I know she stopped then. I felt it. It's an enormous relief, Gibby—it means I can go back to work or anywhere else I want to and she'll be all right, because I can talk to her."

"All we need around here is a couple of spooks," I said, disquieted in spite of myself. I did not like the idea of Lucy's practicing psychic communication on Malory. I wanted nothing murky, shadowed, esoteric, overly passionate, to touch her. When I thought ahead to her growing-up years, I saw sunlight and order and sandboxes and kittens and ponies; children's parties and nurses and starched pinafores and pigtails and family suppers around shining, silver-set tables. It was, of course, my own Buckhead childhood that I saw, or rather the furniture of it; even I knew that I was blithely painting out the pain and fear and treachery of that world, and that it was foolish, perhaps even dangerous, to wish it for Malory. But I did. Order and control— those were the things I most wished for the little girl who bore my name and my nose and my heart; order and control, not the careening, erratic, quicksilver world of excess and privation and kisses and absences and surging subterranean tides that would, I knew, be Lucy's legacy to her. But I knew by then that neither I nor Jack Venable nor anyone else would have much say over the raising of Malory. The symbiosis between her and Lucy was simply too strong.

It crossed my mind not infrequently, in those days before Lucy took the baby home to the farmhouse, that she was most assuredly not the stablest and most responsible mother for this or any other child. I was usually able to bury the notion deep under the knowledge that there would always be other loving caretakers around Malory: Jack, who adored her; the old black woman at the farmhouse, who had a firm and loving way with children; me; even Aunt Willa, who evinced in her granddaughter a sucking, proprietary interest she had never displayed toward Lucy. But once or twice the thought broke free, and the last time it did, it cost me Malory's presence in the house on Peachtree Road.

Lucy had taken to bringing the baby out to the summerhouse to visit in the afternoons, when my reading and note taking were done and she and Malory had had baths and naps. I would make coffee and set out the cake or cookies that Martha Cater brought and light the fire and put Vivaldi or Palestrina on the record player, and Lucy would put Malory's small, fragrant weight into my arms and stretch out on the sofa and light a cigarette. Sometimes she drank sherry instead of coffee, and on these afternoons she grew vivid and voluble and talked once again of the escalating civil rights movement and the never-ended work at Damascus House.

With segregation beginning to crumble in the schools and colleges, black activists were focusing on the still-segregated hotels and restaurants, and scarcely a day passed that spring without a demonstration or picket or sit-in. I knew that Ben Cameron met almost daily with black leaders now. Around that time, a "lie-in" had been held at the Henry Grady Hotel downtown on Peachtree Street—that bastion of middle-class white gentility, where even the cloistered young of Buckhead were allowed to go to the Dogwood or Paradise room to watch an occasional second-class magician or comic—and half the population of Damascus House, including the charismatic Claiborne Cantrell, went happily to the Fulton County jail, singing "We Shall Overcome." Lucy burned with eagerness to be with them.

"I should have been there," she said over and over, through smoke. "I should have been with them. It's my fight, too. I've been away too long."

"Terrific," I said, rocking a sleeping Malory in the old nursery rocker I had had Shem Cater bring from the attic to the summerhouse. "Just what Malory needs. A mother in the Fulton County pokey."

"She'd be okay," Lucy said. "I'd talk to her. She'd have you."

"And Jack," I said. "If he wasn't in jail alongside you."

"And Jack," she said. "He wouldn't be in jail. He's the money man. He's too important. Clay won't let him demonstrate anymore. Jack says he hates being out of the action, but I don't think he does. Besides, Jack would never let himself be arrested. No scotch in jail. No Huntley-Brinkley. No books and records."

But after the news of the arrests from Damascus House, she grew restless and remote, and I would see a light in her bedroom window burning at all hours in the warming nights.

Late in that week, she brought Malory out to the summerhouse wrapped in one of her own blouses, wearing a lace-trimmed blanket of Malory's draped around her own shoulders.

"We're switching off, Gibby," she chortled. "See? She's the mommy and I'm the baby now. It's her turn to take care of me."

She held the baby up gaily, and Malory pawed fretfully at the enfolding blouse, trying to free her tiny feet and fists, and mewled fussily. I felt anger and a tiny lick of the dread I had felt on the morning of Lucy's retreat into depression. I snorted and took Malory out of her arms and jerked the grotesque, trailing blouse off her, and wrapped her in the blanket from Lucy's shoulders.

"Don't ever make her ridiculous, Lucy," I said levelly around the anger.

She stared at me, her eyes burning blue-white.

"Don't you tell me what to do with my own baby," she snapped finally. Her voice was sullen.

I continued to look at her, silently, and presently she dropped her eyes and took Malory from me, and went back into the house. The next evening Jack Venable came and took her and the baby home to the farmhouse in Lithonia, and his joy in his daughter and love for Lucy were so palpable that they almost filled my own hollow heart as I watched the pink-swathed baby being driven away, finally, home.

Lucy went back to work soon after that, leaving Malory in the care of the old black woman, and reported in her soon-resumed evening telephone calls that Malory was as contented with her new nurse and the grudging company of Toby and Thomas as she had been with her mother's and mine.

"She's just one of those rare perfect, unflappable babies, Gibby," she said, inhaling. "Estelle says she never cries. She's getting fat as a little butterball, and she's just as happy to see us when we come in as if we'd been there all day."

And then she would segue from Malory into the work of Damascus House without missing a beat, and I would think again that she seemed deeply content to be back and submerged in the swimming-pool- and park-desegregation plans there, as if her old bone-deep ease and sureness among the activist blacks was a re-

lief after the intense, consuming emotional pitch of her day-to-
day interrelation with Malory. She was soon working longer and
longer hours, and in the middle of the summer Jack left Damascus House—with visible relief, I thought—and took a job with
a large downtown firm of CPAs for shorter hours and slightly
better pay. After that, he had almost sole evening care of the
three children.

I went back to my own work in the summerhouse, and it was
many months before I went into the big house again. It was not
that I was avoiding it, particularly; it was just that, with Lucy
and Malory gone and my father as unresponsive as a drugged
and chained wild animal, there was no reason to do so. I did not
mind. The Peachtree Road house was now as inalterably and indisputably the territory of my aunt Willa as if she, not I, had
been born there. I felt, on my rare forays there to pick up clothing or books I wanted, as if I were burgling a stranger's home.
The very air smelled of her bitter, expensive scent, and the few
times I went to sit briefly beside my mute, grimacing father, the
entire bedroom seemed steeped in it. I knew from that, and from
the occasional generic mutters from Martha and Shem Cater,
that she was still spending many of her free hours sitting with
him, occupying herself God alone knew how—for it surely was
not in conversation with him. He remained as silent and blasted
as a Toltec idol.

It was odd about Willa Slagle Bondurant in those days: She
had, of course, absolutely no more claim to the Peachtree Road
house than she had had while my mother lived, and yet it was
somehow, nail and roof beam, hers. The visitors who drove up
the semicircular drive and left their cards on the old silver card
tray were, now, as often hers as my father's. It was for her that
Shem brought the Rolls around to the front, and for her that
he held the heavy door. Delivery vans brought her orders, and
lawn and linen services arrived at her telephoned command, and
the smart, slender women in wools and silks who came to luncheon and for bridge and drinks were her guests. They were not
the same ones who had come for my mother, but they were, to
all but the fully initiated eye, indistinguishable from them, and
they certainly were not tackpots. High second echelon, one
might have said; the very first echelon had largely been crisped
along with my mother in a ditch at Orly, and in any case, the
ones who had not would not have come to Willa Bondurant. But
I believe that Aunt Willa was, largely, satisfied with them. They
were, as she was now, a long way from the chicken farm.

Her move to establish herself in the house had been as slowly
and delicately accomplished as a cat's tracking of a chipmunk.
Preoccupied with the family of Sarah Gentry and the coming

of Malory, I had not noticed it, although it was I, with my admonition to her on the day I left for Orly that she move into my mother's bedroom, who had given her the implicit permission. And, I suppose, she read my failure to curtail or supplant her in the house as tacit permission to colonize it. I can see now, too, that there was another and stronger license granted: that of queen mother. Aunt Willa was no fool. She must have seen from the first day how I felt about Malory, and she had always known of my immutable and twisted ties to Lucy. I believe she moved into my mother's bedroom and later her house absolutely secure in the knowledge that I would not oust the mother of Lucy and the grandmother of Malory from the house she and Lucy both—and I as well—considered their first home. And she was right.

Shem and Martha Cater hated taking orders from her, I knew, but their sensitive servants' antennae told them, correctly, that I did not wish to hear about it, and would not do anything about it if I did, and so they kept their grievances mostly to themselves. No one else seemed to notice, except perhaps to say, at one time or another, how fortunate it was that my aunt Willa was willing and able to serve as a housekeeper for me and my father, and to wonder what we would ever do without her.

By this time, few of the handsome, middle-aged women who were her contemporaries remembered that they had once laughed with my mother at Aunt Willa behind her back. If she was not one of them she had taken on their patina perfectly and subtly, and in Atlanta appearances have always soothed and charmed. There is not enough genuinely blue blood here to run warm with outrage at the insinuation into its ranks of a Willa Slagle Bondurant. And too, spinning into the mid-sixties, Atlanta was riding the tail of a comet, and Old Atlanta, like it or not, spun with it, gasping and even giggling dizzily among undreamed-of galaxies and constellations. No one had the time or inclination to snub Aunt Willa as they might have done a decade before.

And so she reigned creamily and snugly in the house to which she had come, teetering and faltering in slipshod high heels, a quarter century before, as beautiful and polished and curried as any of the women who had smirked at her at the Driving Club. I was, in the main, grateful enough to let her run the house, as I let canny, abrasive Marty Fox, whom Tom Carmichael and I had hired the year before to manage my father's business affairs, run those. I knew her power over Lucy, but I had also seen her tears and her fear, and so her vulnerability, and I did not think that she had any power over Malory. If she attempted to exercise any in that direction, I could always stop it simply by threatening to put her out of the house, and I would not have hesitated to do so.

For it was in actuality my house now, and not my father's. I don't think Aunt Willa was certain of that, either then or for a long time afterward. I believe she reckoned that it might still be my father's, and that I, too, might well live there on sufferance, and I think that that was why she spent all those hours keeping vigil beside his bed, perhaps thinking, in some corner of her wire-grass soul, that he might reward her by changing his will and leaving her the house, or perhaps simply his insurance.

It would be interesting to know what he thought about her presence beside his bed; we were never sure if he fully comprehended what had happened to my mother, but he must have missed her and concluded at some point that she was dead. If he was lucid enough to grasp it, the splendid futility of Aunt Willa's vigil beside him must have given him a great deal of dark glee. For he had known for many years what I learned only in the days after Orly, from Tom Carmichael: that the house, as well as virtually all the rental property and other Bondurant holdings that my father had tended and maneuvered and multiplied, had been in my mother's name, and that they had passed, at her death, not to him, but to me. I became, in one fiery instant, quite a rich young man and he nominally a paralyzed pauper, and I have always wondered if he did not hate both my mother and me for that knowledge long before it ever became fact. It would explain, at least partly, his cold red distaste for me, and his long retreat from my mother's presence into his study. After the day Tom Carmichael brought Marty Fox to the house and introduced him to me, I never went into that room again.

I did not feel rich, or even different in any way, and forgot for long stretches of time, until Marty brought his monthly sheaf of bills and checks and papers for me to sign, that the reins of the Bondurant holdings rested now in my own vastly unqualified hands. The only significant advantage all that money had for me was its ability to buy me privacy and freedom from onerous duty and detail. I used it shamelessly. Marty Fox virtually ran the business, and Aunt Willa ran the house; I had enough raw Cameron history at my fingertips to keep me absorbed into senility if I wished, and very little outside the summerhouse walls called insistently enough to me to lure me out of it. The smoldering stigma of the Pumphouse Hill fire and the natural preoccupation with young families and fledgling careers kept the Buckhead Boys and their wives at a seemly remove from me now.

If I had truly been one of them, raising a family and pursuing a career and moving with them between the clubs and homes and summer places of our old orbit, I know that I would have been forgiven the fire and taken back into the fold, but I had the mark of the loner on my forehead by that time, and pack animals to their very marrows, they saw and smelled it, and largely let me be. They dutifully, one by one, had me to dinner in their near-identical "starter" houses in the days after my mother's death, and included me in holiday parties and club dances, and other familiar herd rituals, but by then I was outside their ranks, derailed once and for all from the track that would take them to the forefront of the city's corridors of power one day, ready to take up the torches when the Club passed on to them. I did not care. In those days all human encounters seemed collisions, and the dead in the summerhouse received me far more gently than the living in Buckhead. My money bought me seclusion; I could afford to become something of a recluse, and so, gratefully, I became one.

Dorothy Cameron alone in those days tried to lure me back out into the world.

"There's not much excuse that I can see for you to hide out in that summerhouse for weeks on end now," she said, on an evening in the early autumn of 1963, when I loped over in the dusk to see her. "You ought to be out putting some of that money to good use."

I knew that Ben was away; the morning newspaper had said he was meeting that evening with representatives of several black organizations to draft recommendations for a public accommodations act and for laws facilitating open-occupancy housing, fair employment machinery and desegregation of public facilities. He was rarely at home, day or night, in those days. I found Dorothy in the little den of the Muscogee Avenue house, tiny Livvy Gentry playing quietly in the playpen at her feet. Sarah was, she said, practicing for the Junior League Follies, and Charlie was closeted again with Mr. Woodruff, as he was two or three nights a week now.

Dorothy put Livvy into my arms. She was a rather simian baby, as slight in stature as Sarah had been as an infant, but with Charlie's button eyes and long upper lip, and holding her was like cradling a tiny, plucking monkey. After a moment I handed her back to Dorothy; the child might have borne my mother's name, and might be flesh and bone of my lost love, but aside from gratitude at Sarah for thinking to please me by keeping my mother's name alive, I felt absolutely nothing for her daughter except mild regret that she so little resembled Sarah. The powerful, knee-loosening love that I felt when Malory was in my arms was obviously her province alone. I was grateful that with Dorothy I did not have to pretend affection I didn't feel for her granddaughter.

"I'm doing good with all those ancestors of Ben's," I said. "It could be a magnificent book, Dorothy, if I can do it right. It needs a lot of time and concentration. I'm feeling my way. What good is money if it can't buy you the time and privacy to do your work? And besides, what's wrong with a rich recluse? Poverty-stricken recluses get all the good press."

She snorted, taking a Rose Medallion saucer away from the baby. "I don't think there's really any such thing as a poor recluse, not by choice," she said. "The poor man is rarely reclusive by choice. I'll bet you anything the classic, pure recluse is that way because he can't afford to be a rich, corrupt voluptuary."

I laughed. "Well, that's the ticket, then. I'll give up the recluse business and become a rich, corrupt voluptuary, and then everybody will say how money has changed me, and that I'm not the good old plain, down-to-earth hermit I used to be."

"I don't think that idea holds any water whatsoever," Dorothy said. "I've seen an awful lot of money in my life, some of it acquired almost overnight, and the popular theory is that it changes people. Like you said. So-and-so is not the old so-and-so we knew in the lean days. But I think just the opposite is true. Poverty dictates what you will think about the world you live in, and so that's what and who you become. Your poverty defines you. Money lets you choose, lets you buy yourself a persona—indulge your true character, so to speak. People who are most 'themselves' are people who can afford to be. Does that make any sense at all?"

"As much as you ever do, which is a lot," I said. "But if that's true, why is it so awful for me to be a private person? I mean, if that's what I am naturally. What does money have to do with that?"

She shook her head impatiently. "It just ought to be put to work. If you don't want to go out and do it, give it to somebody like Charlie and let him find a use for it. You don't need it, Shep. It's immoral to just sit there playing with Ben's ancestors when some of that money could make such a difference to so many people."

"I cleaned up Pumphouse Hill, Dorothy," I said resentfully. "I'm having Tom and Marty renovate every piece of property we own. I'm not going to waste the money. I'll leave it where it will do good when I die, and right now I'm trying to get some kind of trust set up for Malory."

She looked at me keenly.

"Very generous of you, Shep. I don't imagine Jack Venable thinks too highly of that, does he? And from what I hear, I don't imagine Lucy even realizes Malory needs it, or will. I hear she's harder at it than ever with the movement, and doesn't get home until the baby is asleep, more often than not. It's reabsorbed her like a sponge."

"You hear an awful lot," I said without rancor.

"I do," she said, equally mildly. "People tell me an amazing number of things. Am I right about Jack?"

"Yes," I said. "You are. He flat refused to even discuss a trust for Malory, and said he wouldn't let her touch a penny of it if I went against his wishes and set it up. He'll reconsider, though. He and Lucy don't make enough between them to send her to day camp, much less school and college and . . . whatever else she needs."

"A proud man," she said. "I can see his point, though. She's *his* daughter, after all."

"She's my family, too," I said.

"I know she is," Dorothy Cameron said, and something in her low, rich voice told me that she knew as much as I did or ever would about Malory Venable's patrimony, and had since her birth. But she said no more, then or ever. Dorothy might never cease in her attempt to force perfectibility upon me, but she knew down to a hair when to let me be. It was not the least of the reasons I loved her.

It was that autumn when I first began to worry seriously about Lucy, and consequently, about Malory. From absorption with her work at Damascus House and the civil rights movement, Lucy seemed to sheer over into obsession; from two or three late nights a week, she began to spend three and four there, and often weekend days, and once or twice she slept over on a cot in the business office. I learned this only because, when she made her nightly telephone calls to me, the background noise was indisputably that of other telephones and mimeograph machines and clipped black voices speaking. I don't think she would have told me where she was calling from if I had not asked. She knew, by then, how I felt about her time away from Malory.

"Back off, Gibby," she would say. "Malory is fine; she's wonderful. I just checked on her. She ate seconds at supper and went right to sleep, and Jack says she hasn't cried once tonight. Oh, and he thinks she's about to walk; she's maybe a day or two from real steps. How about that? It's awfully early for walking, you know."

"I hope you're there to see it," I said. "What does this make, Luce, three nights this week? Four? She's going to think Estelle is her mother."

"She knows who her mother is, don't you worry about that," Lucy said defensively. "There's not an hour of the day I'm not talking to her by radar. She always answers. Isn't that good

about the walking? I'll have her marching with us before the
year's out."

"I'd like to come over there and march you home," I said,
exasperated. "She needs her mother, Lucy. It's that simple."

"She needs a world where Negro children aren't blown up in
churches, or bitten by dogs or knocked down by fire hoses and
clubs," Lucy said, in a near-hiss. "It's that simple. Do you think
for one minute I'm not doing this for her?"

"The thought has crossed my mind that you're doing it for
yourself, now that you mention it," I said. The words were un-
fair, but sometimes Lucy veered off into glib, liberal cant, and
that sent me wild. For some reason I could not bear banality
from her.

"Fuck off," Lucy said, and slammed the telephone down, and
did not call again until I telephoned her, two days later, and
apologized. After that I left her hours and her deepening obsession alone, but I did not stop thinking uneasily about them. The
bombing of the black Baptist church in Birmingham in September had sent her nearly mad; she had wept and raged for days,
and, earlier, Jack had been able to prevent her from joining the
Washington March, where Martin Luther King made his electri-
fying "I have a dream" speech, only by threatening to bring Malory to live with me and Aunt Willa if she went. Her emotional
pitch had risen steadily since then; I wondered if, now, that
threat would deter her. I prayed that Jack did not put it to the
test.

In midafternoon of a Friday in November Jack Venable called
me.

"Can you do me an enormous favor?" he said. His voice was
thick and flat, as with great fatigue.

"Sure," I said. "What's up?"

"Could you go down to Damascus House and get Lucy? They
called a minute ago and said she's . . . in some kind of fit, or
collapse, and they can't get her home with all the turmoil, and
I can't leave the children to go myself. If you could bring her
home, I'd be eternally grateful."

Something did not fit, was badly skewed. "What are you doing
at home in the middle of the day?" I said. "Is something the matter with Malory?"

There was a long silence, and then he said, "Don't you know?"

"Know what?" I said, my heart freezing in my chest.

"Kennedy was shot in Dallas around noon. He's dead."

The room swelled and brightened around me, and his voice
faded out, and then came sweeping back like a cold storm tide.

". . . know how she felt about him," he was saying, and what

I had thought was fatigue turned to grief as he spoke. His voice broke and he cleared his throat and went on.

"He was Jesus Christ to King's God with her. And she's been unstable as hell since the baby came. I don't want to pile all three children in the car and go down and get her, and I'd just as soon they don't see her in this state anyway, whatever it is. I don't think they could cope with it, and I'm not sure I could, either. You could always calm her down; I can't tell you how I'd appreciate it if you'd get her and keep her there or somewhere until she's in shape to be around the children. Estelle has taken off someplace and there's nobody but me with them."

"Where was he shot?" I said, numbly and stupidly.

"In a motorcade somewhere in downtown Dallas. Near some kind of schoolbook thing."

"No, I mean . . . where on his . . . was he disfigured?"

It was a horrid and irrelevant question, and I knew it, but all I could think of was the ruin of that splendidly enabling white grin, and the fine shock of red hair, which he had worn with the offhand grace of a battle panache. I did not think I could bear the knowledge of his disfigurement, though I did not know why.

"Christ, Shep, I don't know. The back of his head, I think. What goddamned difference does it make? It killed him, wherever it was."

"I'm on my way," I said.

"Thanks," he said heavily. "Thanks."

But I was not on my way for some moments. My treacherous knees buckled under the loss, even though my overtaxed heart would not acknowledge it, so that I had to sit down on the sofa for a few minutes. I kept shaking my head to clear it. I wondered if I should call Shem Cater to drive me, but I did not want company, and in the end I took the Rolls myself and drove down into the bleak section southeast of Five Points, where Damascus House was, my hands and legs shaking profoundly all the way, as if gripped by an influenza chill.

Claiborne Cantrell was conducting a service in the sanctuary when I arrived, so that there was almost no one about. I could hear sobbing and a peculiar low, timeless keening that lifted the hair on the back of my neck, and an occasional howl of pure grief, doglike and terrible, and the strains of old hymns, sung in cracked voices: "Abide With Me," "The Old Rugged Cross," and that poignant and now heartbreaking anthem of hope and commitment and valor, "We Shall Overcome."

"I don't think we shall overcome this," I whispered to myself, going up the old stone steps and turning right toward the little office where Lucy worked. The music gave searing life to the enormity that lay frozen in my chest, and I felt tears begin to run down my face. I did not wipe them away; it did not seem important to do so.

Lucy was sitting in her desk chair when I entered the tiny, cluttered office, and a vastly fat, middle-aged black woman was sitting beside her, holding both her hands. It did not take me more than a second to realize that she was literally holding Lucy in the chair; Lucy kept struggling to rise, and her head thrashed from side to side, sending the wings of blue-black hair swinging. Her face was the yellow-white of cheap office paper, and there were white rings around her blazing, light blue eyes and deep scarlet patches on her high cheekbones, and she smiled, a terrible, radiant, fixed smile.

"Hey, Gibby," she sang, smiling, smiling. "Did you come for the march? Flora, this is my cousin Gibby. He always knows the best thing to do. He came for the march—I told you people would start coming, if you'd just be patient. Oh, shit, where in *hell* is Claiborne with that bus? We're wasting time. All that singing and yelling can come later. We need to get this show on the road. . . ."

She leaned around the black woman to peer out the door toward the sounds of sobbing and singing. The woman shook her head, her great hands still enfolding Lucy's. The silver tracks of tears had dried on her cheeks, but her face was impassive.

"She think we gon' go to Washington and march on the White House," she said. "She say with the president laying dead an' the biggest march in history, it be the end of the fight, an' there ain't be no more racial injustice. She think he been shot by a bunch of segregationists, and this gon' end it all—"

"It will, it will!" Lucy caroled. Her voice literally shook with excitement, a high tremolo, like a castrato's. "We've won, don't you see? After this, nobody on earth will still believe in segregation—he's the greatest martyr the movement could possibly have! But we have to go now, we have to get there by the time they bring him back. Everybody else will be there already. . . ."

I went and knelt before her and took her hands from the black woman, who touched Lucy's hair gently and went out of the office toward the sound of the singing.

"Lucy," I said, "be quiet and listen to me. You aren't going to Washington. There isn't going to be any march. It wasn't any segregationist plot; it didn't have anything to do with civil rights. I heard on the radio coming down here that they just got the guy, and they think he's some kind of Communist, and he acted alone."

She looked at me quite calmly.

"They want you to think that, of course," she said. "It's all part of it. You'll see—you'll see in the end. Of course they'd want us to think that, but any fool knows it was over civil rights, not some silly little lonesome Communist. . . . Gibby, will you go get Claiborne out of that stupid service right *now?* Every other city in the country will have their people there while we're still sitting on our asses down here, singing!"

"I want you to snap out of this shit right now, Lucy," I said, angry and frightened. "I told Jack I'd bring you home where you belong, with him and Malory, and that's what I'm going to do. Get your things and let's go."

Her smile widened. She looked beautiful and utterly mad. "I'm going to Washington, Gibby, and I'm going to march for my president. Everybody who's got any decency and conscience in the country will be there. I'll bet my father's there. I'll bet he is, right now. . . . Did you ever think how much Jack Kennedy was like Daddy? Don't you think the resemblance was just un-canny? Wouldn't that be something, to run into my daddy there in Washington, at the greatest march in the history of the world—"

"Lucy!" I cried.

"Watch out, Gibby, or I'll really get crazy," she said, sliding her white-ringed eyes sidewise at me, slyly. "You want to see me really crazy? Here we go: DADDY! I WANT MY DADDY! I WANT MY DADDY! MY DADDY'S NOT DEAD! SOME-BODY SHOT THE PRESIDENT!"

Her screams spiraled up and up, so piercing and wild and fierce that they caromed around the little room like mad, trapped birds, and scattered, and flew into the corridors and up to the ceilings of the old building, ringing on and on. She did not seem to need breath for them.

I pulled my arm back as far as it would go and slapped her with all the strength I could muster. I felt the blow into the wing of my shoulder blade. Her head flew sideways, and bounced on her slender neck. She drew in a long, long, sibilant breath, her eyes enormous and unfocused on my face, all pupil, and then she dropped her face into her hands and began to cry. I put my arms around her and drew her against me, and we stayed there, weeping together in that overheated, abysmally cluttered little room, until she literally began to retch from the force of her sobs, and I could no longer feel my knees. I could not see ahead in time; we seemed to have come, at that moment, to the flat, white end of everything.

She was calm after that, a frail, tottering calm, but she could not stop crying. The tears flowed on and on, endlessly, sheeting silently down her ravaged white face and soaking her blouse and sweater. She did not talk on the drive back toward Buckhead,

but she smoked through the tears, and listened in her stillness
to the somber voices on the car radio until I could bear them
no longer and turned it off. Finally, as we passed Brookwood
Station, where, worlds and eons ago, two thin, like-hearted children had rolled under a slowly moving train, hearts in mouths,
she said, "I can't go home. I can stay fairly sane with you, but
if I have to look at those poor, horrible little boys' faces and hear
them prattle about this I'll start screaming like a banshee again.
I know I will. I can't even talk to Malory in my head right now.
I can't listen to Jack's endless analyzing. I'm really afraid to go
home, Gibby."

"We won't go, then," I said. "You can stay with me until you
feel better. We can go out and have some dinner, or I'll fix something for us. I told Jack I might not bring you back tonight."

"Did he mind that?" Her voice was remote.

"It was his idea."

She was silent for a while, and then she said, "Somehow I
don't want to go back to the summerhouse, Gibby. I don't want
to have to associate it with this awfulness later on. And I don't
want to run the slightest risk of seeing Mama. She hated him.
Or even worse, she only said she did, because all her snotty Re-
publican buddies do. I think I'd kill her, literally strangle her,
if she said one word about him right now."

"I know where let's go," I said, as if I had planned it all along.
"Let's go over to the Camerons'. I'll bet you they're there. Somebody will be, anyway. Okay with you?"

All of a sudden I wanted to be there, in the little den of Merrivale House, more than I had ever wanted to be anywhere in my
life. I did not even want any specific one of the Camerons; I just
wanted to be there, in the house that had always seemed so safe
and right and beautiful to me. I realized only at that moment
that whenever I had thought of John Kennedy's Camelot, I
thought, somehow, of it as existing in and around the house on
Muscogee Avenue.

"Okay," Lucy said dully. "Anywhere. Just not home or the
summerhouse."

Ben and Dorothy were not there after all, but Sarah and Charlie were, and Ben Junior and Julia, and Snake and Lelia, and
even Tom and Freddie Goodwin came in just after we did. Others followed. One by one, we came, the Buckhead boys and girls,
from wherever we were, as if summoned out of the November
night; we came to the nearest place Buckhead had to Camelot.

It was a ghastly homecoming. All of us were crying, I remember, even those of us who had not been particularly smitten with
Kennedy. We knew, somehow, that far more than a single visionary life had ended. We knew that we had lost far more than

a president. Our youth had died, our collective childhoods were over, now. This day divided time; forever after we would think of our lives as separated into what had gone before this, and what came after. I suppose that at this, our last great personal transition before our deaths began, on this night of the shattering of time, it was natural that we should gather. I thought, looking at the unabashed tears on these faces I had known literally since my infancy, that except for Lucy and Sarah I had never seen any of these people weep before, and probably never would again, not even at the death of one or another of us. Somehow this night was past and beyond the need or the reach of control. There were no rituals for this.

Sarah met us at the door and brought us back to the little den, her face bleached and scourged with desolation. She had a drink in her hand, and she sipped steadily at it all evening. Like all of us, she was crying. We all drank a great deal, and some of us got frankly drunk for perhaps the first time in our lives. I remembered seeing Ben half carrying Julia up the stairs to his old bedroom at some point in the night, and Tom Goodwin kept stumbling and falling on his way to the drinks tray by the fireplace. Charlie said little, but he wept quietly and steadily, even as he went about his hostly chores, mixing and passing drinks, lighting cigarettes, fetching napkins to mop up spills, taking and producing coats as people came and went. All the while the silent river of tears ran ceaselessly from behind his thick glasses down into his collar.

Sarah brought trays of sandwiches and a platter of cake and set out Dorothy's old Sheffield coffee service, but no one ate. We drank and watched the television set, staring into its flickering maw at images and sounds so unimaginable they did not register, but which were even then being etched in acid in the deepest and smallest folds of our brains: Lyndon Johnson, looming and wolf-like, his hand raised in a cramped airplane cabin. Jackie, erect and stained, alone on a loading dock in Virginia. Flags at half-staff, and people around the world crying in our own horror, and the beginning of the awful voices of the drums.

At about ten, Freddie Goodwin cocked her avian little head and said, "I wonder if this means we'll have to cancel the Junior League Follies? I don't see how on earth we can; we've worked like dogs for months. This would have to happen now—"

"SHUT UP, FREDDIE!" Lucy screamed, coming white-faced out of the chair she had been slumped in all evening, her fingers actually curved into talons before her. I caught her by the back of her sweater before she reached Freddie. She was breathing so hard and rapidly that I thought she was going to faint, or even die. The sound rasped and grated in the room.

454 Anne Rivers Siddons

"You listen here, Lucy Bondurant," Freddie began, but Tom overrode her. "Put a lid on it, Freddie," he said thickly. "Fuck the Junior League Follies. Fuck the entire Junior League, for that matter."

Freddie huffed off into the kitchen, looking sidewise for sympathy as she went, but finding none. No one noticed her. Most of the others were looking sidewise themselves, at Lucy. The outburst had had about it the intensity and swiftness of murder, or madness.

Sometime after midnight, Glenn Pickens came by looking for Ben. His face was wet too, silver-scummed, but I never saw him cry. He sat down with us for a moment, with the looseness and slackness of deathly fatigue, drinking the coffee that Sarah brought him, but saying nothing. Like us, he stared at the television set. Presently he got up to leave, and Lucy saw him and pushed herself heavily from her chair and followed him to the door. She held out her arms, wordlessly, and he hesitated a moment, and then came into them. They held each other briefly, and from where I was sitting, behind him, I saw his shoulders heave, and saw tears start afresh from Lucy's tight-shut eyes.

"I know how you felt about him," Lucy sobbed to him. "I'm so sorry, Glenn. We've lost . . . we've lost . . . God, I don't know . . . everything."

"No, Lucy, you don't know how I felt about him," Glenn Pickens said, in a taut, angry voice. Then he smiled. It looked as if it hurt him as much as the tears must have. "But I know you're sorry. Poor, nice little Lucy. Poor, good little white girl. I wonder if you really know what we've lost."

After he left, Lucy sat back down and quite deliberately and silently drank herself into senselessness. Near dawn Charlie helped me carry her out to the Rolls, and as we slid her long, loose-limbed body, almost birdlike in its lightness, into the backseat, I looked down at her stained face in the light from the Camerons' black iron carriage lamps. It was emptied and blunted and absolutely devoid of the quicksilver life that animated it when she was awake. She looked, suddenly, middle-aged and very nearly ugly, and as if she might be dead. My heart twisted with pain for her. I thought of Glenn Pickens's words: "I wonder if you really know what we've lost."

Much later, months after that night, I read somewhere words that Patrick Moynihan had spoken to Mary McGrory, and wept afresh at that terse elegy for so many and so much: "Mary McGrory said to me that we'd never laugh again. And I said, Heavens, Mary, we'll laugh again. It's just that we'll never be young again."

And it was so. In the rest of her runaway comet's life Lucy Bondurant Chastain Venable laughed a great deal, but she was never again, after that day in November, truly young.

CHAPTER
TWENTY-ONE

L OOKING BACK, I have come to think of the five or so years
after John Kennedy's assassination as the half decade in
which nothing happened. Much did happen, of course: In
that time America was catapulted by Lee Harvey Oswald's bullet
out of the long, doo-wah span of the fifties and into the psyche-
delic nervous breakdown that only ended with the resignation
of Richard Nixon; and Atlanta left its pretty pool of dreaming,
century-old sunlight and leaped into the high, thin, cold sun of
space.

Yes, indeed, much happened. But not a great deal happened,
at least as such things are measured, to us—to me, and to Jack
and Lucy and Malory Venable. I suppose what I really mean
was that Lucy was not, at least overtly, mad in those years, not
visibly out of control. There was no repeat of the scene on the
day Kennedy died. By that time, we were all fairly accustomed
to having our lives defined and the weather of them forecast by
Lucy's emotional state.

So of course, I, of all people, should have known better.

Out and abroad in the country, two centuries' worth of walls
were crumbling, few of them peacefully. The Civil Rights Act
was at last signed. Martin Luther King won the Nobel Peace
Prize. James Meredith was shot in Mississippi. Blacks and
whites marched and sang and were beaten and bitten and jailed
in Selma, Alabama. Watts and Detroit and Newark burned as
angry riots flowered in the dangerous summers. A world away
the feverish green jungles of Vietnam burned, too, and at home
at least half of the riots and rallies decried that sad and sorry
nonwar. The Beatles conquered America, and skirts went thigh-

high and teenagers higher as substances most adults had never heard of slammed through their bloodstreams, and beads and bells and strobes and synthesizers supplanted Japanese lanterns and "Moonglow" at the parties of the American young. America in those years was like an automobile with the governor off its motor and its accelerator jammed to the floor.

In Atlanta, we were almost precisely where Ben and the Club thought we should be. The new major league stadium was begun and built in a record fifty-one days, and the Milwaukee Braves became the Atlanta Braves, and the NFL Falcons came to town, and we played ball. Restaurants and bars were desegregated. An area-wide rapid transit system was authorized. We were, in the middle of those years, the second highest city in the country in terms of new construction. Sleek, sunstruck new hotels and office buildings and apartment houses soared into the sky along Peachtree Street downtown, dwarfing the comfortable Edward Hopper jumble of eight- and ten-story businesses there. New amusement and theme parks opened around and even under the city; new bars and restaurants and clubs sprang up like mushrooms after a summer rain. Malls and strip shopping centers burgeoned. Grady Hospital was desegregated, and the city received a HUD grant for a Model Cities program that encompassed four percent of its land and ten percent of its population. A great new government complex and a flamboyant new governor's mansion went up and the grand old mansions along Peachtree Road began to come down, and in the proper, shabby little Tenth Street section of Peachtree Road historically known as Tight Squeeze, the bearded, beaded, long-haired, perpetually stoned young of the entire Southeast set up camp and renamed themselves hippies. I think that not a few of them swung by there after their sessions with Margaret Bryan, changing into jeans and beads and discarding shoes somewhere along the way.

Atlanta's momentum did not come cheap. Near-riots simmered in the bright, hot days and the thick nights. Ben Cameron met and talked and met and talked until, at one point, he was put to bed in the house on Muscogee Avenue by Hub Dorsey and a determined Dorothy and forbidden to talk for a week on pain of losing his voice permanently. During one particularly spectacular confrontation he climbed atop a parked car, a surging sea of angry, frustrated black faces at his feet, his coppery head a target for any murderous fool within a mile radius, and pleaded through a borrowed bullhorn for order. He finally got it—and his photograph in the newspapers of an entire nation—before he was toppled from the car and ended up in Piedmont Emergency with a sprained ankle and a hole in the seat of his pants. But Atlanta did not blossom into flames as Detroit and

Watts and Pittsburgh and other cities did in those summers, and
as Ben himself said, that was worth a considerable chunk of a
mayor's ass.

In Buckhead, Sarah and Charlie had another little girl, called
Charlsie, and young Ben and Julia Cameron another small red-
haired son, and Ben rapidly became one of the young architects
of the hour and the day, mentioned often in almost the same tone
of voice as Philip Johnson and I. M. Pei. He was out of town
a great deal in those days, and Julia would say, ruefully, that
she supposed he had another family somewhere who was doting
and fussing over him, because she and the boys certainly never
saw him. But her voice was warm with pride. There was no
doubt in the mind of anyone who saw them together that Ben
was absolutely besotted with his sons.

Little Lady had the first of many discreet blackouts and did
a discreet stint at Brawner's while her own small children were
cared for by Atlanta's only, and cordially hated, English nanny,
and Carter grew richer and richer and more remote. Aunt Willa
finally gave up any pretense of working as a buyer at Rich's and
became one of Buckhead's most elegant chatelaines. *The Compleat Georgian* moved ponderously out of my notes and into my
typewriter. And Lucy quit her job at Damascus House and took
one with *SOUTH,* a little foundation-funded, ultraliberal journal
which put her, as she said, far more into the thick of things.

It was, from everyone's standpoint but hers, an appallingly
bad move.

From spending her days and nights within the walls of Damascus House, she was soon traveling all over the South in the little
Austin the journal provided her, hastily gathered clothes strewn
over the backseat and a bearded, cool-eyed, laughably young
photographer in the front beside her, covering the movement.
It was, by then, surging inexorably out of the deep, calm channel
King and his early supporters had dug for it and into the glinting, murderous shoals of radical violence, and we at home feared
both the sniper's bullet and Lucy's own erratic hands on the Austin's steering wheel when she was away. She was by then literally
intoxicated with the momentum and glamour of the movement,
and most of her time was spent in the company of the young
heroes and guerrilla fighters whose names and cold, closed faces
were familiar on television screens and in newspapers on half a
dozen fronts: Little Rock, Selma, Birmingham, Montgomery,
Oxford. More than once she went beyond the bounds of her job
and the instructions of her editors and ended up in jail herself.
Jack and the older children were frightened and resentful, Malory was bewildered, Aunt Willa was predictably outraged and
Lucy herself was as exalted as an avenging angel.

Once, after I had wired bail money yet again, I laid into her on her return. She had brought Malory to the summerhouse for a rare visit, and when the little girl ran out to play by the lily pool I said without preamble, "I guess you think it would be really wonderful to be slain on the altar of the goddamned movement."

"Maybe not slain," she said around her inevitable cigarette. "But I'd love to be beaten or hosed or bitten by dogs. Maybe even shot, if it didn't kill me. I need to know how it feels. I need to go through it all with them. They're my people. It's my fight. You ought to be in it with us, Gibby."

"They're fucking well not your people," I snarled. "Jack is your people. Malory is your people. Toby and Tommy are your people. What good are you to them if you're dead on a dirt road in Mississippi? And I *am* in it with you. I'm financing the damned thing with your bail and fines."

"You're just like Jack Venable," she snapped. "Putting yourselves ahead of the greatest and most . . . morally important . . . movement in history. Why can't you see that I do this for the children? I want Malory to grow up knowing what's really important."

"I want Malory to grow up with a real mother, not a fake honky martyr," I said.

But Lucy was blazing with zeal and exaltation, and did not hear me. She was back on the road the next Monday. She was not eating or sleeping well, and grew thinner and more haggard and incandescent by the day, and drove herself incredibly with her travels and deadlines and the long, passionate talk sessions with the new young black lieutenants now in the movement's vanguard. I do not think that she loved or respected them any more than she had King and his honor guard, but there is no question but that they excited her more. She ran on stimulation, in those days, like a race car on high-octane gasoline.

I think Jack, and certainly I, might have moved more decisively to curtail her activities if the absences and obsession had been having a markedly adverse effect on the children, but they did not seem to do so. The boys, teenaged now, had been indifferent to her at best, and were no doubt glad to have their father to themselves so much of the time. And Malory, at five, was a sunny and self-possessed child, enchanting to look at and adept at pleasing the adults around her, and she showed no signs of missing her mother. She did not lack for company. Wherever she went, Malory charmed. She had an uncanny sense of just what small action or gesture or phrase would most please whom, and had a habit of making vivid little crayon drawings signed, "I love you, Malory B. Venable," and giving them to family, friends and new acquaintances alike. A great many refrigerators around Lithonia and one or two in Buckhead, in those days, wore Malory's drawings. Mine was nearly papered with them. I was not sure I liked or approved of the facility for self-endearment that she displayed; it spoke too loudly of subterranean need. But I was, as was everyone around her, totally captivated by it. Malory Venable midway into her sixth year of life was almost literally too good to be true.

You would often forget, around her, that she was a child. Despite her pointed pixie chin and Lucy's huge, crystal-blue eyes and the silky child's hair, cut in ragged points around her heart-shaped face, Malory had about her the nurturing manner and outward focus of an adult. When I thought about it, I would realize that she had been cast by Lucy's absences into the role of caretaker and helper early on. She brought trays and magazines and slippers and drinks and snacks to Jack, and she fetched and carried for the boys when they would allow her to, and when she was visiting with me she frequently pattered around collecting dishes and fluffing sofa cushions and bringing me astounding treats foraged from my refrigerator. I soon learned to accept them without fuss; if you praised Malory for a service, she would wear herself out finding others to perform.

Perhaps she did not seem to suffer from Lucy's absences because the tenor of her mother's presence, when she was there, was so intense. The old symbiosis still held; an arc of utter attention still leaped between the two of them when they were together, and the old eerie, voiceless communion still prevailed. I have seen Lucy, in front of visitors, stop and fall silent and somehow compose her face, and soon Malory would appear from wherever she was, trotting straight to her mother and looking up questioningly. It was in the nature of a parlor trick, and I hated it when Lucy did it, but it was admittedly startling to see. When Malory was older, she stopped automatically responding, refusing with a lovely and touching natural dignity to allow herself to be exploited, but she still felt Lucy's call, and continued to do so, I know, for as long as her mother lived.

When she was in the city, Lucy was hardly ever away from her daughter. She took Malory into her and Jack's bed in the morning and evenings, brought her along on interviews and into the office and allowed her to sit up late with the blacks and whites in the movement who came, inevitably, to the farmhouse to eat, rest, talk and often stay for a night or a week or more.

"Be brave like that, Malory," she would say often. "Always be brave."

And Malory would nod silently, her whole child's heart in her eyes.

I detested that chaotic nonchildhood for Malory, but I could understand her fascination with her mother. I would try to see Lucy through her eyes, and the vision was irresistible and overpowering: the beautiful, vivid, shimmering mother, rarely seen but constantly felt, swooping in and out of her small life trailing passion and glory and swarms of intense, exotic people in her wake like the cosmic detritus in the tail of a comet. No wonder her father seemed, by contrast, simply dull. I know that she thought him so. How could she not? Sinking into the passivity that would last his lifetime, uniformly silvery gray and amorphous, slumped into his easy chair, mired in the anodynes of scotch and television; the reluctant disciplinarian, the unshining one, always and endlessly *there*—Jack Venable never had a chance with Malory. She loved him, I know, but as one might a great, sweet dog, or her familiar bed. By contrast Lucy burned like Venus on a winter night.

"Jack is a lump," Malory said to me once when she was spending the day with me in the summerhouse. "He sleeps all the time and he smells funny."

She visited fairly often in those years, when Jack had to work on weekends, or when she had a shopping or movie expedition planned with her grandmother. We both loved those days, I because I loved her, by then, with all the passion I could never spend on Sarah or Lucy or my mother, and she, I suppose, because I interested her. She seemed to see nothing odd about an uncle—or cousin, or however she thought of me—who had shut himself up in a summerhouse behind the great house of his birth and saw almost no one. We had long conversations about a startling variety of things: leaping, veering, shining talk that refreshed and enchanted me. It was I who read her Kipling and Malory, and she loved them as her mother had done before her. Lucy had told her about the two books, those icons of safety and magic which had burned so clearly and steadily through our childhood, and when she cried aloud with Mowgli, "Mark my trai-i-i-l!" and, "We be of one blood, thou and I," it was nearly impossible for me to distinguish between mother's and daughter's voices; both resonated, intertwined, in my heart. The words never failed to bring a thickness to my throat: she was, after all, one way or another, of my blood. I like to think that it was, in part, from me that she learned to assess and reflect and think abstractly, and it was from her that I learned again to dream and suppose and play. There was little that she did not say to me. It was hard indeed to remember that she was only five.

"He's not a lump," I said, on the day that she spoke so of Jack Venable. "He works hard all day and he's tired when he gets home. If he didn't rest he couldn't go to work and take care of you."

"Phooey," she said. "He doesn't have to do that. You'll do that. Mama says you will."

"Well, I would if he couldn't for some reason," I said, cursing Lucy silently for that tacit belittlement of Jack. "But he can. It's his job. It's what fathers do. He loves you and your mama."

"You love my mama, don't you?" she said.

"Of course I do," I said, not at all liking where this was going. "But in a different way."

"Well, I think your way is better than Jack's," she said. "He really is a lump. He's a collection of bumping molecules."

I recognized Lucy's voice in that, and said, severely, "I don't want to hear any more talk about your father, Malory. He's a good man. You'd really be up the creek without him around to look after you."

"Maybe," she said equably. "But I could probably look after myself just fine. I wouldn't be afraid."

I knew that she wouldn't. Malory was afraid of almost nothing. Almost. But there was one thing of which she *was* afraid, afraid with a terror so deep and consuming that it sent her into the kind of white, blind hysterics that I had not seen since Lucy's childhood. At first, when she was very small, we could not determine what it was; the fits came at random, once or twice at the Peachtree Road house, more often in the farmhouse. She could only gasp and sob something that sounded like "shoo man, shoo man."

Finally we isolated what it was that sent her into that awful, mindless shrieking: It was the framed photographs that stood about the farmhouse, all taken on the same day, of her grandfather, James Bondurant, Lucy's father. In all of them, he was wearing black and white saddle shoes, and it was only when she was old enough to shape words into sentences that we could fathom why she was so terrified of him. She was afraid he was going to come in his strange, striped shoes and take her mother away. Until she was eight or nine, we could not disabuse her of that notion.

"Did you tell her that?" I demanded of Lucy, the first time the root of the fear came to light.

"Of course not," she said indignantly.

"Well, where the hell else would she get it?"

"Oh, for Christ's sake, Gibby, I might have said something about him coming back to get me one day, but nothing that would make her behave like that."

"Lucy," I said, "sometimes I think you're just plain crazy."

I would remember those words.

The first of her truly bad times came, as we might have foreseen, with the murder of Martin Luther King in Memphis. She was on her way to Pascagoula, Mississippi, in the Austin when the news came over the radio, and the young photographer with her said that she simply dropped her hands from the steering wheel and began to scream, and that if he had not grabbed the wheel they would have gone off the road and been killed. She had screamed until he had gotten her to the emergency room of the nearest little community hospital, where they had had to literally sedate her into unconsciousness, and they kept her that way until Jack and Shem Cater and a trained nurse I had hired arrived in the Rolls to bring her back to Atlanta.

We took her straight to Ridgecrest. It took them two days to get her coherent enough to diagnose her, and even then it was not a unanimous diagnosis. One psychiatrist said flatly that it was schizophrenia and a severe case at that, another opted for manic-depressive psychosis, another favored fatigue and shock and hormonal imbalance and two simply shrugged.

By that time Lucy was talking again, and I gather that what she said had not exactly won friends and influenced people. Between expletives and epithets and the shrill eldritch shrieking, she was obsessed with two separate and bizarre notions: that her father was going to be at King's funeral looking for her and that Jacqueline Kennedy was in Atlanta for the sole purpose of spiriting MLK's body away. It was hard to tell which agitated her more. She strained and struggled against her attendants—seeking to rise and go down to Ebenezer Baptist Church to the funeral, both to meet the phantom father and to confront the treacherous Jackie—until they finally had to place her in isolation.

"Can't you *hear* them, you assholes?" she would cry over and over. "Can't you hear them calling? Are you going to sit here and let her take him and dump him in the ocean at Hyannis Port?"

And when they would not let her go, she subsided, finally, into heartbroken sobs, and then into a muteness that resembled, as it had after Malory's birth, catatonia.

She seemed to surface again in the days following the funeral, but she was dull and lethargic, and grew slovenly and unkempt and had to be bathed and fed by attendants. Jack, exhausted by shuttling between his office and the hospital and home, was forced in the end to send the boys to their aunt back in Nashville, who promptly put them into Castle Heights Military School for the summer, and he gave up and sent Malory to stay with us on Peachtree Road. He was by this time so emotionally and physically depleted that I was relieved to have the children away.

I felt, in some obscure and unexamined way, that for the moment they were, at least, safe.

Lucy began to improve slowly with the administration of a powerful tranquilizer and one of the new tricyclic antidepressants, and begged so insistently to have Malory visit her that the doctors finally decided it might be therapeutic, and so, on a Saturday afternoon in June, I picked Jack up in the Rolls with Malory and drove them there. I had not seen Lucy since we admitted her, but from the little Jack had told me of her condition and appearance, I was apprehensive in the extreme about letting Malory see her. Malory had been strangely unperturbed by her mother's illness during her stay with us; she had said, when I broached the subject with her, only, "Mama is all right. She says so."

But Lucy was not all right, and the sight of her in the hospital's mercilessly lit, plastic-furnished dayroom smote Malory to white-faced silence. I felt enormous red anger at all of them—the doctors, Jack, Lucy herself—but it was too late to do anything at all. Malory walked up to her mother where she was sitting on a green vinyl sofa, an attendant standing behind her, and sat down beside her silently. For what seemed an eternity, she simply stared at Lucy. I could see the rise and fall, rise and fall, of the breath in her thin little chest, but I could not hear her breathing.

It was one of Lucy's bad days, they told us later. She sat dull-eyed and obviously drugged under the sucking lights, her hands clenched motionless in her lap. Her slacks and shirt were spotted with food and stippled with pinpoint cigarette burns, and her fall of heavy, silky black hair had been cut brutally short and square around her fine head, so that there were nicks in the white scalp behind her ears. She had obviously been given shock therapy, for the red stigmata of the electrodes still marred her translucent temples. She was bruised and scratched from her struggles against the restraints, and did not smell clean, and at first she did not speak, only looked into our faces with opaque eyes. Then she put out her hand and touched Malory, and said, in her startling old rich, gay voice, "Hey, sweetheart. Give Mommy a kiss."

Malory put her arms around her mother. She closed her eyes. She whispered into Lucy's dreadful hair: "Mama, I want you to come home. I'll be a good girl if you'll just come home. I won't ever be bad anymore. I'll take care of you, Mama. I'll be the mommy all the time, and you can be the little girl."

"That's right," Lucy said, smiling happily, rocking Malory against her. "You be the mommy and I'll be the little girl."

Even through the great, rushing wind of shock and rage in

my head, I wondered how many times Malory had heard those words, and how deeply the conviction went that Lucy's illness and incarceration were her fault. I seemed to hear, miles and years away, a small Lucy Bondurant pleading with my own father to take care of her, and promising to be a good girl if only he would do so. Beside me, Jack Venable cursed in a defeated monotone.

She seemed to see Jack and me then, for the first time, and the smile widened until it threatened to split her dry, splotched face. I winced. Lucy's fine, fresh porcelain skin seemed to have been tanned like delicate leather, crazing like centuries-old kid gloves at the corners of her eyes and mouth. There were sores at the corners of her lips and the base of her nostrils, where the skin had cracked and bled and healed and cracked all over again. The hands that she clapped in glee were as dry and rough as an old woman's. She held them out to us, and Jack took them in his, and I sat down on the other side of her and put my arm around her shoulders.

"Hi, sugar," Jack said.

"What's happening, Luce?" I said, tasting the ludicrousness of the words as I said them.

"Jack! Gibby!" she cried. "Stick it in your ear!"

We looked at her. She laughed mightily.

"Stick it in your ear, you bastards," she sang. "Stick it in your ear!" And she disengaged her hand from Jack's and put her finger into her ear.

"I think she picked it up from one of the other . . . guests," the attendant said. "We don't think it means anything. But she loves it. Sometimes the only way we can get her to take her medication or go to bed is to play stick it in your ear with her. It works every time, so we don't knock it."

"No," Jack said. "If that's what it takes, I'll go around with my finger in my ear for the rest of my life."

His face was bleached, and he had aged years in the days of her hospitalization, but the look he gave Lucy was still heavy with the freight of his first, dazzled love for her.

"Stick it in your ear, Jack!" Lucy chimed.

He put his forefinger into his ear and smiled, and she laughed and clapped her hands. The dull drug haze seemed to lift with her laughter. She shook her head slightly. The mad rictus became her old smile. Malory crept close to her and Lucy hugged her, and reached up and kissed my cheek, and looked into our faces one by one.

"I've been away a long time," she said. "I'd really like to come home now."

She improved rapidly after that. Her psychiatrist kept her at

Ridgecrest until the antidepressant had time to take effect, but the next two weeks there were uneventful. Lucy was obedient to hospital routine and participated dutifully in the group therapy sessions and the crafts and exercise classes. She attended meals in a group with other adult patients, leaving the large, barred area containing the dayroom and patients' rooms in the company of an attendant three times a day to go down to the sunny, modern cafeteria for meals. Once or twice, she said, they were taken in the Ridgecrest bus to a nearby movie and a bowling alley, and once a day they walked on the paths and sat in the garden, looking, in their slacks and shorts, like vacationers, albeit pale and ill-barbered ones, at some spartan, economy-class resort.

"It's like a big, bland camp for grown-ups; not as fancy as Camp Greystone, by any means, but a hell of a lot more fun," she said on one of my visits that summer. We were sitting in the dayroom, and she had introduced me to nearly every adult patient in the hospital; they came up, one by one, as if drawn to some magnetic force field. I thought, remembering the irresistible light and energy that had played around her in her first youth, that they probably had been. She seemed happy in the hospital, oddly so—somehow safe and shielded and free—and Lucy, when she was happy, had always been irresistible.

She was looking better, too; the harsh, terrible haircut was beginning to soften and fall around her face, and her skin had plumped and smoothed under the rich moisturizing cream I had brought her, and she had asked for her makeup and Tabu to be brought from home. Except for the fading saffron bruises and the red indentations in her temples, she did not look so different from the way she had in the months before her hospitalization. She was even gaining a little weight; the dayroom had its own small kitchen attached, and it was kept stocked with food and snacks of all kinds. All of the patients, she told me, were complaining about getting fat.

Lucy was extremely popular. The other women deferred to her as people do to a natural leader, and the men were teasing and protective of her. I saw none of the instinctive distrust and alarm on the faces of the women who clustered around her that I had seen on female faces surrounding Lucy since her childhood; I supposed that here, in this sheltered place of rules and rituals and schedules and regimens, where aberration was the norm and the outside world kept at bay by bars and strident wellness, Lucy's essential difference did not matter. She was one of them and one with them. Lucy herself bore this out.

"I feel closer to the people in this nuthouse than I ever did to anybody outside but you and Jack and Malory," she said. "England must have been like this during the blitz."

The men out and out adored her, and for her part, she catered to them and coddled them as if she had been hired to do so. Each time I visited, Lucy spent a large part of the time fetching snacks and coffee and cigarettes for me and any other men patients and their guests who were around, trotting in and out of the little kitchen like a slender, elegant servant.

"Why do you do that, Lucy?" I asked her once. "You never used to fetch and carry for me like this, or anybody else, for that matter."

"No, I know it," she said. "It's funny. I don't even believe in it. I don't know where it came from—it sort of emerged, when I got over the worst of the craziness and started feeling better. All of a sudden there I was, needing to wait on these assholes like a damned maid. I guess it's just atavistic, Gibby. This is what we know in our bones, we Southern women. To do it makes me feel sort of . . . mindlessly comfortable and *right,* in a cell-deep way, like I'm plugged into something old and unquestionable, running by remote control on some absolute track. I don't know. It's very comforting. It has nothing to do with what I believe with my mind. Sometimes you need sheer, simple comfort more than anything."

"No wonder so many of you go nuts," I said, taking a plastic tray of empty cups away from her and putting it aside. "It's an awful pull between shagging trays for other people and tending to your own needs."

Lucy squeezed my hand.

"One reason I love you is that you're the only man I ever knew who understood that," she said.

She came home at the end of June, and stayed there, content, under the kiss of the tranquilizer and the benison of the new antidepressant, to read and garden and watch television and sleep. *SOUTH* gave her a leave of absence with half pay, which was hardly a drop in the bucket in light of the staggering debt her illness had incurred, but made her feel as if she was contributing something to the household. Lucy had always been inordinately worried about money, but in those days she did not seem even to think about it—or rather, the lack of it.

Very little penetrated the spell of the drugs and the long, slow summer days on the farm in the company of her beloved Malory. For the first and last time in her life, Malory had her mother completely with her, whole-souled and *there,* and I think she was about as happy as it is possible for a child to be. When they came to see me in the summerhouse, or more rarely, when I drove the Rolls out in the cool of the afternoons, I would notice playing around Malory the same kind of just-glimpsed, dark incandescence that had lit Lucy's childhood. It made of her something entirely magical, an enchantment, but I was not completely easy at the seeing of it. That dark fire had burned, not warmed, her mother.

But for the moment, that glow limned a summer out of time and remembrance for both of them, and they would recall it forever after with love and gratitude. It was not, in the summer of 1968, Lucy and Malory Venable who gave me unease, but Jack.

I knew that he was near distraction with worries about money and Lucy's ongoing emotional state, but he would not talk to me about either, and refused my offer of a loan so tersely that I did not offer again. He took a second job teaching accounting three nights a week at one of our dim, perfunctory local junior colleges, and soon was spending only the few hours after his classes and the weekends, during which he slept most of the time, at the farm. Lucy was strangely blithe about it; more than once I started to pull her up short when she spoke jeeringly of his being away so much she almost thought he had a woman on the side. I could not believe she had forgotten why he took the extra work in the first place. Then I would remember the sheer horsepower of the drugs boiling through her bloodstream, and hold my tongue. Lucy was a long way from being her old self in those days, though she was fey and dreaming and indolent, and seemed happy.

There were other moments in which I thought, again, that some edge had gone from her mind, some cache of clarity and richness erased. She was on Antabuse too, now, because the drugs she was taking were dangerous when combined with alcohol, and I thought that the absence of liquor after so long a time might be taking a temporary toll.

So I was silent, and Lucy moved on in her underwater pas de deux of delight with her daughter, and Jack Venable continued to work himself near to death. It was he, that summer and early fall, who drank steadily through the evenings and into the small hours of the next day, not Lucy.

In October of that year I grew so worried about him that I nagged him into asking his firm for a long weekend, and I took him and Lucy and Malory up to the cottage at Tate. I had lent it to Lucy, who still loved it, on several occasions over the years, but it had been more than a decade since I had been up there, and when the Rolls purred up into the first of the abrupt hills of Pickens County, some long-unnoticed weight lifted from my heart and it seemed to climb straight into the cobalt sky over Burnt Mountain. It was Thursday evening when we got there, and the big old cottages on the hillside overlooking the meadow and the lake were dark. I had called ahead and asked Rafer Spruill, who was the colony caretaker, to get the cottage cleaned and opened for me and lay a fire, and when we walked into the big, vaulted room with its window wall framing the darkening woods beyond the lake, the smell of household cleaner and fresh-cut logs and the dark, loamy earth of the autumn woods was thick in my nostrils. I lit the lamps, and the shabby, familiar old room came leaping at me and closed its arms around me, and I was home in a boyhood that was, in this beguiled and traitorous remembering, as idyllic as any book Lucy and I had loved as children.

Malory was enchanted.

"Oh, Shep, I love this place," she squealed. "Is this ours? Is this mine?"

"Of course not," Jack said impatiently. "You know where your house is, Mal."

"Of course it is," Lucy overrode him gaily. "It's Gibby's, so it's as good as ours too, isn't it, Gibby?"

"It's yours for as long as ever you want it," I said. "And I hope you do, because I never come up here anymore. It's a shame for it to go to waste."

"Why don't you like it, Shep?" Malory said, whirling around in the middle of the floor on one foot. "Is it haunted?"

"In a way, I guess it is," I said, laughing. "Though not by ghosts. This place is haunted by real people. But it's me they haunt, not you or anybody else," for she had looked alarmed. "For you it should be just about perfect."

"Oh, it is, it is!" Malory cried. "I think I want to come live up here forever and ever!"

"Without me?" Lucy said lightly, but her eyes were intent on Malory. Malory felt the look and turned her blue eyes to her mother.

"Well . . . no. Not without you, Mama. But sometime when you could come, too. And Jack. We could live on berries and acorns and honey, like bears do in the mountains, and nobody would have to worry about money anymore."

"Nobody's worried about money now, punkin," Jack said.

She did not reply, but her eyes were full of the lie, and gave it back to him. He turned away.

"I want the martini to end all martinis," he said, "and then I'm going to broil those steaks and eat mine in front of the fire, and then I'm going upstairs and sleep for thirty-six hours. You guys can greet the rosy-fingered dawn over the goddamned beaver dam if you want to. Somebody has to keep ahold of the priorities."

Lucy laughed and kissed him and made him a murderous mar-

tini and brought it to him in the shabby old plaid wing chair by
the great stone fireplace, and Malory curled up in the crook of
his arm, and he was asleep long before the coals on the grill were
ready for the steaks. Lucy led him, mumbling and protesting,
upstairs to the big double bedroom that had been my mother
and father's, though seldom used, and it was noon the next day
before we saw him again. He looked ten years younger when he
came yawning down the stairs, and nearly carefree, and I remember thinking that I really ought to just deed the house over
to him and Lucy. Something in the clear blue air had, in the
night, restored him. It is just possible that, given free and early
access to it, Tate might have healed Jack Venable. It has done
so for other Atlanta wounded.

It was, entirely accidentally, a golden, perfect weekend. On
Friday Charlie and Sarah and the children and Ben and Julia
Cameron and their two little boys came up and opened the big
Cameron cottage, and what had been planned as a solitary retreat turned into an impromptu house party. Tate was that kind
of place; neighbors who would not dream of dropping in unan-
nounced back in the city ambled in and out of each other's
houses as if they were their own, and shared meals and walks
and volleyball games and swims and children, and sometimes
even slept over in unused beds if the hour and the number of
drinks made scrambling back up dark, steep, rhododendron-
shadowed paths problematical.

And so it was on this weekend. On Saturday morning, the four
of them, children in tow, appeared at the back door with blankets
and baskets and a thermos of Bloody Marys and announced a
picnic, Ben Cameron yelling at me to bring my clarinet. By early
afternoon we were sprawled in the deep golden grass of the long
meadow above the lake, winded from volleyball and chasing
dogs and children, the high honey sun warming the earth and
our heads and shoulders, drinking Bloody Marys and laughing.
Even I, to whom the sight of another human being was ordinarily almost tantamount to an invasion, felt washed and nurtured
in old and easy companionship; even Jack, who had never taken
to Lucy's childhood acquaintances and kept himself at a stiff,
formal distance from them, was laughing with Ben and Charlie
and teasing Julia—who was vastly pregnant again—and unfold-
ing like a flower under the warmth of Sarah's old unfeigned
charm.

I don't know why all rules seemed suspended that weekend.
It is the special place-magic of Tate, I think, but I had never felt
it so powerfully and clearly before, perhaps because my parents
had taken me there so seldom. All that blue and tawny amplitude
of wild, singing space; the high, thin pure sun; the wildfire of

the autumn trees on the high shoulder of the mountain above
us; the immense bowl of the sky and the smaller, reflecting cup
of the lake; the symmetry of the cold blue evening shadows falling on the still-warmed earth—Tate was and is larger than the
people who go there, and at the same time intimate and sheltering, so that old tenets and strictures do not seem to apply. It is
as if past and future are left at the gatehouse up on the old macadam highway, and only the intense and pure moment prevails
inside.

There in that high meadow I could watch the lithe, small
beauty of Sarah running in tall grass with her girls and not feel
pain; I could walk with Charlie along the sun-dappled dirt road
around the lake and over the creaking wooden footbridge and
feel nothing in the air between us but old, easy love; I could lie
on my back in the deep grass beside Ben Cameron, my rusty clarinet answering his as smoothly as water pouring over stones, and
see, not the thin, feverish, somehow haunted man he had become, but the old, golden Pan of our childhoods; I could look
at Lucy, filling up with radiance in that enchanted afternoon like
a crystal pitcher with water, and see straight into the soul of her
as I had done when we were young, and hear in the air between
us her unspoken "We be of one blood, thou and I . . ."

That night, after we had put the children to bed in the bunk
bedrooms off the gallery in the Camerons' cottage and sat long
at the old trestle table in the big kitchen over the mortal remains
of Sarah and Julia's lasagna, we moved at last into the living
room and Charlie built up the fire. We sprawled around in the
old furniture sprung by half a century of Cameron rumps, and
Sarah brought cheese and apples and pears and cognac, and
without consciously planning to do so, we replayed our childhoods.

There in the firelit room the invincible Buckhead Boys sailed
again down Peachtree Road on their wind-borne bicycles, Lucy
Bondurant at their head like a dark, slender Valkyrie; we
crawled under a monstrous, creeping black train at Brookwood
Station; we danced at Margaret Bryan's and streamed in packs
across Peachtree Road to the Buckhead Theatre and yelled ourselves hoarse in the cold Friday night bleachers of North Fulton
High stadium; we whirled and dipped and leaped like roseate
trouts on the dance floor at Brookhaven and the Capital City
Club, mimosa in our nostrils and "Moonglow" in our ears. Once
again Charlie and I stood in the punishing flood of a black November wind on the corner of East Paces Ferry, watching Boo
Cutler's Mercury screaming like a devil out of Hell down the
middle of Peachtree Road, trailing immortality and a DeKalb
County black-and-white. Once again he and I pedaled in perfect

despair out night-black Roswell Road toward our appointment
in Samarra and a date to screw Frances Spurling. Once again
all of us—I and Snake and Ben and Tom and Charlie and
A. J. Kemp—suffered a five-year agony of aching testicles and
galloping pulses, and called it love.

I think that all of us, even now, remember that night. Sarah,
her head thrown back on the strong, slender brown column of
her throat, laughed until she sputtered and choked. Julia, pregnant as she was, did a wicked imitation of a Washington Seminary Pink trying to learn to do the Negro bop. Charlie and I
drank an entire fifth of Courvoisier and sang North Fulton fight
songs, leaning against each other so that we would not fall. Lucy,
wrapped in an old sweater of mine, huddled on the couch, literally aflame with incandescence, and cheered them on: "Oh, sing
another one! Tell another story about Freddie Slaton! Tell the
one about A.J. and the Sope Creek bridge, tell what Snake said
to Flossie May that night at the Varsity, tell . . . tell . . . tell . . ."

It was as if the old stories were a rosary, and each telling
brought her closer to deliverance and redemption. It was wonderful to see her flaming face, and hear her old bawdy, lilting
laugh.

Of us all, only Ben Cameron and Jack did not join in the litany. Jack smiled and listened, laughing aloud occasionally, and
Ben drank cognac steadily and quietly, his clever, haggard face
flame-lit into chiaroscuro, looking off into some distance of his
own, his thin hands and feet twitching nervously. Toward the
end of the evening he remembered a phone call he had to make
to a client in Philadelphia, and went out into the still, crystal
moonlight to the feral little Jaguar XKE that he had driven up
behind Julia and the children in the station wagon. We heard
the motor growl into life, and soon he had spurted off down the
gravel road toward the gate cottage, where the sole telephone
was.

"I wish sometimes that he'd just give it up and be a general
contractor," Julia said, watching the XKE's lights careen off into
the darkness. "He drives himself so that he can't even rest on
weekends and holidays. You wouldn't believe the calls that come
at all hours, and the times he gets called away to go hold some
damned fool client's hand—you'd think he was the only architect in the country. He's burning himself up. He's lost I don't
know how much weight this year. And there's another long trip
coming up to Cleveland or somewhere next week."

"He always was as restless as a flea on a hot griddle," Charlie
said. "I don't think you're going to be able to reform him at this
late date."

"And I wouldn't want to if I could," Julia said fondly. "At

least I know he's happy doing what he wants to do. He's an authentic genius—you can't put a fence around him. I know he'd cut back on some of the work if I asked him to, but he wouldn't be happy any way but the way he is. You know Ben, he thinks he can have it all. And I guess he can, at that."

For some reason I looked across at Sarah in the semidarkness, and her face made my breath catch in my throat. There was on it such a still, contained dread that I wondered why the rest of them did not literally feel the force of it. But no one else was looking at her. She turned her head and met my eyes and I read in hers such a naked plea for help that I actually started to rise from my chair, and then she dropped her eyes and reached for her glass and the moment was gone, and I wondered if it had ever been. For the rest of the evening she was as easy and bantering as ever, and I soon came to think that the look was a trick of the firelight and my own solitude-sharpened nerves. But the weight of it remained, cold in my chest.

Ben came back presently, red-cheeked from the chill of the night and glittering like broken glass. He was humming like a fine motor, and for the rest of the evening regaled us with such scurrilous and absurd stories that we wiped tears from our faces and begged for mercy.

"I will leave you with something truly wondrous to think about," he said, standing on the lowest step of the rustic stair, a fresh cognac bottle in his hand. "And I swear it's the God's truth. I heard it from a guy in San Francisco who heard it first-hand. You know those little old watchmakers, the ones who make watches so fine that they have to work under microscopes with little tiny, miniature tools? You know what they lubricate those little tiny watchworks with? Mole sperm. Actual sperm from those little blind moles you see in your front yard after rain. Anything else is too heavy and thick—only mole sperm will do it. But here's the kicker: Where the hell do you think they get that mole sperm? Do you think they have little rooms where they go jerk off the moles one by one? Or do they put 'em in a sleazy motel room and show 'em porn movies and play Ravel's *Bolero* to a bunch of 'em all at once? Anyone with a better idea may submit it at breakfast in the morning."

And he disappeared up into the darkness, leaving us helpless with laughter in the light of the dying fire. From the blackness above us, on the long gallery, his voice drifted down: "As the late, great Harold Ross always said, 'Jesus, nature is prodigal.' "

We went back to Atlanta the next day in midafternoon, Lucy and Jack and Malory and I, and as we drove by the Cameron cottage, I looked up to see if the cars were still there, but they were gone, and the cottage was dark and shuttered.

A week later, on a night of wild wind and rain, Charlie Gentry called to tell me that they had just had the news that Ben had shot and killed himself in a hotel room in Cleveland and that they knew very little as yet, but they did know that he had left a letter for Julia which indicated that he had killed himself for the love, obviously hopeless, of a much younger man.

CHAPTER
TWENTY-TWO

"**D**ID YOU KNOW ABOUT HIM?**"
In the first unspeakable hours after young Ben's death became
known to them, Dorothy Cameron said little else.

She sat in her accustomed chair in the small den,
erect and perfectly groomed and devastated beyond all healing,
and said it over and over to those of us who kept that first vigil
with her: "Did you know? Did you know about him?"

And all of us—Ben Senior, Sarah, Charlie, I—shook our
heads, no. No. We did not, had not, known.

They had the full contents of the letter by then, brought to
them by Julia Randolph Cameron's gray-faced father and left
in the trembling hands of old Leroy Pickens at the front door.
Ben had written Julia that he finally had had to admit to himself
and her that he was and always would be homosexual; and that
he was deeply in love with a young man from his firm with
whom, of course, there could be no future; and that this seemed
to be the only way out of the predicament for all of them. Julia's
father added, in his own hand, the news that Julia had discovered
the relationship while Ben and the young man were away in
Cleveland and had threatened by telephone to take him to court
and divorce him publicly and conspicuously if he did not end
the relationship, and Ben had found that he could not do that.
Nor could he allow the pain of exposure to touch his children.

"Julia lost the baby an hour ago at Piedmont," her father's
note concluded. "Please don't attempt to come or phone or contact her in any way, nor the children. We are taking them away
when she can travel. I will keep you informed."

We sat there into the early hours of the morning, the fire burn-

ing low and being replenished by Charlie or Ben, both moving
like very old men, Sarah crying quietly in the corner of the deep
sofa, wrapped in the old afghan her grandmother Milliment had
knit, Dorothy as erect as a small queen in the tall wing chair
opposite her. I sat in the chair that had been young Ben's.
No one else had moved to occupy it, and somehow I could not
bear to see it empty: a break, eternal now, in the circle around
the hearth of the house on Muscogee Avenue. Rain, driven by
the first of the autumn gales, spattered monotonously against the
leaded windows. The wind prowled and moaned among the
chimney stacks and turrets. Leroy Pickens brought hot coffee
and sandwiches at some point during the night, but no one ate
or drank. His old face was so ashen and crumpled that Dorothy
went to him and hugged him and sent him to bed.

"Ben was as much his boy as Glenn was," she said to no one
in particular. "He's going to sit with the family, Ben; there's not
going to be any argument about that."

She was crying; had been, steadily and silently, since I had
arrived, but her handsome face did not change except to blanch
a deathly white, and her voice and hands were steady. Except
for the wetness on her face, she did not seem fundamentally
changed. Still, I had never seen her cry, and was as moved and
somehow frightened as if some great, primal foundation—a
mountain, the very earth—had shivered and swayed. There are
not a few people in Atlanta who think Dorothy Cameron cold
and unfeeling, but they have always missed the point of her. Her
code, and Ben's, had always had at its core the tenet of strength
and sustenance for others. The tears were the first fissure I had
ever seen in the fastness of that code.

I had seen Ben Cameron weep, in the debris of his very childhood in that charred field at Orly, but he did not weep now for
his only son. I am sure he was an eternity beyond that. At Dorothy's words about Leroy sitting with the family he covered his
eyes with his hand and took a great, shuddering breath, and I
knew he was seeing, as I was, the awful, the unimaginable morning now so near, in Saint Philip's Church and later Oakland
Cemetery, when he laid his firstborn in the earth.

"He never built his own house," he said, eyes still covered.
"Remember, Dottie, he almost started it last year, and then that
job in Houston came up and he didn't? I wish he'd built himself
a house."

"Oh, my dear," Dorothy Cameron said, and went swiftly to
him, and wrapped her slender arms around him. Across the
room Sarah's sobs became audible at last, and the pain of them
turned in my heart until I thought I would scream aloud with

it. Charlie pulled her close, his own face empty and nearly comical with shock. I rose to leave, but Dorothy motioned me down.

"Please, Shep, I want you to stay. Will you stay? We need a head and a heart here that isn't so . . . irrevocably Cameron."

Sarah lifted her ravaged face to me. "Yes. Please, Shep," she whispered. "You're as near to being a Cameron as there is, without being one. You feel like one of us, only better, maybe. Stay."

I wanted, in that moment, to lunge at her and shove Charlie aside and hold her against me so fiercely that pain and loss and monstrousness were literally squeezed out of her; wanted it so badly that my knuckles whitened.

I sat back down in young Ben's chair.

I found, at the bottom of me, that I was not surprised by his suicide. Shocked, grieved, outraged, but not surprised. "Did you know?" Dorothy had cried, and we had said no, but I think that I, at least, lied. I had not known about the homosexuality per se, but I had known that there was in Ben Cameron some unassailable core of shadow and pain, for I had felt my own kin with it. I had known that from our childhood.

I think Sarah had, too. I remembered her face the week before, up at Tate, and the plea in her great brown eyes. We had known, always, of that essential otherness. We had known, just as surely as Ben himself had known. I thought of how it must have been for him when he first began to realize, how it had been through all the desperate years since then. Atlanta was a murderously bad city for a homosexual in the time when Ben Cameron must have first tasted the terrifying truth about himself. Not only the vicious cretins like Boo Cutler, but the others of us, the best, the Buckhead Boys themselves, Ben's own peers—we all sneered and laughed and baited them, the feminine ones, the oblique, the pansies, the fruits, the faggots. Under it all lay the one great taboo: different. We are something of a national mecca for gays now, I am told, but it did not come in time to save Ben Cameron. The Rubicon he crossed had its headwaters in a time as distant, in perspective and ethics, as the first Dark Ages, I thought. My good and beautiful friend. My other.

It was a tragedy all the more unbearable for Ben and Dorothy Cameron, I knew, because it could not be shared, could not be dissipated a bit by the succor of their circle of friends. The code of fineness, service, health and, above all, wholeness with which they had always steered their own lives and attempted to guide those of their children could not permit the aberration, the sheer, self-centered excess of homosexuality. I knew that they would never speak of it. Ben Cameron, Junior, would be eulogized and buried a suicide, but few outside the walls of Merrivale House would ever know why. Julia Randolph Cameron would never

speak of it, either; Ben's sons were likely to know only that their
father chose to leave them by the most radical and irrevocable
means possible, but never why. Over my grief a great, weary,
flaccid anger slumped.

He's the first real casualty of our way of life, our Buckhead
way, our Southern way, I thought. I felt wearily sure that there
would be others. The utter, shadowless simplicity of it, the
rigidity—they were unquestionably the killers of complexity,
delicacy and nuance, those dubious riches which a few children
of that code, like Ben and Lucy and me, had in such abundance.
I knew that it was not any implicit moral lapse that so shocked
the Camerons underneath their searing grief, but the deviation
from the established norm, the lack of straightness and health
and light.

They loved him literally to death, I thought. Love killed him.
The love he could not live up to. The love he could not return
and pass on. The love he could not have. Somehow, illogically,
it was Ben I was sorriest for, dead Ben Cameron, who should
by all rights be safely past pain now. I knew that Julia and her
children and Dorothy and Ben Cameron, Senior, were hardy;
had their undamaged code; would, in the end, survive. Sorriest
for Ben and for sunny, bewildered and diminished Sarah, who
had been taught that willingness, loving kindness and goodness
were enough to ward off demons and monstrousness and loss.

Later that morning, at dawn, when she and Charlie had finally
persuaded Dorothy and Ben to go up to the big, light-washed
bedroom they had shared all their lives and Charlie had gone
to begin the ghastly business of phone calls and arrangements,
Sarah came and climbed into my lap as simply and naturally as
a tired child. I do not even think she knew that she was doing
it. She burrowed her head instinctively into its old place beneath
my chin, and I sat holding the small, wounded weight of her
against me, not speaking, my chin on her curly head, rocking
her lightly to and fro. She had stopped crying, but her voice was
damaged, wrecked. She sounded as if she had been hurt physically.

"I never once asked him what was wrong," she whispered. "I
knew something was, but I just . . . didn't ask. I think I didn't
want him to confide in me. There wasn't anybody for him, Shep.
Nobody to comfort him or support him, or just tell him that he
wasn't . . . awful. . . . He was my brother, and I loved him, and
I let him down. He died without anybody knowing who he was.
He thought he couldn't tell us. He thought it was too terrible.
He died because of that. That's what I don't think I'll ever be
able to bear—that he never had anybody who knew who he was
and loved him anyway."

"Yes he did," I said into the thick, springy curls. "You may
not like who it was, but somebody knew . . . and loved him. He
didn't die unloved."

She sat still, and then, as the realization that I spoke of the
young man in Ben's firm penetrated, scrubbed her head back and
forth against my neck.

"Then why didn't the little bastard save him?" she wept
afresh. "Why in God's name couldn't he be a love worth living
for? Nobody should have to die for love!"

I could have told her that Ben himself chose his death, but
in that bleak, rain-hammered morning it just did not wash. She
was right. No one should have to die of his love. There was nothing I could say to her, and so I said nothing.

We buried Ben Cameron in the family plot at Oakland, down
the hill a bit from the Bondurant plot. The grave site was shaded
by a Japanese maple which was, in the autumn sunlight, so altogether glorious it seemed a sentinel, a beacon fire lit for Ben.
Somehow that radiant, translucent tree gave me comfort in that
otherwise comfortless day. I stood with one arm around Lucy—
behind the mute, bowed ranks of Camerons, with the stricken
Buckhead Boys and their girls and most of the Pinks and Jells
of another, kinder Atlanta around me—bathed in rose-gold light
and as gray as a dead lava field inside, trying to think a good-
bye to him. But I could not. Death still seemed abstract to me
then, the province of the old and used, and I could not particu-
larize it to include this friend of my youth, this young man so
like me. It could have been anyone—old, unknown, man,
woman, even animal—in the casket that lay in its cradle, waiting
to ride into the patient earth. To our crowd, to me and to the
Buckhead Boys and to Ben Cameron, Oakland had meant hi-
jinks and pranks and picnics and illicit drinking and necking;
we did not come here to bury our own. I had the absurd notion
that when the service was over Ben would rise out of the coffin
and go back to Buckhead with us, stopping on the way for a chili
dog and onion rings at the Varsity.

I felt Lucy, beside me, trembling. She had been terribly upset
about Ben and I was a little surprised; they had never been particularly close. Something in each of them had always seemed
to take the measure of the other, and be wary of it. Her upset
had seemed to take the form of an anxiety that bordered on outright terror, and I could not understand it. On the way to the
cemetery from Saint Philip's with her and Jack, I had tried to
allay some of the fear. I thought, perhaps, in light of her emotional fragility, that she was afraid of losing control at the graveside.

"You don't have to go to the grave with us, you know," I said.

"Nobody would think a thing about it if you stayed in the car.
Jack will stay with you. You've already paid your respects at
the church; everybody will appreciate that. It's enough."

"No, I have to go," she said in a small, tight voice, thin with
dread. "I have to see him buried. I won't know for sure until
then that he's really gone."

"Lucy—" I began, feeling the ominous strangeness of the
words, but she overrode me.

"I've been having horrible nightmares ever since he died,
Gibby," she said. "I wake up crying and shaking and can't go
back to sleep. Jack is furious with me. I wake him up every night.
It's always the same dream. I dream that he's in the room with
me—Ben is—and he has the gun in a paper sack or a box or
something, and he's trying to give it to me. For some reason he
can't get close enough to me to hand it to me, and I keep pulling
back from him, till I'm jammed up against the head of the bed,
but I know that soon he'll get to me and put the sack on my
lap or something, and then it will be too late. He's real eager
for me to take it, once he said, 'Come on, Lucy, I can't wait
around here forever.' Jesus, Gibby, I don't want that gun!"

"Sweetie, it's just a nightmare," I said, profoundly disturbed
by her words. It was a terrible image. "What on earth could happen even if he did give you the sack?"

"Then it would be my turn," she said. "The gun is for me.
If he could do that to himself—if he could actually do it—why
won't it happen to me someday? I've got that same . . . thing
in me that he did, Gibby. That darkness, that craziness. I've always known that, and so have you. What he did . . . it makes
it possible, don't you see? I'm more afraid of dying than anything
else on earth. I would do anything . . . *anything* . . . to keep
from dying!"

Her voice had risen, and I remembered that day so long ago
in the living room of the house on Peachtree Road, when she
and I had crept in to watch slides of Rome and she had had the
first of those terrible fits of hysteria when she saw the tombs and
mausoleums of the American cemetery there. She had screamed
then, over and over, "I'm so afraid to die! I'm so afraid to die!"

"You aren't going to die, baby," Jack Venable said. He
sounded very tired. "This is just nerves—you're upset, and
you've been sick. I really don't want you to go to the graveside.
I'll stay in the car with you."

"No," she said. "I have to see him buried."

And she did, and was finally quiet as we heard the benediction
and walked away, as if she had left the terrible fear underneath
the red earth of Oakland with Ben Cameron.

We did not go back to the Cameron house for sherry and cof-

fee and refreshments, as old Atlanta usually does after laying
one of its ranks to rest. There was not even any thought of it.
The crowd at the cemetery—smaller by far than the one that
had come to see Ben Cameron's son married—moved off with
one accord to their big, quiet cars and went home to their big,
quiet houses and closed the great doors behind them. Ben's own
crowd—our crowd, mine—made no move to gather later, as we
might have done following the death of one of us.

For to drink to the dead is to keep them with you for a little
while longer, and I don't think any of us could have borne the
incorporeal presence of that desperate suicide. Lucy was right.
In some fundamental way, dead Ben Cameron frightened us
badly. He had, as she said, made the unthinkable thinkable, the
impossible possible. There had been too much of death in that
terrible year 1968; this last one brought the national horror of
Martin Luther King and Bobby Kennedy home to our very
Buckhead doorsteps. I remember thinking as I watched Lucy
and Jack drive away down the semicircular drive in the battered
Ford that what I felt—what we all must feel now, we golden elect
of an entire generation—was, as well as grief and horror, a kind
of dreary tarnish, the beginning of a subtle, stale cynicism, the
first awful immutable certainty that the rules of the universe do
not always hold.

For the rest of that fall and winter, Lucy seemed to continue
her slow recovery. She saw a new psychiatrist once a week, driving in to his office in one of the twin towers that had risen across
the street from Lenox Square, and she stayed on the Antabuse-
antidepressant regimen. She regained much of her irresistible old
gloss and vitality, and her splendid looks. The doctor discontin-
ued the tranquilizer and her energy and volatility began to seep
back, and by the time the first timid flush of forsythia had appeared the following February, she was restless and prowling
again, pacing the farmhouse and smoking incessantly and drinking gallons of coffee and making endless telephone calls.

"I'll go out of my mind if I don't get out of this backwater
and into something useful again," she fretted to me during one
of them. "I'll end up murdering Jack with a hoe and setting fire
to this dump. I'm sick of reading and I hate television and I don't
want to work in the fucking garden and Estelle is driving me
crazy. She gives Negroes a bad name. She has the IQ of a mess
of collards. I want to go back to work, Gibby, but Jack won't
hear of it. He says I'm too fragile yet. Do I sound fragile to you?
Fragile, shit—I'm not too fragile to cook and clean and wash
his stupid clothes and dig in his pissant garden and fetch his
drinks for him while he watches television every night of the living world."

"Is this the girl who was dying to get away to the clean, pastoral country in a quaint old farmhouse and get her hands into the good earth?" I said. "Give Jack a break, Luce. He's working his butt off. He deserves a hot dinner and a drink or two when he gets home. You know it's you he's thinking about, and he's probably right. You don't seem able just to do a job. You have to work yourself into the hospital."

She was quiet, and I heard the deep inhalation of her cigarette, and then she said, "Oh, I know it. He's right. He's always right. I had gotten myself in bad shape. And he never stops thinking of me—sometimes I wonder why he bothers. I'm really awful to him sometimes, Gibby. But he's gotten so . . . old. . . ."

"Well, he isn't exactly young," I said, near exasperation with her. "He was more than ten years older than you when you married him and he still is. I hope you didn't think that would change. And he works fourteen hours a day most days. What did you expect?"

"I don't know," she said bleakly. "Not this."

"What about Malory?" I said. "Isn't she company for you?"

"Malory is a darling and a dream, but she's in kindergarten now most of the day, and then she has play dates with the little retards around here in the afternoons—Jack makes her go; she hates it—and when he gets home she turns into Mary Poppins, buzzing around here with drinks and trays and newspapers and all till you'd like to trip her. And she *is* five years old. Five-year-olds are not the greatest dinner conversationalists, you know."

"I do know," I said, distinctly annoyed now. "Didn't you, until now? Is this a recent discovery? Mother discovers five-year-old's conversation intellectually lacking? Maybe you should send her to Dale Carnegie. Or me—I think she's terrific company."

"Oh, you're impossible!" she snapped, and hung up the phone, but in a moment she called back.

"It's me who's impossible, not you," she said. "I'm sorry, Gibby. I've turned into a first-class, gold-plated bitch. I'm going to have another talk with Jack tonight about going back to work. He's got to have noticed how miserable I am, and God knows we need the money, and this time I'll find something that's impossible to get absorbed in, like filing or typing or answering telephones."

"I didn't know you could file or type, and I wouldn't let you answer my telephone if it was ringing off the hook," I said. "Jungle drums are more your style."

She laughed, the old dark, rich, fudgy laugh.

"Why is it I only love bastards?" she said. "I can do anything I have to do to get out of God's Little Acre; you'll see how good

I can be. This time it will be different. Will you back me up with Jack if he gives me a hard time?"

I said I would, but in the end I did not have to. She must have convinced him that night that she could hold a job and not let it devour her, for she was phoning her contacts the next day. She eventually persuaded *SOUTH* to take her back, this time as a receptionist working from 10:00 A.M. to 4:00 P.M., and soon she was back in the floodwaters of the civil rights movement again—or at least paddling in the slow, sunny shallows at its borders. She seemed, for a span of months, to be content with speaking by telephone to the disembodied voices of the movement's rank and file, foot soldiers now instead of lieutenants, but as the spring moved into an early inferno summer, I wondered often how long that dutiful new disassociation would last.

I think she might have made it work, eventually made some sort of hard-won transition from activist to onlooker in the movement, if the movement itself had not let her down. If that great, pure, onrushing spate of personal heroism and selfless integrity had not faltered, I think she could have drawn enough stimulus, enough exaltation—who knows?—enough self-validation from simply wading near its peaceful banks. Lucy always did need intimate contact with heroes and legends; had, since the day she stepped into the house on Peachtree Road out of the dragon-infested world. The movement fed them to her by the hundreds for years.

But in 1969, that lusterless year, Richard Nixon took office as the thirty-seventh president of a battered and reeling United States, and a diminished and spent Ben Cameron announced that he would not seek a third term as mayor, and Lucy's fiercely idolized Ralph McGill died of a heart attack in the home of a black friend, and the great civil rights movement divided itself around the mammoth rocks of Vietnam and the youth movement and the drug culture, and never really came together again. It was the very young who raged in the streets now, and they marched and chanted and smoked and sang against the war and their fathers and mothers. The Negro youths who ran in the streets of the South ran largely with the nirvana-bent white young, beaded and fringed and belled and stoned.

In her flaming soul, Lucy did not give a tinker's damn for Vietnam or the hippies. There were no heroes among them; not to her vision-dazzled blue eyes. She did not even care for the budding feminist movement. She found no heroes in those sly jungles, or in the strident bands of bra burners, or in the stoned and supine young. I don't know why I did not anticipate that, lacking heroes, she would eventually go in search of them. It is easier to understand why Jack Venable did not see it; he was, by then, simply so tired that he would have looked the other way if she had put on a suit of armor and brought a white horse around to the front door.

But I, who had watched her quests and even ridden out beside her, on occasion, since childhood; I, who had, when she could not find a hero, tried to become one for her myself; I, who felt her hungers and thirsts, once, as my own—I should have seen. I should have known.

Lucy met Beau Longshore when he came shambling into the office of *SOUTH* looking for funds for his Mississippi mission, and she was probably beyond help by the time he told her what he sought. As terrible as its consequences were, I often thought I would have loved to be there to witness that meeting. Sparks must have danced like fireflies in the overheated air of the dingy little office. I have seen Lucy *connect* before with certain receptive people, and have felt her do it with me; I can testify to the palpability of those invisible explosions of pure light. But they must have been both palpable and visible that day.

It was inevitable that she took Beau home with her to the farmhouse for the night, since he was without cash or contacts or any other resource in the city. She brought him by the summerhouse on the way, to meet me and cadge a sandwich and a drink, and a contribution, and when I was introduced I had the eerie feeling that I was shaking hands with Lucy's twin. The same luminosity looked out of his sunken eyes; the same fever; the same veiled madness. By the time the makeshift meal was over I was almost as captivated by him as she was, but also profoundly alarmed by the meeting of the two of them. I almost called Jack Venable and told him to put an end to the association no matter what it took, but then I didn't. I think perhaps I knew, on some level, that it was already far too late.

Beau's detractors, even then, would have peopled a small county in wire-grass Georgia, but he was personally almost irresistible. Later, after he achieved national recognition, his following gained almost the status and intensity of a religious cult— which, in a very real way, it was—and his detractors feared as well as hated him. He was very tall, and thin to the point of emaciation, and, like Jack Venable, prematurely white-haired, either by hereditary disposition or by bodily abuse. His brown eyes burned in sockets so deep and shadowed they looked like pits in a peat bog in which live coals smoldered. He was deeply tanned from the relentless sun of the Mississippi gulf coast, and the effect was oddly patrician, coupled with his long, graceful bones and good facial modeling. He wore white duck pants and a faded blue denim shirt, and in them he looked as if he had just rowed ashore in a dinghy from the family racing sloop.

In fact, the pants were the white ones he had been issued in the African clinic where he had gone as a medical missionary, and the shirt had come out of the same poor box that clothed his patients in the swamp near Pass Christian. But the aristocratic demeanor was legitimate. He was, Lucy told me later, about as FFV as it was possible to be, having in his ancestry both Custis and Lee blood, and he had graduated from theology school at Sewanee and medical school at Johns Hopkins, both with honors. He did not trade on his family back in Richmond, and they in turn did not acknowledge him. The breach had been opened when he passed up the pulpit of the old gray stone Episcopal church in Richmond to go to Gabon, and had become an abyss when he came home with a shining black, Oxford-educated wife. She had quickly become disenchanted with being a missionary's wife and disappeared back to her people in Bandundu, and he had not seen her again.

"I'm sure we're divorced in her eyes," he told Lucy. "I think they do it by dancing around a chicken, or something. As for God's eyes, he winks at a hell of a lot in Africa."

In Africa he saw that it was disease and passivity, not Godlessness, that was the ancient enemy, and so he came home and put himself through medical school with a stipend from the church and three and four odd jobs at a time. It was inevitable that he would turn to drugs. The whole tenor of that generation was one of chemical exaltation, and he found that the easily purloined drugs gave strength to his intensity and got him through Hopkins. Many medical students of the Age of Aquarius regularly took uppers and downers and Percodan and Demerol; Beau Longshore simply never came down. He graduated to cocaine and flirted with LSD, and in between he drank.

This chemical *pot-au-feu* in his bloodstream did not, for many years, seem to affect him materially. The shimmer of energy and elation in his veins was offset by his lounging, slouching demeanor and his deceptively strong constitution, and in the ten years or so that he had been out of medical school and in Africa and later on the steaming Mississippi gulf coast, he had been able to accomplish an astounding amount of social good on an astoundingly small amount of money. But now he was running out of cash and physical impetus, and his methods of practicing medicine and theology had alienated him from the church and his profession, and so he had come, for the first time, looking for help.

And what he found was Lucy Venable.

"Nobody knows about the work he's doing, Gibby," she caroled to me on the telephone the next day, after Beau had headed back to Mississippi. "He doesn't go looking for publicity, and nobody down there cares about the poor coastal Negroes. They never have. Beau's not a saint, thank God—he's really very realistic about them, and very funny. Cynical, you might say. He says that he never met a noble savage, but he has met an awful lot of sorry ones, and the same thing is true of the Negroes on the coast over there. He says they won't hit a lick at a snake to help themselves and probably wouldn't if they had a million dollars apiece, and what they really need more than money or food or the vote or anything is just to *feel* good. He says that feeling bad is probably the root of all racial oppression; the man who's starved and sick and hookwormy and tired all the time just won't stand up and insist on his rights. He says they need energy as well as legislation, and he probably can't do anything about the latter, but he can the former. So he gives them drugs."

"Holy shit, Lucy," I exclaimed. "Just what the world needs now. A latter-day saint who goes around turning on the poor and the downtrodden. You know, of course, that what he's doing is illegal."

"No it's not," she said hotly. "He's a doctor as well as a minister—he prescribes the drugs he gives them, with a written prescription and everything. And he does an awful lot of other things. He preaches at their little church once a month, and goes around to others, and he marries and baptizes and buries them, and he organizes them for voter registration and takes them to get their teeth fixed, and begs clothes and food and money for them from whoever he can, and he even teaches classes for the smallest ones, and for the ones who can't read. Most of them can't. There's no school for miles and miles. And of course, he runs a free clinic. Nobody has any idea what he's doing down there—I don't even think that miserable little backwater has a name. The nearest big towns are New Orleans and Mobile, but they're hundreds of miles away, and they never heard of him there. His church and the doctors he knows won't help him anymore because of the drugs. What he needs most of all is publicity, and I'm going to get him some. I talked to Chip Turner at *Newsweek*, and he said they'd love to see a piece on him. I'm going to see if *SOUTH* will let me go down and do it, and then Chip can pick it up, and that way it'll get local and national exposure. I'll give Beau whatever Chip pays me, of course. I want you to write him a nice, fat check in the meantime. He doesn't even have enough money to get back. He hitchhiked up here."

"You're out of your mind if you think I'm going to finance the habits of a bunch of black junkies in Nowheresville, Mississippi," I said. "I'll send a truckload of medical supplies and food and clothes or whatever else he needs down there, but I'm not

going to give him money to buy drugs. Marijuana for the masses
is not my idea of an answer to poverty and oppression."

"He doesn't give out downers, only uppers," Lucy said reasonably. "Amphetamines. It's just the stuff in diet pills, it doesn't
hurt anybody. Maybe some tranquilizers for the ones who can't
sleep or have anxiety problems. And pain medication for the
ones who need it. Never any hard stuff. It's not any different
from what any doctor would do."

"Most doctors don't prescribe drugs as a philosophy of social
change," I said. "I guess he's on something himself, isn't he? He
sure looks like a junkie."

"He looks wonderful," Lucy said hotly. "He *is* wonderful.
He's a real hero in an anti-hero age, and I'm going to do a sensa-
tional piece on him. Lord, you sound more like Jack Venable
every day. If you all have so many answers, why aren't you out
somewhere helping people in need, instead of hiding out in front
of a television set or in an overblown dollhouse?"

I bit back an angry reply, largely because she had a point. I
was not exactly proud of my noninvolvement in the great social
issues swirling around me, but I could not seem to fight the en-
tropy that kept me fast in the summerhouse. I could convince
myself for long periods of time that my work on *The Compleat
Georgian* would, in the long run, have greater lasting import than
any sporadic, knee-jerk attempt I might make at social activism,
but I knew very well too, underneath it all, that the only real
value my magnum opus might ever have was that of refuge and
solace for an aging Peter Pan afraid to go out into the world.
So I let her stinging remark about the summerhouse lie.

"I gather Jack is not totally enchanted with Dr. Longshore,"
I said.

"Jack was rude as hell to him the whole time he was here,
and absolutely refused to let me wake Malory up to meet him.
And he made me take him down to the bus station first thing
the next morning; wouldn't even let him sleep late and have some
breakfast, when it was clear the poor man was half-dead for lack
of sleep and malnourished to boot. He said he wasn't going to
have any stray lions of God under his roof; he'd had enough of
my stray black panthers. I was so mad at him I could have really
killed him, Gibby. And Beau was such a gentleman about it. So
graceful and funny. He actually had Jack laughing in the end,
even as he was pointing him toward the door."

"What did he say that made Jack laugh?" I asked.

"He said he didn't blame him. He said the only thing worse
than a professional do-gooder was a professional do-gooder who
was also a stoned-out-of-his-mind fund-raiser who said 'aboot'
and 'hoose.' He said if he were Jack he'd throw him out, too."

I laughed, reluctantly liking Beau Longshore even more than I had the day before. "He's a charismatic sonofabitch, I'll say that for him," I said. "Don't worry about him, Luce. I have a very strong feeling he can take care of himself. Let Chip Turner go down there himself and do a story on him, or send some fresh, bushy-tailed kid. You promised you wouldn't overdo it."

"What's to overdo about a spring weekend on a subtropical beach?" Lucy said gaily. "With a medical missionary close at hand? It sounds like a church retreat instead of a news story. I'm thinking of taking Malory."

"NO!" It was a cry straight out of my heart and viscera, without thought or volition. "I mean it, Lucy! You can go trailing off after that middle-aged Pied Piper if you want to—nobody can stop you. But you are not going to take Malory. I absolutely forbid it."

There was a long pause, and then she laughed softly. "You forbid it, Gibby? You forbid me to take my own child with me on a weekend trip to the beach? Who do you think you are?"

"You know who I am," I said, rage running red and hot in my blood. "If Jack won't stop you, I will. I promise you that."

Another pause. "Oh, calm down," she said, in a lighter, conciliatory voice. "I'm not going to take her, really. I just said I was thinking about it. Lord, you'd think I wanted to take her to a white slaver's den, the way you and Jack Venable are carrying on. *He* threatened to take her to live with you and Mother if she went with me. It's going to be you-all's fault if she grows up scared to take risks or meet new people."

"Good," I thought. "I hope she gets through her entire life without taking your kind of risks or meeting many of your kind of people." But I did not say it aloud. I heard in Lucy's voice an edge of febrile gaiety that could easily spill over into recklessness and worse; I had heard it before, and it did not do to push or challenge it. Not where Malory was concerned.

"So when are you going down there?" I said.

"In the morning. As soon as I can cash a check and pack a bag and rent a car. Chip won't advance me any money, but he's paying for a car for the weekend. I'm going to get a convertible if they have one. The weather on the gulf coast should be beautiful."

"Be careful, then," I said neutrally. I did not want her to hear the unease in my voice. It was an effort to keep it out.

"I will. I'll see you early next week, and tell you all about it. And I'm sorry I snapped at you. I didn't mean that about the summerhouse, or Malory, either. I love you, Gibby, and all I ever do is apologize to you. Please don't ever give up on me, even if I deserve it."

"I won't," I said. "I've got too much invested in you."

"I know it," she said. "I count on that. Good-bye, Gibby."

"Bye, Luce," I said, and then, not really knowing why, "Stick it in your ear."

Her laughter came over the wire, low and full and delighted. "Stick it in your own ear!" And she was gone.

At the end of the two-day weekend she did not come home, and when Jack called Chip Turner at *Newsweek* Chip said Lucy had called and asked to keep the car a few more days, and said that the story was taking longer than she had thought but promised to be wonderful. He was surprised that she hadn't called home.

"But I'm not worried now that I know she's called in," Jack told me when I telephoned to see how the weekend had gone. "I didn't really expect her back after two days. You know Lucy. She gets so caught up in whatever she's interested in she forgets to eat, even. I only hope that asshole is worth it. Malory is really upset this time. She's been fussing and crying off and on ever since Lucy left. She's never done that before."

"Could you put her on?" I said, uneasiness mounting in me like mercury in a thermometer.

"Hey, Shep," Malory said into the wire. Her voice was listless.

"Your daddy tells me you're fussing because your mama's gone," I said. "That doesn't sound like my girl."

"I can't hear her," Malory said softly, as if she was afraid to say the words aloud. "I call her and call her, but she doesn't answer me. She always answers, Shep. You don't think she ran off or died or something, do you?"

"Oh, punkin, of course not," I said. "She's just having such a good time she hasn't got . . . her radio turned on. She'll be home before you know it."

"She always answers," Malory said, and I heard the tears begin. "She always does. She said she always would, no matter where she went."

"She's just fine, you'll see," I said. "Damn you, Lucy," I said under my breath. "Damn you for setting her up as some kind of little psychic receiving station, and damn you for tuning her out after you did, and damn you for going off and leaving her in the first place."

Jack took the telephone then and said, "If she calls you will you let me know? She told Chip she couldn't be reached by phone, but that she'd be calling in. It may be you she calls. She was mad as hell at me when she left. Like I said, I'm not worried, but I'd like to wring her neck for upsetting Malory."

But Lucy did not call me, and she did not come home, and when five days had passed Jack called Chip Turner again. This time there was a long, hollow silence, and then Chip said, "Christ, I thought surely she'd have been in touch, or somebody would have. She . . . Jack, she was sounding so erratic when she called in and asked for more time and money, and then we got word from a stringer down there that she'd been seen in a couple of real badass little backwoods joints, in . . . not very good shape. . . . Well, we took her off the story two days ago. She promised she'd come on home, and said not to call you, that she would. But I should have . . . Jesus. What can I do? What would be the most help to you?"

"Just tell me how to find her," Jack said. "And keep all this as quiet as you can, will you?"

"Of course," Chip said. "Listen, do you want me or somebody from the office to go down with you?"

"No," Jack said in a tight voice. "I have somebody."

He took Malory out of school at noon that day, and brought her, with her pajamas and toothbrush, to stay with Aunt Willa in the big house, and by one o'clock we were on the road southwest toward the Mississippi coast, the Rolls eating up the miles of narrow blacktop in a smooth rush of silence. We said almost nothing to each other beyond consulting the map and asking and receiving directions. I know that in both of us dread hummed like a motor, but we did not speak of it. I thought once, entering the Alabama coastal plain, where ribbons of black ditchwater stood mirrorlike along the margin of the road and the first Spanish moss bearded the trees, that all Jack Venable and I had or ever would have in common was Lucy, and that while it was a bond likely to last our lifetimes and hers, it was not a comfortable one. If it had not existed, we would not have chosen each other for even casual companions.

But I did not think that we would ever be free of each other, now. Going together in search and in aid of Lucy Bondurant seemed to have settled into the very genes of us, as irrevocably as the great marches toward death in the genes of lemmings, and, who knows, perhaps as destructively.

We reached Pass Christian by nightfall, but it was nearly midnight before we found, at the end of a sandy, grass-matted road so dim it seemed a part of the very tangled coastal forest it pierced, the mission and dispensary of Dr. Beau Longshore. It had taken us all those intervening hours of searching and phoning and stopping to ask directions in peeling cinder-block groceries and bait stores, and getting lost at the end of black, moss-hung tunnels and trying to turn the Rolls around in sucking, burr-matted sand, and swatting at vicious coastal mosquitoes, and cursing and squinting in the interior lights at Chip Turner's map, and breathing deeper and harder over the mount-

ing dread, to reach the moment, near-perfect in its awfulness,
that we pulled into that last clearing and saw the leaning, shored-
up frame structure with the raw wooden sign that said: COASTAL
MISSION AND CLINIC. ALL WELCOME. KNOCK OR HONK HORN.
BEAU LONGSHORE, M.D.

The white moon of that gentle, beautiful shore bathed the
leaning building and the four or five disreputable cars and one
filthy new Hertz Mustang convertible in a light so clear and lambent that it seemed palpable, like spring water. The moss in the
live oaks and tall black pines was silver-gray, and shadows were
inky and thick like a photographic negative, and frogs and peep-
ers and other silver-voiced night things called in the murderous
undergrowth, and wild honeysuckle and mimosa was so powerful that it seemed another breath, the living breath of an elemental spirit or God. There was no sign of life about the mission as
we got out of the Rolls, but a dim yellow light, like that of a
kerosene lantern, showed in a back window, and a bluish one
flickered in a front one: television.

We walked together, silently and in a kind of lockstep, to the
porch of the cabin and knocked. The noise of our marauding
knuckles was awful. There was no answer, and presently I took
a deep breath to call out, but Jack laid an urgent hand on my
arm.

"Don't," he said in a whisper. "God, don't. Let me go in."

"Not by yourself," I whispered back.

"Stay out here, Shep," he said in a low, fierce voice. "I don't
want you with me."

"You can't stop me," I hissed back. He glared at me, then
lifted his shoulders and dropped them, defeated, and we went
into Beau Longshore's clinic.

The large main room of the cabin was unbelievably filthy. It
smelled rankly of sweat and spoiling food and something else,
sweet and pungent—marijuana, I supposed, mingled with some
sort of homemade liquor or cheap wine—and illness and despair.
No light burned, but a television set flickered against one wall:
The Tonight Show. On it, a silent, gesticulating Johnny Carson
was interviewing an equally mute black man, bearded and
beaded and wild-haired and fierce; interchangeable with all the
young blacks now in the media's eye. He might have been rock
star, activist, evangelist or felon. On bare, stained mattresses in
front of the set several young black men and women lay sprawled
in drug stupors or liquor comas—it was impossible to tell which,
only that the languors were not those of fatigue and sleep.

No one spoke to us. I do not think anyone even noticed us.
Some of the couples were half-dressed and in disarray, as if they
had been making love, but none were naked, and none were en-

gaged then in sex. Bottles and paper cups and ashtrays and paper
plates half-full of something shining with grease that was turning
fast in the thick, still heat littered the floor beside the mattresses.
In a far corner, over a hot plate, an utterly silent and rather beautiful young black woman stirred something in a dented saucepan,
slowly, slowly. She lifted a sullen, dead-eyed Circe's head and
looked at us, but did not speak or gesture, and presently dropped
her eyes. She wore what looked, grotesquely, like a child's organdy pinafore, translucent over her ripe blackness and far too
small, and nothing else. We walked past all of them and into the
small space behind the main room, and there, by the light that
was indeed that of a kerosene lantern, we found Lucy and Beau
Longshore.

They were naked and intertwined on another mattress on the
floor, and their clothes were piled on one side of it, below black-
framed white rectangles that I suppose were Beau's degrees from
Sewanee and Johns Hopkins. Plates of the same mess that we
had seen in the other room lay beside them, and several empty
fifth bottles. I could not see the labels, but from the shape and
smell of them I knew them to be scotch, and expensive scotch
at that. Lucy's scotch, Haig & Haig, or perhaps Cutty Sark. I
wondered if she had brought them with her, or if some reluctantly scribbled check to Beau Longshore had bought them.
The doctor was bonelessly unconscious, and looked, in the dim,
leaping light, as if he might be moribund or already dead, his
body and face were so thin and slack and livid. But Lucy was
awake, and in her light blue eyes, deeply undercircled now with
black and saffron, I saw the old, icy flame of liquor and madness,
and on top of it a flat, new glitter that I knew must be one of
the visionary young doctor's liberating drugs. I felt only an endless gray annoyance, but I tasted in my mouth the salt of my
own tears.

"Oh, shit, Lucy," I whispered.

"Hey, Gibby," Lucy Bondurant Chastain Venable sang.
"Hey, Jack. Stick it in your ear!"

This time she went to Park Forest, a new psychiatric facility in
the foothills north of the city specializing in alcohol and substance abuse. A stricken Chip Turner insisted that *Newsweek*
cover her bills, even though they had no liability for her, and
Jack gratefully accepted. He was, by then, completely out of
money, and would take none from me. If it had not been for
Chip's offer, Lucy would have had to go to the regional alcoholic
facility in Decatur. I do not think she would have come out. But
Park Forest was experimental and state-of-the-art, and had a
wealth of new therapies and medications to try on her, and did

not, in its jaunty newness, brook defeat. We left her there knowing that what could be done for her they would do. We agreed
not to call or visit for the specified two weeks. We signed the
papers and handed over her bag and kissed her thin, wet cheek
and shut our ears to her cries and pleading and went home to
see what might be done for that other small victim of Beau Longshore's odyssey.

Malory was quiet and docile when Jack picked her up at the
house on Peachtree Road, and went with him obediently after
kissing her grandmother and me good-bye, but the very next afternoon a frantic Jack Venable was on the telephone asking if
I had seen or heard from her, saying that he had just learned
from the old black woman, who had it from her first-grade
teacher, that she had not gotten off the school bus that morning.
Before I had gotten through to the Atlanta police, just as Shem
was bringing the Rolls around to the front door, a yellow cab
drew up to the portico and small Malory Venable got out of the
back and walked hesitantly into my arms.

She had waited until Jack had driven away from the school-
bus stop and walked the few blocks into downtown Lithonia, and
taken the bus with her lunch money and ridden it into the Greyhound terminal in downtown Atlanta, and gotten into the first
taxicab that she had seen outside, and they had brought her to
us. I paid the driver and took her out to the summerhouse while
Martha Cater called Jack. I had not wanted Aunt Willa fluttering around me wringing her hands and excoriating Lucy, and
so had not yet told her that Malory was missing. So far as I knew,
she was still napping in her room. But I took no chances. I sat
Malory down on the summerhouse sofa with a cup of hot chocolate and looked at her, wondering whether to scold or caress or
cry myself, in answer to the great tears that were only then beginning to slide down her cheeks.

"You scared us, you know," I said around the lump in my
throat. "We didn't know what had happened to you."

"I don't want to be there anymore," she said, trying very hard
not to let her small face knot up, struggling to hold back the
tears. "I was scared and Jack doesn't do anything but sleep and
I can't hear my mother. Nobody was taking care of me, and
Mama said you would if nobody else did, and so . . . I came.
If you make me go back I'll just come again."

I took her in my arms then, and sat with her pulled hard
against me in that dying spring twilight, feeling the trembling
and sobbing of relief and release start and swell and then wane
into drowsiness, watching the lights of the big house bloom in

the lavender dusk, and cursed with pain and anger the particular and malevolent world that sent a vivid little girl and, many years later, her own small daughter in the selfsame headlong flight from it.

CHAPTER
TWENTY-THREE

M ALORY RAN AWAY so many times during the next decade that when Willie Nelson recorded "On the Road
Again" in her adolescence, I gave her a gold charm of
the record, and she laughed, and put it on her charm bracelet.

"He should dedicate it to me, shouldn't he?" she said ruefully.
"I guess I'm on the road almost as much as he is. Are you tired
of me?"

"Oh, not yet, I guess," I said lightly. "You add a certain touch
of class to this dump."

For it was to me that she came when the darkening burdens
in the farmhouse overwhelmed her small shoulders, first by bus
and taxi and then, in the heart-stopping manner of her generation, hitchhiking. In time it became Jack and Lucy's custom to
look first for her in the summerhouse of the Peachtree Road
house, and almost always she was there, curled up on the sofa
reading or listening to music, played softly, while I limned the
ancestry of Sarah Gentry. Sometimes, too, she asked to spend
the night at 2500 with her grandmother Willa, who adored her,
and I would take her formally by the hand and present her at
the back door of the big house, and Shem or Martha would bear
her away to the small room next to Aunt Willa's that was kept
for her, smiling broadly in the joy and pride of her presence.
Often she stayed two or three days with us, but always there
came a phone call from Lucy saying that she needed Malory,
and to please have Shem bring her home.

And Malory would go obediently and without protest, for
with her the operative word was and always would be "need."
For the first third of her life, whenever her mother's phone calls

495

speaking of need came, Malory laid aside whatever she was doing and, like the good child she was, went home. The certainty that she would was, I think, one of the few fixed stars in Lucy's careening firmament.

Lucy was in a kind of free-fall by then, not precipitous and horrifying to see, but a kind of sideslipping drifting, a dreaming, spiraling descent, as a sky diver will experience riding the thermal currents before he pulls his cord. I have heard that to the diver, that dreamlike free-fall is more dangerous than the moment of his impact, for it is often so hypnotic, so altogether free and rapturous, that the temptation to prolong it until it is too late to pull the cord is very great. I think perhaps that Lucy found in her long descent something of that freedom and rapture, for she often seemed to retreat into it when the world pierced her too hard and frequently, or she bruised herself upon reality. It was not, I have never thought, that she courted madness and deterioration, but rather that she simply did not seek very hard to elude them. Perhaps she did not, by then, even fully realize when she entered that comfortable fugue. Lucy had lived in the cold land of reality as long as she could bear it; by the fourth decade of her life she was largely an occasional visitor there. It was we who watched, not she, who knew, almost to the moment, when she left it.

I knew by her voice on the telephone. When she was in one of her stretches of smooth water, her voice was rich and slow and husky from her eternal cigarettes, and her drawled "Gibby? It's Lucy, honey" was dark and thick with promised laughter and irony. When she had begun drinking—for it was alcohol now, whatever secret white roots of madness lay still unplowed in her mind, alcohol that began those long, slow spirals, and became the whole of her torment and ours—her voice was as pure and sharp and glittering as broken glass, high and humming with secret glee.

"Gibby, honey?" she would sing out in the crystal voice, followed by a deep, sucking inhalation of smoke. "Are you there, dahlin'? It's Lucy."

I hated that voice. I hated those calls. After a while I stopped wondering, even, what had set her off and braced myself for the litany of anger and terror that would inevitably follow. For after the incident with Beau Longshore on that nameless Mississippi coast, her aberration took a different tack from the hysteria followed by near-catatonic depression that had begun to form a pattern with her, and she became obsessed with fear of, and a terrible rage at, Jack.

She seemed to believe, then, when liquor ushered in her glittering madness, that he was plotting to have her committed to the

state institution for the insane, and was in collusion with Aunt
Willa and the hapless Little Lady to keep her a prisoner there
for the rest of her life. She said, too, with a frail child's terror
that would have been heartbreaking if I had not heard it so often,
that he was abusing her both mentally and physically, often slapping and hitting and kicking her, and she was afraid that someday he would kill her with a gun. I could not disabuse her of
these notions while she was in that state. Nothing, not my insistence that she wake Jack and put him on the phone and let me
talk to him, not my pointing out to her, over and over, that she
had no marks or bruises upon her, nothing brooked the tide of
rage and fear, the nightly recitals of his monstrousness.

"Lucy, he doesn't even have a gun," I said to her once, in the
early days, when I was still trying to reason with her. "He told
me he hated them and that he'd rather be killed by a burglar
than keep a gun in the house with the children there."

"Oh, he has a gun, you'll just never see it," she said in the
crystalline singsong. "But I see it all the time. It's the one he
took away from his first wife once, before she left. Poor woman,
I understand now why she did it. I never did before. I've mis-
judged her terribly, Gibby. Terribly. I'm being punished for
that."

Later in that decade, the calls began to come from other
places. Perhaps three or four times a year the phone would ring
in the evenings, and something about the silence on the other
end of the receiver would alert me even before a laughing, lilting
Lucy told me that she was in one or another of the cut-rate businessmen's motels that ringed the city at the Interstate exits, with
a man she had picked up in the adjacent piano bar.

It was as if that first act of illicit sex with Beau Longshore
had lifted some essential governor off her dark, glinting mind,
and the search for the sheltering father's arms which she had
never found became overt. In her periods of relative health and
rationality, Lucy was as faithful to Jack Venable as some
nineteenth-century farm bride. When the darkness came, it led
her to the scanty sheets and thin mattresses of Holiday Inns and
Howard Johnsons all over North Fulton County. In the beginning Jack would go and get her out, silent and grim, but she became so abusive and strident after a while, when he appeared
to take her home, that he simply stopped going and, when she
called, rolled over and went back to sleep. He knew that she
would call me next, and that I would go. Lucy would usually
come home with me.

I don't know, really, why I made those hopeless night pilgrim-
ages, or why I continued to listen when I heard that increasingly
frequent, high-pitched "Gibby, honey? It's Lucy," followed by

the inevitable threnody of madness and abuse and terror and
pain. We were like two ghosts, I often thought, unable to rest,
doomed to haunt a world we did not even go out into anymore,
talking to each other in the consuming nights over spectral telephones. But I listened, with some degree of patience, no matter
how often she phoned, or how preposterous her accusations
were. Partly it was because she was simply so dependent on me;
so totally, in her sickness, devoted to me; seeming to trust me
with her pain when she would trust no other. And this devotion,
sly and slantwise though it was, warmed and lighted my self-
imposed exile.

But mostly, I listened to the wounded litanies of Lucy Venable
because I knew that it defused her and kept, for a little while
longer, the brunt of her madness from Malory.

For Malory was suffering. By now a serenely beautiful child
with Lucy's straight, black-satin hair and incandescent blue eyes
and the pure young hawk's profile of the Bondurants, she seemed
to have skipped her childhood altogether. With the deepening
of the darkness around her mother she lost most of her old sense
of play and fun; her ridiculous, rich, bawdy laugh, so like Lucy's,
did not ring out often; her mobile, intelligent face did not slip
so naturally into mischief or inquisitiveness as it did into lines
of worry and sunless earnestness. There was in her, had always
been, something of Lucy's old force and intensity, but without
that first lovely leavening of delicious, broad comedy and ridiculousness, it became a thing of fever and insistence, and I worried
to see it. She had wit, but she was by then no longer gay or funny.
Malory, her whole childhood one of reaction to Lucy, caromed
around the spaces of her life like a wildly bounced ball, and I
suppose it was natural that she would curtail, insofar as she
could, whatever elements of surprise and spontaneity she encountered. I did not blame her. Impulse and eccentricity had
cost her dearly all her young life.

At an age when she should have been going to children's parties and running in noisy, yelping groups after school, and ranging free in the long, sweet springs and golden summers and
autumns of the southern Piedmont, she stayed instead inside the
crumbling farmhouse in the loving but limited company of the
old black woman. She read and watched television and kept her
pitiful little vigil over her mother, and waited on her silent, sour-
ing father when he slumped in from work and settled himself
in front of the television set with the newspaper. She brought
him his drinks, and heated and fetched the starchy suppers the
old woman had left for them, and sat silently beside him watching the flickering screen until he fell into a scotch-sodden sleep.
Only then did she pull the afghan over him, brush her teeth and

slip into her own bed and, finally, sleep herself, a thin, used, old woman's sleep.

Because this minimal little routine was of Malory's own choosing, I did not really believe that Jack Venable actually neglected the quiet, lovely little specter in his home. But he could not, somehow, seem to reach out to her, to connect with her in any essential, nourishing way. Perhaps there was in her simply too much of the beautiful, flawed wife who was slipping away from him, or perhaps all real passion had been seared out of him in one too many of Lucy's anonymous motel rooms. Perhaps it had not survived the civil rights movement, which had commanded so much of it. In any case, so far as Malory was concerned, his reasons scarcely mattered. She remained essentially alone in her father's house.

So far as I knew, Jack did not ever think of leaving Lucy, and was not and never had been any of the monstrous things of which she accused him. Indeed, in the considerable periods when she was whole and clean, Lucy obviously adored and depended on him as much as she ever had. His only failing to mother and daughter that I could ever see was, perhaps fatally, his failure to nurture either.

And so Malory Venable ran away. I never once reprimanded her for that. It was perhaps the strongest and wisest thing she could do, under the circumstances. It was when Lucy called and she ran back home, as straight and as true as a silver dart, that my fear for her became, until I knew that she was safe and Lucy sane again, a living thing.

During those first years of Lucy's precipitous journey into aberrance, I fretted often about Malory's presence in the farmhouse. Even in Lucy's "good" periods, when she was home from whatever hospital her current psychiatrist had placed her in and keeping up some pretense of doing free-lance writing, it was a skewed and unhealthy household. At her worst, when she was slipping into still another fen of alcohol and promiscuity and paranoia, it must have been an emotional charnel house. I watched Malory carefully, in the periods when she was with me, for signs of damage, for wounds, but aside from her almost pragmatic running away, I saw few. She seemed to me in her late childhood, on the verge of adolescence, a creature of such miraculous beauty and presence that she might have been gotten by demigods. I literally never, in those days, chided her; I honestly saw nothing to chide. Her emerging habit of simply ghosting away when something displeased or upset her, or of threatening, matter-of-factly and very politely, to run away when Aunt Willa or Jack attempted to make her do something she did not wish to do, seemed to me entirely reasonable and even charming.

It took Dorothy Cameron to open my eyes.

I had taken to visiting her more frequently over the past year, because Ben was slipping slowly into a sly fog of dementia which had seemed to begin with young Ben's death and deepen when his decade as mayor ended, and would be termed, in another decade, Alzheimer's disease. Dorothy was nearly homebound by then; she did not often leave him in the sole company of Leroy Pickens or Minnie, their cook. He was not, yet, continually confused or belligerent, and had long periods of relative alertness and well-being, when the teasing specter of the man he had been flirted through.

But he could go suddenly blank, and it frightened him badly, and more than once he had strayed out of the house and even into his beloved Lincoln, and once had set the woods behind the house afire burning trash and simply walked away from the blaze. It hurt me terribly, and angered me, to see the engaging face and vital sinewy body of this man I loved above all others governed by a frail and flickering intelligence, but I knew that it must be unspeakable for Dorothy, and that she welcomed my visits, largely because Ben still responded almost normally to me. So I went often, and sometimes I took Malory with me. She adored Dorothy Cameron and Ben, who often thought she was Lucy but always remembered her, and they lavished on her almost the same largesse of easy affection that they did on diminutive Livvy and Charlsie Gentry. They did not see Ben's boys much. Julia could not forgive, even those who needed no forgiveness. I knew that the absence of young Ben's sons must be an unhealed and unhealable wound, but neither Dorothy nor Ben spoke of it. It was another reason I took Malory there.

One afternoon when she was ten, we sat with Dorothy Cameron over tea in the little library while Ben napped upstairs, and Dorothy asked Malory what her plans for the rest of the week were. She was spending it with us; Lucy was at Brawner's then, fighting out of the fog that had cast her up at the North Druid Hills Howard Johnson in the bed of a computer salesman from Spartanburg, and not due home for another week or two.

"I forget," she said, smiling at Dorothy and looking quizzically at me. I often planned excursions for her, even if I did not attend them.

"You've got the dentist tomorrow afternoon," I said. "And on Friday your grandmother is going to—"

"No," Malory said.

I looked at her, and Dorothy lifted a dark eyebrow.

"No, what?" I said.

"No dentist. I'm not going to the dentist."

"Sure you are," I said. "You have one more cavity before

you're through. You know that. You made the appointment the last time you were there."

"No I'm not," Malory said, her voice soft and agreeable, her blue eyes level on mine. "I'm not going. If you try to make me I'll run away. You know I will, too, Shep."

I shrugged, knowing that she well might. On the other hand, she could just as easily forget about the threat when tomorrow came, and go willingly to the dentist in the Rolls with Shem Cater. It did not seem important.

"Malory, Pickles has a new litter out in the garage," Dorothy said. "Why don't you go take a look at them? I think their eyes should be open by now."

"I'll be glad to, Mrs. Cameron," Malory said equably, and rose. "Will fifteen minutes be long enough?"

"Quite," Dorothy said, her mouth quirking with suppressed laughter. But when she looked back at me she was not smiling.

"She's almost as frightening as she is charming," she said. "And that's considerable. Listen, you may think this is none of my business, but there's nobody else to tell you. It's time you got tough on her now. She's going to grow up badly wounded if you don't."

"Tough?" I said. The very word tasted hard and queer on my tongue. "What's there to be tough about? She's as proper as a little adult now—"

"And just as stubborn and headstrong as most of them," Dorothy said. "And a good bit more imperious than most. Shep, from what you tell me, literally nobody is raising that child. Her father is either at work or passed out in front of the TV and her mother . . . well. Malory is more than a match for any poor, uneducated Negro I ever met. So that leaves you. You may not realize it, but you've become her primary caretaker. If you're going to be that, then you've got to take care. You can't just dote. This business of threatening to run away whenever she's displeased is serious. And it's the worst kind of manipulation. You need to put a stop to it, and apparently you're the only one who can."

"Jesus, Dorothy, I never asked to be a . . . caretaker," I said weakly.

"Didn't you?" she said. "You set yourself up to be her rock and her refuge. The tough comes with the sweet, my dear."

"How can I get tough with her now?" I said despairingly. "She's been through so much, she goes through so much—she may look self-possessed, but under it she's got to be frail, even damaged already. I don't want to damage her any more. . . ."

"Then you'll be handing her the same awful power her mother has," Dorothy said. "And don't think it's not awful. The power of the weak over the strong. She's already learned the drill. Who do you think she learned it from? You've got to counter that because there isn't anybody else to do it. Or do you want that role for Malory?"

"No," I said, closing my eyes wearily. "No."

And it was true. Much as I would hate it, I knew that I would take Malory aside and talk to her as I never had before. I did not want Lucy's best legacy to her daughter to be a talent for flight or manipulation.

It was a bad afternoon, the one when I broached the subject to her. I did it badly, and she took it badly. She wept and stormed and cried in a manner I had never seen before, so reminiscent of Lucy's early, desperate hysterics that my heart froze within me, and then she ran sobbing out of the summerhouse saying that she would run away and nobody would ever see her again, and only the incorporeal hand of Dorothy Cameron on my shoulder kept me from rushing after her. She did not appear for dinner with her grandmother, and I was on the verge of getting Shem and starting a search through the woods for her—a mirror journey of those her mother had precipitated decades before—when she drifted into the darkening summerhouse, red-eyed and bleared with weeping, and threw her slender arms around me, and said, "I'm sorry. I was being a jerk and you were only trying to take care of me. I won't do it again, Shep."

"No more running away?" I said, hugging her, feeling the lovely, frail cage of her ribs, and my own prickling tears, and a wonderful pride in her.

"I don't think I can promise that," she said after a long pause, still muffled in my neck. "I might have to run away to here some more. But I promise I won't threaten to do it unless I really do mean it."

"Fair enough," I said, over the pride and a dull rasp of rage at the premature adultness she had had forced upon her. Despite my best efforts, Malory Venable was not going to be accorded much in the way of a childhood.

It was not until she was nearly twelve that the other thing that I feared, a specter much slyer and more dangerous, raised its gaudy cobra's head. I had been watching her apprehensively for it for some years: How could it not have touched her in some way, given the thrust of her mother's madness? How not marked or shadowed her? But though I had watched, I had seen nothing.

And then, the week after Christmas, before she turned twelve, she said from the rug in front of the fire, where she was listening to Jimi Hendrix on her headphones while I read Walker Percy, "Why does Mother go to all those motel rooms?" She did not look up at me as she said it, and though her voice was her own, low and sweet, I could see the dull red creeping up the back of her neck.

Dear Jesus, help me now, I thought in pure panic, recognizing in the firelight the old, long-awaited enemy.

Lucy had not had one of her dark times for almost a year. We had high hopes for her new psychiatrist, a wry, warm-voiced woman who had wanted to try her on lithium and a new kind of therapy called cognitive. She thought perhaps the primary trouble might be manic-depressive illness, long concealed under and confused by the alcohol abuse, but thought, too, that Lucy's great anxiety and consequent rage might spring from a bleakly negative way of looking at life. The lithium, she thought, might help with the manic-depressive part and the resulting craving for the anodyne of alcohol, and the cognitive therapy could well address her essential nihilism.

Lucy liked the doctor and had done well on the treatment, even talking of going back to work for *SOUTH* in the new year, and we were beginning to hope, tentatively, that she had left the darkness behind her and was at least approaching the light. Jack's step and voice were lighter than they had been in the past four or five years of doctors and hospitals, and Malory laughed once more, shyly and hesitantly, and had not run away to us since the previous January.

Only I remained skeptical; it seemed to me clear that the darkness in Lucy was a thing of the blood and ran not only in her but through her and back beyond, and was thus out of the reach of drugs and positive thinking. But I did not speak of my doubts to anyone. I was not the clearest of observers when it came to Lucy Bondurant. Enough to let sleeping madness lie. The fact remained that Lucy had not taken a drink or a man for eleven months.

But then she lost it, whatever it was that was bearing her up. As Christmas approached—a time she had, for some reason, come to hate and fear—she grew more and more taut and brittle and crystal-voiced, and though we all tried desperately not to see and hear, none of us was surprised when the telltale call to me came, this time at about midnight of December 17. She had left to go to a nearby suburban mall to do some Christmas shopping and had gone instead to a truckers' motel and road stop up near Duluth, and when she called me, laughing crazily, I could hear the answering laughter of more than one man. When I got to the motel and found her room and let myself in the unlocked door, one was riding her like a bucking mare, and another was kneeling at her head with his fly open, and a third was watching television from the other bed and preparing for his turn with energetic masturbation. They had melted out of the room like dirty snowmen at the sight of me, still adjusting clothing, and Lucy screeched her laughter and defiance all the way to the hospital—not Brawner's this time, for by now they were not anxious to have Lucy back—where the doctor practiced. She had been there ever since.

We had told Malory none of the details, of course; had never done that. We said this time, as we had all those others, only that her mother was ill and in the hospital to get better, and would soon be home. But Malory was light-years removed from a fool and was nearing adolescence, and could have found out the precise shape of her mother's madness in any number of ways. I had, as I said, been waiting for this. I had been watching to see if any taint of that darkness might overshadow Malory— any precocious interest, any prurience, even, God help us, any hint that that same fever might bloom in her own blood. It had appeared in her mother at an age not much past her daughter's now.

But Malory remained as chaste and sexless as a medieval page or a young saint. She had few close acquaintances and no real friends, and none of the former were boys. Jack's boys had long since elected the predictable, if tepid, hospitality of the Nashville aunt; they rarely visited at the farmhouse anymore. She was not overtly uncomfortable in the presence of the boys of her age I saw her with: Snake and Lelia's three, and Freddie and Tom's handsome, stupid Tommy and more rarely young Ben's brace of volatile redheads. But she did not stay long in their presence, melting away as swiftly and silently as spring snow after a moment or so. I had often wondered if she was afraid of boys, and rather hoped, given Lucy's history, that she was. I looked at her on that night in the firelight; she looked, in her tattered, faded blue jeans and fringed vest and boots, like an androgynous Remington sketch. Except for the budding of the sharp, unfettered young breasts and the poreless sheen of her skin, she might have been a young boy.

"I think you ought to ask your daddy about that," I said finally, trying to keep my voice casual. "He'd probably rather talk to you about it than have me doing it."

"I've already asked Jack," she said. She still did not look up. "He said it wasn't anything for me to worry about, and to put it out of my mind. It's Mother's problem, he said, not mine. But that's just crap, Shep. It *is* something for me to worry about. It *is* my problem. It's his problem, too, only he won't act like it is. So I'm asking you."

"Well," I said, on a deep breath, "it's something that liquor and her sickness make her do. Something that she wouldn't do when she was well, and doesn't do then. Something that she won't, when she gets well for good—"

"Yeah, but what's she *doing* there?" Malory asked. I could tell that she was near tears, even though her eyes were veiled by her long lashes.

"Malory, it's not anything so bad, it's just . . . I don't—"

"Oh, Shep, I know she screws men," she said angrily, turning finally to look at me. Her eyes were terrible, bottomless pools of pain. "I know she fucks her brains out with men she never saw before. When Jack wouldn't talk to me I asked the shrink and she told me. What I guess I mean is why? Why does she have to do that? Why isn't Jack enough? Why aren't I?"

The tears started, a slow, silent track down her face, but she did not seem to know they were there, and did not move to brush them away. She stared at me as if the whole of her life hung on my answer. I knew that in a way, perhaps, it did, and hated Lucy in that moment with a hatred as pure and bright as fire, and as undiluted.

"She isn't herself when she does it," I began in dull despair. "I don't think she even knows she's doing it. It may be something to do with brain chemistry, that we don't know about yet, something she can't help. Or more likely it's a way of running away from something that hurts her terribly. . . ."

"You mean like me?" she said, her voice quavering pitifully.

"No, baby, not you, not ever you," I said. "You know that your mother loves you like nothing else in the world, no matter what. Don't you know that? No, it probably all started when she was very small, just a little girl, maybe even before she came to live here. And then finally something, maybe that chemical in her brain, just . . . pulled a kind of trigger. . . ."

"Mama told me once that she had the first . . . sick spell right after I was born," she said neutrally, and I could only think, over the red roaring in my ears, "I would like to kill you for that, Lucy. I truly would."

"Well, she was wrong," I said evenly. "She had some small . . . spells, I guess you'd call them . . . when she was in college, and right after. Maybe she doesn't remember them, but I do. So it couldn't have been you that caused them."

"Dr. Farr said it was a way of looking for her father. My grandfather," she said. The tears still ran, but the awful rigidity had gone out of her shoulders, and she slumped against my knees.

"I think she's right," I said.

"Well, then . . . what I really want to know is . . . does she . . . did she want to do that with her father? I mean, are you supposed to want to . . . you know . . . with your father? Or are you *not* supposed to and it makes you crazy to want to? Or what?"

"Has she ever said anything about that to you?" I asked, already feeling, with crimson pleasure, Lucy's slender throat in my hands.

"Oh no. No, I just wondered. I mean, if she was looking for her father with all those men, and that was what she did with them, was that what she wanted to do with him? All along?"

The truth of it was so absurd and shining and whole that I wanted to laugh aloud. I found that I could not frame a comforting lie for her.

"I don't know," I said on a long exhalation. "I really don't. I doubt if she does, either. It could be."

She sat leaning against my knees for a long time, there in the firelight, and then she put her forehead down on them and rolled it slowly from side to side, as if trying to dislodge the knowledge behind it.

"It's really awful, isn't it? The whole sex thing?" she said.

"It can be," I said. "It can be pretty awful indeed. On the other hand, it can be pretty terrific. It all depends on a lot of things. Who you do it with, mainly."

"Is it awful for you? Is that why you don't . . . you know . . . have a girlfriend or a wife?"

"Me? No," I said, surprised and profoundly uncomfortable. "It isn't awful. It never was. It was . . . pretty great. I just don't have anybody right now I really want to do it with."

"Did you ever?"

"Yes. I did."

"But not now."

"No. Not now."

"Did she go away? Did she die?"

"Malory," I said, "I love you a very great deal, and I will never lie to you, but there are some things that I simply reserve the right not to answer. When it's your business, there is nothing I won't tell you. But this is not your business. This is adult business. You are eleven years old. No matter how well-behaved and mature you are, you are still eleven years old."

"Almost twelve. Twelve in three months and two weeks. How old do I have to be before you tell me?" she said, giggling, and I knew that whatever cliff we had teetered on, we were away from the brink now.

"Thirty-seven," I said. "Maybe forty. Get up now and I'll race you over to the Camerons'. Dorothy said she was going to make tea cakes this afternoon."

"I still think sex is awful," she said, getting up from the floor n one fluid motion of long legs and arms and hair. "I'm not ever going to do it. Not ever. Ugh."

"Famous last words," I said.

"No," she said, turning her face to me. I could see that the laughter and the eleven-year-old child were gone from the blue eyes, and something much older and almost fierce was there, something implacable. "I mean that. I'd rather be dead than go in a room and . . . do that with a man. I'd rather die."

"I hope one day you have to account for that too, Lucy," I said to her, silently, as I jogged with her daughter in the tender dark up Peachtree Road. "I hope one day you get a chance to heal that wound in Malory, because it's gone beyond my ability to do it. And sick as you were, and are, you better make it good."

Lucy stayed in the new hospital, with periodic visits home, for almost a year and a half. At Faith Farr's emphatic insistence, Malory did not visit her there, but she talked to her mother on the telephone and, I suppose, by way of their old silent communication almost every day. She visited often with me and Aunt Willa on Peachtree Road, short visits, but with the boys gone, she was uncomfortable leaving Jack alone for long, and so her primary role in that time of banked turmoil and tough, wiry, greening hope was that of caretaker to him.

He was still working two jobs, and drinking and dozing when he came home, and his waking time with Malory must have shrunk to a matter of an hour or less a day, but she did not seem to mind the long stretches of time alone. Old Estelle still came at noon and stayed until she had prepared their supper, and Malory had discovered early her mother's and my refuge in books. I would have found a way to get her out of the farmhouse for good if I had seen any evidence of loneliness or neglect, but I did not. Malory with something or someone to nurture was Malory fulfilled. So for the time being, I let things ride as they were. Faith Farr, who had drifted into the role of family counselor and confidante as well as therapist to Lucy, seemed to think she was doing relatively well as Jack's housekeeper and companion. But she, as I did, had serious reservations about Malory for the long haul.

"Let's don't try to make plans for her future now," she said more than once, when I cornered her in a new fit of anxiety about Malory. "If we've really got a handle on the thing with Lucy this time, everything may sort itself out just fine. The dependency on Malory may just break itself, and that would be the best way, by far. It if ain't broke, let's don't try to fix it."

"Can you really say it ain't broke?" I would say.

"It may be right now," she said, "but that doesn't mean it always will be. It's all a part of the total dependency package Lucy lugs around, I think. Break one, or find the cause, and the rest will follow. I *think.*"

"You think? Jesus, Faith, if you don't *know* by now, when will you?" I said.

"Probably never," she replied, looking narrowly at me through smoke from her Belair. "No therapist knows. What we do is think. I think better than most. And that's what I think."

So I had to be content with that. But as the months wore on, I had to concede that it did indeed look as though she had a handle of some sort on the monstrous engine that drove Lucy. Lucy looked almost as well as she ever had, except for a permanent webbing of fine lines around her eyes and mouth and the kind of furrows that pain makes between her delicate brows, and had even gained a softening cloak of flesh, and asked for her makeup and favorite clothes once again. She had not had an episode of violence or hysteria or catatonia for months, and had made what the staff shrink termed several significant breakthroughs in her group, and was so well and fully transferred to Faith Farr that Faith said their sessions together were often pure delight.

"She's one of the most charismatic people I've ever met," she said to me and Jack. "It's impossible not to love her. Her charm is immense, and so far as I can see, it's entirely natural now."

"It is," I said. "Everything about her is entirely natural. What you see is what you get, no matter if it's her best or her craziest."

She looked at me. "Lucy has more artifice than anybody I have ever known," she said. "And she's better at it than anybody I've ever seen. That you never saw it is a mark of her skill."

"I simply can't believe that," I said, dumbfounded. "I'd know if she was faking. I've always known when she was."

Jack grinned at me. It was not a pleasant grin.

"Believe it," he said.

A month or so before Lucy was finally scheduled to be discharged, I caught up with Faith in the snack bar of the hospital and asked for an overview of Lucy's condition, and a prognosis. She did not want to give it to me, but in the end she did.

"Understand that I'm talking to you strictly for Malory's sake and no other reason, Shep," she said, blowing on her steaming coffee. "You've really got no business knowing anything about Lucy. It's her business, and Jack's, and Malory's, not yours. I think the interdependency between you and Lucy is as unhealthy as hell, and it's one of the main things I hope to help her break. It isn't all that good for you, and it's dangerous for her. I might even go so far as to say that it's helped her get and stay sick."

"God Almighty, Faith, there've been times that I was literally all she had," I exploded. "What should I have done, walked away from her? And besides, I'm damned well not dependent on her."

"The hell you're not," she said calmly. "And as for walking away from her, yes, that's just what you should have done. It isn't true that you were all she had—she had herself. But she's never learned to use it. That's what we've been working on, like two mules on a sugarcane plantation, for the past year and a half. She's coming along with it. She might even make it if you let her walk by herself. You and Jack and yes, even little Malory. I'm going to talk to them about this before she goes home."

I was silent for so long that she reached over and touched my hand.

"Don't feel bad about it," she said. "You thought you were doing the right thing. Everybody who picks her up and shores her up thinks they're doing the right thing. That's her gift as well as her sickness, the ability to make you think that. It's almost impossible to see the artifice. She even fooled me at first. But try not to bail her out anymore. If you have to help somebody, be there for Malory. Much as she loves her and dotes on her, Lucy can't do that, and Jack . . . oh, poor Jack. He can't even help himself. He's as much a victim of Lucy as she is of herself, and maybe worse. I just don't have any idea if the burnout is permanent. But I do know he's not going to be any good to Malory for a long time. I think that will probably remain to you and her grandmother."

I grimaced, thinking of Malory in the manicured grasp of Willa Slagle Bondurant.

"Do you see any signs of damage?" I said. "I'm worried about her having so few friends and sticking around that house waiting on Jack and Lucy when she's home. And I'm worried as hell about the way she feels about sex. She's really afraid of it. She hates the very thought of it."

"I knew about the waiting on and caretaking," Faith said slowly. "I'm not wild about that, but so far it seems within bounds. I didn't know about the sex thing, though I'm not surprised. It's too early to tell if it's serious, I think. Part of it could be her age—some thirteen-year-olds just haven't gotten there yet. And then, you can understand why she'd feel that way, with her mother in and out of all those beds."

"She's perceptive as hell," I said. "She's already hit on the fact that Lucy, in some entirely unconscious way, was trying to screw her father. Literally, I mean. The only thing she didn't understand was why. I must admit I don't, either."

"Well, a well-fucked man is not so quick to hit the road, Shep." Faith Farr grinned wryly. "That's what this whole thing with Lucy is about, of course. Loss, and the fear of loss. It feels to her that all losses are a replay of that first awful one, her father. She knows better now, but the gut is not long on intellectual knowledge. Changing her reactions to loss, and her fear of it, is going to be a long, long road."

"Loss," I said, old pictures slipping into my mind. "Loss . . ."

"Think back," she said. "Whenever she's lost something valuable to her, or thought she had, she's gone into one of these things. Alcohol is the ignition switch, but it isn't the engine. It only gets her to where the loss doesn't hurt so much. The first one, after Malory was born? She lost her status as a child to be cared for to her own child. Remember her saying, 'I'm the little girl and she's the mother now'? And when John Kennedy and Martin Luther King died, she lost two classic father figures. And not long before she went off with that preacher or whatever he was down there in Mississippi she had lost the movement, which gave her life so much focus and stability, and the hero-fathers in it. . . ."

"And all the other times, when there didn't seem to be anything to trigger it?" I said.

"Loss, as surely as I sit here. Jack for certain, changing before her eyes from the stable, vital, older man, the father figure, to a passive-aggressive child himself, waited on by a child, unwilling even to come to those motels and get her out of the messes she got herself in. You did that. Over and over she tried to get him to take care of her by provoking him with the booze and the men in the motels. And when he wouldn't, the loss was underscored again. A black circle. I think one reason she does so well in the hospital is that the structure and the authority make her feel protected and safe. It's one reason I've kept her here so long this time—to try to give her time to find the weapons to fend for herself and not go back to leaning when she gets home. And to give Malory time to grow up a little, too."

"You think there's going to be trouble for Malory again this time?"

"I think Lucy will try to lean on her again," she said. "I think that famous, eerie old telepathy thing has to do with great need and the response of a hyperreceptive child to it. The need is still there."

"Why, of all people, would she need so to lean on and possess her own child, who's not much more than a baby herself?" I asked. "There was always me. There was Jack. . . ."

She smiled sadly.

"Well," she said. "Lucy never really had much of a mother, did she? Or any female figure who was hers alone. That's the why of that, I think. And that's why it worries me. It's such a primal thing, it goes so deep with both of them. Look at

Malory—she's the classic little alkie-psychotic's child. The perfect little caretaker; the little mother. A great many of them never get free of it. And it can be a life wrecker. That's why I'm talking to you like this. It may never come to that, but watch her closely, and take care of her. If it gets too bizarre, just get her away from there. I may not always be around to watch—I'll have to terminate with Lucy someday, for both our sakes. But I gather you will be."

"You bet I will," I said. "You're damned right I will."

"Well, watch out for yourself, too," she said mildly. "You're almost as vulnerable as Malory is. And I don't do traumatized hermits."

I laughed and kissed her cheek and went back to the summerhouse, but the next evening I called Malory and asked her, casually, if she thought she might like to go away to school somewhere.

"I'd love to send you," I said, as nonchalantly as I could. "Anywhere you think you'd like. We could go the horse route, or the dance route"—her two great passions so far—"or we could get you up in snow country, or even find some place that specializes in pre-pre-pre-vet training. You call it."

"I couldn't do that, Shep," she said, in a brisk, no-nonsense adult's voice that rasped in my ears. "Thanks a million. You're a real angel, but it's just out of the question. There wouldn't be anybody to look out for Jack, and then Mother will be home in a couple of weeks. I can't leave her."

"Malory," I said desperately, "You're only thirteen years old. So far as I can tell, you've never in your life had any real fun."

"My life is perfect for me," she said in prim surprise. "Mother is better fun than anybody my own age when she's . . . you know . . . well, and I know she's well this time. And besides, school is not for fun. Is it?"

"Yes," I said, thinking of North Fulton High when the Pinks and the Jells were in full flower, and of my exhilaration at Princeton. "I think it is."

"Excuse me, but I think I hear Jack's car," she said, politely and inexorably, and hung up the receiver softly.

The next day I called Charlie Gentry and asked if I could come over and see him about a financial matter, and ended up accepting his insistent offer of dinner first with him and Sarah. And on Thursday night of that week, I went to the little house of Sarah and Charlie Gentry for the first time in more than a decade.

They had never moved from the first small house in Collier Hills, as most of our crowd long since had. Charlie, by then administrator of one of the country's mightiest private philan-

thropic trusts and by his own wry admission a sort of "messenger
of the gods" to beseechers all over the country, was not himself
a wealthy man. I know that he probably could have made many
times over his salary in a private law firm, and any one of the
large ones founded and operated by the fathers of our Buckhead
friends and now, increasingly, by those friends themselves would
have gladly snapped him up. It would not have been that ghastli-
est of emerging terms, networking, either. Charlie Gentry was
awesomely good at what he did. His fierce, good heart had found
its home in the genteel, anonymous world of private philan-
thropy, but his old affinity for the law was still alive and leaping,
and I knew he could be employed with full honors and perks
within a day, should he choose to leave the foundation, by making at most three phone calls.

No, money had never been the carrot for Charlie that it was
for many of us, and he had found the perfect wife in Sarah, in
that respect. I knew that she would one day come into the entirety of Ben Cameron's estate, but I knew, too, that it consisted
largely now of the property and house on Muscogee Avenue.
Ben's illness had been long and would be far longer; Dorothy
would not be left rich, nor Sarah after her. Sarah would not care.
Of all the Buckhead girls I have ever known with access to substantial money, Sarah Cameron Gentry cared least for it.

They had added on to the little Cape Cod over the years, and
now it climbed and wandered and tumbled over the steep,
wooded lot and down to a small creek at the bottom of a ravine
behind it. It could have used a paint job, I saw in the lowering
summer dusk, and a few of the shingles were missing from the
steeply pitched roof, but the lawn was green and deep, and flowers rioted everywhere in the wavering miasma of the heat. A battered hose sent a lawn sprinkler whirling, and twin bicycles lay
on their sides in the driveway. The entire house would have fit
into the drawing room of Little Lady and Carter Rawson's, I
thought, and would not have missed it by much in some of the
other homes our contemporaries now occupied, or would come
into, Merrivale House included.

I wondered if Sarah ever missed the sheer space and magnifi-
cence of her first home. I did not, somehow, think so. She had
been ready, after all, to live in that Lower West Side apartment
with me. And as long as his precious relics and his beloved wife
and daughters were there with him, Charlie would have sub-
sisted happily in an igloo. When he and Sarah came out to meet
me on the front steps of the little house, in the hot twilight, I
was struck with how right and organic they looked there, and
how much like one another they had grown. The promise of that
night so long ago at the Plaza, before they were married, when

they had come seeking me and my blessing, had long since been fulfilled; it would not have been possible for any two people to look more married than Sarah and Charlie Gentry. I felt an old, deep pang that I had not thought to feel again, seeing Sarah there in the circle of Charlie's arm, looking down at me from such an unassailable unit, and wondered if the night was, after all, going to be a mistake.

But it was not. That dinner, only the second I had ever had in their home, might have been the two hundredth. Sarah, in shorts and an Agnes Scott T-shirt, her beautiful small body as supple and tanned as it had ever been in her first youth, might have been eighteen again, instead of nearly forty. Only the threads of her father's vigorous iron-gray in her glossy mop told of passing time; the faint webbing of white lines in the tanned skin around her eyes had been there since her late teens. Charlie, on the other hand, looked every day of his years and beyond; he was as padded and settled onto his stocky frame as a good old morris chair, and his glasses were thicker, and the well-creased old chinos strained over his comfortable mound of stomach, and the bald tonsure in his dark, graying hair was larger.

But the eyes behind the glasses were still Charlie's eyes, the eyes of that sweet, ardent, largehearted boy I had first met and ranged the battlefields of the city with, and his smile was as it had always been: open and delighted and innocent still, Charlie's and no other's. We ate good pasta and drank bad wine and laughed at all that had been good and gay between the three of us, and did not speak of the other. I found myself, to my own surprise, loving the night and them—the two of them together, not Sarah and Charlie separately, as I always had before. I determined, as we rose at last from the round maple table, to see them far more often.

Sarah picked up my thought, as she had done so often before.

"This is number one in a series," she said, crinkling the great golden-amber eyes at me. "You take us somewhere for every three dinners here. You simply have no idea how we've missed you, Shep. Charlie has been pining for you for years without knowing it."

"Next one's on me," I said. "Anywhere you say. I don't think I've been out to dinner since Hart's closed."

Sarah snorted her contempt for that.

"On that exceedingly sorry note I'm going to clear away and you-all can get on with your business," she said.

"No need for you to leave," I said. "I just want to see about setting up some kind of trust for Malory, a school or college fund, or something that will be hers alone, no strings, no chance of anybody else getting hold of it. I'd like your ideas, as a matter of fact."

Charlie smiled. "I've often thought I should tell you how great I think you are with her," he said. "I wish I had before. You've been more a father to her than Jack Venable ever has."

Into the long silence Sarah said, energetically, "Well. Let me get at those dishes. Go on down to the basement, you-all, and do your business, and I'll join you when I'm done. Charlie, show Shep that new batch of shells you got from the guy in Louisiana. I'll bet he's never seen anything like that big one before."

Blessing her, I followed Charlie down into the cramped little pine-paneled den he had fashioned for himself in the basement. He switched on the overhead light, and I laughed, entirely spontaneously.

"I know, I know," he said, grinning. "Sarah says it looks like some kind of Civil War toy store for big kids."

It did, and worse. Every surface in the room was covered with the Civil War artifacts and relics that had so beguiled Charlie from that long-ago day in the attic of the Andrews Drive house when he had found his great-grandfather's uniform. They marched in precise rows on shelves and tables, hung in shadow boxes, leaned against furniture, banked the damp concrete-block walls. Shells, minié balls, belt buckles, canteens, spurs, small arms, medals, swords, stirrups, eating utensils, shone with polish and love. A smaller collection of perishable artifacts was housed behind glass cases that covered an entire wall: whole uniforms and parts of them, flags, guidons, regimental standards, gloves, hats, caps, holsters, boots, sashes. . . .

"You've got everything here but the guys," I said. "I wouldn't dare dig in your backyard for fear of who I'd find."

"You might find somebody at that," he said. "The battle of Peachtree Creek took place not three blocks from here. It's one reason I've never wanted to move. Did Sarah tell you that we might be moving?"

"No," I said. "Where to?"

"Her folks' place. Dorothy's gotten to the point that she just can't keep Ben there any longer, even with help. It's too big and too full of pitfalls for him. And the property taxes are eating them up now. She wants to move to that place up on Peachtree Road, the great big, hideous thing that's some kind of fancy retirement condominium. It has an infirmary and maid service and therapy and all kinds of things that Ben will need before long, and she says the inside of it is really quite plush. Restaurants and movie theaters and bridge rooms and libraries, and good-sized apartments. She's trying to give us Merrivale House."

"Well, God, take it," I said. "It's the greatest house in Atlanta. You know it is. Wouldn't Sarah love to be back home?"

"I guess so," he said, without enthusiasm. "We'll probably do that."

"What's the matter, Charlie?" I said.

"It's just that . . . that house is so *Cameron,*" he said slowly. "Everything in it is Cameron. You know them, larger than life. Every time I'm in it I feel like little pieces of me are coming loose and just floating away. If I lived there, I'm afraid I'd turn into a Cameron myself inside a year. Sarah can't understand that, but of course, her Cameronness gets stronger when she's in it, too. I love the Camerons, and I love her more than my life, of course, but I want something around me that says Gentry."

"Then stay here and sell the house," I said, loving him, understanding. "Dorothy wouldn't care. She's never been a sentimentalist. And Sarah would be happy wherever you are."

"I guess she would," he said. "Or if she wasn't, she'd never let me know. But I know she loves that house. She just seems to . . . bloom, somehow, when she goes home. See? I'm doing it. Home is here. Oh, hell. What difference does it make? It's a great house, and like as not we'll be neighbors come fall. At least Sarah and I would love that."

"Me, too," I said, thinking that I would not love it at all. Too close, too near . . . "What's in the box?"

He prodded a large wooden crate in the middle of the floor with a sneakered toe.

"A box of stuff I bought sight unseen from a collector in Louisiana. I know his reputation, though. Shells, mainly, I think. These would be forty-millimeter mortar shells they used in one of the big battles, probably Vicksburg. Did you know that mortars were invented during the Civil War?"

"No," I said, eyeing the box. "They're not live, of course."

"Of course not," he laughed. "Relickers are fanatics about that. Come on and sit down, it's not going to explode. We'll open it after we talk. You said something about a trust for Malory?"

I told him what I wanted, and he listened, nodding thoughtfully, making a note every now and then on a yellow legal pad, chewing his lip.

"That's feasible," he said. "But why me? Wouldn't it be better if Tom Carmichael and your guys down at the bank worked this out?"

"I want it to be separate from all the other Bondurant business," I said. "I don't want there to be anything of anyone else's attached to it. I want there to be no question but that it's hers, from me to her. Airtight and easily getatable. And I don't want anybody else to know about it. You can do that, can't you? I

know you can—you pass out millions every day, with more
strings on them than a kite contest."

"I can do that, sure," he said. "I'll get on it first thing this
weekend. You can sign it Monday, if you like. It will feel sort
of good to practice some law. Sometimes I wonder if I haven't
come awfully far afield from what I'd planned."

"I think you must be the happiest man in America." I grinned
at him. "They pay you to give money away and make people
happy. I know you. You couldn't ask for anything more."

He smiled in return.

"I'm glad I got my foot in the door of the city when I did,"
he said. "It's mattered to me to be able to give something back,
and I don't think one person starting out today could make
much of a difference. The city's just gotten too big. I'm an awfully lucky man, Shep. I got to do exactly what I wanted to do
and what I was meant to do. I got the woman I wanted, and
the kids I wanted, and the life I wanted. Don't you believe I don't
think often about how I got them. Don't think it doesn't bother
me."

"Don't let it," I said. "I think I've ended up doing what I was
meant to do, too."

"And wanted to do?" he said, cocking an eyebrow at me.

"Maybe. Or maybe not. But in the long run, meant to do is
always better than wanted to do—provided they're not the
same."

He closed the legal pad and got up from his desk chair, stretching. "Sarah will be down in a minute with some coffee," he said.
"Or brandy, if you'd rather. Stay and have some and let's open
my new toys."

I looked at him in the lamplight, stooped a little, solid, rumpled, sweet-faced, his head turned to listen up the stairs for the
sound of Sarah, who was his wife and his love and his life. I
wanted to hug him, suddenly. I knew that I would not stay.

They saw me off together, arms around each other's waists,
waving and calling out plans for our next meeting, and then
snapped off the light over the front door and moved out of my
range of vision. It was the last time I ever saw Charlie Gentry.
I remembered later wanting to hug him, there in the dreadful
little basement-den of his funny little house in Collier Hills, and
among all the things in my life I wish I had done and did not,
that is the one I wish most that I had done.

Before I reached Peachtree Road in the thick, still summer
night, Charlie pried open the package from the careful collector
in Louisiana and lifted out the dead mortar shell that was not,
after all, dead, and in a blinding white moment all that was Char-

lie Gentry—glasses and bald spot and paunch and dark, sweet eyes and great and loving heart—was gone into the ringing air of the little house where he had lived with Sarah, and which he had not wanted to leave.

CHAPTER
TWENTY-FOUR

" **F** ROM NOW ON we'll be meeting mainly at funerals,"
somebody—Freddie Goodwin, I think—said at the
small, quiet gathering at Merrivale House after Charlie's. By custom we would have gone back to Sarah's little house
in Collier Hills, but of course, with the damage from the explosion, there was no question of that. Besides, in Buckhead we have
always gathered after the natural deaths, the conventional ones,
if you will, but not usually after the ones that shock and outrage.
We had not gathered after Sarah's brother chose awfulness for
himself. We would not now when her husband, however inadver-
tently, followed him. Not within the walls that still stank with
his leaving.

But Merrivale House—ah, that was different. Merrivale, on
Muscogee: massive, beautiful, cloistered, dignified. Merrivale
House sanctified and sanitized. Here Charlie was and yet was
not; here he remained eternally safe and whole and sweet and
unscandalous; here we could deal with him with fondness and
not recoil. I suppose that I, remembering our last conversation
about that seductive *éminence grise* of his wife's family, was the
only one of us who hated being there. Here Charlie Gentry became, forever, the Cameron he had not wanted to be. They
owned him, now, forever.

I hated Freddie's words, too. They were slick with unwar-
ranted and unearned cynicism—pure Freddie. She spoke as
though we had reached the time when our deaths would come
faster than the other rituals of our lives. That was not true. What
had remained ahead for Charlie, after all the planting and tending years, were the sweet years of harvest. I think of all the

518

deaths I remember, I felt more pure, unadulterated grief at Charlie's than any other.

It was a dreadful day, unredeemed. Unlike the days immediately following young Ben's death, Sarah did not cry. She walked around her father's house devoid of all suppleness and moisture; rigid, dry, robotic. Her cheeks flamed like a circus clown's, or Lucy's long-ago plaster elf, and her great eyes glittered like frozen Coca-Cola. Otherwise she was paper-white from her heart-shaped face to her small, arched feet, as cold and white as carved marble in black high-heeled pumps. To touch her hands was to touch death by dry-freezing. Her white lips were stretched in a smile of terrible entreaty. I could not look long into her face. I could not talk to her; the arid glitter precluded words. They bounced off the surface of her like buckshot off glare ice. One after another we came, Old Buckhead, the Pinks and the Jells, to glance despairingly off the shell of Charlie Gentry's wife.

The two little girls—I say little; they were near Malory's age, but both so elfin, so small—did not cry either, not afterward in their grandparents' house, though both had wept, quietly and almost politely, at the funeral and graveside out at Oakland. They had remained pressed to their mother's sides like small animals then, bewildered and huge-eyed and pathetically still, like exuberant young monkeys gone motionless with grief and enormity. They sat on either side of Dorothy Cameron in the drawing room of Merrivale House later during that hot, gray afternoon, diminutive in short-skirted, severe white cotton—for Sarah would not have permitted mourning's crushing black on her frail-shouldered young—and shook hands and murmured thank-yous and suffered with Sarah's old grace the tearful embraces of their father's friends. But their dark eyes, so like Charlie's, kept darting to Sarah, moving stiff-spined and smiling through the small crowd, and she would feel the glances and turn and widen the awful smile, and nod her approval.

I am sure that almost every man and woman who came to Merrivale House that day was moved by the graceful, seemly daughters of Sarah and Charlie Gentry, and told them that their father would have been very proud of them. And he would have: I knew that Sarah's light, firm and loving hand on the heads of her children, so exactly that of her mother, was one of the things he loved best about her. I would have preferred tears, howling, rage, despair, anything but Sarah's awful glitter and the patrician dignity of the girls and Dorothy's calm endurance, but I knew I was not going to get them. Not in the house of the Camerons.

There were tears there for Charlie, though, and they were, after all, worse than anything, for they fell from the bewildered gray eyes of Ben Cameron. He had not been at the church or at Oakland. I knew that he was beyond large gatherings now, and I wondered who had remained behind with him while we buried his son-in-law. Leroy Pickens, older by far than he had been the day before, and fairly puckered with grief, like a wind-fallen apple, had driven Sarah and Dorothy and the girls in the Lincoln. But sometime after we had all arrived back at the house on Muscogee Avenue Ben, dressed in a silver-gray summer suit which went wonderfully with his copper-gray thatch of hair and his slender, still-erect figure, came down the beautiful old stairs to the drawing room on the arm of Glenn Pickens. We all fell silent and stared at him, and I know we were all thinking and feeling what I was: the outrage, the sheer impossibility, that the man who still walked so lithely and carried his fine, narrow head so high, and whose charming, mobile face was so nearly the same as that of the primary architect of the new Atlanta, was essentially tenanted by a torn and faded mind.

I knew he had been told about Charlie, because tears rolled down the tanned cheeks, silently and ceaselessly, and the gray eyes were as reddened as a child's fist-scrubbed eyes, and he turned his head slowly from side to side, as though looking for someone. It was Dorothy. She got up swiftly from the wing chair beside the great fireplace, where she had been stationed, and went to his side, and took his arm. Glenn Pickens stepped back as though relinquishing a flag, and stood silently, not looking at anyone in particular. His face was impassive.

"Come and sit down and say hello to everyone, darling," Dorothy said. "They've come to pay their respects and tell you how much they love you."

He looked at her, a long, uncomprehending look so full of simple pain that I averted my face.

"Ben is dead," he said pitifully, in a cracked, thin, old voice. "Did they tell you, Dottie? They keep saying that Ben is dead. I don't understand. He was just here."

For the first and last time during that entire awful day, I saw Dorothy Cameron's face twist with naked, powerful sorrow and anguish, and then it slid back into the old lines of gentle, rather austere repose.

"Not Ben, darling," she said. "That was a long time ago. We're all right about that now. This is Charlie. We've lost our dear Charlie, darling. You remember, I told you."

"Charlie?" Ben Cameron said, turning his head to look at all of us, and resting his gaze on Sarah, who had come to stand whitely beside him. "Charlie, that young man who used to hang around here, the one that works for Bob Woodruff? What happened to him?"

"Charlie was my husband, Daddy. He had an accident,"

Sarah said gently, still smiling, and I thought that I would die of the pain of that moment, right there in the drawing room of Merrivale House. Around me I heard murmurings of distress, and the rustle of people withdrawing from something too terrible to look upon.

"Shep is your husband," Ben Cameron said, knitting his iron-gray brows together. "Where's Shep? Tell him to come here. I want to talk to him about that god-awful slum down in Pumphouse Hill. . . ."

I started forward, heart hammering, not knowing what I would say, only wanting more than anything to stop that beloved, insane voice, but then Glenn Pickens moved forward and took Ben's arm and guided him silently out of the room and back up the stairs. Ben shuffled as he went.

"I know you'll forgive him," Dorothy said into the room. Her voice was modulated and clear. "He seemed quite good before we left for the church, and wanted so to come down and greet all his old friends. But I'm afraid it's all been a bit too much for him."

Sarah wheeled and walked on stiff, lamed legs into the kitchen.

Most of us left, then, quietly and with the incomparable and blessedly simpleminded dignity of people who are absolutely sure of the right thing to do, and I knew that the fresh tears on most of the cheeks were as much for Ben Cameron as for his beloved son-in-law.

I followed Sarah into the kitchen, my face stiff with pain. She stood with her own face in her hands, leaning against a counter. I touched her shoulder and she raised her head and looked at me. Her eyes were dry.

"Sarah . . . " I said.

She moved simply into my arms and I held her. I could not feel her heart, or her breath on my neck, but I could feel the chill of her flesh through the dark cotton dress.

"I keep losing my men, Shep," she whispered presently. "There must be something bitterly wrong with me, or about me, because I keep losing my men."

Holding her there in the kitchen of Merrivale House, myself one of those lost men, I thought that she had a point. Little Sarah Cameron, who had had a legion of genuinely adoring men at her side and feet all her life, who had had a bountiful richness of loving brother and father and husband and companions, was now, for all intents and purposes, alone with her mother and daughters in a widow's world of women. In Atlanta, most men will not come poaching in that chaste preserve.

"You've still got me," I said, and winced at the sheer speciousness of it.

"Oh God." Her voice was very tired. "I lost you twenty years ago."

A ponderous, crushing guilt rolled over the grief I felt, as if I had left her, literally, at the church those two decades past.

"I wish it had been me," I said, and found that I meant the words. Charlie Gentry was simply too valuable, and I would not have left behind me this legacy of wrecked women.

"Don't be stupid," Sarah said, and a hint of tartness crept into her voice. "How could Charlie and I have lived with that?"

Soon after, in August, Dorothy moved Ben Cameron into the Carlton House, an imposing, leprous-white retirement condominium on Peachtree Road where the fine old Georgian house of Dr. Thorne Champney had stood from the twenties until recently, and after that the house on Muscogee Avenue stood vacant. Sarah had, to my surprise, set her heels and refused to move out of the house in Collier Hills.

"I just can't," she said one evening in the small living room of Dorothy and Ben's apartment at Carlton House, where I found her when I went to call. Ben slept, and we three sat sipping sherry. "What would we do in that big place, the three of us? We're such . . . *little* people. We'd be like dolls in Versailles."

"You fit just fine when you were much smaller than you are now," Dorothy said, smiling.

"I can't explain it, Mama, but I've . . . shrunk," Sarah said. "I think all that space would simply scare me now. It needs somebody of Daddy's stature to cut it down to size, or yours. You dominated it, even when it was just the two of you. You overflow this silly place now. But I'd be swallowed up. Charlie never really wanted to move there, you know. He would have. We planned to. But in his heart he wanted just to stay on Greystone Road. It was his place, his and mine. And it's still mine. Somehow it wraps around me like a benediction now. Charlie is still there."

She stopped, and gave a little snort of terrible laughter, and said, "Literally, he's still there. There are specks of Charlie everywhere in the basement . . . oh God." She got up and ran out of the room and into the tiny kitchen of the condominium, and I heard her begin to cry.

I looked at Dorothy helplessly.

"Let her cry," she said, tears in her own eyes. "She's only recently begun to. I thought she was going to die of all those unshed tears for a while. She has a lot more to go before she's done."

"It breaks my heart to think of the house empty," Dorothy said later that fall, over coffee in an elegant, discreet little fireside

ook in one of the vast lounges that flourished in Carlton House.
We sat on facing velvet love seats and ate cookies and little sand-
iches; we might have been having one of the legendary teas at
ne Ritz in Boston, or the Plaza, except that everyone in the
ounge was old.

"Martin's people are keeping it up just fine," I said. "I run
y there almost every evening. There's not a blade of grass out
f place, and they're raking the leaves right along."

I did not say that despite the ministrations of the lawn service
he had hired to keep the house up—a cost that, with Ben's spe-
ial nurses and the asking price of the cramped little apartment
nd the property taxes on Muscogee Avenue, I was sure they
ould ill afford—Merrivale House looked just like what it was:
great, yearning, empty house with blind eyes and a cold, dead
eart. I turned my face from it whenever I loped past in the fall-
ng blue dusk.

"I think we might have stayed, Ben and I, despite the cost,
I'd known Sarah wouldn't change her mind about it," she said.
And she still might, of course. But I'll have to sell it if she
oesn't. The taxes are just horrendous, and Ben is probably
oing to live a long time yet, poor darling. And the damned lawn
ervice is costing me an arm and a leg. Oh Lord, Shep, the sheer
xcess of that old way of life, the one that let us build those huge
ld monstrosities, and staff them! I don't know a single widow
n my crowd who isn't looking for a buyer, or a married woman
vho doesn't know in her heart she'll have to one day."

"Well, at least you should be able to get a terrific price," I
aid. "Somebody told me what land on and just off Peachtree
Road was going for. It's just obscene."

"Not, unfortunately, in our immediate area," she replied.
"There's something about the zoning and nobody wants those
ig old houses to live in. They just want the land for commercial
uilding. I'm stuck with it."

"It must be awful for you," I said. "It hurts me to see it. I
an imagine what it must be like for you."

"I hate it, of course, but I'm not a sentimental woman, you
now, Shep," she said. "I'm grateful for this place, awful as it
s. I don't know where else I could put Ben and be with him,
oo. Between this and a nursing home, I'll take this any day. And
'd forgotten what a joy it is just to get around easily. For in-
tance, there's a special little space in the dining room for the
nes of us who're still spry, and another one for all the walkers
nd wheelchairs and such—we call them the Cane and Able
ooms. And a nurse materializes if you lift your hand, only wear-
ng the kind of clothes a good servant would. No, miss it though
do, I don't pine for Merrivale House. That's over; that part

of my life is gone. I just don't go by there anymore. It's Ben who misses it. He doesn't understand why we're staying so long in this hotel. He wants to go home."

"Well, I can see why," I said.

"Of course you can," she said. "My poor, sweet old Ben. This tarted-up geriatric ghetto is not his home. This god-awful place they call Buckhead with the silly, glitzy little shops and the chic little restaurants and those ridiculous little German cars running around all over the place isn't his home. This isn't even his city anymore, not the one he helped build. I wish he *could* go home. I wish he'd just go to sleep one night and wake up . . . home. And I wish, if Sarah doesn't want it, that somebody would just tear that old place down."

I thought it was likely that someone would, in time. Buckhead—or the Buckhead that bordered on Peachtree Road, the one that I thought of when I heard the word—was not a place of living families anymore. Back in the luxe green enclaves of the Northwest, in a cloistered and forested wedge stretching from Buckhead to the Chattahoochee River and now beyond, the great homes of Old Atlanta and the startling ones of the wealthy new still rose, serene and velvety and silent, girded around by mammoth trees and vast lawns and money. But along Peachtree Road itself, that richest and most evocative of arteries, the fine old houses of my youth stood empty or were coming down, falling to prissy, ridiculous, and hugely expensive, ersatz Federal "townhomes" or thrusting glass condominium towers; to thirty- and forty-story office towers and hotels and great "mixed-use" developments, with all three butting up to one another out of the abused red earth. To the south of Buckhead proper, only a scant square block of Peachtree Road where my own home stood was still inhabited by the old houses and their original families. Past us toward downtown not another private home stood. To the north, out Peachtree Road into and past Brookhaven—where the unbroken walls of black-green forest, in which huge old houses hid like reclusive royalty, had once rolled north to Chamblee and Doraville—another minicity like the one in midtown was rising, its towers squeezed onto land that went, in some instances, for $3 million an acre.

And Buckhead proper, that laconic, lunar, jumbled little province of the Buckhead Boys on their bicycles and later their souped-up jalopies, the spiritual home of a generation of Pinks and Jells—what of Buckhead? Well, suffice it to say that I had recently heard Buckhead called, in all seriousness, the Beverly Hills of Atlanta. I had laughed helplessly. Buckhead? Where, at the corner of East Paces Ferry and Peachtree Road, Boo Cutler had written his immortality on the wind in his mighty Merc?

Home of Minhennet's and Wender & Roberts and Tidwell's Barbecue and Burt's Bottle Shop and the Buckhead Men's Shop and four additional drugstores, all with lunch counters? Where dogwood and wild honeysuckle and mimosa handily overpowered automobile exhaust? Where, under the great daytime moon of the benevolent Coca-Cola sign, we had streamed in bright shoals across the five empty, sunstruck converging roads on our way to an afternoon movie at the Buckhead Theatre to eat popcorn and neck a little if we were lucky and cop a terrified feel if we were luckier still?

Buckhead? Where we were young and golden, and the sweating, jostling body of Atlanta proper lay safely to the south, and all that we could see for green, dreaming miles around us was ours?

What had happened to Buckhead? When had the towers and the cafés and grills and bistros and boîtes and wine bars and parking lots and antique shops and collectibles galleries and Mercedeses and BMWs and Jaguars come surging in from the Southside and Cobb and DeKalb counties? When had the gates sagged open and the walls crashed down? While I was not looking, the city had eaten Buckhead. While I was dreaming in the summerhouse, they had come: the feared Yankees and tackpots—and the Arabs and the Lebanese and the Japanese and Germans and South Americans, and the district managers from New York and Scranton and Pocatello and Mill Valley and St. Paul and the small and medium-sized towns and cities of the nation and the world, and we had fallen without a shot, toppled like the dinosaurs we were by the swift, silent defoliant that was money.

I don't know why I was so shocked. The changes had been coming for a long time, first a trickle and then a flood tide, ever since the decade of Ben and the Club had ended almost ten years before and the political and economic base and mix of the city had changed. Ben had predicted it even before he took office, had said that he and his contemporaries were setting out to build a city that would first depose and then eclipse them. I wondered if he had been aware of much of the change, or if the fog in his mind had spared him that. And then I thought that perhaps, after all, he would not have minded, but would have found the transformation exhilarating. Many people did, even though most Old Atlantans were not among them; in its first groping formative days as a Sunbelt city, Atlanta had enormous energy and a kind of brash, raffish charm. And it still was, and is, one of the most beautiful places on earth; to drive into residential North Atlanta in the springtime, or in the bronze and blue of a good October, is to leave the world and move into pure enchantment.

The city Ben Cameron had left behind him in the mists of his wounded mind was a city of severely curtailed white influence, aristocratic or otherwise. Much of Old Atlanta still had money. Our crowd was, in the main, doing almost ludicrously well for ourselves, adding new luster and dimensions to the estates our fathers and grandfathers had amassed. Many of us were so well-dowered initially that it would have been almost impossible to fail. But we were by no means the only money in town now, or even the most substantial. There were hundreds of larger and newer fortunes in the city that rose on the shoulders of Ben Cameron's town, and more streaming in every day. And even these, even a coalition of these, did not buy anything like the political power our fathers had had.

These days, political power and governmental influence lay squarely in the black hands that had stretched out to receive it when the Club had passed the torches. Ben had handed over the symbolic keys to the city to Atlanta's first Jewish mayor and black vice mayor, and since then the South's first black mayor of any real power had been in City Hall for almost an entire term. Blacks dominated all phases of city and county government, and a younger, newer and more worldly echelon stirred restlessly in the wings behind the old street fighters, waiting their turns. Glenn Pickens was one of them. He had left his storefront law practice in 1972 to join the large, prestigious one whose great mahogany doors Ben Cameron had opened for him, and shortly after had run for, and won, a Fulton County judgeship. Now he was beginning to be spoken of as a serious candidate for mayor when the aging and ailing Horace Short stepped down. He kept his own counsel about that, at least publicly, but I could see him as clearly in that second-floor office in City Hall as I had seen him on the day, more than fifteen years ago, of the crash at Orly. Only this time he sat in the chair he had, then, stood behind.

It would not be a city of unity and purpose and wholeness of ethos that he straddled. Atlanta was too big for that now, too fragmented, too much a city of parts and factions and interests. White money and property and, consequently, much of its power had fled the city proper to suburbs stretching fifty miles to the north and west, encamping in great, gleaming, treeless subdivisions that rolled away to the Blue Ridge foothills like tents on the plain of Ilion, and leaving along the way the stigmata of their passing armies: strip shopping centers, malls, fast-food outlets, office and industrial parks turning shabby in the relentless sun even before they were up to full occupancy, wholesale outlets and Honda dealerships.

Behind, in the city proper, the blacks who were left did not move with one body, mind and voice, as Ben and the Club had

done, but snarled and jostled in warring packs. But I thought
that cohesion would come for them, as it had for us before them,
when they finally and fully comprehended that what was at stake
was simply a matter of economics. Atlanta was still, as it had
always been, a business town first and foremost, if by now a riot-
ous and overblown one. Glenn Pickens, groomed by Ben Cameron and raised in the very holy of holies of economic power,
would know that.

All this I saw, in the dying decade of the seventies, when I
raised my head and looked around me. And it seemed to me,
when I did, that only I, in the summerhouse behind the house
on Peachtree Road, and my father, mute and motionless in his
absurd Turkish seraglio upstairs in it, were unchanged, voiceless
ghosts in a city that did not know us.

But the changes did not, in the main, concern me, for the cloistered microcosm that was the house on Peachtree Road and the
summerhouse behind it was by then, as old Omar put it, Paradise
enow. Malory Venable came to live with us when she was fifteen,
and from that time on everyone who came into 2500 walked with
a lighter step and a higher heart.

She came because, ultimately, it was impossible for her to stay
at the farmhouse. Even Lucy, who drove her away while sobbing
her devotion, saw that. Even Jack, whose face as he deposited
her in our care on a flickering April day was that of a man watching the last ship slide away over the cold sea in which he struggled, brought her with gratitude that she had a haven.

"Take care of her for us," he said, his voice as gray and slack
as his heavy face under the scant white hair. "Her mother can't
keep from wrecking her and I can't help her. I don't know what
the hell is going to become of us, but I have to know she's safe."

Malory was crying, unwilling tears streaking the beautiful,
austere young face, so like and yet so unlike Lucy's. She stood
clutching a dreadful, scuffed little aqua Samsonite train case that
had been her mother's and looked from Jack Venable to me, and
I have never seen another living creature so torn.

"Tell Mama I love her and I'll call her every day," she said
in a stricken voice. "Tell her if she needs me I can be there in
an hour."

"I'll tell her you love her," Jack Venable said. "But I won't
tell her you'll call, and I won't tell her you'll come. I won't have
either of those things, Malory. We agreed. There's no point in
your coming here if you're going to stay poised to fly home every
time she yells for you. If you do, even once, until she's a whole
lot better than she is now, I'll put you in boarding school. And
don't think I won't. You have absolutely got to have some kind

of life for yourself, and she's not going to get better until she
stops leaning on you. You know what Faith said."

Malory did not answer. She turned away so we could not see
her tears and I started to put my arm around her, and then
stopped. I knew she would lose her battle for composure if I did,
and Malory at fifteen was as fierce as a young Amazon about
that.

"We'll keep you posted, and you can call her anytime you
want to, or come by," I said. "The coffeepot's always on. It's
going to work out just fine, Jack. We're going to make things
really special for her."

"I hope so," he said dully. "Nothing has been, so far."

He got into the old Ford and drove away, and he did not look
back at us. I watched him out of sight in the omnipresent traffic
on Peachtree Road and then turned to Malory.

"Let's get your stuff upstairs and let your grandmother do her
worst, and then you can come out and have tea with me. Don't
be surprised if she's draped your entire room in pink organdy. I
saw that little chap from Rich's—the one who put your great-
uncle in the harem—floating up the stairs in a veritable cloud
of pink the other day."

She giggled, a weak, watery giggle.

"I know I can't stay out in the summerhouse with you," she
said. "But I don't see why I have to stay just down the hall from
her. That little place up in the attic that you and Mama had when
you were little would be just fine. I don't know if I can take pink
ruffles."

"Give it a try," I said. "A few pink ruffles might do you good.
And besides, your grandmother is so eager to have things perfect
for you that she'll probably let you redo it all in black and worship Satan if you want to. If you just can't stand it, we'll see about
the attic. But I warn you, your mother and I thought it was
pretty awful a good deal of the time. It's no place to be under
house arrest, I'll tell you."

She looked at me gravely, and my heart squeezed afresh at
the clean, severe beauty of her purely carved face and long, light
dancer's body.

"Mama was always in trouble, wasn't she?" she said. "She tells
me funny stories about the Great Captivity, as she calls it, and
how furious Grandmother always was with her, but some of it
must have been her own fault. People don't just . . . persecute
little children. It must have been going on even then—the sickness, I mean."

"I think it was, on a much smaller scale," I said. "Of course,
I didn't think of it like that then. I was right in it with her most
of the time. But yes, the seeds were there, I guess. She was a wild

little thing, always. But probably the most . . . entrancing . . . I've ever known."

"I know," she said. "She still is, to me. There's nobody like her. I wish I had her . . . energy, and her gift for making you feel that the world is a special, magical kind of place, and that you're the most important person in it. And her humor . . . she's just so funny, Shep. I'll never have half her wit, or her . . . vivacity. Is that the right word? It's so much more than that. . . ."

"Thank God you won't," I said, wrestling her bags into the foyer of the big house. "It's wrecked a lot of lives, or nearly. What you've got is a thousand times better, but I don't think you'll be able to see that till you've been away from her for a while."

"What have I got?" She looked at me with grave, curious eyes.

"Goodness," I said, surprising myself. "Integrity. Plus a few million other pretty nice things. You'll be an extraordinary woman, Malory, if you'll let yourself be a teenager first."

She blushed, a deep, vivid rose that stained her translucent skin like summer heat, and smiled shyly.

"That's nice. I hope I will," she said.

"Count on it," I said. "Look out, now. I hear your grandmother coming down in full cry."

Malory herself seemed to realize that she could not live in the house with her mother any longer. It was not a realization that had come easily.

For the first two years after she was home from the last stay in the hospital, it had looked as though Faith Farr had been right, and that Lucy had, this time, really gotten a handle on the illness and drinking. She took her medication faithfully, and continued to see Faith at her office twice a week—much of the time for free, I know, for Faith knew as well as I, by then, what the state of Jack and Lucy's finances was—and got herself a job three mornings a week in the office of the little country weekly published in Lithonia. At first she simply answered the telephone, and then she graduated to some light civic and business reporting, and when her first byline ran she was as exalted as if she had won a Pulitzer Prize.

"It's a start, Gibby," she lilted on one of her evening telephone calls, which had resumed when she came home from the hospital. Her voice was full of hope.

"It's a dinky little story, and the money won't even pay for gas and lunches, but it's a start. And it's a damned good story, if I do say so myself."

"It is that," I said. And it was. Lucy writing county business briefs was like a Lippizaner pulling a plow, but the little job engaged her and kept her mounting restlessness and energy from reaching out to Malory, and there was nothing in the minimal little office, or in that end of the county, for that matter, to either threaten or overstimulate her. For what seemed a very long time, Jack continued to work and sleep, work and sleep, and Lucy spent her afternoons holed up writing something she would neither show nor discuss with anyone, and Malory, poised on the brink of puberty and high school, continued to come home from school and see to the housework and prepare dinner and minister to Jack and Lucy—for black Estelle was simply too old and tired by then to work anymore. I thought that the order and balance of those days were weighted heavily against Malory, but it was a routine she throve upon, and they all three seemed to find a measure of stability and respite in that quiet time.

But then, almost overnight, Malory turned from child into woman, and the stability and respite flew end over end. After her daughter got her first period Lucy bought a bottle of champagne to celebrate and drank the whole thing by herself, and ended up piling the Ford into a stop sign on the way to Wendy's at three o'clock in the morning "to see who might want to come out and play." She was so stricken and remorseful when she sobered up, weeping and apologizing to her white-faced daughter and gray-faced husband when they came to get her in the little county hospital emergency room, that they did not call Faith Farr. For an entire weekend, Lucy was violently ill from the liquor—something that had never happened before—so ill that she swore she never wanted even to smell alcohol again, and Malory, trembling with fatigue from two straight days of holding her heaving, retching mother's bandaged head, believed her. Surely no one would willingly court that awful, gut-tearing nausea again.

But when Malory bought her first brassiere, red-faced with embarrassment and pride, out of the money she had saved from the grocery fund, and came home with her narrow chest thrown elaborately out, Lucy brought home scotch and drank it in her bedroom, while Malory was making dinner and before Jack got home from work. Unlike the champagne, the scotch did not make her sick. They did not even realize that she was drunk until they heard the Ford scratch off into the night, well after she had supposedly gone to bed. This time she did not come home until the next morning, and when she did, she had the look they both knew well by now, the hollowness and flaccidity, the spent and sated look that Jack called her overfucked and underfed look.

And so it started again. The third time she did it she lost the job at the little weekly, and the fourth time Faith Farr terminated the therapy.

"It's the booze by now that's the main problem," she said,

when I finally got wind of Lucy's relapse and called her. Jack and Malory had said nothing to me about the freshening of the illness. It was Lucy herself, in one of the late-night telephone calls from a motel outside Athens, who alerted me.

"She won't go to AA," Faith went on, "and she won't take her Antabuse, and I can't do a goddamned thing for her until she does. Alcohol always gets to be the main problem, sooner or later. I helped her before and maybe I could again, Shep, but I don't do alcoholics. There's no percentage in it. And I'm not going to let her play games with me."

"Then who'll help her?" I said in angry despair, thinking of Malory's strained young face and haunted eyes. "Jack can't handle her. Malory sure as hell can't, though she tries her best. They don't have a red cent between them—they owe everybody in east DeKalb County. She'll have to go to Central State or somewhere if you don't help her. They can't afford anything else, and Jack won't let me pay for her hospitalization."

"Good for Jack," she said. "I guess Central State it is, if they can get her there. They'll have to commit her, though. You know she's not going to let them take her. And I wish you all joy of that. Sorry, Shep. I know you don't believe me, but I love Lucy. I really do. Let's say I love her enough to send her to Central State or wherever it takes. Can you say the same?"

I knew I couldn't. And I knew that Jack, for all his exhausted disengagement, probably could not, either. As for Malory, the mere mention of the name sent her wild. She threatened to run away for good if we put her mother in Central State, and I did not doubt that this time she would do it. I had asked her why she was so violently opposed to it after the third time I retrieved Lucy from a motel.

"It's just a hospital, like all the others she's been in," I said. "Not as fancy, but basically the same."

"They'll give her a lobotomy," she sobbed. "Not many people know it, but that's what they do with their alcoholic patients. Mama told me. Can you imagine Mama after a lobotomy, Shep? I'd rather she was dead. I'll die myself before I let you all take her. I promised her—"

She stopped herself then, but the slip had told me what I needed to know. Lucy's lurid picture of Central State Hospital had had just the effect on Malory that she had known it would. Lucy was safe from Central State or any other hospital after that. She had known she would be. She knew better than perhaps anyone else that Jack and I would do nothing to cause Malory such pain.

"So what was the loss this time?" I asked Faith.

"Malory, of course. Malory growing up and away from her,

starting to date, maybe meeting someone she wanted to marry . . . the first period, and the brassiere—the whole thing. I could kick myself for not anticipating it and at least warning Jack and Malory."

"It wouldn't have changed anything," I said.

"No," she said, sadly. "No. It wouldn't have."

But a time came, as it had to come, when Lucy overstepped herself and lost her daughter, at least for the time being. Always before, she had bought her liquor and met her men away from the farmhouse. The one time she did not—when she brought the stumbling interstate trucker and his half-gallon of Rebel Yell home to her and Jack's bedroom at noon and then fell with him into a long, stuporous sleep—was the one time Malory brought a rare new friend, a shy, straitlaced country girl a grade ahead of her at the county high school, home for Cokes and television until the girl's late bus came.

It was that weekend that Jack brought her to us. Lucy by then was weak and husk-voiced with hysterical weeping and imploring, but this time neither Jack nor I, on the telephone, would relent. And Malory herself, exhausted and desperate, was whitely and silently adamant. It was not until Jack made to drive away and leave her with us that the old, phantom pull began to assert itself and she began to waver. And by that time a team of Clydesdales could not have pried her out of my grasp. Malory was in the house on Peachtree Road at last, and our two lives lifted and deepened and entwined closer than I had ever dared hope they might.

I think she was happy. No, I know she was. As for me, I hummed as I pecked at the old typewriter that was, inch by laborious inch, tracking the spoor of the compleat Georgian, and sang abysmally in the afternoons as I filched snacks and milk and iced tea from a beaming Martha Cater for Malory's and my daily catch-up meeting in the summerhouse, and for the first and last time in my adult life came, washed and pressed, to sit-down dinners in the beautiful old dining room with Malory and Aunt Willa, cooked by Martha and served with a rusty flourish by Shem. We had seldom had family meals there before, but Aunt Willa, thinking, I suppose, to make up for lost time with her elusive granddaughter, insisted on formal table service with candles and the old Redwine damask and proper courses, and I must admit that it pleased me to see Malory's pale, chiseled face glowing with candlelight at my table, to watch her fingering the heavy, intricate old Tiffany sterling and the crystal and porcelain with delicate enjoyment, to hear her talking politely about her day.

For the first time since I had conceded Aunt Willa the field,

I was more than content to sign the checks with which she kept the house running. I was, in fact, eager to do it. The checks bought, now, a safe and privileged haven for Malory, and I thought that I would finance Willa Slagle Bondurant as chatelaine for all eternity and smile as I did so, if it would keep Malory in the house of her great-aunt and her great-uncle and her mother . . . and me. That that mother was now forbidden the house—for Aunt Willa and I had, for once, agreed that Lucy was not to come here—gave me only slight pause. There had been a time once for Lucy here, and might perhaps again. But for now, it was the time of Malory Bondurant Venable at 2500 Peachtree Road, and that time remains, to me and perhaps to Malory herself, as whole and perfect and complete unto itself as a robin's azure egg.

To her credit, Aunt Willa managed to give Malory all she would accept of privilege and near-normalcy. Unlike her recalcitrant daughter, her granddaughter was everything she could have asked for: lovely, graceful, biddable, wellborn enough, unaffected, and with the prospect of infinite eligibility. She was Lucy without the devil in her, Little Lady with brains, a beauty already, a belle waiting to bloom. Best of all, she was the glue that would affix Willa Slagle Bondurant to the house on Peachtree Road once and for all. One look at my face when Malory was near would have told a fool that.

Aunt Willa was in her element. She enrolled Malory in Westminster and saw her safely into the creamy ports of Rabun Gap–Nacoochee and the Junior Cotillion. She gave a small tea for her at 2500 when she turned sixteen, and bought her flocks of pretty clothes, which, I think, pleased Malory even though she remained devoted to her blue jeans. She took her to the symphony and the ballet and the theater and the High Museum, and sometimes to dinner and an early movie. Shem Cater grew so accustomed to bringing the Rolls around that I had to spring for another hideous dark suit and chauffeur's cap. He absolutely refused to drive Malory in the casual clothes that the few remaining chauffeurs of Buckhead had, almost to a man, espoused by now. Shem had his own ironclad notions of propriety, and would no more deviate from them than Aunt Willa would from hers.

When Malory was sixteen Aunt Willa launched a campaign to get her out and about in the social world of what she called her "proper young set," but here Malory set her heels. She did not care for parties and dating, refused with vague politeness the suggestions about spend-the-night parties and turned down the not inconsiderable invitations she had from the young of her milieu, very few of whom I knew, with a sweet and formal distance that discouraged them from asking again. Like Lucy before her, she would not even discuss a debut or the Junior League.

I knew that she was not really shy. It was just that she had been deprived since birth of the flocking instinct and was comfortable only with the nurturing one. Unlike the teenagers around her, she had never truly been young. I was not surprised when she balked at joining any of the clubs and cliques and groups which held, to my mind, so little luster compared to the glittering excesses of the Pinks and the Jells. I was even less surprised when, after I gave her a small Toyota for her sixteenth birthday, she began to spend much of her free time working with a group of young volunteers in a halfway house for teenage drug and alcohol addicts down in the by-now-infamous Tight Squeeze section at Tenth Street and Peachtree. In that time of the flourishing drug culture, when Atlanta was the mecca for the Southeast's forlorn crop of dropouts and runaways and seekers of chemical solace, Malory Venable's tender young face was one of the first many of those wounded pilgrims saw, coming out of their murderous hazes. And it was the last many saw on their way back home or to jobs and schools. Malory had the touch; she healed as well as comforted. She had learned the skill early and indelibly. She loved the work, and it bothered her not at all that she had virtually no social life, even though it drove Aunt Willa wild.

"I don't need it, Shep," she said, when finally, at Aunt Willa's distracted behest, I taxed her with it. "I love this work. It gives me almost everything I need. And I always have you."

"Yes," I thought, looking at her with the weight of my whole unspoken heart in the look. "You always have me."

At the close of that decade, Jack Venable found Lucy in one anonymous rented bed too many, and put her out of the farmhouse. He would not, he said, divorce her, but he would answer neither her hammering on the door nor the frantic phone calls that followed it, and so she came, on a night of bitter, blowing spring rain, to the summerhouse. I knew that she would not have tried the main house. Aunt Willa had been icily adamant about that.

I opened the door to her, of course. In the end I could refuse Lucy almost nothing, and she knew it. So did I.

I sat on the sofa looking at her, my hands dangling despairingly over my crossed knees. She looked dreadful, ill and lamed and old, her glossy good looks thickened and discolored. Her hair was a snarled rat's nest, and her mouth and neck and shoulders were abraded with hard use. The fire-blue eyes were scummed.

She drew deeply on her cigarette and then threw it into the dead fireplace.

"I suppose it's no good telling you about my desperate search for the father I never had," she said, the wounded attempt at cajoling irony curdling in my ears.

"None in the world," I said. "I guess we're lucky it's men you take up with. Women would be more than I could stand."

"Of course it's men," she said, shivering. "Men have all the power. My father taught me that."

I rose stiffly and brought a towel and tossed it to her.

"He sure as hell did a lot for you with that power, didn't he?" I said. "Christ, Lucy, he did exactly zero for you. He wasn't a factor in your growing up at all. That's power?"

"He left," she said matter-of-factly. "The power to do that is the biggest one there is."

She begged me to let her stay for a time in the summerhouse, just until she "got on her feet," and I did let her sleep that night on the sofa, covered with my own comforter and blanket. But the thought of Malory, sleeping unaware and healing in the small white bed that had once been her mother's up in the big house, made anything further impossible. Lucy had not mentioned her daughter, but I knew that that was why, in large part, she had come. In the morning, or the next one, they would meet, and Lucy would send the old dark, glinting hound in her mind sniffing inexorably toward Malory, searching, searching, and then the time of Malory Venable in the big house, and possibly in the world of reality and health, would be over.

"No you won't," I thought. "No you won't."

After she slept I went into my bedroom and called Jack Venable and told him she was with me.

There was a long pause, and then he said, "Ah, shit. Okay, Shep. I'll come get her in the morning. By no means let her near Malory, though."

"No, don't come," I said. "This has got to stop. I'm going to stop it. Don't worry, she isn't going to get within fifty miles of Malory. But I don't want her back with you either, Jack. Not right now. Let me try it my way and see what happens."

He was silent again, and then he burst out, "Holy *Christ,* Shep! She's cost me my boys. She's cost me my daughter. She has all of me—she always did have. What more does she want?"

"She's afraid you'll leave her, so she leaves first," I said. I found that I only half believed the words, and did not care about them. I sounded, even to myself, like a bad recording.

"I wouldn't leave her, not really," he said. He was nearly crying. I had never heard him speak so. Anguish leaped like fresh flame in his bleached voice. "How could I leave her? In her good spells she's totally enchanting, all I ever wanted on earth. Why, after all this, after everything, does she still think I'll leave her?"

You already did that, a long time ago, I did not say, thinking of the ardent, burning man I had met that night many years before at Paschal's La Carrousel.

"I don't know," I said. "I guess it's the old father thing, and Red. And me. It's what men do to Lucy. They leave her. It all goes back to the old man. . . ."

"I'd like to kill the sonofabitch," he said hopelessly.

I thought of that gaudy phantom, sly in his gilded, magical blondness and his striped shoes, who had so devoured and spat out Lucy's childhood.

"So would she," I said.

The next morning I had Shem bring the Rolls around and I drove Lucy down to the only apartment complex I knew, Colonial Homes, where so many of our crowd had begun their post-college lives. It looked dingy and banal in the rain-freshened morning, and the flocks of handsome, sleek people leaving it in their handsome, sleek, expensive cars to go to their jobs were of a world that no more knew me than I did it. I averted my face and shut my ears grimly to Lucy's cries of pain and outrage and entreaty and rented her a studio apartment, paid the deposit and the first three months' rent by check, drove her back out to the empty farmhouse and waited while she packed the few worn things she had, drove her back to Colonial Homes and moved her into the apartment. I said almost nothing to her as I worked. I would, I said, pay her rent and utilities and send her a living allowance until she could get herself on her feet. But she was under no circumstances to try to see Malory. No visits, no letters, no telephone calls. I would enlist Aunt Willa, I said, and have Shem and Martha monitor the telephone, and she would not be allowed to speak to her daughter.

She wept. The fear and despair were real. She still thought Jack had abandoned her, and now not only was I doing the same, I was shutting her off from the child who so succored and fulfilled her.

"I need her, Gibby," she sobbed. "I can't stay in this place alone, you know I can't! Who'll look after me? Who'll talk to me, and . . . you know . . . be with me? Malory could have the pullout bed. I don't mind the chair, or a mattress—"

"No," I said coldly. "Call me if it gets so bad you can't stand it. Or get yourself a roommate. Or join the church. I don't know what you're going to do, Lucy. But you're going to back off Malory. You're going to let her have a shot at growing up straight."

"I love her, Gibby," she whispered.

"Then let her go," I said. She did not answer, and there was not really anything more to say, so I stood to leave.

She came trotting to the door behind me.

"Gibby! I can't live in this place!" she yelped.

"Why the fuck not?" I shouted. "What's wrong with it? It beats the hell out of those roach motels you've been hitting lately."

"It's a singles complex, Gibby," she said, outraged. "It just now dawned on me."

"Well, then, it should be right up your alley now, Luce," I said and grinned mirthlessly, and walked, for the time being, out of her life.

For a few months the telephone calls did not come, and I heard presently from Sarah Gentry, who had run into her at the Colonial Store, that Lucy had started with AA and taken a job with a new Buckhead weekly, and was struggling hard to make a decent life for herself and stay sober. She did both, and so well that in the fall Jack asked her to come home, and she did, with the alacrity of an abandoned dog finding its way home at last. One day not long after that she phoned Malory, and, with hammering heart, I allowed them to speak, and she was so subdued and engaging and remorseful and, above all, loving, that Malory went home that weekend to the farmhouse, and ultimately spent the remainder of her senior year at Westminster there with her mother and Jack, as nearly happy with them as she would ever be again.

I felt, that autumn, like a thin veneer of scourged flesh spread tautly over a howling abyss, but I did not intervene. Malory would be eighteen the next March. Her choices from now on out must be hers alone. I had learned, finally, the value of love held lightly in an open hand.

She graduated second in her class that May, and in the early summer left to begin an accelerated program at Wellesley, where she had won a small tuition scholarship in English literature. I paid with a bursting heart her first year's room and board and expenses, and sent Jack and Lucy with her to Wellesley in the little Toyota, rocking and sagging with a new wardrobe and a cache of books and tapes, all my graduation presents to her. I did not even think of going myself. If they were ever to be a family, it must be cemented now. When she came home again, changed as all the young are who first leave home to go into the world, it would be too late.

It was a lighthearted and almost ludicrously normal little expedition that set off from Atlanta that flawless morning in June, achingly like the one on which my mother and Ben and Dorothy and Sarah Cameron had seen me off for Princeton so long ago, and my best hope and deepest love, except for that stubborn and toothless old passion that Sarah Cameron Gentry still held, all unknowing, went with the slender, newly radiant girl who might or might not be my daughter.

CHAPTER
TWENTY-FIVE

I N OCTOBER of Malory's freshman year at Wellesley my father died in his rotting emir's fastness on the second floor of the house on Peachtree Road, a swift, spasmed, gargling death that he should have died almost twenty years before, and once again Old Buckhead gathered at Saint Philip's and Oakland.

"Are you awfully sad, darling?" Dorothy Cameron said to me in the Rolls on the way through the city, burning in the blue bowl of autumn, toward the old cemetery.

I knew that it was unorthodox that she accompany me in the first family car behind the Spring Hill hearse that bore my father, but she cared little for orthodoxy, and as for me, both my father's friends and my own would have been rather nonplussed if I had, at that late date, observed convention. Shem Cater, wizened and fierce in his new chauffeur's black, was our lone bow to conformity. He drove the shining old car impeccably, and maintained a dignified silence, but an occasional large, rattling sniff gave him away. I wondered how that desiccated old raptor in the hearse ahead of us could have, after all those years of mute and frozen not-thereness, still commanded grief from his chauffeur, but then I remembered that Shem had come to my father as his first employee, and that despite his old primate's agility, he was slightly older than the dead man he had served.

Poor Shem, I thought. He's just plain seen too much change.

I turned to look at Dorothy. In the sunlight streaming through the immaculate window of the Rolls she looked old herself, but still beautiful. Her small body had thinned with advancing age, though she still carried herself as erect as a girl, and her skin had the soft, dull, loose texture of draped silk velvet. The network of wrinkles on her strongly modeled face and throat was cobweb-fine, and her hands were gnarled with arthritis and years of hard work in her garden, but her translucent, golden-sherry eyes glowed with life, and her thick, glorious dark hair, only lightly dusted with gray, shone with the vitality of Sarah's. She wore it in an old-fashioned and becoming French knot now, and looked in it like a miniature Edwardian duchess. She smiled and put her frail hand over mine, and squeezed.

"Maybe I ought to be, but I'm not," I said. "I was sad when he had the stroke, terribly, and I felt miserable for him when Mother died—though it might well have been me I was feeling sorry for, because there was no way to tell how he felt about that. But not now. The past twenty years have been nothing but a long dying for him. I know damned well he must have wanted to check on out every day of his life. If he knew that much, even. Aunt Willa was the only one of us he seemed to want around him. I stopped going up there except about once a month a long time ago. It's like somebody just . . . moved out a piece of furniture. I guess that sounds callous as hell, doesn't it?"

"No," she said, looking at the great city skyline sliding by. "You come to that when the body is still here but the person has gone away. I know how that is. It's a terrible feeling, worse, in a way, than death."

We were silent, looking at the preposterous sunstruck towers whose names we did not know. Then she said, "It was a sad little funeral, wasn't it? Sad not so much for him as for what it represented. So few of us gathered around to see him off. There'll be even fewer to send off my dear old Ben. Sad to see those . . . giants . . . looking like ordinary old men, bewildered and belligerent. I sometimes think the worst thing there is is to live past your time. It's the final obscenity."

"I don't even know whose time it is anymore," I said. "I'm not exactly old, but all that over there might as well be the back of the moon to me," I said, jerking a thumb at the skyline. "It doesn't have anything to do with the Atlanta I know. Knew."

"It's a new day all right, no doubt about that," Dorothy said. She did not sound particularly sad; rather, interested. "A new day, a new world. That's exciting. When you think about what we've seen in the last fifty years . . . Lord! I'd love to live long enough to see what the next fifty will bring, but I'm afraid that will be the province of the young."

"I wonder if they'll even want it," I said. "All the young I know have left to go east or west or even abroad to school. Nobody seems to go to Tech or Georgia anymore. I imagine a lot of them just won't come home again."

She made a slight exasperated sound.

"You sound like the Ancient Mariner sometimes, Shep. I didn't mean Sarah's young, or Malory, or that generation. I meant you. You and Sarah, your crowd. There's still so much time for you, and so much living . . ."

She trailed off, but I knew what she meant. She meant Sarah and me. Together now in our aloneness, with no barriers between us. Shep and Sarah, Sarah and Shep. . . . The old ache that undergirt the two joined names flared up sharp and fresh, briefly, but then it died back down to its welcome dullness.

I had, of course, thought of it, after Charlie's death. But I could see nothing clearly in that country, as if it were shrouded in mist, and the effort to penetrate it was more than I could summon. Maybe, I thought, I had simply lived alone too long, shut away from life and its abrasive passions. Most of us simply give up passion eventually because it presupposes, in its core, intimacy, and we simply get too tired and used up to risk that, and the little deaths that hide in it. Even the passion that I felt for Malory, even that fierce and enduring flame, threatened continually to burn me with its breath, so that sometimes I almost flinched from it. Too hard, now, to lose, too hard . . .

Dorothy picked up my thought in the way her daughter always had.

"Malory didn't come down for the funeral," she observed. "Good. That was wise. I was afraid Lucy would use this to get her home."

I grinned. "Not much gets by you, does it?" I said. "No. Lucy's behaving herself very well these days, but Jack and I agreed there wasn't any reason for Malory to leave school in the middle of the quarter and come home for the funeral of an old man she really didn't know."

"Do you really not want me to come? I can be on a plane in two hours," Malory had said two days before, when I had called her and told her I'd prefer that she stay at Wellesley.

"No," I said. "I'll see you at Thanksgiving. You aren't homesick for Atlanta, are you?"

"No. I thought I might be, but except for you and Mama and Jack, I don't miss it. You know what I do miss, though? I miss Tate. Could we go up there at Thanksgiving? I haven't been since I was a little girl, and I keep thinking of it, for some reason."

I thought of that long-ago weekend of the impromptu house party up at Tate, only days before Ben Cameron shot himself, and of small Malory Venable whirling in a transport of delight in the middle of the cottage floor, exclaiming, "Is it ours? Can we come up here and live forever and ever?"

"We'll go for sure," I said. "Maybe we'll spend the whole

542 Anne Rivers Siddons

weekend, if it's warm enough. Have Thanksgiving dinner up there."

"I'd love that," she said. "Listen—how's Mama, really?"

"She's fine," I said.

"I mean *really*, Shep," she said, and I heard the old, protective fussiness in her voice.

"So do I," I said. "Not a whisper of a drink. Loves her job, and is beginning to do some awfully good stuff for it. She's at AA every Monday night when the doors open, and there's a new young shrink in Lithonia—can you imagine?—who has her on a different medication. She's gained a little weight, and let her hair grow out. It looks pretty. I think you're going to be pleased with her when you see her."

"I can't wait," Malory said. "I hear her calling me all the time. It's hard not to answer."

"Try," I said.

I looked about me during the graveside service at Oakland, at the handful of old people and the smaller scattering of my own friends gathered in the shade of the old oaks and crape myrtles. It seemed to me that I was seeing them for the first time in years, and indeed, in the case of many, I was. "What a long way we've all come," I thought. "We're like survivors of some kind of captive intergalactic journey. And I guess there's more truth than poetry to that."

There were my father's friends and associates, or the ones who were left, the fabled Club of the sixties: old men now, though many were still erect and slender and fit. Some wore the burden of the years badly, and some, like Ben Cameron, mumbling in his shadowland back at Carlton House, were missing from the ranks. Many others were dead. But no matter how well they had weathered the passage of time, I did not think they had weathered so well the profound changes it had brought. There was something in many of those eyes now, something tentative and puzzled, that was hard to countenance in eyes that had so recently seen a great vision for the city and watched it brought to life under their hands. They had, they would be the first to acknowledge, been dethroned by the very people they sought to attract—and also by those they did not: the businessmen of the world and the concerted Atlanta black community. The Club had foreseen and even courted the outside interests, but they had not foreseen the depth and scope of the black power emergence in the city.

I remembered that a social historian from an Eastern university, perhaps my own, once asked Ben Cameron, while he was mayor, if the blacks would ever have full membership in the Club.

"Well." Ben had smiled his famous smile. "They'll always be consulted, of course. But full membership?" and he had spread his hands eloquently, and fallen silent. The national press gave it full play.

But now they themselves were the Club, those blacks who had had to creep in the after-hours darkness of the Commerce Club to a back meeting room in order to help the mayor of their city formulate plans to save it. The inevitable coalition of outside interests and money and sheer physical numbers brought it about. And the mayor of the city now was Glenn Pickens, whose father had driven Ben Cameron's Lincolns and still did, for his family, but who had never owned a car himself. Glenn had won the will-o'-the-wisp mayorship handily in the last election, and had been in office almost two years, and was proving to be a very good mayor indeed, tough and efficient and coolly visionary, though to older Atlantans far too inclined to advocate the razing of the city's old homes and businesses to accommodate the inexorable mercenary army of high rises marching north out Peachtree Road. He was an international mayor for an international city, a new kind of man for a new region called, inelegantly, the Sunbelt.

But the bewildered old Club, watching its venerable social clubs and homes and watering holes come tumbling down, seeing the small, graceful familiar city of their reign swallowed up in concrete and steel and exhaust fumes, could not keep themselves from thinking of him and often speaking of him as "Ben Cameron's chauffeur's boy."

"Ben put him through Morehouse, you know," one would remind another. "Ben virtually raised him. I'm glad he can't see what's come of it."

I thought that, on the contrary, Ben would approve Glenn Pickens's odyssey. Indeed, he had been the architect and the navigator of it. But I *was* glad that he could not see the physical changes in his city; did not have to see his beloved Merrivale House growing dim and tattered in its emptiness, did not have to try to cope with the hordes of newcomers. It gave me physical pain to watch when the old members of the Club occasionally met and attempted to deal with the forceful, no-nonsense, almost laughably rich young outlanders who had the city's reins in their hands now. The old rules, those oblique, graceful, slow rules of order by which they had conducted their business and the city's, no longer worked. The newcomers did not comprehend the need for the graceful rituals of their glory days, the joviality and nuance and offhand courtesy, the ballet of thrust and parry. They did not comprehend the innate specialness of Buckhead that the old lions remembered. There were too many new eyes, hard and flat and canny. They formed a different fulcrum for a new and enormously larger city.

I looked around at my own friends, standing in a tight knot, shoulder to shoulder, as they had stood since childhood and tend to do at all gatherings still. Even if I had not been seated across the new grave with Jack and Lucy and Aunt Willa, they still would have stood a little apart from me. They did not mean to wound with the distance; indeed, in the beginning, it had been I who chose it. Now it seemed to me that a slight pall of the smoke of Pumphouse Hill still hung about me. It did not stink so much as simply obscure me slightly from their view. In the main, I had not minded, and did not now.

"They're what's left of the old Club," I thought, "or what it's turned into. And they're doing okay. Some of them are powerful as hell in their own right. Some of them are right up there with the Arabs and the top blacks and the newcomers, moving and shaking with the best of them. Carter Rawson now, he can buy himself a chunk of any city in the world and tear it down and redevelop it if he chooses. Snake Cheatham has enough real estate, in addition to his income from medicine, to start his own city. And Charlie—in his time, old Charlie had more money at his fingertips than most small nations, even if very little of it was his. Charlie had had more power than any of us, and thought less about it. Oh, Charlie . . .

"But we're not a patch on them, the ones who came before us," I thought. "We didn't pull together. We haven't worn all that well. Ours was the generation that started to question the rules, maybe. Or maybe the blood just thins out in the second echelon. Young Ben Cameron gone. Tom Goodwin stuck out in limbo with his virulent little Freddie; nowhere, really; not even a part of us anymore. Although maybe he could have been, if he'd ditched that little terrier bitch back while he still could. Now, like most of us, he's just too tired. Pres and Sarton Hubbard gone back to Savannah, sick of the whole scene here, gone back where things you know stay the same. A.J. and Lana Kemp working a hundred-acre farm now, and maybe better off than any of us. Charlie gone. And of course, me. The Buckhead Boys' own recluse."

I was not, I knew, a recluse in the strictest sense of the word. I got out now and then to the drug or hardware store or the post office, or to do a small errand. I spent a lot of time in the downtown library and in the archives of the Historical Society, where no one made any fuss over me. I went often out Peachtree Road past Lenox Square to the Carlton House, to see Dorothy Cam-

eron and look at Ben. I jogged five or so miles every morning
at dawn over on the empty North Fulton track, and still made
my loping rounds of Buckhead in the evenings. I attended the
obligatory funerals, though not the weddings, which were, now,
beginning to be the weddings of the offspring of the Pinks and
the Jells. For those, I called Tiffany's and ordered another of the
little enameled boxes that they stocked, and had it sent. I answered with courtesy and promptness the few dutiful invitations
that still came, but only to refuse them. I saw, really, only Dorothy Cameron, Lucy and Jack Venable, Malory whenever I could
and once in a great while, either by accident at Wender & Roberts or at a state occasion such as this, Sarah Cameron Gentry.
Little Sarah, trim and tanned still, lithe as a girl in her skirts
and sweaters and good wool pants, laughing her girl's rich, gay
laugh, only her great amber eyes deeper now with the kind of
pain given only to those who must go on alone. Sarah, once mine,
lost now and speaking to me out of the mists of another, greener
country.

Ben Cameron had told me on the afternoon after the fire on
Pumphouse Hill that my time would come, my day in the sun.
Had it come and gone, I wondered all at once, while I was in
the summerhouse annotating dead Camerons? Could I have
lived comfortably . . . outside? Could I now? No. Not then and
not now. Not yet. Maybe someday . . . But then, what do I have
to show for all those years? Enough notes for the world's longest
Southern genealogy? Who needs another one of those? Nobody,
probably. But I did. I do. It has not been dishonorable work.

What might I have had? During the concluding prayers for
my uncomprehended father, I looked inside myself, deep, deep,
into chambers that I usually kept resolutely shut. I saw nothing.
I felt blinded, bound, tethered, caged. Behind my closed eyes
there was nothing of the present or future, but the past crowded
close: all of us, the Pinks and the Jells, the Buckhead Boys and
our girls, young and golden and untouched, in the coolness of
Wender & Robert's Drugstore; in the high, hot yellow sun of
an April day nearly thirty years ago, beside a great slow, brown
river with the blue sky caught in it. . . . .

The Pinks and the Jells. My eyes stung behind my closed lids.
"We are almost fifty years old," I thought, "and we are lost in
our own country."

Coming up the long hill just past Peachtree Battle Avenue on
the way home from Oakland I lifted my head, as I always did
at this spot, for the first glimpse of 2500's sweet symmetry, and
could not see it. Except for the short block of Peachtree Road
where the house sat, and the small square of untouched woods
behind it, Peachtree Road was lined out of sight with high rises.

Not just the four- and five-story apartment buildings and condo-
miniums that prevailed along some parts of it, but twenty- and
thirty-story office and residential towers, blocking the October
sun off the brow of the house, casting the blazing garden and
the summerhouse into deep blue shadow. My house, that miracle
of proportion and grace and light, looked now like an embattled
old dowager completely surrounded by blind, marching giants.
I drew a sharp breath. The house's extraordinary beauty was
eclipsed now by its air of obstinacy, its ludicrous refusal to accept
the inevitable and fall to the great blind Goths. People not familiar with it must laugh to see it: "Wonder who the holdout is?
Some old geezer out to make a pile off the developers pissing
their pants for that land, probably. Go to it, Pops! Stick it to
'em!"

"When in God's name did all this happen?" I said aloud. It
was a rhetorical question, and Dorothy Cameron and Shem both
knew it was. Neither answered. I knew when it had happened,
of course: I had seen the dozers, had heard the jackhammers.
I had seen the bleeding earth where the great trees and the old
houses of my youth had been torn living from their roots. I could
not have failed to see. It had gone on under my very eyes these
past five or ten years.

But in a larger and deeper way, I had not seen. My very retinas
had rejected those images of devastation.

When I got back to the summerhouse I called Carter Rawson.

"How long have I got before somebody yanks my house out
from under me and puts up a fifty-story Taco Bell?" I said without preamble.

Carter gave the short hyena's bark that passes with him for
mirth. "Forever, from the looks of things. Everybody with any
money in all fifty states and about ten countries has been after
your place. The whole block, as a matter of fact. Me included.
Hasn't Marty Fox told you?"

"No," I said. "After the first three calls five or ten years ago
I had the number changed and the phone unlisted and told him
the answer was no now and forever more, and not to even tell
me about any offers he got."

"Any offers—Holy Mother of God." Carter laughed again.
"Time was you could have bought yourself an emerging nation
with what you could get for that property, with one phone call.
And whatever it was, I'd have doubled it. But right now I doubt
if you could get MARTA fare for it."

"What's the matter with it?"

"It's the zoning. The word is out that it's R-one forever; I can't
count the times a change has gotten past the review board and
into the city council, and every time it's rejected. Unanimously.

No debate, no argument and no explanation. Nobody's going to mess with it until it goes commercial or at least mixed-use."

"Why is that? Who's blocking it?" I said. The cold fear around my heart which had sprung up that afternoon when I had seen, as if for the first time, the house surrounded by sky-stabbing monstrosities eased a little.

"I have no idea. Nobody does, or I'd know it. Somebody awfully high up, who doesn't give a shit about money. And in this town, I simply don't know anybody like that. I'd have said you could buy the entire council for a new BMW, but obviously somebody doesn't need one. It's not that people don't want to sell. Poor old Dorothy Cameron has been trying to unload that old heap of hers for years. So have the Cobbs, and Rhodes Bayliss. Everybody, in fact, but you. You haven't bought off the council, have you?"

"I didn't even know there was one," I said honestly. "So, am I safe, then? Can I count on the house being there for . . . a long time? My lifetime?" And Malory's, I did not say.

"I didn't say that," he said. "In fact, I'd be willing to bet we'll get that zoning changed within five or ten years. Maybe before. We'll get to whoever's blocking it eventually. We always do. Listen, Shep," and his voice deepened and smoothed into his notion of the famous Club drawl, "I meant what I said. When the zoning falls—and it will—I'll go double the best offer you get for it. No matter what it is. Call me first. You won't be sorry. I'll find you another house, one that fits you to a T. Hell, I'll even build it for you and move you in. You won't have to lift a finger."

"I'm not selling, Carter, even if the zoning changes tomorrow," I said. "But just out of curiosity, what would you do with it? Tear it down, I know, but what would you put there?"

"Parking," he said instantly, and I heard the obsessive single-mindedness of the starving man in his voice. "There's not a single public parking lot between Brookwood Station and Lenox Square. The place would mint money. Hey, you want a little piece of it? I can do that—"

"I'm not selling, Carter," I said. "Maybe I didn't make myself clear."

"Oh, you'll sell, when the zoning changes," he said. "One way or another, you'll sell. Willingly or unwillingly. Unwillingly is not usually much fun. I'd hope it was willingly. And to me."

"Carter," I said, "it would please me very much if you would go fuck an I beam."

And I hung up.

Without an instant's hesitation I sat down and dialed City Hall. My index finger knew only milliseconds before my brain who I should be talking to.

"I wondered when you'd be calling," Glenn Pickens said. "You don't catch on very fast, do you?"

"No," I said. "It's never been my long suit. Tell me about my house. How long am I safe, first. And why, second."

He laughed. I did not remember ever hearing him do that, but I recalled that Lucy had said once that they laughed together a great deal when they were very young, she and Glenn.

"Perfect timing, anyway," he said. "There's another application in front of the board right now, and I happen to know that it has the unanimous approval of the council. Like they all have. Which means that I'm going to have to spend another four or five nights and probably a weekend calling and bargaining and making promises and moving and shaking, of which I am getting extremely tired. If anybody ever calls in all my chips I'll have to move to Buenos Aires."

"I don't understand," I said.

The laughter was gone from his voice, abruptly. "Ben Cameron was able to save your asses out in Buckhead until he got sick," he said, "but I'm not in the business of saving Buckhead asses. I want you to know, though, that I'm going to make sure that zoning doesn't go through. I've done it about five million times before, and I'll keep doing it as long as I can. The house is yours for that long. Though it's probably not going to be so peaceful from now on, because it's a matter of time before the money boys tumble to me. You may get a bunch of flak—rest assured I'll get more. But you're safe as long as I'm where I am. I figure I'm good for several more terms. I'm a good mayor. And there are more of us than there are of you."

Tears of simple relief and gratitude stung my eyes, and I was afraid that he would hear them in my voice. I kept it even.

"I can't imagine how I'll ever thank you, Glenn," I said.

"Understand this, Shep," Glenn Pickens said. "This is not sentiment and it sure as hell isn't friendship. The city owes you. You took a bad beating back then after the fire, and you didn't have to. You saved a lot of asses with that, black and white. So this is an old debt. But don't thank me, because it's Ben Cameron you owe, not me."

"Ben?"

He laughed again. "Ben. He's got a long arm. I owe him as much as you do. If I didn't, Buckhead would be solid high rise right now. You think your tax base is anything like what I could make for this city out of that residential real estate out there? No, Ben took me aside when I was getting ready to graduate from high school and said he'd pay my way through college and law school, and take care of my dad for the rest of his life, and he'd make me mayor one day, if I'd do everything he said to, because we were going to have a black mayor as sure as gun's iron, and it ought to be somebody like me. He meant somebody in his pocket, of course, but hell, I didn't care. Every mayor in America is in somebody's pocket, and there are worse by far than his. And in exchange for all that, I was to spare this little hunk of Buckhead real estate that his and your houses sat on when the developers got after it, and later, after the fire, he was doubly emphatic about yours. And he did all those things on his end. And so have I. And so, like I say, you're okay as long as I am. But probably not a second longer."

"Thank you, Glenn," I said.

"Thank him," Glenn Pickens said. "And thank Lucy Bondurant. You I owe. Her, I love." And he hung up the phone.

We did not talk again.

I lay on my back on the sofa in the living room of the summerhouse and stared up into the smoke-blackened old beams. So I'm safe now, I thought. The house is safe—or as safe as anything can be, in this town. But for what, really? Malory will marry; she may not even come home again from Massachusetts. It's a money-eating hunk of junk, when you think about it. It's nothing but an arena for those obscene pretensions Aunt Willa puts on. Lucy can't even come back to it. I don't go into it for months on end. I could go anywhere. I could get an apartment, I could go up to Tate . . . Why stay?

The answer came riding into my mind over her vivid face: Malory. If Malory *should* want to come home to live . . .

She came home for Christmas. It was the first time she had come since she left us the previous June, for she had not, after all, come at Thanksgiving. At almost the last moment she had called me and said that a new friend had asked her to spend the holiday at the family house in Marblehead.

"I'd really love to go, Shep," she said. "The New England coast is really special—I fell in love with it the first time I saw it. There's something about it . . . the *hardness* of it, I think. It's like you can walk right up on the very top of the earth, in all the clean, sharp light and air and wind. At home sometimes your feet seem to just . . . sink into the surface, right up to your knees . . . do you know what I mean?"

"I sure do," I said. I did. The sucking, amorphous surface of the South; the dark, damp pull of old roots. . . .

"Anyway, it's only a long weekend. I'll be home for three weeks at Christmas. And they're really nice people, a big family, and so funny; they laugh all the time. . . . Do you think you could maybe tell Mama for me? I'm afraid if I call her . . ."

She let her voice trail off, but I knew what she feared. I feared it for her. Lucy continued to do well at home, but I knew that she missed Malory fiercely. Jack told me that she had called Wellesley so many times during Malory's first weeks there that he had finally had a long talk with her, and they made a deal that thereafter she would call only once a week. But I thought that the old calls of blood and spirit probably went out almost constantly.

"Unless you think I should come on home," she said. I heard the old anxiety.

"No. I'll tell her," I said. "Don't worry about it. Have a good time with your friend and her family and we'll see you at Christmas."

There was a small silence, and then she said, in a low voice, "Actually, it's a him. But I don't think I want Mama to know that yet. There's absolutely nothing to it—we've just met."

"I got you," I said. "Good thinking. I'll just say friend. Are you sure that's all he is, Mal?"

My voice was teasing, but not my stilled and waiting heart.

"Absolutely," she said. "Don't worry about that. These guys up here are too fast-talking and sharp-edged for me. And there's not a one of them that holds a candle to you. I'm safe."

"See you Christmas, then," I said, and hung up to dial Lucy.

"Oh, shit," she said when I told her that Malory would not be coming home, but then, "Oh well. It's just as well, maybe. I've got a long piece on MARTA due the Monday after Thanksgiving. I was going to have to work all weekend, anyway. But it pisses me off that she calls you instead of me. What did she think I was going to do, have a fit?"

"The thought probably occurred to her," I said.

Lucy laughed.

"No fits," she said. "Absolutely no fits."

So Malory came rushing and glowing back into our lives at Christmas, slender and vital as ever, and with a new layer of Easternness over her that was, I suppose, inevitable, considering how quickly I had acquired my own patina of Princeton at her age. I rather missed the ardent girlishness of her, though. The Malory who returned to Atlanta that winter was all woman, and very lovely indeed.

It was a good Christmas, almost picture-book perfect, at least to me. We had a brief, pretty snow that stuck, and lasted several days. The weather otherwise was clear and blue and sharp: real Christmas weather. With no close friends in the city, Malory spent much of her time with Jack and her mother at the farmhouse, walking in the winter woods and decorating the sagging old house and cooking enormous, elaborate meals that only she and Jack ate. She told me, as we sat before the fire in the summerhouse by the glow of the little tree I had put up just for her, that

Lucy only picked at her food, smoking incessantly and staring at her with her uncanny light blue eyes. Malory spent a lot of time with me that Christmas. I loved the long afternoons and evenings.

"Sometimes I feel like she's trying to memorize my face or something," she said. "And sometimes she just puts her hand on my arm or knee and leaves it there. Poor Mama—there's so little in her life that's fun anymore, with me gone. Jack's practically an Olympic sleeper now. And all she does is work. Just work. But she's not drinking. And she really does look better. I've been awfully worried about her. Sometimes I feel so guilty up there at school, so interested in my courses, and having such a good time, when I know she misses me so awfully."

"Of course she misses you," I said. "We all do. But we all want you to have this experience. You know she wouldn't want you to give that up. She hasn't said so, has she?"

"Oh no. Not in words, anyway. But she wants me home. We have that other language, you know. She tells me that way."

"Turn the receiver off for the next four years," I said. "She may want you home on that level, but she'd be wrecked with guilt if she thought you left college and came home because of her. I'm sure of that. And I've known her a lot longer than you have."

She stretched, a long, luxurious stretch, and sighed deeply.

"You always say the right thing," she said. "The one thing that makes everything all right. Sometimes I wish you were my father."

"Why?" I said, my heart pounding in my throat. "Don't I make a good friend?"

"The best," she said, reaching over and squeezing my hand. "It's just that Jack seems so absent. Like he's nothing to do with me. Like I'm not really there, or he isn't. He's awfully passive, Shep. Sometimes a day or two will go by before he says a complete sentence. I can't imagine him when he married Mama. . . ."

"He's a good man, Malory," I said, not for the first time. "He's had a tough time. He was a fine man then, full of passion, like she was, and if most of it's been burned out of him by now . . . well, you can see how that might be."

"You didn't lose yours," she said.

"Oh, my dear," I thought, "I did—I lost it all but one. But I cannot tell you about that."

"Well, I didn't have to live with your mother, either," I said.

"You lived with her longer than he has," Malory said stubbornly.

"It was different then," I said. "What burns now, warmed then."

"Yes," she said. "I can see that. Oh, poor Jack. Poor Mama. Poor everybody."

"Not so poor," I said. "We've all had you."

"See what I mean, about saying the right thing?" she said, getting up from the sofa to kiss me. "I don't know what I'd do without you."

"You'll never have to find out," I said.

She went back to school three days early, to go skiing at Stowe with her friend and his brothers, and after she had kissed me good-bye and run out to the Ford, which was coughing sulkily in the driveway with Jack at the wheel and Lucy in the backseat, for the trip to the airport, I went back into the summerhouse and shut the door on the cold, pearled light of the dying day and put another log on the fire. If I could have, I would have built a bonfire that roared and bellowed up to the diamond chips of the emerging stars, a conflagration to challenge the very solstice, for the coldness and blackness inside me was nearly total.

I don't know why that twilight was so desperately bleak. Mallory was whole and alive and beautiful in her dark-lit youth, and thriving at her school like a colt in deep bluegrass. She was happy; she was as safe as we could make her; she loved me. I would see her again perhaps at Easter and surely for the long summer vacation. Lucy was inching back toward stability and even Jack Venable seemed a little better, for Lucy's salary at the weekly had allowed him to give up his evening teaching job, and the desperate white exhaustion had loosened its grip somewhat. *The Compleat Georgian* was nearing completion, and a good small university press had gotten wind of it and written expressing interest. It should have been a good time for me, or at least not a bad one.

But the starless darkness that fell down when Mallory ran out of the summerhouse did not lift. I made myself a drink, and put Ella Fitzgerald singing Cole Porter on the stereo, and picked S. J. Perelman off the shelf, and settled with all three before the fire, blackness whirling inside my head like snow. I sat sipping and half listening and staring at meaningless type, a gale of mortality and despair roaring around me, for what seemed hours on end. Old, my mind keened. Old, old, old . . .

I cannot remember a worse time in my life, except one, and I cannot to this day say precisely why it was so.

Until Sarah Cameron appeared in the door of the summerhouse, I did not even realize that it was New Year's Eve.

I blinked at her stupidly, feeling as though I were struggling up through thick, stagnant water toward sunlight. She stood in the open doorway, cold wind rushing in behind her, dressed in a short red satin evening dress with spaghetti straps and in high-heeled silver sandals, and a beautiful dark mink almost the color of her hair was thrown around her shoulders. In one hand there was an unopened bottle of champagne. She was smiling, and her face was so white that the color on her high cheekbones looked like badly applied rouge. From where I sat on the sofa, I could see her lips trembling around the smile.

"It's you," I said witlessly.

"It is. It surely is," she said. "Happy New Year, Shep."

"What are you doing here all dressed up?" My conversation would have seemed dull in a marginal kindergarten.

"I . . . oh, Snake and Lelia talked me into going to that awful thing the club has every year, and it was a mistake. I realized that if I stayed an hour longer I was going to have to kiss about twenty drunk people I loathe. So I pinched a bottle of champagne from a tray and came over here to wish you Happy New Year. And"—her voice broke into a near-operatic tremolo—"and to seduce you. Do you think one bottle will do it?"

She laughed, and I realized with a remote shock that she was not a little drunk. She came across the room and sat down carefully at the other end of the sofa, and then I could see the liquid glitter, like unshed tears, that her great eyes had always seemed to get when she had had too much to drink, back when we both were young. Back then . . .

"You look awfully pretty. Is that a new coat?" I said. The dragging blackness weighed so heavily on me that it was an effort to frame the words. I wanted to put my head into her satin lap and howl. But I sensed that if I made a move toward her, she would bolt like a wild thing. She was, I realized, badly frightened. I could not imagine why, and I could not think what to do about it.

"No. It's Mother's," she said. "She gave it to me when they moved. She said she never intended to go outside when it was cold again as long as she lived. Wouldn't that be wonderful, Shep? Not to ever be cold again . . ."

Tears started down her face, and she turned away and scrubbed at them with her hand.

"I'm sorry," she said. "I'm not a good drunk. I'm sure you remember that. A crying jag is not what I had in mind here."

I took the hand that shielded her face and turned it over and looked at it. It seemed to be made of ice. My own did, too. I could not feel her flesh. There were faint half-moons of dark blue—Prussian, I thought inanely—under the short, buffed bare nails.

"You're painting again," I said dully. "I'm awfully glad. I hated it when you stopped."

"Not really painting," she said, shaking her head as if to clear

it, and smiling even more brightly. A lock of her dark, glossy
hair fell over her forehead. "I'm teaching. Or rather, taking a
few private pupils two or three times a week. I get them on refer-
rals from the school of art at the museum. Some of them are really quite good. And it does feel good to hold a brush again.
Awful on my nails, though . . ."

Her laugh was a stilted social one I had literally never heard
before.

"Have you got a studio now?" I said, just as politely. I did
not seem to know who she was, this satin-shining, tremulous
small woman in my living room, thrumming like a high voltage
wire and smelling of Joy and cold fur. I did not seem to know
who I was, sitting and looking at her.

"I fixed up one in the basement," she said, and then grimaced.
"I know, it sounds grisly. But it was the only place in the house
I could do it."

"Did you ever think of opening the one on Muscogee?" I said.
"Not the house, just the studio. It would be perfect."

"I can't go over there. There's not anybody there that I
know," she said obscurely. Under the despair and strangeness,
my heart twisted.

"Well, at least you're painting," I said.

"At least that," she agreed. "It gives me something to do. Oh
God, Shep. I don't need something to do. I've got plenty to do.
I need the money, that's why I'm doing it. I hate it when I lie.
I've been doing a lot of that lately."

She bit her lip and looked away, and I covered her cold hand
with mine.

"I have more money than God," I said. "I never spend any.
Let me give you some money, Sarah. I can't stand it if you're
giving painting lessons in your basement because you need the
money."

She disengaged her fingers and covered both flaming cheeks
with both hands.

"I don't know what in God's name is the matter with me tonight," she said, and her voice trembled again. "I didn't come
over here to beg money from you. Mother and Daddy would give
me all the money I needed, or Mother would, if I'd let her. I
just didn't want to take it from her. And I'm sure as hell not
going to take any from you. I'm not really poor. It's just that
right now, with both girls in school . . . the painting lessons are
just the ticket. They bring me just enough, and I can stop them
when I don't need the extra anymore. And then, one day the
Muscogee house will sell, and that money will be mine—I'm appalled at myself for even mentioning it to you. I thought I was
coming over to wish you Happy New Year and escape the club

letches. It seemed like a good idea at the time. . . ." Tears were close under the surface of her voice again.

"It was a good idea," I said. "It was a magnificent idea. I was just sitting here feeling sorry for myself, and about a thousand years old. I didn't even realize it was New Year's Eve. I really would have put my head in the oven if I had."

She laughed, a trembling little laugh, and the tears receded.

"I know," she said. "Is there anything worse? All that horn blowing, and frantic smiling and dancing and yelling, and kissing all those people you don't even speak to the rest of the year. . . . Shep?"

"Yes."

"Do you remember that first New Year's Eve you were home from Princeton? And we went to Hart's?"

"And it snowed, and we sat in the bay window looking over Peachtree Street and watched it come down, and drank Taittinger blanc de blanc? Yes," I said, "I remember."

"It was the last really, really good New Year's Eve I can remember," she said.

"Me, too," I said.

"Let's do it again," she said, and fished the bottle from the sofa beside her and held it up. It was Taittinger. The black ice lock in my heart stirred a little, ponderously and far, far down.

"Let's do," I said.

I got a couple of stemmed glasses from the kitchen, and opened the champagne while she watched. It made a wonderful, festive whoosh, and fountained all over the hearth. She laughed, a small, prissy sound, and sat with her hands folded in her lap and her ankles crossed, the old Atlanta Pink posture of genteel repose, watching me pour the fizzing gold into the glasses.

I handed her one and glanced at the clock on the mantel over the fireplace. Twenty of twelve.

"Happy New Year, Sarah," I said.

"Happy New Year, Shep."

We drank. We drank again. The clock moved, the fire spat, Ella segued into "Love for Sale," and we drank again. We finished the bottle of Taittinger in seven minutes flat. We did not speak in all that time. When we both opened our mouths to do so at once, and stopped and laughed, and began again, I suddenly realized that I could not feel my lips, and said, "God, I think I've sat here and gotten drunk as a skunk."

"Oh, I'm so glad," Sarah said. "I don't think I could have done it otherwise."

"Done what?" I said owlishly.

"Seduced you. That really is what I came for," Sarah Cameron Gentry said.

I closed one eye and peered at her, to see if she would stop the slow spin she had begun. She did: The spin stopped and she became Sarah again, sitting bare-shouldered and beautiful and ripe as a small plum in my firelight, and literally terrified. I stared with both eyes, squinting to focus. She was not teasing.

"Can you bear to do that?" I said. "Can you, after all those years and what I did to you and what I've turned into? Can you, Sarah?"

"I can't bear not to," she said, her voice very small, borne out on a long, trembling breath. "I can't bear not to. I've missed you for almost twenty years. And I've just . . . been around women too damned long, Shep."

I stood up, very slowly, my legs unsteady under me, my heart starting a long, dragging, heavy tattoo. I held out my arms to her. I had no idea on earth what I was going to do next.

"Then come here, Sarah Cameron," I said. "Come here and seduce me for New Year's Eve."

She put her glass down and stood herself, looking at me almost defiantly, firelight leaping on her shoulders and face, her eyes glittering with liquor and tears.

"Wait a minute," she said, slurring just a little. She was swaying very slightly, almost imperceptibly. But I had the sense that beneath the protective rush of the champagne she knew exactly what she was about, and it was that which so frightened her.

"I want you to be sure you know what you're getting," she said.

Sarah stepped out of her sandals. She slipped the straps of the red satin dress down off her shoulders, as slowly and delicately as if she were in a pool of blue baby spotlight. She peeled the dress down to her hips and stepped out of it. Underneath she wore a scrap of black satin-and-lace bra, and black panty hose. Her rich, compact little body shone through the black, pale gold like new honey, white only where a recent summer's bikini had shielded her from the kiss of her beloved sun. Good muscles slid in her stomach and arms and shoulders.

"Can you do it with this?" she said, running her hands down her body. "It's not young anymore." I stood staring, blood pounding dully at my temples, ears roaring. I could not speak.

"Can you do it with a middle-aged woman who hasn't done it for years, and only once before with you? Can you?" Sarah whispered. As she whispered she unhooked the brassiere and let it fall to the floor. Her breasts bobbed free in the firelight, sweet and heavy, the heft and fruit of them remembered in my palms and groin. Remembered from a night two decades before, in an apartment on the Lower West Side of Manhattan, in another time and another world altogether. . . . Still, I could not speak.

"Can you, Shep?" Sarah said, and peeled the panty hose down, and stepped out of them. She wore, now, only black lace bikini panties.

"I don't know," I whispered truthfully, strangling on my own voice. I felt paralyzed, drowned in blackness and the heavy weight of time and the sediment of loss. A hunger as old and fierce as the world stirred in me. She was, in the dying firelight, the most beautiful thing I had ever seen, riper and more complete than any young girl. But I had been alone so long, so long. . . . Aloneness ran in my veins and weighed like cold iron in my groin. I did not think I could move.

"I think you can," Sarah said, and came, near-naked, across the floor to me and moved into the wooden arms I held out. "I think you can. . . ."

She moved against me, pressing her body against mine, moving and moving, moving to the beat of the music and the rhythm of her blood, moving, moving. She arched her back and scrubbed her breasts into my chest. Her face was in its old spot in the hollow of my neck, and I could feel the wetness of tears, and the rush of breath as she murmured words I could not hear, soft, crooning words of loss and yearning and old, old love. My arms went around her automatically, and my hands found the smooth, warm hollow in the small of her back, and pulled her into my groin. As if they had life independent of me, they pulled the panties down on her hips, and, still moving against me, she wriggled them down and stepped out of them.

"Please help me," she whispered. "Can you? Can you, Shep?"

Could I? I leaned onto and into her, mindless, moving with her. Could I? Could the cooled blood warm again, the banked heart flame, the body find the old, urgent moves, that long-forgotten ballet of thrust, thrust, thrust? Could the hopeless old love, so long starved and banished, find breath and being in her once again? Could I? Did I dare?

Sobbing softly, she pulled me down onto the sofa with her, and the small body squirmed under mine until it found the core of me, and opened in warmth and wetness and urgency to take me, finally, into the secret center of her. Yes. I could. I could, I dared, I could. . . .

The telephone rang across the room. I knew without a shaving of a doubt, without a silvery hair of uncertainty, who it was. Even as I rocked and plunged, rocked and plunged, liberation from the blackness and the aloneness of two decades gathering inexorably in the starved groin, I knew. I knew, muscle and sinew and bone and blood and skin. My pounding heart knew. My ragged breath knew. My penis knew, and wilted in despair at the knowledge. I lay still atop Sarah, eyes closed, flaccid and finished, desolation and ending bitter in my mouth.

Sarah knew, too. She was out from under me with one smooth, violent movement, utterly and icily white, eyes blinded and unfocused. She was back in the satin dress and the silver sandals, with the coat clutched around her, before I could sit up, and she did not speak until she was at the door of the summerhouse. I looked across the room at her. She looked, in that moment, as old as Dorothy Cameron—older. She looked dead, like an animated corpse, come to call on the remorseless living in her mother's old mink coat.

"I will not bother you again," she said, in a voice to match the corpse-look of her. "I forgot. I truly forgot. But I won't again."

As she turned to go, the bells of Saint Philip's Church just up Peachtree Road began to peal crazily through the wrecked night. Sarah turned back to me.

"I wish," she said conversationally, "that Red Chastain had killed her when he had the chance."

And she was gone into the first pealing moments of a new year.

The phone began ringing again even as the door slammed. I let it ring ten or fifteen times, and then I plodded heavily over and picked up the receiver.

"Hey, Gibby," she said. Pause. Deep, shuddering draw of cigarette. "It's Lucy, honey. Happy New Year!"

CHAPTER
TWENTY-SIX

L UCY NEVER KNEW, after that New Year's Eve, that she had doomed me with Sarah. At least, I do not think she knew in her mind. Her conscious weapons had always been more direct. The midnight telephone call that drowned the ember of hope between Sarah and me was not even coincidental: Lucy had been calling me at midnight on New Year's Eve for years.

But what she knew in her blood was another matter. There in that dark Styx of vivid, indestructible life which sustained Lucy Bondurant Chastain Venable through so much horror, something was that met and knew every inch of me, perfectly. It was not the leaping, singing thing that called between her and Malory, but nevertheless, it knew. The fact remained that twenty years after I had first loved and wanted her, Sarah Cameron was still lost to me, now irrevocably, and even given my own fecklessness, Lucy was the author of that.

Dorothy Cameron knew, too, and unlike Lucy, she knew with the full of her honed and prescient mind. Not far into the new year I took her a first draft of *The Compleat Georgian*, feeling as shy and tongue-tied as if I were calling at Merrivale House to pick up Sarah for a dance when I was fifteen. Ben had had a bad day, roaming and thrashing and falling, and had had to be sedated and moved to the infirmary, so we sat in the downstairs sun-room of Carlton House, drinking tea amid the bamboo furniture and tropical plants and caged birds which had, I suspected, been patterned after the decor of the sun-room at The Cloister on Sea Island, so as to give a dimension of familiar luxury and festivity to this last cloister of privileged old age. In the gray-white light from the window walls, fully half of the population of Carlton House took the winter sun like old turtles.

The light, or more likely the long grief and strain of Ben's deterioration, had leached the high color out of Dorothy's face, that last brave ensign of youth. I wondered if Sarah would ever lose it permanently. She already had, in that last glimpse I had had of her.

"So here it is," she said, hefting the thick folder of manuscript in her thin hands. "The house of Cameron, as seen through the eyes of Bondurant. An unbeatable combination. I'm sorrier than I can say that it's the only one that will ever be."

I knew then that Sarah had told her mother about what happened on New Year's Eve, or at least some of it. What she had not, Dorothy would have filled in for herself. I remembered that long ago, just before I had left on that fatal journey across America after Lucy's frantic call, Dorothy Cameron had warned me about her.

"She is a danger to herself and a worse one to you," she had said. To her credit, she did not remind me now of that conversation. She knew, of course, that it was far too late for that.

"I'm sorry, too," I said. I started to go on, to amplify, justify, explain, offer hope, and then did not. There was nothing further to say, and so I said nothing.

"It would have almost made these last dreadful years worth it," she said, in her usual rich, level voice, but when I looked into her face I saw an anguish that I had seen there only at young Ben's death, and the start of Ben Senior's long decline. Her eyes were closed.

"Oh, Lucy, so many lives," I thought wearily. I could not be angry at her. We were beyond that, too.

"But this is wonderful, darling, just wonderful," she said briskly, and the anguish was gone and only her pleasure in the manuscript remained. I felt foolish elation.

"It is, isn't it?" I said. "I did it, by God. I really did. And I didn't even leave Atlanta. Most of the time if you want to be a creative genius—or ugly, or anything outside the playpen—you have to leave."

"Well, you didn't," she said. "You may have hidden out like a possum in a hollow tree, but you didn't leave."

"I amend that," I said. "If you want to be creative or ugly or happy. You can't stay here and be all of them."

She smiled softly. "But does anybody have all those things, Shep?" she said. "Doesn't everybody have to choose some things over others, no matter where they are?"

"Maybe," I said, feeling an obscure annoyance at her. "But

by God, I don't know many places where your very life has to be one of the choices."

"If you're referring to yourself, you've had an awful lot of privilege," she said.

"You pay so goddamn dearly for the privilege of . . . privilege in this town," I said stubbornly. I did not know why I could not let it go. "Look at Lucy."

"Well, if you insist, then let's do look at Lucy," Dorothy said crisply. "What so terrible has happened to Lucy that she did not bring down on herself? She's been loved, protected, taken care of. . . ."

"But it wasn't enough, and it wasn't the right kind of love," I said. "The original covenant was broken—that her father would take care of her when she needed him—and she's spent her entire life alternately trying to placate and punish him. Privilege didn't help her there."

"Many children have that covenant broken." Her beautiful voice was soft and implacable. The woman who had felt sorrow and pity for little Lucy Bondurant was long vanished.

"But somehow Lucy just couldn't get past it," I said. "At the same time she realized he wasn't going to come and take care of her, she got the message that she herself was essentially worthless and utterly unworthy of care, that nothing she did or ever could do by herself would be enough to keep her whole and safe. That's where all the anger and dependency and self-sabotage comes from."

"Who gave her that message?" Dorothy was stirring restlessly on her rattan love seat.

"The old man," I said. "The South. The South speaking through Willa and all the other women around her. Women, too—women did it to her, too."

"But she's seen strong women," Dorothy said impatiently. "Your mother was a strong woman, in her way. Old Martha Cater was a brick, and loved her dearly. I'm tough in my own way, too."

"Yes, but you're all strong in a man's world, or were," I insisted. "My mother as an accessory to a powerful man, at least to outward appearances. Martha as a servant in that man's house. You were a lioness in that hospital, Dorothy, but it was men who owned and ran it. Lucy happened to want it all. Unheard of, for a Southern woman. Not, of course, for any sorry man in shoe leather, but for a woman . . ."

"And who ever gave her that notion?" Dorothy Cameron said tartly. "Nobody else I know ever had it all, man or woman, past the age of thirteen. Oh, don't bother to answer, it's the Bondurant in her, of course. You always were the wantingest tribe I ever saw."

"Except me," I said.

"Oh, Shep, you most of all! Don't you remember all those passions of yours when you were small? Look at you—you've been in a twenty-year tantrum because you lost part of what you wanted. You've been saying, 'If I can't have it all, I'll reject it all.' You've let an awful lot of good go. You let an entire world go not two weeks ago. It's not Lucy who's the victim, it's you. And God help you, it is quite beyond you to change that now."

I was silent, feeling the old, dead blackness of New Year's Eve well up from its headwater deep within me. Her words seemed to me an immutable condemnation.

"Tough words," I said, finally.

"I wouldn't waste them on many people left on this earth, my dear," she said. "I have loved you most of your life. I wanted better for you than you have chosen for yourself."

"What is this, chopped liver?" I said, attempting lightness. I patted the manuscript in her lap.

"This is marvelous," she said. "A *tour de force*. A fine appetizer. Now, what about the next twenty years?"

"I really hadn't thought about it," I said, the blackness fleeing like fog before a sharp wind of panic. I had not. The pile of pages mounting in their slowness through the years had seemed sufficient, complete in themselves. What *about* the next twenty-five years? I saw whirling whiteness ahead, and nothing else.

"Well, you'd better get your ass in gear," Dorothy Cameron said matter-of-factly. "Because I'm tired and I want to die sometime soon, and I absolutely will not do it until I know you've got something to occupy you. On your head be it if I live to be a miserable, mewling, puking centenarian."

"Dorothy, I think I'd just as soon die when you do," I said, nakedly and honestly. The thought of Atlanta without her was not to be borne.

She was quiet for a long time.

"Please live," she said at last, in a frail, light, infinitely weary voice. There were tears in the corners of her great, hooded amber eyes. "Please find a way, finally, to live."

I left her then, thinking as I loped down Peachtree Road toward 2500, cold in the perpetual blueness of shadows from the beetling, blind-eyed buildings on either side, that when she was gone there would be very few people left in my world who might wear the term "fineness." Only her daughter came to mind.

Lucy continued to do so well in her job and at home on the farm that Malory called me just before Christmas of her sophomore

year and asked if I thought it would be all right to bring her
friend from Boston and Marblehead home.

"I think," she said, and I could hear the tentative joy in her
voice, "that he may be going to ask me to marry him!"

"Oh, Mal—" I said, stricken, and then caught myself. I had
been about to shout at her, "No! No! Too young, you're too
young . . ."

"Does he have a name?" I asked instead.

"John Hunter Westcott the Fourth," she said, laughing a little
over the name. "Is that perfect, or is it perfect? Jinx, of course.
He's tall and blond and cool and beautiful, and he's so impeccably bred that you'd think he had 'Groton-Harvard-Wall Street'
stamped on his aristocratic behind. He doesn't, though. What
he has is a severe case of Long Island lockjaw and a place waiting
for him in his father's and grandfather's impeccable WASP law
firm. You'll probably hate him."

"I can't wait for that pleasure," I said honestly. "I assure you
that I will hate him, and as openly and nastily as I can. I'm going
to tell him all about your many eccentricities and hideous hidden
habits, and send him yelping back to Marblehead, or wherever."

"Lord, don't," she said, only half teasing. "Mother is going
to be quite enough. But they have to meet him, and he wants
to know them. Do you think she can handle it?"

I thought about it for a bit, and then said, "I think she can,
if he doesn't try to count her teeth. I wouldn't say anything about
marriage, though, Mal. It might just be better to let it be a casual
visit."

"I won't. But she's going to know," Malory said.

"Probably. But she won't know for sure unless you talk about
it."

"I won't, then," she said. "You're probably right. Okay, I'll
call her right now. Can I bring Jinx by to meet you the day after
we get home?"

"Oh, by all means," I said. "I'll dig out my old club tie. Would
you like me to meet you at the airport and drive you out? Soften
the first minutes a little?"

"No," she said. "I think she'd rather I brought him there to
them first."

And so I did not go to the farmhouse with Malory and her
cool, aristocratic and altogether perfect captive Brahmin, and
I have regretted that every day of my life since. It was only afterward that I learned what happened that evening, and by that
time Malory was back in Massachusetts determined that she
would never look upon her mother again.

Jack had met their plane and driven them out to Lithonia in
the ancient Ford, and I am sure Jinx Westcott was as gentle-

manly about it as he must have been appalled. Lucy had decorated the farmhouse from rafters to hearth with evergreens from
the woods and the battered ornaments they had bought when
Malory was born, and I think that it probably looked, in its festive dress and the warmth of the leaping fire and candlelight, as
well as it could ever look, though by then the old house had
sagged past genteel shabbiness and into outright dilapidation. I
am certain Jinx was a gentleman about that, too. What, if anything, went on in the elegant brainpan behind the cool blue Nor-
dic eyes, narrowed by the stenosis of centuries of breeding, is
another matter. Malory could not tell me that.

What she did tell me was that it was not she, but Jinx Westcott, who said to Lucy, as she and Malory worked in the kitchen
and Jack nodded with his drink before the television set, "That
looks terrific, Mrs. Venable. I hope Mal got your talent in the
kitchen as well as your looks. None of the women in my family
can cook worth a damn, and I refuse to go through a lifetime
of Stouffer's."

Lucy turned her blue, blue eyes to the blond young demigod
in her ramshackle kitchen.

"Aren't you nice?" she drawled. "I can tell your mama raised
you right. Will you be a sweetie and go see if Lucy's father would
like another drink?"

When Jinx Westcott strode manfully off into the living room,
she turned to Malory.

"Well, darling. Secrets?" she caroled.

"I think maybe he's going to ask me to marry him, Mama,"
Malory said in a subdued voice, her heart hammering.

"Well," Lucy said. "He has a nice ass."

It should have tipped Malory off. It would have me. But Malory was blinded by hope, and Jack was drugged with scotch and
Dan Rather, and no one saw the level in the scotch bottle that
Jack kept on the kitchen counter dropping, dropping, as Lucy
cooked. By dinnertime, when Malory and Jinx Westcott came
in to lay the table, Lucy had turned abruptly and staggeringly
drunk, bestial and hectic and mad-eyed, mumbling and stumbling and laughing and letting herself fall heavily against Jinx.

Malory fled wordlessly to the living room to fetch Jack. It took
her some little time to rouse him. When they returned to the
kitchen, they found Lucy, skirt pulled up and panties down
around her thin white ankles, squirming in the lap of the appalled John Hunter Westcott IV, crying aloud with the shrill
mindlessness of a deranged cuckoo clock, "I want to *come!* I
want to *come!*"

She began to scream then, when Malory and Jack attempted
to pull her off Jinx Westcott's lap, and she screamed long past

the time the ambulance came to take her to Central State—for all the other hospitals in the area had by then declared her unwelcome. Lucy in her madness scratched, kicked and bit; her rage was endless. Her screams still rang in the empty air of the farmhouse when the Lithonia taxi came to take a white, punished Malory and a politely arctic John Hunter Westcott IV to the airport. I thought that Malory would hear them always, in her head.

"I will never see her again as long as I live," she sobbed to me when I called her at school, after the news came from a half-drunk and exhausted Jack Venable that Lucy had been hospitalized again. "I don't care if she's sick—I don't care! I will *not* see her again!"

And she broke down completely, and hung up the phone.

I replaced the receiver in the summerhouse, swearing in my heart that if I could prevent it, she would not indeed. Lucy might be past my help, but Malory would, *must,* be saved.

Something happened to Lucy at Central State. To this day we are not sure what it was. The physician on staff swore he found no evidence of a stroke, and Hub Dorsey, when I called him in, verified that.

"Nothing on the EEG," he said. "Nothing anywhere else to indicate vascular trouble. Whatever it is, it isn't stroke."

What it was was a calmness, a lethargy almost, so profound that she did not require the usual tranquilizers and antidepressants but sat dreaming and nodding in the dayroom for hours at a time, often humming a little to herself, and almost always smiling. It was as if something had, at last, truly eased the flame in her, though when I visited I could see in her blue eyes the small, stubborn spark of intelligence which had not yet, through all the horror and pain, been quenched. She could move as well as ever. It simply seemed that she did not often choose to do so. And she did not speak. We did not know for a long time whether she had lost the function or whether she just considered that matters had gone beyond speech entirely. Whatever it was, she seemed tranquil and docile and quite often content.

I thought then that the electroconvulsive therapy they gave her there had simply short-circuited some intricate and vital circuitry in her fevered brain. I still think that is what happened, although an entire phalanx of overworked young doctors assured us it did not and could not.

I thought it far more probable that they simply did not know whereof they spoke than that they wished to circumvent legal trouble from a patient with a professional husband, for it was obvious to even the casual observer by then that Jack Venable was in no shape to pursue a lawsuit, and besides, he had signed

an elaborate waiver of responsibility when he had committed
Lucy.

So she sat in her silence, smiling and thinking of who knew
what, as lost to us without the connecting bridge of words as
if she had died. I think both Jack and I, in our hearts, were fur-
tively glad to see her so. I, at least, felt simple relief. We, as well
as she, were released from the torment of the fire in Lucy.

In three or four months she began to speak, but she spoke only
in erratic bursts, sometimes muttering abrupt words and sentences that made no sense. I knew that the gibberish had meaning for her, for she often smiled in tender delight after
completing a string of the heartbreaking nonsense, and looked
up at me as if awaiting a reply. I did not know what to say, and
could not bear the wounded sentences that spilled from her
pretty mouth and tumbled to earth like slain birds, so I resorted
to the old anodyne of her early hospitalization.

"Stick it in your ear, Luce!" I would shout gaily, and Lucy
would clap her hands and put her finger into her ear, and her
blue eyes would spill light like kisses, and she would crow, "Stick
it in your ear! Stick it in your ear, Gibby!"

It was the only coherent sentence she made for many, many
months.

They could not keep her indefinitely at Central State, and in
all ways except for the speech she seemed well—or as well as,
now, she would ever be. And so we brought her home. The
sweet, Buddha-like docility persisted, and she seemed to find a
sort of sensual pleasure and comfort in a simple routine of morning television, afternoon naps, hearty meals and short, meandering strolls in the fields and woods around the farmhouse.

Jack could afford no more home caretakers for her, and indeed, was back teaching nights at the floundering little community college in order to try to meet her staggering and unabating
medical bills. But there was no hope that he would ever get ahead
of them, and I thought that if his evening drinking did not stop
and the lethargy that rode him like a succubus did not abate,
he would soon lose one or both of the jobs. The farmhouse was
unspeakable—a pigsty. Finally I could stand it no longer, and
hired, over Jack's objections, a round-the-clock nurse for Lucy.
When she had been on the job for a couple of weeks, I went out
to see how they were faring.

The nurse was a smart, quick, brisk young Trinidadian named
Amelia Kincaid, who handled Lucy with firm competence and
impersonal, unflinching kindness. To my astonishment, Lucy detested her.

"Damned nigger," she spit at Amelia Kincaid and glared

obliquely up at me with sly blue malice. "I hate niggers. Hate niggers!"

Face flaming, I turned to the nurse.

"She doesn't mean that," I said. "She's always loved black people far more than she did white; she's worked all her life for the civil rights movement—"

"Stick it in your ear, Gibby!" Lucy sang.

"It's nothing, Mr. Bondurant," Amelia Kincaid said in her lovely, lilting voice. "A kind of glitch in the brain, I think. I don't take it seriously."

But I could not bear to hear the venom in Lucy's beautiful, rich, drawling voice, which had told me such wonderments; could not bear the mumbled, "Went to the dance and help me, Gibby. Daddy won't like the blood, blood, blood."

I looked in despair at Jack Venable, but Jack had passed out on the sofa in front of a Mary Tyler Moore rerun. It was a house of waste and decay and hopelessness. I would not, I thought, go back to it.

But, incredibly, the phoenix in Lucy's blood struggled up once again, and pulled her partway out of the bonfire of madness with it, enough so that she fetched up once more on a kind of benevolent plateau, calm and tender and childlike, seemingly pleased to drift in the moment, to receive the few visitors who came and gobble the sweet treats they brought, to watch endless blaring television. She grew quite fat, and Amelia Kincaid cut her dry, lusterless hair short so that it would not trail into her food, and it fell sleekly and becomingly about her fine, narrow head. She spent some time each afternoon, in those long late summer and early autumn days, outside in the sun in a lawn chair, and a faint rose flush stained her thin skin, webbed now like spider's silk with a network of tiny lines. She looked quite pretty, though never again beautiful with the old eerie light, and seemed pleased with whatever small lagniappe the minimal days dealt her. Jack was able, at last, to dismiss Amelia Kincaid, and with her went the last of Lucy's strange, isolated rage. And with a sighing and delicately affronted Little Lady Rawson looking in every day or so, Lucy was able once more to stay alone.

I do not think she was unhappy.

I have come to think of the next year as the time in which we all came to terms with our lives, as bitter or minimal as they were and as tenuous as those terms were. We did not so much find peace as we simply stopped struggling, we three: Lucy and Jack and I. Or perhaps I mean Lucy and me; Jack Venable had stopped struggling years before. I think it was why he was still alive.

"Middle age is when you do that, or die," Dorothy Cameron said, when I told her how I felt about that time. "Conventional wisdom has it that you don't grow up until middle age, but old people know that it isn't growing up at all—it's giving up. Just stop fighting and go with the flow, as the hideous saying now goes. Maturity is passivity in fancy dress."

"It sounds like an awful cop-out, when you put it that way," I said. "Just to let go the reins, when you've had charge of your life for all those years."

"But you haven't," she said. "You're grown up, finally, when you realize that you never did. Then you stop squirming like a gigged frog and let the current take you. You get there just as fast, and you feel a great deal better on the trip."

I left her feeling distinctly less noble and more sluglike, but I realized that the free-fall drift we had all found ourselves in was, perhaps, kinder to us than all the desperate, anguished struggles to make ourselves better. We would make no one particularly happy this way, least of all ourselves, but to me and to Jack Venable and certainly to Lucy, her long fires banked at last, the stasis had a certain sweetness, like a safe, if featureless and unlovely, port gained after years of magnificent tempest. I think if there had come for me, at that time, a last great call to life and glory, I would have turned tail and run.

In the course of time the university press that had been interested in *The Compleat Georgian* accepted it, and sent a brace of ghostly, avid scholars to consult with me on it, and after weeks of polite hemmings and "well, actually"'s and "but don't you think perhaps"'s, they left me to begin the satisfyingly long task of revision.

"Well, Dorothy, you don't have to worry about the next year, at least," I thought, sitting down at my desk to begin deciphering the spectral editors' pale notes. "This should last me into next fall, and with luck I can string it out until Christmas."

It was anodyne and anesthetic to go back into that country of dead Camerons. The living ones offered me, now, little but pain. Dorothy Cameron had broken her knee back in the summer, and it was not mending well around the implacable steel pin that held it, and she was growing vague and listless with pain. She could not come down to the lounge at Carlton House anymore, and the times I could go up to the apartment grew further and further apart, for Ben was almost gone from us now, flickering disconnectedly in and out of the raging, blinded body, running on pure will and bitter, empty health. I saw increasingly little of Dorothy, and her voice when I phoned her seemed to have preceded her into another country, one as yet closed to me. And Sarah I simply did not see. Perhaps she had changed her route when she went about her errands in Buckhead, or perhaps she did them in other parts of the city now. Perhaps she did not wish to encounter me, or perhaps she simply did not care. Whatever the reasons for it, I came, finally, to be grateful for her absence from my life. This new, level country of my heart had sealed its borders against pain.

In the spring of that year Martha Cater had a slight stroke in the night in the Caters' quarters over the garage, and awoke with no knowledge of where she was or who the distraught Shem might be. The confusion passed by noon, but what I had resolutely refused to admit to myself now came clear: Martha and Shem Cater were past their determined toiling in the house on Peachtree Road—even the curtailed amount of work that one genteel old beauty and a recluse required—and arrangements would have to be made for them.

I offered to let them stay on in the garage apartment which had been their only home for so much of their lives, but Martha could not manage the stairs with safety, and Shem winced when he climbed them, when he thought he was unobserved. And Martha stubbornly refused to stay in a place where she could not work when she wanted to.

"I ain't gon' set up there on my bee-hind while you an' Miss Willa tries to do for yourselves," she said thunderously. "Ain't neither of you know how to light no stove, even. You starve in a week."

It was not true, but I saw that if she stayed, Martha Cater would die as she had lived, in the service of the Bondurants, and I was not going to have that. When they hemmed and hawed and would not tell me what they wished to do—or perhaps could not—I drove with Tom Carmichael and Marty Fox out to Forest Park, where the feckless ToTo lived with her brood of laconic children, and bought a one-year-old, three-bedroom brick ranch house hard by a new full-service shopping center, framed the deed and hung it over the mantel, and moved the reluctant Caters in. Both professed to hate the house, but Shem's milky old eyes grew liquid with tears when he saw parked in the driveway the immaculate 1972 Buick Marty had found for me. It was as big and heavy a car as we could find, and Shem would look like a gnome peering over a toadstool driving it, but years of the Rolls had left him with a profound contempt for what he called "little old trash cars." The Buick had a heft worthy of his mighty old heart.

And Martha wept and hugged me when she saw her kitchen. I had decreed that it be similar as possible to the one at 2500, and Marty had searched for more than a week until he found the house that harbored this one. I had then duplicated Martha's appliances and cookware down to the baker's rack and the balloon whisks she favored, and added a small kitchen television for good measure, and the oak and rattan rocker from our kitchen, whose seat now cupped Martha's ample buttocks and no others on earth. It was exactly the right thing to do, and I had loved doing it, and if I live to be a hundred—a thought I do not cherish—I will not do so good a thing again. I still smile when I think of Shem and Martha in their first and long-delayed real nest.

But the emptiness that they left was enormous, profound. The house on Peachtree Road cried with it as it never had after the departures of my mother and my father. I had done a loving duty, and in so doing had cut the heart out of my home. I found that I could not abide the efficient, jumpsuited white maids who spilled like circus clowns out of their Clean-As-A-Whistle van twice a week and swarmed into the house. They looked like aerobically trimmed Dunwoody housewives, and probably were. Their eyes, as they came into my house from their scanty, thin-walled Tudors in the suburbs, were avid; they swept the grounds and the summerhouse and me, when I ventured into their line of vision, like homing bats.

I stayed out of their sight after the first encounter. I liked only slightly more the thin, elegant mulatto personal maid Aunt Willa hired to come at ten and hover boredly about her until five or so, when she poured out sherry and passed cheese straws for Willa Slagle Bondurant and whoever shared her ice-crackings. The woman looked and dressed like Jane Fonda, and I did not care for the huge tote she carried. Besides being, I think, a genuine Gucci, I suspected that it harbored its share of Bondurant Lalique and Tiffany as it disappeared into its owner's smart little Honda. But Aunt Willa liked the girl and was satisfied with the maid service, and so I let things go with only a dull and enduring ache in my grateful heart for the Caters. Willa satisfied was Willa out of my hair. She had sulked, delicately and with the air of a highborn sixteenth-century martyr, for weeks when I had refused to hire her a driver for the Rolls.

"I would look absurd driving that big old thing, Shep," she said. "And at my age, I don't think a heavy car is safe."

Since she invoked age and infirmity only when she wanted something, and I knew her to be as healthy and indomitable as a T'ang horse, I smiled affably at her.

"Marty says he'll be happy to drop you wherever you want to go," I said. "His afternoons are pretty much free since we hired Fred Perry. He's a good driver."

She drove the Rolls. I knew she would. Willa would far rather chance ridicule and bodily harm in the old Rolls-Royce than be

driven about Buckhead, even the booming, screeching, runaway
Buckhead that she would not acknowledge, by a slick Jewish
lawyer from Newark. It struck me, watching her slide majesti-
cally away down the drive like an aging queen astride a glacier,
that I had no idea when in her tenure with us Aunt Willa had
learned to drive, or how. She remained into her seventies a creature of infinite surprise. Few of them were as pleasant as that
one.

And so, in our stases, we lived. Jack Venable, in the farmhouse, worked and drank and slept. Lucy, in her new tranquility,
sat in the moonglow of the television and the sun of the spring
and summer and slowly, slowly, slowly, healed herself back to
a fragile and infinitely simpler wholeness. By June her speech
was normal, if what she said was vastly diminished in its essential
Lucy-ness. By August she could read again. By September she
could write a little. The first thing she wrote was a letter to Malory. So far as I know, it was the first communication that had
passed between them since that terrible Christmas past. Neither
Jack nor I knew what she said, or if Malory ever answered.

Malory had meant what she said. She had not been home since
Lucy's last convulsive spasm of madness. She had not called, and
she had not written. I knew because Jack told me. Lucy did not
speak of her daughter. Jack said that she had said no word to
him about Malory since her last illness; it was as if she had simply lost her from her head and heart. She did not seem unhappy
about it, or about anything else. Jack, steeping like an old tea
bag in weariness and apathy and scotch, did not wish to risk his
stale peace by mentioning Malory. It was as if she had never lived
there with them.

She wrote me weekly, dutiful letters with all of her activities
and none of herself in them, and these I passed on to Jack. She
did not phone. When I called her, she was polite and even cordial, but she was no Malory Bondurant Venable I had any ken
of, and so I stopped my calls, miserable but resigned to the tepid
broth of the letters. I knew she must put herself back together
in her own mold after her shattering at Lucy's hands, not in any
image I might create for her. She must come back to me on her
own wings, even if I risked her not coming at all. I thought of
her constantly, and there was a great, empty, wind-scoured plain
within me where she was not, but I answered the dutiful letters
with short, chatty notes of my own, saying essentially nothing,
and I waited to see what she would do and who she would become.

Because she had not wanted to come home, she had gone to
summer school and doubled her course loads, and that, in addition to her accelerated honors program, enabled her to graduate

three quarters early, at the end of August. I knew that she was finishing with honors, but she had not said what she planned after her graduation. Some sort of counseling work perhaps, I thought, but only because her temperament and experience seemed to dictate it, not because she had told me. So far as I knew, Malory's future was as white and featureless as my own.

But in July she called, and her voice was her own, that of the old Malory, or rather, the old Malory but with a new and full dimension I could not name. She wanted more than anything, she said, for me to come and see her graduate. Jack, too, if he liked; she rather thought he wouldn't. But I must.

"And your mother?" I said.

"No, Shep," she said. "Please."

I called Jack Venable that evening and told him of the conversation.

"Can you find a way to tell Lucy?" I asked.

"Oh yes," he said. "It won't be a problem. She knows it's coming up, and she hasn't asked to go. She'll be pleased and interested, but that fire's out, Shep. I think it's out for good. And I think I won't go either. It just seems a bad time to leave Lucy alone. Can you make Malory understand?"

"She'll understand," I said, grateful that I did not have to tell him Malory had forbidden her mother and all but dismissed him.

"I hate being the only one of us there, though," I said truthfully. "It makes me feel as if I'm usurping your places with her."

"Not usurping them. Filling them," he said. "You are. And by rights, you should. You've done more to keep her safe and whole and happy than we ever have. Don't feel bad about it. I'd go if I really wanted to. The truth is, I'm grateful not to have to. I love Mal, of course I do, but I'm just too tired."

And so, in August, I went to Wellesley. I waited for Malory at the stone bench under a great old lilac tree outside her dormitory, and when she came around the corner of the building and ran toward me with her arms outstretched, it was as if a strange and rather terrible young sun had just flamed out of the mists of millenniums of rain.

Because of her pain and devastation when I had last really talked with her, and the long months of ensuing brittleness and silence, I was not prepared for the radiant and complete woman I held in my arms in the close, gray-green morning. She was so like Lucy at that age as to stop my heart, and yet with an otherness about her that I had only sensed before, which was entirely new, her own: a strength, a well-used integrity touching in one so young, a kind of tender gravity for the world, which she had had, in lesser measure, since she was a child. Out of Lucy's face, all October-blue eyes and tea rose skin and silken black hair and brow and lash, my own stubborn chin and high-bridged hawk's nose looked back at me. But of course, she had her own, and legitimate, claim to the Bondurant features through her mother and grandfather.

Over it all sheer, simple happiness shimmered like the flame from a Bunsen burner.

"Oh, Shep," she said, her face finding Sarah Cameron's old spot under my chin, though she had to stoop a bit to accomplish it. "I've never been so glad to see anyone in my life!"

Only then did I see the tall young man at her side. And on seeing him, knew, instantly and without doubt, that Malory Venable had found her future.

It was there in the way their eyes clung to each other's and could not pull away; I remembered that pull. It was there in the numerous tiny, hypnotized brushings of fingertips and hands and shoulders; I remembered those bird's-wing brushings. It was there in the delighted grins that would not let the corners of their mouths rest. My own mouth felt the tremors of that delight. I felt a great stab of pain that was as purely physical as a heart attack, nearly breath-stopping, but over it there crept a great joy, and a warm and boundless relief. Even before I learned his name, even before I took the damp and callused hand, I knew that Malory would be safe with this young man. There was great strength here. And a leavening of humor. And uncannily, out of good brown eyes behind thick, horn-rimmed glasses, Charlie Gentry looked, smiling.

His name was Peter Hopkins Dallett. He was thin, rangy, nutmeg-brown almost all over, hair, eyes and tanned skin, near to being ugly. He had graduated with honors from Yale architecture school in June, after five years spent on full scholarship. He had already had a building erected. He lived in a hamlet on the coast of Penobscot Bay, up in Maine, so small that it did not have a name or a post office; the nearest town of any size was Ellsworth, seventeen miles away. He was the youngest of four brothers, and his father was a lobsterman and ran a small general store during the season. His mother had died when he was twelve. He and Malory had met the previous March, at the wedding of a mutual friend in New Hampshire. They had not spent a weekend apart since. There was no question that they would marry—I had known that before a word was spoken. Only a question of when, and where they would live afterward.

"Will you be taking her away from us?" I said to Peter Dallett over a lunch of champagne and oysters on the half shell. Nobody was hungry, but we drank quite a bit of bad champagne. Peter insisted on buying, and cheerfully ordered what he could afford.

It was by no means Taittinger, but it ran in our veins like sweet fire.

"I don't know yet," he said. "I'd really like to come down and take a look at Atlanta. Malory hates the idea, and I realize why, but she'd be okay there. I can take care of her. It would be all right. And the best designing in the country is coming out of the Sunbelt, or will. . . ."

I flinched involuntarily, and Malory said, quickly, "I don't think we really will, though, Shep. Peter has already got such good contacts here."

She must not come home, my mind shrieked. She must not come.

"Well, good contacts aren't a thing to just toss aside," I said, as casually as I could. "I think you might find that the so-called Sunbelt is not all it's cracked up to be."

"It's a whole new frontier," Peter Dallett said. "There's nothing else like it—it's wide open to a whole new kind of design. We haven't even found a metaphor for it yet. I'd love to be in on that."

I liked the enthusiasm in his voice, but I feared it more.

"If you like strip shopping centers and tanning salons and no real urban centers and solid traffic from Atlanta to Baltimore and endless, endless suburbs, you'll love it. But you should have seen it when it was a real city, when I was Malory's age—"

"That's over," he said, with the casual implacability of the young. "The Sunbelt is what we have now. Enormous vitality. Unlimited growth potential. A whole new set of problems and solutions. Nobody ever designed for it before. Nobody ever worked in it before."

"But could you live in it?" I said. "There is that one little thing, you know."

He laughed, and the glasses bobbled on his short brown nose. I saw that it was peeling.

"I don't know," he said. "But the point is, people won't be actually living in it. Only near it. The cities of the future, especially in the Sunbelt, will be commuter cities. I don't care what the urban renewers and planners say—they will. There's wonderful clear land near Atlanta."

"Tate . . ." Malory said softly, as if she was tasting the word.

Tate. Green, silent, sunstruck and alone, dreaming in its Appalachian eternity on the side of Burnt Mountain, by covenant unchanged and unchangeable. Malory, dancing in the sunlight of Tate on the floor of the big old cottage there, utterly enthralled. Tate . . .

"I could live at Tate," Malory said into her own green distance. "I've been thinking I never wanted to see Atlanta again, but I could live up at Tate. . . ."

She shifted her blue eyes to me, and then dropped them.

"Is Mother all right?" she asked.

"Yes," I said. "She's doing fine. She sends her love. She's very proud of you. You might write and tell her about . . . things. In your own time, of course. She'd love a letter from you."

"Does . . . does she need me?" In a ghost of the old anxious voice.

"No. Really. Just to know that you're happy and taken care of. That you're safe. That's all any of us care about."

"Well, I am that." She smiled. "I truly am that. Shep . . . I thought we'd just have a tiny, quiet wedding, probably up at Peter's little family church, in the fall. I'm going there with him after today and stay. His father has asked me, and it seems just the best thing to go on and get married when the tourist season is over and he can close the store. Nobody but his immediate family. Unless you think we should come home and get married there. I know . . . Mama . . . can't travel . . ."

"No," I said. "You do just that. Come later, after she's had time to digest things. I'll tell both of them for you, shall I? And then you write. It'll be less of a strain for her that way, and for you, too."

She looked at me there in the August light, her young face serious and very beautiful, and then it crumpled, and tears started from the water-blue eyes that were, and were not, Lucy's. She flew into my arms. I felt the tears warm on my face.

"Thank you, Shep. Thank you for everything," she whispered. "Thank you for my whole life."

"You're most welcome, Malory," I said.

The next weekend I took Lucy and Jack up to Tate. It seemed to me somehow that telling them of Malory's wedding up there, in the cool blue hills, shut away from the lingering heat and fever of the September-worn city, might defuse the volatility of the situation a little—if indeed, there was any volatility. There would be none, I knew, from Jack Venable, and looking at Lucy on the seat beside me in the shifting gold light of late afternoon as I drove, I could not imagine madness and hunger washing that tranquil and emptied face. But still, better somehow at Tate. . . .

We heated the pizzas I had brought from Everybody's for our dinner that night, and Jack and I drank raw, thin Chianti with it, and Lucy her endless coffee, which had supplanted the liquor and supplemented the cigarettes, and all of us were in our beds by ten. It was as if, when we turned in between the gateposts

up on the ridge road and dipped down into the bowl of the colony, some great, spiteful hand which had held us fast relaxed
its grip, and ease came flooding in. I lay listening to the night
sounds of those worn old mountains—not many in the exhausted
air of early fall: a few late-lingering cicadas and crickets, a dog
barking over to the west, on some far ridge—and slid into a sleep
so profound that when I awoke, with the early sun spilling across
my face, I was still in the same position in which I had dropped
off.

I was sitting at the scarred old trestle table in the kitchen looking across the meadow to the misted, mirror-still lake and drinking coffee when Jack appeared, sagging and stupefied in a
sweatshirt and pants that were far too big for him. Had they ever
fit? I wondered. How had he shrunk, withered, diminished so
before my very eyes, and I had not noticed?

He looked gray and heavy-faced in the clear, tender light, and
shambled across the kitchen to the table with the tiredness that
was the same in the morning as it was at night. White stubble
dusted his pale jaw. The white hair was utterly devoid of life,
the blue eyes dull and half-shut. It struck me with a pang that
Jack Venable was tired from the soul out. Tired and perhaps ill,
with one of the wasting illnesses despair summons from the very
DNA.

"I'd hoped you'd sleep at least till noon," I said, pouring him
coffee out of the old spatterware pot.

"Lucy was having one of her nightmares, thrashing around
and crying in her sleep," he said. "A rock couldn't sleep through
that. It's funny—there's no agitation in her when she's awake.
And it's not that she's suppressing it, either. I can always tell
when she does that. It's really not there. But then, once or twice
a month, when she's asleep, these things come. . . . I wonder what
she dreams. She says she doesn't remember."

"She's always had them," I said. "They were really terrible
when she was little—awful things about being lost, or abandoned, or in mortal danger, or dying. We'd have an awful time
calming her. I thought she'd outgrown them."

"Poor Luce," he said gently, gently. "Her demons grew up
along with her. She met the enemy and it was her. You know,
there was a time, there at the beginning, that I really thought
I could help her. Be the rock she needed, somebody to lean on.
But after a while I just couldn't seem to take her weight. I never
meant to let her down. I've hated myself for it. But I just . . .
wasn't enough."

"Nobody could have been, Jack. Nobody mortal could have
met all that need," I said, my heart twisting with pity for this
flawed, weary, emptied man whose passion had not withstood

the tidal suck of both the civil rights movement and Lucy Bondurant. I did not think that tragedy was too strong a word for him.

"I guess not," he said. "But God, how I wanted to be the one mortal who did. And now I sit and look at her, one step up from a happy turnip and still just so beautiful to me, and instead of mourning for all that lost light and . . . sorcery . . . I thank God for the happy turnip and go back to sleep."

"Don't beat up on yourself for that," I said. "All of us have blessed the turnip at one time or another. And prayed like cowards for it to last."

"It will," he said. "That devil's exorcised for good. I'm sure of that. What you see now is the Lucy we'll have from here on out. Good luck for us, maybe. Not so good for Luce."

"I hope you're right, at least temporarily," I said. "We're going to have to tell her something today that scares the bejesus out of me. I want to run it past you first."

"Malory," he said, looking up from the coffee. It was not a question.

"Yes. She's going to get married very soon, to a young architect from Maine she met this spring. They'll marry there, with just his folks. I think the family is dirt-poor. His mother's dead. But he's solid rock. I met him at her graduation. You'll like him, Jack. So will Lucy, I think. Malory will be safe with him. And she's crazy about him, and he about her. I . . . none of us will be going, but she'll call her mother, or at least write, when I give her the word that we've told her."

His thin face lit briefly.

"Good for her," he said, smiling. The smile was gray and wounded, like the rest of him. "Good for Mal. I want her happiness very much. I've never seemed to be able to show her that, though. Somehow, everything I had went to Lucy."

"So you think it's safe to tell her?"

"Oh, sure," he said. "Like I said, that fire is out. Whatever they did at Central State cooked it right out of her. You can tell her anything. There's no danger anymore. No matter what I said a minute ago, I almost wish there was . . ."

"Do you want to be with me when I do?" I said.

"No. Do you mind? I'm not afraid. I'm just"—and he grinned, hearing his own words—"tired. I think I'll go back to bed for a while."

He slept for most of the day. Lucy herself slept until noon. When she awoke, she surprised me by wanting to walk around the lake by the sun-dappled dirt road that encircled it. It was our old walk, a smooth and pretty one, but long.

"Can you make it?" I said.

"Yes," she said. "I can if we take it slow, and stop along the way. Let's do it, Gibby. Let's stop by all the old places, and take some sandwiches and have a picnic up in the meadow. Oh, and bring your clarinet—is it up here?"

"The old one is," I said. "The one I learned to play on. Rusted solid, probably. But I'll bring it anyway."

And so we set out, Lucy in blue jeans and a loose old plaid shirt someone had left in her closet, looking, if one did not lean too near, rested and almost young and very close once more to being beautiful. She walked slowly, and she leaned on me, and she did tire, so that we made frequent stops, but when we were seated in the deep shade of a hickory grove, the tawny bowl of the mountains walling us in under the clarion blue of the first autumn sky, she was as delighted as she had been as a child with the old places where so much of our magic and mischief had been wrought, where so much still seemed to hover.

"Tell about the Fourth of July parade, Gibby," she cried, and I spun it out for her in the sunny silence, that joyous long-ago procession of children and adults and teenagers and babies and dogs and banners and bunting and raucous, braying musical instruments.

"Tell about us swimming," she said, and all of a sudden there we were, as thin and supple and slippery as young otters, yelping soundlessly in the hot sun and cold water of the little indigo lake, and there was small Sarah Cameron, pinned against a cobalt July sky in the highest arc of a dive, as beautiful as a young gull.

"Tell about the night the deer jumped over me," she said, and the day darkened into that long-ago magical and terrible night, still and star-struck and moon-dappled, and ahead of me on this very road a will-o'-the-wisp little Lucy Bondurant ran blithely into a pool of utter, soulless blackness, and the spectral shadow of the leaping deer fell down straight upon her like an evil fairy's curse.

I shivered with that one, and not wanting to invoke any more of the small, lost ghosts of Tate, moved with her out into the sun of the high meadow, and played as well as I could on the squawking clarinet that had, so long ago in this same long grass, spilled out "Frenesi" for me like crystal water. I played "Frenesi" again, and "Amapola," and "In the Mood," and several of the other songs we had grown up dancing to, the Pinks and the Jells, on the polished wooden floors of half a dozen clubs, and I finished up, as those vanished dances had, with "Moonglow."

Lucy lay quiet, stretched out on her back in the last of the slanting sun. It gilded her face and struck fire from her dark hair.

"Thank you, Gibby," she said at last. "It was as good as going back."

"You're welcome," I said.

I told her then, told her about Malory, told her with my heart in my mouth and my eyes riveted to her still face and mild blue eyes. But after I was finished, and had fallen silent, all she said was "Oh, Gibby, really? Isn't that wonderful! Tell me about him."

I did.

"Will he be good to her?" she asked.

"Most wonderfully good. Good to her always."

"Then that's okay. That's all that matters."

She was silent, and when I was sure she was not going to speak again, I said, "Lucy . . . I don't think any of us should go. I'm not going. It'll be just his family."

"Oh no," she said, looking up at me with her clear, bottomless blue eyes. "I didn't expect to. I don't deserve to go."

My heart hurt, suddenly and simply and powerfully.

"Oh, honey," I said. "Oh, Luce. It's not that. . . ."

"Oh yes," she said matter-of-factly, and there was in her rich, bronzy drawl nothing of pathos but more than a little of the indomitable small girl who had stubbornly abjured self-pity. "It *is* that. I was awful. I know I was. I drove her away. And I don't deserve to go to her wedding. But that's over, that part of me. Maybe after a while she'll see that, and she'll bring her . . . husband . . . home to us."

"She will," I said. "She's already said she wanted to."

Lucy grinned at me. It was, suddenly and fully, her old grin, quicksilver and devilish and wonderful to see.

"I promise, when she does, to keep my panties on," she said.

"I love you, Lucy Bondurant," I said. I did. I did, in that moment, as much as I ever had in my life.

"I love you, too, Gibby Bondurant," she said.

We sat in the high meadow and watched the sun drop, red and swollen, over the shoulder of Burnt Mountain. Away to the south the coppery cloud of smutch that was Atlanta belching and simmering in its own effluvia came clearer.

Lucy pointed to it.

"Do you still love it?" she asked.

"No," I said. "I guess I never did and I don't even like it anymore now. It's no kind of city that I know or care about. It's loud and it stinks. It's fifty times too big. It has no grace anymore. But I need it, if that makes any sense. You don't have to love something to need it. Dimension and need can come from lots of other things . . . hate, or fear, or anger. . . . I couldn't tell you how, but I know that's so. I just . . . need it."

"You don't have to tell me," she said. "I know. It isn't my town anymore, either. But it has something, Gibby. It has . . . oh, resonance. Passion, energy, and a kind of . . . not noticing quality to it. A carelessness. Impersonality. It doesn't give a shit what you are or what you do. And power—lots of power. I might have amounted to something in a town like that. But I don't love it. I guess I didn't the other one, either, if you get right down to it."

She lit her last cigarette, and inhaled a long, deep lungful of smoke, and let it out into the lavender air of evening, looking through it down into the sour copper breath of the city to the south.

"But, oh Lord," she said, smiling faintly, "it was a wonderful town to be young in, wasn't it?"

Three weeks later, on the first Saturday night in October, the shrilling of the telephone brought me out of a deep, still sleep. It had been hot the past week, as hot as August, and I had turned on the window air conditioner in the bedroom, so that struggling up to the surface of wakefulness was like trying to swim up through pounding black surf. The room was totally dark and without context, and I knocked the telephone from the receiver before I managed to get it to my ear. I had no idea what time it was.

"Gibby?" Pause. Great, indrawn inhalation, deep sigh of exhalation. "It's Lucy, honey."

"Lucy," I mumbled. "What time is it?" My eyes found the digital clock on my bedside table then. "Jesus," I said. "It's almost four o'clock. Is something wrong?"

I knew that something was. The time, of course. Her nightly calls almost invariably came between ten and eleven, after Jack had drowned in sleep. But a wincing, clinching part of me had known when she spoke. The rich, slow voice sang with the honey of the old madness.

"Gibby, did you know Malory was getting married? She's getting married next weekend!" Lucy said in a pouting child's voice.

"Well, yes, I did, Luce," I said carefully. "So did you. Remember, I told you up at Tate two or three weekends ago? We talked about it a long time."

"Well, you obviously told somebody else besides Malory's mother, because it wasn't me. I didn't hear a word about it until Jack Venable just happened to mention it tonight, on his forty millionth scotch. I'm real mad at him. You, too, if you knew and wouldn't tell me."

A vast, trembling, bottomless fatigue settled slowly down over me, like a great, drifting net of cobwebs. I thought it must be what Jack Venable felt a good bit of the time. Oh God, please not again, I said soundlessly.

"I did tell you, sweetie," I said. "I wouldn't not tell you. You said you thought it was wonderful and you agreed that none of us should go because Peter's family is so poorly off, and that you'd be very happy to see them when they came home after the wedding. We were awfully proud of the way you took it."

"Took it, shmook it," Lucy said in fretful annoyance. "You got the wrong lady, toots. I don't think it's fucking wonderful at all. That baby isn't old enough to get married! She hasn't even talked to me about it—I could tell her a thing or two about marriage. I don't know any fucking Peter in fucking Maine. I fucking well did not agree we shouldn't go. Of course I'm going! In fact, that's why I called you. I want you to come out here and get me and take me to the airport. I'm almost packed. No thanks to Jack Venable, I might add. He absolutely refused to take me. He got awfully abusive about it, Gibby."

Her voice slid into an injured child's whine. Something ran lightly up my spine, claws of ice digging into my flesh.

"Put Jack on the phone, Luce," I said neutrally. "Is he awake?"

There was a long pause and then she laughed. The sound tinkled in my ears like shards of crystal ice.

"No," she said gaily. "I don't think you could say he's awake. In fact, I'm fairly sure the sonofabitch is dead. I just shot him in the head with that old gun of his. Not take me to my own baby's wedding! Jesus!"

She had, in her madness, told so many lies about Jack's abuse of her that my first instinct was to hang up on her. But the eerie finger of ice along my spine would not let me do that.

"Are you telling me the truth, Lucy?" I asked. My voice sounded high and silly in my ears.

"Oh yes," she said. "He's bleeding like anything. It's a real mess. That's another reason I want you to come on out here, Gibby. I can't clean this up by myself."

A fine trembling started up deep inside me, and spread from my stomach into my arms and legs, so that I sagged from where I had been standing, naked and perspiring beside the telephone table, down onto my rumpled bed. Even my head shook, and my lips, so that I could not speak for a moment.

"Lucy, I'm going to come out there as soon as I can," I said very carefully, around the ridiculous, waffling mouth. "Just let me get some clothes on. Now listen—don't call anybody else until I get there. Have you called anybody else?"

"Of course not," she said indignantly. "I don't have any friends in this one-horse hick town. Nobody out here even bothered to get to know Malory. I wouldn't let anybody out here take me to the airport to go to my baby's wedding!"

"Well, don't make any more calls," I said. "Tell you what you do. You get dressed, and put on some coffee, and then you sit down and wait for me. Can you do that?"

"Well, of course I can do that, silly," she sang. Delight had crept into her voice, and gaiety. "I'm not paralyzed! You'll take me, then?"

"I'll take you," I said, around the roaring that had begun in my head.

"Oh, Gibby, I could always count on you!"

It was the voice of the delivered changeling, huddled into the corner of a narrow iron bed in a dim attic atop a great, graceful house in a small, beautiful, vanished city, waiting for me to come and vanquish nightmares.

"I'm on my way," I said.

The night was thick and hot and still. No lights showed in the big house. Up on Peachtree Road, winking through the yellowing leaves of the woods around the summerhouse, the eternal cold white lights of the great, hovering buildings burned, useless sentinels of a long-victorious army. The traffic, as I idled at the foot of the driveway, was steady and brisk, as heavy as it had once been at high noon. I found a break in it and slid the Rolls out into Peachtree Road, marveling at my own expertise with the smooth, heavy old wheel. I drove carefully over to the I-85 South ramp at Piedmont, and took that into and through the white-lit city, and then bore off left on I-20 East. Out on the Interstate, once the diminishing lights of the suburban fringes of the city dropped away, the parched October country flowed steadily past in blackness. Only an occasional all-night filling station or motel lit my passage. I bowled silently toward a smudge of lightening gray on the horizon; I was driving east to meet the dawn.

I made a little song as I drove. I sang it over and over, just under my breath, feeling my stiff lips making the nonsense words, hearing nothing but the high roaring in my head, as though a hot wind keened there. I sang it to the tune of "Jada": "Liar, Liar, Liar-Liar-Lie-Lie-Lie. Liar, Liar, Liar-Liar-Lie-Lie-Lie." I think that I sang it all the way to sleeping Lithonia and through it to the turnoff down which, nearly a mile distant, the farmhouse lay.

It was only when I drove out of the tunnel of thin, scabrous woods into the rutted yard and found the house ablaze with lights that I realized I had hoped and halfway expected to find it dark, and Lucy and Jack safely fast in banal sleep. My heart gave a great, sick lurch and dropped in my chest. The song died

on my lips. As I got out of the car and shut the door, precisely
and softly, and walked on unfelt feet up the sagging steps, I whispered, desolately, "Liar, liar, pants on fire." Looking back, I
think that in that moment I was no saner than Lucy.

Lucy had not been lying. In the warmly lit, desperately littered
living room she waited for me, sitting in her accustomed chair
with feet demurely together and hands clasped in her lap, as
Margaret Bryan had taught us all, years ago, to sit when we were
not dancing. The television flickered wildly, an old black-and-
white movie with George Raft, soundless. Lucy wore the good,
if too-big, blue wool dress she had for special occasions, a gift
from Little Lady, who had probably gotten it at Saint Philip's
thrift store; its sheath skirt and short, collared jacket spoke for-
lornly of Jacqueline Kennedy and Camelot. She held a little envelope purse on her lap. A battered fiberglass suitcase sat on the
floor beside her, closed and tagged. A whining, laboring electric
fan was trained on her, but sweat still ran from her hairline and
stood in beads on her collarbone. She wore short white cotton
gloves, but her black hair was wild, a raven's nest, and on her
feet she wore soiled terry scuffs.

Her legs were bare, and they were dappled with dark dried
blood to the knee. More blood had dried in a swooping spatter
across her cheek, and on one forearm. Above the rusty blood
her blue eyes danced, danced. She dimpled, but did not speak.
Her eyes swung from me across the room. My own eyes followed
them with a monstrous, dragging effort.

I could not even flinch at what I saw. I could not back away.

Jack Venable lay on the spavined old sofa across the room
from Lucy. He lay with his back to me, knees drawn up, facing
in toward the stained back cushions of the sofa. I had seen him
lie so many times, safely sunk in his long sleeps. He looked safe
now, tidy and relaxed in rumpled khaki pants and a white shirt
and just his yellowed old crew socks. His scuffed, thin loafers
sat neatly side by side with their toes under the edge of the sofa,
waiting for their owner to get up and shuffle them to bed.

But Jack was not going to rise from this sleep. He seemed immaculate from where I stood, but the blood that had burst from
the ruined temple had soaked through the cushion beneath it,
and spilled in a thin stream down the sofa skirt onto the old,
liver-colored rug, and puddled there, looking for all the world
like black cherry Jell-O only half-congealed.

I did not walk over to the sofa and look more closely at him.
The utter whiteness of the skin of his neck and arms, and the
pure, hopeless stillness of him, and the color and thickness of
the blood told the minuscule part of my mind that stood outside

the hot, howling wind what it must finally know: Jack Venable was dead, and had been for some time.

I looked back at Lucy. In her lap, partly covered by the little debutante's clutch purse, a blunt black gun lay, as ugly and shocking as a snake. She wasn't lying about the gun, I thought dimly. She was right, all those years ago. He did have one.

Lucy looked up at me archly, head cocked, and smiled.

"Hey, Gibby," she said.

My knees unlocked then, and I slumped bonelessly to the floor at her dreadful feet, tailor-fashion. My heart was beating so slowly and thinly that I thought it must surely and simply stop. I was cold, cold, bone-cold, marrow-cold, despite the thick, malodorous heat in the room. An icy lump of nausea rose into my throat at the smell: a smell of burning, and liquor, and sweat, and the sour-sweet, sheared metal smell of turning blood. Something under the blood was too terrible even to register.

I looked blindly into the rug for a while, seeing the tiny lunar desert of a cigarette burn, and the stain of some dark, old liquid. Then I said, in a voice that croaked and scrabbled in my throat, "Lucy, what is going to become of you now? What on earth will happen to you? I can't fix this. This can't be fixed. Who's going to take care of you now?"

She leaned down slightly and peered into my face, and smiled again, as if satisfied at what she saw there.

"Why, you will, Gibby," she said. "You can, too, fix it. You know you can. And Malory. Malory will come. My best boyfriend and our beautiful, beautiful daughter. You knew that, of course, didn't you? That she was our daughter? Of course you did. We be of one blood, we three. So you both have to take care of me, you see. Call Malory, Gibby. Malory will come."

I looked up at the sweet, mad smile and realized that I had no idea whether or not she was lying about Malory, and would never know. Malory. Malory . . . Yes, Malory would come. Like a fierce, beautiful young hawk circling higher and higher in the thin, pure sunlight, only to heed, finally, the falconer's cry and plummet in beauty and mortal peril straight into the snare, Malory would come.

And me? I thought. Yes. As long as Lucy lives, God help me, I will come too. I will come.

I saw us, far back in my ringing head, going on forever, the three of us, locked in a crazy troika of loss and blood and waste and madness. Forever. Forever. . . .

I rose to my knees as stiffly as an old, ill man, and took the gun from Lucy's lap and pressed it into her hands. I closed them around it. They were rough and hot, even against the chill of the heavy steel. They trembled tinily, like the throat of a singing bird. I looked back into her face and she smiled at me again. It was a good child's smile, sweet and simple. Above it her eyes shone, blue, blue, the extraordinary, light-drowned eyes of that doomed child who had stood in the foyer of the house on Peachtree Road, pinning my heart to my ribs with her very presence, and said in a voice like dark honey, "Something stinks."

"Stick it in your ear, Luce," I said.

She laughed, the old rich, bawdy, wonderful laugh.

She put the dark gun to her ear, still laughing, her blue eyes spilling the healing light of redemption and benediction over me.

"Pull the trigger," I said.

Lucy did.

CHAPTER
TWENTY-SEVEN

WELL, AND SO THERE WE WERE again this afternoon, at Oakland. Just as Freddie had said. The aging Buckhead Boys and their girls, come once more to bury one of their own, though only nominally. This one had always walked outside us.

I had an insane desire to rush up to someone and say, earnestly, "We simply have to stop meeting like this." But the three people who would have liked that most, and laughed at it, were under this elegiac October earth now, not atop it with the diminished rest of us. Young Ben Cameron. Charlie. And now Lucy.

Too rich a sowing, for an earth that would yield no harvest.

I remembered the long-ago party in the grand new house out in the Chattahoochee Triangle, when the leathery, discontented Northern woman had asked me where she could find the real Old Atlanta, and I had said, only half jesting, "Oakland Cemetery."

Now, I supposed, we were Old Atlanta, we bewildered and disenfranchised Pinks and Jells of a Buckhead that was deader than Pompeii.

And not a patch on the ones that went before us, I thought again, as I had at my father's funeral here.

I was almost the last one left in the cemetery. Malory, ravaged and mute, had been helped back into the Spring Hill limousine with Peter Dallett's steady brown hand at her back, and would be waiting for me at the Peachtree Road house before flying back to Maine and whatever life awaited her there. She was, of course, devastated; terribly, terribly wounded. I felt her wounds bitterly in my own flesh and heart, atop my own. But it was, I knew,

586

a devastation that had an ending to it. That other wreckage would have been without limit and without end. She could heal, and when she did, Malory Bondurant Venable would be free. Whether she would ever come home to Atlanta did not, somehow, matter to me now. I felt, as deeply as I could feel anything, that she would, in some way and at some time, be a part of this unimaginable city which was no longer a part of me, but I could not justify the feeling, and was content not to probe it. I wished I could have felt sorrier, for all of us, and for everything.

"I'm sorry, Mal," my mouth whispered, but my heart was not sorry. I felt very little on this day but emptiness and a great, poised, focused waiting. I could not have said what it was that I waited for.

Old Willa Bondurant, trailing her cherished Little Lady like a Pekingese, stopped before me and gave me a sly, hooded snake's look, the look of an ancient enemy. I knew she no longer remembered the day in the foyer of 2500 when I told her to move her things out of the attic and into my dead mother's room, and she had wept with deliverance. She could not have afforded that memory.

"I'm a tough old bird, wouldn't you say, Shep?" she said, in her hard-won, genteel drawl. "I'm a survivor. I survived Jim Bondurant, and I've survived two of his three children. God knows it's a terrible thing to be old and lose your looks"—and she patted her lacquered steel-blue hair with the air of one who knows she has kept most of them—"but you can at least take your revenge by outliving everybody."

Something in me, which I had thought long dead, stirred and went into a cold, still crouch.

"How did you know Uncle Jim was dead?" I said. I thought my voice was even and pleasant, but she knew what it sprang from. The basilisk's smile deepened. Old dimples yawned crazily.

"Because he wrote to Lucy for ages," she said with a dreadful arch, conspiratorial lift to her brows. "Ever since she was nine or ten. It went on for years. Of course, I burned the letters. I'd never have let that animal touch my girl in any way. But he kept sending them, the filthy things, and so I finally wrote and told him to stop or I'd have the law on him for desertion, and the letter came back from his last address stamped 'Deceased.'"

I simply looked at her. Speech was impossible. Burned them. She had burned them. Burned them, the letters that might have saved Lucy. Who was to say? There might have been, in those long-awaited words, some deliverance, something that could have fed that monstrous hunger, opened and cleansed that hard bud of madness. . . .

Oh yes. We make our own monsters, but they inevitably have their revenge.

I looked after her retreating figure. She turned and smiled again at me, a bizarre old Junior Leaguer in her simple black dress and her pearls and her "little heels," back to her bridge luncheons at the Driving Club and her pills and her internists and her charities. She was as old and soulless and simple as a Galapagos turtle, there in the waning sunlight, but she looked at that moment younger than the raddled daughter she had just buried.

I knew that she would go back now to the cool, quiet, gracious old house on Peachtree Road—where she, the pretender, had reigned for so long—for the rarely taken cigarette and the thin crystal glass of good sherry served by her elegant mulatto, and the comfort of old women like her. Alive.

Alive.

I turned and followed her back to the line of cars parked on the narrow brick road. When I reached the Rolls, Carter and Little Lady had driven away. I was the last one to leave Oakland.

When I reached the house I left the car in the driveway, door ajar, and went straight to the telephone in the summerhouse and dialed Carter Rawson. For once he answered himself.

"Carter?" I said. "Listen. I've changed my mind about the house. Call Marty Fox tomorrow and give him your best offer. It better be a goddamned good one. There won't be any problem with the zoning."

And I hung up before he could answer.

I dialed the mayor's office at City Hall. When Glenn Pickens's secretary said he was in a meeting and would be glad to call me back, I said, "Just tell him Mr. Bondurant said the debt's been paid in full and to cancel it."

She repeated it back to me, carefully.

"Is that all?" she asked.

"Yes," I said. "That's all."

"Willa," I said aloud into the still, sunny air of the summerhouse, "stick it in your ear."

By seven-thirty that evening I stood at the railing of the old iron bridge over the Chattahoochee River where, thirty years ago, Lucy had shouted my shame across a spring sky before the assembled Pinks and Jells of Atlanta. The Rolls was parked on the weedy apron at the approach to the bridge. There was no traffic on the old road, and the hot silence was complete except for the chorus of cicadas in the fringe of trees along the river, and the sturdy chuckle of the slow brown water far below. It seemed to me very hot and still, and no time at all.

Through the bubble of suspended silence that had wrapped me for the past two days I was suddenly aware of the low-slanting sun on my head and face, and the little twilight breeze which had sprung up off the water. It was soft on my arms and chest and face, though the sharp bones of winter lay just below the surface. I wore jogging shorts and no shirt, and was barefoot, for I was going on a very long journey, and I wanted nothing about me to snag upon the wind of my leaving. I was neither happy nor unhappy, only profoundly aware that I and the world around me were totally stopped and still, frozen on some great axis, and that I did not know or care if either I or it would start forward again. The pale blue arch of the evening sky was reflected perfectly and wholly in the water far below me, just as it had been on that spring day so long ago. The old willows still trailed on its surface, yellow now.

I stood for a while, thinking of nothing at all, and then climbed up onto the railing and looked down at the water. It had been a wet summer and the river was high and running full, but that was down deep; the skin of it was silken and whole. As it had on that other day, the sky wheeled sickly above and below me, and I closed my eyes against the vertigo. From far below and out of time I heard, distinctly, Lucy's silvery, jeering voice: "Come on, Gibby, jump, or we'll think you're a North Fulton fruitcake! Come on! Mark my trai-i-i-l!"

Opening my eyes to slits, I saw below on the willow bank the gleam of white flesh, and the fine shape, under wet black hair, of narrow, beautiful skull. The very air shivered with her vivid aliveness.

I threw back my head and cupped my mouth with my hands and shouted into the wheeling blue emptiness: "Lucy! Lucy Bondurant! Are you listening? Lucy . . . mark my trai-i-i-l!"

Only silence answered. She had gone, leaving to me the emptiness of willows and river. Empty, empty . . . My knees sagged, and the hopeless nausea rose in my throat.

And then another voice also, from far below me, came riding out of our childhood on the little evening wind.

"Shep Bondurant! *I* mark your trail!"

I snapped my head down, space swooping around me.

Sarah Cameron Gentry stood below on the weedy approach to the bridge, her little blue Dodge parked hard beside the Rolls, her red scarf and black hair blowing on the wind. Her cupped hand shielded her eyes from the dazzle of evening light, and even from that distance I could see that she was laughing.

An enormous lightness seized me. Gladness started up in my chest like a lark in the meadow at Tate. The world jerked, shifted, flowed forward again like floodwater. The wheeling space around me bellowed joy. I lifted one fist straight up and out in the old black power salute and, borne up on a great gust of laughter, dived into the sky.

About the Author

Anne Rivers Siddons is the author of JOHN CHANCEL-
LOR MAKES ME CRY, HEARTBREAK HOTEL,
THE HOUSE NEXT DOOR, FOX'S EARTH, HOME-
PLACE, and PEACHTREE ROAD. She lives with her
husband in Atlanta, Georgia.

*Be sure to read
Anne Rivers Siddons'
other Ballantine paperbacks.*

FOX'S EARTH

Beautiful Ruth Yancey rises above her squalid
Georgia milltown roots to become mistress of the
exquisite mansion, Fox's Earth. With masterful
precision, she breaks her descendents' hearts and
bleeds their souls — until another woman attempts
to match her evil, madness, and murder.

> "A lusty Southern saga, this Gothic extrava-
> ganza of greed, madness, and murder is a
> wicked brew, passionate and perverse. . . . It's
> also psychologically astute and excellently
> written."
>
> —*Cosmopolitan*

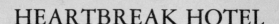

HEARTBREAK HOTEL

Maggie Deloach was a senior at Alabama's Randolph University, the perfect Southern girl, expected to become the perfect society matron. But the summer of 1956, the summer of Elvis Presley's "Heartbreak Hotel"—would change everything.

> "An absolute gem . . . A rare and wonderful book."
>
> —*Richmond News Leader*

HOMEPLACE

Micah (Mike) Winship is going home after twenty years. In 1963, her father forced her to leave her South Georgia home and she's never looked back. But now he's dying and asking for her. Confronting a past that includes an old lover, an overindulged sister, and a plot to seize her family's land, Mike begins to learn—and understand—love and loss, family and forgiveness, and the inexplicable pull of a place called home.

> "A novel to savor."
>
> —*Newsday*